THE
FORTY DAYS
OF
MUSA DAGH

FRANZ WERFEL

THE
FORTY DAYS
OF
MUSA DAGH

Carroll & Graf Publishers, Inc.
New York

Contents

Note

THIS book was conceived in March of 1929, in the course of a stay in Damascus. The miserable sight of some maimed and famished-looking refugee children, working in a carpet factory, gave me the final impulse to snatch from the Hades of all that was, this incomprehensible destiny of the Armenian nation. The writing of the book followed between July 1932 and March 1933. Meanwhile, in November, on a lecture tour through German cities, the author selected Chapter V of Book I for public readings. It was read in its present form, based on the historic records of a conversation between Enver Pasha and Pastor Johannes Lepsius.

Breitenstein, Spring 1933.

Introduction

The Forty Days of Musa Dagh is, first of all, a compelling story of epic dimensions. It was no surprise that Metro-Goldwyn-Mayer should have eagerly paid Franz Werfel substantial option money for the film rights to his novel as soon as it was published here in 1934. A treatment was quickly written, but, although *The New York Times Book Review* considered it a "thrilling" narrative, the film was never made. Why not?

In September of 1935, Münir Ertegun, Turkish Ambassador to the United States, wrote the Secretary of State asking that he exert his "high influence with a view to precluding the carrying out of this project" and stating that the Turkish government had "reasons to believe that this novel, if filmed, would not find a market either in Turkey or in several other European countries."

Wallace Murray, Chief of the Division of Near Eastern Affairs, immediately wrote Will Hays, czar of the film industry, "to solicit such assistance as he might be able to render in disposing of a question which appears to be assuming very large proportions in the minds of the officials at Ankara." Less than a month later, Ambassador Ertegun wrote Murray to say that "Mr. Orr of the Metro-Goldwyn-Mayer called on [him] to . . . admit that the filming of this novel could not but be harmful from every standpoint. Consequently he declared that they would rather drop this scheme altogether." Ertegun thanked Murray profusely for his efforts, "without which the happy conclusion . . . could not possibly have been attained."

For the Armenian survivors of the Turkish genocide of 1915–21, this was, of course, no happy conclusion. Peter Stephan Jungk, Werfel's able biographer, cites an Armenian priest living at the monastery of San Lazzaro in Venice, Father Bezdikian, whose grandfather had fought on Musa Dagh:

> Franz Werfel is the national hero of the Armenian people. His great book is a kind of consolation to us—no, not a consolation, there is no such thing— but it is of eminent importance to us that this book exists. It guarantees that it can never be forgotten, never, what happened to our people.

For someone else the outcome was no more unhappy than it had been for the Turkish government. That outcome was no conclusion for him, however, but rather a beginning. Adolf Hitler, discussing the projected slaughter of an entire people twenty-five years after Musa Dagh, in a remarkable echoing of cipher telegrams of the ruling Turkish triumvirate in 1915, told his commanders: "I have sent to the East my Death's Head Units with the order to kill without pity or mercy all men, women, and children of the Polish race." He went on to say: "Who talks nowadays of the extermination of the Armenians?".

And so things continue. Nations have no souls, but only interests—*raisons d'état*, in the hallowed French phrase. In spite of the evidence of its own files and voluminous other testimony, the American State Department has in recent years deemed it expedient to please our strategically placed Turkish allies by referring to the willed mass extermination of Armenians as an "alleged" event. The Turks, thus encouraged, continue resolutely to deny in life events which Werfel so memorably embodied in art.

Known to Herodotus, the Father of History, the ancient people of Armenia had lived continuously in large parts of what is now Turkey for over two and a-half millennia. They were the first Christian state, their King Tiridates having been converted by Gregory the Illuminator in 301; the Roman Empire followed in 337. Several of the Byzantine emperors were Armenians, notably Basil I, Leo the Armenian, and John Tzimiskes.

After the fall of Constantinople in 1453, the Armenians were recognized as one of several semiautonomous communities, or *millets*, of the Ottoman Empire headed by the Armenian Patriarch of Constantinople. They were known as "the loyal *millet*," and served the empire well, especially as functionaries, merchants, artisans, and architects, in spite of sporadic massacres of the infidel.

Then in 1878, following the Russo-Turkish Wars, the Treaty of Berlin honored nationalistic aspirations within the empire by slicing off substantial chunks of it—Romania, Serbia, Montenegro, part of Bulgaria—and it also ceded other territory to Russia. It gave the Western powers rights of protection over the Armenians on the sensitive Russian border, which made the Christian Armenians an especially manipulable factor in the seesaw game of playing on Turkish fears.

The Turks saw this disturbingly large population as having dangerous nationalistic aspirations. The Armenians—like Jews without the State of Israel—having no diplomatic standing, were also the most available targets for hemmed-in Turkish anger. Their religion and their prosperity made them the natural objects of xenophobia.

In the 1890s, Sultan Abdul Hamid began to encourage wholesale attacks on the Armenian communities. As Christians and therefore forbidden to bear arms, Armenians were at the mercy of the *hamidiyeh*, Kurdish mounted regiments formed by the sultan, counterparts to the Russian Cossacks. This culminated in a massacre of almost three hundred thousand Armenians in 1895.

The year 1908 brought hope to the Armenians in the form of the Young Turk Revolution. The dashing general Enver Pasha declared in a speech in Salonika's Liberty Square that "today arbitrary government has disappeared. We are all brothers. There are no longer in Turkey Bulgarians, Greeks, Serbs, Rumanians, Muslims, Jews. We are all proud to be Ottomans under the same sky." But within a year thirty thousand Armenians had been killed at Adana as the ideology of Pan-Turanism took shape, one not dissimilar from the Aryan ideology soon to emerge in Nazi Germany.

The ruling triumvirate of Enver Pasha, Talaat Bey, and Jemal Pasha was to prove more ruthless than the regime of Abdul Hamid. All three are characters in *The Forty Days of Musa Dagh.* According to British historian Christopher J. Walker, Enver was saved from the Tsarists by Armenian soldiers when he was defeated at the Battle of Sarikamish; yet on April 24, 1915, he and the other two leaders of the Committee of Union and Progress set the genocide in motion.

It was an extraordinarily horrible and not inefficient operation. Before 1915 there had been about two million Armenians in Turkey; afterward, there were well under a hundred thousand; perhaps one out of three of all the Armenians in the world perished.

Pleading the case of the Armenians before Talaat, the American ambassador Henry Morgenthau, another figure revered by Armenians, recounts that he was told:

It is no use for you to argue. We have already disposed of three-quarters of the Armenians; there are none at all left in Bitlis, Van, and Erzeroum . . . We have got to finish with them. If we don't they will plan their revenge.

Morgenthau writes in his memoirs that one day Talaat asked him why he was so interested in the fate of the Armenians. "You are a Jew," he said. "These people are Christians. The Muslims and Jews always get on harmoniously. We are treating the Jews here all right."

There were pockets of resistance to the proclaimed jihad, especially at Zeitoun, at Shabin Karahisar, at Urfa, and at Musa Dagh. French scholar Yves Ternon, in his report to the Permanent Peoples' Tribunal at the session on the Armenian genocide held in Paris in 1984, writes:

. . . In the Jebel Musa, or Musa Dagh, the Armenians refused to submit to the deportation order issued on 13 July. Retreating into the hills they took up a strategic position and organized an impregnable defense. The Turks attacked and were repulsed with huge losses. They proceeded to lay siege to the Jebel Musa with fifteen-thousand men. Fifty-three days later, French and British ships, intercepting signals, picked up the four-thousand survivors and took them to Port Said.

Werfel chose to make the length of the siege forty days. The choice, writes his biographer Jungk, "called up biblical associations: the flood lasted forty days and nights; Moses spent forty days and nights on Mount Sinai; Israel's time in the wilderness was forty years."

In the novel, a cosmopolitan Armenian, Gabriel Bagradian, returns with a French wife and young son to his native village on the slopes of Musa Dagh overlooking the Mediterranean, an hour's ride from the ancient city of Antioch. His intention is to settle the business affairs of his family and return to Europe. "Twenty-three years of Europe, Paris! Years of complete assimilation" when "he had been allowed to live as a scholar, a *bel esprit*, an archaeologist, a historian of art, a philosopher."

Unlike other rich bourgeois who had settled in Europe, Gabriel's grandfather, founder of a world-famous business, had returned home to build "a villa and a church, which formed an entity"; he had lavished his munificence on the seven Armenian villages of Musa Dagh, which one year included a shipment of Singer sewing machines distributed among the poorest families.

On a visit to Antioch, Gabriel, despite his status as a Turkish citizen and a reserve officer who is prepared with pained regret to serve even against his beloved France, experiences an ugly humiliation as an Armenian; he also learns that his government has grisly plans for the Armenians. Though he could escape with his family, he chooses not to, somewhat to his own surprise. Instead, with other leaders, including the remarkable priest Ter Haigasun, he mounts a carefully planned, highly organized, and astonishingly successful resistance to crack Turkish units; though he encourages Juliette, his vacillating foreign wife, to leave in safety, she stays with him until the *deus ex machina* of the allied sea rescue.

Werfel's account of this resistance is vivid with horror as well as Wild West excitement and displays a sophisticated understanding of military tactics. As a child, Franz had loved playing cowboys and Indians and assiduously read Karl May's adventure tales. His intense early attraction to theater and opera in Prague found expression in the novel's cumulatively suspenseful plot. Like his hero, Werfel had been an artillery officer, if a reluctant one, and had won the Iron Cross for bravery on the Russian front in World War I. This experience serves well in Werfel's handling of scenes involving Turkish officers and soldiers among themselves.

Another skill he brings to bear on his exotic material involves research. Werfel, a European, very convincingly re-creates the atmosphere of life among his Armenians of Asia Minor. He succeeds because he has clearly done his homework; but if he were too much the dutiful student taking an examination, it would show. Instead, by scrupulously avoiding an anxious deployment of too many specific and nonfunctional details of local color, arcane custom, tradition, historical background and so on, he makes us forget we are in an alien place. He does this sort of thing so well, along with managing complex events involving "a cast of thousands," so to speak, that his fellow expatriate Thomas Mann described Werfel's 1941 best-seller, *The Song of Bernadette*, not without respect, as "a well-made bad book."

No Armenian of my acquaintance has ever complained that Werfel has got his Armenians wrong—a striking tribute when one considers the intensity of current ethnic sensitivities. There is the gently expressed reservation of Father Bezdikian, cited in Jungk's biography, who was certain that the provincial Armenians of Musa Dagh would never have accepted a leader with a foreign wife, and an unfaithful one at that. But it can be argued that Werfel anticipated this objection with dramatic scenes in which Gabriel's authority was put in severe doubt.

Gabriel's heroic real-life counterpart, Moses der Kaloustian, survived and resided in the city of Beirut until his death seventy years later in 1986 at the age of ninety-nine. A member of the Lebanese Parliament, he is said to have sought the floor only once in the course of many decades. His one-sentence utterance on that occasion was to ask the Speaker if it were not a bit chilly in the hall and could a window be closed. Of course heroes, being heroes, are under no obligation to speak. They have in effect already spoken and don't need to say anything anymore. Der Kaloustian, at the end of his life, seems to have paid Werfel the compliment of imitating his art. During the worst of the Lebanese travail in the 1980s, his family had arranged to leave Beirut for Cyprus. At the last moment, in a gesture reminiscent of the fictional Gabriel Bagradian, he turned away and said, *Go on without me.*

At the front in 1916, sensitive to the frightfulness of war, Werfel devoured Tolstoy. He emulates Tolstoy's methods of juxtaposing important historical characters such as Talaat, Jemal, and Enver with fictional characters, usually to the detriment of the former. Enver, with his Pan-Turanic aspirations, reminds one of the Napoleon of Tolstoy's *War and Peace*, as Gabriel could be a combination of Pierre and Prince Andrei. The historical figures are systematically demythologized, presented warts and all, with accent on the warts. Werfel is equally careful to give his Armenians weaknesses as well as strengths; his schoolteacher would-be hero Hrand Oskanian is a merciless portrait of the blustering coward.

For Werfel, heroes are ordinary people called to unconscious greatness, as his simple Bernadette Soubirous is called to sainthood at Lourdes, in *The Song of Bernadette*. All this simplicity on the parts of both creator and characters must have exasperated an ironic temperament such as Thomas Mann's. To one European critic for whom Werfel was at his best in the short novel form, his strongest fiction (*The Forty Days of Musa Dagh* aside) is the brief *Man Who Conquered Death*, in which an ordinary fellow is called to greatness unexpectedly, somewhat as Tolstoy's quintessentially bourgeois Ivan Ilych is heroically transformed. And here, too, Werfel depicts the passionately decent German pastor Johannes Lepsius as a man who could not possibly have mistaken himself for a hero, which is precisely wherein lies his heroism.

For Werfel, as for Tolstoy and Dostoevsky and against the modern secular current, religious idealism is *the* acutely positive force in the world. The great Rilke's admiration for the young Werfel's first books of poetry may be due partly to a common preoccupation with religion. Hence, for Werfel, the crucial importance of bearing witness in the historical case of Johannes Lepsius as well as in the fictional case of the noble Turkish Sufi, Agha Rifaat Bereket, who in extreme old age does all he can to rescue the Armenians of Musa Dagh; a Turkish patriot, Rifaat attempts to expiate the sin of his regrettably secular fellow Turks.

As unblinking as is Werfel's understanding of the horror of what is going on in his novel, his gentle and idealistic temperament leads him to create good as well as diabolical Turks. There is another reason for this as well, which is that he abjures ethnocentricity.

Yet Werfel's religious yearning does not prevent him from distinguishing between religious conviction and the cynical use of religion, in this case by the ruling triumvirate urging jihad, or holy war, on its people, à la Saddam Hussein. Werfel is cousin to Tolstoy in that for him orthodox religion requires infusions of creative renewal such as that offered by old Rifaat's Sufism or by the unsettling effect of a Bernadette on a complacent Establishment or, say, by anarchic Tolstoyan Christianity.

Perhaps the closest Werfel comes to creating a Dostoyevskyan, or modern alienated figure in the novel, that might satisfy a Thomas Mann is in his characterization of the nihilistic Sarkis Kilikian, who has been through so much horror at the hands of the Turks that nothing can matter; we are left with "the dead, agate shimmer of his eyes." Kilikian, however, like the putatively mysterious but somewhat fustian old witches Nunik, Vartuk, and Manushak, seems more willed than conceived out of some truly black psychic pool within Werfel; it is all so neatly done, and intelligently, too. Such an observation may also hold more pervasively true: When Werfel tries to replicate the inner states of being of his characters, we are occasionally too aware of an intelligent and psychologically sophisticated performance.

It is of course evident that a noble theme, authentic compassion, and a sense of historical urgency do not of themselves make literature. Writing in 1965, critic Frederick Karl finds the book "less a great novel than a portrait of a great ideal." But he adds that "it does wear very well indeed," and that while "it may be lacking as great fiction, it offers us a great vision." No matter how "well made," no matter how willed, this is nonetheless a large, resonant work which strikes transcendent chords, emanating forcefully from the depths of a terribly conflicted but also emblematic psyche. In his personal life, Werfel was pathetically debilitated by this sense of conflict, but the novel's gripping intensity derives from that fact, at least to a degree. If Gustave Flaubert, when asked who his Madame Bovary was in life, could say, "*Madame Bovary, c'est moi*," Werfel could say, "*Les Arméniens, c'est moi*." But Werfel, imploring us to be civilized, is asking us to take a further step, and to declare that we are all Armenians, in a sense.

Anyone who has seen the infamous German photograph of a young boy, arms raised above his head, being led at gunpoint from the Warsaw Ghetto in 1944, may be reminded of it as he reads the remark of one of the Musa Dagh rescuers: "I say, you know, these Armenians! I don't feel as though I'd been looking at people; nothing but eyes." And when at the very end, Werfel has Gabriel thinking that "to be an Armenian is an impossibility," one is tempted to think it could easily be Werfel himself, the European Jew writing under siege, really, in 1933, and thinking desperately how impossible it is to be a Jew.

Though Gabriel was a Christian Armenian, Werfel had much in common with his hero. Both were scions of wealthy businessmen suspicious of their sons' dilettantism. They were both highly educated assimilated Europeans. Where Werfel grew up in Prague and Vienna as the subject of an

Austro-Hungarian Empire in its twilight years, which was comprised of a disparate mix of ethnic groups often in turmoil, Gabriel was a member of one of several *millets* of "The Sick Man of Europe," the sprawling Ottoman Empire. Each had been an officer in an army of people not altogether his own; Gabriel was upset at the prospect of having to do battle against the French, and it is hard to imagine Werfel feeling enmity toward the Allies.

Gabriel's young son dies most hideously and Gabriel's last thought is of him. Werfel's son by Alma Mahler (who was still married at the time to the architect Walter Gropius) is born with a hydrocephalic head and dies in infancy. Strangely, many years later in 1945, a few days before his own death in Beverly Hills, Werfel completed the visionary and mystical novel, *Star of the Unborn*, in which his alter ego, F.W., recognizes the character Io-Squirt as an incarnation of his own long-dead child, Martin Johannes.

Werfel's Alma was the widow of the great composer Gustav Mahler, beloved of the important expressionist painter Oskar Kokoschka, who finally divorced the celebrated Gropius to marry Franz, whereas Juliette Bagradian has no such history. Still, there is an essential similarity between the two wives. The pampered Juliette lives as a Parisian creature of fashion, holding court among the Armenian village luminaries in her tent, or *pavillon*, in a fantastic imaginary world while reality boils over just outside. Alma Mahler-Werfel's chic, lavish parties continue in Vienna even after Werfel's books are being burned to the tune of the songs and marches of the brownshirts and the SS, along with the works of Freud, Marx, Schnitzler, and Stefan Zweig for being "un-German."

Juliette tries to be loyal to her husband's increasing identification with his own people, even to the extent of approving her son Stephan's avid interest in learning Armenian, but is, after all, a product of her environment:

"You may be an ancient people," she kept insisting, "*c'est bien*. A civilized people. No doubt. But in what precisely do you prove it? Oh, of course I've been told all the names . . . But who's ever heard of them? No one in the world except Armenians . . . You've never had a Racine or a Voltaire. And you have no Catulle Mendès, no Pierre Loti . . . Oh, well, I mustn't be too critical! They're really such nice people."

Trying to become friendly with an Armenian woman who has intrigued her, Juliette says: "I can't even bear brunettes at home. But you're not an Oriental, Iskuhi. Right now, sitting there against the light, your eyes look quite blue."

In contrast, Werfel's wife carries her ethnic contempt rather beyond the realm of nuance. The grossly anti-Semitic Alma, while claiming to find her Franz an extremely stimulating fellow, also describes him as a "fat bow-legged Jew," with "thick lips" and "liquid slit-eyes."

Jungk tells us that Werfel was at pains to follow the advice of his friend Ernst Polak not to model his Armenian characters after Jews of his acquaintance. But beyond this general principle, there are also significant, more individual differences between Gabriel and his creator.

While Werfel does not deny his Jewishness, his mistress is Catholicism. Or not? Is it—surprising thought—the other way around? Sometimes one feels that Werfel's *traife* may be Judaism. It is certainly worth noting that Franz, along with the sons of many Jewish families in Prague, attended an elementary school run by the Piarist order. He oscillates between finding a Jewish religious service an embarrassment and, on a trip to Jerusalem, studying the Talmud intensely and relearning Hebrew. In contrast, although Gabriel does once find some Armenian merchants in the bazaar of Antioch repugnant, his attitude toward his Armenian identity is generally not tortuous. If Thomas Mann's Tonio Kröger has a "deepest and secretest love" that belongs to the "blond and blue-eyed, the fair and living," Gabriel doesn't really know about such complexities.

Werfel writes that "Juliette had never observed the least sentimentality in Gabriel," whereas Werfel himself was given to rhapsodically lyrical outbursts, and it was not for nothing that he had an affinity for opera. Gabriel feels an almost fatherly pity for his wife's emptiness; there is no evidence of the infantile need Werfel seems to have felt for Alma, fourteen years his senior.

According to Ernst Polak, as transcribed by Jungk, "Werfel said, quite openly, 'Success! To me, success is practically identical with happiness.' " Werfel was opportunistic and so could not always face facts; Gabriel was not, and readily faced reality, which accounted in great measure for his military success against the Turks. Gabriel, though an artistic type, is not ambitious for himself and readily discovers in himself a capacity for self-transcendent commitment at the risk of his life when the force of circumstance throws this possibility into tragic relief.

It is for this reason that Gabriel stays when he could leave; he has unexpectedly discovered his vocation, like Johannes Lepsius, who was so admired by Werfel. Werfel was slow to leave also, for much different reasons. He temporized with the Nazis much longer than did his colleagues the Mann brothers, Arthur Döblin, Jakob Wassermann and the courageous

Ricarda Huch. It is true that, living in Austria, he was in a position to delay longer; still, he was in a position to see much more than he allowed himself to do. Already the day after the burning of the Reichstag, Werfel's first publisher, the distinguished Kurt Wolff, notes laconically in his journal: "Packed." Wolff left his successful career two days later, immediately penniless. Werfel seems to have found it rather more difficult to give up the imminent prospect of enjoying a best-seller in Germany (instead, he had to experience a hate campaign mounted by the German press), and seems to have relished disproportionately his appointment as Austrian Poet Laureate by his friend Chancellor Schuschnigg.

But it must not be forgotten that it was Werfel who created Gabriel along with an unforgettable gallery of struggling, unconsciously brave victims. He understood the facts and faced them with maturity in his fiction; what he could not resolve in life, he triumphantly resolved in art, and there is a tragic serenity to Gabriel's end that Werfel could not achieve for himself. These anguished figures were not Jews, but Christian Armenians. It is almost as if Werfel, who wanted, perhaps pathetically, to be Christian while remaining Jewish, had found a solution to his dilemma by identifying so resonantly with the Armenians of Musa Dagh. The subject triggered an artistically productive release; he had stumbled on a theme congruent with his own deepest, unresolved inner struggle.

In his biography of Werfel, Jungk describes a walk after school with the nursemaid Barbara Šimunková, a simple Czech Catholic woman in whose company Franz spent so many hours of his early life, long before he ever met Alma:

> They . . . hurried across the rebuilt Karlsbrücke with its statues of saints and a great crucifix encircled by gilded Hebrew letters. The inscription, Barbara told Franz, had been paid for by a Jew as a penalty for mocking the cross.

If we conceive of deep-rooted fear as being a source of opportunism, we may understand Werfel more lovingly than we might otherwise do—in the spirit of his fellow refugees from Hitler, who were fond of him. And it ought to be remembered that, to Armenians at least, he was not only a creator of heroes, but a hero himself. In *The Forty Days of Musa Dagh* he transformed his tormentedness, giving his own voice to mute, maimed children, and thus "snatched from Hades" their "incomprehensible destiny."

—Peter Sourian
Bard College
October 1990

BOOK ONE

COMING EVENTS

"How long, O Lord, holy and true, dost thou not judge and avenge our blood on them that dwell on the earth?"

REVELATION vi, 10

Teskeré

"How did I get here?"

Gabriel Bagradian really spoke these solitary words without knowing it. Nor did they frame a question, but something indefinite, a kind of ceremonious amazement, which filled every inch of him. The clear glitter of this Sunday in March may have inspired it, in this Syrian spring, which shepherded flocks of giant anemones down along the flanks of Musa Dagh and far out across the irregular plain of Antioch. Everywhere their bright blood sprang from the meadow slopes, stifling the more reticent white of big narcissi, whose time had also come. A golden, invisible humming seemed to have encased the mountain. Were these the vagrant swarms of the hives of Kebussiye, or was it the surge of the Mediterranean, audible in the bright transparency of the hour, eroding the naked back of Musa Dagh? The uneven road wound upwards, in and out among fallen walls. Then, where it suddenly ended in heaps of stone, it narrowed out into a sheep-track. He had come to the top of the outer slope.

Gabriel Bagradian turned. His shape, in rough European homespun, straightened itself, listening. He thrust the fez a little back off his damp forehead. His eyes were set wide apart. They were a shade lighter, but not in the least smaller than Armenian eyes usually are.

Now Gabriel saw what he had come from. The house gleamed out, with its dazzling walls, its flat roof, between the eucalyptus trees of the park. The stables, too, and the outhouses, glittered in this early morning sunshine. Although between Bagradian and his property there was now more than half an hour's walk, it still looked so close to him that it might have been following at his heels. And further along the valley the church of Yoghonoluk, with its big cupolas and pointed, gabled minarets at the sides, greeted him clearly. This solemn, massive church and Bagradian's villa formed an entity. Bagradian's grandfather, the fabled founder and benefactor, had built them both fifty years ago. It was the custom of Armenian peasants and craftsmen, after their journeys abroad —to America even—in search of profit, to return home, into the nest. But bourgeois grown rich had other notions. They built their luxury villas along the Riviera from Cannes, among the gardens of Heliopolis, or at least on the slopes of Lebanon, in the neighbourhood of Beirut. Old Avetis Bagradian had drawn a definite line of demarcation between himself and such new-rich. He, the founder of that world-famous Istanbul business, which had offices in Paris, New York, and London, resided, in so far as his time and affairs allowed him to do so, year after year in his villa above the hamlet of Yoghonoluk, under Musa Dagh. But not only Yoghonoluk; the other six Armenian villages of the district of Suedia had basked in the rich blessing of his kingly presence in their midst. Quite apart from the schools and churches built by him—from his summoning of American mission teachers—let it suffice to indicate the gift which in spite of every other event remained, even today, fresh in the memory of his people: that shipload of Singer sewing-machines which after a more than usually prosperous business year Avetis had distributed among fifty needy families in the villages.

Gabriel—he had still not turned his listening gaze away from the villa—had known his grandfather. He had been born in the house down there and spent many long months of his childhood in it. Till his twelfth year. And yet this early life, which was, after all, his own life, seemed so unreal that

4

it almost hurt to think of it. It seemed like a kind of life in the womb, the vague memories of which stir the soul to unwelcome shudderings. Had he really ever known his grandfather, or only read of him and seen his pictures in a story book? A little man with a white goatee, in a long black-and-yellow-striped silk gown. His gold eyeglass dangling from a chain upon his chest. In red shoes he had walked over the grass of the garden. Everyone bowed deeply. Tapered old man's fingers stroked the boy's cheeks. Had it all happened, or was it no more than empty dreaming? To Gabriel Bagradian his grandfather and Musa Dagh connoted the same. When a few weeks ago he had first beheld again that mount of his childhood, that darkening ridge against the sunset, he had been invaded by indescribable, terrifying, and yet delightful sensations. Their depths had refused to reveal themselves. He had at once given up the attempt. Had it been the first breath of a presentiment? Or only these twenty-three years?

Twenty-three years of Europe, Paris! Years of complete assimilation. They were as good as twice, or three times, that. They extinguished everything. After the old man's death his family, absolved at last from the local patriotism of its founder, had escaped this Oriental nook. The firm's head office was, and remained, Istanbul. But Gabriel's parents had lived with their two sons in Paris. Yet Gabriel's brother—he, too, had been called Avetis—about fifteen years Gabriel's senior, had soon disappeared. He went back to Turkey, as active partner in the importing-house. Not unfittingly had he been given his grandfather's name. With him, after some years of neglect, the villa in Yoghonoluk reassumed its seigniorial status. His one amusement had been hunting, and with Yoghonoluk as his base he set forth into the Taurus mountains and to the Harun. Gabriel, who scarcely had known his brother, had been sent to a Paris lycée and then to study at the Sorbonne. No one insisted on putting him into the business, to which he, a miraculous exception in his family, would not have been

5

suited in the least. He had been allowed to live as a scholar, a *bel esprit,* an archæologist, a historian of art, a philosopher, and in addition had been allotted a yearly income which made him a free, even a very well-to-do, man. Still quite young, he had married Juliette. This marriage had worked a profound change in him. The Frenchwoman had drawn him her way. At present he was more French than ever. Armenian still, but only in a sense—academically. Still, he did not forget it altogether, and at times published a scientific article in an Armenian paper. And, at ten years old, Stephan, his son, had been given an Armenian tutor, so that he might be taught the speech of his fathers. At first all this had seemed entirely useless, harmful even, to Juliette. But, since she happened to like young Samuel Avakian, she had surrendered, after a few retreating skirmishes. Their tiffs had always the same origin. Yet, no matter how hard Gabriel might try to concern himself with the politics of foreigners, he was still sometimes drawn back into those of his people. Since he bore a respected name, Armenian leaders, whenever they were in Paris, would come to call on him. He had even been offered the leadership of the Dashnakzagan party. Though he retreated in terror from this suggestion, he at least had taken part in that famous congress which, in 1907, united the Young Turks with Armenian nationalists. An empire was to be grounded in which the two races should live at peace side by side and not dishonour each other. Such an object excited even an alienated enthusiasm. In those days Turks had paid Armenians the most charming compliments, declaring their love. Gabriel, as his habit was, took these compliments more seriously than other people. That was why, when the Balkan war broke out, he had volunteered. He had been hastily trained in the school for reservist officers in Istanbul and had just had time to fight, as the officer of a howitzer battery, at the battle of Bulair. This one long separation from his family had lasted over six months. He had missed them greatly. He may have feared

6

that Juliette would slip away from him. Something seemed imperilled in their relationship though he could not have given a reason for any such feeling. He was a thinker, an abstract man, an individual. What did the Turks matter, what the Armenians? He had thoughts of taking French citizenship. That, above all, would have made Juliette happy. But always, in the end, the same vague uneasiness had prevented it. He had volunteered for the war. Even if he did not live in his country, he could at least always re-evoke it. His fathers' country.

These fathers had suffered in it monstrously and still not given it up. Gabriel had never suffered. Massacre and torture he only knew through books and stories. It is not, he thought, a matter of indifference which country even an abstract man belongs to. So he remained an Ottoman subject. Two happy years in a charming flat in the Avenue Kléber. It really looked as though all problems had been solved and his life taken on its final definite shape. Gabriel was thirty-five; Juliette, thirty-four; Stephan, thirteen. Their lives were untroubled, their work intellectual, they had some very pleasant friends. Juliette was the decisive factor in choosing them. This was chiefly evident in the fact that Gabriel's former Armenian acquaintances—his parents had been dead some time—came less and less frequently to the flat. Juliette, so to speak, insisted relentlessly on her blood-stream. But she could not manage to change her son's eyes. Yet Gabriel seemed to notice none of all this. An express letter from Avetis Bagradian gave a new direction to fate. His elder brother urgently begged Gabriel to come to Istanbul. He was a very sick man, he wrote, and no longer able to manage the business. So that for some weeks he had been making all preliminary arrangements to transform it into a limited company. Gabriel must be there to defend his interests. Juliette, whose habit it was to emphasize her knowledge of the world, had announced at once that she would like to accompany Gabriel and back him up

7

throughout the negotiations. Matters of great importance would be involved. But he was so simple by nature and certainly not up to the Armenian *ruses* of all the others. June 1914. An incredible world. Gabriel decided to take not only Juliette, but Stephan and Avakian, his tutor. The school year was nearly over. This business might prove long drawn out, and the ways of the world are unpredictable. In the second week of July they had all arrived in Constantinople.

But, even so, Avetis Bagradian had not been able to await them. He had sailed in a small Italian boat for Beirut. The state of his lungs had been going from bad to worse in the last weeks, with cruel celerity, and he could no longer stand the air of Istanbul. (Remarkable that this brother of Gabriel, the European, should have chosen Syria, not Switzerland, to die in.) So that Gabriel now, instead of dealing with Avetis, had to deal with directors and solicitors. Still, he soon perceived that this unknown brother had watched over his interests with the greatest tenderness and foresight. For the first time he grew intensely conscious of the fact that his ailing, elderly Avetis had been a worker on his behalf, the brother to whom he owed his well-being. What an anomaly that brothers should have been such strangers. Gabriel was appalled at the pride in himself which he had never managed to stifle, his scorn of "the Oriental," the "business man." Now he was seized with the wish—a kind of longing even—to repair an injustice while there was time. The heat in Istanbul was really unbearable. It did not seem wise at present to turn back westwards. "Let us wait till the storm has blown over." On the other hand the very thought of a short sea voyage was a tonic. One of the newest boats of the Khedival Mail would touch Beirut on its way to Alexandria. Modern villas were to let on the western slopes of Lebanon, of a kind to fulfil the most exacting requirements. Connoisseurs know that no landscape on earth has greater charms. But Gabriel had need of no such persuasions since Juliette agreed at once. In her,

8

for a long time now, some vague impatience had been accumulating. The prospect of something new enticed her. While they were still at sea, declarations of war had come rattling down between state and state. When they stood on the quay at Beirut, the fighting had already begun in Belgium, in the Balkans, in Galicia. Impossible now to think of going back to France. They stayed where they were. The newspapers announced that the Sublime Porte would enter into alliance with the Central Powers. Paris had become enemy country.

The real purpose of the journey proved unfulfillable. Avetis Bagradian had missed his younger brother a second time. He had left Beirut a few days before and undertaken the difficult journey, via Aleppo and Antioch, to Yoghonoluk. Even Lebanon did not suffice him to die in. It had to be Musa Dagh. But the letter in which his brother foretold his own death did not reach Gabriel until the autumn. Meanwhile the Bagradians had moved into a pleasant villa only a little way above the town. Juliette found life in Beirut possible. There were crowds of French people. The various consuls also came to call. Here, as everywhere else, she knew how to gather many acquaintances. Gabriel rejoiced, since exile did not seem to weigh too heavily on her. There was nothing to be done against it. Beirut, in any case, was safer than European cities. For the moment at least. But still Gabriel kept thinking of the house at Yoghonoluk. Avetis, in his letter, had implored him not to neglect it. Five days after the letter came Dr. Altouni's telegram, announcing his death. And now Gabriel not only thought, but constantly spoke of, the house of his childhood. Yet, when Juliette suddenly declared that she wanted to move as soon as possible into the house in which he had been a little boy and had now inherited, the thought scared him. Stubbornly she dismissed his objections. Country solitude? Nothing could be more welcome. Out of the world? Uncomfortable? She herself would see to all that. It was just what so attracted her.

Her parents had owned a country house, in which she had grown up. One of her pet dreams had always been to arrange a country house of her own, to manage it all *en châtelaine*—it made not the least difference where, in what country, it happened to be. In spite of all this vivacious eagerness Gabriel still opposed her till after the rainy season. Wouldn't it be far more prudent to get his family back to Switzerland? But Juliette held to her caprice. She became almost challenging. Nor could he repress a strange uneasiness mingled with longing. It was already December by the time they began to make arrangements to return to the house of his fathers. The train journey, in spite of the moving troops, was quite bearable as far as Aleppo. In Aleppo they hired two indescribable cars. Through the thick mud of district roads they arrived, as by a miracle, in Antioch. There, at the Orontes bridge, Kristaphor, the steward, was awaiting them with the hunting-trap of the house and two ox-carts for the luggage. Less than two hours on, to Yoghonoluk. They passed hilariously. It hadn't been half bad, declared Juliette. . . .

"How did I get here?" These surface combinations of events only seemed to answer the question very imperfectly. Gabriel's solemn amazement still remained. A vague restlessness vibrated through it. Antediluvian things, buried under twenty-three years in Paris, must be re-established in his mind. Only now did Gabriel turn his half-seeing eyes away from his house. Juliette and Stephan must certainly still be asleep. Nor had church bells in Yoghonoluk as yet proclaimed Sunday morning. His eyes followed this valley of Armenian villages a certain way northwards. From where he stood he could still see the village of the silkworms, Azir, but Kebussiye, the last village in that direction, had disappeared. Azir lay asleep in a dark bed of mulberry trees. Over there, on the little hill which nestles against the flank of Musa Dagh, stood the ruins of a cloister. Thomas the Apostle, in person, had founded that hermitage. The scattered stones bore strange inscriptions.

Once Antioch, the regent of the world of those days, had extended as far as to the sea. Everywhere the ground was strewn with antiques, or they rewarded the first turn of the excavator's spade. Gabriel had already in these few weeks gathered a whole collection of valuable trophies inside his house. The search for them was his chief occupation here. Yet, till now, some reverence had protected him from climbing the hill of St. Thomas's ruin. (It was guarded by great copper-coloured snakes, with crowns on their heads. Those who came sacrilegiously pilfering holy stones to build their houses found, as they carried them away, that the stones had grown into their backs, and so had to carry the load to the grave with them.) Who had told him that story? Once, in his mother's room (now Juliette's) old women had sat with curiously painted faces. Or was that only an illusion? Was it possible—had his mother in Yoghonoluk and his mother in Paris been the same?

Gabriel had long since entered the dark wood. A steep, wide gully, which led on up to the summit, had been cut into the mountain slope. They called it the ilex ravine. While Bagradian was climbing this sheep-track, which forced itself painfully upwards, through thick undergrowth, he knew suddenly: I have reached the end of the provisional. Something decisive is going to happen.

PROVISIONAL? Gabriel Bagradian was an Ottoman officer in the reserve of an artillery regiment. The Turkish armies were fighting for dear life on four fronts. Against the Russians in the Caucasus. Against the English and Indians in Mesopotamia. Australian divisions had been landed in Gallipoli, to force the gates of the Bosporus in conjunction with the Allied fleets. The fourth army, in Syria and Palestine, was preparing a fresh onslaught on the Suez Canal. It needed superhuman efforts to keep all these four fronts unbroken. Enver Pasha, that deified war-lord, had sacrificed two whole army corps to his madly daring campaign in Caucasian snows. Nowhere had the Turks enough officers. Their war material was inadequate.

For Bagradian the hopes of 1908 and 1912 were extinguished. Ittihad, the Young Turkish "Committee for Unity and Progress," had only made use of the Armenians, and at once proceeded to break every oath. Gabriel had certainly no reason to give especial proof of his Turkish patriotism. This time things were different in every way. His wife was French. He would therefore have to take up arms against a nation he loved, to which he owed the deepest gratitude, to which he was allied by marriage. None the less he had reported in Aleppo at the district headquarters of his former regiment. It had been his duty. Any other course would have meant that he could be treated as a deserter. But, strangely, the colonel in charge had seemed in no need of officers. He had studied Bagradian's papers very closely and sent him away again. He was to give his address and await his orders. That had been in November. This was the end of March, and still no orders had come from Antioch. Did that hide some impenetrable intention or merely the impenetrable chaos of a Turkish military office?

But, in that moment, Gabriel knew for certain that today would bring him a decision. On Sundays the post arrived from Antioch—not only newspapers and letters, but government orders from the Kaimakam to commoners and subjects.

Gabriel Bagradian was thinking solely of his family. The position was complicated. What was to happen to Juliette and Stephan while he was serving? Gabriel was delighted with Juliette's leniency. But not all her indulgence prevented the fact that his wife and son, if they stayed on alone here, would be cut off from the rest of the world.

The ilex grove was behind Bagradian before he had reached any further clarity on this point. The stamped-out path led northwards, losing itself on the mountain in a tangle of

12

arbutus and wild rhododendron. This part of Musa Dagh was called the Damlayik by the hill-folk. The two peaks to the south rose to about eight hundred metres. The Damlayik did not reach any considerable height. These two peaks formed the last ridges of the central mass, which then, unexpectedly, without regular gradations, fell sheer, as though broken off sharp, in huge stony cliffs, into the plain of the Orontes. Here in the north, where the wanderer was beginning to feel his way, the Damlayik was lower. Then it fell in a saddle-notch. This was the narrowest part of the whole mountainside along the coast—the waist of Musa Dagh. The plateau at the summit narrowed down to a few hundred yards, and the confusion of rocks on this steeply jutting side was thrust far out. Gabriel believed he knew every bush and rock. Of all the pictures of his childhood this place had imprinted itself most vividly. The same wide umbrella-pines, forming a grove. The same creeping gorse, which struggles over the stony ground. Ivy and other clinging plants embrace a circle of white stones, which, like the giant members of a senate of nature, break off their deliberations the instant an intruder's step is heard. A departing tribe of swallows twitters in the midst of the quiet. Excitement ripples the greenish, land-locked sea of air. As of leaping trout. The sudden spread and beat of wings is like the flicker of many eyelids.

Gabriel lay down in a grassy place, joining his hands behind his head. Twice already he had climbed Musa Dagh in search of these pines, these blocks of stone, but had lost his way. So they don't really exist, had been his thought. Now he closed tired eyes. When a human being comes back to any former place of contemplation and inner life, those spirits which he, the returned, once cherished and left there return and eagerly possess him. The ghosts of Bagradian's childhood rushed upon him, as though for twenty-three years they had waited faithfully under pines and rocks, in this charming wilderness, for him to return. They are warlike ghosts. The mad dreams

13

of every Armenian boy. (Could they be otherwise?) . . .
Abdul Hamid, the blood-stained Sultan, had issued a ferman
against Christians. The hounds of the Prophet, Turks, Kurds,
Circassians, rally to the green banners, to burn and plunder,
to massacre Armenian folk. But they had reckoned without
Gabriel Bagradian. He assembles his own. He leads them into
the mountains. With indescribable valour he fights off this
overwhelming power and beats it back.

Gabriel could not shake off these childish fantasies. He, the
Parisian, Juliette's husband, the *savant,* the officer minded to
do his duty as a Turkish subject, and who knew the realities
of modern warfare, was also, simultaneously, a boy who with
primitive blood-hate flung himself on the arch-enemy of his
race. The dream of every Armenian boy. To be sure it only
lasted an instant. But Gabriel marvelled and smiled ironically
before falling asleep.

BAGRADIAN started up with a certain fear. Someone had
watched him closely as he slept. Apparently he had been
asleep some time. He looked up, into the quietly glowing
eyes of Stephan, his son. Some distinctly unpleasant, even if
vague, sensation invaded him. It is not for a son to come upon
his father as he sleeps. Some profound law of custom had been
violated. His voice was rather sharp as he asked: "What are
you doing here? Where's Monsieur Avakian?"

Now Stephan, too, seemed embarrassed at having found his
father asleep. He did not quite know what to do with his
hands. His full lips opened. He was wearing schoolboy clothes,
a Norfolk jacket, short stockings, a wide collar out over the
coat. He tugged at his jacket as he answered: "Maman said
I could go for a walk by myself. This is Monsieur Avakian's
free day. We don't do any work on Sundays."

"We're not in France now, but in Syria, Stephan," his father
somewhat ominously explained. "Next time you mustn't come
straying about the hills alone."

14

Stephan eyed his father eagerly, as though in addition to this mild scolding he were expecting more important directions. But Gabriel said no more. An absurd embarrassment had possession of him. He felt as though this were the first time he had ever been alone with his son. He had not taken very much notice of him since their arrival here in Yoghonoluk and had usually only seen him at meals. True that in Paris or in the holidays in Switzerland he had often taken Stephan for walks. But is one ever alone in Paris? In Montreux, or Chamonix? In any case the limpid air of Musa Dagh contained a releasing element which seemed to bring them close together, in a proximity neither had ever known. Gabriel went onwards like a guide, familiar with all the important landmarks. Stephan came after, still expectantly silent.

Father and son in the East! Their relationship can scarcely be compared with the superficial contact of European parents and children. Whoso sees his father sees God. For that father is the last link in a long, unbroken chain of ancestors, binding all men to Adam, and hence to the origin of creation. And yet whoso sees his son sees God. For this son is the next link, binding humans to the Last Judgment, the end of all things, the consummation. Must not so holy a relationship be timid and sparing of words?

This father, as beseemed him, gave a serious turn to the conversation: "What subjects is Monsieur Avakian teaching you now?"

"We started reading Greek a little while ago, Father. And we do physics, history, and geography."

Bagradian raised his head. Stephan had said it in Armenian. But had he asked his question in Armenian? Usually they spoke French to one another. His son's Armenian words stirred the father strangely. He was conscious that in Stephan he had far more often seen a French than an Armenian boy.

"Geography?" he repeated. "And what continent are you on now?"

"Asia Minor and Syria," Stephan rather zealously announced.

Gabriel nodded approval, as though it was the best thing he could have said. Then, still a little absent-minded, he tried to round off their talk pedagogically: "Think you could draw a map of Musa Dagh?"

Stephan was pleased at so much paternal confidence. "Oh, yes, Dad. In your room there's one of Uncle Avetis's maps, you know. Antioch and the coast. You've only got to enlarge the scale and put in all that they leave out."

Quite right. For an instant Gabriel rejoiced in Stephan's intelligence. But then his thoughts strayed back to marching-orders, perhaps already on their way, or perhaps still buried on a Turkish office desk in Aleppo, in Istanbul even. A silent digression.

Stephan's expectant soul awaited another remark. This is Dad's country. He longed to be told stories of Dad's childhood, that secret time, of which they had so seldom told him anything. His father seemed to make for a definite point. And already they were near that peculiar terrace he had in mind. It extended, jutting straight out from the mountain, into a void. A mighty arm of rock upheld it on spread fingers, like a dish. It is a flat spur of granite strewn with stones, so wide that two houses could have been built on it. Sea storms, to be sure, which have here free play, scarcely tolerate a few shrubs on this rock, and a clump of Mexican grass, tough as leather. This overhanging, freely jutting terrace springs so far out that any suicide who had plunged to destruction from its edge into salt water, twelve hundred feet beneath, could have vanished unwounded by any rock. Young Stephan tried, of course, to run to the edge. His father pulled him sharply back and held his hand clasped very tight. His free right hand pointed out the four quarters of the globe.

"There to the north we could see the Gulf of Alexandretta if Ras el-Khanzir, the Swine cape, weren't in the way. And south there's the mouth of the Orontes, but the mountain takes a curve. . . ."

Stephan attentively followed the movements of his father's forefinger as it traced its half-circle of ruffled sea. But what he asked had nothing to do with the geography of Musa Dagh. "Dad—will you really go to the war?"

Gabriel did not even notice that he was still keeping tight hold of Stephan's hand. "Yes. I expect my orders any day."

"Have you got to?"

"Must, Stephan. All Turkish reserve officers are being called up."

"But we aren't Turks. And why didn't they call you up at once?"

"They say the artillery hasn't enough big guns at present. When the new batteries are set up, they'll be calling all the reservist officers."

"And where'll they send you?"

"I belong to the fourth army, in Syria and Palestine."

It consoled Bagradian to think that he might be sent for a certain time to Aleppo, Damascus, or Jerusalem. Perhaps there would be a chance of taking Juliette and Stephan. Stephan seemed to divine these fatherly cares.

"And what about us, Dad?"

"That's just it. . . ."

The boy fervently interrupted: "Leave us here, Dad—please leave us here. Maman likes our house as much as I do." Stephan was trying to pacify his father as to Maman's feelings here in a foreign country. His delicate alertness was well aware of the two opposing currents in their marriage.

But Bagradian reflected. "It would be best if I tried to send you both to Switzerland, via Istanbul. But unluckily that's also in the war zone."

Stephan clenched his fists across his heart. "No—not to Switzerland. Do let's stay, Dad!"

Gabriel looked at the pleading eyes of his son in some astonishment. Mysterious! That this boy, who never had known his father's home, should feel, none the less, so deeply bound to it. This emotion had lived in him, this affinity with the mountain of the Bagradians; Stephan, born in Paris, had inherited it with his very blood. He put his arm round the boy's shoulder, but only said: "We'll see."

When they got back to the flat plateau of the Damlayik, morning sounds from Yoghonoluk assailed them. It did not take more than another hour to reach the valley. They had to hurry to be in time for at least the second half of mass.

In Azir, the silkworm village, the Bagradians only met a few people, who passed them with morning greetings: "Bari luis"—"Good light." The inhabitants of Azir usually went to church in Yoghonoluk. In front of many houses there were tables with wide boards laid out on them. The silkworms' eggs were spread upon these boards, whitish masses hatching in the sun. Stephan learned from his father that old Avetis had been the son of a silk-spinner and had begun his career very early, at fifteen, by going to Baghdad to buy spawn.

Midway to Yoghonoluk the old gendarme, Ali Nassif, passed them. That worthy saptieh was one of the ten Turks who for many years had lived among the Armenians in these villages in peace and amity with them. Besides himself, the only Turks worth mentioning here were the five gendarmes at his orders, composing his gendarmerie post. They were often changed, but he remained, as firm as Musa Dagh itself. The only other representative of Ottoman authority was the deformed postman, who lived here with his family and on Wednesdays and Sundays brought the post in from Antioch.

Today Ali Nassif looked worried. This scrubby functionary of the Sublime Porte seemed to be in a very great hurry. His pock-marked face glistened with perspiration under his Turkish cap. His martial cavalry sword kept clattering against his bowed legs. Usually the sight of Bagradian Effendi was enough to make him turn a reverent face; today he only

18

saluted stiffly, though even his salute had a worried look. This change of manner struck Gabriel so, that for some minutes he stood looking after him.

A few stragglers were still hastening over the square before the church of Yoghonoluk—the late-comers who lived a long way off. Women in gaily patterned head-scarves and puffed-out coats. Men wearing the shalwar, in baggy trousers, and over these the entari, a kind of gaberdine. Their faces all looked serious and withdrawn. This sun had already the power of summer in it; the chalk-white houses glittered harshly. Most were single-storied and freshly daubed: Ter Haigasun's presbytery, the doctor's house, the apothecary, the big council-house, owned by the chief of Yoghonoluk's notables, that rich mukhtar Thomas Kebussyan. The Church of the Ever-Increasing Angelic Powers was built on a wide pediment. Unbalustered steps led up to its portals. Avetis Bagradian, its donor, had copied on a smaller scale a certain famous national edifice in the Caucasus. The voices of the choir, singing mass, flowed out through its open doorways. Away, beyond the dense congregation, the altar, pale with lit tapers, shone in the gloom. The gold cross gleamed on the back of Ter Haigasun's red vestment.

Gabriel and Stephan went up the steps. Samuel Avakian, Stephan's tutor, met them. He had been waiting impatiently.

"Go along in, Stephan," he ordered his pupil. "Your mother's waiting for you."

Then, when Stephan had vanished through the buzzing congregation, he turned quietly to his employer. "I only wanted to tell you that they've been here, asking for your passports. Travelling passport and passport for the interior. Three officials came from Antioch."

Gabriel glanced sharply at the student's face. He had lived for some years as one of the family. It was the face of an Armenian intellectual. A rather sloping forehead. Watchful, deeply troubled eyes behind glasses. An expression of eternal surrender to fate, but at the same time a sharp look of being on guard, ready every second to parry an attacker's blow. Only after a few instants' concentrated study of that face did Bagradian ask: "And what have you done?"

"Madame gave the officials all they wanted."

"Even the passport for the interior?"

"Yes, foreign passport and teskeré."

Gabriel turned back down the church steps to light a cigarette. He drew a few deeply reflective puffs. The passport for the interior is a document which gives its possessor freedom to move as he pleases over the length and breadth of the Ottoman empire. In theory, without this scrap of paper a subject of the Sultan has no right to move from his village into the next. Gabriel threw away his cigarette and straightened his shoulders with a jerk. "It only means that today or tomorrow I shall have to join my battery in Aleppo."

Avakian stood looking down at a deeply sunken wheel-rut, left by the last rains in the loam of the church square. "I don't think it means your marching orders for Aleppo, Effendi."

"It can't mean anything else."

Avakian's voice had become very quiet. "They made me give them mine, as well."

Bagradian, who had begun to laugh, checked himself. "That only means you'll have to go to Aleppo to be medically examined, my dear Avakian. This time it isn't a joke. But don't you worry. We'll manage the military tax again for you, all right. I need you for Stephan."

Still Avakian did not raise his eyes from the wheel-rut. "Dr. Altouni, Apothecary Krikor, and Pastor Nokhudian certainly aren't of military age, though I may be. They've all had their teskerés taken away from them."

"Are you certain of that?" Gabriel was beginning to lose his temper. "Who demanded them? What sort of officials? What grounds did they state? And where are these gentry, that's the main thing? I feel very much inclined to have a word with them."

He learned that it was nearly half an hour since the officials, escorted by mounted gendarmes, had vanished in the direction of Suedia. Judging by their demands it could only be a question of village notables, since the common craftsman and peasant owns no teskeré, but at most a written permission from the market in Antioch.

Gabriel took a few long strides to and fro, no longer noticing the tutor. At last he said to him: "Go on into church, Avakian. I'll follow you."

But he did not so much as think of hearing the rest of the mass, whose many-voiced choral that same instant came out to him in an especially loud burst of devotion. His head was on one side, sharply reflective, as he wandered back across the square, walked a little way down the village street, and left it where the road forked to the villa. Without even entering the house, he stopped at the stables to tell them to saddle one of his horses, which had once been the pride of Avetis, his brother. Unluckily no Kristaphor was there to accompany him. So he took a stable-boy. He had not yet made up his mind what to do.

But an hour's quick riding would get him to Antioch.

2

Konak—Hamam—Selamlik

THE Hükümet of Antioch, as the government konak of the Kaimakam was often called, stood under the hill of the citadel. A drab but extensive building, since the Kazah Antakiya is one of the most extensive Syrian provinces.

Gabriel Bagradian, who had left his boy with the horses at the Orontes bridge, had already waited some time in the big central office of the konak. He hoped to be received by the Kaimakam himself, to whom he had sent in his card.

A Turkish government office like all the others Gabriel knew so well; on the mottled wall, from which plaster was crumbling, a clumsy portrait of the Sultan and a couple of sayings from the Koran. Nearly every window-pane had been cracked and repaired with oil paper. The filthy deal floor strewn with gobbets of spittle and cigarette-ends. Some minor official sat behind an empty desk, sucking his teeth and gazing out into space. An unopposed legion of portly flies were engaged in a fierce, disgusting concert. Low benches ran round the walls. A few people were waiting—Turkish and Arab peasants. One, not too squeamish, squatted on the floor, spreading his long garments out around him, as though he could not embrace enough of its filth. A sour aroma like that of Russia leather, made up of sweat, stale tobacco, sloth, and poverty, infested the room. Gabriel knew that the district head offices of the various peoples had each its distinctive smell. But this stink of fear and kismet was common to all of

22

them—of little people receiving the impact of the state as a natural and monstrous force.

At last the gaudily patterned doorkeeper conducted him negligently into a small room, differing from the other by its rugs, its intact window-panes, its desk, thickly strewn with documents, its attempt at cleanliness. The walls displayed no portrait of the Sultan, but a huge photograph of Enver Pasha on horseback. Gabriel found himself facing a young man, with reddish hair, freckles, a small, military moustache. This was not the Kaimakam, only a müdir in charge of the coastal district, the nahiyeh of Suedia. The most noticeable thing about the müdir were his long, scrupulously manicured finger-nails. He was wearing a grey suit, which seemed a little too tight even for his measly person; with it a red tie and canary-yellow lace-up boots. Bagradian knew at once—Salonika! He had no reason for knowing it except the young man's outward appearance. Salonika had been the birthplace of the Turkish nationalist movement, of frantic Westernization, boundless reverence of Western progress in all its forms. Doubtless this müdir was a hanger-on, perhaps even a member of Ittihad, that secretive *"Comité pour l'union et le progrès,"* which today held unimpeded dominion over the Caliph's state. He was excessively polite to his visitor. He got up and himself brought the chair to the desk. Most of the time his red-rimmed eyes, with the sparse lashes of red-haired people, looked past Bagradian.

Gabriel rather stressed his name. The müdir nodded, almost imperceptibly. "The highly esteemed Bagradian family is known to us."

It cannot be denied that his tone and words produced a certain glow of satisfaction in Gabriel, whose voice became more assured. "Today certain citizens of my village—I was among them—have had our passports taken away. Is that official? Did you know of it?"

After long reflection and fumbling among documents, the

müdir announced that, with all the press of official business, he found it impossible to put his hand on every trifle directly. At last light dawned. "Oh, yes, of course. The passports for the interior. That's not an independent ruling of the kazah—it's a new order from His Excellency the Minister of the Interior."

Now at last he had found the crumpled sheet, which he spread in front of him. He seemed willing, on request, to read the full text of this decree of His Excellency Taalat Bey. Gabriel asked if the order were to be generally applied. The answer sounded rather evasive. The mass of people would scarcely be affected by it, since usually only the richer shop-keepers, merchants, and such like owned a pass for the interior.

Gabriel stared at the long finger-nails. "I've lived most of my life abroad, in Paris——"

Again the official slightly inclined his head. "We know that, Effendi."

"And so I'm not very used to these deprivations of liberty."

The müdir smiled an indulgent smile. "You over-rate the matter, Effendi. This is war-time. And nowadays even German, French, and English citizens find they have to submit to a great deal to which they used not to be accustomed. All over Europe it's much the same as it is here. May I also remind you that this is the war zone of the fourth army, and therefore a military area? It's absolutely essential to keep some control of people's movements."

These reasons sounded so cogent that Gabriel Bagradian felt relieved. That morning's event, which had brought him to Antioch, suddenly seemed to lose its astringent quality. He had been hearing rumours everywhere of traitors, deserters, spies. The state had to protect itself. Impossible to judge such measures as this by the hole-and-corner methods of Yogho-noluk. And the müdir's further observations were of a kind to allay Armenian mistrust. The Minister had, to be sure, withdrawn all passports, but this did not mean that, in certain

24

cases, new ones might not be procurable. The vilayet office in Aleppo was the competent authority for these. Bagradian Effendi must know himself that the Wali, Djelal Bey, was the most just and benevolent governor of the whole empire. A request, backed by recommendations from these offices, would be sent to Aleppo. . . . The müdir broke off: "Unless I'm mistaken, Effendi, you're liable for military service."

Gabriel gave a short account of the matter. Yesterday, perhaps, he might still have asked the official to find out why no marching-orders had reached him. But the last few hours had altered everything. The thought of war—of Juliette and Stephan—oppressed him. His sense of duty as a Turkish officer had evaporated. He hoped now that the battery in Aleppo had forgotten him and he felt no desire to attract attention. But it struck him how well informed these Antioch officials seemed to be, of all that concerned him.

The müdir's red-rimmed eyes transmitted his satisfaction. "So that now, Effendi, you are, so to speak, a soldier on leave. So, for you, there can be no question of any teskeré."

"But my wife and son . . . ?"

As he said this (it seemed to mystify the müdir), Gabriel felt for the first time: "We're in a trap. . . ."

That same instant the double doors into the next office were pushed open. There entered two gentlemen. One was an elderly officer; the other, doubtless, the Kaimakam. This provincial governor was a big, puffy-looking man, in a grey, crumpled frock-coat. Heavy, dark-brown pouches under the eyes, in the sallow face of a dyspeptic. Bagradian and the müdir rose. The Kaimakam paid not the least attention to the Armenian. In a low voice he gave some directions to his subordinate, raised a hand carelessly to his fez, and, followed by the major, walked out of the office, since he seemed to have finished his day's work.

Gabriel stared at the door. "Are you making distinctions between officers, then?"

25

The müdir had begun to tidy his desk. "I don't quite know what you mean, Effendi."

"I meant, are Turks and Armenians to be given separate treatment?"

This seemed to horrify the müdir. "Every Ottoman subject is equal before the law."

That, he continued, had been the most important achievement of the revolution of 1908. That certain habits of pre-revolutionary days should still persist—as for instance the preferential treatment of Ottomans in military and government offices—that was one of the things that could never be altered by act of parliament. Peoples did not change as quickly as did their constitutions, and reforms were far easier on paper than in reality. He concluded his excursion into political theory: "The war will bring a great may important changes."

Gabriel took this for a hopeful prophecy. But the müdir suddenly jerked his freckled face, which, for no apparent reason, was twitching with hate.

"Meanwhile let us hope that no incidents will force the government to relentless severity with certain sections of the populace."

WHEN Gabriel Bagradian turned into the bazaar at Antioch, he had made up his mind on two points. If they called him up, he would not shrink from any sacrifice to buy himself clear of the army. And he would await the end of the war in the peace and quiet of his house at Yoghonoluk, unmolested and unperceived. Surely, since this was the spring of 1915, it could only be a few months before peace was signed. He reckoned on September or October. Surely none of the Powers would dare another winter campaign. Till peace he would have to make the best of things and then—back to Paris, as fast as possible.

The bazaar bore him along. That deep surge which knows none of the ebb and flow, the hurry, of a crowd along a European pavement, which rolls on with an irresistible, even motion, as time flows on into eternity. He might not have been in this God-forsaken provincial hole, Antakiya, but transported to Aleppo or Damascus, so inexhaustibly did the two opposing streams of the bazaar surge past each other. Turks in European dress, wearing the fez, with stand-up collars and walking-sticks, officials or merchants. Armenians, Greeks, Syrians, these too in European dress, but with different headgear. In and out among them, Kurds and Circassians in their tribal garb. Most displayed weapons. For the government, which in the case of Christian peoples viewed every pocket-knife with mistrust, tolerated the latest infantry rifles in the hands of these restless mountaineers; it even supplied them. Arab peasants, in from the neighbourhood. Also a few bedouins from the south, in long, many-folded cloaks, desert-hued, in picturesque tarbushes, the silken fringes of which hung over their shoulders. Women in charshaffes, the modest attire of female Moslems. But then, too, the unveiled, the emancipated, in frocks that left free silk-stockinged legs. Here and there, in this stream of human beings, a donkey, under a heavy load, the hopeless proletarian among beasts. To Gabriel it seemed always the same donkey which came stumbling past him in a coma, with the same ragged fellow tugging his bridle. But this whole world, men, women, Turks, Arabs, Armenians, Kurds, with trench-brown soldiers in its midst—its goats, its donkeys—was smelted together into an indescribable unity by its gait—a long stride, slow and undulating, moving onwards irresistibly, to a goal not to be determined.

And Gabriel smelt the savours of his childhood. The whiff of seething oil of sesame, which came in sharp gusts across the street through crevices in the herbalists' vats, the onion-laden reek of mutton fricassees, simmering over open fires. The stench of rotting vegetables. And of humanity, more noisome than all the rest, which slept in the clothes it wore by day.

He recognized the yearning cries of the street-venders: Jâ rezzah, jâ kerim, jâ fettah, jâ alim—so the boy who offered for sale his rings of white bread from a basket still chanted sentimentally.—"O All-Nourisher, O All-Good, O All-Provident, O Knower of all things." The ancient cry of the ages still proffered fresh dates—"Thou brown one, O brown of the desert, O maiden." The salad-vender retained his throaty conviction: "Ed daim Allah, Allah ed daim"—that the Everlasting alone was God, that God alone was the Everlasting—some consolation, in view of his wares, to the purchaser. Gabriel bought a berazik, a little cake spread with grape syrup. This "food for swallows" also brought its memories of childhood. But the first bite of it turned his stomach, and he gave the sweetmeat to a youngster who had stood in rapture, eyeing his mouth.

His heart sank so, that for an instant he had to close his eyes. What could have happened to change the world so completely? Here, in this country, he had been born. Surely he ought to feel at home here. But—the irresistible, evenly moving crowd in the bazaar seemed to put his home at enmity with him. And that young müdir? Surely he had been scrupulously polite. . . . "The highly esteemed Bagradian family . . ." Yet in a flash Gabriel knew for a certainty that this suavity and its "highly esteemed family" had been no more than a single piece of insolence. It had been worse—hate masked as courtesy. This same hate flowed around him here. It seared his skin, galled his back. And indeed his back was suddenly panic-stricken, with the panic of a man hunted by enemies, without a soul to befriend him in the world. In Yoghonoluk, apart, in the big house, he had known nothing of all that. And before, in Paris? There, in spite of all his prosperity, he had lived in the cool spaces surrounding aliens, who strike root anywhere. Had he struck root here? Here for the first time, in this mean bazaar, at home, he could measure fully the absolute degree of his alien state upon this earth. Armenian! In him an ancient blood-stream, an ancient people. But why did his thoughts more often speak French than Armenian—as for instance now? (And yet that morning he had felt a distinct thrill of pleasure when his son answered him in Armenian.) Blood-stream, and people. To be honourable. Were not these mere empty concepts? Human beings in every age have strewn the bitter bread of existence with a different spice of ideas, only to make it still more unpalatable. A side-alley of the bazaar came into view. Most of its venders were Armenians, standing before their shops and booths: money-changers, carpet-sellers, jewellers. So these were his brothers, then? These battered faces, these glistening eyes, alert for custom? No, many thanks, he refused such brotherhood, everything in him rebelled against it! But had old Avetis Bagradian been anything other, or better, than such as these?—even though he were more far-sighted, gifted, energetic. And had he not his grandfather alone to thank that he was not forced to live as they? He went on, shuddering with repugnance. Then he was suddenly conscious of the fact that one of the great difficulties of his life sprang from the circumstance that nowadays he saw so much through Juliette's eyes. So that not only in the world was he an alien, but within himself, the instant he came into contact with other people. Jesus Christ! Couldn't one be an individual, free from all this seething, stinking hostility, as one had that morning on Musa Dagh?

Nothing more unnerving than such a test of one's reality. Gabriel fled from the Usun Charshy, the Long Market, as the Turks called the bazaar. He could no longer endure its hostile rhythm. He found himself in a little square, composed of new buildings. A pleasant-looking house leapt to his eyes, hamam, the steam-bath, arranged, as everywhere in Turkey, with a certain luxury. It was still too early to call on the old Agha Rifaat Bereket. And, since he felt no inclination to go into one of the dubious restaurants, he turned into the bath.

He spent twenty minutes in the big steam-room amid slowly mounting vapours, which not only made the other bathers look like far-off ghosts, but seemed even to divorce him from his own body. It was a kind of minor death. He could feel this day's impenetrable significance.

In the cooling-room next door he lay down on one of the bare couches to submit to the usual treatment after a bath. Now he felt more naked than he had before in the steam. An attendant hurled himself upon him and began, according to all the rules of his art (which truly is one), to knead his flesh. With resonant smackings he played on Gabriel's rump as on cymbals, humming and panting as he did it. A few Turkish beys, on the other pallets, were undergoing similar treatment. They surrendered to it with gasps of dolorous pleasure. At intervals, interrupted by grunts of pain, their voices talked in broken phrases through the angry zeal of the masseurs. Gabriel had at first no wish to listen. But, mingled with the hummings of his torturer, their voices assailed him inescapably. They sounded so individual, so sharply distin-guished from one another, that he felt as though he could see them.

The first, a well-fed bass. No doubt a very self-assured gentle-man, to whom it was highly important to know the ins and outs of everything—if possible, even before the officials con-cerned. This man of information had secret sources. "The English sent him in a torpedo-boat, from Cyprus to the coast. . . . That was near Oshalki. . . . The fellow brought money and arms and was seven days nosing about the village. . . . Of course, the saptiehs didn't know anything. . . . I can even give you the names . . . Köshkerian is the name of the unclean swine."

The second voice, high and flurried. An elderly, peaceable little gent, who always did his best to be optimistic. The voice seemed somehow not so tall as the other, as though it were looking up at it. Its interjections of pleasurable pain were framed to an august verse of the Koran: "La ilah ila 'llah. . . . God is great. . . . We can't have that sort of thing. . . .

But it may not be true . . . la ilah ila 'llah . . . one hears all kinds of things . . . This is probably only a rumour."

The well-fed bass, contemptuously: "I have very serious letters from a highly placed personage . . . a close friend."

Third voice. That of a strident amateur politician, who seemed to find it highly satisfactory that things in the world should be so unsettled. "We can't let it go on much longer. . . . We shall have to finish it. . . . What's the government there for? What about Ittihad? . . . The unfortunate thing is this conscription. . . . We've even armed the curs. . . . Now, how do you think we'll be able to deal with them? . . . The war . . . For weeks I've shouted myself hoarse."

Fourth voice, heavy with the cares of state: "And Zeitun?"

The peaceable voice: "Zeitun? Why, what do you mean? . . . Good heavens. . . . What's been happening in Zeitun?"

The politician, ominously: "In Zeitun? . . . Why, the news has been posted up in every reading-room of the Hükümet. . . . Anyone can convince himself . . ."

The informative bass: "The reading-rooms established everywhere by the German consulates . . ."

A fifth voice, interrupting from the farthest pallet: "We ourselves established them."

An indistinct tangle of obscure allusions: "Köshkerian— Zeitun . . . We've got to finish it . . ."

But Gabriel understood, without knowing the details. As the bath attendant dug his two fists into his shoulders, these Turkish voices roared in his ears like water. Acute shame. He who a short time ago had passed the Armenian shopkeepers in the bazaar with such a shiver of repugnance felt himself now to be involved, answerable for the destiny of his people.

Meanwhile the bather farthest away from him had heaved himself, groaning, off his pallet. He gathered up his burnous, which served as a bath-gown, and, on toddling feet, ambled a few steps about the room. Gabriel could see only that he was

31

tall and stout. His consequential way of speech, the respect
with which they heard him out, made Gabriel conclude that
this was a very wealthy man.

"People are unjust to the government. Impatience alone
does not suffice to determine policy. The true state of affairs
is very different to what the uninformed masses suppose it to
be. Treaties, capitulations, considerations of all kinds, foreign
opinion. . . . But let me assure the beys in confidence that
orders have just been issued by the War Office, by His Excellency Enver Pasha in person to the district military authorities,
to disarm melun ermeni millet (the treacherous Armenian
race)—that is to say, to recall Armenians from the firing-line
and degrade them to the basest tasks—road-making, carrying loads. . . . Such is the truth. . . . But it must not be
mentioned."

"I can't let it pass. I won't swallow that," Gabriel said to
himself. Another voice warned him quietly: "You yourself
are the persecuted." But some dark force, which drew him up
from the pallet, decided the struggle. He pushed the attendant
to one side and sprang on to the tiles. He tied the white
towel around his loins. His face aglow with rage, his hair
disordered from the bath, his broad chest, seemed not to belong to the gentleman who, that morning, had worn tourist's
tweeds. He planted himself squarely before the rich man.
Suddenly, by the dark bags under the eyes, the liverish face,
he knew the Kaimakam. The sight only served to increase his
fury.

"His Excellency Enver Pasha and his whole staff had their
lives saved in the Caucasus by Armenian troops. He was as
good as taken prisoner by the Russians. You know that as
well as I do, Effendi. You also know that His Excellency, in
a letter to the Catholicos of Sis, or to the Bishop of Conia,
praised the valour of sadika ermeni millet (the loyal Armenian
people). This letter was posted up by government order. That
is the truth. And whosoever poisons that truth by spreading

rumours is weakening the conduct of the war, destroying our unity, is an enemy of the empire, a traitor. I, Gabriel Bagradian, tell you this, an officer in the Turkish army."

He stopped, and waited for the answer. But the beys, non-plussed by this wild outburst, did not utter a word—not even the Kaimakam, who only drew his burnous more tightly around his nakedness. So that Gabriel could get out of the bath victorious, although still shaking with excitement. As he dressed, he was already aware that this was the stupidest thing he had ever done. Now the way to Antioch was barred. And it was the only way in, or out, of the world. He ought, before offending the Kaimakam, to have considered Juliette and Stephan. Yet he could not altogether reproach himself.

His heart was still beating fast as the Agha Rifaat Bereket's servant conducted him into the selamlik, the reception-room of this cool Turkish house. Gabriel walked up and down over wide vistas of carpet lost in the gloom. His watch, which, idiotically, he still kept set to European time, pointed to the second hour of the afternoon. It was, therefore, the sacred domestic hour, the hour of kef, the never-to-be-encroached-on midday peace, in which every visit was a very serious piece of tactlessness. He had got here far too early. And the Agha, a stickler for the forms of old-Turkish etiquette, allowed him to wait.

Bagradian walked to and fro, from one end to the other of this almost empty apartment, in which, besides two long divans, there were only braziers and a little table for cups. He justified his discourtesy to himself.—There's something brewing, I don't quite know what it is, but I haven't a minute to waste till I get it clear.—Rifaat Bereket had been a friend of the house of Bagradian from its origins, even in the palmy days of old Avetis. Some of Gabriel's pleasantest, most respectful memories centred upon him. He had called on him twice since coming to stay in Yoghonoluk. The Agha had not only helped him to make purchases, but from time to time would send him agents with offers, at absurdly low prices, of rare finds for his collection of antiques.

The master of the house, who entered noiselessly on thin slippers made of goatskin, found Gabriel talking to himself. The Agha Rifaat Bereket, over seventy, with a white goat-beard and thin features, half-shut eyes, and small, shimmering hands, wore a yellow scarf around his fez. It was the emblem of the Moslem who performs his religious duties more exactly and regularly than the many. This old man's little hands waved in ceremonious welcome; they touched his heart, his mouth, his forehead. Gabriel was equally ceremonious. No impatience would have seemed to tighten his nerves. The Agha came nearer and stretched forth his right hand towards his visitor's heart, so that his finger-tips just rested on Gabriel's chest. This was the "heart-felt contact," the closest form of personal sympathy and mystic usage, which pious men of a certain order of dervishes have adopted. The small white hand gleamed whiter still in the pleasant twilight of the selamlik. Gabriel fancied this hand a face, even perhaps more sensitive and delicate than the actual one.

"Friend, and son of my friend"—the long-drawn emphasis of this was still a part of the ceremony of welcome—"your visiting-card has already come to me as a pleasantly unexpected gift. Now your presence itself brightens the day for me." Gabriel, who knew his manners, found the right formula for reply.

"My deceased parents very soon left me alone. But in you I find a living witness of their memory and fond attachment. How happy am I to possess in you a second father."

"I am in your debt." The old man led his guest to the divan. "Today you honour me for the third time. It has long been my undischarged duty to await you as a visitor in your house. But you see in me an old and infirm man. The road to Yoghonoluk is bad and long. And, besides, a long and urgent

34

journey lies before me for which I must spare my limbs. Forgive me, therefore."

This ended the ritual of reception. They sat down. A boy brought coffee and cigarettes. They sipped and smoked in silence. Custom ordained that this young visitor must wait for the old man to give him an opening to direct the conversation as he desired. But the Agha did not yet seem inclined to emerge out of his own twilit world into any reality of the day. He signed to his serving-boy, who handed the master a small leather case, which he held in readiness. Rifaat Bereket pressed a spring, and the case flew open; his thin, old fingers stroked the satin, which embedded two ancient coins, one silver, the other gold.

"You are a very learned man, who has studied at the Paris university, a decipherer and knower of inscriptions. I am only an uneducated lover of antiquity, who could never vie with you. But in the last few days I have had these trifles prepared as a gift for you. The one, the silver coin, was struck a thousand years ago by that Armenian king whose name resembles that of your family, Ashod Bagrathuni. It comes from the neighbourhood of Lake Van, and they are rarely found. The other, the gold, is of Hellenic origin. You can decipher the profound and beautiful inscription, even without a magnifying-glass:

" 'To the inexplicable, in us and above us.' "

Gabriel Bagradian rose to take the gift. "You shame me, Father. Really I do not know how to thank you. We have always been proud of bearing a similar-sounding name. How plastic the head is! A real Armenian head. And one should wear the Greek coin round one's neck as an admonition. 'To the inexplicable, in us and above us.' What philosophers those must have been who paid their way in coins like these. How low we have sunk!"

The Agha nodded, pleased indeed with so conservative a sentiment. "You are right. How low we have sunk!"

35

Gabriel laid the coins back on the satin. But it would have been impolite too soon to change the subject of the gift. "I would beg you to choose yourself a present in exchange from among my collection of antiques. But I know that your belief forbids you to set up any image that casts a shadow."

On this point the old man lingered with unmistakable satisfaction. "Yes, and for that very reason you Europeans despise our holy Koran. Is there not supreme insight concealed in this law, which forbids all statues that cast shadows? The imitation of the Creator and His creation is the first beginning of that wild pride in men which leads on to destruction."

"These times and this war seem to show us that your prophet was in the right, Agha."

This conversational bridge extended its curve towards the Agha. He began to cross it. "Yes, so it is. Man, as the insolent imitator of God, as technician, falls into atheism. That is the deepest reason for this war into which the West has dragged us. To our misfortune. Since what have we to gain by it?"

Bagradian tested the next step. "And they have infected Turkey with their most dangerous pestilence—racial hatred."

Rifaat Bereket tilted his head a little backwards. His soft fingers were playing listlessly with the beads of his amber rosary. It was as if these hands emitted a faint aureole of sanctity. "It is the worst of doctrines, to bid us seek our own faults in our neighbours."

"God bless you! To seek our own faults in our neighbours. This doctrine has possession of all Europe. But today, alas, I have had to learn that it has its adepts even among Turks and Moslems."

"To which Turks do you refer?" The Agha's fingers suddenly ceased to tell his beads. "Do you mean that absurd pack of imitators at Istanbul? And the imitators of those imitators? The apes in frock-coats and dinner-jackets? Those traitors, those atheists, who would annihilate God's universe itself, merely in order to get money and power? Those are neither Turks nor Moslems. They are mere empty rascals and money-grubbers."

Gabriel lifted the tiny coffee cup, in which by now there was only thick sediment. An embarrassed gesture. "I admit that years ago I sat together with these people, because I expected good things from them. I took them for idealists, and, perhaps, in those days they really were so. Youth always believes in everything new. But today, alas, I am forced to see the truth as you see it. Just now, in the hamam, I heard a talk which troubles me greatly. That is the reason why I visit you at this unseemly hour."

The Agha's perspicacity needed no closer indication. "Was this talk of the secret army order degrading Armenians to street-sweeping and service as porters?"

Gabriel Bagradian deciphered the flowery riddle of the carpet at his feet. "Even this morning I still awaited orders to join my regiment. . . . Then there was also some talk of the town of Zeitun. Help me. What exactly is happening? What has occurred?"

The amber beads were again flowing evenly through the Agha's fingers. "As to Zeitun, I am well informed. What has happened there happens every day in the mountains. Some affair of thieving hordes, deserters and saptiehs. There were a few Armenian deserters. Before, nobody noticed such things." His voice was more deliberate as he added: "But what are occurrences? They are only what interpretation makes of them."

Gabriel seemed about to lose control. "That's just it. In the solitude in which I live no news of it reached me. The basest interpretations are being attempted. What does the government intend?"

The sage put aside these indignant words with a weary movement of the hands. "I will tell you something, friend and son of my friend. A karmic destiny hovers over you, since a

37

part of you belong to the Russian empire, the other part of you to us. The war has cleft you. You are dispersed among the nations. . . . Yet since, in this world, all things interpenetrate, we too are submitted to your destiny."

"Would it not be better to do as we did in 1908 and strive to reconcile and adjust?"

"Reconcile? That is no more than an empty word used by worldlings. On earth there is no reconciliation. We live here in corruption and self-assertion."

And, to confirm this view, the Agha, in prescribed singsong, quoted a verse of the sixteenth sura: "And He created the earth diverse in colour; see, there is in this truly a sign, for those that can take warning."

Gabriel, who could no longer sit quiet on the divan, stood up. The old man's astonished eyes, reprimanding so arbitrary a movement, forced him to sit again.

"You wish to know the government's intentions? I only know that the atheists in Istanbul need racial hatred for their purposes, since the deepest essence of all godlessness is fear, and the sense of having lost the game. So that now, of every little city, they make a sounding-box of rumours, to spread abroad their evil will. It is good you have come to me."

Gabriel's right hand tightened round the case with the coins. "If it were only I . . . But, as you know, I am not alone. My brother Avetis died without issue, so that my thirteen-year-old son is the last of our family. Moreover, I have married a Frenchwoman, who must not be dragged into this calamity, which does not concern her."

The Agha dismissed this plea with some severity. "She belongs to your nation, since you have married her, and cannot be absolved from its karma."

It would have been a vain attempt to explain to this confirmed Oriental the feminine independence of the West. So Bagradian ignored this objection. "I should have sent my family abroad, or at least to Istanbul. But now they have taken away our passports, and I can expect nothing good from the Kaimakam."

The Turk placed his right hand on his guest's knee. "I must seriously warn you not to go to Istanbul with your family, even if you should find the journey possible."

"What do you mean? Why? In Istanbul I have friends of all kinds, even in government circles. There our business has its central office. My name is very well known there."

The hand on Gabriel's knee became heavier. "For that very reason—because you are so well known there—I would warn you against even a short stay in the capital."

"Because of the fighting in the Dardanelles?"

"No. Not because of that." The Agha's face became inscrutable. Before continuing, he listened to some inner voice. "No one can tell how far the government may go. But this much is certain—the great and respected among your people will be the first to suffer. And it is equally certain in such a case that arrests and accusations will be begun in the capital."

"Do you speak by hearsay, or have you any certain grounds for your warning?"

The Agha let his amber beads vanish into his wide sleeve. "Yes, I have certain grounds."

Now Gabriel could no longer control himself and sprang up. "What shall we do?"

"If I may advise you—go home to your house in Yoghonoluk, stay there in peace, and wait. You could not have chosen a pleasanter place of sojourn for yourself and your family, in the circumstances."

"In peace?" Gabriel cried out scornfully. "It is already a prison."

Rifaat Bereket turned away his face, perturbed by this loud voice in the quiet selamlik. "You must not lose your self-control. Forgive me if my candid words have wounded you. You have not the least reason for anxiety. Probably it will all vanish in sand. Nothing bad can happen in our vilayet, since,

God be praised, Djelal Bey is the Wali. He submits to no high-handed measures. Yet whatever is to come is there already, enfolded within itself, like bud, blossom, and fruit within the seed. What will happen to us has happened already in God."

Riled by these flowery theological commonplaces, Bagradian, careless now of forms, paced up and down. "The most horrible thing is that there is nothing to hold on to—nothing to fight against."

The Agha approached the distraught Gabriel, to hold his two hands firmly within his own. "Never forget, my friend, that the blasphemous knaves from your Committee are no more than a very small minority. Our people is a kindly people. If again and again blood has been shed in anger, you yourselves are no less guilty of that than we. And then— there are enough men of God who live in the tekkehs, in the cloisters, and fight for the purity of the future within their holy circles of prayer. Either they win or we all perish. I must tell you, too, that my journey to Anatolia and Istanbul is to be made on behalf of the Armenians. I implore you to trust in God."

The Agha's little hands were strong enough to pacify Gabriel. "You are right. I will do as you say. Best to creep back into Yoghonoluk and not stir again till the war is over."

Still the Agha did not let go of his hands. "Promise me that at home you will say no word of all these things. After all, why should you? If all goes as before, you will only have frightened people unnecessarily. If any evil should come upon you, the fear of it will have been of no avail. You understand me—trust, and keep silence."

And in taking leave he repeated urgently: "Trust, and keep silence. . . . You will not see me again for many months. But think that in all that time I shall be working for you. I received much kindness from your fathers. And now, in my age, God is permitting me to be grateful."

40

3

The Notables of Yoghonoluk

THE ride home took some time, since Gabriel seldom galloped his horse and kept letting it slow down to its own pace. This also led to his straying off the shortest road and remaining on the highroad along the Orontes. Only when, beyond the clustered houses of Suedia and El Eskel, the far sea-line came into sight, did the rider start out of his dream and turn off sharply northwards, into the valley of Armenian villages. He reached the road—if the rough cart-track could be called one—which linked the seven to one another, just as the long spring dusk was gathering.

Yoghonoluk was nearly in the centre. Therefore he had to ride through the southern villages, Wakef, Kheder Beg, Hadji Habibli, to reach home, which would scarcely be possible before darkness. But he was in no hurry.

In these hours the village streets round Musa Dagh were crowded. People all stood out in front of their doors. The gentleness of a Sunday evening brought them together. Bodies, eyes, voices, sought one another, to enhance, with family gossip and general complaints about the times, the pleasure of being alive. Sex and degrees of age made separate groups. Matrons stood eyeing each other askance, the young wives joyous in their Sunday best, the girls full of laughter. Their coin-ornaments tinkled. They displayed their magnificent teeth. Gabriel was struck by the numbers of able-bodied young men, fit for the army, but not yet called up. They joked and laughed as though no Enver Pasha existed for them. From vineyards and orchards came the nasal twangings of the tar, the Armenian guitar. A few over-industrious men were preparing their handiwork. The Turkish day ends with dusk, and so the Sabbath rest ends also. Settled, industrious men felt the urge to fuss over odd jobs before going to bed.

Instead of calling them by their Turkish names, it would have been possible to christen the villages by the handicraft which distinguished each. All planted grapes and fruit. Scarcely any, grain. But their fame was for skill in handicraft. Here was Hadji Habibli, the wood-workers' village. Its men not only cut the best hardwood and bone combs, pipes, cigarette-holders, and such like objects for daily use, but could carve ivory crucifixes, madonnas, statues of the saints, which were sent as far as Aleppo, Damascus, Jerusalem. These carvings had their own style, achieved only in the shadow of Musa Dagh; they were not mere rough peasant handiwork. Wakef was the lace village. The delicate kerchiefs and coverlets of its women found buyers even in Egypt, without the artists knowing that this was so, since their wares were sent only to the markets in Antioch, and that not more than twice a year. Of Azir and its silkworms we have spoken. The silk was spun in Kheder Beg. In the two largest villages, Bitias and Yoghonoluk, all these various crafts worked side by side. But Kebussiye, the most northern, isolated village, kept bees. The honey of Kebussiye, or so at least Bagradian considered, had not its equal anywhere on earth. The bees sucked from the innermost essence of Musa Dagh, from its magic dower of beauty, which set it apart from all the other melancholy peaks in the land. Why should it have been Musa Dagh which gushed forth such innumerable springs, most of whose waters fell, in long, cascading veils, to the sea? Why Musa Dagh, and not Turkish mountains, like Naulu Dagh and Jebel Akra? Truly it seemed as though, miraculously, the divine quality in water, offended in some unknown previous time by Moslems, the sons of the desert, had withdrawn from off these arid, imploring heights to enrich with superabundance a Christian mountain. The flower-strewn meadows of its eastern slopes, the fat pasturage of its many-folded flanks, its lithe orchards of apricot, vine, and orange around its feet; its quiet, as of protecting seraphim—all this seemed scarcely touched by the fall of man, under which, in rocky melancholy, the rest of Asia Minor mourns. It was as though, through some small negligence in the setting up of the divine order of the world—the good-natured indulgence of an archangel open to persuasion, and who loved his home—an afterglow, a reminiscent flavour of Paradise, had been allowed to linger on for ever in the lands around Musa Dagh. Here along the Syrian coast, and a little farther, in the country of four rivers, where experts in Biblical geography are so fond of locating the Garden of Eden.

It goes without saying that the seven villages round the mountain had retained their share of this benediction. They were not to be compared with the wretched hamlets which Gabriel had passed as he rode through the plain. Here there were no loam huts, which had not even the look of human dwellings, but of caked deposits into which someone had bored a dark hole for living-room and stable, humans and beasts. Most of these houses were built of stone. Each contained several rooms. Little verandas ran round the walls. Walls and windows sparkled with cleanliness. Only a few huts from the dark ages, observing the custom of the East, had no windows turned towards the street. As far as the dark shadows of Damlayik extended, sharp across the plain, so far this friendly prosperity was evident. Beyond these shadows began the desert. Here, wine, fruit, mulberry, terrace upon terrace; there the flat, monotonous fields of maize and cotton, revealing in places the naked steppe, as a beggar shows his skin through rags. But it was not only the blessing of the mountain. Here, after half a century, the energy of old Avetis Bagradian had borne full fruit, the love of this one enterprising man, who had concentrated such stormy energies on this, his strip of native earth, despite all the enticements of the world. That man's grandson watched with astonished eyes this people invested in some strange beauty. The chattering groups became silent a few minutes before his approach; they turned towards the centre of the street and greeted him with loud evening salutations: "Bari irikun!" He believed—it may have been fancy—that he saw in their eyes a brief flicker of gratitude, not towards him, but towards the ancient benefactor. Women and girls stood looking after him; the spindles in their hands twirled in and out, like separate beings.

These people were no less foreign than the crowd that day in the bazaar. What had he to do with them—he who a few months ago had gone out for drives into the Bois, attended Bergson's lectures, talked of books, published articles on art in precious reviews? And yet, deep peace enveloped him from them. Because he had seen the threat of which they knew nothing, he felt some strange fatherliness towards them. He bore a great load of care in his heart, he alone, and would keep it from them as long as he could. The old Agha Rifaat Bereket was no dreamer, even though he wrapped his shrewdness in flowery sayings. He was right. Stay in Yoghonoluk and await the event. Musa Dagh stood beyond the world. No storm would reach it, even if one should break.

A warm love of his people invaded Gabriel. May you long continue to rejoice; tomorrow, the day after . . .

And, from his horse, he raised his hand gravely in greeting.

In cool, starry darkness he climbed the road through the park to the villa. He entered the big hall of his house. The old wrought-iron lamp hanging from its ceiling rejoiced his heart with its pale light. In some incomprehensible cranny of consciousness it seemed like his mother. Not that old lady who, in Paris, in a standardized Parisian flat, had welcomed him back from the lycée with a peck, but the mildly silent mother

44

of days as impalpable as dreams. "Hokud madagh kes kurban" —had she really ever spoken those Eastern words as she bent down over her sleeping child? "May I be as a sacrifice to your soul."

There was only one other benediction from that primal age —the little lamp under the Madonna in the niche on the stairs. Everything else dated from the time of the young Avetis. And those, in so far at least as the hall was concerned, had been days of war and of the chase. Trophies and arms hung on the walls, a whole collection of ancient bedouin rifles, with very long barrels. That this solitary master had been more than a man of one crude passion was proved by some magnificent bits of furniture—chests, carpets, lustres, which he had brought back home with him from his travels, and which delighted Juliette.

As Gabriel absent-mindedly went upstairs, he scarcely heard the babel of voices from the rooms on the ground floor. The notables of Yoghonoluk were assembled. In his room he stood some time by the open window and stared, immobile, at the black silhouette of the Damlayik, which at that hour seemed twice its size. It was ten minutes before he rang for his valet, Missak, whom, on his brother's death, he had taken into his service, along with Kristaphor, the steward, Hovhannes, the cook, and all the other house and outside staff.

Gabriel washed from head to foot and changed. Then he went into Stephan's room. The boy was already in bed and so childishly fast asleep that not even the glare of an electric torch could wake him. The windows were open, and outside the masses of plane tree crowns rustled in some slow presentiment. Here, too, the black, living mass of Musa Dagh invaded the room. But now the crest of the mountain glowed against some gently shining depths, as though there had been no salt sea behind it, but a sea composed of the gleaming essence of eternity. Bagradian sat on a chair beside the bed. That morning the son had watched his father asleep. Now it was the father who watched his son. But that was permitted.

Stephan's forehead (it was Gabriel's forehead over again) shimmered translucent. Below it the shadows of closed eyes, like two rose leaves blown from outside on to his face. Even asleep, you could see how big these eyes were. The pointed, narrow nose was not his father's; it was Juliette's legacy, exotic. Stephan breathed quickly. The walls of his sleep encased a rushing life. His folded hands were pressed against his body, as though he had to keep tight hold of reins or galloping dreams might run away with him.

The son's sleep became restless. The father did not move. He drew his son's face into himself. Did he fear for Stephan? He could not tell. No thoughts were in him. At last he stood up, unable, as he did so, to stifle a sigh, so depressed he felt. As he fumbled his way out, he bumped a table. The dark intensified the short noise. Gabriel stood still. He was afraid he had waked Stephan. A boy's drowsy voice in the dark murmured: "Who's that . . . Dad, is it you?"

At once his breathing became quiet again. Gabriel, who had switched off the electric torch, after a while switched it on again, blinding its little light with his hand. The beam caught the table, on which lay drawings. Stephan had already got to work and begun a sketch of Musa Dagh, as his father suggested. A hesitant sketch. Avakian's many red pencil-corrections intersected the lines.

Bagradian did not at first remember the stimulus he had given his son, when they met that morning. Then he recollected the stormy eagerness with which his son had sought and tried to persuade him. The uncertain sketch had become a symbol.

THE reception-room of the villa led out into a wide room, which opened into the hall. It was barely furnished and used only as an anteroom. Old Avetis had built his residence with a view to numerous descendants, so that neither the solitary

46

hunter nor this small family, now remaining, could use more than a few of the rooms. An oil lamp, screwed down to the floor, lit this bare anteroom. Gabriel stopped for an instant and listened to the voices next door. He heard Juliette laugh. So she was pleased, then, with the admiration of the Armenian villagers in there. Something gained.

Old Dr. Bedros Altouni was just opening the door on his way out. He lit the candle in his lantern and took up his leather bag, which stood on a chair. Altouni only noticed his host when Bagradian called to him softly: "Hairik Bedros"— Bedros, little Father. The doctor started. He was a small, shrivelled man with an untidy goatee, a survival of those Armenians who, unlike the younger generation, seemed to bear on their shoulders the whole load of a persecuted race. In his youth, as Avetis Bagradian's protégé and at his expense, he had studied medicine in Vienna and seen the world. In those days the benefactor of Yoghonoluk had cherished vast projects, which even included the building of a hospital. But he had gone no further than to install the district doctor, though this was much, considering the general state of affairs. Of all living people Gabriel had known this old doctor longest, this "hekim" who had brought him into the world. He felt tenderly respectful towards him, another legacy of his feelings as a child. Dr. Altouni was struggling into a rough serge overcoat, which looked as though it might have been a relic of his student days in Vienna.

"I couldn't wait any longer for you, my child. . . . Well, what did you manage to get out of the Hükümet?"

Gabriel glanced at the shrivelled little face. Everything in this old man was angular—his movements, his voice, even the occasional sharpness of what he said. He had been sharpened, inside and out. The road from Yoghonoluk to the wood-carvers' village on the one side, the beekeepers' village on the other, seemed damnably long when you had to travel it several times a week on the hard back of a donkey. Gabriel recognized

47

the eternal leather bag in which, besides sticking-plaster, thermometer, surgical instruments, and a German medical handbook dated 1875, there was only a pair of antediluvian obstetrical forceps. The sight of this medical bag made him swallow down an impulse to confide his experiences in Antioch.

"Nothing special," he answered, dismissing it.

Altouni fastened the lantern to his belt and buckled it. "I've had to renew my teskeré at least seven times in my life. They take them away to get the tax which you've got to pay on every new one. It's an old game. But they won't get any more out of me. I shan't need any more passports in this world." And he added caustically: "Not that I even needed the others. It's forty years now since I moved out of here."

Bagradian turned his head to the door. "What sort of a people are we, who submit without a murmur to everything?"

"Submit?" The doctor seemed to relish the word. "You young people don't know what submitting means. You've grown up in very different times."

But Gabriel stuck to his question: "What sort of people are we?"

"My dear child, you've lived all your life in Europe. And I should have, too, if only I'd stopped in Vienna. It was my great misfortune I ever left it. I might have become somebody. But you see, your grandfather was as big a fool as your brother, and he wouldn't so much as hear of an outside world. I had to sign a promise to come back. It was my misfortune. It would have been better if he'd never sent me away."

"One can't always go on living as a foreigner." The Parisian Gabriel felt surprised at his own words.

Altouni laughed harshly. "And here—can one live here? With uncertainty always in the background? I suppose you fancied it all very different."

Suddenly the thought came to Bagradian: "We shall at least have to do something to defend ourselves."

48

Altouni set down his bag on the chair again. "Curse it! What are we talking about? You're dragging the old stories out of me again. I'm a doctor, and I've never believed particularly in God. And yet, at one time, I was always having arguments with Him about it. You can be a Russian, or a Turk, or a Hottentot, or God knows what—but to be an Armenian—why it's impossible."

He seemed to jerk himself back from the edge of a gulf to which he had strayed. "That's enough. Let's leave all that. I am the hekim. That's all that matters to me. And I've just been called away from this pleasant company to a woman in labour. You see, we still keep putting Armenian children into the world. It's crazy."

Grimly he seized his leather bag. This talk on the threshold, which had gone to the roots of the matter, seemed to have riled him. "And you? What's wrong with you? You've got a very beautiful wife, a clever son, no worries, all the money you want—what more do you need? You live your life! Don't bother yourself with all this filth. Whenever the Turks have a war, they leave us in peace—we've always known that. And after the war you'll go back to Paris and forget all about us and Musa Dagh."

Gabriel Bagradian smiled as though he were not taking his own question seriously.

"And suppose they don't leave us in peace, little Father?"

GABRIEL stopped an instant on the threshold of the big reception-room. About a dozen people were assembled. Three elderly women sat together round a little table, in silence, with the tutor keeping them company, presumably at Juliette's orders. But even he seemed to take no trouble to get them to talk. One of these matrons, Dr. Altouni's wife, was also a survival of Gabriel's childhood. Her name was Mairik Antaram, little Mother Antaram. She wore black silk. Her hair, drawn back off her forehead, was not yet quite grey. Her wide bony

49

face had a look of daring in it. Even though she said nothing, she sat at her ease, allowing her inquisitive glances to travel freely about these people. The same could not be said of her neighbours, the wives of Harutiun Nokhudian, the pastor of Bitias, and of the village mayor, the Mukhtar of Yoghonoluk, Thomas Kebussyan. It was enough to look at them to see how embarrassed they felt, how much on their best behaviour, even though they had taken all their finery out of the wardrobe so as not to be shamed by the Frenchwoman.

Madame Kebussyan had the worst time, since she could not understand a word of French, though she was one of those who had been to school in the American mission at Marash. She blinked up at this extravagant candlelight, from lustres and chandeliers. Ah, Madame Bagradian had no need to economize! Where did she buy such thick wax candles? They must have come from Aleppo or Istanbul even. The Mukhtar Kebussyan might be the richest man in the district, but in his house, apart from petroleum, they only burned thin tallow candles and tapers of mutton-fat. And over there, next the piano, in tall candlesticks, there were even two painted candles, as in church. Wasn't that going a bit too far?

The pastor's wife, who was feeling equally ill at ease, asked herself this very same question. To her honour be it said that, in her case, no squinting envy coloured her feelings. The women's hands were folded on their laps. This evening, in honour of the soirée, they had left their sewing at home. The wives of the pastor and the mukhtar eyed their husbands in astonishment at these two old men.

And indeed both gentle pastor and massive mukhtar had changed completely. They formed only a part of the masculine group around Juliette. (She was just then displaying the antiques which Gabriel had collected and set up in this room.) Among this group were the two schoolmasters, one of whom, Hapeth Shatakhian, had once spent a few weeks in Lausanne and ever since been conscious of the fact that he

50

had an unusually good French accent. The other, Hrand Oskanian, was a dwarf, whose black hair grew very low upon his forehead. As Gabriel entered the room, he heard the loud-voiced French of the proud Shatakhian: "But, Madame, we should be so grateful to you for bringing a ray of culture into our wilderness."

That day Juliette had had an inner conflict to sustain. It had been so hard to decide in which clothes to receive her new fellow-countrymen. So far, on such occasions, she had always dressed very simply, since it had seemed to her both undignified and superfluous to attempt to dazzle "ignorant half-savages." But even the last time she had noticed how the magic she could shed upon her guests was reflected back upon herself. So that today she had yielded to temptation and chosen her most elaborate evening frock. ("Oh, well," she had thought as she examined it, "it dates from last spring, and at home I shouldn't dare show my nose in it.") After some hesitation, since the frock itself was so resplendent, she had also decided to wear jewellery. The effect of this deliberate decision, of which she had at first been rather ashamed, surprised even her. It is pleasant enough to be a beautiful woman among many, but the feeling soon wears off. In lighted restaurants one is only a pretty member of a beauty chorus. But to be the unique, the yellow-haired châtelaine, among all these dark, glittering-eyed Armenians—that surely was no everyday fate! It was an experience, bringing back the flush of youth, a glow to the lips, a light of triumph to the eyes.

Gabriel found his wife surrounded by humble, dazzled admirers. When Juliette moved, he recognized again her "sparkling step," as he once had called it. Juliette, here in Yoghonoluk, seemed to have found her way into the hearts of his simple-minded compatriots, though in Europe she had often jibbed at the society of the most cultivated Armenians. And strangest of all . . . In Beirut, overtaken by the war, without any chance to get back home, Gabriel had been

51

haunted by the fear that Juliette would be devoured with homesickness. France was fighting the worst battles in her history. European newspapers seldom reached that corner of the world. One was entirely cut off, could find out nothing. Till now only one letter, dated November, had reached them, by many long detours. From Juliette's mother. Lucky that at least she had no brothers. Her marriage with a foreigner had estranged her a little from her family. Be that as it might, her present tranquil frivolity had come as a great surprise to Gabriel. She seldom seemed to think about home. In this fourteenth year of their married life the unhoped-for seemed to have taken place.

And indeed there was something essentially new in her, as she put her arms round his neck. "At last, *mon ami,* I was just beginning to be anxious."

She began to be concerned with his hunger and thirst, almost to the point of exaggeration. But Gabriel had no time to eat. He was surrounded. Naturally that morning's official inspection had not passed without leaving some trace on people's minds. The very fact that the Turkish authorities should have chosen a Sunday—the hour of high mass—for their visit, might itself be considered a hostile sign. An omen of intricate hostility.

But the Musa Dagh colony had been almost spared in the bloody events of 1896 and 1909. Yet such men as Kebussyan and the little pastor of Bitias were sharp-eared enough to become alert at the slightest suspicious rustling. Only this evening-party and Juliette's radiant presence had been enough to distract them from such troubling of their peace. Now, as, remembering his promise, Gabriel repeated the müdir's words —that this was no more than a general war-time measure— they all, Kebussyan, Nokhudian, the schoolmasters, had of course long since answered the riddle themselves. They became light-heartedly optimistic. The most hopeful of all was Shatakhian. He drew himself up to his full height. The Middle

Ages were over, he opined, addressing his glowing words to Madame Bagradian. The sun of progress would rise, even over Turkey. This war was its crimson dawn. The Turkish government was under the surveillance of its allies. Shatakhian glanced expectantly at Juliette. Had he not acclaimed progress in faultless French? His hearers, in so far as they understood them, seemed to share his views. Only the silent Oskanian, the other teacher, smiled sarcastically. But he always did when friend Shatakhian let himself go and revelled in his own linguistic verbosity. Another voice made itself heard: "Never mind the Turks. Let's talk about something more important."

This had been said by Krikor, the apothecary, the most remarkable person in the room.

KRIKOR's very garb denoted the fact that his character was subject to no change. All the other men, even the mukhtar, wore European dress (a tailor, back from London, lived in Yoghonoluk). Krikor had on a kind of light-blue Russian blouse, but made of the softest raw silk. His face, without a wrinkle in spite of the fact that he was sixty, with its white goatee and rather slanting eyes, was more that of a wise mandarin than an Armenian. He spoke in a high, but oddly hollow, voice, which sounded as though much learning had exhausted it. And in fact Apothecary Krikor owned a library surely unequalled in all Syria—and was moreover himself a walking library, a man of encyclopædic information, in one of the remotest valleys on earth. Be the subject the flora of Musa Dagh, desert geology, an extinct species of bird, copper smelting, meteorology, the fathers of the Church, fixed stars, cooking receipts, the Persian secret of extracting oil of roses— Krikor's hollow voice could supply information, and that in a careless, casual manner, as though it were rather an impertinence to have asked him such a trivial question. There are many "know-alls" in the world. But Krikor's genuine

53

personality could not have shown itself by this alone. No, Krikor was like his library.

This was composed of only a few thousand volumes, most of which were written in languages which he himself was unable to read. Providence had set many obstacles in the way of his ruling passion. Such French and Armenian works as he possessed were the least interesting. But Krikor was more than learned, he was a bibliophile. The bibliophile is more enamoured of the very existence of a book than of its form and contents. He has no need to read it. (Is not all true love much the same?) The apothecary was not a rich man. He could not afford to give expensive orders to book-sellers and antique shops in Istanbul or abroad. He could scarcely have paid the freightage. He had to take what came his way. The foundations of his library, he insisted, had already been laid in his boyhood and his years of travel. Now he had agents and patrons in Antioch, Alexandretta, Aleppo, Damascus, who from time to time sent him a parcel of books. What a red-letter day when they arrived! Whatever they might be —Arabic or Hebrew folios, French novels, second-hand rubbish—what did it matter, they were always so much printed paper. Krikor contained within himself that deep Armenian love of culture, the secret of all very ancient races which survive the centuries. This queer, and most of it unread, library would scarcely have sufficed to supply the apothecary's vast store of information. His own creative audacity filled in the gaps. Krikor completed his universe. Any question, from statistics to theology, he answered out of his plenitude of power. The innocent happiness of poets glowed in his veins each time he threw out a few major scientific terms. That such a man had disciples goes without saying. Equally obvious that they were composed of the schoolmasters of all seven villages. Apothecary Krikor was the Socrates of Musa Dagh—a peripatetic who, usually in the night, took long walks with these, his disciples. Such walks offered many chances to increase his followers' respect. He would point up at the starry sky.

"Hapeth Shatakhian, do you know the name of that reddish star, up there?"—"Which? That one there? Isn't that a planet?"—"Wrong, Schoolmaster. That star is called Aldebaran. And do you know what gives it that reddish tinge?"—"Well—perhaps our atmosphere."—"Wrong, Teacher. The star Aldebaran is composed of molten, magnetic iron, and that's what makes it look so red. Such at least is the opinion of the famous Camille Flammarion, as he writes in his last letter to me."

And that great astronomer's letter was no mere empty fabrication. It existed in fact. Krikor, in the person of Camille Flammarion, had written the letter to himself. To be sure, he rarely sent himself such letters; only on the most solemn occasions. Usually the disciples heard nothing of them, since even Voltaire and Raffi, the great Armenian poet, had several times been inspired to exhaustive answers to Krikor's questions. Krikor was therefore a corresponding member of Olympus.

All the educated families in Musa Dagh took an annual holiday, if only to Aleppo or Marash, to the American, French, German missionary schools there, in which their education had been completed. Not a few among the village elders had returned from America to enjoy their earnings. Almost as war broke out, a batch of émigrés had crossed the Atlantic. Only Krikor had remained where he was. It was rare for him even to visit a neighbouring village. In his youth, he declared, his bodily eyes had seen enough wonders of the world. Occasionally he hinted at these journeyings, which had lost themselves in remote distances, eastwards and westwards, but in which he had, on principle, taken no train. It is uncertain whether they were of the same nature as Flammarion's letter. Nothing in Krikor's tales savoured in the least of exaggeration or bragging. His accounts were steeped in shrewd observa-

55

tion and consistency, so that even such a man as Bagradian might not have suspected. But Krikor was always insisting on how little need he saw for travel. All places were alike, since the outside world is contained in the inner. The sage sits, quiet as a spider, in the net which his mind has spun round the universe. So that, when the talk was of war or politics, of any burning question of the hour, Krikor would begin to get restless. Last arrogance of the mind! He despised all wars not contained in books. That was why Krikor had snubbed the political observations of the schoolteacher. And he concluded:

"I can't make out why people must be for ever eyeing their neighbours. War, government orders, Wali, Kaimakam —let the Turks do as they please. If you don't worry about them, they won't worry about you. We have our own earth here. And it has distinguished admirers. If you please . . ."

With this Krikor introduced a young man to his host, a foreigner, who had either been hidden by all the others or whom Gabriel had failed to notice. Krikor rolled out the young man's sonorous name: "Gonzague Maris."

This young man, to judge by his appearance, was a European, or at least a distinctly Europeanized Levantine. His small black moustache, on a pale, highly alert face, looked as French as his name sounded. His most distinctive trait were the eyebrows, which forked upwards in a blunt angle. Krikor played herald to the foreigner: "Monsieur Gonzague Maris is a Greek."

At once he improved on this, as though he were afraid of demeaning his guest: "Not a Turkish Greek, but a European."

This stranger had very long eyelashes. He was smiling, and these feminine lashes were lowered almost over his eyes. "My father was Greek, my mother's French. I'm an American."

The quiet, almost shy approach of this young stranger favourably impressed Bagradian. He shook his hand. "What extraordinary combination of circumstances—if you don't mind my calling it that—brings an American with a French mother here—of all places?"

Gonzague smiled again, lowering his eyes. "It's quite simple. I had business for a few weeks in Alexandretta and got ill there. The doctor sent me up to the hills, to Beilan. Beilan didn't suit me. . . . In Alexandretta they told me so much about Musa Dagh that I felt inquisitive. It was a great surprise to me, in the God-forsaken East, to find such beauty, such cultured people, and such comfort as I'm enjoying with my host, Monsieur Krikor. I like everything strange. If Musa Dagh were in Europe, it'd be famous. Well, I'm glad it belongs only to you."

The apothecary announced, in the hollow, indifferent voice which he used for giving important information: "He's a writer, and he's going to work in my house."

But Gonzague Maris seemed embarrassed. "I'm not a writer. I send an occasional article to an American newspaper. That's all I do. I'm not even a real journalist." Vaguely, with a gesture, he indicated that his scribbling was no more than an attempt to make money.

But Krikor would not let go of his victim, who must be used as an asset. "But you're also an artist, a musician, a virtuoso. Haven't you given concerts?"

The young man's hand was raised in self-defence: "That's not quite right. Among other things I've been an accompanist. One must try all kinds of things." His eyes sought Juliette's assistance.

She marvelled: "How small the world really is. How strange that I should have met a compatriot here. You're half French."

THANKS to Juliette's verve the evening was a very successful one, not to be compared with former gatherings in Villa Bagradian. Most of these rustic Armenians lived Orientally, that is to say they foregathered only in church or in the

57

street. Visits were for state occasions. This cloistered domesticity was the true cause of the women's uneasiness. But this evening they thawed, little by little. The pastor's wife forgot to warn her husband, whose life she devoted her energies to prolonging, and whose sleep must therefore never be encroached upon, that it was time to go home. The mukhtar's wife had come close up to Juliette, to finger the silk of her dress. Mairik Antaram, however, had suddenly vanished. Her husband had sent a small boy to fetch her, since he needed her help in a difficult delivery. It was one of her duties to chase away the old spey-women, who at every childbirth besieged a house to sell magic potions to the mother. In the course of decades Madame Altouni had become the doctor's valued assistant and had ended by taking over most of his practice. "She's better at it than I am," he always said.

The host took longest to unbend. But little by little he grew convivial. He eyed discontentedly the long table laid with plates of cakes, tea and coffee cups, and two carafes of raki. He sprang to his feet. "My friends, we must have something better than this to drink." He went down to the cellar with Kristaphor and Missak to fetch up wine. The younger Avetis had laid down an ample store of the best years' vintages. The steward had charge of them. It is true that the heady wines of Musa Dagh did not keep long. This may have been because they were not bottled, but kept, in accordance with old tradition, in big sealed jars. It was a dark golden drink, very heady, similar to the wines which flourish at Xara on Lebanon.

When they had filled their glasses, Bagradian rose to give a toast. It came out as uncertainly and ominously as everything else he had said that evening: It was good that they should all be sitting here, happy, tonight. Who could tell whether next time, or the time after that, they would still be so carefree! But nobody must let such thoughts spoil his evening. They brought no good with them. . . .

This toast, or rather this veiled warning, Gabriel had given in Armenian. Juliette raised her glass and looked across at him. "I could understand every word you said. But why so gloomy, my dear?"

"I'm such a bad speaker," he excused himself. "I should never have made a leader of the people."

"Rafael Patkanian," the apothecary interjected, turning to Juliette, "Patkanian was one of our greatest popular leaders, a real inspirer of the Armenian people—and he was the worst speaker you could imagine. He stuttered worse than the young Demosthenes. As a young man I had the honour of knowing and hearing him speak. In Erivan."

"You mean," Gabriel laughed, "that everything's possible."

The heady wine was producing its effect. Tongues wagged. Only the schoolteacher Oskanian still kept the embittered, dignified silence due to himself and his importance. Nokhudian, the man of God, who carried his liquor poorly, defended his glass against the onslaughts of his spouse as she tried to take it away from him. He kept saying: "Why, woman, this is a feast day, isn't it?"

As Gabriel opened a window for a glance at the night, he felt Juliette behind his back.

"Are you having a nice time?" she whispered.

He put his arm about her waist. "Whom have I to thank for it, if not you?" But his strained voice was unsuited to the loving words.

Wine brought the desire for song. Several people pointed out a young man, one of the teachers—a disciple of Krikor. His name was Asayan. This wisp of a man was known to have an excellent voice and memory for Armenian songs. Asayan showed all the diffidence of amateurs. He couldn't possibly sing without accompaniment, and his house was too far away to fetch a tar. Juliette had already thought of sending upstairs for her gramophone; to be sure most of the natives of Yoghonoluk already knew this triumph of technical skill. But it was Krikor who settled the matter, with a significant

59

glance at his foreign guest: "We have a professional among us."

It did not need too much persuasion to make Gonzague Maris sit down to the piano. "One of the twelve pianos in Syria," announced Gabriel. "It was sent from Vienna for my mother a quarter of a century ago. But Kristaphor tells me that my brother Avetis had an expert in from Aleppo to tune it and put it to rights. In the last weeks of his life he played a good deal. And I never even knew he was musical."

Gonzague struck a few chords. But, as often happens, the professional could not find the right tune for this late hour, the unusual relaxation, the need these people felt to be amused. Carelessly, his head bent forward over the keys, he sat there, cigarette in mouth—but his fingers became more and more involved in macabre sounds. "Out of tune," he murmured, "horribly out of tune," and was perhaps for that reason unable to disentangle himself from howling discords. A veil of boredom and fatigue descended upon his face, which had looked so handsome. Bagradian quietly observed this face; it seemed no longer boyishly shy, but dissipated and disingenuous. He looked round for Juliette, who had pulled her chair nearer the piano. Her face was suddenly sagging and middle-aged. Softly she answered his questioning expression: "Headache.—It comes from this wine."

Gonzague suddenly stopped, and shut down the piano-lid. "Please excuse me."

Although, to let the others see he was musical, Shatakhian began in highly technical language to praise the foreigner's playing, the evening was really at an end. Pastor Nokhudian's wife a few minutes later set the example for breaking up. To be sure they were to stay the night with friends in Yoghonoluk, but they must set out for Bitias at sunrise. The silent Oskanian stayed on longest. When the others were already in the park, he turned back, to approach Juliette on his short legs, so resolutely, so severely, that she felt a little scared. But he had only come to present her with a big and imposing manuscript roll, written in different coloured inks, in Armenian letters, before he vanished.

It was a passionate rhymed declaration of love.

JULIETTE awoke in the night to find Gabriel sitting bolt upright at her bedside. He had lighted his candle and for some time must have been watching her asleep. She could distinctly feel that his eyes, not the candlelight, had awakened her.

He touched her arm. "I didn't mean to wake you. But I wanted you to wake up."

She shook back her hair. Her face was amiable and refreshed. "I shouldn't have minded your waking me. You know that. You know I always like to talk in the night."

"I've been thinking things out . . ." His voice was hesitant.

"And I've been having a simply marvellous sleep. So my headache can't have come from your Armenian wine. It must have been brought on by the playing of my—*comment dire?* —my semi-compatriot. What a coincidence! Fancy using Yoghonoluk as a spa, and Monsieur Krikor's house as a hotel. But the funniest one of all was that little black-haired schoolteacher who gave me his rolled-up poem. And that other teacher, drawling through his nose. He seemed to think he was speaking such good French—and it sounded like a mixture of stones being ground and whining dogs. You Armenians have such a funny accent. Even you, *mon ami,* have it slightly. Oh, well, I mustn't be too critical! They're really such nice people."

"Poor people. Poor, poor people."

Juliette had never observed the least sentimentality in Gabriel. All the greater, therefore, her astonishment. She looked across at him in silence. The candle behind his head made her unable to study his face; she could see only the upper

61

half of his body, like a dark mass of carved stone. But Gabriel
—since now, not only candlelight, but the first starry dawn-
light fell upon Juliette—was in the presence of a tenderly
radiant being. "Fourteen years in October. The greatest happiness in my life. And yet it was a bad mistake. I ought never
to have dragged you away . . . thrust you into a foreign
destiny."

She felt for matches to light her own candle. But he snatched
her hand and prevented it. So that again she heard him speak
through the formless dark. "It would be best if you could
escape. . . . We ought to divorce."

A long silence. It simply did not occur to Juliette that this
mad, incomprehensible suggestion had any serious reality.
She shifted nearer him. "Have I hurt you, wounded your feelings, made you jealous?"

"You've never been so kind as you were tonight. It's years
since I've felt so much in love. . . . That makes it all the
more horrible."

He sat up more stiffly, so that the dark mass of his body
looked stranger still. "Juliette, you must take what I'm going
to say seriously. Ter Haigasun will do whatever he can to get
a divorce put through as fast as possible. And the Turkish
authorities don't put many obstacles in the way of that sort
of thing. Then you'd be free, you'd have ceased to be an Armenian, you could get away from the ghastly fate of my people, in which I've involved you. We could go to Aleppo. There
you can place yourself under the protection of a European consul, the American, or the Swiss, it doesn't matter. And you'll
be safe, whatever happens here—or there. Stephan'll go with
you. You'll be able to leave Turkey without difficulty. Of
course I'll make over my property and the income to
you. . . ."

He had said all this with difficulty, but quickly, so that she
should not interrupt. But Juliette's face came close to his.
"And are you really taking this madness seriously?"

"If I'm still alive when it's all over, I'll come back to you."

"But yesterday we were quietly discussing what was to happen when you got called up. . . ."

"Yesterday? Yesterday was all an illusion. The world's changed since."

"What's changed? This business with the passports? We shall be given new ones. Why, you yourself said that in Antioch you heard nothing terrible."

"I heard all kinds of disturbing things—but that's not the point. Perhaps, really, very little may have changed. But it always comes suddenly, like a desert storm. It's in my bones. My ancestors in me, who suffered incredible things, can feel it. My whole body feels it. No, Juliette, you can't understand! Nobody could understand who hasn't been hated because of his race."

Juliette jumped out of bed, sat down beside him, and took his hands. "You're just like Stephan. Whenever he's had a bad dream, he only half wakes up and can't shake it off for the next hour. Why should we ourselves be in danger? What about all your Turkish friends, those charming, sensitive people we knew in Paris, who called so often? Have *they* suddenly changed into cunning wild beasts? No. You Armenians have always been unjust to the Turks."

"I'm not being unjust to them. There are some very fine people among them. After all, in the war I got to know the poor people, how good and patient they are. It isn't their fault and it isn't ours. But what difference does that make?"

The dawnlight had kept increasing; the crest of Musa Dagh, beyond the windows, had begun to sharpen. Gabriel stared up at the mountain. "I've been thinking how odd it is that we should have come here in pursuit of Avetis, who kept escaping us. As though he'd meant to lure me to Yoghonoluk by his death. . . . But no—really it was you who insisted on coming here."

It was getting chilly. Juliette's bare feet were freezing. She

63

did not want to argue. "Well—you see! It was just my obstinacy. That ought to calm you."

But Gabriel's thoughts were pursuing another object. "Yesterday, for an instant, I felt unshakably convinced that I'd been brought here by some supernatural power, that God has something or other in store for me. My feeling really was unshakable, though it only lasted an instant. The life I've been leading so far can't have been right. It's so pleasant to imagine oneself an exceptional personage—the only grain in a wheat sheaf, not subject to the law of gravity, but free to wander, without obligations. . . . And so, by His will, through Avetis, God brought me back here. . . ."

He stopped. For some time she had been peering into his indistinct face. "This is the first time I've seen you afraid."

Still he did not turn away his eyes from the sharpening crest of Musa Dagh. "Afraid? As I should be of anything supernatural. As a child I used sometimes to imagine a tiny star in the sky growing bigger and bigger, swelling up, coming nearer and nearer, and crushing the earth."

He shook himself to regain his self-control. "Juliette. It's not for me. It's for you and Stephan."

Then at last she got very angry. "I simply don't believe in all your bogies. This is 1915. I've never met with anything in Turkey, or anywhere else, but friendship and civility. I'm not frightened of people. But, even suppose there should be danger, do you really think I'd be such a low-down coward as to run away and leave you here to face it? . . . I couldn't even do that if I'd stopped loving you."

He said no more and shut his eyes. Juliette already wanted to get up quietly. But Gabriel let his head sink into her lap. His forehead was damp and cold. In a sudden burst the birds struck up their shrill dawn twitterings.

4

The First Incident

THIS sudden weakness and surrender passed as quickly as it had come. Yet Gabriel was transformed since that day in Antioch. He, who for hours together had worked in his room, had now begun only to sleep at home. But then he was so tired out that he slept like a corpse. He did not say another word of the menace which had shaken him so profoundly that Sunday night. Juliette, too, avoided the subject. She was convinced that there was really nothing to fear. Already, in the course of their marriage, she had been through three or four such crises with Gabriel—days of depressed, apparently causeless brooding, of heavy silences, which no affection served to dissipate. She knew it of old. At such times a wall grew up between them, and they were strangers, so unapproachable to each other that Juliette felt appalled at the childish recklessness which had let her join her destiny to this strange blood.

To be sure, in Paris things had been different for Juliette. Her own world, in which Gabriel was the foreigner, had supported her like a higher power. In Yoghonoluk their positions were reversed, and it is very easily understood that Juliette, for all her irony, should have striven to fortify in herself her feeling of being well disposed towards the "half-civilized" people with whom she was living.

Gabriel must be left to his own devices. That painful talk in the night seemed no more to Juliette than one of the moods she already knew. For this Frenchwoman, grown up amid immeasurable security, could not imagine in the least what

65

Gabriel had meant by his "desert storm." Europe was now a battlefield. Even in Paris people were having to spend the night in cellars, taking refuge from enemy aircraft. But here she lived amid paradisaic spring. A few more months of this would be delightful. Then, sooner or later, they would be sure to return to the Avenue Kléber—and meanwhile Juliette's days were fully, and very pleasantly, occupied. She had not the time to do much thinking. Her ambitions as a châtelaine were aroused. These servants must be trained to civilization. She soon found herself admiring the natural talents of Armenians; within a few weeks Hovhannes, the cook, had developed into almost a *cordon bleu.* The butler, Missak, was so versatile that she had thoughts of taking him back with her to Paris. Her two maids bade fair to become expert ladies' maids. The villa on the whole was in good condition, yet sharp feminine eyes could pick out many points where decay and dilapidation threatened. Workmen invaded the house. Their master, Tomasian, undertook to do all the carpentering. But Tomasian must never be called a master-carpenter to his face. He described himself as a "builder and contractor," wore a heavy gold watch-chain across his middle, hung with a big medallion of his late wife, that had been painted by the schoolteacher Oskanian, and never let slip a chance of telling people how his two children, a son and a daughter, had been to school in Geneva. He was tediously thorough and insisted on engaging Juliette in endless discussions. In compensation, however, he succeeded in repairing any structural damage the house had sustained and could even make certain additions and improvements necessary to European habits. His men worked fast and with astonishing quiet. By the beginning of April, Juliette was already proudly aware that here, on the remotest coast of Syria, she possessed a country house which, apart from its rather primitive lighting and sanitation, could easily compare with any in Europe.

Her chief delights were the rose garden and orchard. Here

her inherited instincts found expression. Is there not in every Frenchman an inborn gardener and fruit-grower? But Armenians also are born gardeners, especially those round Musa Dagh. Kristaphor, the steward, was an expert. Juliette had never conceived of such fruit. No one, without having tasted them, can have any idea of the sweetness and juiciness of Armenian apricots. Even here, beyond the watershed of the Taurus, they retained all the savour of their home up along the shores of Lake Van, so rich in gardens. Juliette kept making the acquaintance of more and more new kinds of fruit, of flowers and vegetables of which she had never heard. She spent most time in pruning rose trees, on her head a sombrero, a vast pair of Kristaphor's gardening-scissors in her hand. For such a rose-lover the delights of this could not have been equalled. Long beds of rose trees, shrub after shrub, tree after tree, not in stiff European lines, but a tangled tumult of scent and colour, on dark green waves.

Apothecary Krikor had promised that, if she would send him enough baskets of the real moschata damascena, he would extract for her a tiny vial of that attar, the receipt for which goes back through the centuries. And he told her a legend. A single drop of the genuine essence has such power that a corpse, on to whose hair it has been sprinkled, will still be perfumed with it at the Last Judgment, and so will influence the recording angel in his favour.

Sometimes Juliette went for rides with Stephan. Behind them rode a stable-boy, for whom she had designed picturesque livery. The instinct to embellish, to decorate, possessed her completely. When she rode forth with Stephan and the decorative groom down the village street and across the church square of Yoghonoluk, she felt like the princess of this fairy-tale world. She sometimes thought of her mother and sister in Paris. What a much better time she was having! Wherever she went, she was greeted with the deepest obeisance, even in the Mohammedan villages, which she touched on her longer rides. It was obvious. Poor Gabriel had another of his *crises de nerfs*. She, Juliette, could see not the slightest sign of a changed world.

GABRIEL BAGRADIAN left the house early every morning, but no longer to explore Musa Dagh. He went through the villages. His hankerings after memories of his childhood had been replaced by more adult cravings. He was determined to get to know these people thoroughly, their way of life, their needs, their comings and goings.

At the same time he had sent a batch of letters to Istanbul, to Armenian friends in the Dashnakzagan party, and some to former friends among the Young Turks. He shrewdly hoped that, though the metropolitan censorship might prevent most of these from being delivered, some at least would get to their destination. The answers that came must decide the future. If everything was as usual in the capital, or if it were simply a case of general military control, he would, he had decided, break up this household and dare the journey to Istanbul, even without the necessary passport. If no answers came, or unfavourable ones, the old Agha's fears must be well founded, his fate sealed, retreat cut off. Then there would remain only the hope that such a friend of Armenians as the Wali Djelal Bey might tolerate no "incidents" in his vilayet, and that a peasant community like this round Musa Dagh would be left unmolested by the firebrands, who, after all, congregate in big cities. In that case the house in Yoghonoluk might, as the Agha had said, be an ideal refuge.

In so far as the absence of marching-orders was concerned, Bagradian fancied he could perceive the exact workings of the minds of the Turkish High Command. Why were Armenians being retired from the line and disarmed? Surely the Turks feared that defeat would mean that a strong minority, armed with all the latest weapons, might be tempted to demand certain rights from the dominant race. But where there

68

could be no soldiers, officers, who at the proper moment might snatch up the leadership of such a movement, were still less to be tolerated.

Valid as were all these reasons, Gabriel had not a second's real peace. Yet now his unrest was no longer neurotically on edge, but fruitful and purposeful. He found in himself a meticulous sense of detail, so far known only in his scientific work. It was useful as a means of discovering exact relationships. He did not once ask himself to what object his new exertions were being directed or to whom he imagined they might be useful.

His first step was to investigate the village of Yoghonoluk. It was the largest village. In its communal house the municipal business of all seven villages was transacted, particularly their dealings with the authorities. Mukhtar Kebussyan was away. The village clerk let Gabriel in with many bows; a visit from the head of the fabulous Bagradian family was a great distinction.

Was there a register? The clerk pointed ceremoniously to the dusty shelves round the walls of his little office. Naturally there were lists. And not only had every inhabitant been entered in the proper church register—these were not Kurds or nomads, but Christian folk—only a few years ago the mukhtars had taken an independent census. In 1909—after the reaction against the Young Turks and the big massacre in Adana—Armenian party leaders had given orders for lists to be taken in the villages. By a rough calculation there must be about seven thousand Christians. But if the Effendi so desired, he could have the exact figures within a few days. Gabriel did so desire.

His next inquiry was more delicate. How were those young men placed who were liable for military service? The village clerk had begun to squint a little, like his master, the mukhtar. So far the order had concerned all able-bodied men between twenty and thirty, though legally twenty-seven was the age-limit. About two hundred men in this whole village district had been affected. Just one hundred and fifty of these had paid their bedel, the sum which bought them clear of the army—fifty Turkish pounds a head. The Effendi knew how thrifty people were in the villages. Most fathers began to save for the bedel the instant their sons were born . . . to spare them the horrors of Turkish barrack-life. The Mukhtar of Yoghonoluk, in conjunction with the gendarmerie station, had to collect it as every batch received its marching-orders and pass it on to the Hükümet at Antioch.

"But how is it," Bagradian asked, "that in a population of six thousand there should only be two hundred men fit for service?"

The answer did not come as a surprise. The Effendi must remember that this lack of able-bodied men was a legacy from the past, a consequence of the blood-letting to which, at least once every decade, the Armenian people was subjected. But that was only a euphemism. Gabriel himself had seen over two hundred young men in the village streets. There were other ways of avoiding conscription, without having to pay the bedel. The pock-marked saptieh, Ali Nassif, was no doubt fully conversant with these other methods.

Bagradian came back to the point: "Well, then . . . Fifty people were sent to barracks in Antakiya. What's happened to them?"

"Forty were kept for service."

"And in which regiments, on what fronts, would they be serving?"

That was uncertain. It was weeks, months, now, since the families had had news of their sons. The reliability of the Turkish field-post was all too well known. Possibly they were in barracks in Aleppo, where General Jemal Pasha was reconditioning his army.

"And does nobody say in the villages that they're going to

use the Armenians as inshaat taburi, as depôt soldiers?"

"They say all kinds of things in the villages." The clerk looked rather uneasy as he answered.

Gabriel eyed the little bookcase. A *List of Householders* stood next a copy of the *Imperial Ottoman Book of Laws,* and next that a pair of rusty scales for weighing letters. He turned suddenly: "What about deserters?"

The harassed village clerk tip-toed to the door, opened and shut it again mysteriously. Of course there were deserters, here as everywhere. Why shouldn't Armenians desert, when Turks were setting them the example? How many? Fifteen to twenty. Yes! They'd been after them, too. A few days ago. A mixed platoon of saptiehs and regular infantry, led by a mülasim. They'd looked all over Musa Dagh. Made fools of themselves.

The pointed face of the blinking little man was suddenly craftily triumphant. "Fools of themselves, Effendi. You see, our lads know their own mountain."

Ter Haigasun's presbytery was the third best house in the church square of Yoghonoluk. Only the mukhtar's house and the school buildings could compare with it. With its flat roof and single-storied, five-windowed façade, it might have stood in any small town in the south of Italy. Ter Haigasun was Gregorian chief priest to the whole district. His province even included hamlets with mixed inhabitants and the small Armenian communities in such Turkish towns as Suedia and El Eskel. Ter Haigasun had studied in the seminary at Ejmiadzin, at the feet of the Catholicos, in whom all Armenian Christianity acclaimed its chief spiritual head, and was therefore in every way the chosen vicar of his district.

And Pastor Harutiun Nokhudian? How did a Protestant pastor suddenly come to inhabit such a remote Armenian village? The answer is that Syria and Anatolia contained a great

71

many Protestants and that the Evangelical church had those German and American missionaries who had cared so well for Armenian orphans and victims to thank for these proselytes. The worthy Nokhudian had been such an orphan, sent by these compassionate mission-folk to Dorpat in East Germany to study theology. But in everything that was not of strictly spiritual concern Nokhudian submitted to Ter Haigasun. In view of the constant danger besetting Armenians theological differences became of comparative unimportance, and Ter Haigasun's spiritual leadership—he was, in the truest sense, a spiritual leader—remained uncontested and uncriticized.

An old man, the sacristan, led Gabriel into the priest's study. A bare room with a wide carpet. Against the window a small writing-desk with, beside it, a tattered, straw-seated chair for visitors. Ter Haigasun stood up behind the desk and came round it a step nearer Bagradian. He could not have been more than forty-eight, yet his beard had long grey streaks on either side. His big eyes (Armenian eyes are nearly always big; big with a thousand years of terror) had a mingled look of shy isolation and resolute knowledge of the world. The priest was wearing a black alpaca cassock with a hood that rose to a point over his head. His hands were hidden in wide sleeves, as though they were freezing even on this warm, spring day. Was it a shiver of humility? Bagradian sat down carefully on the rickety straw-seated chair.

"I much regret the fact, reverend Father, that I am never able to greet you at my house."

The priest cast down his eyes; both hands waved a gesture of apology. "I regret it even more than you, Effendi. But Sunday evening is the only time we priests have free in the whole week."

Gabriel looked about him. He had hoped in this presbytery study to find some documents and records. Nothing at all. Only a few written papers on the desk. "I can well believe that you carry a heavy burden."

Ter Haigasun did not deny it.

Gabriel tried to arrest the eyes of the priest. "Don't you agree, Ter Haigasun, that these are not the days for social gatherings?"

A brief, attentive glance was his reply. "On the contrary, Effendi. This is the right time for people to come together."

Gabriel at first said nothing in answer to these strange words with their double meaning. It was a while before he observed: "It really is surprising that life here should go on so calmly, and that nobody seems to be perturbed."

Again the priest was sitting with downcast eyes, as though he were prepared to accept any scorn with humility.

"I was in Antioch a few days ago," Gabriel very slowly observed, "where I heard a good deal."

Ter Haigasun's freezing hands slipped out of his sleeves. He joined his finger-tips. "The people in our villages only very seldom go to Antioch. And that is good. They live within their own boundaries and know little of things in the world outside."

"How long will they still be able to live at peace in their own boundaries, Ter Haigasun? . . . What will happen, for instance, if all our leaders and rich men in Istanbul get arrested?"

"They have already been arrested," the priest answered very softly. "For the last three days they have been in the prisons of Istanbul. And they are many, very many."

So that Gabriel's fate was sealed, the way to the capital blocked. Yet for the moment this major fact impressed him less than Ter Haigasun's calm. He had no doubt that the news was reliable. The clergy, in spite of the liberal Dashnak-zagan, was still the one great power, the only real organization of the people. The priest was the first to learn, by quick and secret ways, of any new and dangerous factor, long before the newspapers of the capital had dared report it. Gabriel wanted to convince himself that he really had understood.

73

"Actually arrested? And who? . . . Are you perfectly sure?"

"I'm certain."

"And yet you, the head priest of seven large villages, keep so calm?"

"Excitement would be of no use and would probably only injure my people."

"Have any priests been arrested?"

Ter Haigasun doubtless perceived the guile in this question. He nodded gravely. "Seven, so far. Among them Archbishop Hemayak and three highly placed prelates."

For all this devastating news Gabriel craved a cigarette. He was given one, and a light. "I ought to have come to see you before, Ter Haigasun. You have no idea how hard it has been to keep silence."

"You did very well to keep silence. And we must continue to keep it."

"Would it perhaps be better to prepare these people for what may happen?"

Ter Haigasun's face, as though carved in wax, showed no emotion. "I can't tell what may happen. But I know the dangers of panic in a community."

This Christian priest had spoken to almost the same effect as had Rifaat, the pious Moslem. But in Gabriel's mind a lightning vision came and went: a huge dog. One of those stray mad curs that make all Turkey dangerous ground. An old man on a road, stopping in terror of the dog, swaying on his feet, and turning, with a sudden jerk, for flight—but already the rabid fangs are in his back. . . . Gabriel passed his hand across his forehead.

"Fear," he said, "is the surest way of exciting our enemy to slaughter us. But isn't it rather sinful, and perhaps even more dangerous, to keep the people ignorant of their fate? How long can the secret be kept?"

Ter Haigasun seemed to be listening into the distance. "The

74

papers are still not allowed to report these things, so that foreign countries may not know anything of them. And in the spring there's so much work to do that our people have no time and scarcely go anywhere. So that, with God's help, we can be spared anxiety for some little while. But one day it will come. Sooner or later . . ."

"Will come? How do you see it coming?"

"I don't see anything."

"Our soldiers disarmed? Our leaders arrested?"

Ter Haigasun, in the same quiet voice, as though it gave him secret pleasure to torment both himself and his listener, concluded his story. "They have even arrested Vartkes, the bosom friend of Talaat and Enver. Some of them have been deported. They may be dead by now. All Armenian newspapers have been shut down, all Armenian shops and businesses closed. And, as we sit here, there are fifteen innocent Armenian men hanging on fifteen gallows on the square before the Seraskeriat."

Bagradian rose so excitedly that he overturned the straw-seated chair. "What's the real meaning of all this madness? Can you make it out?"

"I can only see that the government is planning such a stroke against our whole people as even Abdul Hamid never dared."

Gabriel glared as angrily at Ter Haigasun, as though he had been faced with an enemy, a member of Ittihad. "Are we really so helpless? Must we really hold out our heads to the noose in silence?"

"We are helpless. We must bow our heads. We may perhaps be allowed to cry out."

This damned East, with its kismet, Bagradian thought in a flash of rage. At the same instant his consciousness was invaded by a thousand names, connexions, possibilities—politicians, diplomats, his personal friends, Frenchmen, Englishmen, Germans, Scandinavians. They must arouse the whole world! But how? The trap had closed. The mists returned. His words came out very subdued. "Europe won't stand for it."

"You see it through foreign eyes." Ter Haigasun's passive calm was unendurable. "There are two Europes. The Germans need the Turkish government more than it needs them. And the others can't help us."

Gabriel stared at the priest, whose alert cameo-like face nothing could disturb. "You are the spiritual father of thousands of souls"—Bagradian's voice had almost a military sharpness—"and your whole skill consists in the ability to withhold the truth from people, just as we hide it from children, or the old, to spare them. Is that all you can do for your flock? What else can you do?"

The attack seemed to have pierced the priest to the quick. His hands on the table slowly clenched. His chin sank on to his chest.

"I pray . . ." Ter Haigasun whispered, as though ashamed of letting be seen by a stranger the spiritual struggle which day by day he waged with God for the safety of his flock. Perhaps this grandson of Avetis Bagradian was a freethinker, a scoffer. But Gabriel paced the room, breathing heavily. He struck the wall with the flat of his hand, suddenly, so hard that plaster came flaking down. "Pray then, Ter Haigasun"— and still like an officer giving an order—"pray . . . But God helps those who help themselves."

THE first incident which revealed these secret happenings to Yoghonoluk occurred that very same day. It was a warm, cloudy day in April.

Gabriel, at Stephan's request, had had a few roughly carpentered gymnasium fittings set up in the park. Stephan was naturally athletic. His father often joined his exercises. Shooting at the target was their favourite, though Juliette, to be sure, preferred croquet. Today, immediately after lunch, at which

Gabriel had still not said a word, Avakian, Stephan, and his father went out to the range set up outside the park enclosure on a little woody hillock of Musa Dagh. There Gabriel had had a transverse gully, about fifty feet long, cleared of its undergrowth. Under a high oak there was a lying-board wedged down into the soil, from which to aim at the target fixed to a tree at the farther end of the gully. Avetis had left his brother well supplied with arms—a box of eight hunting-rifles of various patterns, two Mauser infantry rifles, and a full supply of ammunition.

Gabriel was a fairly good shot, but for five cartridges he got only one bull's eye. The very short-sighted Avakian kept clear of the contest, so as not to put too hard a strain on his pupil's respect. But Stephan proved a crack shot, since, of seven cartridges fired out of the smallest of the hunting-rifles, six pierced the playing-card which served as bull's eye to the target, and four hit the face of the figure. It excited Stephan greatly to beat his father. He would have liked to go on shooting till the evening, had Gabriel not suddenly broken off: "That's enough."

Gabriel's state of mind was one he had never before experienced. He could not think of anything quite like it. He felt insipid. His tongue was dry and heavy in his mouth. His hands and feet were cold. All the blood seemed to have left his head. But these were the mere outward signs of some change at the very centre of his being. "I don't feel ill," he reflected, having waited some time to see what would happen. "All I feel is that I'd like to get out of my skin, strip off my body." At the same instant came the senseless longing to run away, far away from this, no matter where. "Let's go for a short walk together," he decided. He did not want to be left alone. If they left him, he would have to walk on and on in short, quick steps, farther and farther, and never turn round till he had walked right out of the world.

Avakian undertook to carry the rifles back to the house.

77

The son and father left the park and went down the road to Yoghonoluk, not ten minutes' walk. Suddenly Gabriel felt like a very old man, his body so heavy that he leant on Stephan. They could hear the noisy buzz of voices even before they came into the church square.

Armenians, in contrast to Arabs and the other clamorous races of the East, are quietly reticent in public. Their ancient destiny in itself is enough to inhibit their taking part in noisy gatherings, or themselves producing them. But here and now about three hundred villagers had collected in a wide half-circle, besieging the church. Among these men and women, peasants and craftsmen, there were several who emitted long, hoarse objurgations and shook their fists. No doubt these curses were aimed at the saptiehs, whose shabby lambskin busbies rose above the heads of the crowd. Apparently these protectors of law and order were trying to clear a space before the church, so as to leave the steps and entrance free. Gabriel seized Stephan's hand and forced a way through the shoal of people. At first they saw only a tall, ragged fellow, who had crowned his black cap with a straw wreath, and whose right hand waved the head of a sunflower, broken off short. This apparition, obeying some rhythm of its own, executed with deathly seriousness a dance of wearily thudding steps. But this was in no sense the dance of a drunkard; that was at once plain.

The crowd did not even notice this dancer, waving his sunflower-head. Their eyes were set on another picture.

On the steps of the church four people squatted. A man, two young women, a little girl of twelve or thirteen. All four were staring out into the distance with a dazed expression—their eyes seemed unaware of their surroundings, of the excited crowd, the apothecary's house immediately opposite.

The man, still young, with a thin, crazed-looking, unshaven face, wore a long, grey alpaca cassock, of the kind worn here by Protestant pastors. His soft straw hat had rolled down the

78

steps. The ends of his trouser-legs were tattered. His broken boots, the thick coating of dust on his face and cloak, showed that he must have trudged for several days. The women, too, wore European dress, and not by any means the cheapest, as far as could be judged by their present state. The one sitting beside the pastor—doubtless his wife—looked as though she might faint or go into convulsions at any minute, since suddenly she fell backwards on to the steps and would have bumped her head against the stone had her husband not put out an arm to support her. This was the first, still strangely jerky movement of the group.

The other woman, still in her earliest youth, looked beautiful, even in such a plight. Her little face was thin and livid, but the eyes had in them a feverish shimmer of vitality; the full, soft lips were parted, gasping for air. She was in obvious pain, must be wounded or have met with an accident, since her left arm, which looked contorted, hung in a sling. Finally the child, a perky, sparrow-like little creature, had on the striped smock worn by children in orphanages. This little girl stretched her feet convulsively out from under her frock, obviously concerned to touch nothing with them.

"Like a hurt animal," Gabriel thought, "stretching its wounded paws away from its body." And indeed the poor child's feet looked very swollen, purple, and covered with open wounds. Only the dancer with the sunflower-head seemed sound of limb and full of strength.

An older man came running across the square. Apparently he had been called away from his work, since he still had on a blue apron. Stephan recognized Tomasian the builder, who had supervised the improvements in the villa. Young Stephan had often loitered round him inquisitively, and Tomasian had proudly told him of Aram, his son, a very respected man in the town of Zeitun, a pastor, and the head of the orphanage there. So this must be the son, thought Stephan. Old Tomasian stopped, with raised inquiring arms, in front of the group.

Pastor Aram came back to his surroundings with difficulty, sprang to his feet with forced agility, and did his best to wear an appeasing smile, as though nothing very serious had happened. The women, too, stood up, but not so easily, since one had a broken arm and the other, it was apparent, expected a child. Only the little girl, in her striped orphanage smock, sat on, squinting suspiciously up at her fellow-sufferers. Impossible to make out the sense of their sudden questions and sounds of woe. But for an instant, as Pastor Aram embraced his father, he lost control. His head sagged on to the old man's shoulder, and a short, hoarse sob of grief became fully audible. It came and went, and still the women did not speak. But it spread, like an electric shock, through the crowd. Whimperings, sobs, loud clearings of the throat. Only oppressed and persecuted peoples are such good pain-conductors. What has befallen one has been done to all. Here, in the church square of Yoghonoluk, three hundred Armenians were shaken by a grief, the story of which they had not yet heard. Even Gabriel, the stranger, the Parisian, the cosmopolitan, who had long since overcome his origins—even he had to force down something which throttled him. He glanced surreptitiously at Stephan. The last tinge of colour had faded out of that crack marksman's face. Juliette would have been startled, not only at her son's pallor, but at the wild look of uncomprehending horror in his eyes. She would have been scared to see her child look so Armenian.

Meanwhile Dr. Altouni had joined the group, as well as Antaram Altouni, the two schoolmasters, who had been called away from their classes, the mukhtar Kebussyan, and, last of all, Ter Haigasun, just back from a visit to Bitias, on his donkey. The priest called out a few words in Turkish to the saptieh, Ali Nassif. None of the crowd were to be let into the church. He, however, bundled the Tomasian family and the little orphan through the door. The doctor and his wife, the teachers, and the mukhtar followed. The crowd and the sunflower-dancer, who sank down on the steps and went to sleep, remained in the square.

Ter Haigasun led the exhausted people into the sacristy, a big, light room containing a divan and some church benches. The sacristan was sent for wine and hot water. The doctor and his wife got to work at once. The girl with the broken arm —Iskuhi Tomasian, the pastor's sister—was examined. So were the wounded feet of Sato, the little orphan whom Pastor Aram had brought from Zeitun.

Gabriel Bagradian stood apart, holding Stephan's hand, a stranger—for the present at least. He listened to the confused questions, the broken answers. Thus, bit by bit, he heard the disordered tale of Zeitun, the tragic history of this town, of Pastor Aram, and of his flock.

ZEITUN is the name of an ancient hill town on the northern slopes of the Cilician Taurus range. Like the villages around Musa Dagh, it was almost entirely inhabited by its original Armenian population. Since, however, it was a town of some importance, of about thirty thousand inhabitants, the Turkish government had garrisoned it with considerable numbers of troops and saptiehs, officers and officials, with their families— as they did wherever it seemed necessary to keep non-Turks under surveillance. Only such people as Bagradian, whose lives had been spent in Paris or some other capital in the West, could still have hoped for any reconciliation of opposites, any stilling of a hatred in the blood, or "triumph of Justice," under the Young Turkish banner. Gabriel had once been friends with a certain number of journalists and lawyers whom the revolution had helped into the saddle. In the days of conspiracy he had sat up all night, arguing with them till dawn in Montmartre cafés, with assurances of eternal friendship, messianic prophecies of the future, exchanged between Turks and Armenians. In defence of a fatherland with which he had had very little to do, he, a married man, went to the war—a notion which had not even occurred to most of the Turkish patriots in Paris. And now? Their faces were still in his mind; some flame, still not quite extinguished, of reminiscent friendship made him ask himself: "What? Can such old friends be my mortal enemies?"

Zeitun was the crude answer. It should be pictured as a high, many-creviced rock, crowned by a savage-looking citadel, honeycombed with the streets of an ancient town. A haughtily repelling pyramid of ways piled one above the other, only its modern quarters spreading their tentacles a little way out into the plain. Zeitun had been a perpetual thorn in Turkish flesh. For the earth has both its holy places, its sites of pilgrimage, which frame the human mind to devotion, and its natural fortresses, redolent of hate and defiance, whose spirit is such as to rouse to seething-point the blood of an opposing racial fanaticism. In Zeitun such hate had its definite reasons. First, until far into the nineteenth century the city had governed itself. But more unpardonable still was the memory of its astounding conduct in the year 1896.

In those days the good Sultan Abdul Hamid had called into being the Hamidiyehs—predatory bands of nomads, robbers, convicts, let out of jail for the purpose—with their sole object the formation of a troop of valiants restlessly bent on provoking "incidents," with which he hoped to stop the mouths of the Armenian reformers. Everywhere else these bands were distinguished for their successes—in Zeitun only did they encounter bloody defeat instead of achieving what had been promised them, an enjoyable and remunerative massacre. Worse still, even the battalion of regulars hurried to their assistance was driven back with heavy losses out of the narrow streets. Not even the siege with full armament following this rout brought the least success. Zeitun remained impregnably rebellious. When at last European diplomacy intervened on behalf of these brave Armenians, and ambassadors to the Sublime Porte, which, spattered with dishonour, had no alternative, achieved full amnesty for Zeitun—the Turk set his teeth, abysmally humbled.

All military races, not only the Ottoman, have encountered defeat at the hands of their own kind and forgotten it. But to have been beaten by a race of merchants and craftsmen, people whose ideal had never been military—a race of bookworms —it was more than any soldierly people can forget. So that the new government, now that the old had been disposed of, still had old scores to pay off in Zeitun.

And what better chance of paying off old scores than the Great War? Martial law and a state of emergency were proclaimed. Most young men of Zeitun were at the front or in distant barracks. Repeated house-to-house searches, in the earliest days of the war, had entirely disarmed such inhabitants as remained.

Only one thing was lacking: a pretext.

The mayor of Zeitun was a man named Nazareth Chaush. He was a typical Armenian mountaineer—haggard, bent, sallow, with a drooping bushy moustache and a hooked nose. But he was ailing, no longer young, and had long done his best to avoid election. He could scent the reek of future holocausts. The lines from his nostrils sharpened daily as he toiled up the steep hill to the Hükümet, to receive the latest orders of the Kaimakam. His hand, round a rough stick, was deformed by rheumatic knots. Nazareth Chaush was highly intelligent. He had seen at once that in future there could be only one policy —that of being on guard against provocation. Nothing should be allowed to cast any slur on the patriotic integrity of Armenians. All traps must be skilfully avoided. One was, and remained, a thoroughgoing Ottoman patriot. Not that Nazareth Chaush really bore any grudge against Turkey, nor did any other inhabitant of Zeitun. Turkey was the destiny of the race. It is futile to bicker with the earth on which one has to live, with the air one breathes. He cherished no childish dream of emancipation, since, after all, the choice lay between Tsar and

Sultan and it was as hard to make as it was superfluous. He remained in agreement with the words which had achieved a certain celebrity with Armenians: "Better perish physically in Turkey than spiritually in Russia." There was no third way.

A clearly defined line of conduct towards Turkish authorities was therefore laid down. The living example of their leader, Nazareth Chaush, forged iron discipline among the inhabitants of Zeitun. So far no longed-for "incident" had assuaged the secret itch of the High Command. A medical board, eager for blood-letting, passed cripples and invalids for the army. Good! They reported for duty without a murmur. The Kaimakam imposed illegal taxes and war levies. Good! They were punctually supplied. This same Kaimakam used the most foolish pretexts for arranging victory celebrations and mass demonstrations of patriotism. The townsfolk mustered in full force, their faces aglow with honest loyalty, to bawl the prescribed hymns and victorious anthems to the braying of Turkish army bands.

So nothing was to be done along such lines. But what mass-provocation had failed to achieve might yet be managed by petty tyranny. Suddenly the cafés, the bazaar, every street and square, the inns of Zeitun, became infested with strange Armenians, soon on gossiping terms at every corner, taking a hand at cards and dominoes, even worming their way into private houses, to bemoan with peculiar acrimony this intolerable and increasing Turkish oppression. Such grains of sedition as they could gather hardly paid these spies' personal expenses. The first winter of war descended without one "incident" having been angled out of the still waters of Zeitun, though a certain exalted quarter urgently needed one. At last the Kaimakam decided to take over the part of *agent provocateur*.

It was Nazareth Chaush's good fortune—or indeed, as things turned out, his bad—to have a very clumsy player to deal with. This Kaimakam was no blood-smeared tyrant, but a mediocre petty official in the style of the old régime, who, on the one hand, wanted a quiet life, on the other, to "keep in" with his superiors. These superiors began with the Mutessarif of the sanjak of Marash, to which the kazah of Zeitun was subordinate. This Mutessarif was a very sharp-eyed individual, a dauntless member of Ittihad, resolute to enforce without compunction all decisions of Enver and Talaat as to the fate of the "accursed people"—even against the orders of his superior, the Wali of Aleppo, Djelal Bey. The Mutessarif overwhelmed the Kaimakam with questionnaires, warnings, acrid reprimands. So that the portly chief justice of Zeitun—who would far rather have lived at peace with Armenians—found that he must trump up grounds of complaint, if only against a single prominent personality. It is the essence of a good negative civil servant that, having no character of his own, he should mirror that of any temporary superior. The Kaimakam therefore addressed himself to the mukhtar, Nazareth Chaush, whom daily he invited to come to see him, overwhelmed with cordial civilities, and even offered the chance of a very good business deal with the government. Not only did Chaush turn up punctually whenever he was required, but, with the most innocent expression, made the most of these business-like inducements. Naturally such constant visits gave rise to more and more heart-felt conversations. The chief justice kept assuring the mayor how passionately fond he was of Armenians. Chaush begged him earnestly not to exaggerate: all peoples had their faults, and not least his compatriots. It was for Armenians to win their position in the fatherland by the services they rendered in the war. What newspapers did the mukhtar read to get the true account of the situation? Only the *Tanin,* the official Ottoman newspaper, answered Chaush. And, as for truth, these were the days of world-shaking military events—surely truth was one of the prohibited weapons. The Kaimakam, in his helpless simplicity, grew plainer. He began to abuse Ittihad, the power behind the power. (Probably

85

he meant what he was saying.) Nazareth Chaush was visibly horror-stricken. "They are great men, and great men always act for the best."

The Kaimakam lost his temper at being laughed at. "And Enver Pasha? What do you think of the Enver, Mukhtar?"

"Enver Pasha is the greatest general of our time. But what else can I think of him, Effendi?"

The Kaimakam began to blink, whine, and implore. "Mukhtar, be frank with me. Have you heard the Russians are advancing?"

"What are you saying, Effendi? I don't believe it. There's nothing about it in the papers."

"Well, I tell you they are. Be frank, Mukhtar. Wouldn't that be the solution?"

Nazareth Chaush interrupted, noisy with horror: "I warn you, Effendi. Such a highly placed man as you. Please say no more, in Heaven's name. It sounds like high treason. But have no fear. Your word shall be buried within me."

When such ruses had failed, open aggression could not be far off. Naturally, even in Zeitun, and in the wild country surrounding it, there were "elements." Their numbers, the longer the war lasted, kept being increased from without. Besides Armenians there were at least an equal number of Mohammedans escaped from the barracks at Marash. The jagged mountain range, Ala Kaya, was a safe and pleasant retreat for deserters of all kinds, or so the rumour went in all the barracks. But these deserters were inoffensive: apart from the usual country pilferings, they harmed nobody, were even anxious not to cause trouble.

One day, however, a Turkish muleteer was attacked in the mountains, whether by deserters or others remained unknown. Some incredulous people even suggested that this lousy patriot had let himself be thrashed half to death for the baksheesh of the Imperial Ottoman government. In any case the man was discovered in a ditch, half unconscious. Here was the longed-for "incident." Müdirs and petty officials began to wear a look of inscrutability, all saptiehs were ordered to patrol the streets of Zeitun in pairs, and this time Nazareth Chaush was commanded, not invited, to attend the Kaimakam.

Revolutionary unrest, the Kaimakam mourned, seemed increasing to a most alarming extent. His superiors, in particular the Mutessarif of Marash, were demanding extra measures to deal with it. If he delayed any longer it would be all over with him. Therefore he counted implicitly on the help of his friend, Nazareth Chaush, so highly respected all over the district. It ought not to be difficult for the mukhtar, in the interests of the whole Armenian people, to give up a few firebrands and criminals; there must be a great many in the neighbourhood, even in the town itself. And here this clever man walked into the trap set by the stupid one. He ought to have said: "Effendi, I am at your orders and those of the Mutessarif. Command me, what I am to do." Instead he made his first real blunder: "I know nothing of criminals or revolutionaries, Effendi."

"So you can't even tell me the place where you hide your rabble to molest honest Turks in full daylight?"

"Since I know of no rabble, I am also unaware where it is to be found."

"That's a pity. But the worst of it is that you yourself, in the last few days, have received some of these scoundrelly traitors in your house."

Nazareth Chaush raised gouty fingers to heaven and denied it. But he could not manage to sound very persuasive.

The Kaimakam had an inspiration, not born in the least of cunning, merely of his own inertia, which instinctively shunned anything troublesome: "I'll tell you what, Mukhtar. I have a request. I'm really getting to loathe all these difficulties between us. I'm a peaceful man, I'm not a police-hound. You take all this business off my hands. I beg you to go to Marash. Speak to the Mutessarif. You're the city elder, he's the responsible man. He's got my report on what's been happening here. You two will soon find the right way to deal with it."

"Is this an order you're giving me, Effendi?"

"I told you—it's a personal request. You can refuse, but it would hurt me very much."

"If I go to Marash, I shall be in danger."

The Kaimakam grew reassuringly benevolent. "Danger? Why? The road's quite safe. I'll give you the use of my own carriage and two saptiehs for a guard. And I'll give you a letter of personal recommendation to the Mutessarif, which you can read before you go. If there's anything else you want, I'll let you have it."

The wrinkled face of this Armenian mountaineer turned ashen-grey. He stood there as old and dilapidated as the weatherbeaten rocks of Zeitun itself. Desperately he sought some valid excuse. But his lips, under the overhanging moustache, could frame no more words. An unknown power lamed his will. He only nodded weakly, at last. Next day he took quiet leave of his family. A short journey. He would not be away more than a week. His eldest son went with him to the Kaimakam's carriage. His swollen feet and hands made it hard to climb into it. The young man supported him. As Chaush set one foot on the step, he said in a low, casual voice, so as not to be overheard by the coachman: "Oglum, bir, daha gelmem." My son, I shall not come back.

He was right. The Mutessarif of Marash made short work of Nazareth Chaush. In spite of his cordial letter of introduction he was received as a criminal, whose crime however was kept secret from him, and finally, as an enemy to the state and member of a treasonable secret society, he was placed in the jail of Osmanieh. Since no further inquiries elicited any information as to the secret organization of an Armenian revolutionary movement, nor even as to deserters in Zeitun, he was condemned to the highest degree of the bastinado. After which corrosive acid was poured upon his bleeding feet. This was too much for his failing body. He died after an hour of indescribable agony. A brass band of janizaries played outside the windows of the jail. Their drums and fifes were to drown the shrieks from his cell.

And not even this martyrdom brought the expected results. At first nothing happened. Only the grief, the sullen desperation, of these townsfolk became an almost physical miasma. A darkness of the human spirit brooded upon this dark mountain town, stifling people's breath like a black fog. It was March before at last two events gave the government its excuse to fulfil its intentions. The first of these was a shot fired out of a window. A police patrol in the Yeni Dünya quarter of the town, as it passed the house of the dead mukhtar, was fired upon, and one of them was slightly wounded. Instead of holding the usual inquiry, the Kaimakam declared at once that his life was in danger in Zeitun and, having sent telegrams right and left, moved his residence to a barracks outside the town. This mode of procedure was entirely consonant with his character, slyly stupid, and anxious not to take trouble. At the same time, to protect the Mohammedan population, he gave orders for a "civil guard" to be armed—that is to say, a few quickly drummed up hooligans received, quite in the manner of Abdul Hamid, a green armlet each and a Mauser rifle. Worthy Turkish citizens in Zeitun, dignified and law-abiding souls, were the first to lodge angry complaints against their "protectors." They besieged the Kaimakam and demanded the instant disbanding of their guardians. It availed them nothing. A paternal government was obstinately concerned for their security. At last the civil guard gave a good, clear pretext for the second incident, which brought matters to a head. In the afternoons, Armenian girls and women liked to frequent the Eski Bostan, a small public garden in the suburbs. Wide plane trees shaded a few benches. Children played about round the fountains, the women sewed and gossiped on the seats. A sherbert-seller pushed his stand. This garden was suddenly invaded by the raggedest members of the civil guard. These panting vagabonds flung themselves on the Armenian women, held them, and began to strip off their clothes. For, no matter how intense the itch to slaughter the men of the accursed race, the Turks had always longed for their women, those soft-limbed, full-lipped creatures with alien eyes. Shrieks and children's howls filled the air. But help came the next instant. A much stronger force of Armenian men, who, scenting evil, had crept out after the town's protectors, thrashed them until they were lame, with bare fists, straps, and cudgels, and took away their rifles and bayonets.

To their own disaster. Open rebellion against the state! This disarming of the civil guard by rebels furnished all the proof that was wanted. It could not be denied. That same evening the Kaimakam issued a list of names for arrest to be handed over by the municipality. The men affected came together in desperate rage, swore not to separate, and took refuge, half an hour east of the town, in an old tekkeh, an abandoned cloister of pilgrims and dervishes. Some deserters on Ala Kaya and other points in the nearby mountains got wind of this and came down to join the fugitives. This little fortress contained about a hundred men.

The Mutessarif in Marash, the government agents in Istanbul, had all they had planned for. The time for petty provocations was over and a very effective little rebellion well under way. Neutral and allied consuls should no longer be allowed to keep their eyes shut to Armenian lawlessness. Within two days military reinforcements had reached Zeitun—two provisional infantry companies of the line. The bashi, the major in command, laid siege at once. But—whether because he was a hero or merely a fool—when he rode forth, disdainful of any cover, on a plunging horse at the head of his men, towards the tekkeh, to subdue its garrison in this very frank and warlike manner, he and six of his men were shot down with well-aimed bullets. This was even more than had been desired!

The major's heroic death was broadcast at once, with a blare of trumpets, to all four corners of the empire. Ittihad worked feverishly to get the exact note required into the cries of indignation that arose. In about three days Zeitun had become an armed camp. A contingent of four battalions with two batteries had been summoned to clear out this little nest of despairing fugitives. All this, moreover, at a moment when Jemal Pasha needed every man and every gun for his fourth army. In spite of this vast surrounding force a private was sent with a white flag to admonish the rebels to surrender. He received the classic answer: "Since we have to die, let it be fighting."

But the surprising, the miraculous, thing was that they lived. For scarcely had the siege artillery dropped its fourth superfluous shell against half-ruined walls when the order came from some mysterious quarter to cease fire. Were the few Moslems among the besieged a sufficient reason for such misplaced humanity? The townsfolk of Zeitun did not suppose it—they saw in this constricting truce the omen of some more than usually gruesome evil. They had reason to do so. And in their terror they sent a deputation to the Kaimakam, begging him that the valiant troops might free them of these cursed rebels as soon as possible. They had nothing to do with them. The Kaimakam moaned and sighed. It was too late now to see reason. All future decisions were in the hands of the commander of the occupying regiments. He himself was now no more than a tolerated cipher.

One radiant morning in March a terrifying rumour spread through the town. The besieged deserters, leaving their dead, whom they had however disfigured past recognition, had escaped from the fortress and disappeared into the mountains. Those Zeitunlis who did not believe in miracles asked: How could a hundred tattered, highly suspicious-looking men have got through lines of over four thousand trained soldiers? And the questioners knew well what their question meant. The blow had already fallen by midday. The commandant and the Kaimakam called the whole town of Zeitun to account for the disappearance of this hundred. The profoundly treacherous Zeitunlis had, in some devilish fashion, contrived to spirit the besieged garrison past sentries, through lines of peacefully slumbering Turkish troops. News of this crime had brought the Mutessarif in person, in his carriage, all the way from Marash. The münadirs, the drummers-up, passed with a dull rattle down all the streets. Strings of official messengers followed them, whose business it was to summon the elders and notables of Zeitun to "a conference on the situation with the Mutessarif and the commanding officer." The summoned, fifty of the town's most respected inhabitants, doctors, schoolteachers, priests, large shopkeepers, business men, appeared without delay at the place appointed, most of them still in their working clothes. Only a few of the most far-seeing had hidden any money about them. The "conference" consisted in this—that these elderly and highly respected citizens were brutally herded together on a barrack square by sergeants and counted like cattle. This had ended the matter, they were informed, and the very next day they were to set out along the Marash-Aleppo road, on their way to the Mesopotamian desert, to Deir ez Zor, to which they were to be "migrated." They stared at one another without a word. Not one of them had a stroke, not one of them wept. Half an hour ago they had been the chief citizens of a town; now, at one blow, they were degraded to almost inanimate lumps of clay, livid of face, half bereft of will. The new mukhtar, their spokesman, begged almost voicelessly for one favour: that their families, in the name of divine compassion, might at least be left in peace in Zeitun. Then they would meet their fate quietly. The answer came with a cruel sneer. Certainly not—the Armenians were already sufficiently known, and nobody had any desire to separate the respected fathers of families from their nearest relatives. On the contrary, the order was that all present should by tomorrow, an hour before sunrise, have handed in a written declaration of readiness to march, with all their relatives, their goods and chattels, wives, sons, daughters, children of every age. Orders from Istanbul explicitly stated that the whole Armenian population, to the last baby in arms, was to be evacuated. Zeitun had ceased to exist. From now on its name was to be Sultanieh, so that no memory might remain of a township which had dared open rebellion against the heroic Turkish people.

Next day, at the hour assigned, the first piteous convoy did in fact set out, beginning one of the cruellest tragedies that ever in recorded history has overwhelmed a whole people. Military guards followed the emigrants—it was suddenly evident now that this vast force, summoned to reduce a hundred fugitives, had other minor, but all the more treacherous, duties assigned it. Every morning now the same heart-rending pageant was staged. Those fifty chief families of the town were followed by fifty others, less well-to-do, and, as the exiles sank in the social scale, their numbers increased. To be sure the vast war zones along every European front were equally crowded with refugees. But, hard as was the fate of these homeless people, it was nothing compared with that of these poor townsfolk.

For many people it is depressing even to move house. A lost fragment of life always remains. To move to another town, settle in a foreign country, is for everyone a major decision. But, to be suddenly driven forth, within twenty-four hours, from one's home, one's work, the reward of years of steady industry. To become the helpless prey of hate. To be sent defenceless out on to Asiatic highroads, with several thousand miles of dust, stones, and morass before one. To know that one will never again find a decently human habitation, never again sit down to a proper table. Yet all this is nothing. To be more shackled than any convict. To be counted as outside the law, a vagabond, whom anyone has the right to kill unpunished. To be confined within a crawling herd of sick people,

93

a moving concentration-camp, in which no one is so much as allowed to ease his body without permission.—Who shall dare say he can measure the depths of anguish which invaded the minds of these people of Zeitun, in that long week between the setting out of the first transport and the last! Even so young a man as the pastor Aram Tomasian, who, since he was not a native of Zeitun, had better prospects than all the others, became almost a wraith in those seven days.

Pastor Aram—he was called only by his Christian name— had for over a year been the pastor of the Protestant congregation of Zeitun and head of the big orphanage. His appointment, at scarcely thirty, to the directorship of that institution was due to the fact that the American missionaries in Marash had considered Aram their most promising pupil and hoped great things of him. They had even sent him with a stipend for three years to Geneva, to finish his studies there. His French, therefore, was fluent, his German and English both very good. The orphanage of the American missionaries was one of the most pleasing results of their civilizing work of fifty years. Its large, bright rooms gave shelter to over a hundred children. There was a school attached to it, also open to children from the town. A small farm surrounded the institute, so that the orphanage supplied its own goat's milk, vegetables, and other provisions. Therefore, to be director of this orphanage required not only scholastic ability, but sound, business-like common sense. Pastor Aram, attracted like most other young men by the thought of being independent, had embraced his new duties with enthusiasm. He had spent a very happy and active year and was full of projects. He had married, in the previous spring, shortly before beginning his new duties, Hovsannah, an old flame, a girl from Marash, the daughter of a pastor of the first generation of the seminary there. Whereas most Armenian women are soft-limbed and not very tall, Hovsannah was tall and well-developed. She moved slowly, never had much to say, and often gave the impression of complete detachment from her surroundings. Iskuhi, however, had once suggested to her brother that Hovsannah's quietness had sometimes a dash of malice and stubbornness in it. It was said as a joke, and seemed to be an unjustified observation, since what really malicious and obstinate married woman would ever have had her sister-in-law to live with her? The relationship was peculiar in the case of the nineteen-year-old Iskuhi. Aram worshipped his young sister. In her ninth year, after their mother's death, he had already fetched her away from Yoghonoluk to place her in the missionary school in Marash. Later he sent her to Lausanne, where she spent a year in a finishing-school. The cost of this select ambition on his younger sister's behalf he had paid by many cleverly contrived economies. He could not imagine life without Iskuhi. Hovsannah knew it and had herself proposed this *ménage à trois*. The girl had been given a post as assistant teacher in the orphanage. She taught French. It was not surprising that Iskuhi should have inspired love, and not only in her brother. Apart from her magnificent eyes, the most beautiful thing about her was her mouth. Her deeply tinged lips had always a glistening, smiling sheen upon them, like her eyes, as though her mouth could see. The three had contrived a pleasant life together, quite unlike the usual life around them. The pastor's quarters were in the orphanage. Their bare look had soon vanished under Hovsannah's hands, for she had a gift for decoration and a sharp instinct for beautiful things. She made excursions into the town and surrounding villages to bargain with the Zeitun women for fine tapestries, wood-carvings, household gear, with which to enliven these rooms—a pursuit which took up weeks of her time. Iskuhi was fonder of books. Aram, Hovsannah, and Iskuhi lived for each other. This orphanage and its school were such worlds away from the rest of the town that the three flourishing people had scarcely noticed the oppressive atmosphere of Zeitun. The pastor's Sunday sermons had expressed, until well

95

on into March, a heartening cheerfulness, more redolent of the peaceful joys of his own existence than of any clear-sighted estimate of what the government might intend.

The blow almost stunned him. He saw his work all gone for nothing. But then he was seized with frenzied hope that the government would not dare close down the orphanage. Aram had soon pulled himself together. A word from Hovsannah, in the very first days of banishment, gave him back his strength. Only at such a moment as this did the full meaning of the Christian priesthood become evident. Thus spoke the pastor's daughter. Heartened by her admonishment, Pastor Aram began to put forth superhuman energy. He not only kept his church open day and night, to give spiritual comfort to groups of exiles as they departed—he went from house to house among his flock, from family to family, mingled with the sobbing people, helped them with every penny he possessed, organized a certain order in the convoys, wrote cries for help to all the missions which lay along their route into exile, and carefully worded petitions to Turkish officials, wherever he considered them well disposed, begging letters and testimonials; attempted to obtain delays, haggled with Turkish muleteers—in short did everything he could possibly have done in these grievous circumstances. Then, when he could do no more, could no longer console with the sufferings of the gospel, he would sit in silence, beside these people, dazed with grief, shut his eyes, close convulsive fingers, and cry aloud in his soul to Christ.

The town emptied from day to day. The roads to Marash filled with long serpentine convoys, whose marchers seemed unable to advance. A watcher from the citadel of Zeitun might have seen them far into the mountains, and nothing could have aroused more horror in him than the creeping quiet of these lines of death, rendered more piteous still by the shouts and laughter of the armed escort. Meanwhile the dying streets of Zeitun were reanimated by carrion birds, pilferers, professional thieves, the dregs of the town, and robbers from the country round it. They infested the deserted houses and began in them a vigorous search for plunder. Carts and barrows trundled through the streets, sumpter mules came clattering in. Carpets, clothes, bedsteads, heaps of linen, furniture, mirrors, were all piled up, in leisurely, undisturbed tranquillity, as though it were an ordinary, lawful house-moving. The authorities did nothing to prevent it. They even seemed to look upon such plunder as the natural reward of Turkish scum— always providing that the Armenians were made to go peacefully into exile. The order that, of every craft, six representatives should remain in "Sultanieh," so that the drifting wreck of daily life might not be left entirely without its crew, had the ring of some barbaric fairy-tale. These lucky ones were not chosen by the authorities; the commune was ordered to elect them, a cunning intensification of punishment, since it inflicted a new, acute, mental agony.

The fifth day had already dawned, and Pastor Aram had still received no summons. All that had so far happened was the visit of a Mohammedan mullah, a stranger, moreover, to Zeitun, who had come to demand the keys of the church. This Protestant church, as he courteously informed its pastor, was to be reconsecrated as a mosque, before evening prayer. Yet Tomasian still clung to the hope that his orphanage would be left in peace. He ordered that, from now onwards, everyone was to keep indoors, neither teacher nor child to show himself at the windows, and no loud word was to be spoken. The shutters were to be kept bolted all day, no lights were to be shown in the evening. A strained, death-like rigidity descended on this house, as a rule so alive. But it is just such mockeries of fate which provoke its onslaught. On the next day, the sixth, one of those official messengers who sped, like angels of destruction, gruesomely up and down the streets of Zeitun summoned the pastor instantly before the town-commandant.

97

Aram set forth in his priestly gown. His prayer had been heard. Not a trace of fear or excitement ruffled his dignity. He came, quietly erect, into the staff-officer's presence. In the present case, unluckily, this bearing of his was a great mistake, since the bimbashi enjoyed the sight of tearful cringers. Then he was sometimes ready to wink, ameliorate, show himself kindly and humane. But Aram's certainty of manner stifled this benevolence at its source, since it was born of the contrast between his greatness and the miserable writhings of worms.

"You are the Protestant pastor, Aram Tomasian, native of Yoghonoluk, near Alexandretta?" The colonel growled this warrant of apprehension before he hurled himself on the victim. "You leave with the last convoy, tomorrow morning. In the direction Marash-Aleppo. You understand?"

"I'm ready."

"I didn't ask if you were ready. . . . Your wife and other relatives to accompany you. You are to take only such baggage as you can carry. You will receive, as far as it is possible to supply it, a daily ration of one hundred direms of bread. You are permitted to purchase extra supplies. Any attempt to leave your column of march without permission will be punished by the officer in charge; with death, in the case of a second infringement. The use of vehicles is forbidden."

"My wife is expecting a child," said Aram quietly.

This seemed to amuse the bimbashi. "You ought to have thought of that before." He glanced again at his papers. "The pupils of your orphanage, as Armenian children, are naturally not exempt from transportation. They are to hold themselves in readiness punctually, and in full muster—they and the whole staff of your institution."

Pastor Aram retreated a step. "May I ask if any provision is to be made for these hundred innocent children? A great many of them are under ten years of age, and have never undertaken a long march. And children need milk."

"It is not your place to ask questions, Pastor!" the colonel shouted. "You're here to take my orders. For the last week you've been living in a military area."

Had this bellow made the pastor break down in terror, the bimbashi, from superlative heights, might perhaps have conceded him his goats. But Aram continued, quietly stubborn: "I shall therefore arrange for our herd of goats to be driven out, so that the children may get their milk as usual."

"You'll keep your insolent mouth shut, Pastor, and knuckle under."

"Moreover, Effendi, I make you personally responsible for the orphanage building, which is the inalienable property of American citizens, under the protection of their ambassador."

At first the bimbashi could find no answer. This threat seemed to have had its effect. Such gods subdue their tinny voices as soon as higher gods come into sight. After a long and, for a colonel, rather disastrous pause, he spluttered: "Do you know that I can tread on you like an insect? I have only to breathe, and you never so much as existed."

"I won't prevent you," said Pastor Aram, and meant what he said, for a monstrous longing for death had overwhelmed him.

Later, when Aram, Hovsannah, and Iskuhi were asked which moment of their exile had seemed the worst, they all three answered: "The minutes when we were waiting for our transport to get under way." It was an instant in which their actual, concrete wretchedness seemed only half as acute as a kind of heavy desolation, a primitive horror within their blood, some awakened memory of a dim primal age before security of domicile had been won as a legal right, so that now this mass of a thousand people, dishonoured, helpless, fused into one, not only felt the final loss of all its possessions, the onslaught of the perils of life, but became aware beneath all this of itself as a collective entity, a people robbed of the rewards of centuries of effort, the cultural fruits of a thousand years. Pastor Aram and the two women had fallen a prey to this general, unfathomable melancholy.

An overcast day of low-hung clouds, which veiled the familiar heads of the mountains of Zeitun: far better than a sunny day to march on. But this outward gloom of the day seemed to load down the backs of the exiles more heavily than any of the bundles they had been permitted to take with them. This first step had something deeply significant, something sacred, in its sheer terror, and which flashed upon every soul like lightning. Families herded close together. Not a word, not even the crying of a child. But already, after the first half-hour, when the last outlying houses were behind them, these people felt a certain relief. The primitive childishness of all humans, their poignant, frivolous faculty of forgetfulness, gained the upper hand for a certain time. As a single timid chirrup is heard at daybreak, and instantly the whole choir has joined it, soon, above the heads of this whole transport, there arose an entangled skein of jagged children's voices. The mothers quieted them. Even the men called out this or that to one another. Here and there a faint laugh was already heard. Many old people and children were riding donkeys, also laden with bedding, coverlets, sacks. The officer in charge allowed it to be. He seemed, on his own responsibility, at his own peril, to wish to mitigate the harshness of this order of banishment. Aram, too, had procured a donkey for his wife. But most of the time they walked beside it, since she feared the joltings of the ride. Although it would have been more prudent to send them on to the head, the orphans brought up the rear of the convoy. After them came only the herd of goats, which the pastor, neglecting orders, had fearlessly caused to be driven forth. At first the children enjoyed it all as an adventure, a delightful change. Iskuhi, who kept among them, did her very best to encourage these high spirits. Nobody could have seen the strain of her sleepless nights. Her face showed only delight in the moment, the joy of life.

Tender and weak as her body seemed, the all-powerful resilience of her youth had surmounted everything. She even tried to get the children to sing. It was a pleasant song from Yoghonoluk, where people sang it at their work among vines and orchards. Iskuhi had introduced it into the school at Zeitun.

> "Days of misfortune pass and are gone,
>   Like the days of winter, they come and they go;
>   The sorrows of men do not last very long,
>   Like the buyers in shops, they come and go."

But Aram Tomasian came hurrying back at once to forbid their singing. The young pastor covered twice or three times as much ground as the others. He would be seen at the head of the convoy, then at the rear, among the stragglers, always with his big gourd hung from a strap, out of which he kept offering drinks of raki. And he gave out courage, cracked jokes, adjusted differences, doing his best to bring some shape and order into life, even such life as this. Everyone had a duty assigned him. Among the craftsmen, for instance, shoemakers were entrusted with the task, during every halt, of quickly repairing all broken shoes. Though there were very few Protestants in the convoy, Tomasian was the only priest, since all the Gregorians and Catholics had been sent forth in the first days. So that the pastor had charge of all these souls. He evolved his own particular method of making these exiles keep up their courage. Only what seems aimless is unbearable; he knew that by his own experience. Therefore he kept repeating, in a voice full of the stoutest confidence: "We shall be in Marash by tomorrow evening. There, it will all be different. Probably we shall stay there some time, till orders come to send us home again. And it's as good as certain we shall go home. The Istanbul government can't possibly be behind all this. After all, we have deputies and national representation. In three weeks from now it will all be arranged. But what matters most is that you should all be well when we get to Marash and that we should keep up our strength and courage."

Such speeches had a soothing effect, even on the naturally pessimistic, on those who were too intelligent to believe in the innocence of the central government. Despairing faces began to brighten. The miracle was due not only to this rosily pictured future, but to an aim, a definite, firmly defined thought: "We shall be in Marash tomorrow." In the long rests the young officer in command of the Turkish escort showed himself a very decent fellow. As soon as his men had finished their cooking, he offered the pastor the use of their field-cookers, so that warm food could be cooked for the weak and ailing. But, since tomorrow they would be in a big town, even the strong did not trouble to economize their supplies. And for the next few hours the march took on a new ease and confidence.

And when that evening they encamped in the open fields and stretched out, weary to death, on their blankets, they could thank God that the first day had passed off tolerably. Not far from their camp there was a big village, called Tutlissek. In the night a few mountaineers, yailadjis, came out of the village to visit the Turkish guards. The men squatted together in dignified conference, gravely smoking, and seemed to be discussing a serious matter. When, just before dawn, the Zeitunlis awoke and went to collect their goats and donkeys, to water them, all the beasts had vanished.

This was the first stroke of a cruel day. They had marched two hours when the first death occurred in their ranks. An old man suddenly sank to the ground. The convoy halted. The young and, as a rule, so friendly officer came riding up in anger. "Get on!" A few tried to lift the old man up. But they soon had to let him slip to the ground. A saptieh prodded him with his foot. "Come on. Get up, you swindler." But he still lay on, with open mouth and turned-up eyes. His corpse was flung into the ditch. The officer harried them: "No standing about. Forbidden. Get on. Get on." Not all Aram's prayers, nor the howls of the family, could procure either leave to carry the corpse, or a quick burial. It must suffice that they raised the old man's head a little and placed big stones on either side of him. There was no time left even to cross his hands on his chest, since the saptiehs brandished their cudgels, cursing and driving on the hesitant crowd. Panic descended on the transport—a trotting run, like a stampede, which only ceased when the corpse had been left far behind and carrion birds from the Taurus came circling nearer it.

Scarcely had the horror of this first sacrifice been surmounted when a yayli, a ponderous two-horsed coach, held up the convoy. It thrust the exiles off the narrow highroad, into swampy fields. Inside it a portly young gentleman of about twenty-five, with many rings on his fingers. Carelessly he thrust a bejewelled hand through the carriage window to present a document to the officer. It was a government order, duly stamped, giving him the right to select one or several Armenian girls for domestic purposes. Since his coach happened to be surrounded by orphans, his jaded, benevolent eyes alighted on Iskuhi. He pointed his stick at her, beckoned her to him with a smile. This important gentleman did not consider himself in the least a violator of women, but their benefactor—was he not ready to snatch one of these dirty creatures from her fate, take her to his bosom, to that of his highly respected family, in his dignified and secure town house? All the greater therefore his amazement when the fair one, instead of taking happy refuge in his sheltering arms, ran away from him with loud shrieks of "Aram." The coach pursued her. Perhaps no reasons with which the pastor strove to protect his sister would have availed. That he should have mentioned her European upbringing was a mistake, born of desperation, since this served only to put an edge on the ardour of her would-be protector. Only the sharp intervention of the young commanding officer settled the matter. He most unceremoniously tore up the suitor's government order, adding that, as officer in charge, he alone had power to dispose of Armenian convoys. Unless the Effendi instantly made himself scarce, both he and his yayli would be arrested. He emphasized all this with a cut of his riding-switch on the flanks of the horses. The corpulent benefactor, wounded to the quick at having been balked in a good deed, clattered on at a remorseless trot. Iskuhi soon recovered from the incident. Soon she was seeing it as a joke, so that certain of its comic details made her shout with laughter. But her amusement was not to last long.

That same afternoon it began with the sufferings of the orphans. It is strange that these children should not singly have noticed their wounded feet, but all together—so that a sudden howling, whimpering, wailing, which tore the women's heart-strings, filled the air. The easy-going young officer, however, was ruthlessly in earnest on one point—no rests or delays over and above the regulations. He had orders to reach Marash with his convoy two hours after sundown. This he was determined to carry out punctually, though in all the rest he might use discretion, often against the clear indications of his superiors. His professional pride was involved in this. There could therefore be no question of any halt for the children's bleeding feet to be dressed with oil.

"All that's no good to you. See that we get to Marash in time, then you can dress your wounds. Forward."

There was nothing for it. Some of the children had to be carried. Here even the weak Iskuhi distinguished herself, though soon she too was involved in disaster.

Her brother had repeatedly warned her not to lag in the rear of the convoy, or even among the orphans who composed it. It was certainly the unsafest part of the transport, immediately in front of the ill-disposed soldiers of the escort and the many varieties of hideous vagabond which straggled inquisitively out of villages. But Iskuhi refused to listen, for she felt her place to be with the children, especially now that, with every fifteen minutes, they became more weary, ill, and footsore. The other teachers of the orphanage little by little went on ahead, leaving only Iskuhi doing her best to shepherd and encourage, with various arts, her yelping infants. They stumbled more and more miserably, and for this reason the line was often broken, till at last there was a fairly wide gap between the rear and the main body. At such a juncture as this Iskuhi felt herself gripped from behind. She screamed and tried to wrench herself free. Over her there appeared a terrible face, gigantic, with filthy stubble, snorting, rolling its eyes, stinking, inhuman. She let out another piercing scream and then struggled silently with the man, whose spittle dripped into her face, whose brown claws were tearing her dress to shreds, to fasten themselves into naked breasts. Her strength failed. The face above her swelled into a mountainous, shifting hell.

She sank into its horrible breath. . . . It was Iskuhi's good fortune that, attracted by the piercing howls of the children, the officer came galloping sharply back to them. The brown claws flung her to the ground. The tramp tried to run away but did not escape a final stroke with the flat of the sword on the back of his head.

Iskuhi struggled to her feet but could not even manage to cry. At first she only supposed that her left arm had been numbed in the struggle. "As though it has gone to sleep," she thought. Then, suddenly, wild pain flamed up in it. Speechless with this, she could not tell her brother what had happened. Hovsannah and Aram led her. Not a sound passed her lips. Everything in her became unconscious—only not her feet, which still took quick, little steps.

It is still a riddle how they ever managed to reach Marash. As soon as the town was in sight, the desperate pastor went to the officer and even ventured to ask him how long he thought the exiles would be allowed to halt there. That, he was plainly told, would depend on the Mutessarif. He might safely reckon on a halt of several days, since most of the out-going transports were still in the town. There would be some regrouping. Aram raised imploring hands. "You see what a state my wife and sister are in. I beg you to let us go to the American mission, for this evening."

The young officer was a long time thinking it over. In the end his pity for poor Iskuhi overcame all official considerations. Still on horseback, he scribbled a leave-chit for Pastor Aram and the two women.

"I haven't the right to let you go. If you're caught escaping, I shall be held responsible. You are ordered to report to me daily, in the concentration-camp."

The mission fathers received their three protégés and pupils with compassionate love. They had devoted their whole lives to Armenian Christians—and now this thunderbolt, which might be the merest indication of the devastating storms to come! A doctor was sent for at once, unluckily a very young, inexperienced one. He jerked Iskuhi's arm backwards and forwards. The infernal pain of this, added to all that had gone before it, made her really faint for a few minutes. No bones were broken, said the doctor, as far as he could see, though the arm looked curiously disjointed. The hurt was in the shoulder. He put on a big, tight bandage and gave her a draught to dull the pain. It would certainly be as well, he advised, if she could keep her arm stiffly resting for at least three weeks. Iskuhi did not sleep a wink that night. Hovsannah, in the room assigned to the women, had dropped at once into a sleep which was like unconsciousness.

Aram Tomasian sat at the missionaries' table, discussing what was to be done. The vote was unanimous. The rector, the Reverend E. C. Woodley, said decisively: "Whatever else may happen, you can't go back into that convoy. Hovsannah and Iskuhi would be dead long before you reached Aleppo.

And, apart from that, you aren't natives of Zeitun, but were sent there by us."

Pastor Aram had one of the hardest spiritual conflicts of his whole life to sustain. "How can I leave my people, at the very time when they need me most?"

How many Protestants were there in the convoy? they asked. He had to admit that, apart from a tiny minority, they all belonged to the Old Armenian or the United churches. But that did not console him in the least. "In such circumstances I can't worry about trifles. I'm the only priest they have."

Mr. Woodley calmed him: "We'll send someone else with them. But you're to go to your home. You must wait there till we have another cure for you."

"And what's to happen to my orphans?" groaned Aram Tomasian.

"You can't help the children by dying with them. The orphanage in Zeitun is our property. You've done more than your duty by bringing the orphans to Marash. Leave all the rest to us. It's ceased to be your affair."

A teasing voice in Aram was not to be silenced. "Am I not bound to more than just my duty?"

Old Woodley showed impatience, though his heart was rejoicing over Aram. "You surely don't imagine, Aram Tomasian, that we intend to submit to this treatment of our orphanage so tamely? It's not decided yet, by any means, what is to happen to these children. But you're getting in our way, my dear boy. As the pastor of Zeitun you're compromised. Understand? Good. I release you formally from your charge as director of the orphanage."

Aram felt that, if only he could hold out a few minutes longer, Woodley would not only cease to oppose, but would bless him for his Christian courage in sacrifice. But he said no more, in spite of this distinct sensation, and submitted to the mission father's arguments. He believed he was doing this

107

for Hovsannah and Iskuhi. And yet, every time he woke out of a sleep crowded with images, he was filled with the heavy sensation of defeat, of having betrayed his vocation to the priesthood, with the shame of weaklings.

Next morning the Reverend E. C. Woodley, accompanied by the American vice-consul, went to the Mutessarif and procured for Tomasian and his wife and for Iskuhi an official permit to travel to Yoghonoluk. But this would be valid for only fourteen days, within which they must have reached their destination. So that, in spite of the serious state of Iskuhi's arm, they were forced to set out three days later. They might have chosen the shorter route, via Bagche, the nearest railway station along the Anatolian line. They were advised most strongly against it. The Taurus line was crowded with transports for Jemal Pasha's fourth army. Nowadays prudence forbade any unnecessary contact with Turkish troops, especially with Armenian women to escort. Since the pastor had already submitted to the Marash fathers' decision, he was equally ready to let them choose his route. Instead of the short railway journey they began a very difficult carriage drive, of several days' duration, on mountain roads. First into the mountains, to Aintab, then along the wretched winding tracks over the passes of Taurus, down to Aleppo. The mission fathers placed a large two-horse carriage at Aram's disposal, and an extra horse, which could also be used as a mount. They wired to their representative in Aintab to prepare relays.

But the travellers were not yet past the suburbs of Marash when pursuing, imploring howls drowned the clatter of hoofs. The orphan girl Sato and the house-boy Kevork came running up behind them, clamouring. Fortunately it was early morning, there was still no one out in the streets to betray this scene. Inconvenient as it was to have to do so, nothing remained for Pastor Aram but to rescue these two unwanted additions to his party. The little vagabond Sato had always been a very difficult child and a burden on the Zeitun orphanage. About every three months she would be overcome with longings for vagabond life. Then she would vanish for days, to come back in an almost subhuman state, lousy and caked with dust and very subdued. And before these attacks she was quite unmanageable—incapable of connected speech or any other laboriously acquired attainment. Nor was it any use to lock her up. She seemed to get through walls like a ghost. But, if she could not manage to get away, Sato would be possessed by devils and could alarm the whole house with her genius for malicious damage. Iskuhi had been the first to influence her to the point at which her malice could be restrained and perhaps at last even exorcized—and this not by any specifically educational means. Iskuhi knew very little of pedagogic methods. For this little tramp was devoured with love for young Iskuhi, love which wrought sad confusion in Sato's already bewildered brain, and even seemed to have the power to engender that most dangerous of emotions—self-contempt. Now, in her pleated orphanage smock, Sato came pattering down the street with many cries.

"Küchük Hanum! Miss! Please don't leave Sato alone," this skinny little waif besought, with eyes widened by deathly fear and yet at the same time insolent—eyes which concealed inescapable resolution within their depths. Neither Iskuhi nor Hovsannah had ever really been able to repress a shudder of instinctive repugnance at the sight of Sato. Even when she was clean and kempt, she inspired a certain physical disgust.

Yet now this unwelcome acquisition had to be stowed away on the back seat. The house-boy Kevork took his place on the box beside the driver. Kevork came from Adana. Ever since, as a half-grown lad, he had been hit over the head with a rifle-butt, in the course of one of the numerous "incidents" there, he had remained a good-natured cretin. He could only talk in a stutter. And when, like Sato with her uncontrollable longings to run wild, he was seized with his mania for dancing, he too was impossible to control. This solemn fit had caused him to be named "the dancer." It was a quiet and very harmless peculiarity, which seldom possessed him altogether, and then only when something had stirred his mind. Otherwise Kevork faithfully discharged his duties as stoker, water-carrier, wood-chopper, gardener, and with mute zeal did the work of two grown men. How many promising children and useful adults (the thought flashed into Aram's mind) were there to rescue—and yet God sends me a little criminal girl and an idiot. It seemed to him a significant answer to his lukewarm shrinking away from sacrifice on behalf of the banished folk of Zeitun. Sato, however, was shaken by eerie, boisterous merriment. She wriggled up, with her pointed knees, against Iskuhi; she laughed and jabbered all day long, as though exile were the best conceivable holiday. Perhaps it was her first ride in a carriage. She let her thin little hand, with its big, filthy nails, hang out, as though over the side of a boat, drawing it after her with delight through the cool wake of surrounding air. These high spirits only annoyed and alarmed the others. Iskuhi jerked away her knees. The pastor, riding beside the carriage, threatened Sato that, unless she could sit still, he would either put her down without compunction or tie her hands.

The exhausting journey to Aintab—their nights had to be spent in wretched village khans—passed without catastrophe. In Aintab itself they rested three days. The Armenian colony there had received Mr. Woodley's wire and the relay horses were waiting. On the previous day the first convoy from Zeitun had reached the town. The people of Aintab had seen these miserable people and now awaited their own fate in despair. They scarcely went out of doors. Horrible rumours kept circulating. It was said that the government intended to give even shorter shrift to Aintab—that the Armenian quarter was simply to be set on fire, its inhabitants shot in batches. Yet the Aintab commune could not be kind enough to the pastor. It was as though the sight of these rescued victims inspired in them the hope of themselves being saved. Aram Tomasian tried to find a home in the town for Sato. But she clung in such strident terror to Iskuhi that he ended by taking her back into the carriage, perhaps as an act of penance for his own sin.

Things still went smoothly as far as Aleppo, though they spent four days crawling down the passes of the Taurus, had the greatest difficulty in finding relays at the post-houses, and had twice to sleep in empty barns. But the big town, with its many bazaars, its well-paved streets, its government and army buildings, pleasant gardens, and opulent mission-houses, inns, and hostels, acted like a charm on these ailing and dispirited people. In spite of sharp inquisition by saptiehs at the octroi—Sato and Kevork, after several minutes' palpitating fear, were passed as "servants"—the very sight of these streets, with their streams of undisturbed-looking people, gave bondsmen the illusion that they were free. Their reception, however, by the missionaries and heads of the commune was very different from those at Aintab and Marash. The fathers here were so overburdened with business and worries of all kinds, they were so bureaucratically organized, that Aram shrank from demanding their help. All he asked was two small rooms for himself and his family. The Armenian colony here was very rich, and so more timid, more hard-hearted, than the smaller people in Aintab. Their terror was intensified by the fact that they had so much more to lose than the others. Worse still, when the pastor mentioned Zeitun, he perceived at once that the very name of this town of revolt aroused mixed feelings in these city-brethren. They did not wish to seem, in official eyes, to have any connexion with such folk, pilloried now as stubborn rebels. The pastor's very presence in their offices was enough to compromise them. At present, if one hoped to save one's skin, it was necessary to seem a fanatical devotee of the state and scrupulously shun all suspected company. Aram was offered a sum of money. They could do no more for him. He refused it with thanks.

Time pressed, and Tomasian found himself obliged to hire a yayli for himself—a two-horse cab, of which there were dozens on every rank. At first the owner refused even to think of facing all the discomfort of such a journey. As far as the coast behind Antioch? He clutched his fez, astounded at such foolery. However, after many protestations, many "Inshallahs" and "Allah bilirs," a price was settled, two-thirds of which he insisted on being paid in advance. Since Aram knew that every other cabman would have acted in exactly the same way, he gave him the money. The pastor chose the road to Alexandretta in spite of its windings. He hoped in a day and a half of quick driving to reach the place where it forks to Antioch, and from there to be at home within twenty-four hours. But, just before sunset on the first day, the driver climbed down off his box, inspected damaged hoofs, wheels, axles, and declared that he had had quite enough. His horses were fagged, his carriage overloaded, it wasn't his business to cart Armenians all over the world—and so he was going straight back home, to be sure of getting to Turont, where he had relatives, in reasonable time. No prayers availed on him, not even the offer of almost double his fare. He had had his money in advance, it was all he wanted, the Turk magnanimously announced. He would do even more; he would take them back all the way to Turont for nothing, where they could spend a delectable night in the excellent beds of the first-class khan of his relations. Tomasian raised his stick and would have given the insolent brute a thrashing had not Hovsannah held his arm. Upon which the man threw their luggage out of his yayli, jerked his reins, and left these five people stranded in the midst of a wilderness. For an hour they walked on along the road in the hope of coming to a village or getting a lift. But, far and wide, there was nothing, no cart, not even a barn, no huts, no village. They had to spend another night in the open, and it passed more slowly than the first, since no one had reckoned on it. The curve of the road shone under the faint moon like a dangerous scimitar. They lay down as far from it as they could, on the bare earth. Yet even that mother of all proved ill disposed towards Armenians. Damp forced its way up through the rugs; poisonous airs from the swamp, alive with insects, enveloped them. Kevork and Aram kept guard, the pastor tightly grasping the hunting-rifle which the Marash fathers had given him for the journey.

But the depths of their misery was touched only in the next fifty hours, during which these wanderers reached Yoghonoluk. It was a miracle that no harm came to Hovsannah, that Iskuhi did not entirely collapse. The pastor made the mistake of not sticking to the highroad, off which he struck far too early on to a cart-track, in the south-westerly direction. After a few miles along it, the cart-track trailed off into nothing. They were lost and wandered for hours. In the last stage of their way of agony Kevork displayed great physical strength and carried the women by turns on his back for long distances. (They had soon had to leave their luggage.) The pastor plodded on with only one thought—not to lose direction, given him by the clouds above the mountain along the coast. Again and again they discovered cart-tracks, which they could follow for a couple of miles and which spanned the waterfalls in little bridges of rotting planks. Here and there a kangni, an ox-cart, would also give them a lift for some long distance. They were not molested by human beings. The few peasant Moslems they came across were friendly, gave them water and cheese. They would not have defended themselves had they been attacked. Numb to the pain of their aching limbs, their bleeding feet, they stumbled on in a coma of exhaustion. Even the sturdy Aram walked half in a dream, lost in a world of juggling images. Sometimes he burst out laughing. Sato showed remarkable indifference to pain. She limped on agonized feet, swollen black and blue, behind Iskuhi, as though all her vagabond escapades had been meant to harden her to such toil.

When Gabriel saw the five, on the church steps, they were still possessed by exhausted dreams. Yet, since they were young, since the sudden sense of having been rescued rose within them, since faces of people whom they knew, the pastor, the priest, the doctor, hovered before them, since tremulous words were in their ears, and all the warmth of a home-coming enveloped them, they came quickly to themselves, and this leaden, superhuman strain melted without transitions into a state of excited animation.

PASTOR ARAM TOMASIAN kept insisting: "Don't think of the old massacres. This is far worse, far more gruesome, far more relentless, than any massacre. And, above all, it's far slower. It remains with you, day and night." He pressed his hands against his temples. "I can't get the horror out of my mind. . . . I keep seeing those children. . . . If only Woodley can save them. . . ."

Dr. Altouni was in silent attendance on Iskuhi. But the other men kept questioning Aram. A confused outburst of only too natural inquiries: "Will it stop at Zeitun? . . . Isn't the colony in Aintab already on the road? . . . What do they say in Aleppo? . . . Any news from the other vilayets? . . . And we . . . ?"

The doctor had unrolled the bandage and was bathing the darkly suffused arm in warm water. He laughed sharply. "Where can they deport us to? We're already deported on Musa Dagh."

The noise of the crowd in the square had become audible in the room. Ter Haigasun cut short these confused inquiries. He turned his timid, yet at the same time very resolute, eyes on Bagradian. "Will you be so kind as to go out and say a few words to the people? Make them go home."

114

What had made Ter Haigasun light on Gabriel, the Parisian, who had nothing in common with these villagers? It should by rights have been the duty of Kebussyan, the mukhtar, to speak to the crowd. Or had the priest his own secret reasons for his request? Bagradian started and felt embarrassed. None the less he did as Ter Haigasun told him, though he took Stephan out with him by the hand. Armenian was his native language, yet in this first instant, as he found himself facing this crowd—which meanwhile had increased to about five hundred—it felt like impertinence to use it, an unwarranted interference with their affairs. He would almost rather have spoken Turkish, the army language. But only his first words made him feel embarrassed, and then came a clear rush of syllables, the ancient speech within him began to germinate, to spin itself out. He asked the inhabitants of Yoghonoluk, and whoever else had assembled here from the other villages, to go home quietly. So far the only irregularities had occurred in Zeitun, and nowhere else, and their true cause would be investigated. Every Armenian knew that Zeitun had always been exceptional. For the people round Musa Dagh, who belonged to an entirely different district, and had never been mixed up in politics, there was not the very slightest danger. But in just such times as these law and order were more than ever necessary. He, Bagradian, would see to it that from now on every important event was regularly reported in the villages. And, if necessary, all the communes should meet in an assembly of the people to discuss the future.

Gabriel, to his own surprise, found that he was speaking well. The right words came of themselves. A pacifying strength went out of him to his hearers. Somebody even shouted: "Long live the Bagradian family." Only one woman's voice wailed: "Asdvaz im, my God, what's going to happen to us?"

If the crowd did not disperse immediately, it at least broke up into smaller groups and no longer besieged the church. Of the saptiehs only Ali Nassif still prowled; both his comrades had already made themselves scarce. Gabriel went across to the pock-marked Ali, who for some time had seemed to find it hard to make up his mind whether to treat the effendi as a great gentleman or a khanzir kiafir, an unbelieving swine, who, in view of the latest turn of events, was officially not even worth answering. This very indecision caused Bagradian to take a high-handed line: "You know what I am? I'm your master and official superior. I'm an officer in the army."

Ali Nassif decided to stand to attention. Gabriel felt significantly in his pocket. "An officer gives no baksheesh. But you will receive from me these two medjidjeh in payment of the unofficial service which I am about to explain to you."

The rigid Ali was becoming more and more acquiescent. Bagradian jerked his hand to let him know he might stand at ease. "Lately I've been seeing some new faces among you saptiehs. Has your post been increased?"

"There were not enough of us, Effendi, for the long roads and the heavy service. So they sent us some extras."

"Is that the real reason? Well, you needn't answer unless you like. But how do you get your orders, your pay, and so on?"

"One of the boys rides to Antakiya every week and brings back the orders."

"Well, Ali Nassif, listen to your unofficial service. If ever you get any orders, or hear any news of your command, which seems to be important to this district—you understand?—you're to come to me at once, at my house. There you'll receive three times what I'm giving you now."

Then, with the same negligent haughtiness, Bagradian turned away from the saptieh and went back to the sacristy.

Dr. Altouni had finished examining the arm; he was saying scornfully: "And to think that in Marash they've a big hospital, instruments, an operating-theatre, medical libraries—

and yet that ass of a doctor didn't so much as dress it properly. What can I do? I've got nothing here but a rusty forceps for pulling out teeth. We shall have to put the arm between two slats. It seems in an awful state. She must have a good long rest in bed, in a pleasant room. And the same, of course, for your wife, Aram."

The old builder, Tomasian, was in despair. "I've so little room since I sold my house. How shall we ever manage?"

Gabriel at once offered Mademoiselle Tomasian a room in the villa—one with a pleasant view out on to the mountain. Dr. Altouni's instructions should be carefully followed.

The old doctor was overjoyed: "Koh yem—splendid, my friend. And this poor little creature—Sato, isn't it?—will you take her, too, so that my honoured patients may be together? My old bones will thank you."

It was arranged. Aram and Hovsannah went with Tomasian's father, taking with them Kevork the dancer, whom the old man suggested that he could use in his workshop. Gabriel sent Stephan ahead to bring Juliette news of all these events.

The boy came breathless into the house.

"Maman! Maman! Something's happened. We shall be having people in to stay with us. Mademoiselle Iskuhi, the sister of the pastor at Zeitun. And a little girl, with her feet all bleeding."

This surprising news affected Juliette strangely. Gabriel had never before brought strangers to stay in the house without having asked her permission. His relationship to her had in it a kind of hesitation where guests were concerned, especially Armenians. But when, within the next ten minutes, he arrived with Iskuhi, the Altounis, and Sato, Juliette was kindness itself. She, like so many pretty women, fell an easy prey to feminine charm, especially the charm of a young girl. The sight of poor Iskuhi moved her and aroused in her all the instinct to help of an elder sister. As she gave all the necessary orders, she kept saying to herself with satisfaction: "She's really unusual. One seldom sees such delicate-looking faces among them. She looks like a lady, even in those ragged clothes. And she seemed to speak such good French, for an Armenian." The room was soon ready. Juliette herself came to wait on Iskuhi; she even brought her a very pretty lace nightdress of her own. Nor did she hesitate to sacrifice her own expensive scents and *eaux de toilette,* although these treasures were irreplaceable.

Altouni again inspected Iskuhi's arm, with many bitter little jokes on the subject of the doctors in Marash. "Is it very painful, my dear?" No, she felt no pain in it now, only a kind of feeling, a numb feeling—she tried to think of the word—a feeling of not being able to feel it. The old doctor could see that all his skill would be of very little use to her. Still—he could do nothing else—he smothered her arm in a wide bandage, which sheathed her shoulders, up to the neck. The nimble dexterity still preserved in his old brown, wrinkled fingers became apparent as he did it. Soon after this Iskuhi was comfortable in bed, clean, cared for, and at peace. Juliette, who had helped with all this, was about to leave her. "If you need anything more, dear, all you have to do is to swing this big hand-bell hard. We'll send you up something to eat. But I shall be coming in to see you first."

Iskuhi turned the eyes of her people upon this bene-factress—eyes which still looked out into terrifying distances, and did not seem to notice this pleasant safety.

"Oh, thank you, Madame—I shan't need anything. . . . Thank you, Madame." Then came the thing which had never happened in all that fearful week in Zeitun, nor in the days with the convoy, nor on the journey. Iskuhi burst into storms of tears. The outburst was not convulsive, it was sheer weeping, without a sob in it, a grief, so to speak, without hill or valley, a release from rigidity, vast and inconsolable as the Asiatic steppes from which it came. As Iskuhi wept on quietly, she kept repeating: "Forgive me, Madame. . . . I never meant to do this. . . ."

Juliette would have liked to kneel beside her, kiss her, and tell her she was an angel. Yet something made these conventional words of comfort quite impossible. Some remoteness still enveloped this young girl, her experience wrapped her like a chrysalis. Juliette could not follow her own warm impulse. She contented herself with lightly stroking Iskuhi's hair and waiting in silence by her side till this quiet grief had fully spent itself, till the eyelids drooped, and the girl sank down into merciful nothingness.

Meanwhile Mairik Antaram had dressed and bandaged Sato's feet. The child was put to bed in one of the unused servant's bedrooms. Scarcely had she dropped into heavy sleep, when she let out her first blood-curdling scream. Her screams continued. In all these days she had never once shown signs of fear, but now, as she dreamed life over again, a hundred whips seemed to swish around her. It was no use shaking her repeatedly. She slept too heavily to be waked, so that after a time her moans and piercing howls began again. Sometimes these long-drawn wailings sounded as though the voice were clinging desperately to one saving name: Küchük Hanum.

As these hair-raising howls forced themselves out of the distant bedroom, Juliette met her son coming up the wide steps to the front door. Stephan was glowing with excitement. This new thing, this unknown, with its threat, electrified him and set his nerves pleasantly tingling. In November he had celebrated his thirteenth birthday and so was just reaching the age when sensations kindle most boys' enthusiasm. He would even stand at the window watching some unusually heavy thunderstorm, filled with the unholy longing that something out of the ordinary might happen. Now he stood and listened, agreeably horror-stricken.

"Maman, listen to Sato screaming."

"Iskuhi's eyes—my boy has the same kind of eyes as Iskuhi."
Juliette perceived it in a flash. And the subterranean snares and
entanglements of life revealed themselves. She felt her first
great terror for Stephan. She hurried him into her room and
kissed him hard. Sato's screams still rang in the empty hallway.

LATER that evening Gabriel Bagradian had invited the priest
Ter Haigasun, Bedros Altouni, the doctor, and Apothecary
Krikor to come to see him. They sat together, in the dimly
lighted selamlik, over chibuks and cigarettes. Gabriel wanted
to know how these highly educated and very worthy notables
of Yoghonoluk really viewed the position, how they intended
to act in the event of an order of banishment, and what means
the commune of Musa Dagh had at its disposal to avert the
worst.

He could get nothing out of them. Ter Haigasun stubbornly
kept his mouth shut. The doctor announced that, since he was
already sixty-eight, the three or four short years he had still
to live would be got through somehow. If anything happened
to bring the end a little sooner, then so much the better as far
as he was concerned. Ridiculous to trouble one's head for the
sake of a few scurvy months. Was the whole of life really
worth a single worry? The main thing was to save people
anxiety as much, and for as long as, one possibly could. That
he considered his chief duty, which he meant to fulfil, whatever happened. All the rest was no business of his. Krikor
smoked his nargileh, profoundly at peace—he had very
prudently brought it with him. He selected, with an air of
profundity, from among the glowing coals those which appealed to him most and pressed them down with his naked
fingers on a roll of tobacco in the hubble-bubble. Perhaps he
wanted to symbolize to the others that he could grasp fire
without being burned by it. Thought alone gives any right to
reality—not vice versa. Why want to *do* anything? All action
is already in vain, and only thought thinks on for ever. He

cited a Turkish proverb, which might equally well have issued from the lips of the Agha Rifaat Bereket: "Kismetdén zyadé olmass." Nothing happens unless predestined.

These words afforded the opportunity of evading the troublesome problems of the hour. And Krikor's hollow voice became eloquent on the various theories of predestination, the relationship of Christendom to Islam, the Council of Chalcedony. The very words inebriated. The priest should be made to hear with amazement how much theology Apothecary Krikor had acquired.

It was too much. Gabriel rudely sprang to his feet. All the European in him was up in arms against these sleepers, these gossips, who would sink down into death without a protest, as they rotted their lives away in filth. He interrupted Krikor, with a contemptuous wave of his hand: "I want most urgently to submit an idea of mine to you gentlemen. It came to me today as I talked to the saptieh, Ali Nassif. I'm still, after all, a Turkish officer, a front-line soldier, decorated in the last Balkan war. Now suppose I get into uniform and go to Aleppo? How would that be? Years ago I happened to make myself useful to General Jemal Pasha——"

The old doctor almost gleefully interrupted: "Jemal Pasha moved his headquarters some time ago to Jerusalem."

But Bagradian was not to be put off. "It makes no difference. Djelal Bey, the Wali, is even more important than Jemal Pasha. I don't know him personally, but we all know about him, who he is, and that he'll do whatever he can for us. Well, now, suppose I go to him and remind him that Musa Dagh is right out of the world, and that therefore we can't possibly have had anything to do with politics, perhaps . . ."

Gabriel said no more and listened to the imperturbable silence. Only the bubbling water in Krikor's nargileh broke it at irregular intervals. It was some time before Ter Haigasun laid down his chibuk.

"The Wali, Djelal Bey"—he thought it over, staring out in

front of him—"is certainly a great friend of our nation. He has shown us repeated kindness. And under his government we never needed to fear the worst. . . . Unfortunately his friendship for us has done him very little good. . . ." Out of his wide sleeves Ter Haigasun drew a folded newspaper. "Today is Friday. This is Tuesday's *Tanin*. It's a paragraph in very small print, pushed away into the corner of the paper." He held up the sheet, far from his eyes.

"'According to information received from the Ministry of the Interior, His Excellency the Wali of Aleppo, Djelal Bey, has been permanently placed on the retired list.' . . . That's all it says."

5

Interlude of the Gods

At the very instant when, urging his cabman to greater speed, Dr. Johannes Lepsius reached the great bridge across from Pera, the garden suburb, to Istanbul, the automatic signal started to ring, the barrier sank, the bridge trembled like a live thing, broke groaning in two, and its rusty halves, this side and that, rose slowly up, to allow a warship to proceed into the innermost harbour of the Golden Horn. "This is really dreadful," Dr. Lepsius said, aloud and in German, closing his eyes and sinking back on to the frayed upholstery of his araba, as though he had given up the struggle. Yet he was out of the cab in the next instant, had thrust a few uncounted piastres on the driver, had run (nearly slipping up on a fruit skin) down the steps and on to the quay, where a few kayiks, little ferryboats, plied for hire. There was not much choice; only two phlegmatic old ferrymen drowsed in their boats, not seeming in the least to want a fare. Lepsius jumped into a ferryboat and waved across, in sheer, scurrying desperation, to the Istanbul side. He had still six minutes till his appointment at the Seraskeriat, the War Ministry. Even if his boatman rowed with a will, he would need a whole ten to cross the sound. On the other quay—so reckoned the impatient Dr. Lepsius—there could not fail to be a cab-rank. So that from there it need only take another five minutes to the Ministry. Six from fifteen minutes, if all went smoothly— nine minutes late. Very unfortunate, but still not so bad as all that. . . . And, of course, everything went wrong. The

boatman, pushing like a gondolier, was not to be roused by
admonitions, nor by imploring prayers, from his calm meditation. The boat danced up and down but would not go forward. "It's the tide, Effendi. The sea's coming in." Thus did
the weatherbeaten Turk define fate, against which there can
be no striving. To make bad worse, a fishing cutter crossed
their bows—which meant the loss of two more minutes.
Dully resigned, impotent as only a man can feel who finds
himself tossed on waves, the German sank into reflections.
He had, for the sake of this one appointment, undertaken all
the fatigue of this journey, come to Constantinople from
Potsdam, besieged the German ambassador day after day, and
not him alone, but every neutral representative. This one
appointment had sent him hurrying to meet every German or
American in from the interior, in every possible quarter of
the town, to get further details. This one appointment had
kept him sitting for whole days in the American Bible Society's offices, had caused him to make himself a nuisance to
the people of the various orders, had sent him, by carefully
thought-out routes, avoiding spies, to meet Armenians in
secret rooms. All so as to be prepared for the great encounter.
And now fate played this practical joke of making him late
for it. It was almost enough to inspire belief in some direct,
Satanic intervention. How hard that very pleasant German
naval commander attached to the military mission had worked
to get this conversation arranged! Three times it had been
conceded, three times postponed. Enver Pasha is the Ottoman
war god. He does not care to be ceremonious with such an
insignificant antagonist as Dr. Johannes Lepsius.

So—the ten minutes had slipped away. Enver would by
now have given orders not to admit this querulous German
on any pretext. The game was lost. Let it be lost! "My own
country is fighting for dear life. The dark rider with the
scales flies above us also. What do Armenians really matter
to me?" Johannes Lepsius discarded these spurious consola-

tions with a short, dry little gasp. No! These Armenians meant a great deal to him—even more if he dared rigorously to examine his heart—more perhaps than even his own countrymen, mad and sinful as that no doubt might be. Ever since Abdul Hamid's butcheries, since the massacres of '96, since that mission to the interior, his first days of missionary experience, he had felt himself especially sent to these unfortunates. They were his task on earth. And at once he could see a few of their faces. Such faces as only those beings have who must empty the chalice to its dregs. Christ on the cross may well have had just such eyes. It was perhaps for them that Lepsius loved these people so dearly. An hour ago, in the eyes of the Patriarch, the Armenian chief priest of Turkey, Monsignor Saven, he had seen, or rather had had to keep turning his face away from, an ardent hopelessness. And this visit to the Patriarch had made him late. It had of course been stupid to go back to Pera after calling on him, to the Hotel Tokatlyan, to change. Yes, but—he had had to call on the Patriarch in the long black cassock suitable to a Protestant clergyman. And, with Enver, he did not want to stress his position, was most anxious, in that fateful interview, to avoid any appearance of formality. He knew these Ittihad people, his opponents. A casual tone, a grey lounge suit, certainty of manner, the hint of powers behind—that was the proper way to deal with adventurers. And now, the grey lounge suit had caused all this.

He ought not to have stopped so long with the Patriarch, could have got away in a few minutes. Unluckily Dr. Lepsius's forte had never been systematic concentration. Even his success in helping Armenians at the time of the Abdul Hamid massacres had been less a matter of thought-out policy than of passionate insistence on being received. He was still far too much at the mercy of that youthful vice, of thinking graphically—"dances of death," "the eternal Jew," "John Bull," etc. Improvisation, a tendency to rely on the minute—these, as he knew, were his worst faults. So that today he had not been able to free himself from the aspect of that piteous cleric. "You'll be with Enver in an hour." The faintness of Monsignor **Saven's** voice told its own story of sleepless nights; it seemed to be dying, along with his people. "You'll stand before that man. God bless you! But not even you will be able to do anything."

"I'm not so pessimistic, Monsignor," Lepsius had striven to reassure.

But his words had been stopped by a gesture of agonized submission. "We've just heard today that, after Zeitun, Aintab, Marash, the same threat of deportation is to be suspended over the East Anatolian vilayets. So that up to now, apart from the west of Asia Minor, only Aleppo and the strip of coast from Alexandretta have been spared. You know better than anyone that deportation is a more painful, more long-drawn-out kind of death by torture. They say that not one inhabitant of Zeitun has survived." And the Patriarch's eyes had forbidden Lepsius any protest. "Leave the impossible and concentrate on the possible. You may succeed—I don't suppose you will—in getting a respite for Aleppo and the country along the coast. Stress German public opinion, the newspapers you intend to inform. Above all, don't moralize. It merely provokes him to contempt. Stick to political facts. Threaten him economically—that's your most likely way to make an impression on him. And now, my dear son, you have my blessing for your noble work. Christ be with you." Lepsius had bent his head, but the Patriarch had signed his chest, with a wide cross.

So that here he sat in this heavy boat, ploughing its way through the waters of the Golden Horn, under its stolid, meditative oarsman. And when at last they arrived, it was more than twenty minutes late. With one glance Dr. Lepsius was aware that no arabas waited along the quayside. He broke into a wry little laugh—since more than hazard must conceal itself somewhere within this chain of hindrances. Some opposing power had taken a hand in the Armenian business, which no doubt must be left to go on unopposed, and was thrusting a stave in between his legs. He made no further attempt to find a cab, but began to run, stout, elderly, conspicuous-looking as he was.

He did not get far. The squares and alleys of old Istanbul were thick with holiday-keeping crowds. Along past shops and cafés, gay with bunting, under beflagged windows, thousands in fez and tarbush jostled and shoved. What was it? The Allies driven out of the Dardanelles? Lepsius thought of the distant gun-fire which he heard so often in the night. The big guns of the British fleet, hammering on the gates of Constantinople. But he remembered that this was the anniversary of some triumph of the Young Turkish revolution—perhaps of that glorious day on which the Committee had killed off all its political opponents, to seize power at last. Not that it mattered what they were celebrating; any crowd shouts and brawls. A solid mass of people in front of a shop. Boys, hoisted on ready shoulders, clambering up along the shop-front. Next minute a big sign-board came clattering down. Lepsius, wedged in the crowd, asked his neighbour, who wore no fez, what all this was about. "No more foreign signs," he was told. "Turkey for the Turks. All sign-boards, names of streets, and advertisements to be written exclusively in Turkish from this day on." And this neighbour (a Greek or Levantine) giggled spitefully. "This time they've demolished an ally. It's a German business-house."

A long line of halted trams crawled on. "Really it doesn't matter," Lepsius thought, "when I get there now. It's all over." None the less he put on a spurt, thrusting into the crowd, shoving relentlessly. One more side-alley, and the square opened out before him. The vast palace of the Seraskeriat. High rose the tower of Mahmut the Second. And now the pastor took his time. He walked slowly, so as not to come

127

breathless into the lion's den. When, fagged out with endless stairs and corridors, he whipped out his card at the offices of the Ministry of War, it was only to be informed by a smartly uniformed and very amiable aide-de-camp that His Excellency Enver Pasha deeply regretted that he had found it impossible to wait and begged the Herr Doktor to do him the honour of calling at the Ministry of the Interior within the Seraglio.

So Dr. Johannes Lepsius had to set out on an even longer journey. But now the malign spell was broken. The demons had thought out another method. They almost forced him to be at his ease. Outside a cab had just set down its fare. The driver had his eye on an easy journey, he avoided crowds, and so, in a magically short time, fully reposed, and invaded now by a self-confidence for which he could have given himself no reason, the crusader entered the quiet world of the Seraglio and clattered thunderously on across the ancient cobbles to the Ministry. Here they were expecting him. Even before he could show his card, an official had greeted him with the question: "Dr. Lepsius?" What a good omen! More stairs, and a long corridor. But, borne on the wings of happy presentiment, the pastor almost felt he hovered along it. The quiet Ministry of the Interior, Talaat Bey's fortress, made a pleasantly dream-like impression. These official rooms seemed almost enchanted—without doors, only divided by billowy curtains. This, he could not tell why, soothed him with the assurance of coming success. He was conducted to the end of a passage, into a special suite. Enver Pasha's headquarters in the Ministry. Here, doubtless, in these two rooms the dice of the Armenian fate had been cast. A large apartment, seemingly a waiting- and audience-room. Next it, a study, containing only a big, empty writing-table. The curtain into this study had been pulled back. Lepsius saw three portraits on the wall behind the empty table: right, Napoleon; left, Frederick the Great; an enlarged photograph of a Turkish general in the middle. Doubtless Enver Pasha, the new war god.

The expectant pastor seated himself beside the window. His eyes, over the rims of pince-nez, drew in peace from the beauty of heaps of ruins, shattered cupolas, broken columns, sheltered by umbrella-pines. Beyond, the Bosporus, whose toy steamers thrust their way on. The pastor's blue, myopic gaze, his full and childish lips pouting through the short grey beard, his severe cheeks still rosy with haste and perturbation—all this produced an image of long-suffering, of a soft heart, inflexibly hard upon itself. A servant brought in a copper coffee pot. Lepsius greedily gulped three tiny cups. This coffee gave him an advantage, his nerves tightened, his veins pounded fresh blood to his brain. When Enver Pasha came upon him, he had just emptied his fourth cup.

BEFORE leaving Berlin, Johannes Lepsius had asked for minute accounts of Enver Pasha, yet he felt surprised that this Turkish Mars, this one of the seven or nine arbiters of the life or death of the world, should be so unimposingly diminutive. He instantly saw the reason for those portraits of Frederick the Great and Napoleon. Heroes five feet tall, little conquerors, always on tip-toe, who force a way to power to spite their inches. Lepsius would have wagered anything that Enver Pasha wore high heels. He did not, in any case, take off his lambskin képi, which certainly looked much taller than dress regulations allowed. The gold-tabbed marshal's (or fancy-dress) uniform, beautifully moulded to the waist, lent added majesty, by the smart, stiff perfection of its line, investing this figure, in conjunction with gleaming rows of medals, with something almost frivolously young, ornately bold. "The gipsy-king," reflected Lepsius and, although his heart was pounding, he could not escape a rampant waltz of his early youth:

> "All this and more
> You may be sure
> I'll do."

129

Yet this text, which now assailed him at the sight of the spick-and-span magnificence of the uniform, was in sheer contradiction to the glance and manner of this youthful commander-in-chief. Enver Pasha looked shy, almost embarrassed; from time to time he would open his eyes like a young girl. The narrow hips and sloping shoulders gave his movements a certain delicate grace. Lepsius felt heavy and obese.

Enver's first attack took the form of arousing a sudden sympathy with his tripping person, a feeling he knew how to awaken in visitors. He did not, having welcomed Lepsius, conduct him to the adjoining study but, begging him to stay where he was, pulled up a chair for himself from the table to the window, not troubling that his face was in the light while his visitor's was shaded.

Johannes began the interview (he had thought this out, in deciding his plan of campaign) with greetings from an admiring German lady, which he laid at the general's feet. The general smiled his peculiar, shy little smile and said in a pleasant tenor, which, vocally even, gave full effect to the winsomeness of his whole personality, and in excellent German: "I have the very deepest respect for Germany. There can be no doubt that you are one of the most astonishing peoples in the world. Personally, I'm always delighted to get a chance to receive a German."

Enver, Pastor Lepsius knew, had been pro-French on the Committee and perhaps, in private, continued to be so. He had stubbornly tried not to come into the war on Germany's side, but on that of the Allies. All that did not matter at present. Lepsius went on feeling his way, with civilities: "Your Excellency has so many devoted German admirers. We all expect you to astonish the world with your victories."

Enver opened his eyes. A little movement of the hand seemed wearily to defend him against the demands which always lie hidden within such flatteries. A silence, implying

130

more or less: "Well now, my dear fellow, look out whom you're dealing with." Lepsius turned his head to the window, listening, though out there no noise was audible save the faint hoots and signal-bells on the Bosporus.

"I've been noticing how enthusiastic the people seems to be, here in Istanbul. Especially today. I was most impressed by the crowds."

The general, in his pleasant, but by now quite indifferent voice, decided on a pithy little saying, in the style of patriotic pronunciamentos: "The war is hard. But our people is aware of what it owes itself."

The German made his first sortie: "Is it quite the same in the interior, Excellency?"

Enver glanced with delight into the farthest corner of the room: "Certainly. Great things are happening in the interior."

"Excellency, these great things are well known to me."

The war-lord refused, with a hint of surprise, to understand. For the leader of a great empire, his cheeks looked surprisingly fresh and young. "The position on the Caucasian front improves every day. It is of course a little premature to speak of the southern army under Jemal and your countryman Kress."

"Most encouraging, Excellency. But, by the interior I mean the peaceful vilayets, not the war zone."

"While a state is at war, all its government districts are war zones, more or less."

This was discharged with a certain delicate crispness. So that the outpost skirmish had gone against Dr. Lepsius, who was forced to open frontal attack: "Your Excellency is aware, perhaps, that I'm not here as a private individual, but as representative of the German Orient Society, who will require my report upon certain happenings."

A surprised Enver sat wide-eyed. What exactly is an Orient Society?

"Our Foreign Office, indeed our Chancellor, is in active

131

sympathy with my mission. On my return I am to deliver a lecture in the Reichstag on the Armenian question, for the information of the German press."

Enver Pasha, listening in routine patience, his eyes cast down, looked up at the words "Armenian question." The sulkiness of a spoilt child whom heavy grown-ups will not stop pestering with their stale old nonsense clouded his face for an instant. It passed at once. Yet Dr. Lepsius's heart already failed him. "I come to you in my need, Excellency, because I'm convinced that a leader of your distinction will not do anything which might besmirch his name in history."

"I know, Herr Lepsius," Enver Pasha began, in the softest, most indulgent voice, "I know that you've come here, and asked for this interview, to demand my explanation of all these matters. And although a number of urgent questions require my attention, I'm perfectly willing to spare you whatever time you may need and give any information you choose to ask for."

Lepsius was forced to acknowledge this sacrifice with a deeply grateful little bow.

"Ever since my friends and I have controlled the government," the general continued, "we've always striven to grant the Armenian millet's requests, and see that absolute justice was meted out to it. There was an old understanding. Your Armenian friends acclaimed our revolution most cordially; they swore all kinds of oaths of fidelity to us. Unfortunately they broke them overnight. We shut our eyes as long as possible, as long as the Turkish people, the ruling people, was not in danger. We are living in Turkey, are we not? But when, after war was declared, cases of high treason, felony, and subversive tendencies kept increasing, when desertion assumed alarming proportions, when it came to open revolt—I'm only thinking, mind, of the great revolt in Zeitun—then we found ourselves obliged either to take action to repress it or lose our right to direct the war and remain the leaders of our people."

Lepsius nodded, as though he were well on the way to becoming convinced. "In what, Excellency, did these legally proved cases of treason and sedition consist?"

A broad gesture from Enver. This plenitude of crimes could never fully be exhausted. "Conspiracy with Russia. Sasonov's speech praising Armenians in the Petersburg Duma was clear enough. Conspiracies with France and England. Intrigue, espionage—all you can think of."

"And these cases have been legally investigated?"

"By court martial, naturally. It would be just the same in your country. Not long ago fifteen of the worst offenders were sentenced and publicly executed."

"Clumsy insolence," Lepsius mentally decided. He leaned back and tried to control his unsteady voice. "According to my knowledge those fifteen Armenians were arrested long before the war. So they can scarcely have been found guilty of treachery by usual military law."

"We ourselves derive from the revolution." Though the general did not answer to the point, he did so with the gleefulness of a schoolboy who remembers a most amusing escapade. "We know exactly how all that's done."

Lepsius swallowed down a very expressive description of the revolution and all its works. He cleared his throat for the next inquiry: "And these Armenian notables and intellectuals, whom you've arrested here in Istanbul and deported—are they also convicted of treachery?"

"You must see for yourself that we can't keep even possible traitors so near the Dardanelles."

Johannes Lepsius did not contradict, but plunged, in a burst of sudden temperament, into the main issue: "And Zeitun? I'm very anxious indeed to hear Your Excellency's view of Zeitun."

Enver Pasha's blankly gleaming suavity was overcast with a sudden disapproval. "The revolt in Zeitun is one of the worst mutinies in the history of the Turkish empire. Unfortunately

133

our troops lost heavily in their struggle to subdue the rebels, though I'm afraid I can't give you exact figures."

"My reports of Zeitun differ from those of Your Excellency." Lepsius planted this blow in hesitant syllables. "My accounts make no mention of any revolt of the population there, but of provocative oppression, lasting over a period of months, by the district and sanjak officials. They speak of some trifling disorder, which could easily have been checked by strengthening the town police, whereas any fair-minded person can easily perceive a deliberate intention in military reinforcements of over a thousand strong."

"You've been given false information." Enver was still quietly well behaved. "May I inquire who your informants were, Herr Lepsius?"

"I can name a few of them, but I may as well say that no Armenian sources are included. On the other hand I have the specific memoranda of various German consuls, reports from missionaries, the eye-witnesses of the worst atrocities. And finally I've been given a most consistent account of the whole business by the American ambassador, Mr. Morgenthau."

"Mr. Morgenthau," said Enver brightly, "is a Jew. And Jews are always fanatically on the side of minorities."

Lepsius gasped at the graceful evasiveness of this. His feet and hands were cold as ice. "It isn't a question of Morgenthau, Excellency, but of the facts. And you neither will, nor can, deny them. A hundred thousand people are already on their way into exile. The officials talk of nothing but resettlement. But I suggest to you that, frankly, that's a misnomer. How can a people of peasant mountaineers, craftsmen, townsfolk, professional people, be resettled by a stroke of the pen in Mesopotamian deserts—empty plains? In waste country, hundreds of miles away from their homes, which even bedouin tribes refuse to inhabit? And that object is simply a blind. The district officials are conducting these deportations in such a way that, in the first eight days' march, these wretched people either collapse or go mad of hunger, thirst, disease, so that helpless boys and defenceless men get slaughtered by Kurds and bandits, if not by the military—and young girls and women are literally forced into prostitution. . . ."

The attentive general listened scrupulously, though his languid pose most clearly indicated: This is the kind of rigmarole one has to hear at least twelve times a day. "All very regrettable. But the supreme commander of a great military power is responsible for the security of his war areas."

"War areas?" Lepsius cried out—and at once controlled himself, trying to manage Enver's calm. " 'War areas' is the one fresh nuance. All the rest—Zeitun, high treason, intrigues —was there already. Abdul Hamid made masterly use of all that, if the Armenians cared to believe it all over again. I'm an older man than you are, Excellency, and I saw it all on the spot. But when I think of these deportations, I almost want to apologize to that old sinner. He was a bungler, a harmless child, compared to this new method. And yet, Excellency, your party only took power because it wanted to replace the bloodshed of the old Sultan's time by justice, unity, and progress. The very name of your Committee proclaims it."

This stroke was daring, indeed rash. For an instant Johannes Lepsius sat expecting the war-lord to stand up and conclude the interview. Yet Enver sat quietly on, not the lightest shadow clouding his suave serenity. He even bent forward, confidentially. "Dr. Lepsius, may I show you the other side? . . . Germany, luckily, has few, or no, internal enemies. But let's suppose that, in other circumstances, she found herself with traitors in her midst—Alsace-Lorrainers, shall we say, or Poles, or Social-Democrats, or Jews—and in far greater numbers than at present. Would you, Herr Lepsius, not endorse any and every means of freeing your country, which is fighting for its life against a whole world of enemies without, from those within? . . . Would you consider it so cruel if, for the sake of victory, all dangerous elements in the population were simply to be herded together and sent packing into distant, un-inhabited territory?"

Johannes Lepsius had to hold on tight by both hands to keep himself from springing to his feet and giving full rein to his indignation.

"If my government," he said very distinctly, "behaved unjustly, unlawfully, inhumanly" ("in an un-Christian way" was the expression on the tip of his tongue) "to our fellow-countrymen of a different race, a different persuasion, I should clear out of Germany at once and go to America."

A long, wide-eyed stare from Enver Pasha. "Sad for Germany if many other people think as you do there. A sign that your people lacks the strength to enforce its national will relentlessly."

At this point in the interview the pastor was overcome by a great fatigue. It was born of the sensation that, in his way, this little, closed-up fellow was in the right. The hoary wisdom of the world is always, in its way, right against Christ's wisdom. But the worst of it was that Enver's rightness infected, at this instant, Johannes Lepsius, and lamed his will. The uncertain destiny of his fatherland descended on his soul with the weight of a mountain. He whispered: "It's not the same thing."

"Quite right. It's not the same thing. But it's we who gain by the comparison. We Turks have a hundred times harder struggle to assert our rights than you Germans."

Lepsius, tortured and absent-minded, pulled out a handkerchief, which he held up like a parliamentary banner. "It isn't a question of protecting yourselves against an enemy in your midst, but of the planned extirpation of another race."

This he jerked out in a sullen voice; his eyes, no longer able to endure Enver's cool detachment, strayed towards the study with its three heroes on the wall. Had Monsignore Saven, the Patriarch, no right there? Lepsius suddenly remembered that he was here to discuss economics. Quickly he gathered strength

136

for a fresh encounter: "Excellency. I won't presume to waste your time in empty discussion. But may I venture to draw your attention to certain rather grave drawbacks, which you yourself perhaps may not yet have considered very carefully —naturally enough, weighed down as you are by your burden as commander-in-chief. I may perhaps know the interior, Anatolia, Cilicia, Syria, better than you do, since I worked for years under difficult conditions in all that territory. . . ."

And so, in hurried words—he felt time ebbing away—he developed his plea. The Turkish empire, without the Armenian millet, would be bound to go to pieces economically, and its army would, as a consequence, be endangered. Why? He did not care to insist on the export trade, ninety percent of which was in Christian hands, and His Excellency knew as well as he did that most of the foreign trade was conducted by Armenian firms, so that in consequence one of the most essential branches of war industry, the provision of raw materials, as well as of manufactured goods, could only be successfully managed by these firms—for instance, by such a world-established business as Avetis Bagradian and Sons, which had branches and representatives in twelve different European cities. And as to the interior itself, he, Lepsius, years ago, on his journeys there, had seen that Armenian agricultural methods in Anatolia were a hundred times ahead of Turkish small landholding. In those days Cilician Armenians had imported hundreds of threshing-machines and steam-ploughs from Europe and, by so doing, given the Turks a strong incentive to massacre, since they not only slaughtered the ten thousand inhabitants of Adana but also broke up the machines and ploughs. In that alone, and nowhere else, lay the real mischief. The Armenian millet, the most progressive and active section of the Ottoman population, had for years been making vast efforts to lead Turkey out of its old-fashioned, primitive methods of agriculture into a new world of up-to-date farming and budding industrialization. And it was for just this very beneficent pioneering work that Armenians were being persecuted and slaughtered by the vengeful violence of irritated sloth.

"Let's admit, Excellency, that craftsmanship, trade, and peasant industry, which in the interior are almost exclusively Armenian, could be taken over by Turks—who is to replace all the numerous Armenian doctors, trained in the best universities in Europe, who care for their Osmanli patients with the same skill as for their own people? Who's to replace all the engineers, all the solicitors, all the export traders, whose work so indefatigably drives the country forwards? Your Excellency will perhaps tell me that, at a pinch, a people can live without intellect. But it can't live without a stomach. And at present the stomach of Turkey is being slit open, yet you hope to survive the operation."

Enver Pasha heard this out, his head inclined gently on one side. His whole aspect, incisive, youthful, subdued only by that hint of shyness in him, displayed as few unintentional creases as did his uniform. The pastor, on the other hand, was already beginning to look dishevelled. He was sweating, his tie was askew, his sleeves worked their way up his arms. The general crossed his short but slim legs. The glittering riding-boots fitted as though they were on trees.

"You speak of the stomach, Herr Lepsius." He smiled effusively. "Well, perhaps after the war Turkey may have rather a weak one——"

"She won't have any stomach left at all, Excellency."

Unruffled, the commander continued: "The Turkish population is forty millions. Well, now—try to see it from our point of view, Herr Lepsius. Is it not a great and worthy policy to try to weld these forty millions together and establish a natural empire, which henceforth will play the same part in Asia as Germany does in Europe? This empire is waiting. We have only to grasp it. I agree that among Armenians one finds an alarming proportion of intelligence. Are you really so much in favour of that kind of intelligence, Herr Lepsius? I'm not. We Turks may not be very intelligent in that way, but on the other hand we're a great and heroic people, called to establish and govern a world empire. Therefore we intend to surmount all obstacles."

Lepsius twisted his fingers but said not a word. This spoilt child was the absolute master of a great power. His finely modelled, attractive little head brooded on such statistics as might have amazed all who knew the reality. He could produce none to blind Dr. Lepsius, who was precisely aware that in Anatolia there were scarcely six million pure-bred Turks; that, if one went into Northern Persia, to the Caucasus, to Kashgar and Turkestan, he would not be able, even by including all nomad Turkic tribes, the vagrant horse-thieves and steppe-dwellers spread across a land as wide as the half of Europe, to trump up as many as twenty millions. Such dreams, he reflected, the narcotic of nationalism engenders. Yet at the same time he was moved to pity for this porcelain war god, this childlike Antichrist.

Johannes Lepsius's voice became soft and surcharged with wisdom: "You want to found a new empire, Excellency. But the corpse of the Armenian people will be beneath its foundations. Can that bring you prosperity? Could no more peaceful way be chosen, even now?"

Here for the first time Enver Pasha laid bare his deepest truth. His smile had no longer any reserve in it, a cold stare had come into his eyes, his lips retreated from a strong and dangerous set of teeth.

"There can be no peace," he said, "between human beings and plague germs."

Lepsius came down on this in a trice: "So you openly admit your intention of using the war to extirpate the Armenian millet?"

The War Minister had decidedly said too much. He retired at once within his impregnable fortress of discourteous courtesy. "My personal opinions and intentions are all contained in the memoranda published by our government on the subject. We are acting under the force majeure of the war, in self-defence, after having waited and observed as long as we could. Citizens who work to destroy the state render themselves liable in all countries to be dealt with by the sharp process of law. So that our government is within its legal rights."

They were back at the beginning. Johannes Lepsius could not manage to stifle a sound like a groan. He could hear Monsignore Saven's voice: "Don't moralize! Be matter-of-fact! Arguments!" Oh, if he could but remain matter-of-fact and use only arguments keen as razor-blades! But this very necessity to keep sitting, the impropriety of springing to his feet to answer, set his nerves despairingly on edge. He, the born speaker on committees, at public meetings, needed room, freedom to move in.

"Excellency"—he pressed a hand against his wide and finely shaped forehead—"I'm not going to speak to you in platitudes. I won't say that a whole people can't be made to suffer for the misdemeanours of a few individuals. I won't ask why women and children, small children, as you yourself were once, must suffer a bestial death for the sake of a policy of which they haven't so much as heard. I want you to look at the future, your people's future, Excellency! Even this war will end some day, and Turkey will be faced with the necessity of concluding peace terms. May that day be a good one for all of us! But, if it should be unlucky, what then, Excellency? Surely the responsible head of a people must take some measures against the possibility of an unfavourable ending of the war. And in what position will the Ottoman peace commission be to negotiate if it finds itself faced with the question: 'Where is your brother Abel?' A highly painful situation. The victorious Powers—may God prevent it!—might use this pretext of a great crime that has been committed to share out the booty remorselessly among themselves. And General Enver Pasha, the man who, in such a case as that, would be the greatest among his people, the man who had shouldered all responsibility, whose word had been all-powerful—how would he defend himself then against that people?"

Enver Pasha's eyes had begun to dream; he said quite seriously: "Thank you for this very excellent hint. But any man who goes into politics must possess two special qualifications: first, a certain levity, or, if you like, indifference to death—it comes to the same thing; and, secondly, the unshakable belief in his own decisions, once they are taken."

Herr Pastor Lepsius stood up. He crossed his arms upon his breast, almost in the fashion of the East. This guardian angel, sent by God to shield the Armenian people, was in a pitiful state. The big handkerchief hung out of his pocket, his trousers had worked up almost to his knees, his tie wandered nearer and nearer his ear—even his pince-nez seemed to have vanished utterly.

"I implore Your Excellency"—he bowed before his seated interlocutor—"let it end today. You have made such an example of this enemy in your midst—who is not one—as history has never recorded. Hundreds and thousands are dying on the highroads of the East. Make an end today. Give orders to keep back these new edicts of transportation. I know that not all the vilayets and sanjaks have been depopulated yet. If, for the sake of the German ambassador and Mr. Morgenthau, you still hesitate with the great deportations in Western Asia Minor, spare Northern Syria, Aleppo, Alexandretta, Antioch, for my sake. Say: 'This is enough.' And when I get back to Germany, I'll sing your praises wherever I go."

And still the pastor would not sit down again, although the general's patient hand had several times pointed to his chair.

"Herr Lepsius," Enver declared at last, "you overestimate my competency. The carrying into effect of such government decrees is a matter for the Ministry of the Interior."

The German snatched his pince-nez from off red eyes. "But

that's just it—the way in which the thing's being carried out. It isn't the Minister, or the Wali, or the Mutessarif, who puts these decrees into execution, but bestial, heartless subordinates and sergeants. Do you, for instance, or does the Minister, intend that women and children should collapse on the highroad and be driven on at once with cudgels? Is it your intention that a whole area should be infected with rotting corpses, that the Euphrates should be thick with dead? I know for a fact that that's how it's being carried out."

"I'm aware how well you know the interior." Enver Pasha came a little way to meet him. "And I should be very glad to have your written suggestions as to how these matters can be improved. I'll examine them carefully."

But Lepsius stretched out his arms. "Send me down there. That's my first suggestion. Not even the old Sultan refused me that. Give me full powers to organize these transports and convoys. God will lend me the strength, and I've had more experience than anyone. I don't need a piastre from the Ottoman government, I'll get hold of the necessary funds. I shall have German and American relief commissions behind me. Once before I succeeded in a great work of assistance. I helped to establish numbers of orphanages and hospitals and more than fifty industrial societies. In spite of this war I can do the same again, and better—and in two years you yourself will be thanking me, Excellency."

This time Enver Pasha had listened with not merely his usual attention, but intense eagerness. And now Herr Lepsius saw and heard a thing he had never experienced in his life. It was no sneering cruelty, no cynicism, that transfigured the boyish look on this war-lord's face. No. What Herr Lepsius perceived was that arctic mask of the human being who "has overcome all sentimentality"—the mask of a human mind which has got beyond guilt and all its qualms, the strange, almost innocent naïveté of utter godlessness. And what force it had, that a man could not hate it!

"Your estimable suggestions interest me," said Enver appreciatively, "but it goes without saying that I must reject them. This very request of yours shows me that up to now we have talked at cross-purposes. If I let a foreigner help Armenians, I shall create a precedent which will admit of the intervention of foreign personages, and so of the countries they represent. I should be destroying my whole policy, since its object is to teach the Armenian millet the consequences of this longing of theirs for foreign intervention. The Armenians themselves would be bewildered. First I punish their seditious hopes and fantasies, and then I proceed to send one of their most influential friends to reawaken them. No, my dear Herr Lepsius, that's impossible. I can't let foreigners benefit these people. The Armenians must see in us their sole benefactors."

The pastor sank down into his chair. Lost. All over. Words were superfluous. If only the man were malicious, if he were Satan! But he had no malice, he was not Satan; this quietly implacable mass-murderer was boyishly charming. Lepsius had begun to brood and so did not see at once the whole effrontery of Enver's offer, made in a cheery, confident tone:

"Shall I suggest something, Herr Lepsius? You get money! Get as much money as ever you can, from your societies, a lot of money—in Germany and America. Then, when you've collected it, bring it to me. I'll use it all as you want it used, according to your suggestions. But I must point out that I can't allow any supervision by Germans or other foreigners."

Had Johannes not been so perturbed, he would have burst out laughing, so amusing was the thought of those devious channels by which his collected funds, disposed of by Enver, would travel in Turkey. He did not answer. He was beaten. Although he had been without much hope, even before the interview began, he realized only now that a world lay shattered. He summoned his wits together and, to bring himself back to self-control, made himself look a trifle more presentable, mopped his glistening forehead several times, and stood up.

"I can't bear to think, Excellency, that this hour which you have been so kind as to grant me has been quite fruitless. There are a hundred thousand Armenians in North Syria and along the coast, living far away from any battlefield. I'm sure Your Excellency agrees that punitive measures which have no object are better left in abeyance."

Again the boyish Mars bared a row of smiling teeth. "You may be sure, Herr Lepsius, that our government will avoid all unnecessary harshness."

This on both sides had been empty formality, an aimless juggling, to enable this political discussion, like every other, to ebb away in vague inconclusiveness. Enver had not made the least concession. It was still his affair what harshness he might think necessary. And Lepsius, too, knowing that his last words were meaningless, had said them merely to end the interview. The general, who, in contrast to the pastor, looked at that moment especially spick and span, stood back to give his visitor the *pas*. He even went with him a little way and then, in his slightly surprised inscrutability, watched the pastor's unsteady steps bear him out of sight, down a long corridor, with billowing curtain-doors on either side.

ENVER PASHA went into Talaat Bey's office. The clerks sprang up. Hero-worship shone out of their faces. That almost mystic love had still not waned which even these paper-gentry felt for their dainty war god. Hundreds of boastful stories of his mad daring were current here in all the departments. When, for instance, during the war in Albania, an artillery regiment had mutinied, he, cigarette in mouth, had stood before the muzzle of a howitzer and challenged the mutineers to pull the firing-cord. Round Enver's delicate, silky features, his people saw a messianic aura. He was the man sent by God, who should re-erect the empire of Osman, Bayazid, Suleiman. The general greeted his clerks with a merry shout, evoking over-emphasized delight in them. Too-hasty hands snatched open the doors which led on into Talaat's sanctum through outer offices. The little room seemed far too small for that Minister's crushing personality. When, as he did at this instant, this Hun stood up behind his desk, he darkened the window. Talaat's mighty head was grey at the temples. Above the pursy lips of the Oriental there hovered a small, pitch-black moustache. Fat double chins thrust out of a stick-up double collar. A white piqué waistcoat, like the symbol of candid open-heartedness, curved over a jutting expanse of belly. Each time Talaat Bey beheld his co-ruler in this duumvirate, he felt the urge to place his great paws in fatherly tenderness on the narrow shoulders of this youth blessed of the gods. Yet each time, the aura of glacial shyness surrounding Enver impeded such familiar proximity. Yet Talaat was the exuberant man of the world, the talker, whose heady, confident way could dispose of five diplomats at a time, whereas Enver, the demi-god of his people, the consort of an imperial princess, would often at great receptions stand for half an hour shyly aside, lost in his dreams. Talaat dropped his big, fleshy hand again and contented himself with a single question: "So the German's been seeing you?"

Enver Pasha turned his eyes on the Bosporus, with its jocund waters, its little hurrying tugs, its tiny kayiks, its cypresses, which looked so unconvincing, so badly painted, at that hour —its theatrical ruins. Then he glanced back and let his eyes stray through this empty office till they paused on an old-fashioned Morse apparatus set on a little carpeted table, like some very valuable curiosity. On this wretched machine, before the Ittihad revolution had raised him up to be the first statesman in the Caliph's empire, the young Talaat, the minor post-and-telegraph official, had fingered out Morse code. Let every visitor admire this proof of a giddily steep ascent, the reward of merit. Enver, too, seemed to view this significant

145

telegraph apparatus with benevolent eyes before he quite remembered to answer the question. "Yes, the German! He tried to threaten a little, with the Reichstag."

This remark showed how right Monsignore Saven had been—how mistaken, from the very start, those humanely imploring tactics of Dr. Lepsius. A secretary brought in a sheaf of dispatches, which Talaat began to sign without sitting down again. He did not look up as he was speaking: "These Germans are only afraid of the odium of being made partly responsible. But they may have to come begging to us for more important things than Armenians."

This might have ended that day's discussion of the banishment, had Enver's inquisitive eyes not rested on the dispatches in casual scrutiny. Talaat Bey noticed his glance and made the papers rustle as he waved them. "The precise directions for Aleppo. Meanwhile, I suppose, the roads will be clearer again. In the next few weeks Aleppo, Alexandretta, Antioch, and the whole coast can begin to move out."

"Antioch and the coast?" Enver repeated interrogatively, as though he might have something to say on the point. He did not speak another syllable but stared enthralled at Talaat's fat fingers, which, irresistible as a storming-party, kept scribbling signatures under texts. These same forthright and stumpy fingers had composed that order, sent out to all walis and mutessarifs: "The goal of these deportations is annihilation." The short pen-strokes showed all the impetus of complete, implacable conviction; they had no scruples.

The Minister raised up his bent torso. "That's done. In the autumn I shall be able to say with perfect candour to all these people: '*La question arménienne n'existe pas.*'"

Enver stood at the window and had not heard. Was he thinking of his future caliphate, which was to reach from Macedonia to India? Was he worried about the munitions supplies for the army? Or dreaming of fresh acquisitions for his magic palace on the Bosporus? In its great banqueting-hall he had caused the wedding throne to be set up which Nadjieh Sultana, the Sultan's daughter, had brought with her dowry. Four silver-gilt pillars and, over them, a starry canopy of Byzantine brocade.

JOHANNES LEPSIUS was still creeping through the alleys of Istanbul. It was long past midday. He had missed his lunch. The pastor dared not go back to the Hotel Tokatlyan. An Armenian house. Terror and despair were in all its inhabitants, from the host and guests down to the last waiter and lift-boy. They knew his ways and had known of his undertaking. The spies and confidence men who, by order of Talaat Bey, followed him everywhere might track him now as much as they liked. It hurt him that his friends should be somewhere waiting for him in a well-considered place of security. Davidian, the president of the former Armenian National Assembly, would be one of them; an arrested person who had, however, managed to escape and remain illegally in Istanbul. Lepsius had not strength or courage to face them. The fact that he did not come would be enough to show them the truth, and it was to be hoped that by now they would have separated. Even the worst pessimists among them (they all were pessimists, and no wonder)—even they had not considered it out of the question that the pastor might get a permit for the interior. Much would have been gained by it.

Lepsius came to a public garden. Here, too, festivity. Garlanded benches. Half-moon pennons fluttering out from poles and lamp-posts. The jam of idlers, thick, slab, unpleasant, oozed its way along gravel paths between the grass-plots. Lepsius, dazed and unsteady, caught sight of a bench. He found a seat on it, beside others. A half-circle, vivid with waving colours, curved out before him. That same instant, over in the grandstand, a Turkish military band burst forth with clashing janizary music. Cornets, flutes, raucous clarinets, clashing brass, ascending and descending the short intervals

147

with the sharp unity of a razor-blade, mingled with the fanatical yelps of taut-strung drums, the incessant clattering, clinking rattle of tambourines, the shivering hatred of cymbals. Johannes Lepsius sat in this music up to his chin, as in a bath of glass splinters. But he wanted to suffer, not to free himself, and pressed handfuls of glass splinters into his consciousness. That which Enver Pasha had refused was now conceded him. In the long deportation convoys of this people, given into his charge, he dragged his way down the stony, marshy highroads of Anatolia. Let not his own condemn him —they who in the trenches of the Argonne, on the battlefields of Podolia and Galicia, at sea and in the air, were being decimated. Were not those endless hospital trains, at the sight of which a man had to cry out, more terrible still? Had not the eyes of German wounded and dying become Armenian eyes? Lepsius, under this janizary band, let his head, dull with fatigue, sink lower and lower. He had not been chosen to care for his own, but for that which was not his. A new note was forcing its way into this strident, wrathful Turkish music, a vibrant clatter which rose and rose. And it came from above. A Turkish air squadron was on its way across Istanbul, dropping swirling clouds of proclamations. Though he could not tell why, it grew clear to Johannes Lepsius that these planes above him should be named "Original Sin and Its Pride." He wandered about within this perception as he might have in a huge building—in the Ministry of the Interior. Curtains fluttered out from before the doorways; they waved, like flames, and he thought of a passage in the Apocalypse, which he had meant to use in his next sermon: "And the shapes of the locusts were like unto horses prepared unto battle . . . and they had breast-plates, as it were breast-plates of iron, and the sound of their wings was as the sound of chariots of many horses running to battle. . . . And they had tails, like unto scorpions, and there were stings in their tails, and their power was to hurt men five months."

Johannes Lepsius started up. New means, new methods must be thought out. If the German Embassy failed, perhaps the Austrian Markgraf Pallavicini, a most distinguished man, might have more success. He might threaten reprisals—the Mohammedan Bosnians were Austro-Hungarian citizens. And, so far, papal admonitions had been too tepid. But then Enver Pasha approached him, with his never-to-be-forgotten smile. No—shy was not the word to describe this boyish (or girlish) amiability of the great mass-murderer.—We intend, Herr Lepsius, to pursue the policy of our interests to the very end. Only a power which stood above all interests could prevent us, a power never tainted with any rascality. If you should happen to turn up the name of such a power in the diplomat's register, I shall be so glad to receive you again at the Ministry.

Lepsius shifted and fidgeted so wildly that his veiled neighbour on the bench, becoming scared, got up to go. He did not notice, since now he was weighted hand and foot with his leaden conviction: "No more to be done." There was no more help. What the priest Ter Haigasun in Yoghonoluk had known for weeks was just beginning now to dawn on Pastor Johannes Lepsius: "There's only one thing left—to pray."

And so, amid the press of these folk on holiday, jostled by laughing women and squalling brats, as the janizary music brayed again, as his head, with his eyes closed, rolled impotently about from side to side, the pastor folded, or at least believed he folded, his hands, as petitioners should. And his soul began speaking: "Our Father which art in heaven, hallowed be Thy name. . . ."

But how had the "Our Father" changed? Each word was a gulf deeper than the eye could measure. Even at the words "us," "ours," his head swirled. Who dare still say "us," since Christ, who first bound the "us" together, created it, went to heaven on the third day? Without Him it is all no more than a stinking heap of shards and bones, as high as half the universe. Lepsius thought of his mother, of the words which, after his baptism, she had written fifty-six years ago in her diary: "May his name, Johannes, for ever remind me that it is my sacred duty to bring him up a true Johannes, one who really loves his Lord and walks in His footsteps. . . ." Had he become a real Johannes? Was he really full to the brim of that deep trust in God which cannot be named? Alas, such trust threatens to crumble as the body declines. His diabetes had come back again. He would have to be careful what he ate. Above all, nothing sweet, no bread or potatoes. Perhaps Enver, by forbidding his journey to Anatolia, had prevented his becoming any worse. But what was the hotel porter of the Tokatlyan doing here? And since when had he worn that lambskin officer's kepi? Had Enver sent him? Politely the porter handed him a teskeré for the interior. It was an autographed photo of Napoleon. And yes, of course, the first convoy of exiles must be waiting for him outside the hotel. All his friends would be there, Davidian and all the others. They were smiling and beckoning to him. "They all look jolly well," thought the pastor. And indeed the worst, most horrible reality has always a compensation at the heart of it, if only one can look at it steadily. On the banks of a river they halted, under wildly overhanging rocks. Why, they even had tents with them. Perhaps, sub rosa, Enver had made a few small concessions. When they had all lain down to rest, a tall Armenian man, his clothes thickly caked with slime, came over to him. He spoke queer, ceremonious, broken German: "See—this charming river is the Euphrates, and these are my children. But you are to stretch your body across it, from bank to bank, so that my children may have a bridge to cross by."

Lepsius pretended this was a joke, and retorted: "Well, you and your children'll have to wait a bit, till I've grown a little." But at once he began to grow, with delightful celerity. His hands and feet spread endlessly far away from him. Now he could fulfil the Armenian man's request with pleasant nonchalance. And yet, in the end, it didn't work, because Johannes Lepsius lost his balance and almost slipped down off his bench.

"This is really terrible," he said to himself, for the second time that day. But actually, more than anything else, what he meant was the thirst that tormented him. He shook himself, hurried to the first drink-shop, and, without any thought of medical warnings, greedily swallowed down a sweet iced drink. With his enhanced sense of well-being new and courageous plans began to invade him. "I'll never let go," he laughed absent-mindedly to himself. And this vague laugh was a declaration of war on Enver Pasha.

In that same instant Talaat Bey's private secretary was handing the representative on duty at the Ministry of Post and Telegragh an official dispatch concerning Aleppo, Alexandretta, Antioch, and the coast.

6

The Great Assembly

EVER since the day on which Djelal Bey, the estimable Wali of
Aleppo, had refused to carry out in his province the government decrees of banishment—since that spring day there had
been no further hindrances, no annoying recalcitrance.

Apart from those directly affected by it, the heaviest burden
of this tragic measure lay on the müdirs. Their nahiyehs, the
districts they administered, comprised wide stretches of territory, with scarcely a railway line, with little telegraphic communication, where even carriage driving along the cruellest
highroads and tracks was an agony. So that really the müdirs
had no choice but to sit all day and half the night in the saddle,
till every Armenian village over every square mile of country
had been sent packing at the proper time. This "proper time"
was often the midnight before the morning of setting out. It
had been easy enough for the Wali, the Mutessarif, the Kaimakam, to give their orders and "hold responsible." In the towns
it was child's play. But when one had ninety-seven small districts, villages, hamlets, parishes, to control, it looked very
different. So that many a müdir, who was both unable to
work miracles and not scrupulous as to the letter of the law,
decided without much hesitation to "forget" this or that remote village. Many müdirs were inspired by good-natured indolence. In others such easy-going mildness had in it a dash
of cunning. These "overlookings" might prove remunerative,
since the small Armenian, even the peasant, is not unprosper-
ous. Indulgence was only perilous in districts in which there

was a standing gendarmerie post. The saptiehs wanted to make a little themselves, and what better, more fruitful method than legalized plunder, at which the authorities winked both eyes? To be sure, the possessions of exiles were legally the property of the state. But the state was well aware that it had not the means rigidly to enforce its just claims and could see the advantage of not allowing the zeal of its executives to flag.

Whereas in all provincial selamliks, cafés, baths, places of assembly, the progressives—all, that is to say, who read a newspaper, who had been to Smyrna or Istanbul and there seen, instead of karagös, the old-Turkish shadow-theatre, a couple of French comedies, and who had heard the names "Sarah Bernhardt" and "Bismarck"—whereas these cultured ones, the highly progressive urban middle class, stood to a man behind Enver Pasha's Armenian policy, the simple Turk, peasant or town proletarian, felt differently. Often, as he rode about his district, a surprised müdir would pull up in the village street, where he had just read out his decree of banishment, to watch Turks and Armenians mingle their tears. He would marvel as, before an Armenian house, its Turkish neighbours stood and wailed, calling after its dazed and tearless inhabitants, who without looking back were leaving the doors of their old home: "May God pity you!" And more, loading them with provisions for the road, with costly presents, a goat, or even a mule. The amazed müdir might even have to see these Turks accompany their wretched neighbours for several leagues. He might even behold his own compatriots casting themselves down before his feet, to beseech him: "Let them stay with us. They haven't the true faith, but they are good. They are our brothers. Let them stay with us."

But what use was that? The very best-natured of müdirs could overlook no more than a few unnamed desert villages, where secretly he tolerated the presence of some remnant of the accursed race, cowering into the shelter of its own terror of extinction. Otherwise it went stumbling along field-paths, turned off on to cart-tracks, mingled and jostled along the roads, to come at last, after days, to the great highway which leads south-west over Aleppo into the desert. A hesitant, million-footed rhythm, such as the earth had not yet known. The route-march of this army had been sketched out and was being followed with real strategic foresight. Only one department had been neglected by its invisible commanders—the commissariat. In the first few days there was still a little bread and bulgur, dried wheat, available, when most had still not exhausted their own supplies. In these early days every adult had still the right to draw from the onbashi, the paymaster-sergeant of the convoy, legal pay amounting to twelve paras, less than a penny. But most were wise enough not to make the demand, which could only have drawn down the hatred of the all-powerful upon their heads; and then, for twelve paras, with the cost of living risen to what it was, the most one could hope to buy would be a couple of oranges or one hen's egg. So that with every hour the faces became more hollow, the million-footed steps unsteadier. Soon no other sounds forced their way out of this dragging throng along the roads than groanings, pantings, whimperings, with sometimes a wild, convulsive scream. With time this being shed more and more component parts; they sank to earth, were bundled into the ditches, and there perished. The saptiehs' clubs came thudding down on the backs of hesitant throngs. For these saptiehs foamed with irritation. They themselves were having to live like dogs till such time as they could hand over their convoys at the frontiers of the next kazah, the next gendarmerie district. At first, roll-calls were still taken. But, as death and sickness gained the upper hand, as more and more half-dead and corpses, especially children's corpses, were flung into the ditches, this keeping of lists seemed highly onerous, and the onbashi relinquished superfluous scribbling. Who cared to know that Sarkis, Astik, or Hapeth, that Anush, Vartuhi, or Koren, were rotting somewhere in the open? These saptiehs were not all brutes. It is even probable that most of them were good, plain, middling sort of people. But what can a saptieh do? He is under stringent orders to reach such and such a point with his whole convoy by such and such a scheduled hour. His heart may be in perfect sympathy with the screaming mother who tries to snatch her child out of a ditch, flings herself down on the road, and claws the earth. No use to talk to her. She's wasted minutes already, and it's still six miles to the next halt. A convoy held up. All the faces in it twisted with hate. A mad scream from a thousand throats. Why did not these crowds, weak as they were, hurl themselves on the saptieh and his mates, disarm them, and tear them into shreds? Perhaps the policemen were in constant terror of such assault, which would have finished them. And so—one of them fires a shot. The rest whip out their swords to beat the defenceless cruelly with the blades. Thirty or forty men and women lie bleeding. And, with this blood, another emotion comes to life in the excited saptiehs—their old itch for the women of the accursed race. In these helpless women you possess more than a human being—in very truth you possess the God of your enemy. Afterwards, the saptiehs scarcely know how it all had happened.

A shifting carpet woven with the threads of blood-stained destinies. It is always the same. After the first few days on the roads all the young men and the men in the prime of life get separated off from the rest of the convoy. Here, for instance, a man of forty-six, in good clothes, an engineer. It needs many cudgel blows to get him away from his wife and children. His youngest is about one and a half. This man is to be enrolled in a labour battalion, for road-making. He stumbles in the long line of men and shuffles, gibbering like a half-wit: "I never missed paying my bedel . . . paying my bedel." Suddenly he grips hold of his neighbour. "You've never seen such a lovely baby." . . . A torrent of sentimental agony. "Why, the girl had eyes as big as plates. If only I could, I'd crawl after them on my belly like a snake." And he shuffles on, enveloped in his grief, completely isolated. That evening they lie down to rest on a hillside. Long after midnight he shakes the same neighbour out of his sleep. "They're all dead now." He is perfectly calm.

In another convoy a husband and wife. Both still quite young. The bridegroom's upper lip has scarcely a trace of down on it. Their hour is approaching, since all the active men are to be separated. The bride gets an inspiration to disguise her young husband in women's clothes. These two children have already begun to laugh, delighted at the happy disguise. But the others warn them against any premature triumph. On the outskirts of a big town some strange chettehs, armed roughs, come out to meet them. They are out on a woman-hunt. Among several others, they choose the bride. She clings fast to her husband. "For God's sake, leave me with her. My sister is deaf-mute. She needs me." "That's no reason, janum, little soul! The fair one shall come with you." The couple get taken off to a filthy hut. And there the truth is soon made manifest. The chettehs kill the young man instantly, and mutilated his corpse in a fiendish mockery of the disguise which he had assumed. Then, after the most horrible abuse, the girl is tied naked to her groom—face to face with his mutilated corpse.

A shifting carpet, woven of lives which none can unravel. . . . There, again and again, the mother who for days carries her child, dead of starvation, in a sack on her shoulders, until at last, unable any longer to bear the stench, her own people complain to the saptiehs. There, too, the crazed mothers of Kemakh, who, bawling hymns and with sparkling eyes, as though this were a blessed work in the sight of God, cast their children down from a rock into the Euphrates. Again and again some bishop, some vartabed, approaches. He gathers up and spreads out his robes, casts himself down before the müdir, sobs: "Have pity, Effendi, on these innocent." And the müdir has to give the official answer: "Priest, do not meddle in politics! The government respects the church. I am only concerned with you in ecclesiastical matters."

In many convoys nothing in particular seems to be happening, no apparent suffering, only hunger, thirst, wounded feet, and disease. And yet one day a German deaconess stood outside the hospital of Marash, at which she had just arrived to go on duty. An endless, mute convoy of Armenians came dragging onwards past the hospital, and she stood waiting to let them pass. She could not manage to stir till the last had vanished. Something which she herself could not understand had begun to stir in this nursing-sister—not pity, no, and not horror either; something vast and unknown, almost exultation. That evening she wrote home to her people: "I ran into a long convoy of exiles, who had only just been turned out of their villages and were still in quite a good state. I had to wait a long time to let them get past me, and I never shall forget what they looked like. Only a sprinkling of men, the rest all women and children. A lot of them had light hair and great blue eyes, which stared at me with such deathly solemnity, such unconscious grandeur in them, that they might have been the angels of the Last Judgment." These poor avenging angels had come from Zeitun, Marash, Aintab, and the vilayet of Adana. They came plodding down from the north, from the provinces of Sivas, Trebizond, Erzerum. They came out of the east, from Kharput and the Kurd-infested Diarbekr, from Urfa and Bitlis. Before the Taurus, before Aleppo had been reached, they all mingled in the one endless, shifting carpet of lives. And yet in Aleppo itself nothing had happened, nor in the teeming sanjaks and kazahs of its vilayet. The coast lay peaceful and untouched. Musa Dagh was at peace. The mountain seemed not to notice this gruesome pilgrimage which passed not so very far away.

157

GABRIEL BAGRADIAN pursued his investigations in the villages. He even extended their scope. Southwards he often got as far as Suedia, and northwards, after several hours' ride, he once even touched Beilan, that deserted villa-pleasaunce of rich Armenians from Alexandretta. He only dared one other journey to Antioch. Gabriel found the ancient doors of the Agha Rifaat Bereket's mansion closed. He pounded the knocker several times against the copper-inlaid wood, but nobody answered. So the Agha was not back yet from Aleppo. Though Gabriel knew he was travelling in aid of the Armenians, the absence of this friend of his father depressed him.

On his return he decided that henceforth in all his journeyings he would not go beyond the farthest precincts of Musa Dagh. Some compelling magic emanating from the mountain of his fathers, becoming stronger and stronger the longer he stayed here, forced him to this. The same solemn amazement still descended on him as each morning he opened his window wide to greet the mountain. He could not understand. The huge mass of Musa Dagh, changing its aspect every hour, now firmly compressed, now almost on the point of evaporation into downy sunlight—the very essence of this mountain, eternal amid all this mutability, seemed to renew Gabriel's strength and give him courage for the torturing hither and thither of thoughts which had robbed him of sleep ever since the arrival of Pastor Tomasian. But the instant he left the shadow of Musa Dagh the courage to think such thoughts ebbed out of him. Meanwhile, his industrious excursions through the villages had born good fruit. He got what he was after—not only a fairly consistent general notion of the day-to-day lives of the peasants, fruit-growers, silk-spinners, weavers, beekeepers, and wood-carvers, but many glimpses into the more closed circles of their minds, into the nature of their family relationships. Not that it was easy. At first many of these country folk could only see a wealthy foreigner, no matter how much he might be bound to them by racial ties and common ownership But with time their trust in him grew, and even a secret hope they had of him. The effendi was, to be sure, a powerful man, who knew foreign parts and was feared by the Turks because of his influence. As long as he stayed on in Yoghonoluk, the worst might perhaps be spared the villages. No one scrutinized the real worth of such hopes. But another instinct helped to feed them. Though Gabriel spoke as little of the future as they themselves, many could sense, in his eyes, his restlessness, his gestures—in the notes which he kept taking—some purposeful thought, a special activity, which distinguished him from everyone else. All their eyes were on him when he came among them. He was asked into many houses. Though the rooms were bare, according to Eastern custom, their clean comfort always surprised him. The clay floors were strewn with clean carpets. Divans covered with pleasant rugs took the place of chairs. Only in the poorest houses were the stables anywhere near the living-room. The walls were by no means bare. Old illustrations and little pictures saved from calendars were pinned up beside the pictures of the saints. Many housewives decorated their rooms with cut flowers—a very unusual habit in the East—laid out as a rule in flat dishes. When the guest was seated, a big wooden stand would be set before him, on which were placed the wide tin dishes of cakes, honey-fingers, and sweet cheese biscuits. Gabriel could remember their taste from his childhood. In those days they had been forbidden luxuries, since his parents were not supposed to know that the servants took young Master Gabriel into village houses. But, now that they were being heaped upon him, Gabriel's digestion began to protest, especially when they insisted on bringing melon slices and sugared fruit into the bargain. To have refused would have been an outrageous breach of hospitality, so he, the guest, in self-defence, had to keep giving dainties to the children whom they always brought in to be introduced, and occasionally munching a sweet himself. It moved him to see how clean and well looked-after these children were, the smallest especially. The mothers took their greatest pride in the cleanness of the little white smocks, tiny coats and aprons. Later, as these children grew up, even they, it is true, could not keep their boys from running wild, on warlike expeditions after booty, over Musa Dagh and into the gorges of the Damlayik.

Gabriel made many friends in these frequent excursions into the villages. The closest of them all was the staid, respectable Chaush Nurhan, or, more correctly, Sergeant Nurhan. Next to the elder Tomasian, this Chaush Nurhan owned the best craftsman's business south of Yoghonoluk—he was a smith and locksmith and besides owned a saddlery, a carriage-building establishment in which he built the kangnis used in these parts, and finally, a holy of holies, a shop where he worked alone, without any witnesses. Initiates knew that in secret he repaired hunting-rifles and made the cartridges for them. But his occupation was best kept secret from Ali Nassif's inquisitive eyes.

Chaush Nurhan was an ex-regular. He had served seven years in the Turkish army, which he had spent in the war and in an Anatolian infantry regiment in the huge barracks at Brussa. He looked the hardened regular that he was, with his straight, iron-grey moustache twisted into very long points, his continual, forceful use of army expletives, and above all his stiff respectfulness with Bagradian, whom he greeted only as his superior officer. He may perhaps have sensed certain qualities in Gabriel, who did not himself know he possessed them. Chaush Nurhan, who had already worked for the younger Avetis, agreed to inspect the extensive gun-room of the villa and make sure that everything was ship-shape. He took away the guns to dismember and oil them in his secret workshop. Gabriel often came to see him at work. Sometimes he would bring Stephan with him. They reminisced about the army like keen professionals. The chaush was full of coarse barrack-room stories and quirks, of which the *bel esprit* Gabriel never wearied. So that, incredibly, in these months of banishment, two Armenian men became engrossed in their memories of Turkish army life as though they had been in a Turkish barracks. Chaush Nurhan was a widower, like old Tomasian. But he had a promising brood of half-grown children, whom he himself seemed to find it hard to distinguish. He scarcely ever troubled his head with his progeny. This erstwhile tyrant of recruits, with the awe-inspiring, iron-grey moustache, was placid good nature itself when it came to his own flesh and blood, and he let them run wild without a qualm. In the evenings, when his only journeyman had handed over the workshop keys, he neither entered his own house, full of children, nor knocked at any neighbour's door. With a pitcher of wine in one hand, in the other an infantry cornet, pilfered from a quartermaster's store, he would go into his apricot orchard. There, in the dusk, unsteady howlings rent the air. They were well known to the other villagers. Turkish bugle-calls, halting and kicking, would rattle forth, as though, before night came, Chaush Nurhan meant to rally the folk in all the villages.

THERE had been some slight disagreement on educational policy in the villages. The scholastic programme of the Miazial Engerutiunk Hayoz, the General Armenian Schools Association, that recognized scholastic authority for the whole Armenian people, had laid it down that the school year was to end in the first days of early summer—that is to say, in the first week of May. But Ter Haigasun, as district head-superintendent of schools, gave sudden orders that this year teaching was to begin again after only one short week of holidays. The priest's decision sprang from the same motives as did the dully frantic industry of the whole population in these days. The deluge was at hand. This approaching dissolution of all order must be opposed by twice the normal regularity; utter helplessness, which all awaited as something inevitable, should be countered by the severest order and discipline. And besides, in these harassed days, the wild, unconscious clamour of children on holiday would have been an unbearable nuisance about the land. And clearly every grown-up in the district would have sided with Ter Haigasun, had the teachers not bitterly opposed him. These teachers, above all Hrand Oskanian, did not want to be robbed of their free time, guaranteed them by contract. They appealed to the mukhtars, they warned the parents—the poor little mites would be getting brain-fever if they had to work on in this grilling heat. Oskanian, the ever-silent, vented a perfect torrent of spite against Ter Haigasun. It was all no good. The priest was inflexible. He called a meeting of the seven mukhtars of the villages and convinced them in a few short words. So that the new school year, in spite of the heat, began more or less where the old had ended. The teachers, as a last resource, tried to bring in Bagradian on their side. Shatakhian and Oskanian, serious and formal, called at the villa. But Gabriel plainly and ruthlessly declared for the continuation of studies. He welcomed it, not only as a matter of general policy, but in his own interests, since he meant to send his son Stephan to school with Monsieur Shatakhian. He should at last be able to mix with boys of his race and age.

On the first day of term Gabriel arrived at the school-house of Yoghonoluk with Stephan. Sato came, too; her wounded feet were already healed. It had meant a tiff with Juliette. She was worried about Stephan, she told him. Why should he have to squat on the same benches as these unwashed boys in an Oriental stable? Even in Paris, Stephan had never had to go to the public primary school, where after all there had been less danger of infectious disease and lice. Gabriel had stuck to his decision. If one looked at things as they really were, such dangers as that, which any day now might give way to real ones, were certainly not worth taking seriously. As a father he considered it far more important that Stephan should at last get to know the life of his people from its beginnings. In former days, in another atmosphere, Juliette could have raised a hundred objections. As it was, she gave in at once and said no more. It was a silent acquiescence which she herself could understand least of all. Ever since that talk in the night, when Gabriel had seemed so very upset, something incomprehensible had been happening. Life on a basis of mutual confidence— the gathered harvest of a marriage that had gone on now for fourteen years—seemed to evaporate more and more. At present, when Juliette woke in the night, she felt as though she and the sleeper beside her were no longer sharing the same past. Their marriage had been left behind in Paris, in glittering towns all over Europe; they had lost it, were cut off, it was theirs no longer. What was this thing that had been happening? Had Gabriel altered, or had she? She could still not take the future possibility really seriously. It seemed to her almost absurd that a deluge should not gallantly retire from before her feet—the Frenchwoman. Surely it was simply a question of getting through the next few weeks. And then—back home! Whatever might or might not happen in these weeks was trivial child's play. So she said no more about Gabriel's decision that Stephan should go to the village school. Yet when in her most secret soul she suddenly was aware of that tepid sensation—"Oh, well, what business is it of mine?"—she felt startled and stirred to an unknown grief, not only for herself but for Stephan.

Young Stephan naturally rejoiced at the very thought of this new arrangement. Lately, as he admitted to his father, he had scarcely been able to fix his mind on what the good Avakian was saying. He, the boy from the Paris lycée, the Hellenist and Latinist, much preferred an Armenian village school. Such complaisance was not due merely to the boredom of Stephan's lessons with Avakian. His very soul had become confused, and yet alert, ever since Iskuhi and Sato had been

163

their guests. Sato had already got him into mischief. One morning she and Stephan had suddenly vanished into the wilds, not coming back till well after lunch. Since Sato seemed to be threatened with dire consequences, Stephan had gallantly taken all the blame, insisting that they had lost their way on the Damlayik. Juliette had "made a scene" not only with Avakian, but also with Gabriel, and had forbidden her son so much as to speak to Sato in future. The waif had been banished from the drawing-room and told to stay in her room when she was home. All the more frequently therefore had Stephan found himself drawn to Iskuhi, who was still not cured, though she too had long been out of bed. He would squat at her feet as she lay in a deck chair in the garden. He had so many things to ask her. Iskuhi had to tell him all about Zeitun. Yet whenever Maman came upon them, they were silent as a pair of conspirators. "How they all draw him to them!" reflected Juliette.

The school-house of Yoghonoluk was imposing. As the largest school of the Musa Dagh district, it comprised four classes. Ter Haigasun had entrusted their superintendence to Shatakhian. That teacher, on his own initiative, had added continuation classes to those of the usual village school. In these he taught French and history while Oskanian taught literature and calligraphy. But even this was not enough. There were evening classes for grown-ups. Here such a universal sage as Apothecary Krikor displayed his light. He lectured on stars, flowers, beasts, on geology, and on the nations, poets, and sages of antiquity. As his habit was, he drew no clear distinctions between these things, but bathed them all in the effulgence of one magnificent fairy-tale of science.

Shatakhian drew Gabriel aside. "I don't quite understand you, Effendi. What can you expect your son to learn here? I should say he knew more than I do about most subjects, though I did study for some time in Switzerland. But I've vegetated here for years. Just look at all these children. They're

164

like Hottentots. I don't know whether they'll be a good influence."

"It's just their influence that I don't want him to miss, Hapeth Shatakhian," Gabriel explained—and the teacher wondered at this father who seemed so stubbornly set on turning his son from a good European into a little Oriental.

The room was full of children and of parents come to enter their names. An old woman, pushing a little boy in front of her, approached Shatakhian. "Well, Teacher, here he is. Don't thrash him too much."

"You hear?" Shatakhian turned to Gabriel, with a sigh over this wilderness of superstition, medievalism, and darkness of the spirit, which he had to spend such laborious days in combating.

It was arranged that Stephan should come to school three times a week. His chief task would be to put the finishing touches to his written and spoken Armenian. Sato was consigned to the infant's class, composed mostly of girls and all much younger than the sorry orphan of Zeitun. Even after his second day at school Stephan came home in a very bad temper. He wasn't going to let them go on ragging him about these stupid English clothes. He was going to wear exactly the same as all the others. In a towering rage he insisted that the local tailor should be commissioned to make him the usual entari-smock, with an aghil-belt, and the loose shalwar-trousers. These demands entailed a long dispute with Maman. It remained undecided for several days.

Now that he had no Stephan to teach, Samuel Avakian had another, entirely different occupation. Gabriel passed him all the rough notes which he had been collecting for many weeks and asked the student to reduce them to one comprehensive, statistical statement. Avakian was not told why. His first job was to classify under various headings the population of all the villages, from Wakef, the lace village in the south to Kebussiye, the bee-keeping village in the north. The information gathered by Bagradian from the village clerk of Yoghonoluk and the other six village elders was to be arranged and checked. By next morning Avakian had the following precise table for Gabriel:

Population of the seven villages, classified according to sex and age:

       583 babes in arms and children. .under 4 years of age
       579 girls........................between 4 and 12
       823 boys.........................between 4 and 14
      2074 females.....................over 12
      1556 males........................over 14

This census included the Bagradian family, with dependants. But, besides such lists, more exact classifications were drawn up, giving the number of families in each village according to occupation or craft, indeed from every conceivable angle. But it was not only a matter of human beings. Gabriel had tried to find out the number of head of cattle in the district. That had been by no means an easy task, an only partially successful one, since not even the mukhtars knew the exact figures. Only one thing was certain. There were no big livestock, no oxen or horses. On the other hand, every well-to-do family owned a couple of goats and a donkey, or a riding and sumpter mule. The larger herds of sheep, owned by individual breeders or communes, were driven, in the fashion of all mountaineers, up on to the quiet meadow pasturage—sheltered meadows where they stayed from one shearing to the next in the care of shepherds and shepherds' boys. It proved impossible to get any exact idea of these herds. The industrious Avakian, to whom every task was a boon, went zealously forth into the villages and had already transformed Bagradian's study into a kind of statistics bureau. Secretly he rather scoffed at this very elaborate hobby, by which a rich man was attempting to fill up the days of an indefinite period of suspense. Nothing seemed too trifling for this pedant, who had obviously conceived the idea of writing a scientific memoir on the village life around Musa Dagh. He even wanted to know how many tonirs, kneading-troughs walled into the ground, there were in the villages. He investigated the harvests minutely and seemed to be worried by the fact that the mountain folk imported their maize and the reddish Syrian wheat from Mohammedans down in the plain. It seemed to annoy him that there should be no Armenian mills, either in Yoghonoluk and Bitias or elsewhere. He even ventured to trespass on Krikor's preserve and inquire as to the state of the drug supplies. Krikor, who had expected to display his library, not his pharmacy, traced the curve of the roof with a pair of disillusioned fingers. On two small shelves bottles, jars, and crucibles of all kinds were set out, painted with exotic inscriptions. It was all there was to suggest a chemist's shop. Three big petroleum jars in a corner, a sack of salt, a couple of bales of chibuk-tobacco, and some cheap ironmongery indicated the more active side of the business.

Krikor proudly tapped one of the mystic jars with his long bony fingers. "The whole pharmacopœia, as St. John Chrysostom pointed out, can be reduced to seven primary substances: lime, sulphur, saltpetre, iodine, poppy, willow-resin, and bay-oil. It's always the same thing in hundreds of different disguises."

After such a lesson in contemporary pharmaceutics Gabriel made no further inquiries. Luckily he had a fairly extensive medicine chest of his own. But, more significant than all this, was the incident of the small-arms. Chaush Nurhan had already dropped some dark hints on the subject. Yet, the instant Gabriel tried to broach it with village notables, they beat hasty retreat. One day, however, he assailed Mukhtar Kebussyan of Yoghonoluk in his best parlour and pinned him down:

"Be frank with me, Thomas Kebussyan. How many rifles have you, and what pattern are they?"

The mukhtar began to squint horribly, and wagged his bald pate. "Jesus Christ! Do you want to bring ill-luck on us all, Effendi?"

"Why should I, of all people, seem so unworthy of your confidence?"

"My wife doesn't know it, my sons don't know it, not even the schoolteachers know it. Not a soul."

"Did my brother Avetis?"

"Your brother Avetis certainly did, God rest his soul. But he never mentioned it to anyone."

"Do I look the sort of person who can't keep his mouth shut?"

"If it comes out, we shall all be slaughtered."

But since Kebussyan, for all his squintings and waggings of the head, could not manage to get away from his guest, he ended at last by double-bolting the parlour door. In a frightened hiss he told his story. In 1908, when Ittihad had gone over to revolution against Abdul Hamid, the Young Turkish agents had distributed weapons to all districts and communes of the empire, especially to the Armenian districts, which were regarded as the chief supporters of the revolt. Enver Pasha had of course known all about it and, when war broke out, his instant order had been to disarm the Armenian population. Naturally the character and methods of the government officials concerned had made a great difference to the way in which the order was carried out. In such vilayets as Erzerum or Sivas, hotbeds of provincial zeal for Ittihad, unarmed people had been forced to buy rifles from the gendarmes, simply to hand them back to the government. To possess no arms in such a district was merely considered a cunning attempt to evade the law. But here, under Djelal Bey, it naturally had all gone far more smoothly. That admirable governor, whose humane instincts were always in rebellion against the edicts of the pretty war god in Istanbul, carried out such orders very negligently, where he could not simply allow them to disappear in his waste-paper basket. This mildness usually found its echo in the administrative methods of his subordinates, with one harsh exception—the Mutessarif of Marash. The red-haired müdir of Antioch had arrived one day in January in Yoghonoluk, with the chief of the Antioch police, to collect all weapons. He had gone away again quite peacefully on receiving the smiling assurance that no such weapons had been distributed. Luckily the mukhtar of those days had not given the Committee's agents a written receipt.

"Very good"—Gabriel was delighted with the mayor—"and are these guns worth anything?"

"Fifty Mauser rifles and two hundred and fifty Greek service-carbines. Each has thirty magazines of cartridges, that is, about a hundred and fifty shots."

Gabriel Bagradian stood reflecting. Really that was scarcely worth talking about. Had the men in the villages no other firearms of any kind?

Kebussyan hesitated again. "That's their business. Lots of them hunt. But what use are a few hundred old blunderbusses, with flint locks?"

Gabriel rose, and held out his hand to the mukhtar. "Thank you, Thomas Kebussyan, for having trusted me. But, now that I know, I'd like you to tell me where you've hidden them."

"Must you really know that, Effendi?"

"No. But I'm curious, and I don't see why you should keep that secret, now that you've told me all the rest."

The mukhtar writhed in inner conflict. Apart from his brothers in office, Ter Haigasun, and the sexton, there was not a soul who knew that secret. Yet there was something in Gabriel against which Kebussyan could not hold out. He unburdened himself, after desperate admonitions. The chests containing these rifles and supplies were in the churchyard of Yoghonoluk, buried in what seemed the usual graves, with false inscriptions on the crosses.

"So now I've put my life in your hands, Effendi," the mukhtar moaned as he opened the door again for his visitor. Gabriel answered him without turning round:

"Perhaps you really have, Thomas Kebussyan."

THOUGHTS at which he himself began to tremble kept haunting Gabriel Bagradian. They had such power to move his heart that he could not escape them, day or night. Gabriel saw only the first steps, only the parting of the ways. Five paces on from where they branched, and all was darkness and uncertainty. But in every life, as it nears decision, nothing seems more unreal than its own aim.

Yet was it easy to understand why Gabriel, with all his roused-up energy, should have moved only about this narrow valley, avoiding any avenue of escape that might still have been open to him? Why are you wasting time, Bagradian? Why let day after day slip by? Your name is well known, and you have a fortune. Why not throw both these into the scales? Even though you are faced with danger and the greatest difficulties, why not try to reach Aleppo, with Juliette and Stephan? After all, Aleppo is a big town. You have connexions there. At least you can put your wife and son under consular protection. No doubt they've been arresting notables everywhere, banishing them, torturing them, putting them to death. Such a journey would certainly be a terrible risk. But is it any less of a risk to stay here? Don't lose another minute, do something before it's too late to save yourself! . . .

This voice was not always silent. But its cries came muted. Musa Dagh stood serene. Nothing changed. The world around seemed to show that the Agha Rifaat Bereket had been right. Not a breath of outside trouble reached the village. His home, which even now he could still sometimes mistake for a van-

ished fairy-tale, kept fast hold of Gabriel Bagradian. Juliette
lost reality in his eyes. Perhaps, even if he had tried, he might
not have freed himself now from Musa Dagh.

He kept his solemn promise not to say a word of the hidden
small-arms. Even Avakian had learned nothing. On the other
hand that tutor was suddenly given a fresh task. He was
appointed cartographer. That map of the Damlayik which
Stephan, with clumsy markings, had begun early in March,
to please his father, gained fresh significance. Avakian was
instructed to make an exact, large-scale map of the mountain
in three copies. "So he's come to the end of the valley, with
all its livestock and people," thought the student, "and now
he has to go to the hills." The Damlayik is, of course, the real
heart of Musa Dagh. That spur of mountain disperses itself
in many ridges towards the north, where they peter out in
the vale of Beilan in dream-like natural citadels and terraces,
while southwards it suddenly descends, disordered, embryonic,
into the plains around the mouth of the Orontes. In its centre,
Damlayik, it gathers all its strength, its concentrated purpose.
Here, with mighty fists of rock, it drags the vale of the seven
villages, like a many-folded coverlet, to its breast. Here its two
crests rise almost sheer over Yoghonoluk and Hadji Habibli—
the only treeless points, grown over with short crop-grass.
The back of the Damlayik forms a fairly wide mountain
plateau; at its widest point, between the ilex gorge and the
steep, shelving rocks along the coast, it is, as the crow flies
(by Avakian's reckoning), more than three and a half miles
across. But what most of all preoccupied Avakian were the
curiously sharp demarcation lines which nature seemed to
have set round this mountain plateau. There was, first, the
indentation towards the north, a narrow defile laced to a ridge
between two peaks, even directly approachable from the valley by an old mule-track, which, however, lost itself in undergrowth, since here there was no possibility of reaching the sea
across walls of rock. In the south, where the mountain broke

off suddenly, there rose, above a sparse, almost arid half-circle of rocky banks, a towering mass of rock fifty feet high. The view from this natural bastion dominated a sweep of sea and the whole plain of the Orontes with its Turkish villages as far as away beyond the heights of the barren Jebel Akra. One could see the massive ruin of the temple and aqueduct of Seleucia, bent under the load of its green creepers; one could see every cart-rut on the important highroad from Antioch to El Eskel and Suedia. The white domino-houses of these towns gleamed, and the big spirit factory on the right bank of the Orontes, in nearest proximity to the sea, stood livid in sunlight. Every strategic intelligence must perceive at once what an ideal place of defence the Damlayik was. Apart from the arduous climb up the side facing the valley, which exhausted even leisurely sight-seers by its rough, uncompromising ascent, there was only one real point of attack—the narrow ridge towards the north. But it was just here that the terrain offered defenders a thousand advantages, and not least the circumstance that the treeless declivities, strewn about with knee-pine, dwarf shrubs, tussock grass, and wild bush growths of every kind, provided a difficult series of obstacles.

Avakian's map-drawing efforts took a long time to satisfy Gabriel. Again and again he discovered fresh mistakes and inadequacies. The student began to be afraid that his employer's hobby had little by little become a mania. He had still no inkling. Now they spent whole days on the Damlayik. Bagradian, the artillery officer of the Balkan war, still possessed field-glasses, a measuring-gauge, a magnetic compass, and other, similar surveying-instruments. They came in very useful now. With stubborn insistence he made certain that the course of every stream, each tall tree, big block of granite, was being marked. And red, green, and blue markings did not suffice him. Strange words and signs were added. Between the dome-shaped peaks and the northern saddle there was a very extensive gentle declivity. Since it was overgrown with lush and excellent grass, it was here that they always found themselves in the midst of herds of sheep, black and white, with shepherds who, like the shepherds of antiquity, drowsed above their flocks in sheepskins, summer and winter. Gabriel and Avakian, counting their steps, got the exact boundaries of this pasturage. Gabriel pointed out two streams which, above, on the verge of the meadow, forced their way through thick growths of fern. "That's very lucky," he said; "write above that, in red pencil: 'town enclosure.'" There was no end of such secret terminology. Gabriel seemed to be looking with particular zest for some spot which he would choose for its quiet, sheltered beauty. He found it. And it, too, was near a well-spring, but nearer the sea, in a place between high plateaux of sheer rock, where a dark-green girdle of myrtles and rhododendron bushes extended.

"Pick that out, Avakian, and write over it, in red: 'Three-Tent Square.'"

Avakian could not manage not to ask: "What do you mean by 'Three-Tent Square'?"

But Gabriel had already gone on and did not hear him.

"Must I help him dream his dreams?" the student thought. Yet only two days later he was to learn exactly what was meant by "Three-Tent Square."

When Dr. Altouni took the bandages off Iskuhi's arm and shoulder, he sounded morose: "Just as I thought. Now, if we were in a big town, it could still be set right. You ought to have stayed in Aleppo, light of my eyes, and gone into hospital there. Still, perhaps you were right to come on here. Who can predict, in times like these? Now, my soul, you mustn't get depressed—we'll see what else we can do."

Iskuhi pacified the old gentleman. "I'm not worrying. It's lucky it should be my left arm." But she did not believe the doctor's feeble reassurances. She glanced down swiftly at herself. Her arm hung limp, distorted, too short for the shoulder. She could not move it. At least she was glad it no longer hurt her. So that now, she supposed, she would be a cripple all her life. But what did that matter, when she considered the fate of most of the convoy? And she had only been with them two short days! (She, too, like all those people, was now deeply aware that she had no future.) In the night she was still in the midst of horrible sounds and terrifying images. The shuffling, scraping, creeping, tapping of thousands of feet. Exhausted, whimpering children fell to the ground, and she with her broken arm had to snatch up two or three of them at a time. Crazy shrieks from the end of the column, and already saptiehs with bloodshot eyes, brandishing cudgels, came dashing furiously. Everywhere the face of the man who had tried to rape her. It was not made of one, but thirty different faces; many of them she knew by sight, and they were of people who had not even seemed repugnant. But mostly it was a filthy, stubbled face, spotted with blood, that kept bending over her. Bubbles of spittle broke on the tumid lips. . . . In such detailed clarity could she see that kaleidoscopic surface larger than life. It bent above her and enveloped her in an anæsthetic vapour of oniony breath. She fought, fleshed her teeth in hairy, simian hands, which closed on her breasts. I've only got one arm, she reflected, as though it were a kind of extenuation to the fact that she surrendered to this horror, and so lost consciousness.

The days that followed such nights were like those of a malaria patient, whose temperature runs down without transitions from high fever to well below normal. Then there would be a veil upon her senses, and perhaps that was the reason why she took her misfortune so easily. Her lame arm hung at her side like an impediment. But her body, young and full of sap, surmounted its hurt more skilfully, day by day. Without quite knowing how she managed it, she accustomed herself to doing everything with her right hand. It pacified her deeply to think she needed no help from anyone.

Iskuhi had by now been living some time with the Bagradians. A short while back, Pastor Aram Tomasian had called, thanked them for all their kindness to his sister, and announced that he had come to take her away. He had furnished an empty house near his father's. The suggestion deeply wounded Gabriel. "But why, Pastor Aram, do you want to deprive us of Iskuhi? We're all so fond of her—my wife more than anyone."

"Visitors who stay too long end by becoming a nuisance."

"Please don't be so proud. You know yourself that Mademoiselle Iskuhi is the kind of person whom, unfortunately, one notices all too little in the house, she's so quiet and reserved. And then, aren't we all sharing the same fate here? . . ."

Aram glanced slowly at Gabriel. "I hope you don't imagine our fate to be rosier than it is in reality." These carping words had in them a kind of suspicion of the foreigner, of this rich man, who seemed to have no idea of the horrors by which he lived surrounded.

But this very mistrustful reserve made Bagradian feel intensely friendly. His voice sounded cordial: "I only wish you were staying with us, too, Pastor Aram Tomasian. But I beg that, whenever you feel like it, you'll come in and see us. I'll give orders that from today they always lay two extra places for you and your wife. Please don't let my invitation annoy you, and come here to meals if it isn't too much exertion for her."

Juliette showed even more reluctance to let Iskuhi move into other quarters. A very curious relationship had arisen between these two women, nor can it be denied that Juliette sought the favours of the Armenian girl. Iskuhi, for a girl of nineteen, was still strangely unawakened, especially for the East, where women ripen so early. In Madame Bagradian this young girl saw only a *grande dame,* infinitely above her in beauty, background, and knowledge of life. When they sat together in Juliette's room upstairs, Iskuhi, even in such intimacy, seemed unable to conquer her shyness. Perhaps, at such moments, she also suffered from the idleness to which she was condemned. Juliette, on her side, seeking Iskuhi, never felt quite certain of herself when they were together. This seems absurd, and yet it was so. There·are people who need in no way be distinguished, either by position or personality, and who yet infect us with a feeling of timidity in their presence. Perhaps that constraint which always seemed to get hold of Juliette in Mademoiselle Tomasian's society had its origins in some such source as this.

She would watch Iskuhi for some time and then burst forth more or less as follows: "*Ma chère,* do you know, as a rule I detest Oriental women, their laziness, their languid movements? I can't even bear brunettes at home. But you're not an Oriental, Iskuhi. Right now, sitting there against the light, your eyes look quite blue."

"You say that, Madame!" Iskuhi was startled. "You, with your eyes, and your blond hair? . . ."

"How often am I to ask you, *chérie,* to *tutoyer* me and not to call me 'Madame'? Call me 'Juliette.' Must you always keep rubbing it in that I'm so much older than you?"

"Oh, no—really I wasn't. . . . Forgive me, please." Juliette had to laugh at so much guilelessness, which answered a coquettish little joke with startled, almost terrified eyes.

Iskuhi had had to leave nearly everything in Zeitun and the rest along the road. Juliette fitted her out with a whole new wardrobe. It was a process she thoroughly enjoyed. At last that cabin-trunk packed with garments, the trusty fellow-traveller from Paris via Istanbul and Beirut to this wilderness (you could never be certain), justified the trouble it had given. True that women's clothes are like summer leaves and wither in the autumn of fashion, no matter how good and expensive the silks and materials may have been. Juliette knew nothing at all of the present fashions in Paris. She invented a few of her own "by sheer intuition" and began to remodel all her apparel for her own as well as Iskuhi's benefit. This occupation, eagerly embraced, pleasantly filled up the afternoons after a morning's work in house or garden. Juliette had really scarcely the chance to come to herself. The modiste's workshop was set up in an empty room. She chose two skilful girls from the village as her seamstresses.

Poor Iskuhi could only sit looking on. But she made an admirable fairylike mannequin for the display of Juliette's handiwork. Dull shades suited her especially. She was for ever having to try on this or that, let down her hair and put it up again, twist and turn round. She did not mind doing it. Her zest for life, shaken by the Zeitun experiences, began to revive, her cheeks to flush a little.

"You really are a fraud, *ma petite*," Juliette remarked. "One might have imagined you'd never worn anything all your life but your smock, and perhaps a Turkish veil in front of your face. And yet you put on your clothes and move about in them as though you could think of nothing but fashions. You didn't come out unscathed from your stay at Lausanne and your contact with French culture."

One evening Juliette asked her to put on one of her *"grandes toilettes,"* a very low-necked frock without arms. Iskuhi flushed. "But it's impossible. I can't—with my arm. . . ."

Juliette looked immeasurably concerned. "It's true. . . . But how much longer will all this business last? Two—three months. Then we shall all be back in Europe. And I'll take you with me, Iskuhi. I give you my word. In Paris and Switzerland there are clinics that will soon put you right."

Almost at the same hour in which Gabriel Bagradian's wife was expressing so audacious a hope the remnants of the first convoy reached their journey's end at Deir ez Zor, on the edge of Mesopotamian sands.

Juliette was again full of a theme which had caused her

husband many bitter hours. Strangely enough, Iskuhi, in Gabriel's absence, seemed particularly to inspire her to dwell on it. It took the form of a series of depreciatory remarks on the Armenians, viewed in that brilliant light of Gallic culture, which Juliette turned on their obscurity.

"You may be an ancient people," she kept insisting, *"c'est bien*. A civilized people. No doubt. But in what precisely do you prove it? Oh, of course, I've been told all the names— again and again. Abovian, Raffi, Siamanto. But who's ever heard of them? No one in the world except Armenians. No European can ever really understand or speak your language. You've never had a Racine or a Voltaire. And you have no Catulle Mendès, no Pierre Loti. Have *you* read anything of Pierre Loti's, *ma petite?*"

Iskuhi, hit by these shafts, looked up intently. "No, Mad— No. I've never read anything."

"Well, they're all about distant countries." Juliette seemed scornfully to suppose that this in itself was a good enough recommendation for Iskuhi. It was not precisely magnanimous of Juliette to work with such overwhelming comparisons. But she was now in the position of having to defend her own against the superior forces of her environment, so it was not unnatural.

From Iskuhi's eyes it was evident that she might have said much. But after a while she answered in one simple sentence: "We have some old songs that are very beautiful."

"Won't you sing one of them, Mademoiselle?" begged Stephan, who sat watching her from a corner. Iskuhi had scarcely known he was there. And now she felt more clearly than ever before that the Frenchwoman's son was a real Armenian boy, without any trace of foreigner in him. It may have been this perception that made her overcome her reluctance and begin to sing "The Song of Coming and Going," which, less on account of its text than it flowing melody, had become the working-song of the seven villages:

"Days of misfortune pass and are gone,
  Like the days of winter, they come and they go;
The sorrows of men do not last very long,
  Like the buyers in shops, they come and go.

"Persecution and blood lash the people to tears·
  The caravans, they come and they go,
And men spring up in the garden of earth,
  Whether henbane or balsam, they come and they go.

"Let the strong not be proud, let the weak not look pale,
  Since life will transpose them; they come and they go.
The sun pours down fearless, for ever, his light,
  While clouds from the altar, they come and they go.

"The world is an inn on the road, oh, singer,
  The people, its guests, they come and they go.
Mother Earth embraces her well-taught child,
  While ignorant nations may perish, and go."

During this song Juliette could feel quite clearly in Iskuhi
that impenetrable something, presented as shyness, as grief,
even as the reluctant acceptance of gifts, but which stubbornly
resisted all her blandishments. Since she had not understood
all the words, she asked for some of the song to be translated.
The last verses brought from her a cry of triumph: "Well,
there you see—how proud you all are! The well-taught child,
to whom Mother Earth behaves so obligingly, is Armenian.
And the ignoramuses are all the others. . . ."

Stephan asked, almost peremptorily: "Something else,
Iskuhi."

But Juliette insisted on hearing something amorous. Nothing too solemn. And nothing more about "well-taught children" and "ignorant nations." "A real love song, Iskuhi."

Iskuhi sat very still, bent slightly forward. Her left hand,
with its crooked fingers, lay in her lap. The deep-hued sun
behind her filled the window-space, so that her face was

dark, its features indistinguishable. After a short silence she seemed to remember something. "I know one or two love songs which they sing round here. One especially. It's quite mad. Really it ought to be sung by a man, though the girl's the chief thing in it."

Her little girl's, or priestess's, voice seemed to come from a void. To this cool voice the wild song was in strangest contrast:

> "She came out of her garden
> And held them close against her breasts,
> Two fruits of the pomegranate tree,
> Two great and shining apples.
> She gave them me, I would not take.
> Then, with her hand, she struck—
> Struck with her hand upon her breast-bone.
> Struck three times, six times, twelve times—
> Struck till the bone was broke."

"Again!" Stephan demanded. But Iskuhi could not be persuaded to repeat, for Gabriel Bagradian was quietly standing in the room.

In those days the Bagradian villa grew more and more animated. There were guests at nearly every meal. Juliette and Gabriel both of them welcomed this animation. It was becoming hard for them to be alone together. And guests made the time pass more quickly. Every evening meant a fresh victory, since it strengthened a hope that with it the perpetual shadow had moved its threat a little way farther off. July had almost arrived. How much longer could this menace last? There were rumours that peace was soon to be signed, and peace meant safety. Pastor Aram was now a regular guest. Hovsannah, who still had not quite managed to recover, had asked him to go and take care of Iskuhi. She, after all, knew how accustomed he was to living always with his sister, that he became restless when he had been a few days without having seen her. But there were other frequent guests at Gabriel's table. The main group was composed of Krikor and his satellites. The apothecary's tenant, Gonzague Maris, was among them. This young Greek was not merely welcome as a pianist. He could appreciate beauty and pretty frocks. He "noticed things"; Gabriel Bagradian no longer, or very seldom, "noticed" them. Juliette's dress-making hobby, which after all was no more than an aimless method of whiling away her time with thoughts of Paris, found its applause in Gonzague Maris. He could always, while eschewing vapid flatteries, manage to say something delightful, not only about Juliette's appearance, but in skilful praise of the inspirations with which she tried to enhance Iskuhi's charm. Nor did he ever speak as a blind enthusiast; it was as an artist, an initiate, that he raised the thick eyebrows which slanted at so wide an angle. So that Juliette's workshop, by virtue of Gonzague Maris's insight, was lifted out of the region of hobbies on to a plane of acknowledged values. His æsthetic sense had also been applied to his own appearance. Gonzague was doubtless poor and a man with a, presumably, chequered past. But he never mentioned this. He avoided Juliette's questions on the subject —not because of any special secretiveness, or because he really had much to hide, but because he seemed to regard whatever had been with a contemptuous shrug, as unimportant. In spite of, or because of, his small means, he was extremely well-dressed whenever he called at Villa Bagradian. Since it was certain to be some time before he got another chance of replenishing his European wardrobe, he took scrupulous care of his clothes. This spick-and-span-ness of Gonzague affected Juliette very pleasantly, without her ever knowing that it was so. Its effects on the two schoolteachers, Shatakhian and Oskanian, were not so gratifying. Gonzague aroused splenetic rivalry in them. The diminutive Hrand Oskanian was invaded by a reckless jealousy. Neither his poetical calligraphy on parchment nor his so distinguished, portentous silences had yet succeeded in winning Madame Bagradian's attention. She ignored his inner worth, his reserve, his dignity. And yet this conceited half-breed, by his vain sartorial display, had managed instantly to attract her. Oskanian made up his mind to take up the unequal struggle in this department. He hurried off to the village tailor, who, half a generation back, had practised in London for two years.

On the walls of this English maestro's establishment there were fashion-plates of impeccable "lords" of that period. But there was not much choice of material—only a few yards of thin, grey cloth, hoary with age, scarcely good enough to use for lining. That did not deter Oskanian. He chose a lord from among the models, one whose male svelteness was neatly moulded into a long swallow-tailed morning-coat. The first fitting revealed the fact that the swallow-tails reached down to little Oskanian's heels. He did not object, though the tailor seemed rather doubtful. When the masterpiece was ready to wear, Oskanian stuck a white flower in his buttonhole—it too in imitation of the "lord." Unluckily his own inspiration was allowed to supply the finishing touch. He hurried to Krikor, from whom he bought the strongest scent in the shop, a good half-bottle of which he proceeded to sprinkle about his person. So he did, at last, for the first five minutes, manage to get himself noticed by Madame Bagradian, and by all her guests—the consequence being that Gabriel had to take him on one side and tactfully ask him to wear another coat for a couple of hours, while the grey *chef-d'œuvre* was being hung out to air in the kitchen garden.

One fine morning in July Gabriel made a suggestion. How would it be to spend tomorrow evening and the following night on Musa Dagh? To see the sunrise. It seemed a very European notion—the genuine inspiration of a tourist whose life is spent between concrete walls, among business letters. But here? The guests, all down the table, were perturbed.

Only Hapeth Shatakhian, anxious not to put his foot in it, appeared to welcome the delights of a night spent in the fresh air. But Gabriel Bagradian disillusioned him: "We shan't have to sleep in the fresh air. I've found three tents in one of the attics here, all of them perfectly fit to use. They belonged to my late brother, who took them on his hunting-expeditions. Two of them are perfectly modern hunting-tents, they're big enough to hold two or three people. The third is a very beautiful Arab pavilion. Either Avetis must have brought it back from one of his journeys or else it belonged to our grandfather. . . ."

Since Juliette rather welcomed this break in the monotony and Stephan was already jumping for joy, the following morning, a Saturday, was fixed on for the expedition. Apothecary Krikor, to whom there was no new thing under the sun, since he had already done and experienced everything from fruit preserving to comparative theology, began to reminisce about the days when he had lived and slept in the open.

Iskuhi seemed unenthusiastic. No wonder! She had too much knowledge of the cruelty of sleeping out of doors—of unsheltered earth. Not three hundred miles east of this diningroom the dying convoys toiled along the roads. Bagradian's heartless game annoyed her. She had no inkling of its purpose. "I'd so much rather stay here," she begged.

Gabriel turned to her rather sharply. "Impossible, Iskuhi. You don't want to spoil our sport, do you? You must sleep in the pavilion with Juliette."

Iskuhi stared at the cloth and struggled with words. "I've . . . I'm afraid . . . You see, every night, I feel so glad I can sleep in a house."

Gabriel tried to make her look at him. "I've been counting especially on you."

Iskuhi still did not look up. She bit her lips; Bagradian seemed very set on a trifle. "I really insist on it, Iskuhi."

Her face had already begun to twitch. Juliette signed to her husband to stop worrying Iskuhi. She made him understand that later she herself could soon persuade the child. But it proved harder than she had thought. She attempted womanly advice. All men were really children, *au fond*. Any woman who cared to direct life found it best to give them their boyish way whenever possible. A real man was never so grateful for anything else, and consequently never so easy to manage. If one wanted to have one's way in the important things one ought never to mind giving way in trifles. These maxims sounded as if Juliette were advising herself, the married woman. But what, after all, had Iskuhi to do with the little masculine foibles of her host, Gabriel Bagradian?

She turned away her embarrassed head. "This isn't a trifle for me."

"After all, it may be very jolly. At least it's new . . ."

"I have too many recollections of the novelty."

"Your brother, the pastor, doesn't mind."

Iskuhi drew a deep breath. "It's not just my obstinacy."

But Juliette seemed to have thought of another way. "If you stop here, I won't go either. I should hate to be the only woman among all those men. I'd rather stay here."

Iskuhi cast a long glance at Juliette. "No. Impossible. We can't do that. I'll come if you want me to. I've got over my first feeling already. I'd love to do it for you."

Juliette looked suddenly fagged out. "Well, we've time enough till tomorrow morning. We can think it over ten times if we like."

She clasped her forehead and shut her eyes. She felt vaguely faint, as though certain of Iskuhi's memories had at last begun to invade her consciousness.

"Perhaps you're right, Iskuhi, in what you feel. We all live such a safe kind of life."

NEXT morning they were up early. Because of the ladies they did not choose the short cut up through the ilex gorge, but the gentle, if rather tedious, long way round, over the northern saddle. Today, for all its clefts, rocky bastions, wildness, Musa Dagh proved a well-disposed mountain, which showed its best side to the climber. Iskuhi's quiet was lost in the general hilarity. But even she seemed, little by little, to cheer up.

Gabriel Bagradian could observe with what astonishing celerity his son was shedding his European habits ever since he had begun going to Shatakhian's school. "I can scarcely recognize him," Juliette had recently said to Gabriel. "We shall have to be very careful. He's already begun to speak that dreadful, hard Armenian French, like stones being broken. Just like his wonderful teacher." By now Stephan knew the Damlayik nearly as thoroughly as his father. He played the guide but could never manage to stay on the road, since he kept looking out for every difficult short cut to climb and exercise his gymnastic skill on. Often he was far ahead and often well behind the rest, so that his voice could only just be heard when they called him.

They reached the beautiful meadow sooner than Gabriel had reckoned. The tents were already set up. There was even a flag, waving above the Arab pavilion of the sheikh, or Grandfather Avetis. It was embroidered with the arms of ancient Armenia—Mount Ararat, the Ark, and the dove fluttering in its centre.

This pavilion was indeed the resplendent relic of a prouder, more magnificent age. It was eight paces long and seven wide. Its scaffolding was of poles thick as an arm, of precious woods; its interior walls were the finest carpets. It had one great disadvantage. It was impregnated with the reek of camphor and musty cloth. The walls had been rolled up and sewn into sacks, which from time to time the steward Kristaphor had buried under mountains of camphor and insect powder. The modern tents, brought back from London a few years ago by Avetis the younger, aroused far more admiration, though

185

they were only made of the usual canvas. But they were "replete" with every convenience which the perspicacity of an experienced hunter could have desired. Nothing had been forgotten in these tents: collapsible field-beds, far from uncomfortable, silk sleeping-bags, featherweight tables and chairs that fitted into one another, cooking-sets, tea sets, pots and plates, all of aluminium. Rubber bathtubs and wash basins. Not to mention wind-proof lamps for petroleum and methylated spirit.

They began to sort themselves for the night. Juliette refused the sheikh-pavilion and took up her quarters in a modern tent, with Iskuhi. Krikor and Gonzague were given the other canvas tent. Teacher Oskanian explained, with a sombre glance at Juliette, that he preferred, for reasons of his own, to sleep under the open sky—apart. As he said it, he threw back his woolly head, as if expecting a general chorus of approbation at so proud and resolute a decision, while at the same time a cooing, feminine voice would beseech him to relent and change his mind. But Juliette did not so much as mention the wild beasts and deserters to which he exposed himself for her sake.

Bagradian secretly thought of this night out of doors as a dress rehearsal. But it passed without any incident—like hundreds of picnics of the same kind. Nothing romantic—unless indeed it were the fact that the cook Hovhannes prepared supper over an open fire. The daring house-boy Missak had ventured a few days back to go to Antioch, where a well-disposed army contractor had sold him a whole mule-load of English tinned foods, which they sampled that night. Sato had followed the party at a distance. She lurked in the dusk beyond the fire, and during the meal Stephan jumped up from time to time to take her some of his own food. They sat round the fire on rugs, like all picnickers. Missak had spread out a tablecloth on a flat knoll for the dishes. The evening was pleasantly cool. The moon was near its first quarter. The fire began to burn more faintly. They drank wine, and the strong mulberry brandy distilled by the peasants of the district. Juliette soon broke up the party. She had a queer feeling of disquiet. Now at last she could understand Iskuhi's reluctance. All round her glowered the savage, unpeopled earth—so horribly in earnest. This was perhaps a rather malicious game that Gabriel played at. The others also said good-night. Oskanian strode off, with head erect, to pay for his vanity with a chilly night, as near the encampment as possible. Gabriel posted sentries. Two men together for three hours were to keep guard around the tents. Gabriel gave out rifles and ball-cartridges. Kristaphor and Missak had gone on hunting-expeditions with Avetis and were quite used to handling firearms. At last Gabriel lay down. Neither he nor Iskuhi could sleep.

The girl lay taut, not moving a limb, anxious not to wake Juliette. But Gabriel twisted and turned for hours. The reek of camphor and mildew stifled him. At last he dressed again and came outside. It was about fifteen minutes to twelve. He sent the sentries, Missak and the cook, to bed. Then he paced slowly up and down, sole guardian of the "Three-Tent Square." Often he switched on his pocket-torch, but it only lit up a tiny circle. Bats flapped through the dark. As the moon rode seawards out of a cloud, a nightingale began singing in the deathly quiet with such bubbling energy that Gabriel was stirred. He tried to find out how it had happened that his deepest thought was already taking so clear a shape. There they were externalized—three tents against the dark sky. How had it come about? Thinking was impossible now. His soul was too full. As Gabriel lit a fresh cigarette, he saw a ghost standing not far off. This phantom wore the lambskin cap of a Turkish private, and was leaning on an infantry rifle. Its face was invisible—probably a very hollow-cheeked face, against which its cigarette had begun to glow. Gabriel hailed the ghost. It did not move, even at his second and third call.

He drew his army revolver and snapped the catch with a loud click. It was sheer formality, since he felt quite certain that the man had no intention of molesting him. It hesitated a while before it moved, and then a queer, long-drawn, indifferent laugh came rattling out of it. The cigarette-end vanished, the ghost with it. Gabriel shook Kristaphor awake. "There are one or two people hanging round. Deserters, I think."

The steward did not seem in the least surprised. "Oh, yes, there'll be some deserters. The poor lads must be having a bad time."

"I saw only one."

"That may have been Sarkis Kilikian."

"Who's Sarkis Kilikian?"

"Asdvaz im! Merciful God!" Kristaphor in a vague, helpless gesture indicated that really it was impossible to say exactly who Sarkis Kilikian was. But Bagradian ordered out his men, by now all awake: "Go out and find this Kilikian. Take him something to eat. The chap looked hungry."

Kristaphor and Missak set out, with tins of food and a lantern, but came back in the end without having found him. Apparently they had ended by feeling scared.

THE evening had been anxious, the morning was deceptive. The world looked vaporous. They all felt restless. Sunrise was quite invisible. All the same they climbed one of the treeless knolls, from which they could scan the sea and surrounding country emerging gradually through the haze.

Bagradian turned. "One could manage to hold out here for a few weeks." He said it as though in defence of the maligned beauties of Musa Dagh.

Gonzague Maris seemed to have passed a better night than anyone else, he looked so fresh and full of life. He pointed out the big spirit factory near Suedia, its chimneys just starting to belch forth smoke. This factory, so he told them, was owned by a foreign company. Its manager was a Greek, whom he had got to know in Alexandretta. He had seen him only the other day and heard some rather interesting rumours. First, a combined peace effort by the American president and the Pope was well under way. The second concerned the Armenian transportations. These were only intended to affect the Armenian vilayets, not Syria. He, Gonzague, could not tell how much all that was to be relied on, but this factory-owner was considered a most reliable sort of man and had private interviews every month with the Wali of Aleppo on army supplies. Gabriel was filled for a few seconds with the conviction that all danger was past, and what had seemed so near was already retreating into the distance. It felt as if he himself had beaten back fate.

He burst forth, in gratitude: "Just look! Isn't it lovely here?"
Juliette was impatient to get back home. She hated being seen in the early morning, by men especially. In the morning, she insisted, only ugly women look their best, and no ladies exist at 6 a.m. Besides, she wanted at least half an hour's rest before mass. When she had got engaged to Gabriel, she had obliged him by ceasing to be a Roman Catholic and entering the Armenian Orthodox Church. This had been one of the many sacrifices which she never forgot to mention when they quarrelled. She picked holes, as her habit was. The Armenian rite was not nearly ornate enough to please her. But what shocked Juliette most was that Armenian priests should all wear beards, and usually long ones. She could not abide a bearded man. Their way back was down the shorter path, which led through the ilex grove to Yoghonoluk. Krikor, Gabriel, and Shatakhian went ahead. Avakian stayed. He took this chance of making a few improvements on his maps. Bagradian had given orders not to strike the tents for the time being. Some of the stable-boys were to stay up on the Damlayik to guard them. Perhaps they would soon be having another picnic. One reason for this was Gabriel's superstitious

fancy that such preparedness might help to break the power of fate. The wretched donkey-track lost itself here and there in shrubs and undergrowth. Juliette in thin shoes, and with pampered feet, kept voicing her horror of such impediments. Then Gonzague would assist her, with a resolute grip. They had begun a vague and often interrupted conversation:

"I can never stop remembering, Madame, that we're the only two foreigners here."

Juliette anxiously tested the earth she trod. "You at least are a Greek. . . . That's not quite so foreign."

Gonzague let her surmount her difficulties unaided. "What? . . . I was brought up in America. . . . But you've been a long time married to an Armenian."

"Yes. I've got some reason for living here. . . . But you?"

"Usually I find my reasons afterwards."

A steep place had set them running. Juliette paused to get her breath. "I've never really understood what you want here. . . . You aren't very frank about it, you know. . . . What can an American who's not trading in lambskins or cotton or gallnuts find to do in Alexandretta?" . . .

"Though I may not be frank—careful just here, please— I'm perfectly willing to tell you that. . . . I was engaged as accompanist by a touring vaudeville troupe . . . not much of a job . . . even though my host Krikor seems to think so highly of it. . . ."

"I see. . . . So you left all your actress friends in the lurch. . . . And where's the vaudeville troupe now, then?"

"It had contracts for Aleppo, Damascus, Beirut. . . ."

"And you simply left them?"

"Quite right. . . . I just ran away. . . . It's one of my foibles."

"Ran away? . . . A young man like you? . . . Well, you must have had some good reason. . . ."

"I'm not so very young as you seem to think."

"*Mon Dieu,* this road! . . . My shoe's full of stones. . . .

Please give me your hand. . . . Thanks." With her left hand she kept a firm hold on Gonzague. With her right she shook out the shoe.

He, however, stuck to his question: "How old do you think I am? . . . Guess."

"I'm really not in the mood for guessing just now."

Gonzague, serious, as if conscience-stricken: "Thirty-two."

Juliette, with a short laugh: "For a man! . . ."

"I'm sure I've seen more of the world than you, Madame. When one gets pushed about as I have, one comes to see the truth. . . ."

"Heaven only knows where all the others are. . . . Hullo . . . I do think they might answer us."

"We're getting on all right. . . ."

Juliette stopped again, as the road became steep and full of shrubs.

"I'm not used to climbing about like this—my legs ache. Let's stop a minute."

"There's nothing here for us to sit on."

"I tell you, Gonzague, you'd far better get away from Yoghonoluk. . . . What can they do to you? You're an American citizen. . . . And you don't look the least bit Armenian. . . ."

"But? French?"

"Oh, you needn't go and imagine that!"

The little stream that flowed through the ilex gorge lay across their path. Not so much as a tree-trunk to cross by. Gonzague lifted Juliette over, big as she was, with an easy swing. His narrow shoulders had not looked as though he could do it. She felt his cool fingers around her hips, but they did not stir her. The path was becoming less steep, and they quickened their pace.

Gonzague broached the essential question: "And Gabriel Bagradian? What makes him stay on? Hasn't he any chance to get out of Turkey?"

"In war-time? . . . Where? . . . We're Turkish subjects. . . . Gabriel is liable for service. . . . They've taken our passports. . . . Who can make out these savages? . . ."

"But, really, Juliette, you look sufficiently French. . . . No, really, you look more like an Englishwoman."

"French? English? . . . Why, what do you mean?"

"Well, with a little courage you—I mean you especially—could get anywhere."

"I'm a wife and mother."

Juliette was walking so fast that Gonzague had to keep a little behind her. She seemed to feel the breath of his words: "Life is life."

She turned abruptly. "If that's your way of looking at it, why do you stop in Asia?"

"I? It's war-time now for all the men in the world."

Juliette's haste increased again. "It's easy for you, Gonzague. If only we had your American passport . . . You could easily follow your troupe to Damascus or Beirut. Why waste your time in this God-forsaken hole?"

"Why?" By now Gonzague could keep close up behind Juliette.

"Why? If I really knew that, perhaps you'd be the last person I could say it to, Juliette."

TRULY the spirit had guided Gabriel to stage his eleventh-hour "dress rehearsal." In the hall of the villa the pock-marked Ali Nassif awaited him. "Please, Sir, I've come for those medjidjehs you promised me when you gave me something on account."

Gabriel drew forth a Turkish pound and with a steady hand gave it to Ali, as though, now, all were in order, and he could hear what he had paid for without impatience.

The old saptieh took the money cautiously. "I'm going clean against my orders. But you won't give me away, Effendi?"

"You've taken your money. Say what you have to say."

Ali Nassif blinked around dubiously. "In three days the müdir and the police chief will come to the villages."

Bagradian leaned his stick in a corner and freed himself from the field-glass slung over his shoulders. "I see. And what good news will the müdir and police chief have to bring us?"

The policeman rubbed his stubbled chin. "You'll be having to leave here, Effendi. The Wali and the Kaimakam have commanded it. The saptiehs are to collect you and your people from Suedia and Antakiya and lead you eastwards. But I can tell you you won't be allowed to halt in Aleppo. That's because of the consuls."

"And you—will you be one of the saptiehs, Ali Nassif?"

The pock-marked Ali protested noisily: "Inshallah! I thank God! No! Haven't I been living twelve years among you? As commandant of the whole district? And there's never once been any trouble. Yes, I've kept order day and night. And now, because of you, I'm losing my good job. Oh, ingratitude! Our post is being disbanded altogether."

And Bagradian, to comfort the poor fellow, pressed a few cigarettes into his hand. "Now tell me, Ali Nassif, when is your post to be disbanded?"

"I have orders to march to Antakiya this very day. The müdir will come here with a whole company."

Meanwhile Juliette, Iskuhi, and Stephan had reached the house. The sight of Ali Nassif aroused no suspicion in them. Gabriel shepherded the saptieh out of the hallway and into the gravelled square in front of the house. "According to what you've been saying, Ali Nassif, the villages will be left without police supervision for three days."

Gabriel seemed to consider that suspicious. The saptieh anxiously lowered his voice. "Oh, Effendi, if you give me away, I shall be put to death, and worse. I shall have a scroll pinned on my chest with the inscription, 'Traitor.' . . . All the same I'll tell you everything. For three whole days there won't be

193

a single saptieh in the villages, because the post is being re-conditioned in Antakiya. And then you'll all be given a few days to pack up in. . . ."

Gabriel glanced at the windows of the house, as though fearful that Juliette might be looking out of them. "Have you had to send in lists of inhabitants, Ali Nassif?"

The pock-marked face blinked with sly fidelity at Gabriel: "Hope nothing for yourself, Effendi. They're going to be particularly hard on the rich and learned. They say: 'What use is it to us that poor, hard-working Armenians should die off, if the effendis, the money-bags and lawyers, stay on in our country? There's a special bad mark against your name. You've been reported at headquarters, Effendi. They've talked of you again and again. And don't go and imagine they'll spare your family. You're to be taken together as far as Antakiya, but after that they mean to separate you."

Bagradian eyed the policeman almost joyously. "You seem to be one of the great and initiated. Has the müdir opened his heart to you, Ali Nassif?"

Ali nodded solemnly. "Only for your sake, Sir, did I labour so. I stood in the offices of the Hükümet and, remembering you, I strained my ears. Oh, Effendi, in spite of your miserable paper pound, I have earned a great reward in the hereafter. What is a paper pound worth today? Even if they will change it in the bazaar for you, they cheat you. And see, my successors will have more than a hundred gold pounds, and all the medjidjehs they find in the villages. Your house will be theirs alone, with all that is in it. You can take nothing with you. And your horses also will be theirs. And your garden, and all its fruits. . . ."

Bagradian stopped this flowery enumeration: "May they have joy of it."

He drew himself up. But Ali Nassif would not stir from his disconsolate place. "Now I have sold you all this for a scrap of paper."

And so, to get rid of him, Bagradian emptied all the piastres out of his pockets.

WHEN Gabriel entered the presbytery, he saw to his great surprise that Ter Haigasun must have known of the catastrophe several hours before Ali Nassif brought him the news. Thomas Kebussyan was with him, together with the six other mukhtars, two married village priests, and Pastor Nokhudian from Bitias. Grey and waxen faces. This thunderbolt had not cleared away that cloud of morbid coma in which for weeks these people had been creeping about their business; it had only thickened it. They stood leaning against the walls, seeming to grow against them like plants. Only Ter Haigasun was seated. His face was bent back, almost in shadow, but his hands, resting quietly before him on the desk, flamed white, in a rigid shaft of sunlight. When anyone spoke, it was in a scarcely audible whisper, not moving his lips. Even Ter Haigasun only whispered, as now he turned to greet Bagradian:

"I've told these mukhtars to call their people together, the instant they get back to their villages. This very day, and as soon as possible, all the grown-ups, from Wakef to Kebussiye, must come together here in Yoghonoluk. We shall hold a big meeting to decide what's best to be done."

Pastor Nokhudian's tremulous voice came out of a corner: "There's nothing to be done. . . ."

The mukhtar of Bitias came a few steps out into the room.

"Whether it's any use or not, the people must come together to hear speeches and speak themselves. It'll make it easier."

Ter Haigasun let these interruptions pass as he sat there frowning. He went on to tell Gabriel of his decisions: "In this general assembly the peoples are to choose delegates whom they trust and who will take over the leadership. Discipline is the only weapon left us. If we keep law and order, even out there, perhaps we shan't die."

195

As he said "out there," Ter Haigasun opened his half-shut eyes to glance searchingly at Gabriel.

Thomas Kebussyan wagged his bald head. "We can't hold a meeting in the church square. Nor in the church. There are the saptiehs. . . . And others, too. God knows who wouldn't creep in and listen, and then betray us. And besides the church is too small for all of us. So where?"

"Where? That's very simple." Bagradian spoke for the first time. "My garden has a high wall all round it. The wall has three doors which you can bolt. There's enough room for ten thousand people. It's as good as a strong fortress."

This suggestion of Gabriel's decided it. Those who, from despair or will-less passivity, longed to let themselves be destroyed without any irksome show of resistance—and those who made heavy weather of everything—could raise no objections. And what serious objection could they have had against the proposal that folk of this Armenian valley should get together, in this death-agony of their race, and choose leaders —even leaders as helpless as they? This place of assembly was secure, they need fear no intensification of punishment. Perhaps what contributed to this feeling was the superstition that Bagradian had powerful connexions, which he might use in behalf of the seven villages. With dead movements and dragging steps, the mukhtars left to assemble their communes. Since Yoghonoluk was the central village, the last stragglers would be in Bagradian's garden by four that afternoon. The mukhtars themselves were to undertake to guard the entrances, so that no outsider should be let in. Ter Haigasun stood up. The bells were already ringing. He would have to get ready to vest for mass.

Of all the masses used by Christian sects the Armenian takes longest. The time from the Introit to the priest's last sign of the cross may easily be an hour and a half. No instruments, only tinkling bells and cymbals, accompany the choirs, which, on any impatient Sunday, increase their tempo to hurry the priest. But today the choirs were not successful. Ter Haigasun took longer than ever before over each sacred paragraph and act. Was he striving to hitch his prayer to the miracle of some incomprehensible rescue? Did he want to put off as long as possible the instant at which this flash of lightning would strike down on his unwitting flock? All too soon came the last blessing and the words: "Go in peace, and the Lord be with you." The benches began to rustle with departure. But Ter Haigasun came down to the edge of the chancel steps, spread his arms, and called:

"What we have all been fearing has happened."

Then, in a quiet voice, in a few words, he explained. Nobody must get unnecessarily excited, or let himself be carried away. The deathly silence of this instant must remain unbroken through the next days. No confusion, no losing of heads, no weeping or wailing, was of any use. It would only make things worse than they were already. Unity, resolution, discipline. They were the only means of avoiding the worst. There was still time to think out every step. Ter Haigasun invited the communes to the great assembly in Bagradian's garden. No healthy adult of sound mind, man or woman, should stay away.

In this assembly it would be for the seven communes not only to decide collectively what line it was best to take, but to elect leaders to represent the people before the authorities no matter what happened. This time the usual show of hands at parish elections would not be enough. So let everyone bring pencil and paper to record his vote in proper form.

"But now go quietly home," the priest implored them. "No standing about. Don't make disturbances. Perhaps they've sent spies to watch you. The saptiehs mustn't notice that you're warned. Don't forget to bring voting papers. Quiet, above all."

He need not have given his second warning. Like dead people, or people already touched by death, they silently groped their way out into the daylight as if they had never known it.

No man knows himself until he is tested. Gabriel's biography till that day: The son of a well-to-do family; brought up in comfortable surroundings; his life that of a leisured "intellectual" spent here and there in Europe, in Paris. Long since absolved from any ties which bind a man to his family, to the state, from any sense of community with the masses; a sheltered, an abstract human being. Very few angles to bark his shins on. An elder brother—an invisible, imperceptible benefactor—who, as head of the house, provided for every need. Then, strangely enough, the first interruption of this thoughtful, sensitive, introverted life—the episode of the military training-school and war. That patriotic idealism with which the contemplative suddenly found himself imbued is not so easy to account for. The general political fraternization of Turkish and Armenian youth could not be a sufficient explanation. Perhaps something more was involved then: some secret restlessness, the attempt to get away from his own, all too well-ordered, easy-going life. And during that short campaign Gabriel Bagradian had discovered unsuspected capacities in himself. He was not only, as till then he had supposed, a man whose eyes were exclusively set on invisible worlds. He showed himself surprisingly equal to demands made on his powers of action, presence of mind, foresight, courage, and to a far higher degree than most of his Oriental comrades. He was promoted quickly, several times mentioned in dispatches, praised in commanders' reports. True that in the days which followed all that had seemed a thing of the past, an almost illogical memory, since his earlier nature resumed its sway, more mature, far more balanced than previously. But today—it was the twenty-fourth of July—made all the years of his life seem a pale preliminary.

Samuel Avakian was amazed when he saw how the artificial foibles of weeks, the hobbies of a bored idler, dovetailed together into one startlingly vivid plan of defensive action. They sat in Bagradian's study behind locked doors, which were opened to no one. The mysterious strokes, crosses, dotted lines, on the three maps, at which the student had smiled as at a dreamy testing of his patience, revealed themselves now as a unified, precisely thought-out system. The thick blue line along the northern saddle meant a long trench set back against the stone barricades (indicated in brown) of the rocky side. The thinner blue line behind denoted a reserve trench; the little squares to the sides of these trenches, flank-protection or outposts. Those figures, too, from two to eleven, which filled up the side of the Damlayik facing the valley, ceased to be meaningless numbers and became well-thought-out sectors of the defence. So, too, did various inscriptions take on a meaning: "Town Enclosure," "Dish Terrace," "Headquarters Peak," "Observers I, II, III," "South Bastion." The last was the best inspiration of the whole scheme. A garrison of two dozen men posted here ought to be enough to hold off any number of assailants. Even women might be able to hold it.

Gabriel's face was aglow with eagerness. It had never looked so like the young face of his son Stephan. "I'm starting to feel very hopeful." He measured out a distance with Stephan's compasses. "I know what Turkish soldiers are like. And all their best troops are at the front. The sort of territorial off-scourings they'll have mustered up from Antioch, with saptiehs and the irregulars in the barracks, are only good for a little safe looting."

Suddenly confronted with this strange new military work, Samuel Avakian's high, receding forehead took on a dull white look in contrast to the colour in Gabriel's cheeks. "But at best we can only count on a thousand men. I don't know how many rifles and munitions they've got. And there are regulars in every Turkish town—not only in Antakiya, but everywhere. . . ."

"We have a population of about five thousand five hundred,"

interrupted Bagradian. "We need expect no mercy, only slow death. But Musa Dagh isn't so easy to surround."

Avakian stared goggle-eyed through the window. "But will these five thousand all want the same thing as you do, Effendi?"

"If they don't, they all deserve to perish together in Mesopotamian dust. . . . But I don't want to live. I don't want to be rescued. I want to fight! . . . I want to kill as many Turks as we have cartridges. And, if necessary, I'll stay on alone on the Damlayik. With the deserters!"

It was not precisely hate. It was a kind of sacred, and at the same time exultant, wrath that glittered in Bagradian's eyes. It was as though he rejoiced at the thought of standing out single-handed against Enver Pasha's army, a million strong. It lifted him out of his seat and urged him up and down the room, like a madman. "I don't want to live, I want to have some value!"

The crumpled Avakian still refused to be talked round. "Very good. We can defend ourselves for a time. And then . . . ?"

Gabriel halted his excited pacing and quietly sat down to his work again. "Anyway, within the next twenty-four hours we've got to solve all sorts of problems. Which would be the best place for the stockyard, the munition dump, the hospital? And what kind of shelters can we raise? There are enough springs, but what will be the best way to economize water? Here are some rough notes in which I sketched out the routine for the armed troops. Make a fair copy, will you, Avakian? We shall need them. In fact, get all these notes here into shape. I don't think there's much I haven't thought of. For the present it's all still theoretical, but I'm convinced that most of it can be worked out. We Armenians are always priding ourselves on superior brains. That's one of the things that's riled them so. Now it's for us to prove that we really are so much cleverer."

Avakian felt profoundly disturbed. More even than by this general catastrophe was he confused by irresistible waves of strength which now seemed to emanate from Gabriel. There was about him not a shining atmosphere so much as a hot, glowing one. The less he spoke, the more quietly he worked, the more overpowering it became. Avakian felt this influence so strong on him that he could not concentrate his thoughts, could find no more words to express his doubts, had to keep on staring at Gabriel's face, deeply engrossed over war maps. In this silent paralysis he even failed to hear Bagradian's next order, and had to have it impatiently repeated:

"Go downstairs now, Avakian. Say I shan't be coming in to lunch. Ask them to send Missak up with something. I can't waste a second. And—I'll see no one before the meeting. You understand? Not even my wife."

By one o'clock the people had begun to arrive. The mukhtars, according to arrangements, personally supervised the doors of the park wall, to test the credentials of every member of the assembly. This precautionary measure proved superfluous, since Ali Nassif and his gendarmes had already set out for Antakiya without having cared to say good-bye to acquaintances of many years' standing. Nor had either the Turkish postman's family or any of the Moslem inhabitants of nearby villages secretly joined the throngs on the roads to Yoghonoluk. Long before the time given out, the last groups had been filtered through the sieve. Then the main entrance gates were closed, and finally the garden doors. The people massed on the wide empty space in front of the house. About three thousand men and women. There was a big stable-yard just beyond the left wing, but at Ter Haigasun's request this was roped off with clothes lines and kept free of people. The notables had assembled on the raised terrace before the house. The few steps leading up to it formed an excellent tribune for speech-making. The village clerk of Yoghonoluk had placed his little scrivening-table at the foot of these steps, to take down any important resolutions.

Gabriel Bagradian stayed as long as possible in his room, the windows of which were turned away from the crowd. He was anxious not to fritter away the plenitude of emotion which possessed him in haphazard talks. He came out of the house only when Ter Haigasun sent for him. Sallow, despondent faces stared up at his, not three thousand, but one face only. It was the helpless face of exile, here as in hundreds of other places at this hour. The mass, without needing to do so, stood there so painfully jammed together that it looked far smaller than it was. Some way beyond it, where ancient trees bounded the open space, there lay or squatted a few stragglers, cut off from the rest as though their lives had ceased to matter.

As Gabriel scanned this people, his own people, a sudden horror began to invade him. His scared heart missed a beat. Once again reality looked quite different from any concept which he had formed of it. These people here were not the same as those he had seen day by day in the villages, the object of all his daring calculation. A deathly severity and bitterness stared at him from wide-open eyes. Such massed faces looked like shrivelled fruits. Even the cheeks of the young were drawn and wrinkled-looking. He had sat in these peasants' workshops and parlours but had seen as little of the truth as a traveller driving through a village. For the first time now, in this instant of overwhelming attention, was a deep contact re-established between this uprooted "European" and his own. All he had thought and worked out in his room was losing validity—so alien, so uncanny, the sight of these whom he wanted to impel his way. Women still in their Sunday clothes, with silk head-scarves, strings of coins round their necks, and clattering bracelets on their wrists. Many were wearing Turkish dress. Their legs were in wide trousers, and they had drawn the feredjeh round their foreheads, although they were devout Christians. Proximity made such assimilations inevitable, especially in the border villages such as Wakef and Kebussiye. Gabriel stared at the men in their dark entaris, on their bearded heads fezes or fur caps. It was hot, and some had pulled their shirts open. The flesh under their tanned and crowsfooted faces looked strangely white. The white, prophetic heads of blind beggars, here and there in the mass, stood out like searching assessments of guilt at a Last Judgment. In the very front stood Kevork, the sunflower-dancer. Even this half-wit no longer wore an expression of slobbering eagerness to be useful, but of reproach, which included this and the other world. Gabriel passed an ice-cold hand down the English tweed of his jacket. It felt as though he were stroking nettles. And the question rose in his mind: "Why me, of all people? How shall I speak to them?" The responsibility he was shouldering chilled him, like a sudden eclipse—a shadow of bats' wings. The shameful thought: "Get clear of all this. At once, today. . . . No matter where. . . ." Ter Haigasun had begun slowly hammering his first words into the crowd. They sounded clearer and clearer in Gabriel's ear. Words and sentences took a meaning. The eclipse had passed across his sky.

Ter Haigasun stood motionless on the top step. Only his lips and the cross on his breast moved very slightly as he was speaking. The pointed hood shadowed his waxen face; his black beard, with its streaks of grey, stood out from deeply furrowed cheeks. His eyes, which he kept half shut, formed mysterious shadows. It looked not as though he were experiencing at that moment the first stirrings of infinite thoughts, but as though he had already lived through them, had weighed and pondered, and now, arrived at his conclusion, was at last able to seek repose. Although, like all Eastern languages, Armenian lends itself to tropes and images, he spoke in curt, almost arid sentences.

They must see exactly what the government meant to do. There could scarcely be any among the elder people present who had not had a taste of the earlier massacres, if not in their own persons, then at least through the deaths and sufferings of their kindred over in Anatolia. Christ had watched over Musa Dagh with undeserved mercy. For many long and blessed years the villages had been left in peace while Armenians in Adana and other places were being killed off in their tens of thousands. But they must clearly distinguish between massacre and exile. The first lasted four or five days, perhaps a week. A brave man had almost always the chance to sell his life dearly. It was easy to find a place in which women and children could hide. The blood-lust of excited soldiers soon died down again. Even the most bestial saptieh sickened at the thought, once it was over. Though the government had always arranged such massacres, it had never admitted having done so. They were born of disorder, and vanished in disorder again. But disorder had been the best part of such rascally business, and the worst to fear from it had been death. Banishment was a very different story. Anyone might think himself lucky who was released from it by death, even the cruellest. Banishment did not pass, like an earthquake, which always spares a certain number of people and houses. Banishment would go on till the last Armenian had either been slaughtered, died of hunger on the roads, of thirst in the desert, or been carried off by spotted typhus or cholera. This time it was not a case of unbridled, haphazard methods, of whipped-up blood-lust, but of something far more terrible—an ordered attack. It was all to go according to a plan worked out in the government offices of Istanbul. He, Ter Haigasun, had known of such a plan for months, even long before the misfortune of Zeitun. He also knew that not all the efforts of the Catholicos, of patriarchs and bishops, all the threats of ambassadors and consuls, had availed. The only thing that he, a village priest, had been able to do had been to keep silence, no matter how hard it had seemed to do so, so that the last happy days of his poor flock might not be destroyed. That time was over at last. Now they must look things squarely in the face. Nobody, in these discussions, need make the futile suggestion of sending petitions and delegations to the authorities. All that would be a waste of time. "Human compassion is at an end. Christ crucified demands of us that we follow Him in his passion. There is nothing left us but to die. . . ."

Here Ter Haigasun paused for a scarcely perceptible instant, before concluding on a new note: "The one question is—how?"

"How?" shouted Pastor Aram Tomasian, and pushed his way quickly out beside the priest. "I know how I mean to die —not like a defenceless sheep, not on the road to Deir ez-Zor, not in the filth of a concentration camp, not of hunger, and not of the stinking plague—no! I mean to die on the threshold of my own house, with a gun in my hand. Christ will help me to it, Whose word I preach. And my wife shall die with me, and the unborn child in her womb. . . ."

This outburst had almost broken Aram's chest. He pressed his hands on his midriff, to get his breath again. Then, more quietly, he began to tell them what life had been in the convoy, what he himself had had to suffer, though only in the mildest form, for a very short time.

"No one can possibly know what it's like, beforehand. One only begins to realize at the last minute, as the officer gives the order to move off, as the church and houses, when you look back on them, get smaller and smaller, till they vanish. . . ."

Aram described the eternal route, from stage to stage, with one's feet getting worse every day, one's body swelling—with fainting people left to die on the roads, with people who dragged themselves along, till gradually they got to be like beasts, with people who perished one by one, under daily thrashings from the saptiehs. His words themselves descended on the crowd like cudgel-blows. . . . Yet, strangely, not a cry had risen from the agonized souls of these thousands, not one wild outburst. They stood, still staring up at the small group

205

of people round the house door, as they might have at a group of tragic actors playing what did not directly concern them. These vine- and fruit-growers, wood-carvers, comb-makers, bee-keepers, silkworm-breeders, who had felt so long that this would happen, could not grasp it with their minds, now it was here. The haggard faces still looked puzzled and concentrated. The life-force in them was still struggling to pierce the sick chrysalis stage of the last few weeks.

Aram Tomasian shouted: "Blessed are the dead, for with them it is all over."

Here, for the first time, an indescribable moan passed through the listeners. It was not an outcry, but a long, sighing, groaning breath, a huge, swelling sigh, as though not human beings were sighing, but the suffering earth itself.

Aram's voice sharply capped this threnody: "We, too, want to get death over as fast as possible. Therefore we must defend our homes, so that all of us, men, women, children, may find a quick death."

"Why death?"

This had come from Gabriel Bagradian. A light, somewhere deep down in his consciousness, seemed to ask him, even as he heard himself: "Is that I?" His heart beat quietly. The strained vacillation was past and gone—for ever. Great certainty possessed him. All the muscles of his body were relaxed. He knew with his whole being: "For this one second it's worth while to have lived." Always, when talking to these villagers, his Armenian had seemed laboured and embarrassed. But now it was not he who spoke to them—and this knowledge brought him complete peace—it was the force which had brought him here, down the long, winding road of centuries, the short, twisted path of his own life. He listened in amazement to this power, as it found the words in him so naturally.

"My brothers and sisters, I haven't lived among you. . . . That's true. . . . I was a stranger to my home and no longer

206

knew you. . . . And then . . . no doubt because of this, God sent me back from the big cities of the West to this old villa, which was my grandfather's. . . . And so now I'm no longer the guest, almost the stranger, I was among you, for my fate will be exactly the same as yours. . . . With you I shall either live or die. . . . The government means to spare me less than any of you, I know that. . . . They hate and persecute my kind worst of all. . . . I'm forced, just like all of you, to protect the lives of my wife and family. . . . And so, for weeks now, I've been carefully thinking out what possible ways we have of defending ourselves. . . . Listen here, I was terribly scared at first, but I'm not now, any longer. . . . I'm full of hope. . . . With God's help, we aren't going to die. . . . I'm not telling you this as a vain fool, but as a man who's seen what war is, as an officer. . . ."

His thoughts found clearer and clearer words. The intense, concentrated labour of the last few weeks was coming in useful. The number of fully thought-out problems gave him more and more inner certainty. This certainty of systematic thought—thought, as he had learned it in Europe—raised him far above these dully resigned prisoners of fate. This same sensation of playful mastery had been his as a young man when at examinations he found that he could answer some question with an exhaustive knowledge, which at the same time selected its own method of answering. He disposed of Aram's desperate speech without once mentioning it directly. It would be a senseless attempt, to defy the saptiehs in the streets, at house doors. It might perhaps be surprisingly successful for a few hours, but would only lead all the more inevitably, not to a quick death, but to a slow one, by torture, with the rape and befoulment of all the women. He, Bagradian, also wanted resistance. To the last drop of their blood. But there were better places to fight in than the valley, the village streets. He pointed in the direction of Musa Dagh, whose peaks, towering behind the roof, seemed to look down and take part in the great assembly. They probably all remembered the old stories in which the Damlayik had offered help and protection to escaping Armenians. "And it would need a very big force really to surround and storm the Damlayik. Jemal Pasha needs every man he can get. He has something more important to do than turn out a few thousand Armenians. We shall easily finish off the saptiehs. A few hundred determined men with rifles are all we need to defend the mountain. We have the men, and the rifles too."

He raised his hand, as though for an oath. "I engage myself, here, before you all, to lead that defence in such a way that our women and children will live longer than they would on a convoy. We can hold out for several weeks, maybe for months. Who knows? Perhaps by then God will grant that the war may be over. Then we're certain to be relieved. And, even if peace doesn't come, we've still always got the sea behind us. Cyprus, with its French and English battleships, is near. Mayn't we hope that one day one of those ships will come down the coast, and that we shall reach it with our signals, and get help? But, even if there's no such good fortune in store for us, there'll still be plenty of time for dying. And then at least we shan't need to despise ourselves as defenceless sheep."

The effect of this speech was by no means clear. It looked as though now, for the first time, these people were being roused out of their torpor to the full consciousness of their fate. Gabriel thought at first that either they had not understood him or were rejecting his scheme with howls of rage. This solid mass fell apart. Women screamed. An impact of hoarse, masculine oaths. A lurching, this way and that. Where were the furrowed and resigned grief-stricken peasant faces, and where the veils of deathly quiet? A savage brawl seemed to begin. The men yelled at one another, they shouted and tugged at each other's clothes, each other's beards even. Yet all this was far less disputation than it was a wild unburdening, a blowing sky-high of the rigid impotence, the stealthy consciousness of death—violently released by these first words of trust and energy.

What? Among these thousands, who now bellowed and raved in this unchained torrent of desperation, had there not been one to conceive this very simple thought in the long days of suspense allowed them? A thought so close to them by tradition? Had it needed a "gentleman from Europe," a "strong man," to come and speak it? Yes, the same thought had occurred to many among these thousands, but only as an idle day-dream. Nor, in their most secret conversations had it ever forced its way to utterance. Till a few hours before they had all still told themselves, lost in their artificial stupor, that this nemesis might draw in its claws and drift away across Musa Dagh. After all, what were they? Wretched villagers, a persecuted race on a beleaguered island, without a city at their backs. There were few Armenians in Antioch, and such as lived there were money-changers, bazaar merchants, speculators in grain, and so by no means the right sort of agitators and allies. And again, in Alexandretta there was only a very small, rich colony—bankers and war contractors—who lived in ornate villas, just as they did in Beirut. Such anxious magnates had not even a thought for the petty mountaineers of Musa Dagh. There was not one such individual as old Avetis Bagradian among them. They bolted the shutters of their villas and crept into the darkest corner to hide. Two or three, to save their lives and property, had gone over to Islam, submitted themselves to the blunt, circumcising knife of the mullah. Oh, those people in the far north-east had an easy time of it—those citizens of Van and Urfa. Van and Urfa were the two big Armenian towns, full of weapons and traditional defiance. There were clever people there, the deputies of the Dashnakzagan. There it was easy to talk of resistance and to organize it. But who would dare speak such impious thoughts in wretched Yoghonoluk? Armed resistance to the civil and military powers? Everyone born in these parts felt in his bones a respect, mingled with terror, of the state. The state, the hereditary enemy. The state—that is to say, the saptieh, who could arrest or thrash you for no reason; the state—that is to say the filthy government office, with its picture of the Sultan, its text from the Koran, its spittle-covered tiles, where one paid one's bedel. The state meant huge, forbidding barrack squares, where one served as a private under the fists of the chaush, the onbashi, and where a special form of bastinado had been devised to punish Armenians. So that therefore it is more than comprehensible that—apart from Pastor Tomasian's futile outburst—it should have been a stranger, a freed man, not a native, who hurled down the first systematic thought of resistance into this crowd. Only such an emancipated foreigner had the necessary freedom from guilty feelings to enable him to speak out such a thought. And the people was still far from feeling at home in it. It looked as if this brawl would never end. It kept increasing. Voices snarled, and fists were shaken, in a fashion altogether incongruous to these usually shy women and grave men. Naturally, too, the children, whose mothers were either nursing them or carrying them pickaback, sharpened the general hubbub with their wails. No doubt even they could sense in their souls the peril of this moment and with shrill sobs struggled against impending death. Gabriel looked down silently into the whirlpool. Ter Haigasun came towards him. He touched Bagradian's shoulder with all ten finger-tips. It was the embryonic attempt at an embrace, a gesture at once of blessing and abnegation. Gabriel may perhaps have read in the depths of those resolute, humble eyes: "So we've joined forces then, without saying a word to each other." This attempt at an embrace at once embarrassed and held Gabriel rigid. Ter Haigasun's emaciated fingers slipped down off his shoulders.

Meanwhile Pastor Harutiun Nokhudian was doing his best to subdue the crowd. The small, spare man had to struggle with his wife as he was doing it, who thrust herself against him and did her best to prevent his saying anything imprudent. He could only manage to make himself heard by degrees. His reedy voice had to strain itself to its highest pitch: "Christ strictly enjoins us not to withstand authority. Christ strictly enjoins us not to resist evil. My office is the gospel. As the shepherd of my flock, I must disapprove of all recalcitrance."

This pastor, whom Bagradian always considered as an ailing, timid little man, showed great resolution in defending his own point of view. He described the consequences of armed resistance as he foresaw them. Such a revolt would at last give the government its right to change an infamous decree into a ruthlessly vindictive extermination. And then death would have ceased to be a meritorious discipleship to Christ's passion, it would have become the lawful punishment of rebels. Not only would the souls of all these here assembled be cursed by God for impious rebellion, but its last effects would inevitably be felt by the whole people—it would be used against all Armenian sons and daughters. They would have given their masters the welcome pretext to brand the Armenian millet before the whole world as disturbers of the common peace—as traitors. A good woman, even if her husband ill-treats her, has no right to surrender her house to strangers. Such was the view of Harutiun Nokhudian—whose own domestic arrangements did not go very far to bear out his contention, since the wife of his bosom was his tyrant, and not only in what concerned his health. His strained vocal cords nearly gave out.

"And which of us shall say for certain that our banishment must necessarily end as Ter Haigasun and Aram Tomasian prophesy? Are not God's decrees inscrutable for them also? Has He not the power to send help from all sides? Are there not human beings everywhere, who can pity, even among Turks, Kurds, Arabs? If we keep our trust in God, shall we not find food and shelter everywhere? Even among strangers? Is it not possible even now, while we despair, that help may be on its way? If it does not reach us here, at least it may reach us in Aleppo. If not in Aleppo, at least we may hope for the next halting-place. Our bodies may have to suffer bitterly, but our souls will be free. If we have to choose between sinful and innocent death, why should we choose to die in sin?"

Nokhudian could not finish his speech, for his thin voice was thrust out of the way by the deep, decisive tones of a woman. Could this bellicose matron in black really be little mother Antaram, the doctor's wife? Was it really Mairik Antaram, the helpful, the succouring, the little mother of village mothers, from whom the very people she helped and advised scarcely ever heard a long speech? She was so excited that her black lace shawl had slipped half off her hair, not yet entirely grey and parted down the centre. Her bold nose jutted imperiously from her flushed face. That vigorous torso, springing up from between wide hips, held high her erect head. The clear blue eyes were netted in a thousand belligerent wrinkles. And yet Antaram Altouni's magnificent wrath made her look young again.

"I'm a woman." The full voice, by its sheer challenge, got absolute quiet with its first sounds. "I'm a woman, and I speak for all the women here. Many of us have suffered. My heart has failed me again and again. It's a long time since I've cared whether I die or not. I don't mind how soon I do die. But I'm not going to die like a cur on the highroad. I'm not going to lie out rotting in the fields. Not I! Nor do I mean to go on living in a concentration camp, among all those rascally murderers, and the poor women they've befouled. None of us women means to do it—no, not one of us! And if you men are so cowardly that you'd rather stay on here and be slaughtered, we women alone will arm ourselves and go up on Musa Dagh with Gabriel Bagradian."

This spirited appeal raised a far noisier tumult than the last. It looked as though at any minute now these madmen might whip out knives against each other and so anticipate Turkish blood-letting. The schoolteachers, headed by Shatakhian, were already preparing to rush the crowd and act as police—Ter Haigasun quietly beckoned them back. He knew his people better than all these teachers and mukhtars. Such vociferations were not vindictive. Empty excitement. The mind of these thousands had still not really digested the thought of banishment. Now it had slowly to assimilate the challenging voices of the speech-makers. A glance from the priest said: "Just leave them alone." He watched the tumult with patient eyes. Women's voices, roused by Antaram, were more and more gaining the upper hand. Ter Haigasun also prevented would-be orators—Oskanian, the teacher, for instance—from saying more. He was right. The din, with nothing there to fodder it, died down, sooner than was expected. In a few minutes this tumult had stifled itself, and only grunts and sobs were left over. Now was Ter Haigasun's chance to clear things up and bring them speedily to a head. He waved his right hand to get them quiet.

"It's all quite simple." He did not use too much of his voice but scanned each syllable very sharply, so that his words bored their way into the dull comprehension of the mass. "Two proposals have been made to you. Those are the only two ways we can go. There's no other way for us except these two. The one, Pastor Nokhudian's way, takes you eastwards with the saptiehs. The other, Gabriel Bagradian's way, leads us up, with our own weapons, on to the Damlayik. Each of you is perfectly free to choose for himself which way to go, as his will and understanding may dictate to him. There's nothing more to say about that, since all that's been said already. I want to make the decision very easy for you. Pastor Nokhudian will be so good as to stand over there in the empty yard, on the other side of those ropes. Let everyone who agrees with

213

the pastor, and would rather go into exile, go across and stand with him. Those on the side of Gagriel Bagradian, stay here, where he is. No need to hurry. There's plenty of time."

Sudden, deep silence. Only Madame Nokhudian's rapid, almost yelping sobs became audible. The old pastor bowed his head, in its little cloth cap. A heavy load of thoughts seemed to bow his shoulders, drag him to earth. He remained a very long while in this thoughtful posture. And then his legs began to move. He trotted, in hesitant steps, to the place to which Ter Haigasun had assigned him. He lifted the clothes line with a clumsy movement over his head. The stable-yard reached almost to the villa. Only a stretch of grass, with a wall of magnolia bushes, lay in between. The big yard was completely empty. Stable-boys and house servants had both crowded to the meeting. Nokhudian's short little legs made the most of this way of decision; they needed quite a while to reach the magnolia bushes, where he took up his position, his back to the crowd. His wife, shaken with sobs, came after him. Another, still longer, emptier pause, with not a word in it. Only then did one or two people free themselves from the centre of the crowd, force a way out of it, and, measuring out the intervening space with the same gentle, thoughtful steps, take up their stand beside Pastor Nokhudian.

At first there were only a few—the elders of the Protestant congregation of Bitias, with their wives. But, little by little, the number of those who had chosen exile increased, until at last the pastor had almost his whole congregation, young and old. A few more joined them, from other villages; but these were old and burdened people, whose strength to resist had already failed them, or who, at the very end of their lives, really feared to set heaven against themselves. With their hands over their breasts as if in prayer, they took the first steps of the road to Calvary. All this happened so deliberately, in so gently introverted a manner, that it looked less like a decision pregnant with consequences than a religious ceremony.

It was as though these people were stepping modestly, slowly, into the grave, without first having stretched themselves out to die. One. And then another. A couple. And then several. Then another couple. Nokhudian's disciples at last increased to something like four hundred souls, not counting those of the Protestant congregation who, from sickness or some other cause, had had to stop away from the meeting. With him the pastor took a fair proportion of the inhabitants of Bitias, the second largest commune of the valley. The mass of people watched with fascinated eyes the hesitant steps of these others, resolved for obedience. Not a word of comment. Until, last of all, very late in joining Nokhudian's band, came a little, shrivelled-up man, lurching over his stick like a drunkard, and talking to himself. This figure of fun, well known to all the people of Kebussiye, who did not really seem to know what was happening, provoked a cry of arrogant hatred in the crowd. At first it was no more than the sight of a half-wit producing the usual malice. Then came the arrogance: Here were the brave, and there the cowards. Here the strong, the men of sterling worth, and there the cripples. It was only that one young man had bawled something derisive, and that a gust of laughter shook the crowd. But Ter Haigasun was already pushing his way into the densely packed mass, which he thrust away from him with both arms, as though he would reach to very heart of this baseness, pounce on the giber, drag him out, and thrash him. His face looked dark with anger. His hood fell back off his close-cropped, iron-grey hair. Murder was glinting in his eyes: "What cur dared? What brutes are laughing?"

Vehemently he beat upon his breast, again and again, to punish at least himself for the mocker and still his rage. Then, in the resumed stillness, he went across to Harutiun Nokhudian and his band, stopped a little distance away from them, bowed very low, and said in his resonant, priestly voice: "To us you will always be holy. May we be holy to you."

Bagradian was thinking feverishly. An unstemmed rush of new ideas swept him along. The great work of defence went ardently forward in his mind. Ever since the decision had fallen, he had been only half listening to what happened. His whipped-up thoughts noted and reflected simultaneously. What a giant of inspiration this Ter Haigasun had shown himself to be! "It's invaluable," the thought flashed through him, "that I should have this authority rooted in the soil behind me." And it seemed a further stroke of fortune that the good No-khudian, and a few hundred more non-combatants, should have chosen otherwise. "They'll be useful in keeping our movements and decisions from the saptiehs till the very last minute. The villages mustn't be empty. The Turks mustn't begin to suspect before we're ready for them." Gabriel's plan went on unfolding itself. His forbears' calculating intelligence, all the shrewdness of grandfather Avetis, were uppermost now in this, their other-worldly grandson, that simple idealist at whom his more distant relations, hard-headed merchants, had always smiled. From every considered actuality there spun forth its inevitable series of ghostly threads of future consequence, and not one thread was inessential. An impetuous ambition took hold of Bagradian. So, according to Ali Nassif's report, the müdir would arrive with his escort three days after this present Sunday. By Wednesday, therefore, all the foundations would have to be laid, from which to build in the days that followed. Now was the moment to test what he had always believed, that mind must triumph over matter, even in its highest, most intense manifestations—force and chance.

No wonder that, held fast by his scheming thoughts, intoxicated with self-reliance, he should have forgotten even his wife, been scarcely conscious of all the bustle surrounding him. All this was sheer waste of time. A few village speech-makers were still talking. But what, now that the great die was cast, did their clumsy, empty words matter to him? They were all equally bellicose—not a single voice in opposition. Ter Haigasun gave the people plenty of breathing-space for this spirit of valiant resolution to take deep anchorage in their midst, so that the hesitant and timid might be drawn in. But, before the first wave of exhaustion threatened, he stepped forward, interrupting the speaker, and decreed that they should at once choose representatives. The village clerk of Yoghonoluk went round with a basket, collecting voting-papers. The schoolteachers, helped by Avakian, lost no time in beginning the count inside the villa.

It goes without saying that the majority of votes went to Ter Haigasun. Immediately after him came the doctor. Then the seven mukhtars and three village priests, with the votes of their congregations. Then, with a considerable gap, Apothecary Krikor, and some of the schoolteachers, among whom, of course, were Shatakhian and Oskanian. Gabriel got about the same number of votes as Pastor Aram Tomasian. Among the non-official villagers old Tomasian and Chaush Nurhan, the ex-regular sergeant, were elected to leadership. One woman, Mairik Antaram, received a large number of votes—in these parts a decided innovation. She energetically refused to accept. Shatakhian read out the results. Those selected retired into the house to draw up their rules as a corporate body. Gabriel had told Kristaphor and Missak to have everything ready for a sitting in the big selamlik—cold food, wine, and coffee. The crowd—even those mothers with small children at home to be looked after—remained in the grounds, encamped here and there in the big garden. Comestibles were sent for, from Yoghonoluk. The master of the house sent out a ration of water, wine, fruit, and tobacco. Soon gossip, mingled with cigarette smoke and the bubbling of comfortable chibuks, rose in the evening air, as though nothing had happened. Pastor Nokhudian's adherents left with their leader to go home to Bitias. It was a quiet and dreary setting forth. A few of the younger of this band turned back at the garden door and joined the main encamped body of the people, whose zest for life, after

weeks of coma, seemed for the first time now to have returned.
Now in this short, fugitive interval between everyday routine
and the unknown, incomprehensible pleasure invaded their
souls. Why? Because more than mere suffering lay before
them, because, though they suffered, in and above their pain
there would be action.

THE night of Musa Dagh quickly absorbed the July twilight.
Eastward, a horizontal half-moon pushed off from the ragged
peaks of the Amanus and sailed into open sky. The doors of
Villa Bagradian stood wide open. The inquisitive might go in
and out unhindered. The leaders of the people had gathered
in the big selamlik. This council of leaders, a group of thirty,
seemed to itself at first very helpless. The mayors of the other
villages, the priests and schoolteachers, who were in this house
for the first time, sat or stood about in awkward silences.
Some may only now have become aware of the full audacity
of this step to which the unexpected, impetuous course of
the great assembly had committed them. Gabriel instantly
sensed an acrid stink of flickering courage, given off by certain
of the chosen. The lukewarm must on no account be allowed
to "come to their senses"; no fundamental "if's" or "but's"
must be spoken. The people had taken its lawful decision;
there could be no vacillations now; these fires of defensive
resolution should be fanned into a towering flame. It was
Bagradian's job as master of the house to put an end to this
shapeless hanging about of tepid men, to get the people's council under way, and to have fruitful tasks ready for all. Every
advantage of his Western education must make itself felt. He
did the only thing that was to be done. He turned with
solemnity to Ter Haigasun.

"Ter Haigasun, it was more than the people outside that
elected you. I speak for all here, when I say this: We beg you
to be the supreme head of our struggle. In peace-time you held
an office of leadership and, as spiritual head of the communes,

218

you have done your duty with the greatest self-sacrifice till today. It is God's will, by the cruelty of men, to extend your powers. We all want to make you the solemn promise that, in every decision we may make, in every precautionary measure on which we decide, we will submit to your final veto without a murmur. Not until you have endorsed them, shall the resolutions of this council of leaders become valid and so be given the power of laws, binding on our whole people."

This little speech brought its self-evident result. Nobody else but Ter Haigasun could possibly have been chosen supreme head. Not even Mr. Schoolmaster Hrand Oskanian would have ventured a secret sneer at this established fact. And Gabriel's words sounded agreeably in the ears of his listeners, especially of those to whom he was still a mistrusted foreigner. Two trains of thought brought this soothing effect: Many had been expecting that "the Frenchman" would snatch the leadership on the strength of his Western superiority. And then—an even deeper reason—Bagradian's speech, its solemn form as well as its legal content, prepared the ground on which all future decisions could be built up. These few words had quite imperceptibly laid down the fundamental law for this newly constituted entity about to form itself. Ter Haigasun made the sign of the cross in silence, to show that he consented to take office, with all its heavy responsibility. From this moment there were two legal powers—the Council of Leaders and the Supreme Head of the People, who, though he presided over the council, had alone the power to make its resolutions legally valid. Every member came up to Ter Haigasun to kiss his hand, according to custom, and took the oath. Only when this ceremony was over, did a wide circle take form along several tables set end to end. Gabriel Bagradian had war maps and complete data in front of him. Samuel Avakian stood behind him, ready to be consulted. When Gabriel, with a look, had asked for silence, he stood up.

"My friends, the sun went down two hours ago, and it will

have risen again in another six. We have only about six hours to get through the whole of our thinking. When we go out tomorrow morning, to face the people again, there must be no more uncertainty. Our will must be clear and unanimous.

"But this is the most necessary measure. In the very first hours of tomorrow morning all who are young and strong enough must go up to the Damlayik and begin to build the fortifications. I beg you, therefore, to save time. It is an advantage to all of us that some time ago I worked out all the details of our plan of defence. I can give you my suggestions at once. I think that in these sittings it will be best to work by the same rules as those at our communal meetings. I ask Ter Haigasun's leave to explain my plan. . . ."

Ter Haigasun, as his habit was, half shut his eyes, giving his face a tired and agonized look. "Let us hear Gabriel Bagradian."

Gabriel spread out the best of Avakian's three maps. "We shall have a thousand minor tasks to perform, but, if once we look at the thing correctly, we find that they all come under two main headings. The first and most important is our actual method of defence. Even our second, the way we organize our life together, must serve that struggle above all. I'll begin with it. . . ."

Pastor Aram Tomasian raised a hand to interrupt. "We all know that Gabriel Bagradian, as an officer, knows most about military matters. The fighting leadership goes to him. . . ."

All hands went up in assent to this. But Pastor Aram had not done yet: "For some time Gabriel Bagradian has been concentrating his whole mind on the plan of defence. It would be best to leave him to arrange our resistance. I therefore suggest that we postpone all discussion of his tactical scheme till we've a clear idea how, and for how long, five thousand people, cut off from the rest of the world, can live on the Damlayik."

Gabriel, who had been in full spate, sighed and let his maps fall back on the table. "My arrangements included that problem. I've made notes on these maps for everything necessary to maintain life. But, if Pastor Tomasian likes, I'm perfectly ready to put off explaining my scheme of defence."

Bedros Altouni, the doctor, had not long managed to sit quietly in his parliamentary seat. He wandered, growling, about the room, to suggest that, at this moment of urgent peril, debates, with a show of hands and speeches, seemed to him ridiculous frivolity. His growling impatience was in sharp contrast to the dignified impassivity of Krikor, who sat immobile, in an attitude which seemed to ask: "When shall I be free to escape in peace from this barbarous encroachment on the one thing in life which beseems me or makes it worth living?" The doctor, fidgeting round the room, made a sudden remark, which had nothing whatever to do with present business: "Five thousand people are five thousand people, and the heat of the sun's the heat of the sun. And cloudbursts are cloudbursts."

Gabriel, to whom these problems of housing, of the town enclosure, the care of the children, had caused so many sleepless nights, took up this remark of the doctor. "It would be best for our protection to keep all the children between the ages of two and seven in one shelter."

The hitherto silent Ter Haigasun rejected this suggestion most decisively. "What Gabriel Bagradian has just advised would mean the beginning of very dangerous disorders. We must not sunder what God and time have bound together. On the contrary, it seems to me highly essential that single parishes, and in fact, single families, should not be separated more than is absolutely necessary. Relations ought all to have their own separate encampment, every village its camping-ground. The mukhtars to be responsible to their own people, as usual. We ought to change the relationships to which we are accustomed down here as little as possible."

Emphatic, unanimous assent, which implied a minor failure for Bagradian. Ter Haigasun had guaranteed them as close an approximation as possible to their normal life. The prospect had a very soothing effect. For, to peasants, the worst, most cruel thing that can befall them is expressed in the one word—change. But Gabriel would not give way so easily. He sent round the map, with his drawing of the town enclosure. Everyone recognized the wide meadow pasturage of the communal flocks. It began to dawn on them that this big, stoneless expanse of grass was the only possible camping-ground. There would have been room enough for two thousand families, let alone one thousand, on it. Gabriel skilfully compromised with Ter Haigasun. The allotment of family and communal camping-grounds could easily be arranged as the priest desired. And he found himself agreeing with Ter Haigasun. On the other hand, they would have to admit that the thousand families could not possibly run separate establishments; that it would never work if the common resources were not pooled. They need only work out the saving in food and fuel, the gain in free labour power. Apart from this, there would really be no possibility of holding out for a long time if it were not arranged that beasts must be slaughtered, bread and grain distributed, goat's milk allotted to children and invalids, only according to strictly determined regulations. Whatever else might be done to classify people according to family, the ticklish question of private ownership could not be got round. Since he, Bagradian, was willing to place his whole possessions, in so far as they were obtainable and divisible, at the disposal of the common defence—all the cattle on his farm, all the supplies in his house and cellar—everyone else must contribute his share. These circumstances imperatively demanded the communal distribution of goods. It would be quite impossible for each individual family to slaughter its own sheep. Milk must go to those who needed it, and not, for instance, to any strong, well-fed people who happened to own a couple of goats. The notion, which some perhaps still cherished, that up on the Damlayik it would still be possible to buy certain privileges for money, was a childish dream. From the instant the communes arrived in camp, money would cease to have the remotest value. And all barter would have to be strictly forbidden, since from that day on all goods would be the goods of the people, to be used to defend their lives in battle. No one who had clearly perceived that exile meant the loss of all he possessed would surely think the demands of Musa Dagh worth another second's hesitation.

But at once it was plain that in making these just demands Gabriel had erred most sadly. It had not so much as entered these peasant minds—though a few hours back they had known with such inevitable certainty that they stood face to face with exile and death—that now their own would cease to belong to them. It was more than the mere loss that produced their obstinacy—it was the disciplined inevitability, the "European," in Gabriel's words. This led on to a time-wasting argument, which was fruitless, if for no other reason than that the most determined peasant skull could conceive no alternative. A bandying of words which only served to vent disgruntlement. Ter Haigasun waited a certain time. A short, warning glance across to Gabriel: "It's necessary to be rather careful in making these people see the obvious." Then he interrupted their empty chatter:

"We are going up to the mountain and shall have to live there. Many things will arrange themselves which we needn't bother our heads discussing at present. It would be better if you mukhtars would begin to think out the most urgent matters: Will it be possible to have enough supplies taken up there? For how many weeks do you think they'll be likely to last? Is there any possible means of supplementing them?"

And here Pastor Tomasian had another, very feasible suggestion. It was the mukhtars' business to get together and work out their own estimate of provisions, and scheme for the commissariat. And this not only applied to the commissariat, but to all other matters to be discussed. This general council was unwieldy. They were not here to talk and argue, but to work. He, Aram Tomasian, therefore proposed that the various departments should get together, and each form a separate committee. Each of these committees to be presided over by a head, named by Ter Haigasun. The heads to form a closer, separate council which should have in its hands the actual management of affairs. There would be five departments: First, Defence; second, Legislation, which concerned Ter Haigasun alone; then came Internal Order; then all that concerned Public Health and Sickness; and lastly the special affairs of single communes, as against those of the whole community. Gabriel enthusiastically welcomed the young pastor's inspiration, and for the first time Dr. Altouni also gave some signs of assent. No one demurred. Ter Haigasun, to whom the inevitable chatter of a big council was an uncongenial as to Aram, at once endorsed this legislative arrangement. Chaush Nurhan, the teacher Shatakhian, and two younger men, whom he selected, were assigned as a military committee to assist Gabriel. Aram Tomasian also made one of this Committee of Defence. In the same way Gabriel was himself a member of the Committee of Internal Order, led by the pastor. This committee made itself responsible for everything connected with the obtaining and rationing of supplies. Therefore, Thomas Kebussyan and the other mukhtars were members. The elder Tomasian, the builder, found himself solely entrusted with the business of erecting huts. It need scarcely be said that Dr. Altouni and the detached apothecary, Krikor, had to form the Committee of Public Health. With that they had all achieved a rough and ready division of labour. In the next few hours these isolated groups were to make what provision they could for their departments. So that then, in the early morning, a short sitting of the General Council would be enough to estimate results. The mukhtars went outside to get directly from their villagers a possible estimate of supplies.

Gabriel was to follow them later and, with their help, to muster the youngest, strongest men, who, early next day, were to begin digging-operations on the main line of trenches between the north peaks. Meanwhile, map in hand, he eagerly explained his plan of defence to Ter Haigasun, Aram Tomasian, and the rest. Even Krikor began to be curious and came across to listen.

Only one person stood aside, with inscrutably folded arms—Hrand Oskanian, naturally. That sombre schoolteacher had met with yet another rebuff. No leading role had been allotted him—no, not even a fairly respectable second. While his colleague Shatakhian had been given a seat on the Committee of Defence, Ter Haigasun, in his deep hatred of the other, silent pedagogue, had condemned him to go on "teaching school" and keeping the children in order. That was the priest's revenge for the fact that at the communal elections Hrand Oskanian, the poet of Musa Dagh, had been elected by hundreds of votes. Icily reserved, Oskanian was already wondering whether or not to leave the assembly and go home. Then he grew proudly conscious of the fact that the many by whom he had been chosen looked up to him with trustful eyes and that, moreover, the priest would be more riled by his presence than by his absence.

Shortly after midnight the council was suddenly suspended. As often happens in such cases, it had occurred to no one to make sure of that on which the whole future would depend. Fifty Mausers and two hundred and fifty Greek service-rifles still lay buried in a grave in the cemetery. They must be dug up instantly and carried up the Damlayik before morning, with the munitions. Though Gabriel did not mistrust Ali Nassif's report, there was still always the possibility that in the course of the next twenty-four hours fresh saptiehs might come to the villages, to make a sudden search for arms. A deputation of six went off, post-haste, to the churchyard of Yoghonoluk, situated beyond the village on the road to Habibli. The two grave-diggers came last. The rifles, thanks to Nurhan the armourer's foresight, had been laid in bricked graves. They awaited their glorious resurrection enveloped in rags, in air-tight coffins, bedded in straw. Only four weeks previously Chaush Nurhan had inspected them summarily by torchlight and found them in perfect condition. Scarcely one breech-lock had rusted. Nor had the cartridges suffered in any way. That night these heavy chests, fifteen in all, were hauled up for ever out of the graves. It was hard work. Since not many hands were there to do it, Ter Haigasun, who had flung off his cassock, did a muscular share. Later a couple of the strong shaggy donkeys of the district were fetched, so that at last, towards morning, led by Chaush Nurhan, a secret caravan set out for the northern mountain pass through the deserted villages of Azir and Bitias.

Not till an hour before sunrise could Ter Haigasun get back to the selamlik of Villa Bagradian. The garden looked like a corpse-strewn battlefield. Not even the people of Yoghonoluk had gone home. Ter Haigasun, like a general among the dead, had to step across the motionless sleepers.

Thanks to the energy of Bagradian—who kept urging them on—the members of the sub-committees had done some very useful work. The main lines of the conditions of defence and rationing had been laid down. A muster of the fighters had been drawn up and approximate calculations made of the amounts and kinds of obtainable foodstuffs. Provision had also been made for the building of a colony of huts, a hospital shelter, and a larger government barrack. With Ter Haigasun's return the General Council reassembled. Gabriel briefly reported decisions taken to the chief. With Aram Tomasian's energetic support he had managed to get nearly all his suggestions accepted. Ter Haigasun gave his assent to everything, with an absent-looking face and half-closed eyes, as though he did not believe that this new life would be made subject to resolutions. Both lights and men were on the wane, yet their eyes still showed more excitement than fatigue. A glorious morning began to glitter, deep silence descended on them all. The men stared out of the window at the gentle light of this bud of dawn, unfolding petal by petal. The pupils of their eyes shone, strangely dilated. No sound in this selamlik of the night watch save the scraping of two pencils—Avakian's and the communal clerk's—engaged in drafting a protocol of the most important resolutions.

When the sun shone full and golden into the room, Gabriel put an end to this comatose dreaming. "I think we've all done our duty tonight, and that nothing's forgotten."

"No. We've forgotten one thing—the most essential thing." Ter Haigasun remained seated as he spoke, but his resonant voice brought all who had risen back to the table. The priest raised deep, significant eyes. He stressed each syllable:

"The altar."

Then added with calm matter-of-factness that a great wooden altar must be set up, in the centre of the camp, as the holy place for prayer, the service of God.

Towards five o'clock—the sun was high by now—Gabriel came into Juliette's room on the top story. He found there a number of people who had sat up all night with Madame Bagradian. Stephan, for all his mother's commands and entreaties, had not gone to bed. Now he lay on the sofa, fast asleep. Juliette had spread out a rug over him. She was standing leaning out of the window, with her back to the people in the room. Everyone here gave the impression of being alone, apart from the others. Iskuhi stiffly sat by the sleeping Stephan. Hovsannah, Pastor Tomasian's wife, whose fears towards morning had driven her to the villa, sat sunk in an armchair, staring out at nothing. Mairik Antaram, less affected than any of the others by this night of alarums and excursions, listened at the open door to the buzz of voices from the council-room. But a man was also in the room. Monsieur Gonzague Maris had been keeping the ladies company all night and, although at the moment nobody noticed him, he seemed to be the only person present who was not lost in his own thoughts. His beautifully brushed hair shone in the sunlight, unruffled by either his vigil or these events. His observant, indeed alert, velvet eyes, under the blunt angle of their brows, strayed here and there among the women. He seemed to be reading every wish, as it passed across these haggard faces, in order, gallantly, to fulfil it.

Gabriel came a few steps nearer Juliette, but stopped and stared at Gonzague. "It's a fact, isn't it, that you have an American passport?"

A mocking, rather scornful twist crept across the lips of the young Greek. "Would you care to look at it, Monsieur? Or my registration papers as a journalist?"

His cool, slender fingers strayed to his pockets. Gabriel had ceased to notice him. He had hold of Juliette's hand. The hand was not cold, but the life had gone out of it, it was shamming dead. All the more vivacious, therefore, the eyes. There was in them a *va et vient,* an ebb and flow, as always at moments of conflict. Her nostrils quivered a little—a sign of resistance well known to Gabriel. For the first time in twenty-four hours a cloud of fatigue began to descend on him. He hesitated. Within him, hollowness and the void. They watched each other's eyes in a long scrutiny, man and woman. Where was Gabriel's wife? He could still feel her hand in his, like an object, like unyielding porcelain—but she herself had slipped away from him. How many days' marches and sea journeys away? But this time-devouring distance, longer and longer every second, not only increased from her to him, but from him to her. Here stood Juliette's tall and beautiful body, so near, so entirely a part of his. Every inch of it must remember his kisses, the long neck, the shoulders, the breasts, the knees and shins, the very toes. This body had born Stephan, had endured for the future of the Bagradians. And now?

He could scarcely recognize it. He had lost the image of its nakedness. It was like having forgotten one's name. But bad enough as it was to find some French lady standing here, with whom one had once had a liaison—this lady had become an enemy, she was on the other side, had a seat on the exterminators' councils, although she was herself an Armenian mother. Gabriel felt something huge and hard rise in his throat, without really noticing it. Only in the last half-second did he free himself of this choking sensation.

"No . . . that isn't possible . . . Juliette."

She put her head slyly on one side. "What isn't possible? What do you mean?"

He stared at the vivid colours outside the window, could distinguish no shapes. For several hours he had been making Armenian speeches, and French now crept back into his mind, outraged. He began, in a hesitant voice, in a hard, unusual accent, which seemed to set Juliette's nerves still more on edge: "I mean . . . you're right, I think . . . you mustn't be dragged into this. . . . Why should you? . . . You remember our talk that night? . . . You must get away. . . . You and Stephan."

She seemed to be weighing her words: "I remember exactly what we said . . . that time. . . . Unheard of as it is, I'm in this with you. . . . I said so, then." She had never used such a tone before, but that was a matter of indifference. She threw a reproachful glance at Hovsannah and Iskuhi, as though in them she recognized the responsible parties.

Gabriel passed his hand twice across his eyes. He was again the man and leader of last night. "There's a way out for you and Stephan. Not a safe or easy one. . . . But you've got a very strong will, Juliette."

A sharp, testing look came into her eyes. Roused wild beasts have such a look before they spring, in one long bound, away past a man or a danger into freedom. Perhaps, now, every impulse to flight was crouched, ready to spring, in Juliette.

229

But scarcely did Gabriel begin speaking when the glowering tension left her face; she became uncertain, dismayed, and sly.

"Gonzague Maris will be leaving us today or tomorrow," said Bagradian with the unanswerable decision of a leader. "He has an American passport. It's invaluable in circumstances like these. I'm sure, Maris, you won't refuse to get my wife and son into safety. You can take the hunting-trap. It's summer, and the roads in the valley are still passable. And I'll give you reserve wheels and all four horses. Kristaphor will go with you, as well as the coachman; those two can get away as your servants. Via Sanderan and El-Maghara it's only five or six hours to Arsus. I reckon you'll have to walk the horses most of the way. The fifteen English miles to the coast, from Arsus to Alexandretta, are a trifle, because you can trot for hours along the sandy beach. In Arsus, I believe, there's a small garrison. It won't be hard for Maris to frighten the onbashi there with his passport."

Kristaphor had come in to ask his master for orders. Gabriel turned to him sharply. "Kristaphor, is it possible to get to Arsus, via Alexandretta, in ten hours with the hunting-trap?"

The steward opened his eyes wide. "Effendi, that depends on the Turks."

Bagradian's voice grew sharper still. "I didn't ask you that, Kristaphor. What I really mean is: Would you trust yourself to get the hanum, my son, and this American gentleman to Alexandretta?"

Sweat stood out on the steward's forehead. He looked like an old man, although he was only forty. It was not quite clear what it was that moved him—fear of a hazardous adventure, or the sudden prospect of saving himself. His eyes strayed from Bagradian to Gonzague. At last a furtive look of wild joy came into them. But this he controlled at once, either out of respect for Bagradian or so as not to give himself away. "I could do it, Effendi. If the gentleman has a passport, the saptiehs won't be able to touch us."

After this explanation Gabriel sent Kristaphor back to the kitchen to prepare a copious breakfast for everyone. He continued his instructions to Maris. Unluckily there was no American consul in Alexandretta, only German and Austro-Hungarian vice-consuls. He had made inquiries some time previously about these two. The German was called Hoffmann, the Austrian, Belfante; they were both well-disposed European business men, who might be expected to do all they could to help. But since they were both Turkish allies, it would be necessary to use the greatest discretion.

"You'll have to make up some story . . . Juliette is a Swiss, who has lost her passport in a travelling accident. . . . The vice-consuls must get you a railway passport from the local military authorities. . . . In the next few days they'll be opening the branch line to Toprak Kaleh. . . . Hoffmann and Belfante will be sure to know whether the commandant can be bribed. If so, it'll be all right. . . ."

Gabriel had passed a great many sleepless nights thinking out these directions for escape—rejecting, altering, taking up again. There were various alternatives: one in the Aleppo direction, another to Beirut. Yet now his jerky indications sounded as though he had only just thought of them. Juliette stared; she seemed not to be understanding a single word he said.

"You must think out some plausible tale, Maris. . . . It won't be so easy to make them believe in the accident and the lost passport. . . . But that isn't the main thing. . . . Juliette . . . the main thing is that you, an obvious European, won't be suspected of belonging to us. And that in itself is enough to save you. . . . You'll be taken for an adventuress, or at worst for a spy. . . . There's certainly the danger of that. . . . You may be subjected to inconveniences and even perhaps have to suffer. But, after all, compared to what we're suffering here— it's scarcely worth mentioning. . . . You must keep the one main object before your eyes—a way out of this. Free yourself from this people under a curse, with whom you've got involved through no fault of your own."

With these words, which he brought out in a loud staccato, Gabriel's face suddenly lost its look of desperate strain. Juliette bent the upper half of her body a little backwards, an involuntary movement, which seemed to suggest that she was ready to do her husband's will. Gonzague Maris came a few steps nearer the couple—perhaps to suggest that, though he was ready, he did not want to force any decisions. All the others seemed to accentuate the stiff lifelessness of their attitudes, as if to mitigate their inconvenient presence at such a scene. Gabriel had regained his self-control.

"Troop trains are the only ones still running. You'll have to bribe the commandant of every section of the line. . . . They're usually old people, who've stuck to the old ways, and have nothing to do with Ittihad. . . . Once you're in the train, you'll have gained a good deal. . . . The hindrances will be frightful. . . . But every mile nearer Istanbul will improve matters. . . . And you'll get to Istanbul even if it takes you weeks. . . . Juliette, there you must go straight to Mr. Morgenthau. . . . You still remember him? . . . The American ambassador."

Gabriel felt in his pocket and drew out an envelope bearing a legal seal. This, too, his last will, he had for weeks been keeping ready for Juliette without her knowledge. He held it out, silently. But slowly she drew back her hands and put them away behind her back. Gabriel, with a slight tilt of his head, pointed through the window at Musa Dagh, which stood as though molten in the strong morning sunlight. "I must go up there. The work's beginning. . . . I'm afraid I shan't be able to get back today."

The outstretched hand, with its sealed letter, sank to his side. What kind of tears were these? . . . "And Juliette can't control them," marvelled Gabriel. "Is she crying about herself? Or about me? Is she saying good-bye?" He sensed her grief,

232

but could not recognize it. He glanced round quickly at the others, those silent ones, still scarcely venturing to breathe lest perhaps they influence this decision. Gabriel longed for Juliette, who was standing only a few paces away from him. He spoke clearly and urgently, like a man who must talk to the woman he loves, across foreign countries, into a telephone: "I've always known it would come, Juliette. . . . And yet I've never known it would come like this . . . between you and me."

Her answer came obscurely, drawn up out of depths, outraged, and not torn by any sob. "And so that's what you really thought of me!"

Nobody knew how long Stephan had been awake, nor how much he had clearly heard and understood of this conversation between his parents. Only Iskuhi suddenly stood up, in a startled movement. Juliette knew, and had often marvelled at the fact, that between Gabriel and her son there was a relationship as shy as it was profound. Stephan, usually eager and voluble, was mostly silent in Gabriel's presence, and Gabriel's manner with Stephan was also peculiarly reserved, serious, and sparing of words. Their long stay in Europe had obscured Asia, and yet not stifled it, in the souls of the two Bagradians. (In every house of the seven villages sons, no matter what their age, kissed their fathers' hands every morning and evening. There were even a few strict houses in which, at meals, the father was not waited on by his women, but by his eldest son. And, on his side, the father honoured his eldest in a fashion tenderly severe, in accordance with a very ancient tradition, since a son is the next step on the shimmering staircase of eternity.) True that, in the case of Stephan and Gabriel, this relationship had ceased to express itself in the ancient rituals prescribed; but it remained in a shyness which bound and separated them. Gabriel's attitude to his own father had been the same. He, too, in his father's presence, had always felt this constraint, this solemn shyness, so that he never dared a tender word or a caress. All the more shattering, therefore, the effect of the cry uttered now by Gabriel's son, as he realized that separation threatened them. He flung off the rug, rushed across to his father, and clung to him.

"No, no . . . Father . . . You mustn't send us away. I want to stay . . . stay with you!"

What was it that looked at the father out of his son's almond-shaped eyes? This was no longer a child whose life one arranges, but an adult impelled by his will and blood, a destiny fully shaped, no longer susceptible to moulding. He had grown and developed so much in the last few weeks. And yet this new perception did not exhaust the thing which his father encountered in Stephan's eyes. He dissuaded feebly: "What's coming, Stephan, won't be child's play."

Stephan's cry of alarm changed to a defiant challenge: "I want to stay with you, Father . . . I won't go away."

I, I, I! Jealous rage had hold of Juliette. Oh, these Armenians! How they stuck together! She herself had ceased to be there. Her child belonged to her, as much as to him! She wasn't going to lose him. Yet, if she stood up for her rights, she'd lose Stephan. She came a decisive, almost an enraged, step nearer father and son. She caught Stephan's hand to pull him towards her. But Gabriel knew only that Juliette had come to them. "And so that's what you really thought of me?" In that malicious question there had still lurked a hint of indecision. But this angry step was decisive for Gabriel. He drew wife and child within his embrace.

"May Jesus Christ be our help! Perhaps it's better this way." As he strove to calm himself with these words, he was invaded with a kind of dull horror, as though the Saviour he invoked had caused some door to shut against Stephan and Juliette. Before their embrace had achieved any real warmth and life, he let fall his arms, turned away, and left them. He stopped again in the doorway. "It goes without saying, Maris, you can have one of my horses for your journey."

Gonzague deepened his attentive smile. "I should accept your kindness most gratefully if I didn't have another request. I want you to allow me to share your life up on Musa Dagh. I've already talked it over with Krikor. He's been asking Ter Haigasun's permission for me, and he hasn't refused."

Bagradian considered this. "I suppose you realize that later on the best American passport won't help you in the least."

"I've lived here so long, Gabriel Bagradian, that I shouldn't find it easy to leave you all. And, besides, I'm a journalist, you know. I may never get another chance like this."

Something in Gonzague gave Bagradian a sense of hostility, repelled him even. He tried to think how to refuse the young man. "The only question is, will you ever get the chance of making any use of what you write?"

Gonzague answered not only Gabriel, but all the people in the room: "I've often found that I could rely on my intuition. And I feel almost certain that things will turn out all right for you in the end. It's only a feeling. But it's the kind of feeling I can trust." His alert velvet eyes glanced from Hovsannah to Iskuhi, from Iskuhi to Juliette, on whose face they rested. And Gonzague's eyes seemed to be asking Madame Bagradian if she didn't find his reasons convincing enough.

7

The Funeral of the Bells

For two days and nights Gabriel stayed up on the Damlayik.
Even on the first evening he had to send Juliette word not to
expect him. A variety of circumstances forced him to remain
so long on this mountain ridge. Suddenly the Damlayik had
ceased to be that idyllic mountain slope familiar to Gabriel,
first as a place on which to dream, intimate in spite of its
ruggedness, then as a strategic possibility. For the first time
it showed him its true, unvarnished face. Everything on earth,
not man alone, shows its reality only when we make demands
on it. So too the Damlayik. That after-glow of Paradise, those
solitudes whose laughing well-springs made them alive, had
vanished now off its wrinkled, forbidding aspect. The defence
terrain chosen by Gabriel comprised a surface area of several
square kilometres. This surface, as far as the fairly level town
enclosure, was a difficult up-and-down of hills, depressions,
knolls, and gullies, which roughly made one aware of its in-
equalities once it was necessary to visit its various points many
times a day. Gabriel wanted to avoid the waste of time and
energy entailed in any not absolutely necessary descent into
the valley. All the same, he had never felt so toughly vigorous
in his whole life. His body, too, now that unsparing demands
were being made on it, showed him both what he was and
of what he was capable. By comparison the weeks he had
spent as a front-line soldier in the Balkan war seemed slack
and boring. In those days one had been mere human material,
to be pushed forward under fire, seemingly by some natural

236

force, or to drift back in the same constant danger, with the same will-less passivity. In the last few years Gabriel had often suffered from stomach trouble and palpitations. These derangements of a pampered body were now as though blown away by a single breath of necessity. He no longer knew that he had a heart or a stomach, and simply did not notice the fact that three hours' sleep on, or under, a blanket fully sufficed him, that a roll and some kind of tinned food stilled his hunger for the whole day. But, even though he thought very little about it, this proof that he was really a strong man filled him with a glow of pride. It was the pride which tingles through our substance only when our minds have defeated it.

His was occupied with much else. Most of those men intended as fighters had already forgathered on the mountain, together with a few of the stronger women and a few half-grown boys to be used as workers. All the rest had been shrewdly kept in the valley. There daily life was to seem to be going on quietly as usual, so that no rumour should spread of deserted villages. And these villagers had undertaken the task of getting as many stores as possible up the mountain in the dead of night. These could not all be loaded on to mules. The long beams and struts of old Tomasian's workshop, for instance, had to be carried up on their own shoulders by his apprentices. This wood was to build the altar, the government hut, and the hospital. The younger of the people's representatives, above all Pastor Tomasian and the teachers, were needed by Gabriel on the Damlayik, while the General Council, under Ter Haigasun, continued its business in the valley.

At that time there were about five hundred men encamped on the Damlayik. With the shock troops and élite, it was a question not only of spurring on this work to the exhaustion point, but of fanning to higher and higher flame the passionate fighting-spirit already in them. When at night with exhausted bodies they gathered round the fires in the town enclosure, Pastor Aram, in long exhortations—which had, however, little of the sermon in them—would explain the real meaning of this resistance. He proclaimed the divine right of self-defence, spoke of the mysterious way of blood which Armenians have trodden all through the ages—of the value of this one brave attempt, as an example which might fire their whole people to resist and so save itself. He described all the cruelty of the convoys, all he had himself seen or heard described, giving such atrocities as an instance of the way in which these thousands of villagers would have been certain to perish in the end, and, with equal conviction, he kept assuring them that the great deed in which they were united was a certain way to freedom and victory. To be sure, he was never very explicit as to how they were to gain their victorious liberty. Nor did anyone ask him. The very sound of his stormy words was enough to fire the blood of the young men; the meanings behind them mattered less.

Sometimes Gabriel spoke instead of the pastor. He was less rhetorical, more exact. They must never, he urged them, waste a second, eat one unnecessary mouthful; must concentrate every pulse-beat on the one aim. Let them think less of inevitable misfortune than of the sorry pain and degradation with which the Turks were befouling their Armenian subjects. "If once we manage to drive them down off the mountain, we shan't have merely wiped off this insult, we shall have humbled and dishonoured the Turks for ever. Because we're the weak, and they're the strong. They despise us as a set of merchants and always boast of being soldiers. If we beat them once, we shall have poisoned their self-esteem and given them a lesson they'll never get over."

Whatever Gabriel and Aram may really have been thinking at this time, they insisted again and again on the glorious outcome of resistance, hammering fanatical belief and, more important still, fanatical discipline, into young, impressionable minds.

No more than Gabriel had ever been aware that he possessed

an iron constitution, had he suspected his gifts as an organizer. In the milieux in which he had so far lived "sound practical sense" had always connoted limited and acquisitive thinking. Therefore he had striven all too successfully to be on the side of the unpractical. But now, thanks to preliminary work, he succeeded in the first few hours in building up the most feasible division of his army into skeleton "cadres," into which reinforcements from the valley could very easily be incorporated. He built up three main divisions: a fighting-formation; a big reserve; and a cohort of youth, for all half-grown lads of from thirteen to fifteen, only to be used as a last resort in case of very heavy losses on a harassed front, but otherwise to act as scouts, observation corps, and liaison runners. The full strength of this front line of defence worked out at eight hundred and sixty men. This, not including the less fit, the totally unfit, and a certain number of the most indispensable "experts," comprised all the men from sixteen to sixty. All others, elderly men still able to work and a certain proportion of girls and women, were lumped together as reserve—so that his second strength was somewhere between a thousand and eleven hundred. The third branch, the scouting-brigade of his cohort of youth, the cavalry of the Damlayik, consisted of over three hundred boys. On the second day Gabriel sent his adjutant Avakian down to the valley to fetch Stephan. He was not certain that Juliette would let him go so easily. But the student punctually returned with a radiant Stephan at his heels, to be enrolled at once as a scout by his father. Of the eight hundred and sixty men of his main defence, it is true that not more than three hundred could be armed with what infantry rifles they had. Most, unfortunately, had either ordinary hunting-guns or the romantic flint-locks to be found in nearly every house in the villages.

Gabriel had ordered every gun from his brother's chests that was in any sort of working order, to be distributed. Luckily most of the men, not only those who had served as Turkish conscripts, knew how to handle a rifle. Yet, for all that, the main defence was lamentably armed. Four platoons of regular infantry, even without the usual machine-gun, would have been a far superior force. The most essential part of the defence had naturally not been thought of as one vaguely uniform mass; Gabriel had split it up strategically into definite sections of ten men each, that is to say, minute battalions, which could be moved and disposed independently. He had also taken care that each of these decads should be composed of men of the same village, if possible of the same family, so that comradeship might be as strongly cemented as possible.

The command presented greater difficulties, since one in each of these ten must be given authority, just as the bigger units must have their commanders. Gabriel chose these leaders from among men of various ages who had seen service. The invaluable Chaush Nurhan undertook the business of general, chief ordnance officer, fortress engineer, and sergeant-major all in one. The twisted ends of his grey, wiry moustache bristled, the huge Adam's apple on his stringy throat worked up and down. Nurhan seemed heartily grateful to the Turks for having arranged a few deportations and so provided his opportunity, so passionate was the zeal with which he hurled himself on military duties so long forgone. For hours he drilled those men who were not at work, without once resting or letting them rest. He had the notion, with the help of Armenian quick-wittedness, of working in a few days through the whole Turkish drill-book, as laid down for an infantry-training of several years. His main preoccupations were fighting-manœuvres, heads "up" and "down," quick entrenchments, the use of terrain, and storm attack. He was disgusted with Bagradian for having forbidden any rifle practice, even though it was most understandable, and not merely to save munitions. Elderly as Nurhan was, he raced from one drilling company to the next, instructing each platoon instructor, shouting and raving in the bluest of barrack-room

Turkish. Armed to the teeth with sword, army revolver, rifle, cartridge-belt, he had also slung on the infantry bugle, scrounged from a quartermaster's store, and used its kicking, strutting bugle-calls at any instant to rally his men. A startled Gabriel hurried the whole long way from the north ridge to the drilling-ground to put a firm stop to these reckless tootings. Was it absolutely necessary, he asked, to give the saptiehs and Mohammedan villages of the neighbourhood strident warnings of manœuvres on the Damlayik?

During the first day all the deserters on Musa Dagh had begun to join forces with the garrison. In the course of the next few days their number increased to the very respectable figure of sixty. Nurhan's bugle seemed to have rallied these lads from the hills around, from Ahmer Dagh and the barren Jebel el Akra. To Gabriel, although they were well armed, they were welcome, yet unwelcome, reinforcements. There could be no doubt that this pitiful mob contained not only the usual recalcitrants—cowards, bullied men, haters of discipline —but sinister elements, fellows with as much to fear from the civil authorities as the military. There were crooks among them, who spuriously assumed the deserter's halo, whose real profession was that of foot-pad, who seemed to have come, not from any barracks in Antakiya, Aleppo, or Alexandretta, but from the jail at Payas. It was hard to distinguish sheep from goats in this reinforcement of sixty-odd, since all looked equally scared, shy, famished. It was not surprising that they should, since day and night they had had to keep a look-out for gendarmes and could never venture down into the villages before two or three in the morning to beg a crust from their scared compatriots. The skeletons of these deserters— they could scarcely any longer be said to have bodies—were hung with the rags of desert-hued uniforms. What still was visible of their faces, under a matted growth of hair and bristle, was tanned almost black with sun and dirt. Their Armenian eyes expressed not only the general pain, but with it a peculiar agony, the sullen pain of the shady outcast slowly sinking back to the level of beasts. The pack looked as though humanity had cut it off. Only to the deserter Sarkis Kilikian, whom they called "the Russian," was this inapplicable, outwardly at least, though he of them all seemed the most irrevocably cut off from the safety of the human family. Gabriel recognized him at once as the ghost which had risen that night in "Three-Tent Square." The problem of enrolling these sixty vagrants without imperilling the gradually forming discipline of the rest was one that could not be solved immediately. For the present, in spite of their disillusioned grimaces, they were sent to drill under the iron supervision of Chaush Nurhan, who made them sweat for their keep through the very same drill-book, to avoid which they had escaped. More essential even than Nurhan's drilling was the other task of these wildly industrious days—the building and digging of fortifications. The blue and brown lines marked by Gabriel on Avakian's map were being changed into realities. Since for the time being the Damlayik had more hands than spades, shifts of diggers were formed. Bagradian's eventual aim was to use only the reserve for labour—that is to say, the eleven hundred men and women who would not be at their posts unless there was fighting, and whose task would otherwise be all the necessary work of the camp. But these people were still down in the villages.

By Gabriel's reckoning there were thirteen different points at which the Damlayik could be threatened. The most open point of attack was in the north, that narrow indentation he called the North Saddle, which separated the Damlayik from the other portions of Musa Dagh which lay dispersed in the Beilan direction. The second, but far more vulnerable, spot was the wide path above Yoghonoluk up through the ilex grove. Further danger zones on the western extremities of the mountain resembled this in a lesser degree, wherever, in fact, the slopes became less steep, and where flocks and herdsmen had trodden out a natural track. The only points of differentiation were the strong, towering rocks to the south, the "South Bastion" of the map, which dominated the broad, stony slopes rising out of the plain of the Orontes in abrupt, terraced ridges. Down in the plain stood the remnants of a fallen human world, the fields of Roman ruins of Seleucia. These stony leavings of a civilization crashed to earth aped the southern flank of the mountain, with its tier upon tier of heaps of stone. Under Samuel Avakian's supervision and Bagradian's precise directions two fairly high walls composed of great blocks of stone had been put up, not only on this rocky incline itself, but right and left of it. The student marvelled that such complete walls should be thought necessary for the mere purposes of cover. His strategic insight was still very imperfect in those days, and he seldom understood his master's intentions. But the hardest work was that demanded in the north, the most vulnerable point of the defence. Gabriel Bagradian himself worked at the long trench— several hundred paces long—with all its chevrons and supports. In the west it was backed by the rocky confusion of the side overlooking the sea, which, with all its obstacles, natural entrenchments, caverns, formed a labyrinthine fortress. Eastwards Bagradian strengthened his entrenchments with outposts and tree-entanglements. It was lucky that the greater part of this terrain should have been composed of soft soil. Yet the spades kept jarring against big blocks of limestone and dolomites, which impeded the progress of the work so that they could scarcely hope to complete these trenches in less than four working days. While muscular diggers, aided by a few peasant women, turned up the soil, boys with sickles and knives felled the scrubby undergrowth at certain points in front of the trench, that the fire-zones might be unimpeded. Bagradian stayed there all day, supervising. He kept running up to the indentation and the counter-slope of the saddle to make sure, from every conceivable angle, that the trench was

243

being properly dug. He gave orders that the thrown-up earth was always to be flattened into the soil again. His whole aim was to assure himself that this wide groove should be fully camouflaged, that the thick-shrubbed slope along which it ran should seem to be still untouched by human hands. When it is remembered that, aside from the reserve trench in the next wave of ground, there were still to be completed twelve smaller positions, Bagradian's stubborn concentration here must have filled every intelligent observer with anxiety.

It was evening. Gabriel lay on the earth exhausted, staring at the uncompleted altar-frame, which looked to him disproportionately high. Then, in his half-sleep, he noticed that he himself was being stared at. Sarkis Kilikian, the deserter! The man was probably his junior, perhaps scarcely thirty years old. Yet he had the sharp, emaciated look of a man of fifty. The skin of his face, livid for all its tan, seemed to be tightly, thinly stretched over a sardonic skull. His features appeared less to be hollowed out by endurance than by life itself, lived to its very last dregs. Sated—satiated with life, that was the word! Though his uniform was just as tattered as those of the other deserters, it gave an impression of elegance run wild, or of elegant wildness. This was mainly due to the fact that he alone of them all was clean-shaven, and shaven freshly and closely. Gabriel felt a chill and sat up. He thrust a cigarette at the man. Kilikian took it without a word, pulled out some kind of barbarous tinder-box, struck sparks which, after many vain attempts, at last set light to a strip of tow, and began to smoke with a jaded indifference which seemed to suggest that Bagradian's expensive cigarette was his usual brand. Now they were both staring in silence again, Gabriel with increasing discomfort. The Russian never turned his indifferent, and yet scornful, eyes away from Bagradian's white hands.

Gabriel at last could bear it no longer. He stormed: "Well, what do you want?"

Sarkis Kilikian blew out a thick cloud of smoke, not changing one nuance of his expression. The worst of it was that he still kept his eyes on Gabriel's hands. He seemed lost in profound reflections upon a world in which such white, undamaged hands could exist. At last he opened his lipless mouth, disclosing decayed, blackened teeth. His deep voice had less hate in it than his words: "Not the thing for such a fine gentleman."

Bagradian sprang to his feet. He tried to think of a sharp, effective answer. To his deep discomfort he could not find one. The Russian, slowly turning his back on him, said, half to himself, with a fairly good French accent: "*On verra ce qu'on pourra durer.*"

That night, round the campfire, Gabriel made several inquiries about Sarkis Kilikian. The man had been well known for several months in the whole district round Musa Dagh. He was not one of the local deserters, and yet the saptiehs seemed especially eager to track him down. In this connexion Shatakhian told Gabriel the Russian's history. Since, as a general thing, the schoolmasters in the seven villages were a highly imaginative set, Bagradian almost suspected that Shatakhian was piling up horrors of his own invention to spice his story. But Chaush Nurhan was sitting beside him, nodding grave assent to every detail. Chaush Nurhan was in bad odour in the neighbourhood, as a special patron of deserters and the intimate knower of their ways. And he at least was not suspiciously imaginative.

SARKIS KILIKIAN had been born in Dört Yol, a large village in the plain of Issus, north of Alexandretta. Before he had quite completed his eleventh year, massacres on the classic pattern arranged by Abdul Hamid had broken out in Anatolia and Cilicia. They fell out of a cloudless sky. Kilikian's father had been a watchmaker and goldsmith, a quiet little man who set great store by civilized living and on having his five children well brought up. Since he was well-to-do, he intended Sarkis, his eldest, for a priest, and would have sent him to one of the seminaries. On that black day for Dört Yol, Watchmaker Kilikian shut his shop early, at midday. But that did not help him since, scarcely had he sat down to dinner, when a band of roughs came thundering on the shop door. Madame Kilikian, a tall, yellow-haired woman from the Caucasus, had just brought on the dishes when her white-faced husband left the table to unlock his shop again. The few minutes of timeless experience that followed this will still be part of Sarkis Kilikian's being for as long as a created soul must remain itself through all migrations and metamorphoses within the universe. He ran out after his father into the shop, which by now was crowded with men. A picturesque storm troop of His Majesty the Sultan's Hamidiyehs. The leader of this band of storm troopers was a young man with a rosy face, the son of a minor official. The most noticeable things about this rather portly young Turk were the many strange medals and decorations strewn here and there about his tunic. Whereas the solemn, matter-of-fact Kurds at once proceeded to get down to business, carefully emptying out the contents of drawers into their bags, this spruce and dauntless son of a petty official seemed to view his mission in its purely political aspect. His loutishly juvenile face glowed with conviction as he bellowed at the watchmaker: "You are a usurer and a money-lender. All Armenian swine are usurers and money-lenders. You unclean giaours are responsible for the wretchedness of our people."

Master Kilikian pointed quietly to his work-table, with its magnifying-glass, pincers, little wheels, and springs. "Why do you call me a money-lender?"

"All this here is lies which you use to hide your bloodsucking."

Their discussion did not get any further, since shots cracked out in the low, narrow room. For the first time in his life little

Sarkis smelt the narcotic reek of gunpowder. He did not at first in the least understand what had happened as he saw his father, bending over his table to his work, pull it down on to the floor with him. Without a word Sarkis flitted back to the parlour. His yellow-haired mother stood drawn up, with her back to the wall, not daring to breathe. Her hands, right and left, were clutching her small daughters, two and four years old. Her eyes were fixed on the basket-cradle containing her baby. The seven-year-old Mesrop was staring greedily at the appetizing mutton kebab, which still stood peacefully smoking on the table. But when the armed men came crowding in on them, Sarkis had already seized the dish and hurled it, steaming, in one desperate jerk, straight into the leader's plump, rosy face. That dauntless youth ducked with a howl of pain, as though he had been hit by a hand-grenade. Brown gravy streamed all down his resplendent tunic. The big, clay pitcher followed this first hit, with still better effect. The leader's nose had begun to bleed, but this did not prevent his urging on his men in an anguished bellow. Little Sarkis, armed with a carving-knife, stood in front of his mother to protect her. This miserable weapon in the hands of a boy of eleven was enough to decide the dauntless Hamidiyehs not to let it get as far as a hand-to-hand battle. One of them flung himself, swift and cowardly, on to the cradle, snatched out the screaming baby, and cracked its skull against the wall. Sarkis pressed his face into his mother's stiffening body. Strange, whispering sounds kept forcing their way through her tight-pressed lips. And then began the deafening crack and rattle of many revolver bullets, all emptied into a woman and four children, a salvo which should have been enough to set a whole regiment in retreat. The room was thick with fumes, the brutes aimed badly. It was of course predestined that not one of these bullets should hit Sarkis. The first to die was the seven-year-old Mesrop. The bodies of the two little girls hung limp in the hands of their mother, who did not let go of

247

them. Her full, round face was rigid and motionless. A bullet hit her right arm. Sarkis felt, through his back, the short, convulsive movement which she gave. Two more shots pierced her shoulders. She stood erect, still not letting go of her children. Only when two more had blown half her face away, did she topple forwards, bend over Sarkis, who still wanted to keep fast hold of her, pour out her mother's blood upon his hair, and bury him under her body. He lay still, under the warm, heavily breathing load of his mother, and never stirred. Only four more shots bespattered the wall.

The pudgy-faced leader felt he had done his duty. "Turkey for the Turks!" he crowed, though no one echoed his cry of victory.

While Sarkis lay protected, as in a womb, his senses were strangely alert. He could hear voices which made him conclude that the leader was behaving repulsively in a corner.

"Why are you doing that?" someone reproved. "There are dead people here."

But this fighter for the national principle refused to let himself be so balked. "Even as corpses they've still got to know that we're the masters, and they're dirt."

A profound quiet had been established before Sarkis, covered in blood, dared to creep out from under his mother. This movement seemed to bring Madame Kilikian back to consciousness. She had no recognizable face left. But the voice was hers, and so quiet: "Fetch me water, my child." The pitcher was broken. Sarkis stole out with a glass to the courtyard fountain. When he got back, she was still breathing but could neither drink nor speak again.

The boy was sent to live with some rich relations in Alexandretta. In twelve months he seemed to have got over it all, though he scarcely ate, and though nobody, not even these kindly foster-parents, could get him to say more than the most indispensable words. Teacher Shatakhian had precise information about all this, because this same Alexandretta family had

paid for his own stay in Switzerland. Later they sent Sarkis
to Ejmiadzin, in Russia, the largest theological college of the
Armenian nation. Pupils of this famous establishment could
aspire to the very highest offices of the Gregorian church. The
intellectual drill to which these students had to submit was
on the whole not so very rigorous. And yet, before the end
of his third school year, Sarkis Kilikian, in whom a savage,
a diseased, longing for freedom had slowly developed, ran
away from the seminary. He was almost eighteen when he
wandered the dirty lanes of Baku, possessed of only his shabby
seminary cassock and the appetite of several days. It did not
occur to him to apply to his foster-parents for funds. From the
day of his flight from Ejmiadzin, these good people lost all
track of their protégé. Sarkis Kilikian had now no choice but
to look for work. He got the only work of which there was
plenty in Baku, servitude in the huge oil-fields along the bare
coasts of the Caspian Sea. There, in a very few months,
through the effects of oil and natural gases, his skin turned
yellow and shrivelled-looking. His body dried up, like a dead
tree. Considering his nature and his book-learning, it is not
surprising that he should have become involved in the social-
revolutionary movement, which in those days was beginning
to take hold of the workers of the Russian Near East: Geor-
gians, Armenians, Tatars, Turkomans, and Persians. Though
the Tsar's government did its best to egg on these various
peoples against each other, it did not succeed in breaking
their solidarity against the oil kings. From year to year strikes
became more widespread and successful. In one of them Cos-
sack provocation led to fearful bloodshed. The reply to this
was the assassination of the district governor, a Prince Galitzin,
come on a tour of inspection. Among those accused of conspir-
ing this was Sarkis Kilikian. Almost nothing could be proved
against him judicially. He had neither made speeches nor
"worked underground." No one could give definite evidence
against him. But "escaped seminarists" were a class apart—it

bred the most stubborn agitators. That alone was enough. Sarkis strayed, for life, into the convict prison of Baku.

He would certainly have died off soon enough in that den of filth and disease, had fate not had more cunning benefits in store for him. The murdered Galitzin was succeeded by a Prince Vorontsov. This new, unmarried governor was later joined by his sister, also celibate, in the government residence at Baku. Princess Vorontsova bore her virginity with iron self-abnegation. Energetic and full of the best intentions, she was in the habit of instituting in every government district to which her brother was appointed a unique mission of reform. Those who are relentless with themselves are apt to be equally so with others, and so in time this exalted lady had developed into a veritable sadist of neighbourly love. Her devout eye, wherever she might happen to be, was first directed upon the prisons. The greatest poets of the Russian land had taught that the nearest thing to the kingdom of God is often a den of thieves. In the prisons it was usually the young "intellectuals" and "politicals" who aroused her zeal. Along with other selected convicts Sarkis Kilikian was now marched off every morning to an empty barracks where, in accordance with Irene Vorontsova's curriculum, and under her active co-operation, his spiritual healing was briskly attempted. Partly it consisted in strenuous gymnastic exercises, partly in a series of moral lectures. The princess saw in this young Armenian the attractive child of Satan himself. It was worth while fighting for such a soul! So that she herself took a hand in disciplining him. When that dried-up satanic body had been broken in by several hours of exhausting drill to the bridle-rein of salvation, the soul was led out to grass. To her great delight she was soon able to note the amazing pace at which Kilikian came cantering down the paths of virtue. Her hours with this taciturn Lucifer produced in her, too, a feeling of divine illumination. At nights she dreamed of the next few pages of the catechism. And, of course, so apt a pupil must be rewarded. She procured him more and more special privileges. It began by their taking him out of irons and ended by his being moved from prison into a small, empty room in barracks. Unfortunately he did not long make use of his privileges. By the third morning after his removal he had disappeared—and so, by one more bitter experience, enriched Princess Vorontsova's knowledge of how hard it is to fight the devil.

But where can one escape to from the Russian Caucasus? To the Turkish Caucasus. It was not a month before Kilikian had to admit that he had acted rashly in exchanging Paradise for hell. When, half famished, he tried to find a job in Erzerum, the police soon had him in charge. Since he had neither come up for inspection nor paid his bedel, the local magistrate soon condemned him to three years' hard labour as a deserter. Scarcely had a Russian jail released him when a Turkish one offered him hospitality. In the jail of Erzerum the inscrutable moulder of our destinies put his last touch upon Kilikian. He was invested there with that enigmatic indifference, sensed by Bagradian in the ghost outside "Three-Tent Square," an "indifference" which the word itself can only suggest, without expressing it. They let him out in the last months before war was declared. Though the army doctor marked him unfit for service, Kilikian was promptly enrolled among the recruits of an Erzerum infantry regiment. The life he led in it bore some remote resemblance to a human life. It also proved that his outwardly weedy body had reserves of inexhaustible toughness. And army life, in spite of all its restraints, seemed in a way to suit Kilikian. His regiment in that first winter of the war did its share in Enver Pasha's memorable Caucasus campaign, in the course of which that pretty war god not only used up a whole army corps, but was himself almost taken by the Russians. The division which covered the staff's retreat, and so saved Enver's liberty and life, was composed almost entirely of Armenians. It was an Armenian who bore that Supreme Commander on his back

251

out of the line. (When Shatakhian placed Sarkis among these Armenians, Gabriel, who suspected him of embellishment, glanced inquiringly at Chaush Nurhan; but the old man nodded with measured seriousness.) But, whether or no Kilikian fought with these brave men, Enver Pasha's gratitude, at least to the whole nation to which Kilikian belonged, had soon expressed itself. Scarcely had Private Kilikian's frostbites begun to heal—scarcely, that is to say, had he moved his army blanket from the brick floor of a very congested hospital to the brick floor of an equally congested barrackroom—when the War Minister's order was read out to them. It thrust all Armenians out of their companies in disgrace, disarmed them, degraded them to the rank of inshaat taburi, the despised labour battalions. They were herded together from every hole and corner, their rifles taken, and they themselves sent in wretched droves south-west, to the hilly neighbourhood of Urfa. There, starved, and threatened at every turn with the bastinado, they were set to work heaving blocks of stones for a road that was being built in the Aleppo direction. A special order forbade them to protect themselves with carrying-wads against the jagged edges of their loads, though in the very first grilling hours of work their necks and shoulders streamed with blood. Whereas all the rest groaned and complained, Sarkis went stumbling in silence from quarry to road, road to quarry, as though his body had long ago forgotten what pain meant. One day the captain summoned all the men of the inshaat taburi, among whom, by chance or as a punishment, there happened to be a few Mohammedans. They were told off from the rest. But this unarmed herd of Armenians was marched under the escort of an officer about an hour's distance from its quarters into a pleasant valley, tapering between two low hills. "Those are the hills of Charmelik," an innocent happened to remark, who came from these parts and was thankful for the day's freedom. But on the gentle slopes of this valley more awaited them than thyme

252

and rosemary, orchids and pimpernels and melissa—strangely enough, they found themselves facing an armed platoon. They suspected nothing. They were ordered to form up in one long rank along the hillside—and still did not suspect. Then, suddenly, without ceremony or preparation of any kind, the platoon on their right wing opened fire. Cries filled the air, less of fear than boundless amazement. (A woman among the listeners here interrupted Teacher Shatakhian: "Can God, among His angels, forget those screams?" She began to sob and only with difficulty controlled herself.) Sarkis Kilikian was clever enough to fall with the others. The bullets zipped over him. For the second time he escaped a Turkish death. He lay on, among corpses and helplessly dying men, till it should be dark. But, long before dusk this flowery valley, consecrated to the practical application of Enver Pasha's national policy, was visited a second time. The corpse dismantlers of the neighbourhood were anxious not to waste any government property still worn by these "executed" men. They had a special eye on sound pairs of army boots. As they quietly worked they kept grunting out one of those songs inspired by the recent decree of banishment. It began with the onomatopœic line: "Kessé kessé sürür yarlara."—"Killing, killing, we rout them out." They came to Kilikian's boots. He kept his legs stiff, almost to cracking-point, to imitate rigor mortis. The pilferers tugged—cursed—if it had been a little harder than it was, they might easily have hacked off his feet to save themselves trouble. But at last even these industrious fellows departed, with another song on their lips: "Hep gitdi, hep bitdi!"—"All away, all away!" In that night Kilikian began his monstrous wanderings. His days were spent in many hiding-places; at night he strayed along unknown paths, over steppes and marshy ground. He lived on nothing, that is to say, on what grew everywhere out of the earth. Very seldom did he venture into a hamlet to knock in the dark at the door of an Armenian house. Truly it was proved

253

beyond doubt that Sarkis had a devil's body, superhumanly strong. The skeleton cased in leather that he was managed not to perish on the roads but reached Dört Yol in the first days of April. Without caring about the danger Kilikian went straight to his father's house, out of which weeping people had led him twenty years ago. The house had remained faithful to his father's trade; a watchmaker and goldsmith was living in it. The well-known sounds of filing and tapping came from the shop. Sarkis went in. The frightened watchmaker was already trying to hustle him out when he gave his name, whereupon the new owner consulted his family. The deserter got a bed in the same parlour where the horror had been. After twenty years there were still bullet-marks on the wall. Kilikian stayed two days in this place of refuge. Meanwhile the watchmaker had procured him a rifle and some cartridges. When they asked if there was anything else they could do for him, he begged only to be given a razor, before vanishing through the·dark again. A few nights later he met two other deserters, in the village of Gomaidan. They seemed reliable and experienced in the ways of life. They recommended Musa Dagh as a good and safe place on which to hide.

That is the story of Sarkis Kilikian, "the Russian," as it emerged from Teacher Shatakhian's account, Chaush Nurhan's assenting silences, and the occasional comments and additions of other listeners, and as it was formed and reflected in Bagradian's sensitive mind. The European could only marvel and be aghast at the fateful burden of such a destiny and at the strength which had not broken down under it. But this respect was tinged with horror and the desire to see as little as possible of this victim of jails and barrack-squares. That night, after long consultation with Chaush Nurhan, Gabriel decided to assign the Russian and the other deserters to the defence of the "South Bastion." It was the strongest part of his whole defence, and also the farthest from camp.

On the third morning they all went back to the villages. Only a few dependable sentries stayed on the Damlayik with the stores and munitions. Ter Haigasun himself had given the order. The saptiehs, come to look for arms, must find no empty or half-empty houses. Any noticeable absence of young men could have been masked neither by Pastor Nokhudian's band of the devout in Bitias nor by a part of the people left in the valley for that purpose. Bagradian had expected the priest to give this order. Perhaps it had also an educational intention concealed in it. The young men of Musa Dagh, who so far knew of atrocities only by hearsay, must now come face to face with the living reality; their subsequent fight must be to the last point of desperation.

At the exact hour foretold by Ali Nassif the saptiehs entered Yoghonoluk, about a hundred strong. There was obvious contempt in this. The authorities had sent a handful of men to clear a considerable district. The Armenian sheep would be certain not to put up a fight when led to the slaughter. The few instances to the contrary, so welcome to the government, proved nothing. How could a weak, mercantile people hope to stand up to the warrior race? The answer to this question was the hundred gendarmes detailed for Yoghonoluk. But these were no longer stout assassins in the genre of Abdul Hamid. No more trusty, pock-marked faces, whose loyally menacing wink had often indicated that a quid pro quo would make them easier to deal with. Now it was plain, inhuman cruelty—quite single-minded. These saptiehs did not, like their predecessors, wear lousy lambskin bonnets, nor the trumped-up uniforms, composed of a tunic and nondescript mufti, of the good old days. They were all clothed in the same yellowish-brown field uniform recently issued. Round their heads, in the manner of bedouins, they had bound the long, trailing sun- and sweat-cloths, which gave them an unmistakable aspect of Egyptian sphinxes. They arrived in regular formation, not marching perhaps with the true

255

mechanical step of the West, but still, no longer in the uneven roll of the East. Ittihad had exercised its power even on
these Antioch saptiehs, so far from Istanbul. The sporadic
flames of religious hatred and fanaticism had been skilfully
fanned to the cold, steady flare of nationalism. The deportation
squad was commanded by the muafin, the police chief of
Antioch. The young müdir with the pink, lashless eyes and
freckled hands came with it. The men, whose arrival had long
been heralded, came swinging at midday into the church
square of Yoghonoluk. Strident Turkish bugle-calls resounded,
and drums were tapped. But in spite of these commanding
admonitions, the Armenians still remained indoors. Ter
Haigasun had issued the strictest orders to all seven villages
that people must show themselves as little as possible, must
avoid all crowding together, and walk into no provocative
traps. The müdir read out his long decree of banishment to
a public consisting of saptiehs, a number of stragglers with the
troops, and the closed windows of the church square. This
order was at the same time posted up in several places on
the church walls, on the council house, and on the school
building. After which administrative measure the saptiehs,
since now it was dinner-time, encamped where they stood, lit
fires, and began to cook up their kettles of fuhl, broad beans
with mutton fat. Then, squatting and chewing, as with flat
cakes of bread they scooped up their portion of the stew,
they looked round them idly. What well-built houses! And
all made of stone, with firm roofs and carved wooden verandas! Rich people, these Armenians—rich everywhere! At
home in their own villages they were thankful when the roofs
of their hovels, black with age, did not give way under the
many storks' nests. And the church of these unclean pigs
was as massive and imposing as a fort—with all its angles
and buttresses. Ah, well, Allah was about to pay them back
something for their pride! They've had a finger in everything,
haven't they—governed in Istanbul, raked in the money like

a harvest. Other people had had to put up with anything, till at last even the sleepiest patience gave out. Not even the müdir and the muafin could conceal their interest in the splendours of this village square. Perhaps, for the space of half a second the police chief felt the insecurity of a barbarian confronted with a superior civilization. But then he boiled with redoubled hatred, remembering Talaat Bey's famous words, quoted again by the Kaimakam as they mustered to set out: "Either they disappear, or we do."

The quiet, which in spite of many soldiers lay over this square, was odd and unnatural. Nor was it broken perceptibly by the presence of a certain number of roughs, who had joined the saptiehs on their way. The off-scourings of Antakiya and the bigger villages on its outskirts poured their dregs into the valley of seven villages. On bare, dirt-caked feet the scum came pattering—from Mengulye, Hamblas, and Bostan. From Tumama, Shahsini, Ain Yerab, and, further still, from Beled es Sheikh. Eyes of unbridled covetousness darted up and down the houses. Arab peasants from the El-Akra mountains in the south waited, quietly squatting on their heels, on the fat event. Even a little group of Ansariyes had come along—the lowest pariahs of the prophet, nationless half-Arab mobs of underlings, waiting to make the most of this rare chance of feeling superior to somebody. There were also a few Mohajirs, even now; war refugees sent by the government to the interior and invited cordially to indemnify themselves with Armenian property. And, with such simple plebeians, strange to relate, a ring of heavily veiled ladies, in a half-circle of glowing timidity. There could be no doubt that they came of the better classes. It could be seen by a glance at the costly material of the cloaks drawn down over their faces, the texture of their veils, the tiny mules or lacquered slippers which embellished their braceleted feet. These women were the avid clients of the bargain sale about to begin, and they waited impatiently. For weeks the whisper had gone the rounds of the women's

257

quarters of Suedia and El Eskel: "Oh, haven't you heard? These Christians have the most marvellous things in their houses, things we've never so much as heard of—far too expensive to buy."—"Have you ever been inside an Armenian house, dear?"—"I? No. But the mullah's wife has been telling me all about it. You'll find cupboards and cabinets with little towers on the top of them and pillars and crowns. And you'll find very few sleeping-mats of the kind you lock away in the daytime, but lots of real beds with carved flowers and forbidden carved children's heads on them, beds for husband and wife as big as a wali's carriage. You'll find clocks with gold eagles sitting on them, or cuckoos jumping out of their insides and calling."—"Well, there's another proof that they're traitors, otherwise how could they ever get furniture from Europe?" But it was just such household gear as this that so powerfully attracted these ladies, to whom beautifully wrought brass dishes, woven carpets, and copper braziers meant nothing.

The weird stillness was suddenly broken. The police chief, for some time eager for a victim, had thrown himself on a villager imprudent enough to come to his house door. The man was thrust into the middle of the square. This police constable's face was characterized by two entirely different eyes. His right eye was large and staring, the left little and nearly closed up. His military moustache might threaten as fiercely as it liked, his chin protrude itself as murderously—his unequal eyes condemned this police chief to a role of ferocious comicality, of comic ferocity. Since he was always conscious of this defect, his fear of making himself ridiculous caused him to exaggerate the authoritative side of his personality. Therefore, though already by nature a bully, he had also to play the bully's part. His staring eye did its best to roll, as he bellowed at the captured villager:

"What's your priest called? What's the name of your mukhtar?"

The villager whispered an answer. The next minute a hundred voices were shouting across the square: "Hullo, Haigasun! Come out of your hiding-place! Come on out, Kebussyan. Out with you, Haigasun and Kebussyan!"

Ter Haigasun had awaited the summons inside the church. After the holiday mass, without having taken off his vestments, he had remained kneeling before the altar with his deacons. He intended to face the saptiehs in the glamour and sublimity of his office. This intention was entirely characteristic. There was more in it than an empty gesture of ceremony, there was a keenly psychological object. Every Oriental is filled with sensations of holy awe by ceremonious pageantry and the splendour of religious vestments. Ter Haigasun reckoned that his appearance as a fully vested priest would mitigate the saptiehs' brutality. Slowly, in purple and gold, he emerged from the doorway of his church. On his head sparkled the tall Gregorian mitre, in his right hand he bore the doctor's wand of the Armenian rite. And in fact this consecrated figure served to dampen the spirits of the police chief, whose brutal voice lost some of its certainty.

"You're the priest. You'll be answerable to me for everything that happens. Everything! You understand?"

Ter Haigasun inclined his bloodless face in answer. In the strong sunlight it looked like carved amber. He bowed his head and did not answer. The head constable felt himself in danger of being polite—that is to say, of becoming slack. His left, swollen eye had started to twitch. These two sensations filled him with rising irritation. It was high time to remind the müdir, his saptiehs, and this priest of his own pulverizing authority. So with clenched fists he bore down on Ter Haigasun but found that he had to halt in an uneasy posture of respect. All the more, therefore, did his voice feel obliged to spread consternation, the due effect of his own authoritative person.

"You'll deliver up all your weapons—all of them! You understand? You can look like a bazaar juggler all you want, but you're personally responsible for every knife there is in the village."

"We have no weapons in the village."

This was perfectly true. Ter Haigasun spoke very quietly and steadily. Meanwhile, in the dark hallway of the mukhtar's house, there was in progress a minor tragi-comedy, which ended when the old village clerk with the sly goatee came flying out of the door, which quickly slammed after him. In this primitive fashion did Mukhtar Kebussyan, at this, the most difficult juncture of his mayoralty, appoint his clerk to represent him. The luckless pseudo-mukhtar, white as chalk, came stumbling into the arms of the saptiehs, who thrust him forwards to their leader.

The clerk babbled an echo of Ter Haigasun: "We've got no weapons in the village."

The head constable was greatly relieved by the sight of this trembling, stuttering mukhtar. It fully re-established his own thunderous divinity. He snatched a leather whip out of the hand of the nearest saptieh and swished the air with it. "All the worse for you if you've got no weapons."

Here, for the first time, the red-haired müdir took a hand. This young man from Salonika was anxious to show the Christian priest what a world of difference there existed between his like and a loutish police chief of the worst provincial variety. Ittihad did not stand for out-of-date massacres. Ittihad's methods were of the subtlest. Ittihad, with iron resolution, gave irresistible effect to the necessary *raison d'état,* while endeavouring, in so far as this could be managed, to avoid superfluous harshness. Ittihad was so modern. It disliked the crude blood-baths of former days; it was in fact quite proud of possessing "nerves." All of which inspired the young müdir to a glance at his beautifully red-tinged finger-nails before he turned towards Ter Haigasun, full of that dangerous amiability which all official persons invested with the powers of life and death know how to use so tellingly.

"You know what we've decided to do with you?"

The priest looked him steadily in the face, still not answering.

The müdir, a trifle disconcerted, waved at a placard. "The government has decided to migrate you. You're to be allotted other territory."

"And where is the other territory situated?"

"That's neither your affair nor mine. My only business is to collect you, and yours is simply to march."

"And when must we leave?"

"It will depend on how you behave how much time I give you to get your belongings into order and make yourselves ready to march according to exact stipulations."

The village clerk had by now managed to control himself. He asked in a voice of expectant humility: "And what are we allowed to take with us, Effendi?"

"Only what each individual can carry for himself on his back, or in his hand. All the rest, your fields, gardens, landed property, your houses, with all such movable and immovable furniture as belongs to them, goes to the state, by ministerial decree of the fifteenth of Nisan of the present year. The Migration Law of Mayis the fifth provides that you be allotted fresh holdings of ground in exchange for what you have vacated. Every holder to produce the registered extent of his property, to obtain a legal substitute from the government. Such a document must bear stamps to the value of five piastres. These stamps are obtainable at the district police headquarters."

This official chant came forth so mildly and melodiously from the lips of this young, carroty müdir that it sounded like some regulation for fruit-growers. The benevolent müdir raised his forefinger. "It will be best for you all to create as little disturbance as possible—not to destroy any property, but to hand it over entire, just as it is, to the state."

Ter Haigasun opened his hands and spread them out towards the diplomatic young man from Salonika. "We don't

261

want to keep anything, Müdir. What good would it be to us? Take whatever you find. Our doors are open."

The müdir's smooth tone had begun to rile the head constable. It was undermining his authority. After all, in the last resort, he was the head of this expedition, and this quill-driver a mere accessory person sent by the Kaimakam. If he let this mealy-mouthed clerk go on much longer, everyone would cease to believe that he was chief of police of the town of Antakiya. He opened the staring eye a little wider, with bloodshot, buffalo ferocity, came two steps nearer Ter Haigasun, and seized him by the thickly embroidered stole. "Now you'll get together six hundred rifles and have them piled up here before me!"

Ter Haigasun stared a long while at the place where the rifles were to be stacked. Suddenly he took a step backwards, with a violent jerk which almost overturned the head constable. "I've already told you that there aren't any rifles in the villages."

The müdir smiled. It was his turn now to get what they wanted, without any shouting and rolling of eyes, by sheer astute political methods. His voice had a kind, thoughtful note in it, as though he were trying to give the Armenian his excuse. "How long have you been head-priest in the village, if you'll forgive my question, Ter Haigasun?"

The vague benevolence of this put Ter Haigasun on the alert. He answered softly: "About fifteen years next autumn, after the vintage."

"Fifteen years? Wait. So, in the year of the great revolution, you'd been just eight years in Yoghonoluk. Now try and remember. Didn't you receive some chests of rifles in that year, allotted you to do your share in the struggle against the old government?"

The müdir asked this by sheer intuition; he had only been in office since the war broke out. He supposed inductively that Ittihad would have sought the same allies in Syria as in

Macedonia and Anatolia. He did not know he hit the mark. Ter Haigasun turned his head to his acolyte, who had still not dared to come down the church steps. This quick movement beckoned the other priest as witness. "Perhaps your priests may have to do with weapons, Müdir. That is not the case with us."

At this dangerous juncture the village clerk began to whine: "But we've always lived here in peace. This has been our country for thousands of years."

Ter Haigasun stared absently at the müdir. He seemed to be trying hard to remember. "You're right, Müdir! The new government did distribute arms at about that time, in various places all over the empire—even to Armenians. If you're old enough, you'll also recollect that all communes receiving them had to give a written acknowledgment when they arrived. The Kaimakam, who was a müdir like yourself in those days, organized the distribution. He'll be sure to have kept all the receipts—one doesn't throw away an important document of that kind. Well, I don't suppose if there'd been any weapons in the villages, he'd have sent you to us without the receipt for them."

This was undeniable. And it was true that in the last few days the Record Office of Antakiya had been turned upside down to find such receipts. Most of the nahiyehs had delivered them—only the Nahiyeh of Suedia and the surrounding district seemed really to have been sent no weapons in 1908. The Kaimakam certainly declared that he seemed to remember the contrary but could give no proof of it. So that Ter Haigasun had quietly found the right way out.

The conviction he displayed envenomed the pleasantly diplomatic smiles of the müdir, whose voice became edged. "What's a written receipt? A mere scribble. What does that prove, after all these years?"

Ter Haigasun waved an indifferent hand. "If you don't believe us, look and see for yourselves."

The police chief, eager to put an end to this long, superfluous discussion, brought down his whip with a swish on the priest's shoulders. "Yes, we'll look all right, you son of a bitch. But you two are under arrest, you and the mukhtar. I can do what I like with you. Your lives are at my sole discretion. If we find any weapons, you'll be nailed up on the door of your church. If we don't, I'll have you roasted over a fire."

The saptiehs bound Ter Haigasun and the clerk. The müdir took out a little nail file and got busy on his exquisite fingers. This scraping and polishing worked like a gesture of regret at the necessary harshness of government measures, the indication that he, a civil servant, had nothing at all to do with the armed executive. That, however, did not prevent his giving a bored hint to the policeman.

"Don't forget the churchyard. That's a very favourite hiding-place for munitions."

Having said so much, he turned off for a little constitutional, down the village street, leaving all the rest to the skew-eyed muafin. At a word from that ferocious commander the saptiehs split up into little groups. A few remained to guard the prisoners. Ter Haigasun was made to sit on the church steps in his heavily embroidered vestments. Meanwhile, with wild vociferations, the saptiehs began to invade surrounding houses. From behind the walls came the instant din of cracking furniture, splintering glass; windows flew open. Rugs, blankets, cushions, mats, straw chairs, icons, and all the numerous other articles of household gear came whizzing down—to be surrounded at once by the looting populace. More fragile objects came out after them—oil-lamps, looking-glasses, shades, pitchers, jugs, crockery, which smashed under a chorus of regretful yammering from the eager bargain-basement ladies. All the same they grabbed up the fragments and bundled them together in their charshaffes. This din and devastation crept round the square, from house to house, before it continued along the village street. For three horrible hours the two bound men crouched on the steps, before the saptiehs returned from their expedition. Its results were worse than disappointing—two old blunderbusses, five rusty sabres, thirty-seven sheathed knives, which really were no more than pruning-knives or large-sized penknives. The saptiehs, either because they had no spades, or were too lazy to have used them, had refrained from desecrating the churchyard. The police chief bellowed and raved. This cunning swine of a priest had cheated him of a report which ought to have bristled with arms. What a setback for the Antakiya police! Ter Haiga-sun was jerked to his feet again. The staring and the swollen eye both glowered on him. The breath that came puffing in his face stank of hate and ill-digested mutton fat. He turned his head, with a little grimace of disgust. In the next instant two blows with the hard butt of a leather whip had caught him full across the cheek.

For a few seconds the priest lost consciousness, swayed, came awake again, stood amazed, waiting for the blood to flow. At last it gushed out of his nose and mouth. A strange, almost blissful sensation possessed him as he stood there, bending his head far forward, that his poor blood might not stain the garment of Christ's priest. Some distant angelic voice seemed to say in his mind: "This blood is good blood."

And it was, in effect, good blood, since the sight of it made a certain impression on the young müdir from Salonika, just back from his afternoon siesta. He was a fiery advocate of extermination but did not like to have to witness it personally. Ittihad, in this müdir, had by no means its most relentless exponent. He struck a balance, avoiding any display of senti-mentality. Time pressed. There were six more villages to visit. And, since even the muafin had stilled the itch to assert his position and prove his authority, he waved magnanimously. The priest and clerk were set free. They were sent home. So that, in Yoghonoluk, the day had passed off smoothly enough, far more smoothly than such days usually did, in these towns and villages. Only two men, who made some show of resisting domiciliary inspection, were shot in the process—only two young girls got raped by the saptiehs.

GABRIEL BAGRADIAN had to wait a full twenty-four hours before it became the turn of himself and his house. Once again they sat up all night. Exhaustion forced its way through their limbs, like a soft mass, stiffening slowly. The many inhabitants of the villa—Juliette, Iskuhi, Hovsannah, Gonzague Maris, who had recently taken up his quarters there—kept dropping off to sleep for minutes together, where they sat. This vigil was entirely aimless, since the saptiehs' visit was not expected before next morning, nor indeed even before midday. Yet nobody thought of leaving the others and lying down. Bed— that soft kingdom of pillows, that cool security protected by its draped mosquito-net, that loving mother, protector of the civilized human being—how remote it seemed, even now! They had lost their right to such oblivion. When, early next morning, the cook Hovhannes sent fresh coffee, eggs, cold chicken, on fine porcelain dishes, into the dining-room, they were almost uneasy in spite of their hunger and thirst. They ate quickly, as if the house might fall about their ears before they had finished. Had they still any right to eat up such good things in the old way, without a thought? Surely it was unwise to encroach on the provisions of the Damlayik. All their thoughts were centred on Musa Dagh. Gabriel had on his Turkish officer's uniform. He was wearing his sword and medals. He would receive these saptiehs as their superior.

Gonzague Maris advised most strongly against it: "Your military fancy dress will only get on their nerves. I don't think it'll be to your advantage."

Gabriel was unmoved: "I'm an Ottoman officer. I've duly reported at my regiment, and so far no one has degraded me."

"That'll be done soon enough."

So Maris spoke, but his thought added: "There's nothing

266

you can do for these Armenians. They're solemn lunatics—always will be."

At about eleven that morning Iskuhi suddenly collapsed. First a brief faint, then uncontrollable shivering. She dragged herself out of the room, insistently refusing any help. Juliette wanted to go after her, but Hovsannah raised a warning hand.

"Let her be. . . . It's Zeitun. . . . She's terrified. . . . She wants to hide. We're having to go through it all a second time." And the pastor's young wife hid her face in her hands, her heavy body shaken with sobs.

This was about the moment at which the police squad, the muafin and the müdir turned into the grounds of Villa Bagradian. The sentries posted by Gabriel came breathlessly scurrying to announce them. Six saptiehs were placed outside the doors of the garden wall, six more in the garden, six in the stable-yard. The müdir, the muafin, and four men came into the house. The Turks looked fagged. In the last twenty-four hours they had played havoc in the villages, looting and breaking up the insides of houses, arresting men and thrashing them till they bled, they had done a little raping, and so in part actually realized the festive programme arranged for them by the government. Luckily, therefore, their thirst for action was somewhat slaked. This huge Bagradian family mansion, with its thick walls, cool rooms, full of strange-looking furniture, its silencing carpets, acted no doubt as a kind of restraint. The red window curtains of the selamlik had been drawn. Intruders into the rich dusk of the room found themselves in the midst of what looked like an august gathering of European ladies and gentlemen, respectfully surrounded by their servants. This impressive company waited stiffly and never moved. Juliette kept fast hold of Stephan's hand. Only Gonzague lit a cigarette. Gabriel came a step nearer the committee, his sword caught up, in prescribed officer's fashion, in his left hand. The field-uniform, which he had had made in Beirut before he left, made him look taller. He was certainly the foremost man in the room, and this quite apart from his inches. Gonzague seemed to have been wrong. The uniform was having its effect. The police chief glanced uneasily at this officer with the row of medals on his tunic. The fierce eye clouded with melancholy, the half-shut one closed up altogether. Nor did the freckled müdir seem altogether happy in his part. It had been far easier to be a convincingly watchful providence in the stuffy rooms of wood-carvers, silkweavers. Here in these civilized surroundings the delicate nerves of Salonika were proving a handicap. Instead of striding pitilessly on to take possession of this cursed house in the name of his race, of Ittihad, of the state, the young gentleman nodded and clutched at his fez. He began uncomfortably to remember a certain talk with Bagradian in his office. His moral conflict caused delay and prevented his finding the right opening. Gabriel watched him with such contemptuous gravity that really the tables seemed almost turned—it was as though a tall, war-like Armenia were facing a red-haired, cringing, half-breed Turkey. Bagradian seemed to grow and grow, as the müdir suffered under his dwarfishness, which so inadequately embodied the heroic quality of his race. In the end he could manage to do nothing but produce a vast official document, against which, so to speak, to steady himself, and rap out his business as brusquely as possible.

"Gabriel Bagradian, born Yoghonoluk? You are the owner of this house, the head of this family? As an Ottoman subject you are liable to the decrees and enactments of the Kaimakam of Antioch. You, together with the rest of the population of this nahiyeh, from Suedia to Musa Dagh, are ordered to set out eastwards, on a day shortly to be specified. Your entire family to go with you. You have no right to raise objections of any kind against the general order of migration—neither as concerns your own person, nor those of your wife and children, nor for any other member of your establishment. . . ."

The müdir so far had behaved as though he were reading an incantation; now he squinted up, over the document. "I am to draw your attention to the fact that your name is on the list of political suspects. You are closely connected with the Dashnakzagan party. Therefore, even on the convoy, you are to be subjected to close daily inspection. Any attempt at escape, any insubordination against government or executive orders, or infringement of transport discipline, will render, not only you, but your relatives, liable to instant execution."

Gabriel seemed about to reply. The müdir refused to let him speak. His stilted and involved official phrasing, in such contrast to the usual floweriness of the East, seemed to inflate him with satisfaction.

"By extraordinary edict of His Excellency, the Wali of Aleppo: Armenians on the march are not permitted to make use of such conveyances, sumpter or saddle animals as they may think fit. In certain exceptional cases leave may be obtained to make use of any customary vehicle of the country-side, or of an ass, for the weak and ailing. Have you any requests for such special treatment?"

Gabriel pressed his sword-hilt against his thigh. The words dropped like stones from his lips: "I shall go the way of my whole people."

By now the müdir had entirely shed his first embarrassment. He could put some suave concern into his tone. "So as not to expose you to the dangerous temptation of either trying to absent yourself, or, later, of leaving the convoy—I hereby take possession of your horses, your carriage, and all other beasts of transport."

Then came the usual procedure, but slightly modified. The police chief was still not quite sure how to deal with the uniform, sword, and medals of this prospective deportee. He growled out the usual question about arms. Gabriel sent Kristaphor and Missak to fetch in the long-barrelled Bedouin flint-locks hung up as ornament in his hall. (This had of course been arranged; all the useful weapons in the house were by now safely on the Damlayik.) Scornful laughter bubbled out of the police chief, as out of a kettle on the boil.

The müdir thoughtfully tapped these romantic flintlocks. "You surely aren't going to tell me, Effendi, that you live here in this solitude without weapons?"

Gabriel Bagradian sought the lashless stare of the müdir and held it steadily. "Why not? This is the first time my house has been broken into since it was built in 1870."

The freckled one shrugged regretful shoulders. Such recalcitrance made it impossible to do anything to mitigate Bagradian's fate. And so, much against his will, he was forced to leave the field clear for the sharper process of armed authority. The house to be searched for arms! The muafin metaphorically rolled up his sleeves, though the officer's uniform worn by this outcast still troubled his sergeant-major's mind, filling him with a puzzled irritation. The staring right eye could not detach itself from the medals on Bagradian's chest; apparently the chap had served with distinction. It was quite impossible to decide how this deportee ought to be handled by an Imperial Ottoman employee. To hide these irritable doubts he conducted the search with as much din and pother as he could—went stumping at the head of his saptiehs, with the müdir close upon their heels yet still refusing to be involved. Gabriel, Avakian, and Kristaphor followed. The Turks nosed in every corner, knocked on the walls, overturned the furniture, smashed whatever was breakable. Yet it was easy to see that this vandalism, perpetrated as a matter of course, as if by mistake, hurt their self-esteem. They were used to making a straight, clean job of it. But now their method of smashing bottles in the cellar, with their rifle-butts, was most perfunctory. Nor was there any real *brio* in their method of dealing with whatever flasks, jugs, dishes, wine-jars they found. (The most important provisions had all been removed.) And these disillusioned saptiehs had expected a better cellar in such a palace.

Since these were all they could find, they took away a couple of empty petrol-tins, on which glittering toys the Oriental sets great store. Then, sweating and disgruntled, the warriors took the staircase by assault and began to rummage the upper story. Here they did most in Juliette's bedroom and dressing-room, the scents of which had attracted them so sharply from a distance that the other rooms were entirely forgotten. The big wardrobe was prised open. Dirty brown fists snatched last year's Paris models off their pegs—frocks like the softest petals, which now lay strewn in crumpled twists and heaps about the floor. A particularly evil-looking gendarme pawed them with both feet, like a stolidly rampaging bull, as though set on stamping these European reptiles into earth. Night-dresses, batiste underwear, shifts, and stockings met the same fate. The sight of these intimate garments was too much for the police chief. He plunged both hands into the white and rose-coloured foam and buried his punchinello face in it. The müdir, to indicate the fact that the legislature had nothing in common with the executive, went dreamily over to the window to look at the garden. An especially zealous saptieh had flung himself on the untouched bed and was engaged, since he could think of no other method, in tearing open the pillows with his teeth. Perhaps there was a bomb among the feathers. There was always so much talk of Armenian bombs. Another swung his club over the washing-stand. Crystal flasks, bowls, powder boxes, saucers, came smashing down, giving out wave on wave of heady perfume.

Gabriel equally watched this desecration. Poor Juliette. . . . But what was this by comparison with the next hours, days, weeks? He felt deeply troubled. He remembered Iskuhi, creeping away to hide in her bed. She was nothing to him—and yet he pitied her most of all. These beasts had crippled her, and she had to face this horror a second time. Bagradian tried to think of a method for getting the muafin and saptiehs past Iskuhi's door.

And, indeed, heaven seemed well disposed. Iskuhi, who had crept under the sheets, heard the trampling steps and rumbling voices of the worst of all deaths come closer and closer. She stretched herself out stiff and covered her lap with her right hand, while she ceased to breathe, and the ravaged, kaleidoscopic face bent nearer and nearer over hers. But this ravager only snuffled her for a second and vanished. Outside, the steps clumped on past her door, the voices rumbled farther and farther off; they seemed to be going downstairs again. Then she heard them dimly on the ground floor. Sudden, perfect quiet. Had they gone? Iskuhi sprang out of bed. To the door on her stocking feet. She pushed open a chink of it. Christ Saviour, were they really gone? She almost fell back into the room again as she heard the cracking of a lash. . . . Voices—men's voices raised. She recognized Gabriel's among them. Holding her lame arm tight, that it might not hinder her, she dashed to the staircase. Below, the following had occurred.

Thinking that now the worst was over, Gabriel had pointedly stopped in the hall. He had said to the müdir: "You see, we've got nothing hidden. Anything else?"

That freckled political idealist had done his duty. He had seen to it that the Armenian effendi and his family should at least not escape the Turkish government. The Kaimakam's special instructions concerning Bagradian had been to the effect that he was to march with the first convoy, under drastic supervision, to Antakiya, where that district authority in person, as he himself put it, would "take a squint at them." In the müdir's view this ended official proceedings. Such illustrious victims ought not to be goaded too soon to desperation. Far better to give them a certain confidence in the government's inscrutable designs, while intensifying, little by little, the sharpness of what they would have to experience. Today ought to be mild—preliminary. So again the müdir hesitated, trying to think out effective exits, scrutinizing his beautiful finger-nails. Unluckily he had reckoned without the police chief.

That troubled mind was still unreconciled to the fact that this insolent giaour should be strutting about in a padishah uniform, with padishah medals and sword. But he still did not quite know what to do about it. Nor had he managed to shake off his ignoble embarrassment. Since nothing more effective occurred to him, he tried to roll the staring eye. He planted himself, corpulent and challenging, before Bagradian.

"We haven't seen everything yet. . . . Up there. . . . There were several doors we didn't open."

If Gabriel had managed to control himself, all would no doubt have ended happily. But he sprang on to the lowest step of the staircase, spread his arms out wide, and shouted: "That's enough!"

Now, at last, the muafin had his case. He bore down with obvious pleasure on Bagradian, to hold a fist up under his nose. "What's enough, you pig of an Armenian? Say that again. What's enough, you unclean swine?"

That second, in Bagradian's mind, completed one of those highly complicated mental processes which engender our fates. It was an instant of the sheerest reflection. Gabriel realized clearly that his life, and not only his, was now in the balance. "Give in," he thought, "and step aside. Let them go up again, and up there bribe the animal with ten pounds. . . ." While his reason debated all this with impressive clarity, he himself was shouting, as never before: "Step back, gendarme. I'm a front-line officer."

This brought the muafin to the very centre of his aim. "An officer, are you? For me you aren't even a stinking dead dog." And with a quick tug he wrenched the silver medals off Gabriel's tunic.

Later Bagradian asserted that his hand had never touched his sword. The fact was that, in less than a second, he found himself sprawling on the ground. The sword splintered against the wall. One saptieh was kneeling on Gabriel's chest, the rest were tearing off his uniform. Gonzague and the women rushed

273

out of the selamlik. Stephan's shouts mingled with the tugging grunts of his father. It was not a minute before Gabriel lay there stripped to his boots. He was bleeding from a few flesh wounds. His life would not have been worth a para, had Gonzague Maris not saved him from instant slaughter by turning all the attention to himself. Though his gesture was careless, it told with the sharpest effect. His voice had that impressive note in it which obtains the iciest quiet in the midst of commotion. He had pulled out his papers and stood holding them high above his head. This gesture caught everyone's eyes. The müdir stared at him, perturbed. The police chief turned in his direction; even the saptiehs let go of Gabriel.

Gonzague unfolded his documents with all the calm of a secret agent sent by Ittihad to keep a sharp eye on the conduct of local authorities. "Here you are. Passport of the United States of America, with a visa from the General Consulate in Istanbul." He stressed these insignificant words in such an authoritative staccato that he might have been apprising them all of some secret diplomatic mission of decisive importance to Turkey. "Here—teskeré for the interior, autographed by His Excellency in person. You understand me, Effendi?"

It was not this empty flourish with a passport that had saved Bagradian's life—it was the desperate trick which made them forget him. For some minutes it confused the müdir. In the various instructions issued for the guidance of deportation authorities, it was indicated over and over again that the methods of applying this measure must be kept as unobtrusive as possible in the presence of Allied and neutral consuls. For an instant the müdir really imagined that he must be dealing with a confidential agent of the American embassy. A glance at the papers, however, assured him that this person was harmless. But he was really glad that the foreigner's interference had prevented bloodshed. He returned Gonzague his papers, with mocking ceremony.

"What do your passports matter to me? You'd better make

yourself scarce as soon as possible—or I'll have you arrested."

The constable's confusion abated more slowly. Blood impressed him far less than paper. In the course of his career documents had often been inconvenient. You were never sure what they might not do to you in the end. He decided to let Bagradian go on living, at least for the present. The thing could be done just as well on a highroad, without witnesses who held American passports. The muafin put his revolver, already primed, back in its case, took another swollen and staring glance at this naked officer, spat a huge gobbet, and gave his saptiehs the curt order: "Get along now for those horses and mules."

The müdir had missed his effective exit. He had to content himself by following the armed executive in as thoughtful and detached a manner as possible, leaving no resonant echo of personality.

Gabriel, breathing hard, had scrambled up. Shame, and no other sensation, possessed his mind. Juliette had had to witness this horror—she and Stephan. His eyes sought his wife, who stood there rigid, her face averted. Gabriel tottered, then controlled himself. Behind his back he felt something tremble— Iskuhi. Then his few scratches began to burn. They were not worth mentioning. Iskuhi, silent, on stocking feet, crept close. Her imploring eyes sought Samuel Avakian. The student came with a coat to cover Gabriel's sweat-streaked body.

A FAVOURABLE turn of events. The müdir, the police chief, and the saptiehs left the villages that same day to turn their attention to Armenians in Suedia and El Eskel. It was one of the best-considered nuances of the Turkish government's migration policy that it never specified the exact day and hour of a given march. Since the deportation was officially a wartime measure of military necessity, and since also it was semi-officially punitive, the "moment of surprise," which gave banishment its peculiar poignancy, must not be neglected in either

275

of these interpretations. But Pastor Harutiun Nokhudian had managed by heavy bribes to elicit the fact that the first convoy had been fixed to leave on July 31. Between then and now a hundred extra saptiehs would reinforce the first contingent. The thirty-first would be a Saturday. Counting today, Thursday, that was two days. The Council of Leaders decided on the night of Friday to Saturday to move their populations up to the Damlayik. They had good reasons for their decision. Friday was the Turkish day of rest. Past experience made it extremely probable that saptiehs in the Christian villages would vacate them on Friday for the Turkish and Arab villages in the plain, in which there were mosques, relations, amusements, and women. And, with the saptiehs, the plundering riff-raff would also probably vanish for the day, since they felt with a certain amount of justice that, once there was no saptieh to interfere, the Armenians, in spite of being unarmed, would make quick work of them with scythes, axes, and hammers.

These special circumstances, therefore, exactly predetermined the choice of time. The Council of Leaders reckoned on the following developments: The returning saptiehs, arriving on the morning of Saturday, would find, instead of the whole people, only Pastor Nokhudian with his five hundred Protestants in Bitias. The pastor—this ruse came from Gabriel —was to tell the müdir a long story of how, notwithstanding his supplications, all the people had packed their belongings in the night and set out of their own accord into exile. Their reason for this had been their terror of the saptiehs, and of the police chief especially. He could not say exactly which roads they had taken, since people had set out in small groups in every conceivable direction: one group towards Arsus and Alexandretta, another southwards, but all with the intention of avoiding inhabited places. The largest group had certainly meant to find its way to Aleppo, to take shelter in the big town. Pastor Nokhudian, whose mildness and Christian spirit of obedience had caused many to mistake him for a coward, revealed his heroism. This deception which he undertook to practise meant at the least death, as far as he was concerned. The instant the Turks discovered the stratagem, it would be all over with him. He shrugged his shoulders. Where was there no danger of death? The fighters on the mountain had to gain time. This feint would postpone discovery several days and give them sufficient grace to complete the defences.

The Council met in Ter Haigasun's presbytery. The priest was very disfigured from the blow of the constable's whip. His right eye and cheek were swollen; a violet weal striped his whole face and half-way up his forehead. He had lost two teeth, and it was easy to see he was in great pain. Gabriel's scratches, on the other hand, could scarcely be felt under Altouni's plaster. The physical brutality he had suffered—the first, in all his sheltered, remote existence—had drawn him even closer to all the rest. At this sitting the Council discussed a very disquieting, adverse circumstance, which unluckily it was already too late to remedy. In peaceful years the villagers had been in the habit of buying grain in July, after the harvest, from Turkish and Arab peasants in the plains. They themselves scarcely grew any grain. This year, dazed with the threat overhanging, they had put off buying their usual provisions against the winter. This delay was now a serious matter. The villagers had flour, potatoes, and maize, but in very insufficient quantities. To hold out with these for any time would necessitate the greatest economy. And since Armenians were used to much bread and little meat, this lack of it was a terrible problem for the leaders. Added to which, for the first few days there would be no chance on the Damlayik of baking, since the brick ovens would have to be dug into the earth. Pastor Aram therefore decreed that, till Friday evening, every tonir must be kept alight in the villages, so that as many flat cakes as possible might be ready before they left the valley.

Ter Haigasun concluded the session with the announcement of a solemn mass of petition for the following morning,

Friday. After mass the bells were to be taken out of the church tower, carried to the churchyard in solemn procession, and buried. There the whole people should take leave of them, praying before the graves of its fathers. Ter Haigasun further announced that he intended to take several barrel-loads of consecrated earth up to the Damlayik. Those who died up there, in the camp or in battle, should not have to lie quite abandoned in the merciless wasteland, but should be given a handful of their ancient, consecrated ground on which, at least, to rest their heads.

On the Friday morning the saptiehs did in fact take their departure, to the last man, into Mohammedan country. Müdir and muafin had ridden to Antioch. The Church of the Ever-Increasing Angelic Powers was fuller, long before the appointed time, than it ever had been since it was consecrated. The atrium and the square nave over which rose the tall central cupola, the two side aisles, and even the platform upon which rose the high altar could scarcely hold the congregation. Since the church, according to very old custom, had no windows, sharp amber blades of sunlight, like the eyes of the Trinity, pierced the oblong slits in the wall, shaped like arrow-slits in a fortress. But these crossed shafts of light did not illuminate; they merely served to dim the candles and cast a network of curious shadows upon the crowd. Today there were not only hundreds of faithful, come to Yoghonoluk to mass from the smaller villages, but also all the priests and choir-singers, to assist at this last high mass "on solid ground." Never yet had the choir sung its choral, announcing at the foot of the altar the vesting of the priest in the sacristy, in so full a voice:

"Deep secret, incomprehensible, without beginning!
Thou hast adorned with glory
The host of the beings of fire."

Never had Ter Haigasun bowed more deeply, nor made more complete and shuddering an admission of sin before

278

the people. Under his gold mitre the weal of the whip stood out on his face. And never before had the secret of the kiss of peace, the reunion of the community in Christ, bound the souls of these faithful in holier ties. At other masses, when after the sacrificial prayer the deacon, at the words: "Greet ye one another with the holy kiss," had held the thurible up to the lips of the chief singer (Teacher Asayan)—when this singer had kissed the one next to him, so that the embrace might continue through the choir and from the choir through the people—it had usually been in a series of quick little touches, mere slack formality. But today they held each other close and really kissed on cheeks or mouth. Many were in tears. When after the communion the assistant priests, at a sign from Ter Haigasun, began stripping the altar, a wild, un-expected pain flung the whole congregation on its knees. Un-controllable grief, groans, wailings, rose above the glimmering play of shadows, above the crossed, flaming seraphim swords of the sun, up into the tall, dim cupola. Each of the holy vessels was held up high before it disappeared in a straw-plaited basket: chalice, paten, ciborium, and the great book of the Gospels. The sacristan packed the censers, the silver candle-sticks and crucifixes, into another box. At last there was only the lace altar-cloth. Ter Haigasun crossed himself for the last time, let his hands—their hue that of yellowish church tapers —hover for a while over the altar-cloth till, with a sudden jerk, he lifted it. The unveiled stone stood bare, which had once been hewn out of the grey rock of Musa Dagh. In the same instant old Tomasian's workmen were letting down the bells, the big one and the smaller one, by pulleys from the campanile. It needed all their strength to raise the heavy metal on to the two biers, each of which were to be carried by eight men.

Acolytes bearing the tall Greek cross headed the procession. Then, with their bells, the stumbling coffin-bearers. After them, Ter Haigasun and the other priests. It took a considerable time for this funeral cortège to reach the graveyard of Yoghonoluk. The train of mourners really seemed to be escorting an honoured body to the grave. The heat was deadening. Only at the rarest intervals did a breath from the Mediterranean find its way across Musa Dagh to mitigate the Syrian summer. Swirling dust-clouds ran before the procession, like spectral dancers before the Ark, a thin, degenerate variety of the sacred pillars of cloud which went before the Israelites in the wilderness. The churchyard lay far along the road to Habibli, the wood-carvers' village. Like most graveyards in the East, it crept up the slope of a hill and was not surrounded by any wall. This, together with its gravestones, either fallen or slanting deep in the soil, their weatherbeaten limestone crudely chiselled with inscription and cross, gave it almost the look of a Turkish or Jewish burial-ground in the Near East. As the procession turned into it, there was a grey, bat-like fluttering and scurrying, hither and thither, between cairns and monuments. These were old women, whose flimsy garments were held together only by their substratum of dirt and dust. Old women everywhere feel drawn to cemeteries. In the West also, we know these pensioners of death, tomb-dwellers, keening wives, guardians of corruption, whose begging is often only their second trade. But here in Yoghonoluk this was a recognized class, a close corporation of nestlers in churchyard mould, wailing women and helpers at a birth, who, according to the tradition of these villages, had to live on the outskirts of each community. One or two old beggar-men, with biblical, prophetic heads, were among them, and a few cripples, fantastically deformed, such as only the East engenders. The people protected itself against the dross of its own loins by banishing it, in the absence of any institutions or homes for the aged poor, into its cemetery, a place both sacred and unclean. So that now nobody felt scared when two mad women rushed to hide, with heart-rending shrieks, up the graveyard hill. This churchyard and its neighbourhood formed the alms-house, hospital, and mad-house of Yoghonoluk. It was even more; it was the place to which sorcery had been relegated. The torch of enlightenment, in the hands of Altouni, Krikor, Shatakhian, and their predecessors, had driven magic beyond the confines of the villages and yet not killed it. These keening spey-wives, under the leadership of Nunik, Vartuk, Manushak, had fled so far before the hatred of the doctor, but no farther. Here they awaited their clients, to be summoned not only for death vigils and corpse-washings, but far more often to an obstinate illness or a child-birth, since many trusted less in Altouni's science than in the herb-potions, magic formulas, and prayers for health of Nunik, Vartuk, Manushak. In this ancient quarrel science did not always come out best. That was undeniable. Superstition had an incalculable advantage in the variety of its potions and old wives' cures. And Altouni had no bedside manner. Once he had given up a case, he sharply refused to raise false hopes. A creature like Nunik, on the other hand, could never get to the end of her stored-up knowledge, nor would she bow before death. If a patient died on her, he had only himself to blame for having sent, in a moment of weakness, for Altouni, and so brought all her skill to naught. Nunik was the living emblem of her art. The village women told each other how, in the days of the first Avetis, she had been seventy, just as she was today. The enlightened persecuted these spey-wives, and chased them from among the living. But that did not prevent their creeping at night from their haunt of death to go about their secret business in all seven villages. Now, however, they were all collected in the churchyard, to take their share of alms with the blind and the halt. Sato had left the cortege and run on ahead. She had long had many cronies among the grave-folk. These border people attracted her borderline soul. They were so easy to live with! It was so hard to live with the Bagradians! Though gifts of clothes from the great hanum might feed Sato's vanity, in reality she felt as uncomfortable in them, in shoes, stockings, in a clean room, as a wild dog in a collar. With beggars and spey-wives, and with mad people, Sato could give free rein to her thoughts, in words that had no special meaning. Oh, how delightful to kick off the speech of the great, like a tight shoe, and talk with bare feet! Nunik, Vartuk, Manushak, had secrets to tell her which made her whole soul shiver in unison, as though she too had brought them into this world with her, from the life of her ancestors. Then she would sit still and listen for hours, while the blind beggars beside her fumbled over her thin child's body with alert, sensitive fingers. Had there been no Iskuhi, Sato might have let the others go up to the Damlayik, while she lived at ease among the grave-folk. These happy souls were not to be taken into the narrow confines of the mountain camp. The leaders had passed the resolution, with one dissentient, Bagradian. He, though as commander he saw clearly that every superfluous mouth would enfeeble resistance, had not wanted to exclude any Armenian. But these outcasts seemed neither unhappy at this decision nor especially scared. They stretched out hands and snouts to their compatriots with all the usual beggars' litany.

The sky was so scorchingly empty that the very notion of a cloud might have seemed a story-teller's fable. This inexorable blue seemed never to have known a drop of rain since the Deluge. The people crowded about the open grave to take leave of the bells of Yoghonoluk. In peaceful days their sound had scarcely been noticed. But this was like the silencing of their own lives. The mother bell and her daughter were low-ered into earth amid breathless quiet. The muted ring of scat-tered clods upon the metal was like a prophecy to these people that now there could be no more going back home and no resurrection from the dead. After a short prayer said by Ter Haigasun, the communes dispersed among their graves, si-lently, and the separate families went to take a last look at their fathers' resting-place. Gabriel and Stephan did the same and wandered to the Bagradian mausoleum. It was a small, low house, under a cupola, shaped like the mounds in which Turks bury their worthies and saintly men. Grandfather Avetis had built it for himself and his old wife. The founder of all their splendour lay, by Armenian tradition, without a coffin, in his shroud, under stone slabs, slanted against each other like praying hands. Apart from him and his wife, there was only one other Bagradian buried here—Avetis the brother, faithful to Yoghonoluk, not long a dead man. "There wouldn't have been room for any more of us," reflected Gabriel, who oddly did not feel in the least serious, but rather amused. Stephan, bored, shifted from foot to foot. He felt so many æons away from death.

Surrounded by a little knot of people Ter Haigasun stood at the top of the slope on the last outskirts of the dead land. Some diggers had shovelled out a wide spare pit, like a *fosse commune*. Five barrels were filled with the earth they dug, and when these were ready, Ter Haigasun went from one to the other and made the sign of the cross over each. He stopped before the last and bent down over it. This was not black loam, but poor and crumbling earth. Ter Haigasun dipped into the barrel and laid a handful of consecrated ground against his face, like a peasant testing the soil.

"May it suffice," he said to himself. Then in surprised cogitation he stood looking down over the graveyard, already almost deserted. Most of the villagers had long since set out for home. It was getting on towards midday. In the larger villages such as Bitias and Habibli, similar ceremonies were being performed. But the Council had appointed the hour after sunset for setting out.

GABRIEL made the most considerate arrangements for Juliette. Drawn into this Armenian gulf, she should miss her own world as little as circumstances could possibly allow. True that this European world of hers was also engaged in a dog-fight, compared to which all else of the kind seemed a pointless, haphazard brawl. But there the dog-fight was being conducted with all modern conveniences, according to the most advanced scientific principles, not with the innocent blood-lust of the beast of passion, but with the mathematical thoroughness and precision of the beast of intellect. If we were still in Paris— Gabriel might, for instance, have told himself—we should not, it is true, have to sleep on the stony earth of a Syrian mountain, we should still have a bathroom and W.C. But, for all that, we should be liable at any hour of the day or night to leave these comforts for the dark cellar, to hide from aerial bombs. So that, even in Paris, Stephan and Juliette would still be exposed to a certain risk. None of which reflections occurred to Gabriel, for the simple reason that for months he had seen no European newspapers, and knew next to nothing about the war.

On the previous night he had sent Avakian and Kristaphor, with all his household servants, up to the Damlayik, so that Juliette's quarters might be got ready. They were prepared with the very greatest care. "Three-Tent Square" must have its own kitchen and scullery, with every usual arrangement. Gabriel had ordered that Juliette should have all three tents at her disposal. She was to say which she would like to live in. With endless labour, carpets, braziers, divans, tables, armchairs, had been dragged up the Damlayik, and an astonishing collection of smart luggage—wardrobe-trunks, shiny leather suitcases, baskets for crockery and silver, a whole collection of medicine bottles and toilet articles, hot-water bottles, thermos flasks. Gabriel wanted Juliette to take comfort from the sight of these European conveniences. She was to live like an adventurous princess, travelling for a whim, surrounded with toys. And for just this reason his own life, in the eyes of the people, must seem twice as Spartan. He had made up his mind not to sleep in a tent, nor eat food cooked in "Three-Tent Square."

Back from their graves the Yoghonoluk villagers took a last

look at houses no longer theirs. Each of them had a huge corded bundle, heavier than his strength, to carry up with him. Dazed and unhappy, fidgeting and straying about their rooms, they awaited the night. Here was the mat one had had to leave, here stood a lamp, and there, Christ Saviour! stood the bed. The expensive bed, saved up for through hard working years, so that one might become a better man by the possession of this fortress of family life. And now the bed must be left standing, mere loot for Turk and Arab scum. The hours dragged on. And in these homes everything was unpacked and packed again, to see if room could not be made for this or that unnecessary object in the bundle. Even in the craziest tumble-down hovels there took place these poignant separations from the household gear that envelops the human being in his illusions and in his love.

Gabriel, like all the rest, went straying late that afternoon through the rooms of his house. They were dead and empty. Juliette, with Gonzague Maris and her establishment, had set out hours ago for the mountain. Since the day was intolerably hot, she had longed for the coolness she expected to find there. Nor had she wanted to be caught in crowds of villagers on the move. Gabriel, who could feel some passing regret at leaving the most casually slept-in hotel bedroom (since everywhere one leaves a bit of oneself, a beloved departed), was quite unmoved. This house of his fathers, the place where he had been a child, had lived through these last decisive months, had nothing to say to him. He marvelled at this lack of all emotion, but it was so. The only things he regretted even a little were his antiques, those collector's joys of the first happy weeks in Yoghonoluk. He kept turning from Artemis and Apollo to the glorious Mithras, stroking the faces of gods with a tender hand. Then, at the selamlik door, he turned sharply away and gave up the house, its lares and penates, for ever.

In an innyard, leftwards from the villa, an unusual scene was being played. Those dregs of Yoghonoluk not permitted to follow the others into camp had gathered together there. The keening women, the beggars with prophetic heads, a few stray brats escaped from their parents, formed an excited group. That Sato, the orphan of Zeitun, should have been with them is not to be wondered at. One personality stood out from them, whose impressive power even Gabriel could not manage to ignore. This was old Nunik, chieftainess of magic healers and conjuring women. The dark face of this female Wandering Jew, whose origins were lost in the grey of ages, was distinguished by more than a nose half eaten away. It was informed with the ferocious energy by which Nunik had raised herself to the invincible leadership of her caste. The story that she was well over a hundred might be mere fraud, a rumour set going by Nunik for advertisement, and yet her very appearance of timeless age seemed almost the indestructible guarantee of the worth of her cures and of the healing quality in the rough life she led. Nunik held between her hard, stringy thighs a black lamb, no doubt strayed from the herds, and she was slitting its throat open from underneath. It seemed a very workmanlike slit, done with the quietest of hands, while her lips parted under the horrible, lupus-eaten nose from over a gleaming set of magnificently youthful teeth. It gave her such a look of grinning relish that Bagradian lost his temper at the sight.

"What are you all doing here, you set of low thieves?"

A prophet tapped his way to the front, to inform him with unapproachable dignity: "It's the blood-test, Effendi, and it's being done on your behalf."

Bagradian nearly flung himself on the rabble. "Where did you steal that lamb from? Don't you know that anyone who touches the people's property can be shot or hanged?"

The prophet seemed not to notice the base aspersions. "Better watch, Effendi, to see which way the blood will flow. Towards the mountain or towards the house."

286

Gabriel saw how the lamb's dark blood came throbbing out of it, collected on the flat, smooth place below it into a thick pool, which rose and rose in a growing circle until the last drops fell. Still the puddle seemed undecided, as though it had some secret injunction to obtain. At last, three little tongues edged charily forwards, but stopped at once, till suddenly an impetuous rill wound itself out, wriggling quickly on—towards the house. The mob went mad with excitement.

"Koh yem! The blood goes to the house!"

Nunik bent down close over the blood-pool—as though from its nature and the tempo of its course she could tell with the greatest precision something of importance. As she raised her head, Gabriel saw that the twisted grin which had so roused him was the usual look of her ravaged face. But she spoke in a curiously soft, old voice that did not seem to be her own: "Effendi, those on the mountain will be saved."

In that instant Gabriel remembered the coins given him by the Agha, and left forgotten in the villa. "I'll have those at least," he thought; "it'd be a pity . . ." He went back. At the door of the villa he hesitated. Should one ever turn back again from a journey? Then he hurried on, in long quick strides, to his bedroom, and took the coins from their case. He held the gold one up to the light; Ashod Bagrathuni's head stood out from it in the finest chiselling. The Greek inscription round the edge of the silver coin ran, without divisions into words, into an almost unreadable circle of letters:

"To the inexplicable, in us and above us."

Gabriel put them in his pocket. He left the garden through the west door in the park wall without turning back to look at the villa. A few steps farther, he stopped to look at his watch, still absurdly set to European time. The sun was already above the Damlayik. Gabriel Bagradian noted carefully the hour and minute at which his new life had begun.

287

Soon after sundown the people of the seven villages, heavily laden, had moved out in groups or families to toil up the steeps by all the most available paths.

A dense moon, incredibly metallic, rose behind the jagged grey peaks of the Amanus, in the north-east. It sailed on visibly through the sky, nearer and nearer. It was no longer something flat stuck against the vault of heaven. The black depths behind it grew more and more distinct. Nor was the earth, for Gabriel, the usual stable abiding-place, but the little vehicle through the cosmos that it is in reality. And this stereoscopic cosmos not only extended beyond the plastic moon, but forced itself down into the valley to bathe in coolness every pore of Gabriel's resting body. The moon was already half-way over the sky, and the panting groups still toiled on past him. It was always the same silhouette. In front, grimly prodding the ground with his stick, the father, loaded with baggage. A gruff call, a lamenting answer. The women stumbled under loads which bowed them almost to the earth. In spite of these, they had to keep a sharp look-out, to see that the goats were not straying. And yet, now and again, under these burdens, there came a little spurt of young girl's laughter, an eye sparkling encouragement. Gabriel started out of a half-sleep. Innumerable children were lifting up their voices to weep. Hundreds of squalling children—as though they had all at the same instant discovered that their parents had gone away. And in the midst of this the short grunting voices and shrill reproofs of many grandmothers. But no—they were not abandoned infants, only the cats of Yoghonoluk, Azir, and Bitias. Cats have seven lives and as many souls, and each soul its own voice. Therefore, to kill a cat, you must kill him seven times (Sato had long had this wisdom from Nunik). In real truth their masters' absence did not move the cats of Yoghonoluk, Azir, and Bitias in the least, for cats serve only the house with their seven lives, not its human beings. Perhaps they were even squalling for joy in their new, unbridled lease of life. The

288

dogs really suffered. Even the wild dog of Syrian villages never quite gets away from men. He can never find his way back to himself, to fox, jackal, wolf. He may have been wild for countless generations, he is, and remains, the dismissed employee of civilization. He snuffles longingly round houses, not merely for a bone, but to get himself taken back into slavery, to be set to the tasks he has forgotten. The wild dogs of the villages knew all this. Already they had nosed out the camp on the Damlayik. But they also knew that this camp, unlike the village street, was strictly forbidden them. Madly they scurried up the forbidden mountain, grovelled their way through brushwood, rustled like snakes under myrtle and arbutus bushes. Not one of them got the bright idea of going off to Moslem neighbourhoods, to beg bones in Chalikhan or Ain Yerab. They still adored this faithless people which had now abandoned its common dwelling-place. Their souls seemed to perish in wild grief, yet few of them dared to utter their monosyllabic bark, which has long since lost the extensive, much inflected, civilized vocabulary of European house dogs. These dogs' whole grief was in their eyes. Everywhere round him in the dark Gabriel caught glints of the green fire of these eyes, rapturously curious, which dared not venture nearer forbidden ground.

The moon had vanished behind the back of Musa Dagh. A faint wind had come into being. "They're all up there by now," reflected Gabriel, past whom, over an hour before, the last group had plodded its way. And yet, either from weariness or the sheer need to be alone, he could still not tear himself loose from this dark observation post. How could he tell that this might not be the last time in his life at which he would be able to be alone? And had not this power to be alone always seemed to him God's best gift? He granted himself another half-hour of this extra-mundane peace—then he would have to push on up to the north defences to superintend and hurry on the trench-digging. He leaned back against the oak

behind him and smoked. Out of the darkness came a very
tardy straggler indeed. Gabriel heard the clip-clop of hoofs,
and stones rolling away. He saw a lantern, then a man with a
donkey, both piled up with towering burdens. Each step the
donkey took was almost a fall. Yet the man dragged a monstrous sack, which every few minutes he set down, panting
and gasping. Gabriel recognized the apothecary only when
Krikor's sack came thudding at his feet. Krikor's face looked
distorted; the impassive mandarin's countenance had become
the mask of some furious warrior divinity. Sweat streamed
over the polished cheeks into the long goatee, which jerked up
and down for want of breath. He seemed in great pain, and
hunched his shoulders, bending far forward.

Gabriel revealed himself: "You ought to have given your
drug-sack to my people, instead of trying to drag your whole
chemist's shop alone."

Krikor still strove to get his breath. Yet, even so, he could
put a certain aloofness into his answer: "None of this has
anything to do with my drugs. I sent those up several hours
ago."

Gabriel had by now observed that both the chemist and his
ass were laden exclusively with books. For some vague reason
this annoyed him and inspired him with the wish to mock.
"Forgive my mistake, Apothecary. Are these the only provisions you've managed to bring?"

Krikor's face was again impassive. He eyed Gabriel with all
his usual detachment: "Yes, Bagradian, these are my provisions—unluckily not the whole of them." A coughing-fit
shook him. He sat down and mopped his sweat with a monstrous handkerchief. The starlight twinkled. The donkey
stood with its heavy load and melancholy knock-knees on the
pathway. Minutes elapsed. Gabriel regretted his unkind impulse. But Krikor's voice had regained all its old superiority.

"Gabriel Bagradian, you, as a Paris *savant*, have had very
different chances from mine, the Yoghonoluk chemist. Yet

perhaps one or two things have escaped you, which I have perceived. Possibly you never heard the saying of the sublime Gregory Nazianzen, nor the answer he received from the pagan Tertullian."

No wonder Gabriel was unacquainted with St. Gregory Nazianzen's saying, since Krikor was the only man who had heard it. He related it in his usual lofty voice, with supreme, lordly detachment—though, to be sure, his confusion of Tertullian, the Church Father, with a pagan of the same name was a sign that Jove can nod.

"Once the sublime Gregory Nazianzen was invited to dinner by the august pagan, Tertullian.—Have no fear, Bagradian, the story is as short as it is profound. They spoke of the good harvest and the fine white bread which they were breaking together. A sunbeam lay across the table. Gregory Nazianzen lifted up his bread in his hands and said to Tertullian: 'My friend, we must thank God for His great mercy—for see, this bread which tastes so delicious is nothing else than this golden sunbeam which, out in the fields, has changed itself into wheat for us.' Tertullian, however, stood up from table and drew down a work of the poet Vergil from his shelves. He said to Gregory: 'My friend and guest—if we praise God for a mere slice of bread, how much more, then, must we not praise Him for this book. For see, this book is the transformed sunbeam of a far higher sun than that whose beams we can watch with our eyes across the table.' "

After a while Gabriel asked in melancholy sympathy: "And your whole library, Krikor? This can be only a sample of it. Have you buried the books?"

Krikor rose as stiffly as a wounded hero: "I did not bury them. Books perish in the ground. I left them, just as they were."

Gabriel took up the lantern which the apothecary had forgotten. It was getting lighter, and Krikor could not hide the fact that tears ran down his inscrutable parchment cheeks.

Bagradian shouldered the old man's sack: "Do you really think, Apothecary," he said, "that I was only born for service-rifles, cartridge belts, and trench-digging?"

Though Krikor protested again and again, Gabriel carried his heavy sack to the North Saddle.

BOOK TWO

THE STRUGGLE OF THE WEAK

"And the winepress was trodden, without the city . . ."

REVELATION xiv, 20

1

Life on the Mountain

MUSA DAGH! Mountain of Moses! At its summit, in the grey dawn-light, a whole population set up its camp. The mountain top, the windy air, the sea surge, put such new life into this people that the toil of the night seemed dispersed and forgotten. No more strained and exhausted faces, but only excited-looking ones. In and around the Town Enclosure they ran past one another, shouting. No consciousness whatever of the underlying reality of it all, only a pugnacious stir. Like a spring torrent, small and overwhelming urgencies swept away all thoughts of the whole. Even Ter Haigasun, decking the wooden altar at the centre of the camp, and so engaged in getting things ship-shape for eternity, was shouting impatiently at the men who helped him in the work.

Gabriel had climbed the point selected by him as observation post. From one of the rocky knolls of the Damlayik, it offered a clear look-out to sea, across the Orontes plain and those undulations of the mountain which ebbed away towards Antioch. You could see the valley itself from Kheder Beg as far as Bitias. The outlying villages were hidden by bends in the road. Of course, besides this chief observation post, there were ten or twelve thrust-out spying-points, from which single sections of the valley could be closely observed. But here, well shielded by ridges of rock, he had a clear view of the general outlines. Perhaps because, from his position, he stood above the general scurry of the camp, Bagradian found himself suddenly, sharply confronted, pierced to the quick, by its reality. There in the north, the east, the south, as far as Antakiya—no, as far as Mosul and Deir ez-Zor—destruction, not to be evaded! Hundreds of thousands of Moslems, who would soon have only one objective—the smoking out of this insolent wasps' nest on Musa Dagh. On the farther side an indifferent Mediterranean, sleepily surging round the sharp declivities of the mountain. No matter how close Cyprus might be, what French or English cruiser would take the least interest in this arid length of Syrian coast quite out of the war zone? Certainly the fleets only put out in threatened directions, towards Suez and the North African coast, always sailing away from the dead Gulf of Alexandretta. Bagradian, looking over the desert sea, realized how impossibly—demagogically— he had behaved both towards himself and his hearers, when he tried, at the general assembly, to raise hopes of a rescuing gunboat. The scornfully empty horizon crushed his arguments. All round them, incalculable death, with not the narrowest cranny of escape—such was the truth. A huddled, piteous crowd of villagers, inescapably menaced on every side. And even that was not the whole truth. For should death from without—though not even a madman would have supposed it—remain benevolently inactive; though no attack should come, not one shot be fired—even so, another death, from within, would rise in their midst, to destroy them all. They might scrape and spare as much as they pleased, herds and supplies could not be renewed and, within measurable time, they would be exhausted.

Down in the valley the thought of the Damlayik had seemed a release, since in bitter need the prospect of any kind of change works as an assuagement and a cure. But now they were firmly ensconced, the healing thought no longer sustained Gabriel. He had the sensation of having been hurled out of space and time. No doubt he could keep the inevitable at arm's length for a few seconds, yet in exchange he had had to sacrifice the hundred cracks and loop-holes which chance

296

presents. Had not Harutiun Nokhudian made a wiser decision for his flock? An icy compulsion had hold of Gabriel. What an unforgivable sin against Stephan and Juliette! Over and over again he had let slip the moment of escape, nor once seriously tried to shake Juliette out of her fool's paradise, though he had known, even on that March Sunday, that the trap was closed. Violent giddiness, sudden emptiness in his head, succeeded this incredible feeling of guilt. The two horizons, land and sea, had begun to swirl. The whole earth was a twirling ring, and Musa Dagh its dead, fixed focus. But the true centre of that focus was Gabriel's body, which, high though it stood, was in reality the lowest point of rigidity above which swung this inescapable vortex. All we ask is to keep alive, he reflected horror-stricken. Instantly there followed the still thought: "But—why?"

Gabriel rushed down to the Town Enclosure. The separate committees of the Council were sitting already, since the myriad tasks of the first day were not yet apportioned. He insisted that every active person, man or woman, should set to work instantly on the trenches and outposts already begun. This whole line of defences must be as good as complete by tomorrow evening. Who could tell whether the first Turkish assault might not be delivered within two days? He had to keep on urging again and again that defence, and all that appertained to it—the sharpest fighting discipline—must take precedence of all other things. Since they had chosen him to lead their resistance, it followed as the inevitable consequence that he must be given a free hand, not only over the front-line fighters, but the reserve—that is to say, over fighters and workers—the whole camp. Pastor Aram, who was unfortunately very touchy, kept saying that it was equally urgent to control the inner life of the community. At present it was all chaos—each family jealous of the living-space assigned to every other, and the separate communes equally dissatisfied with their camping-ground. Bagradian seized on the pastor's words. There must be no such thing as dissatisfaction, this was a state of acute emergency. Grousers must be dealt with out of hand, and ruthlessly punished. Kebussyan and the other mukhtars at once began siding with the pastor. Even Dr. Bedros Altouni obstinately insisted that the bodily needs of the people were the first thing to be considered, that work on the hospital-hut must be started at once, so that the sick might not get any worse. Then, one after another, teachers and mukhtars made rambling speeches—each on the particular urgency of his own particular job. Gabriel perceived with terror how hard it is to get a deliberating body to pass the most essential and obvious measure. But the constitution he had given them soon proved its efficacy. Ter Haigasun had the necessary authority to determine undecided cases. He made such skilful and unobtrusive use of it that their counsels had soon ceased to be troubled with dangerous and confusing suggestions. Gabriel was perfectly right. Everything else must give way to the work of defence. The rules of discipline laid down several days ago by the council must be read out instantly to the decads and, as from that moment, come into force. Everyone owed unconditional obedience to the chief. He had the definite advantage over all the other representatives of having learned to know war as a front-line officer. The Council therefore must give him complete authority in all which might concern defence, fighting preparations, and camp discipline. Gabriel Bagradian and the members of his Defence Committee were in no way bound to submit their decisions to the General Council. Pastor Aram Tomasian had been given a seat on that committee, and Gabriel on the Committee for Internal Discipline, so that unnecessary friction might be avoided. And naturally the commander must have his own powers to inflict punishment. He must be able to deprive recalcitrants and lazy people of their rations, have them put in irons, punished with the bastinado, mild or severe, as he might see fit. Only one punishment—death—remained at the sole discretion of Ter Haigasun, the Council having unanimously endorsed it. Every inhabitant of the camp must be made to realize, from this first hour, the seriousness of a war situation. The chief tasks of the Camp Committee would be to provide for strict law and order, to make these difficult circumstances seem natural, and to direct every effort towards the development of a normal, ordinary daily routine, just as much up here as down in the valley. Ter Haigasun kept stressing the words "normal" and "everyday." On these unobtrusive powers, more than on any deed of heroism, would depend the strength and duration of their resistance. So that not one pair of hands must be left idle. Not even children must be without their regular work. No holiday wildness should encroach on this life-or-death struggle. School must still be taught in a place assigned to it, and in as disciplined and serious a manner as ever. Teachers, as they came off duty, must take their turns in holding classes. Only unremitting work, concluded the priest, would enable people to sustain this life of deprivations. "So get to work. Let's waste as little time as possible on talk."

The mukhtars assembled their communes on the big square before the altar, already marked out as the Town Enclosure. Bagradian ordered Chaush Nurhan to form up the eighty-six decads of his first defence. That tyrant of recruits soon had them drawn up in front of the still unconsecrated altar, in neat square formation. Ter Haigasun climbed the altar tribune, a broad space raised fairly high above the square. He asked Bagradian, but no other leader, to stand beside him. Then he turned to the men and in a resonant voice read out the rules, as taken down by Avakian. These he supplemented with a few threatening words of his own. Anyone who disobeyed, or set himself up against, his chief would bring down instant punishment on himself. Let all newcomers from Turkish barracks take that to heart. It was not an understood thing that they should be taken into camp and fed out of communal supplies.

It was an act of brotherly kindness by the communes, of which they would have to show themselves worthy. Ter Haigasun took up the silver crucifix from the altar and came down into the ranks, along with Gabriel. Slowly he administered the oath. The men had to repeat, with uplifted hands:

"I swear before God the Father, the Son, and the Holy Ghost that I will defend this encamped people to the last drop of my blood; that I subordinate myself to my commander and all his edicts, in blind obedience; that I acknowledge the authority of the elected Council of Leaders; that I will never leave the mountain for my own purposes—as God the Father shall help me to my salvation."

After this oath had been administered, the front-line men marched behind the altar. The eleven hundred reservists, men and women, divided into twenty-two groups, took a shorter oath of obedience and willingness to work. This reserve shouldered the main burden of entrenchment and camp-building. It had nothing with which to ward off an attack but those scythes, pitchforks, and hammers which it had carried up with it from the valley. Lastly the three hundred adolescents, the "light cavalry," marched forward. Ter Haiga-sun made them a short speech of admonishment, and Gabriel explained their duties as scouts, signallers, and liaison-runners. He divided these youngsters up into three sections, by "picking them out." The first were to garrison the observation posts and concealed look-outs, and send a report every two hours to headquarters. The hundred oldest and most reliable boys were chosen for this very important duty. It would also be their job to post sentries, day and night, on the "Dish Terrace," to use their sharp young eyes to keep a look-out for the smoke (vain hope!) of passing ships. The second section were to do orderly work. This hundred must always be somewhere about around headquarters, to take the commander's orders in any direction, and keep him in touch with the various sectors of the defence. Samuel Avakian was put in command of this corps of orderlies, and Stephan enrolled in it. Finally, the third hundred were to be at Pastor Aram's disposal, for general use about the camp and, for instance, to carry rations out to the line.

This dividing up of the villagers by Bagradian instantly revealed its advantages. The martial self-importance which swelled the breasts of the various decads, the pricking itch to command, with which lower officers were at once infected, the childish delight in forming ranks and playing soldiers—all these human traits served to veil completely, in the beneficent ardour of a game, any deeply uneasy sense of the inevitable. As, soon after this, the ranks marched off to trench-building, there arose here and there, shyly yet stubbornly, the old workers' song of the valley:

> "Days of misfortune pass and are gone,
> Like the days of winter, they come and they go;
> The sorrows of men do not last very long,
> Like the buyers in shops, they come and go."

Gabriel summoned Chaush Nurhan and the heads of the most important decads. But meanwhile Ter Haigasun had left the altar square for that of the Three Tents, near a great well-spring. Sheltered on three sides by fern-grown rocks and myrtle bushes, its beauty was a signal proof of how carefully Juliette was looked after. Ter Haigasun asked to speak to the hanum Juliette Bagradian. Since Kristaphor, Missak, Hovhannes, and the other servants were all engaged in setting up the adjacent "kitchen square," the priest found only Gonzague Maris to take his message. That young man was pacing rapidly up and down, as passengers walk for exercise up and down the narrow deck of a liner. The Greek went to Juliette's canvas tent and struck the little gong which hung at the entrance. But the hanum kept them waiting a very long time. When at last she appeared, she asked Maris to bring out a chair for Ter Haigasun. He refused to sit down, regretted that he had no time to spare. He let his hands slip out of sight into his wide sleeves, and cast down his eyes. What he said, in his stiff French, was charged with formality. Madame's kindness was known to everybody. He therefore begged Madame to honour his people by undertaking a special duty. It was necessary that a very large white banner, with a red cross, should be set up on the ledge of rock jutting out to sea, on the steep side behind the mountain, to give any ships which God, in His mercy, might choose to send them knowledge of their desperate plight. Therefore the banner must bear an inscription in French and English: "Christians in need. Help!" Ter Haigasun bowed as he asked Juliette whether, with the help of some other women, she would be willing to get this banner prepared. She promised; but tepidly, indifferently. It was queer —the Frenchwoman seemed to have no inkling of the honour Ter Haigasun was paying her, as much by his visit as this request, which he framed with all possible courtesy. She had grown indifferent again to all things Armenian. But when Ter Haigasun quickly left her, with nothing more than a curt nod, she suddenly became very restless, and herself sought out two big linen sheets, to be sewn together on the machine.

GABRIEL insisted again, to Chaush Nurhan and the other platoon leaders, on the need for the very strictest discipline. From now on let no one leave his post without permission. Nor must any man in the front line be allowed to sleep in the Town Enclosure with his family. Nights must be spent in the trenches unless special leave were given by the commander. Bagradian also set up his headquarters at a place where all could easily reach him. There, every day, two hours before sunset, he would hold a session, which every section and group commander must attend. He would be ready to hear requests, complaints, and denunciations, arrange for reinforcements, and give out the following day's orders. That completed the broad outlines of military organization. Now it would all depend on

302

will and endurance to get things going. Gabriel, map in hand, discussed the disposal of his thirteen sections of defence. Three of these required larger garrisons—the others were mainly strong observation posts, for which, provisionally, one or half a decad sufficed. To the trenches and rock barricades of the North Saddle, on the other hand, Gabriel assigned a skeleton force of forty decads, with two hundred rifles in good repair. He himself was to command this important sector. His immediate subordinate was Chaush Nurhan, to whom the command of the positions above the ilex gully and the task of general inspection were entrusted. His responsible duties comprised especially the renewal of munitions and supplies and the proper care of rifles. Chaush Nurhan had the invaluable faculty of being in ten places at once, and had indeed made all his preparations for a workshop and cartridge factory. All the necessary tools and material had been carried up from his secret store in Yoghonoluk. All that now remained was the question who should command the South Bastion. The garrison of this most distant sector would be composed of fifteen decads. For reasons already stated, deserters, both authentic and bogus, had been detailed off to make up this force—a very large one, considering the fortress strength of the point. Provisionally these men were being commanded by a reliable native of Kheder Beg. But Bagradian pursued a definite object. Sarkis Kilikian was, after all, a gallant soldier, with very recent trench experience in the Caucasus. He was both intelligent and educated. He had suffered unheard-of cruelties from the Turks and, if he still had anything like a soul in him, it must be parched with an inhuman thirst for revenge. Gabriel therefore intended to keep a sharp, provisional eye on Kilikian, and entrust him with this command if he proved satisfactory. He hoped that this might not only release a valuable force, but give him full power over the deserters, unreliable people in the main. So, when the decads marched off, he had kept back the Russian. All this while Kilikian had stood scrutinizing Gabriel, with a kind of rigid detachment that seemed too bored even for insolence. This figure, emaciated by slavery in the oil fields, by jails, by a hundred gruesome adventures, clothed as it was in earthy rags, and the face like a young death's-head stretched with tanned hide, looked aristocratic, imposing, in spite of everything. Since he never once turned his light, contemptuous, observant eyes away from Bagradian, he may have sensed a kind of respect even in this pampered, well-dressed "boss." Perhaps he mistook for simple fear what in reality was the tribute to his own indescribable fate and the strength that had managed to surmount it. But his very inkling of a fear, in conjunction with the appearance of this bourgeois, who could never in all his life have known a second's real want, degradation, terror, aroused all the malice in Kilikian. Bagradian called sharply, like an officer, to him:

"Sarkis Kilikian, report to me in two hours, in the north trenches. I've got a job for you."

The Russian's eyes (he had still not turned them away from Bagradian) took on the dull shimmer of an agate. He replied with a jerky laugh: "I may come, and again I mayn't. I really don't know what I'd care to do."

Gabriel knew that everything would depend on his reply. He must make quite sure of his rank. His authority would be gone for ever if he struck the wrong note, or fate went against him. They were all listening eagerly; many a hidden, unholy joy flared up. Gabriel had made for himself a uniform, out of a hunting-kit, scarcely worn, which had belonged to Avetis. With it he wore leggings and a sun-helmet. This he put on before bearing down, in slow, swinging steps, upon the Russian. The helmet made him taller by half a head. He struck at his leggings with a cane.

"Listen to me, Sarkis Kilikian—and keep your ears wide open."

His approach had been so direct that it forced the Russian a step back. Bagradian paused. His heart was thudding; he could feel that his voice was not quite steady. This good luck he conceded his opponent. He waited, therefore, never taking his eyes off this death's-head, till he could fill to overflowing with clear, cold will-power.

"I myself give you leave, Kilikian, to do whatever you think you must. But before you leave here, you'll have to have made up your mind. . . . You're free. You can go to the devil, no one's keeping you. People of your sort are the very last we need in this camp."

Gabriel paused, as though expecting Sarkis Kilikian to avail himself immediately of this permission and slouch off in his usual slow, contemptuous way without another glance at the Damlayik. But the Russian stood rooted. An inquisitive glint had found its way into the dead, agate shimmer of his eyes.

Bagradian's voice became coldly pitying: "I intended to distinguish you, who've been a soldier, from your comrades, by entrusting you with a post of leadership, since I know you've had more to bear from the Turks than most of us. You might have taken bloody revenge on your own behalf, and on theirs. . . . But—since you really don't know whether you'll care to —since you're really nothing but a skulking coward of a deserter, who can't even see his duty to his own people, after having taken a solemn oath—get out! We don't need a slacker, an insolent hound, eating the food of our wives and children. If you ever dare show yourself here again, I'll have you shot. Go over to the Turks. Their regiments will soon be here. They're expecting you."

For such a man as the Russian there should really have been nothing left after this but to rush on this "capitalist" and bash his face in. But Sarkis Kilikian never moved. His eyes lost their staring calm and strayed from man to man in search of supporters.

Gabriel let five seconds elapse, seconds which raised his

305

authority like a wave before bellowing with unrestrained harshness: "You seem to have made up your mind. Well— quick march. Get along."

It was curious how this sudden cracking of the whip could transform the Russian into the old jail-bird he was. His head sagged down between his shoulders, his sulky eyes glowered up at Gabriel, now much the taller of the two. Kilikian's whole weakness lay in the clarity with which he could estimate his position. He was fully conscious that this was a moment of nauseating defeat—yet all violence depends on a spirit so drunk with hate that the will is not lamed by a previous calculation of consequences. For months he had lived secure on Musa Dagh. He had begged enough to eat in the villages. This general migration on to the heights came as an unforeseen improvement in his condition. But, should he get turned out of camp, his last chance of finding human sustenance would have vanished. He would not dare show himself in the valley, while even the surrounding hill-country would be invested, in a hand's turn, by the Turks. Death, which had so often passed by him carelessly, might snap him up. The least he could expect from the Turks would be to be flayed alive, killed by inches. All this had flashed, in the fraction of a second,. upon Kilikian, and neither his pride, his hate, nor his defiance prevailed against such certain consciousness. He attempted another laugh, but could manage only a piteously degraded sneer.

Gabriel did not budge an inch: "Well? What are you still hanging about for?"

Sarkis Kilikian's face, the cowering face of an old convict, turned. "I want . . ."

"Well . . . ?"

The Russian looked up, but with different eyes, no longer of a pale untroubled agate, but the eyes of a hesitating school-boy. Gabriel had to remember the boy of eleven, with a carving-knife in his hand, shielding his mother. It was some time before Kilikian could manage to announce his defeat: "I want to stay."

Gabriel reflected. Would it not be as well to force this recalcitrant to his knees, make him whine out his petition before the assembled decads, and oblige him to take a more rigorous oath? He decided against it, not merely out of pity (his vision of the boy of eleven) but because his deepest instinct forbade. It would have been beneath any leader's dignity to make too much of this puny victory, and unwise to burden his own defence with the hate of a profoundly humbled enemy. He allowed a tinge of kindness to creep into his officer's growl: "This time I don't mind letting you off, Kilikian, and I'll watch your behaviour for a bit. But you aren't worth the slightest responsibility. Look out! You'll be under surveillance. Dismiss!"

So the South Bastion was to be manned only half by deserters. As Kilikian's insolence had shown, they needed a martinet in command of them. A poisoned thorn would have to be driven into their flesh. Bagradian felt certain that in Oskanian, the self-opinionated dwarf, he had found the right kind of commander. So he offered that sombre little schoolmaster the leadership of the South Bastion. He was to enforce impeccable service, the sharpest discipline—was, above all, instantly to report the most trifling slackness or sabotage.

Hrand Oskanian puckered his low forehead, so that his thick, black eyebrows formed a single line above his nose. He appeared to be magnanimously considering whether this half pedagogic, half punitive job was beneath so considerable a man. At last he stated his conditions: "If I'm to take charge of the South Bastion, I must be very well armed, Bagradian Effendi. The fellows'll have to see I'm not to be trifled with."

So Teacher Oskanian arranged with Chaush Nurhan that he was to be given, not only a rifle with a double belt of five cartridges, but a huge holster-pistol and a large, broad-bladed fascine-knife. Thus, armed to the teeth, he hurried off to Three-

Tent Square, where he advanced pompously on Juliette to announce his rank. He did not deign a glance at Gonzague Maris, convinced that this smooth-tongued weakling would vanish at the sight of him—the warrior.

DURING this first day on Musa Dagh work on the trenches advanced so well that there was every hope of completing all the essential defences before sunset. This fever of industry so enthralled them that past and future alike were forgotten in laughter and songs.

The morale of the Town Enclosure turned out to be far less satisfactory. Ter Haigasun and Pastor Aram had their work cut out to deal with the crop of problems that arose. Gabriel's suggested solution, at the first sitting of the council, of that major problem, private property, had already displeased the mukhtars and the rich. But now these hard-headed peasants saw for themselves that no life would be possible on the Damlayik without communal ownership of the herds. So and so many sheep must be slaughtered daily, by precise regulation of supplies, and therefore it would be quite impossible to consider individual owners of flocks. Every reasoning person could also see that the slaughtering must be done by communal butchers on ground set apart; that the delegates of the Council of Leaders must superintend the daily distribution of meat to decads and families, unless there were to be injustice, and so, dangerous discontent. Since one thing leads to another, the mukhtars had at last been got to consent even to a communal kitchen. And this was still not enough! Their duty demanded that not only should they provide these common necessities, but should supervise their distribution, and make them palatable. Such recent converts found it no easy matter to struggle to establish a social order whose ingrained opponents they were themselves. The housing question was solved more easily. Ter Haigasun had always insisted that too rigid and constricting a community, from which there could be no escape, would seem unnatural, and be bound sooner or later to bring its own nemesis. To adapt oneself with the minimum of friction to a new day-to-day life—such was the formula which he championed. So that living-quarters were to be made as extensive as possible. Even to-morrow, as soon as hands and tools could be spared from trench-building, Tomasian senior was to start work on the new settlement of huts, to be built of branches as designed by Aram. There were about a thousand families on the Damlayik, so that a thousand of such huts were intended, planned according to the numbers each must contain. There was abundant wood, to be cut down. Gabriel, even today, had released a certain number of men for tree-felling.

All this was hard, but the real difficulties only began with bread and flour. Here, in view of the urgent necessity to econ-omize, Ter Haigasun was implacably communist. Every sack of grain which single families still possessed—oats, bulgur, maize, potatoes—all that they had baked in their own ovens and laboured to carry up the mountain must be surrendered without mercy. Out of this communal store, at the morning distribution of meat, each family would receive a minute ra-tion. And not only flour was to be sequestered, but salt, coffee, tobacco, rice, spices—all the precious things which careful housewives, with the greatest labour and wisest foresight, had got together for their own use. Opposition to this drastic decree continued for hours. At last Aram Tomasian and the mukhtars, by prayers and curses, had got so far that a few of the more virtuous fathers of families reluctantly set out for the depot, with their bread and flour, their coffee and tobacco. These confiscated goods of the people were classified and ar-ranged there for distribution. Such exemplary self-sacrifice brought imitators, till, little by little, spurred on by shame (since the open camp afforded no means of concealment), the majority followed. Sacks of flour and maize were piled up one beside the other. Old Tomasian was commissioned to build, early next morning, a roof for protection over these stores. Five armed guards were posted round the depot. Ter Haigasun chose these five from the poorest families in the villages.

Ter Haigasun, Gabriel, and the Council had planned, without self-deceiving optimism, against the annihilation of Musa Dagh from all four quarters of the globe. But one danger-spot had so far escaped their calculations. And so, shortly before sunset on the following day, it was just this quarter that delivered an irreparable onslaught, the effects of which were never to be made good. That day the work was going better and better, if only because the sun was overcast. It refrained from slanting its grilling rays across the bent backs of these poor robots, and no one was forced to seek shelter. But, although the sun was covered, there was not a cloud in the whole sky, nor was it any cooler than yesterday. The air was saturated in some composition of dreary mist, some hog-wash rinsings of the universe, surrounding the world like an un-clean conscience; instead of the blazing heat, sultriness lay mountainous over all things. The sea was glassy; from time to time a hot puff of wind came from the west, without ever rippling its firm surface. Yet, for all its heavy immobility, from midday onwards surf kept leaping upon the rocks, with more strength, more suppressed anger, each minute. The work-ers, their minds fast set on their own care and labour, had paid no heed to the evil squintings of the sky. So that the sud-den deluge fully achieved its aim. Four, five gusts of rattling wind, like a short ultimatum of war. The whole Damlayik— every rock, every tree, every myrtle and rhododendron bush— became alert with terror. A terrific thunder-clap—war was declared! And already this southern storm, bristling with flashes, and itself as swift as any lightning, swept on to the attack, enveloping all things in its stifling thicknesses of dust. Mats, coverlets, beds, cushions, white sheets, headkerchiefs, pots and jugs, lamps, heavy things, light things, clattered and swirled past one another, were upset, caught up, and swept away. The people, lifting up their voices, chased malevolently fugitive gear, ran into one another's arms, trod one another's goods into the soil. This noise of assault drowned the wailing voices of many babes, who had all seemed to sense the deeper meaning of this celestial thrashing on their first day. Almost at once this mad chase of vanishing possessions was cast to earth by such a hailstorm as few among these mountaineers could remember. After vain efforts to stand up to it, many lay down flat on the steaming earth, offering their backs to the bastinadoing skies. They bit the ground. They longed to perish. A sudden shout—the munition dump! But luckily Gabriel Bagradian had had the cartridges moved into the sheikh's tent, while Chaush Nurhan had found means for keeping the loose gunpowder dry. Provisions! came the second thought. The men rushed shouting to the grain depot. Too late! The flat cakes were reduced to a sticky mass, the loaves to eviscerated sponges. All the meal-sacks steamed like slaking lime. This destruction was a very serious matter. Most of the salt had melted into the ground. Many began to think of that age-old threat, that on Judgment Day a man shall pick up with his eyelids whatever salt he has spilt during his life. This disaster made them cease to struggle. Drenched to their skins, whipped with hailstones, they huddled on the marshy earth, indifferent to the deluging clouds which poured down swathes an inch thick. Not even their women complained and yammered. Everyone wrapped himself up in brooding solitude, nursing unutterable wrath against Ter Haigasun and the Council, who had this food depot on their consciences, this thrice-accursed order to give up stores. Nothing so much relieves the pent-up breast of a human being as to make individuals responsible for a natural disaster and heap reproaches. Nor did the glowering folk on the Damlayik consider, till long after this, that disaster was in no way the result of Ter Haigasun's command to deliver supplies, since in private hands it would have been just as impossible to rescue them. In the minds of these peasants Heaven seemed, by this punishment, to make manifest its wrathful dislike of communal ownership, its championship of private property. The converted mukhtars, with squinting Thomas Kebussyan at their head, relapsed at once to their first persuasion. They mingled their growls with the reproaches which now assailed the priest from every side.

Ter Haigasun, as the rain ceased, stood with bent head, confronting their fierce hostility, his cassock clinging to his body, the drops pouring off his beard. Bread and flour were utterly spoiled. The priest could not escape the terrible question why God, within the space of ten minutes, should have thought fit to confound the human reckonings of innocent and persecuted men. And this before the end of their first day on Musa Dagh! The sun sank in jagged mountains of crimson, oblivious of the whole incident. Birds sang on till the last instant of light, as though they were making up for lost time. All the humans had been struck dumb. Men, women, children, wandered half naked past one another. Housewives tied ropes between the trees and hung up the dripping clothes to dry. Nobody wanted to sit on the ground, though, before the moon was up, this thirsty soil had sucked in its last gout of moisture. None the less the campfire would not burn, since thick drops still clung to the logs and faggots. Single families squatted, bunched together, turning ill-tempered backs on their next-door neighbours. They must manage to sleep on the bare earth, since mattresses, coverlets, cushions could not possibly be dry till tomorrow night. But they slept in heaps. In misfortune one body needed another to touch, each grief to make quite certain of its neighbour.

PASTOR ARAM TOMASIAN sat in an observation post which the scouts' division had set up in the branches of a very wide and shady oak. From this point one could get a clear view of the church square and village street of the large village of Bitias.

The pastor had borrowed Bagradian's field-glass, so that the dust-swept square and road were clearly visible. Nokhudian's band of Protestants stood in marching order, outside the church. There seemed a surprising number of them; many of his co-religionists must secretly have gone over to Nokhudian. Surprise at finding every nest of Armenians empty as far as Bitias may have caused the müdir and the police chief to hold back their convoy from Saturday to this present Sunday. Saptiehs were scurrying in and out, brandishing their truncheons or guns. Impossible to make out exactly which. A distant zigzag of tiny shapes. Perhaps the gendarmes were already striking right and left. But no sounds of pain or rage drifted so far. Distance had toned down any horror to a framed, faintly animated miniature. Tomasian had to make a conscious effort to realize that this was not a puppet-show which he watched so detachedly through the round end of his glass, but his own destiny. He might tell himself again and again that he had escaped from among the outcasts who down there in the dust-clouds of the valley were setting forth on their road to death, only to prolong his own earthly life by a few days. Up here, among oak leaves, the shade was so pleasant. Rest and comfort filled him from top to toe. The reality of that horror below him was being dispersed in tiny movements, which teased the eye, but left the heart more indifferent than any dream. Pastor Tomasian started, as he realized his own cold-hearted guilt. Down there was his place, and not up here! He thought of the mission house in Marash. The Reverend Mr. Woodley, sent him by God to test his heart, posed again his enigmatic question: "Can you help those children by dying with them?" The trap was set. But later, over there in Bitias, he had let slip his chance a second time, of adding to the pains by which he must bear witness to Christ.

It was a long, a painfully long while, before the convoy, with his old, yet so much juster brother in God, Nokhudian, began to move off. And the freckled müdir seemed certainly to have made a few concessions. A line of sumpter mules walked in the train, the rear of which was even being followed by two carts, their high wheels jolting through the dust-cloud. Pastor Aram saw what he had seen so often in those last seven days in Zeitun: a sick, worming line of human beings, feeble to the point of extinction; a blackish caterpillar, with tremulous feelers, bristles, and tiny feet, winding its piteous length through the landscape, without ever seeming to advance. This mortally wounded, forsaken insect seemed to seek in vain for a place to hide in, among the open windings of the valley. Its peristaltic back thrust forward the foremost sections of its body, drawing the rear ones painfully after it. So that deep notches kept being formed, and often the creeping insect got split up into several parts which, urged by scarcely visible tormenters, grew jaggedly together, as best they might, to break once more when the join had scarcely healed. It was not the wriggle, it was the twitching death throes, of a worm, a last, writhing, stretching, convulsive shudder, as though already carrion flies were creeping up to the open wound.

It seemed almost to be a miracle that, little by little, a gap should form between this worm and the last houses of the village, through which it dragged so unbearably slow a way. "They have several pregnant women," Aram reflected. The instant thought of Hovsannah weighed on his heart. By various signs it was apparent that his wife was very near her time. Nothing had been done, or could have been done, to help her. So that his first child would be born as roughly as any beast on Musa Dagh. Bad as this was, a deep presentiment burdened Tomasian still more heavily—a fear lest this child in its mother's womb should have to suffer for his sin. He lowered his field-glass and, suddenly giddy, clung with both arms to the solid prongs of the fork within which he was sitting. When, after a while, he looked again, the miniature in the telescope had changed. Now the worm was wriggling on through Azir, the silk village. And a party of saptiehs had de-

314

tached itself and was marching north-east, away from Bitias, towards Kebussiye. Pastor Aram sent instant warning to headquarters. The danger soon passed. The saptiehs did not wheel in the direction of the North Saddle of the Damlayik, but disappeared up the rising ground at the foot of the valley. They were on the wrong track, thanks to Nokhudian. The country lay quiet. A few hundred Moslems were prowling the squares and streets of empty villages—mohajirs from the north-west, brought by the scent of booty, and the native riffraff of the plain. This scum still seemed not to have possession of the houses. Perhaps some government order had dulled its appetite. These gentry buzzed, like indolent horseflies, along the streets. The saptieh detachment was lost to sight, eastwards, down a side valley, before it had come as far as Kebussiye—another proof of how it had been outwitted. The sudden hope —perhaps we'll be left in peace for days . . . perhaps the Turks will leave Musa Dagh on their left for ever.

Pastor Aram jumped down from his spying-post. Woodcutters' hatchets rang out on every side, in the dark groves. If he had not been able to prove himself God's priest, let him at least prove himself God's soldier. He almost ran the whole way back into camp, in his haste not to miss an instant's duty.

THE camp looked incredibly industrious. Long lines of burdened donkeys, piled high with heavy loads of oak branches, nodded past young Tomasian. Great stones for laying foundations were being trundled by on wheelbarrows. Father Tomasian's assistants were measuring out streets with lines of cord and marking off the spaces for the huts. Already, here and there, there had arisen the vague scaffolding of a hutment. Families competed in speed. Children, and even the very old, worked beside the strongest men and women. The "public buildings" were already surprisingly far advanced—the hospital-tent, under Bedros Altouni's supervision, and the big granary. But Father Tomasian in person supervised the government barrack, a work on which he had set his heart. It covered a wide space, with two side-cabins, provided with doors that could be locked.

Meanwhile Juliette had installed herself in Three-Tent Square. Gabriel had expressly begged her to think of nothing and of nobody but herself, not even of him. He had brought up the matter for discussion at a Council sitting: "My wife has the right to lead her own life, even up here, on the Damlayik. She must live here just as she chooses. We others are of the same blood and so are subject to laws on which we've all of us decided. But she remains outside our laws. She's French —the child of a more fortunate people, although she's compelled by fate to share our dangers. And therefore she has the right to our most generous hospitality."

All the members of the Council of Leaders had responded to Bagradian's appeal. The three tents exclusively reserved for Juliette, the heaps of luggage, her special kitchen and separate household, her tinned food, her two Dutch cows, bought by Avetis the younger—all these exceptional possessions and special privileges would have to be made acceptable to the people. Gabriel had indeed given orders that most of the milk was to be distributed among the children of the camp, with whatever else could be spared from Juliette's kitchen. But these were very minor concessions, which left her still a highly privileged person.

Enemies, or ill-disposed friends, to demonstrate the gap between precept and practice, needed only to point to Juliette's luxury when Gabriel urged the necessity for a careful sharing-out of supplies. They could not have denied that their leader did not sleep in a tent, but at his post; that he drew the same rations as all his men; that his property had gone into the general pool and been of the greatest advantage to the community—however, it remained equally undeniable that, for Juliette's sake, he withheld a great many luxuries from the common stock. This discrepancy might foster dangerous con-

316

flicts. But at present none of the leaders seemed to be thinking anything of the kind.

And yet, not an hour before, the mayor of Yoghonoluk had had to submit to an acid lecture from his wife on the subject of Three-Tent Square. Wasn't she, the pupil of the Missionary Sisters at Marash, as much a lady as this Frenchwoman? Was she so very much beneath her that she had to live, just like all the common village women, in a wretched hut made of branches? And was he, her husband, Thomas Kebussyan, really such a poor little worm that now there was no difference between him and any beggarly Dikran or Mikael, whereas the difference was so immense between him and that inflated Bagradian? These wifely exhortations ended in Kebussyan's slyly contriving that he and his family should not have to live in a draughty hut, but in a spacious log-house, especially built for them, close to the altar. That no bad blood might be caused by this stately edifice, the mukhtar had made up his mind to hang out a sign over the door, with the inscription "Town Hall." So that, remembering his intended ruse, he nodded approvingly to Bagradian's appeal on behalf of Juliette.

Ter Haigasun looked Gabriel full in the face before lowering his eyes, as he always did when he was speaking: "Gabriel Bagradian, we all hope your wife may escape, even if sooner or later the rest of us perish. May she say a good word for us to the French."

Juliette lived in one of the two hunting-tents. She had asked Hovsannah and Iskuhi to share the second. Hovsannah, in sombre anxiety, awaited her child. In the sheikh-pavilion, half of which was used for stores and luggage, there were three beds. Stephan slept in one, the second belonged to Samuel Avakian, who, however, as staff-officer and adjutant, always passed his nights within reach of Bagradian. Since the latter had curtly renounced all comfortable living, Juliette placed the third bed in the sheikh-tent at Gonzague Maris's disposal. She felt under some obligation to that young man for the very

317

discreet homage with which he surrounded her, especially in these last, trying days. He had saved Gabriel's life. Also he was the one European, besides herself, on the Damlayik. There were many moments when this bond between them grew so intense that they eyed each other like conspirators, prisoners in the same jail. Juliette felt a dangerous inclination to slackness. Gonzague was still dressed out of a bandbox. She came upon him sometimes unawares, brushing a suit, with scrupulous care, outside the tent, sewing on a button, polishing shoes. His nails were always clean, his hands well cared for; he shaved, in contrast to Gabriel, every day. Yet this scrupulous care of himself suggested no particular vanity, seemed rather to be an active dislike of whatever was soiled or ill defined. A spot on his clothes, mud on his shoes, would cause Gonzague real unhappiness. It was as though by nature he could not tolerate anything fusty or half unconscious, as though, if he were to live at all, it must all be raised into the light of a clear purpose of his own. This meticulous approach to life, which refused to give way before any circumstance, impressed Juliette. All the less intelligible, therefore, Gonzague's placid decision to share the death of a set of foreigners.

Once, when he had not been near her all day, she routed him out: "Have you begun to write your descriptive articles?"

He watched her, surprised, and yet half quizzical. "I never take notes. My memory is my only real asset. I shan't need to save a few smudged papers."

The young man's cocksureness annoyed her. "It remains to be seen if you'll manage to save your head—memory and all."

He answered with a short laugh; really he was expressing a deep conviction: "You don't surely imagine, Juliette, that Turkish soldiers, or anything else, could prevent my leaving this if I really wanted to?"

Both this and the tone in which he said it displeased Juliette. This decisive biding of his time which Gonzague so often let her see in him repelled her. But there were other moments at which he could seem as lost as a stray child. Then a motherly pity would well up in her. And it did her good.

Near Three-Tent Square, beyond the beeches, Kristaphor and Missak had set up a table with benches. This nook was as charmingly peaceful as though it had been the remote corner of a garden with alleys all round it, not part of an inaccessible mountain camp. Here of an afternoon sat Juliette, with Iskuhi and Hovsannah, receiving her guests.

Usually these callers were the same as those who had frequented Villa Bagradian. Krikor was a regular visitor, and the teachers, whenever they happened to be off duty. Hapeth Shatakhian did his uttermost, as he expressed it, "to delight Madame by the purity of his French conversation." But Oskanian had ceased to appear as the maestro of poetry and calligraphy; he was now a fierce and impassioned warrior. For "afternoon calls" he still always wore his grey "milord's" morning-coat; under it he had slung his trench-knife to a belt, out of which the butt of a saddle-pistol fearsomely lowered. He would neither lay aside his weapons nor remove his martial lambskin kepi.

Juliette "received" not only gentlemen; the wives of the notables also frequented her. Mairik Antaram, the doctor's lady, came in whenever she had the time; the mukhtar's wife, Madame Kebussyan, less frequently, though when she did her alert curiosity was insatiable. Madame Kebussyan insisted on seeing all there was to see. Almost with tears in her eyes she begged Juliette to show her the inside of the sheikh's pavilion —the rubber tubs, the dinner-sets, the furniture which could be taken to bits, the expensive cabin-trunks. With the deepest, most prescient emotion, she stuck her nose into chests of supplies, airing her opinions on sardine-tins, patent foods, soap, and sugar. Juliette could manage to rid herself of this worthy lady, whose quick, mouse eyes ferreted in and out of every corner, only by offering her gifts out of the stores, a tin of food, a cake of chocolate. Then Madame Kebussyan's thanks, and promises of fidelity to her friend, exceeded even her praise of all these good things.

Mairik Antaram, on the other hand, never came without bringing a small gift, a pot of honey, a cake of "apricot-leather," that reddish brown fruit preserve, indispensable to the Armenian breakfast table. She bestowed her gift secretly. "When they're gone, djanik, little soul—you eat this. It's good. You shan't have to go without things while you're with us."

But often Mairik Antaram would look very sadly at Juliette, through her fearless, and never self-pitying, eyes: "If only you'd stayed at home, my pretty!"

ISKUHI TOMASIAN saw less of Juliette on the Damlayik than she had in the villa in Yoghonoluk. She had asked Ter Haigasun to use her as assistant schoolteacher, and the priest had welcomed the suggestion.

Juliette scorned this resolve: "Why, my dear, when we'd just begun to make you really well again, do you want to go off and work yourself to shreds? Whatever for? Placed as we are, it seems ridiculous."

Juliette was still in the strangest relationship to Iskuhi. She seemed, by dint of the many acts of kindness which she had shown her from the very first, to have conquered, one after the other, both that stubborn shyness and eagerness to be of use, behind which the real Iskuhi was hiding. Iskuhi had even shown signs of shyly returning this affection. When they said good-morning or good-night, she would put her arms round this elder friend. But Juliette could feel distinctly that these *tendresses* were mere imitations, adjustments, just as in speaking a foreign language we may often use its idioms without really knowing their shade of meaning. Iskuhi's hardness, the centre crystal of her being, that which was for ever strange in her, remained untouched by all endearments. And it cannot be denied that Juliette suffered at this soul's impregnability, since every wound inflicted on her sense of power seemed to infect her whole estimate of herself. Even this business of "teaching school" meant a defeat for her.

Now Iskuhi spent many hours a day on what was known as the "School Slope," far removed from Three-Tent Square. There was a big blackboard, an abacus, a map of the Ottoman empire, and quantities of spelling books and readers. Several hundred benches. A whole army squatted, sat, or lay in the shade of a clearing, filling the air with shrill sparrow chirrupings. Since usually the whole male teaching-staff was on duty in the trenches or in camp, Iskuhi would often be left for hours at the mercy of rampaging brats. To keep order, or even establish peace, among four- to twelve-year-old savages was impossible. Iskuhi had not the strength to take up the struggle. Soon she would cease to hear her own voice and wait, resigned, for the arrival of some trusty male pedagogue, say Oskanian, to scare the little devils to wan submission. That teacher, iron militarist that he was, strode in among them rifle in hand, since by military law he had now the right to shoot them all for insubordination in the field. The switch he carried, in addition to all his other accoutrements, swished round the shoulders of guilty and innocent indiscriminately. One unlucky group was put to kneel on pointed stones, another to stand for fifteen minutes with heavy objects held above its heads. After which Oskanian would leave his female subordinate to enjoy the fruits of his pedagogic method—a deathly silence.

Juliette saw at once that these strenuous efforts were very bad for Iskuhi's looks. Her cheeks had begun to lose their colour, her face was peaked, her eyes as huge as when she had first emerged from the hell of the convoy. And Juliette strove with all her might to rid Iskuhi's heart of its zeal for duty. She only managed to shock and puzzle her. How, in this crisis of her whole people, could she shirk so absurdly easy a task? On the contrary! She wanted more work for the afternoons. Juliette turned her back on her.

321

At present Juliette spent half the day lying on her bed. The narrow tent stifled her. Two pestering sunbeams forced their way through chinks in the canvas door. She had not the energy to get up and cover them. "I shall be ill," she hoped. "Oh, if I were only ill already." Her pounding heart threatened to burst, with unassuageable longings—longings for Gabriel. But not for the present Gabriel—no! For Gabriel the —*Parisien,* that sensitive, gentle, and considerate Gabriel, whose tact had always made her forget the things which are not to be bridged over. She longed for the Gabriel of the Avenue Kléber, in their sunny flat, sitting down good-temperedly to lunch. Her distant world enveloped her in its sounds: its hooting cars, the subterranean rattle of the Métro, its delicious, chattering bustle; the scents of its familiar shops. She buried her face in the pillow, as though it were the one thing left, the one handsbreadth of home that remained to her. She was seeking herself in its odorous softness, striving with all her senses to hold fast to these fugitive memories of Paris. But she did not succeed. Rotating splotches of sunbeam forced themselves in, between closed lids. Coloured disks with, in the centre of each, a piercing eye—eyes that reproached and suffered, forcing themselves in on her from all sides; Gabriel's and Stephan's Armenian eyes, which would not let go of her. When she looked up, the eyes were really bending over her, in the wildly bearded face of a strange man. She stared in alarm at Gabriel. He seemed remote, his nights all spent out of doors, the reek of damp earth clinging to him. His voice was the hurried voice of a man between two urgent duties.

"Are you all right, chérie? Nothing you want? I've just looked in to see how you're getting on."

"I'm all right—thank you."

She offered him a dream-enveloped hand. For a while he sat next her, saying nothing, as though there was nothing they could discuss. Then he stood up.

But she sat up irritably. "Do you really think me so empty,

322

so materialist, that you only ever need worry about externals?"

He did not understand at once. She sobbed: "I can't go on living like this."

He turned back with a very serious face. "I quite see you can't live like this, Juliette. One just can't live in a community, when one puts oneself entirely apart from it. You ought to do something. Go into the camp, try to help. Be human!"

"It's not my community."

"Nor mine as much as you seem to imagine, Juliette. We belong far less to what we've come from than to what we're doing our best to reach."

"Or not to reach," she wept.

When he had gone, Juliette pulled herself together. Perhaps he was right. It really couldn't go on like this. She begged Mairik Antaram to ask the doctor to let her work in the hospital hut. The thought that a thousand Frenchwomen were doing the same, at that very minute, for their wounded, helped her to come to this decision. At first the old doctor jibbed, then he accepted her. Juliette, that very same day, made her first appearance in the hut (it was still in process of being built) suitably attired in coif and apron. There were luckily very few cases of serious illness on the Damlayik. One or two fever patients swathed in rags lay on mats and cushions, still stiff with damp from the recent storm. They were mostly very old people. Grey, mysterious faces, already half out of the world. "Not my sort," felt Juliette, with a certain pity, a vast repugnance. She could see how unsuited she was to such works of mercy. It was as though she had been lifted above herself. She had all the available bedding brought from the tents—anything she could possibly spare.

TILL midday, the fourth of August passed like the days that had preceded it. When in the early morning Gabriel scanned the valley with his field-glass, the villages looked quiet and deserted. It seemed almost a permissible thought that everything would work out smoothly, world peace be signed, and the return to normal life secured for them. So that he left his observation post in quite a hopeful frame of mind, and went on from sector to sector on a surprise inspection of the work and discipline of the decads. Towards midday, entirely satisfied, he returned to his own headquarters. A few minutes later scouts came running in from all sides. Report: a big dust-cloud on the road from Antioch to Suedia—lots and lots of soldiers —in four detachments—behind them saptiehs and a big crowd of people! . . . They were just turning into the valley and already marching through Wakef, the first village. Gabriel dashed to the nearest observation post and established the following: the column of march of an infantry company at war strength was on its way down the village street. He recognized them at once as regulars, from the mounted captain who led them, and the fact that they were marching in four platoons, which seemed almost able to keep in step. They came swaying onwards. They must therefore be trained, and perhaps even front-line troops, garrisoned in the barracks of Antakiya, part of Jemal Pasha's newly conditioned army. About two hundred saptiehs dribbled along, far behind the company, while the scum of the plains, the human dregs of Antioch, raised its dust on either side of this column of march. The advance of so war-like a contingent of nearly four hundred rifles, including the saptiehs, was carried out in such God-forsaken indifference to exposure through this open country that Gabriel was inclined for a time to think that these troops had another objective. Only when the column, after a short pause and officers' consultation, moved forward north-west, behind Bitias, into the mountains, was it quite certain that this was a campaign against the villagers. The Turks seemed to imagine that they were doing policemen's work, less dangerous even than the usual hunt for deserters—that all they would have to do would be to surround an unarmed encampment of miserable villagers, smoke them out, and herd them into the valley. For such a task they must have felt superlatively strong, as indeed they were, when one considers that the Armenians only had a hundred good rifles, scarcely any munitions, and few trained men. By the time they were in Yoghonoluk, Gabriel had sounded the major alarm, practised daily with his decads and the camp. The münadirs, the drummers, gathered together the Town Enclosure. The orderly group of the cohort of youth went darting all over the mountain plateau with orders to the section-leaders. A few of these lads even ventured down into the valley, to find out the formation and movements of the enemy. Ter Haigasun, the seven mukhtars, the elder members of the council, stayed with the people, in the centre of the camp, as had been arranged. No one dared to breathe. Even babes in arms seemed to stifle their wailings. Reservists, armed with axes, mattocks, and spades, encircled the camp in a wide ring, to be ready in case they were wanted. Gabriel stood with Chaush Nurhan and the other leaders. The whole event had been foreseen.

But, since this was a first encounter, and no other point was directly menaced, he emptied his supports of all but their most necessary defenders, and threw every decad at his disposal into the trenches of the North Saddle. The system had four lines. First and foremost the main trench, which blocked the entrance to the Damlayik, on the uneven summit of the left slope of the Saddle. A few hundred yards behind it the second trench, dug along very uneven ground. On the frontal side of slope, beyond the trenches, flank-protection, with thrust out sniping-posts. Finally, on the side facing the sea, the barricades, luckily too high to see across, of jagged limestone rock.

About two hundred, armed with the best rifles and, it was to be hoped, the best of the fighters, manned the front-line trench. Bagradian himself was to lead them. Nor had he allowed Sarkis Kilikian, or any other deserter, into this garrison. Men from carefully picked decads were placed under

Chaush Nurhan, in the rock barricades. Another two hundred stood in the second trench, ready in case things should go badly. Every fighter received three sets of five cartridges—only fifteen bullets apiece.

Bagradian insisted: "Not one unnecessary bullet. Even if the fighting lasts three days, you've all got to make your three cartridge-clips do. Save—or we're done for. And—listen carefully—this is the most important thing of all. No one to open fire without my orders. All keep your eye on me. We must let the Turks, who won't even know we're there, come on, till they're ten paces off us. And then—aim steadily at the head, and fire steadily. And now, keep thinking of all the horrible things they've done to us. And of nothing else."

Gabriel's heart, as he said it, beat so hard that his voice shook. He had to pull himself together to prevent their noticing. It was more than any excitement of coming battle; it was the clear knowledge of this crazy, monstrous defiance of the forces of a world-army by a handful of half-trained men. There was not a trace in him of hatred. He awaited an impersonal enemy, no longer the Turk, no longer Enver, Talaat, the police chief, the müdir—simply "the enemy," whom one slaughters without hate.

And, as Bagradian felt, so did all the rest. Tension seemed to have stopped their very heartbeats when the boys came crawling back out of the thickets and, with wild gestures, announced the near approach of the Turks. This excitement froze at once to a glacial calm as the sound of infantry boots came nearer, over crackling twigs, with bursts of most imprudent noise, without any prescience of danger in it. Little by little, puffing from the climb, their column of march broken up, the Turkish soldiers approached the Saddle. The captain in charge seemed quite persuaded that this was a job for the police. Otherwise he would surely not have neglected the most obvious precautionary measures, the basic tactical principles for a force in enemy country. Unshielded by any patrols, advance guard, flank or rear protection, a disordered swarm of laughing, gossiping, smoking infantrymen had come straggling up, to collect on the ridge, and get their breaths after the climb.

Chaush Nurhan crawled to Bagradian, down the trench, and tried, in a sharp, loud whisper, to persuade him to attack, surround the Turks, and cut them off. But Gabriel, clenching his teeth, merely put a hand over Nurhan's mouth, and pushed him away. Their captain, a stout, good-looking man, had taken off his lambskin kepi, with the half-moon, and was dabbing up the sweat that streamed down his forehead. His lieutenants collected round him. They stood disputing over a sketch-map, all arguing, in rather unsoldierly fashion, as to the probable hiding-place of the wasps' nest. Fiery eternities for Bagradian. The puffing captain would not so much as take the trouble to climb the highest point and survey the terrain. At last he ordered his bugler to sound the "fall-in," in several strident repetitions, no doubt in order to put the fear of Allah into cringing Armenians. The four lines formed up two deep, in extended order, as if on a barrack-square. The corporals dashed in front of the men and reported to the officers. A lieutenant drew his sword to report to the captain.

Gabriel took a good look at this captain's face. It was not an unpleasant one. It was a broad, friendly face, in gold-rimmed pince-nez, planted well up the nose. Now the captain, too, was drawing his sword and, in a high, weak voice, giving his order: "Fix bayonets." A clatter of rifles. The captain twirled his sword once round his head, before thrusting its point towards the ridge of the Armenian Saddle. "First and second platoons, in extended order—follow me." The senior lieutenant pointed his sword in the opposite direction: "Third and fourth platoons, in extended order—follow me." So that the Turks were not even certain whether the fugitives had encamped on the Damlayik or the northern heights of Musa Dagh. The Armenians stood breast-high in their trenches.

The thrown-up escarpe in front of them, in the slots of which they rested their guns, had been fully camouflaged, as had also the lines of visibility, hewn out in the undergrowth and knee-high grass which strewed the incline. In ragged extended order the unwitting Turks toiled up the height. The first-line trench was so brilliantly masked that it would have been perceptible only from a much higher observation point; a point which, however, did not exist, except in the tallest tree-tops of the counter-slope. Gabriel raised his hand, and drew all eyes in his direction.

The Turks were making slow progress through the undergrowth. The captain had lit a fresh cigarette. Suddenly he started and stopped. What was the meaning of that turned-up soil, over there? It was still a few seconds before it flashed upon him—that's a trench. And it still seemed to him so incredible that again he delayed, before he shouted: "Get down! Take cover!" Too late. The first shot was already fired, and indeed before Bagradian's hand had dropped for it. The Armenians fired reflectively, one after another, without excitement. They had time to aim. Each of them knew that not one cartridge must be wasted. And since their victims, rigid with surprise, were still only a few paces off them, not one bullet missed its mark. The stout captain with the good-natured face shouted again: "Down! Take cover." Then he looked up in amazement at the sky, and sat on the ground. His glasses tumbled off, before he sank over on his side. Discipline suddenly broke in the Turkish ranks. The men, shouting wildly, ran down the slope again, leaving dead and wounded, among whom were the captain, a corporal, and three onbashis. Gabriel did not fire. Suddenly he felt raised above the earth. Reality around him had grown as unreal as it always is, in its truest essence.

The Turks took a long time to collect themselves. Their officers and non-coms had a hard job to hold up the retreat. They had to chivvy back their protesting men with blows from the flats of their swords and rifle-butts. Meanwhile, the two

ranks which had taken no fire were advanced. But, instead of
first discovering a practical line of attack, these riflemen sought
their cover haphazard, behind bushes and blocks of stone,
without the vaguest inkling of an Armenian trench almost
under their rifles. A mad shower of spattering bullets was
released from behind bushes and dwarf shrubs, which did the
trench not the slightest damage. Only now and again did a
stray shot ping over the heads of the defenders.

Gabriel sent an order down the trench: "Don't shoot. Take
good cover. Wait till they come back."

At the same time he sent word to his flank positions; anyone
daring to fire a shot, or even so much as show his face, would
be punished as a traitor. No Turk must have the smallest suspicion of the presence of any flank protection. The Armenian
slope seemed as dead and empty as ever. It looked as though
all its defenders had succumbed to the fierce peppering of
the Turks. After an hour of this savage wasting of munitions,
the company, four madly daring extended lines of it, attempted
a fresh assault. The Armenians, now surer than ever of themselves, again allowed them to come up close before they again
opened fire: a fire far worse, far bloodier, than the last. Now
the non-commissioned officers found it impossible to keep
control of a wild retreat. In an instant the whole Saddle was
swept clear. Only the cursing of wounded came out of the
bushes. A few Armenians were about to climb out of their
trenches when Gabriel shouted to them that no one had had
orders to leave his post.

After a while some Turkish stretcher-bearers gingerly advanced between the trees and began to wave a red-moon flag.
Gabriel sent Chaush Nurhan a few steps out to them. He
beckoned them nearer; then he bellowed: "You can take away
your dead and wounded. Rifles, munitions, packs, cartridge-
belts, bread-rations, uniforms, and boots to be left here."

Upon which, under the threat of barrels turned on them,
the stretcher-bearers were forced to undress each corpse, and

329

leave all this, in untidy heaps. Then, when they had cleared away these victims—it took a long time, because they had always to keep coming back—all the fighters, including Chaush Nurhan, were of opinion that the attack had been routed, and that no further attempt need be feared. Gabriel did not heed these deceptive voices. He ordered Avakian to collect the nimblest lads among the scouts and some of his own group of orderlies. These were sent out to collect the plundered stores and scramble back behind the line with them. He picked out the slipperiest of his spies. They were to follow the companies and watch their movements very closely. Even before the orderlies finished collecting, Haik, a youngster not much older than Stephan, was already back with his report. Some of the Turks were climbing the mountain, farther north, at a place where there was nothing for them to find.

This could only be an attempt at envelopment from the coast side. So much was clear not only to Gabriel, but to Chaush Nurhan and all the rest. Gabriel deputed his command to his most reliable decad commander, and left the trench, taking Nurhan with him. They climbed up to the men posted among the rocks and itching to fight. The natives of Musa Dagh knew every stone, every jutting ledge, every grotto, bush, and aloe of this bare, indented, limestone promontory, below which, three or four hundred feet to the sea, the jagged cliff fell sheer, or in ledges. This knowledge was of incalculable advantage against troops who could not find their way here, no matter how much the stronger these might be. Bagradian left it to his mountaineers to dispose themselves so cunningly in the crevices and behind rocks that communication was kept intact and there would be no danger of one receiving the other's fire. Their task was the same as that of the others—to lure the enemy on to destruction by means of complete invisibility and absolute quiet.

But this time the enemy was more alert. He advanced his main force slowly along the counter-slope, facing the Saddle,

330

and opened fire at the very edge of the wood, well-protected by trees. It was a fire at once vehement and nervous, directed against the main trench, but, as before, not answered by its defenders. And, during this, announced by scouts, a patrol of four men advanced, very gingerly indeed, among the rocks. It was evident that these were not mountain-dwellers. They came stumbling on across the stones, ducking their way from cover to cover. They reconnoitred very carefully, looked into every hole, behind every ledge. The Armenians saw with relish that they were saptiehs. The soldiers were strangers. But the saptiehs! Now was the moment to pay back in some of its own coin this lowest by-product of militarism, these bestial skunks, valiant in their dealings with old women, scared of a man, until they had disarmed him three times. Gabriel noticed a crazy glint in many eyes.

The onbashi of the saptiehs must have imagined that he was already past the line of entrenchments, and so in the rear of the Armenians. Noiselessly he sent back one of his men, who began to signal with a red flag. It was still some time before this enveloping force came slowly on, at a stumbling, ever-retreating pace, as though they were advancing through boiling water. This group was half infantrymen, half saptiehs. Urged by its officers, it reached the place to which the onbashi had already reconnoitred the ground. Then, at a moment when most of them were without cover, the Armenians opened fire, from all sides. They leapt about in scurrying confusion. They forgot their rifles. The Turk, the Anatolian especially, is a good soldier. But this attack seemed to come from nowhere. Not even the brave knew how to defend themselves. By the time the Armenians dashed out from their hiding holes and among their rocks, the air was thick with groans and yelps of pain. With Chaush Nurhan at their head they at once drove in a wedge between saptiehs and infantry. Of the first a number were cut off, and driven outwards, towards the cliffs. They got lost among the inexorable rocks, and cringed helplessly against the stone waiting for a bullet, or remained desperately caught, clinging to the thorny acanthus plants. Many began to slip, turned head over heels, and bounced from rock to rock, like balls, before they went hurtling into the sea. But the main body of the Turks tried to escape from amid this rocky confusion by the shortest cut, and leapt, stumbled, rushed towards the Saddle, chased by the mountaineers.

These were no longer sane. Unintelligible, throaty growls came out of them as they tracked this enemy. Gabriel himself had long since lost the clear-headedness of a leader, was the wild prey of some intoxication, a crazy rhythm come suddenly to life in his blood that had slumbered a thousand years. He, too, let out these short, slavering sounds, a savage speech which, if he had been conscious, would have horrified him. Now the world was a hundred times more impalpable. It was nothing! Less solid than the humming of a dragonfly. It was a reddish, skipping ballet, in which the dancer could feel no pain. Pastor Aram Tomasian, who had been one of the fighters among the rocks, was swept along by the same madness. He, like a crusader brandishing a crucifix, howled: "Christ! Christ!" But the warrior-Christ of his battle-cry had very little indeed in common with that stern, suffering Lord, by whose Testament the pastor as a rule strove to guide his days. Oddly, these shouts of "Christ" brought Gabriel back to his senses with a jerk. He began to observe the fight, but as though he himself were not engaged in it, much less its commander.

This noise of a battle among the rocks was the signal for the Turkish firing-line, on the edge of the wood along the counter-slope, to advance in a frontal attack. They came out in extended lines, shooting at nothing, threw themselves on the ground, shot in the air again, sprang up again, ran on a few steps, and then ducked down. At just this minute the last of the routed, would-be envelopers had been driven out from among the rocks. Therefore their pursuers' fire took the attacking lines in the flank.

Gabriel stood on a rock, but did not shoot. He watched one of the Turkish lieutenants intercept a disordered group to rally a defence around it. The line was already flinging itself down to open fire. But Chaush Nurhan sprang at the Turkish officer, and felled him with a crack of his rifle-butt. The Turks threw away their guns, as though they had just seen the devil, and indeed the old sergeant was not unlike him. He let them see what a perfect soldier the Turkish infantry had lost. His face was purple. His huge grey moustache bristled wildly. He had not even a hoarse crow left in his throat. He did not seem in the least to realize that he must take cover or be shot down. Sometimes he stopped, to raise his bugle and force out of it a long, jerky call, whose ferocity had its effect on both friend and enemy.

When Bagradian saw that the Turks were trying to turn their front towards the rocks, he swung his rifle round his head, to give the men in the long trench the galloping-signal. Their decad commanders had had their work cut out to hold them. They came rushing with a bellow over the top, spattering the new Turkish flank with bullets, without throwing themselves down, or any longer trying to save supplies. So that the company was helplessly caught between the two blades of a shears. With more presence of mind and experience, Bagradian might have wiped them out or taken them prisoner. As it was, by a wild scurry, they could escape, though both flank-protecting decads blocked their way, and then shot after them. This wild Turkish scurry down the mountain did not even halt at the foot of the Damlayik, but only in the church square of Bitias, where at last they rallied.

Nine soldiers, seven saptiehs, and one young officer had fallen into the hands of the defenders. These, as a matter of course, and with the most frigid ferocity, set to work to demonstrate to their prisoners exactly what it feels like to die in an Armenian massacre. Two of the saptiehs Gabriel could no longer rescue. But he, Pastor Aram, and a few more of the elder men threw themselves before the other prisoners—though Chaush Nurhan, and with him the overwhelming majority, could not in the least understand such mercy shown to the butchering tyrants of a hundred thousand of their race. It was very hard for Bagradian to make the disappointed men see reason.

"We shan't get anything out of killing them, nor out of keeping them here as hostages. They'll sacrifice their own without thinking twice about it. And then we should have to feed them. But it would be to our advantage to send them with a message to Antakiya."

He turned to the white-faced lieutenant, who could scarcely manage to stand upright. "Well, you've seen how easily we can deal with you. And you can send us regiments instead of companies—it's all the same to us. Look up at the sky. The sun's not down yet. And, if we'd really wanted it to happen, not one of you would still be alive. Go and say that to your commandant in Antakiya. Tell him how much more mildly than you deserved we've handled you. Tell him, in my name, he'd better keep his regiments and companies for war against the enemies of Turkey—not against her peaceful citizens. We want to be let live up here in peace. That's all we want. Don't molest us in future, unless you'd like some even worse experiences."

The swaggering undertones of this, the certainty with which he seemed to be threatening, the pitiful fear these prisoners showed of being slaughtered—all this assuaged the blood-lust of the decads. They forced the Turks not only to leave behind their arms, their boots and uniforms, but to strip to the skin. In this miserable state they were released, and had besides to drag their dead and wounded down the mule-track of the Damlayik. That day's booty was considerable: ninety-three Mauser rifles, abundant munitions, bayonets. Of the sixty-five decads not fully armed, about ten could now be armed completely. This did most of all to raise morale. Such success had

334

been gained without one loss—the Armenians had only six wounded, and none of them seriously.

It is not surprising that so stupendous a victory should have been very much overrated, both by the decads and the people. A few poor, exiled villagers, insufficiently clad and scarcely housed, nesting on the summit of their hill, had—as it were with their bare fists—with the certainly of death in their souls, routed a company at war-strength, a hundred Turkish regulars, trained for months and armed with the very latest rifles. And not only routed, but almost finished them. This fierce but easy struggle had not lasted four hours. It had all been accomplished in a hand's turn, without a casualty worth the name, thanks to a well-considered plan, a magnificent system of defences.

But Gabriel had no joy in it all, only a kind of weary embarrassment. Nor did he feel he had rendered any extraordinary service. Any other officer who knew war could have put the Damlayik in just the some state of defence. It was not unusual acumen, it was the natural advantage of the mountain, that had given them their victory. The grey heads of the mukhtars swayed before his eyes, since even these uncongenial peasants, who had always behaved so pawkily towards "the foreigner," were now clutching at his hand to kiss it as though he had been their father. This hand-kissing filled him with dismay. His right hand struggled against it desperately. He longed to thrust it into his pocket. Slowly he forged a way through the dense crowd. He looked round for help, for a face that meant something, and at last he discovered Iskuhi. She had followed him all this time, but always keeping behind his back. Now, as he drew her hand towards him, he seemed to feel that her fragile body could give support.

"Juliette's waiting; she's got everything ready," Iskuhi whispered.

He did not heed her words; he heeded her touch. Iskuhi

335

walked at his side, as though leading the blind. Suddenly he felt astonished that all this blood and death should not have moved her.

At last, in the tent, he could wash all over, luxuriously, after a village barber had shaved him. Juliette waited on him. She had heated up the water in kettles, poured it into the rubber bath, laid out the towels and the pyjama-suit which she knew to be his favourite. She stayed outside the tent until he had dried himself. Never, in their long married life, had they lost the last vestige of shame before each other. It took him a long time to get clean. He scrubbed with a hard brush, till his skin was red. But, the more attention he gave to this, the more impatiently he strove to get this day scrubbed well out of him, the farther away he seemed to be from himself. Into this marvellous cleanness in which he revelled the "abstract man" refused to return—the "individual," the man he had brought with him from Paris. He saw the same face in Juliette's looking-glass, flanked by its candles. And yet, deep in his soul, there was something wrong. He could not make it out.

Her voice outside softly reminded: "Are you ready, Gabriel? . . . We'll carry the bath-water outside," she was saying zealously, not having called in one of the servants. They bore the rubber tub out between them, to empty it behind the tent. Gabriel sensed a yielding readiness in Juliette. She had suffered no other hand to serve, had come more than half-way to meet him, with deep emotion. Perhaps the hour had arrived in which the stranger in her would melt away, submit, as he, over there in Paris, had submitted his to her alien self.

"How much longer?" he thought. For now, after today's fighting, he had no more hope that they would survive. He laced up the entrance to the tent. Gently he drew Juliette to the bed.

They lay very close, but could say nothing. She displayed a new, and reverent tenderness. Her eyes made no effort to

336

keep back tears as, tremulously, she kept repeating: "I've been so terrified about you."

He stared as absently at her as though her grief were incomprehensible. Strive as he might, his thoughts were savagely swept away by fierce powers to his trenches. "If only the sentries weren't slack tonight, didn't go to sleep, weren't late in relieving each other. . . . Who could tell that the Turks might not be planning a night-attack." Gabriel had ceased to belong to Juliette—and to himself. For the first time in their married life he could not manage to show he loved her.

2

The Exploits of the Boys

THIS devastating rout of a front-line infantry company on Musa Dagh came as a painful surprise to the Hükümet in Antioch. It was a lasting stain on the Turkish escutcheon. The power of any warrior race is dependent on magic belief in invincibility, and the morale engendered by it. So that, for those who take the sword, every value totters with a defeat, and their very foundations seem to crumble when a race of puny intellectuals succeeds in routing professional soldiers in successful, so to speak, amateur competition. This had undeniably been the case in the sortie of August 4.

And what—Allah is great!—was to be written and read about Musa Dagh! Politically it was far less significant than the news of it was likely to prove dangerous. It would need only a few more Bagradians here and there to get Turkey into serious difficulties. Since every Armenian was in actual fact condemned to death, since some still had weapons at their disposal, such complications would have to be reckoned with.

The worthy citizens of Antioch, from whom this humiliation was being provisionally withheld, saw lights at a very late hour in the windows of their Kaimakam's council-chamber and feared the worst. That district councillor presided over the major provincial assembly, usually composed of fourteen members. At the moment his bloated body seemed to long, with every breath it drew, to shove away the conference table. The Kaimakam's liverish face, with its dark-brown pouches under the eyes, looked sallower than ever in the discreet il-

338

lumination of an oil-lamp. Councillors became more and more verbose. He, however, sat silent and full of cares. His loose, well-shaven cheeks sagged over the wide stick-up collar; the fez had been pushed askew on his left temple, a sign of evil-tempered drowsiness. On his right the commandant of Antioch, a grey-bearded colonel, with small eyes and rosy, innocent cheeks, a bimbashi of the good old school, who would, it was obvious, stand out to the last drop of heroic blood in defence of his own peace and quiet. His deputy sat beside him, a younger yüs-bashi, a major of barely forty-two, his antithesis, as so frequently happens in military double harness. This major was wiry, hatchet-faced, with very determined features; his deep-set eyes glinted with suppressed ire. They seemed to proclaim to all and sundry: "It's my misfortune to be yoked to this unconscionable old dug-out. You all of you know me, you know I'm keen enough for anything, and always do whatever I set out to do. I belong to the Ittihad generation!"

A lieutenant of the routed company, the sole commissioned survivor of August 4, he who had been sent naked to Antakiya with Gabriel Bagradian's message, stood giving his report to these superiors. He could scarcely be blamed for doing his best to make disaster seem more palatable by the wildest exaggerations of Armenian strength. There must be quite ten—or even twenty—thousand of them on Musa Dagh, hidden within the strongest defences. And there could be no doubt that for years they had been collecting munitions and supplies, enough to hold out, up there, indefinitely. He, the mülasim, with his own eyes had seen two machine-gun emplacements. It was machine-guns which, apart from their ten-fold outnumbering, had decided the unfortunate event.

The Kaimakam said nothing. He rested his heavy head on his right hand and stared down at the map of the Ottoman empire spread over the table. Though such high matters concerned none of them, the Hükümet officials found it delightful to stick in little flag-pins along the fronts. But, for all their loyal manipulations, the future of the war seemed not of the rosiest. The little pins kept pricking further and further back, into Turkish flesh. These fronts perhaps scarcely justified Enver Pasha's glittering reputation. His Caucasus army, his best material, strewed, as a field of unburied skeletons, the passes and slopes of those pitiless highlands. And already the Russians stood on the boundaries of Persia, their faces set towards Mosul, driving Djevded Pasha, Enver's cousin and a general renowned for his massacres, further and further into retreat. The English, with their Gurkhas and Hindus, threatened Mesopotamia. Jemal's grandiose Suez expedition had literally melted away in sand. Men and stores lay covered by the desert. All this time, on the Gallipoli peninsula, the Allies with their big naval guns had been battering on the gates of Istanbul. Huge stores of arms and war material had already been wasted on all these occasions. And Turkey had no, or next to no, war industry. She depended on the bounty of Krupp in Essen, Skoda in Pilsen. These production centres of destruction could scarcely keep pace with the huge demands of immediate clients. Only a small percentage of that huge output of new cannon, howitzers, mortars, machine-guns, hand- and gas-grenades came through to Turkey, and had to be hurried straight to the various fronts.

The old, good-tempered bimbashi with the rosy cheeks put on his glasses, although there was nothing for him to read. He may simply have wanted to point out that he was the most far-sighted man in the room. He nodded severely at the mülasim. "This misfortune is the direct result of your stupidity and carelessness. It's down in regulations that you've got to reconnoitre any enemy position before advancing on it. But, now that it's got so far, I ask the Kaimakam: What's to be done about it? Must we sacrifice even more of our men? Or shall we leave these cursed swine in peace, to starve on their mountain? What harm do they do us? This deportation is your business, not ours. Why don't you civilians get on with it? If they really have got ten thousand rifles . . . ?"

The red-haired müdir raised his hand to speak. "They haven't five hundred, not even three—I ought to know, since I'm in charge of that nahiyeh, and went to the villages."

The bimbashi took off his glasses, as purposelessly as he had put them on. "I think it would be best to suppress the incident. They've deported themselves. What more do we want? You've got all sorts of people along the coast, Greeks and Arabs. . . . Am I to be asked to make myself ridiculous by waging a little war under their noses? If I sweep up every detached unit in the kazah, I shan't get together four regular companies. And the Chettehs, the Kurds, and whatever other scum I could lay hands on wouldn't only go for the Armenians—they'd go for us! Believe me, it's far wiser to say no more about it."

The morose yüs-bashi with the deep-set eyes had for an hour lit one cigarette from the last. He had not said a word. Now he stood up, and respectfully fronted his superior. "Bimbashi Effendi, will you allow me please to express my most respectful surprise at what you've just said? How can we possibly hush this matter up when a company commander, three officers, and a hundred men have all been slaughtered? Even now I suggest it's unforgivably slack of us to have delayed so long with our report. The instant this conference is over, I shall have to draw it up, at your orders, to be sent on to G.H.Q."

The bimbashi collapsed. His cheeks turned rosier still; first because the major was right—he always was—and second because he was a Satan.

Now at last the Kaimakam seemed to rouse himself from his long, impersonal meditations: "I shall liquidate this affair within my own province."

This was his astute bureaucratic way of proclaiming a highly involved decision, to which fear of the Wali of Aleppo mainly contributed. Sharp daily instructions kept demanding that the

341

deportation order should be enforced with an almost apoplectic zeal. The resistance of these seven villages might break the Kaimakam, since it implied slack surveillance and incomplete disarmament. Should the Wali receive a plain unvarnished tale of the affair, the Kaimakam might look for the worst from him and from Ittihad. His civil report would have to be most delicately phrased.

The old bimbashi remarked obtusely: "How can you liquidate it, when your saptiehs are all on convoy duty, and your soldiers all at the front?" He blinked, and glowered at the major. "As for you, Yüs-Bashi, I order you, in your report to G.H.Q. to ask for four battalions and field artillery. We can't surround a huge great mountain of that sort without troops, and without guns."

The yüs-bashi did not seem to notice the old man's rage. "Bimbashi Effendi, I quite understand your order. His Excellency General Jemal Pasha has all such matters personally explained to him. I think you may be certain he'll back you up. These Armenian deportations are, after all, the work of his friends. He certainly won't let a few lousy Christian peasants play about with you."

The Kaimakam, who meanwhile seemed to have fallen asleep again, had already decided his course of action. He must ally himself with the strongest man in the room, the major, and, to that end, throw the old bimbashi to the wolves. So the Kaimakam nearly yawned his head off, and rapped the table with the ivory handle of his cane: "I dismiss this session, and would request a few minutes' private conversation with the yüs-bashi, to decide on our joint report to the civil and military authorities. Bimbashi Effendi, I'll submit mine to you for endorsement."

Next day two long and involved accounts left Antioch. The very severe acknowledgments took five more days in which to arrive. Musa Dagh, so these orders ran, must be taken with what material was to hand, and instantly cleared, whatever happened. The only concession to the bimbashi was the loan of a couple of 10 cm. howitzers, already on their way to Aleppo from Hama, and now to be diverted to Antakiya. It was seven days before this artillery arrived. A very callow young lieutenant, three corporals, twelve old reservist artillery-men, and a few filthy privates for dragging purposes, composed the crew. It would be almost impossible to use howitzers of this pattern in the mountains.

IN a sense Stephan had a more difficult time of it than his father, whose earliest memories linked him to Musa Dagh. Yet Stephan, in this short time, seemed to have forgotten his previous life, his fourteen years of Europe. He had sunk, if one is to call it sinking, back into his race. But not so Gabriel. Gabriel's very marriage had placed him between two blood-streams. At first he had even felt it rather tactless that he, a foreigner, should force a plan to save them upon these na-tives. Perhaps that was the deepest reason for those solemn, yet disconsolate emotions which invaded him on the night of August 4.

Stephan was different. Though two blood-streams ran in his veins, his mother's seemed to have lost all influence. He had become what all the others he mixed with were—an oriental schoolboy. Why? He could not have asserted himself among them otherwise. These pompously conceited, apishly pliant schoolboys were not in the least impressed by the well-brought-up young Stephan's western attainments. The most fluent written and spoken French was no use here. When he told them of European cities, they only ragged him. Howls of derision greeted his habit of carrying school books under his arm instead of on his head as they did. What other way could you possibly carry books? Had Stephan been soft, he would at once have gone running to his father and begged to be taken away from school. As it was, he took up the challenge. He had had to quarrel for several days with his mother to get permission to wear Armenian dress. In his new clothes Stephan, who was a handsome boy, looked like the young prince on a Persian miniature. This Juliette could feel, but she felt more strongly that this prince had nothing to do with Stephan, her boy. So they struck a bargain. Stephan might go to school in "fancy dress," but must wear ordinary clothes at home. Since after the flight to the Damlayik there was no longer any "home" to be normal in, the contract fell through.

Yes, Stephan was completely changed. But no one knew what efforts it had cost him to go back, in this fashion, to the primitive. He could wear the same clothes as the others. But at first they were disastrously clean, and without one rent in them. This cleanness was a serious drawback—and he admitted that he had only himself to thank. He still found it hard not to dislike himself for having dirty hands and feet, thick black nails, and uncombed hair. When one day, still in Yoghonoluk, he had managed to get lice in his head, so that Maman, with squeamish hands, tied a napkin soaked in petrol round his hair, he had felt thoroughly miserable. Stephan had permanent disadvantages, as compared to the other village boys. His feet, for instance, no matter how much trouble he might take with them, dabble them as he would in slime and dust—to how many dangerous climbs had he not exposed them?—remained white and pampered. He could achieve no more than tan, blisters, kibes, which, besides being very painful, gave Maman her pretext for keeping him in the house. How he envied the other boys their impervious feet; brown, shrunken claws, vastly superior to his. Stephan had really to suffer before he could establish his position. The village boys let him feel he was not their equal, that not all the splendours of Villa Bagradian, including Avakian and the household staff, impressed them enough to make him acceptable. What assets had Stephan to strengthen him in this curious struggle? Ambition, energy, which he usually turned against his own body, and one other quality which these village boys

344

did not possess. Even Haik, already past fourteen, muscular, tall, and well set up, the undisputed head of the gang, could not boast the purposeful concentration, the planned logical thought, which Stephan had brought with him from Europe. As a rule these Orientals forgot a scheme before they had half carried it through; they were swirled about by their short-lived notions, instinctive urges, like leaves in the wind. Any-one watching them after school might have fancied them a pack of excited young animals, rushing here and there to no end, impelled by one vague impulse after another. When, like a swarm of birds, they alighted on some wide, unguarded orchard, this might be considered a purposeful enterprise—but far more often they would all go darting off into mountain thickets, urged on by demons, or cluster about a stagnant pond, or rush through the fields, to twirl and wallow in their sensations. Such excursions often ended in a religious, or better, a kind of pagan ritual, but of this they themselves were, of course, unaware. It began by their forming a ring, clasping each other, humming faintly, till their heads began to loll, till their voices, their swaying rythm, rose and rose, till at last they all burst forth in a howling tumult, beyond description. On many this rite was of such potency that their eyes turned up, and foam stood out on their lips. They, in their simplicity, only practised the ancient, well-known attempt of certain dervishes to get into secret touch with the primal force of the universe, by means of such epileptic self-conquest. They had seen no grown-up do anything like it, but their need for such exultant self-conquest was in the very air of this countryside. Naturally Stephan, the European, was the puzzled, hopeless spectator of these ecstasies. He, of necessity, lacked one strength —the very faculty most predominant in the lives of all these other boys—a kind of clear-sighted rapport with nature, im-possible to put into words. Just as a good swimmer can lie, sit, stand, walk, or dance, entirely "in his element," in the waves, with a physical ease that is indescribable, so were these children of Musa Dagh indescribably "in their element," in the country that lay around it. They were interwoven with the very nature in which they lived. Their hills were as much a part of them as their flesh, so that to differentiate between outward and inward became impossible. Every leaf that stirred, every fruit that dropped, the rustling of a lizard, the faint plash of a far-off waterfall—these myriad stirrings had ceased to be mirrored by their senses; they formed the very heart of those senses themselves, as though each child were himself a little Musa Dagh, creating it all with his own body. These bodies were like carrier-pigeons, whose inhuman sense of direction can never err. They were like slender, pliant dowsing-rods; their twitchings proclaimed the hidden treasures of the earth. Young Stephan, who for far too long had had his feet upon dead pavements, had, it is true, an adroit and active, but a numbed, body by comparison.

But when the villages set up their camp on the Damlayik, when these aimless rovings came to an end, and discipline and purposeful activity were required of schoolboys, Stephan's prestige increased by leaps and bounds. The reflected glory of his father's leadership contributed. This cohort of half-grown boys ranged from ten to fifteen years of age. Of the few girls none were older than eleven, since girls of twelve in eastern villages are already considered to be ripe. And Ter Haigasun had given orders that even the elder among the boys must go to school in their hours off duty. They seldom managed it, since either their masters were in the trenches, or shirked classes, which they considered entirely unnecessary. Hapeth Shatakhian led the scouts' group, Avakian set the orderlies their tasks, but, apart from these, the three hundred or more boys of the "cavalry" were left to their own devices most of the day. They strayed about the Damlayik plateau, making every knoll, crevice, gully insecure. They would even dare to play in the trenches and embitter the lives of the decads, drilling under Nurhan's scourge, by inquisitive and sardonic hang-

346

ing about. These aimless wanderings were forbidden. Then they grew impudent, and began to break the bounds of the camp, strayed off on to the heights beyond the Saddle, which faced the valley, or into the rocks and stream-beds of the coast side. It was strictly forbidden on the Damlayik to go outside the Town Enclosure. But the gang managed never to be caught. Stephan and Haik, of course, were involved. Sato, too, had slipped in among them, and now she was not to be got rid of. Although the Bagradian family had given shelter to this strange bastard, the villagers still objected to having her in contact with their children. So that Sato depended entirely on the good, or bad, temper of the gang. One day they thrashed her, the next they let her come along. She lived on the verge, here as everywhere. She scurried over sticks and stones with them, never close behind the rest, but always a good way to the side. When the gang squatted together in the ilex gully, or in any other place out of bounds, bragging, thinking vaguely of new schemes, or only, as its habit was, intensifying the quality of existence by wild, collective swayings of the body, Sato's thirsty eyes would stare across from out of her solitude. Then the eternal, gabbling pariah mingled her voice with that of the choir and, still apart, gave imitations of their wild swayings.

There was another doubtful member besides Sato. His name was Hagop, and Stephan protected him. Hagop's right foot had been amputated a few years previously by the army doctor in Aleppo. Now this boy hopped on a rough crutch; it was only a stick with a wooden cross-piece. But, in spite of this rickety support, Hagop could move with a certain vehement eagerness, the wild nimbleness of gait often to be seen in cripples. He was refusing to let these two-legged boys get the better of him, and when he followed their stormy chase there was not a hand's breadth between him and the last of them. Hagop's parents were well-to-do, and he was related to Tomasian. He had thoughtful eyes and, what was very

347

rare among the villagers, dark yellow hair. He read avidly whatever he could lay hands on, stories in almanacs and so forth. But he did not want to be a scholar. He wanted to run, play, climb, and swagger and, since this was war-time, do the same scout duty as all the rest. Stephan, already attracted by his light hair, protected him, and not merely out of pity. But Haik toughly opposed all Hagop's ambitions. Without the slightest sentimental compunction he made him feel that cripples are not worth considering.

Haik was a case apart. At fourteen and a half he was already fully representative of that dour being, the Armenian mountaineer. His deliberate slouch, muscular slimness, the huge hands which swung so heavily at his sides, expressed all the overweening pride of this firmly self-sufficient race—a physique which set him well apart from the other members of the gang, with their rippling, eastern restlessness of body. The Armenian living in the cities of his diaspora may have all the pliancy of Ulysses—it is not for nothing that the *Odyssey* makes cunning and homelessness go together in its protagonist—the Armenian mountaineer, the pick and core of the whole race, is arrogant and impatient. These very exasperating traits he opposes, together with unremitting industry, to the lazy dignity of the Turk. Such a clash of fundamentals explains a good deal.

Haik's family came from the north, from the Dokhus-Bunar mountains. His mother, the widow Shushik, a blue-eyed giantess, was by no means popular in her village, indeed people shunned her almost in terror. Though she had lived for years under Musa Dagh, she still counted as a stranger. The story went that once Widow Shushik had throttled with her bare hands an impudent assailant of her virtue. Whether this was true or false, her boy Haik had in any case inherited both her muscular body and flinty, arrogant disposition. Arrogant people always diminish others' self-esteem. Haik did this constantly to Stephan. It was because of him that the young Bagradian forced himself to one exploit after another, to make quite certain he was genuine. This urge to convince the dour, sceptical Haik took, as it always does in ardent natures at such an age, the most poignantly self-lacerating forms. Samuel Avakian, as his tutor, kept an eye constantly on Stephan, anxious lest he should get into dangerous mischief. This fussy carefulness of his elders shamed young Stephan in his own eyes, and in Haik's degraded him to the level of a pampered, sheltered mother's darling. Haik refused to be convinced, in spite of Stephan's constant, strenuous efforts, that Bagradian's son could really be "all right." The worst of it all was that any preference shown to Stephan made Haik a little more cocksure, since Widow Shushik's son had a searching eye, not to be taken in by mere externals. When Stephan, as often happened about that time, lay tossing from side to side in his tent, kept awake by his own doubts and questionings, his restless mind burned with the one question: "Oh, God, what can I do to show Haik something!" But this fight for Haik's esteem was only one front in a war waged for its own renown by the ambitious soul of the young Bagradian.

Ar about this time—it was now the ninth day on Musa Dagh —the camp began, at first without really knowing it, to suffer from its unmixed diet of meat, the almost total lack of fruit and vegetables. A drastic order had already restricted the milk ration so that only invalids, hospital patients, and children under ten now drew their share of the thin goat's milk still available, leaving over a very small quantity for cheese and butter-making. Everyone growled at having to pool supplies, and in fact, by some incomprehensible law, that summary measure seemed to have worsened the general stock and diminished rather than evenly distributed it. Though Juliette, now that she worked with Dr. Altouni, had placed at the disposal of his hospital more than a fair share of her supplies, her tinned food, her sugar, her tea and rice, she still had enough cake and biscuits to enable her, and those who lived with her, to supplement this diminishing bread ration. Stephan had not yet suffered the least privation. Haik, on the other hand, was already beginning to growl at the eternal, stringy mutton he had to gulp down. It was not even hung, it was half raw. There was nothing to go with it. "Oh, if we'd only got a few figs or apricots." Stephan had a vision of the wide orchards around the foot of Musa Dagh. But he still said nothing.

The cohort was continually on duty. A group of orderlies had always to be within call of the thirteen teachers; others around the numerous observation posts. Teacher Shatakhian inspected his scouts every day, and gave unexpected practice-alarms. So that a major, unofficial enterprise could only be carried out in the sheltering dark, when the boys were off duty and not being supervised. In the course of this same day on Musa Dagh, Stephan was already explaining his scheme to the ever-unapproachable Haik. How miraculous that a foreigner should have thought of it, not a real Armenian! Since the villages moved up on to Musa Dagh one or two daring people had already ventured down into the valley, in the hope of completing supplies. Always they had come back empty-handed, since strong patrols of saptiehs paraded the villages, day and night. Stephan's plan was that the cohorts should replenish the diminishing common stock by a night raid into the orchards. Haik eyed his ambitious rival thoughtfully, as a finished artist might an amateur, who has no idea of the real difficulties. Then he at once began to organize this secret rally and pick out raiders. Stephan was naturally afraid lest his father should get to hear of the scheme and curtail his liberty. He admitted his fears. But Haik, who seemed to have forgotten that the whole suggestion had come from Stephan, answered in the insufferable voice which he knew so perfectly how to use:

"You'd better stay up here if you're scared. I think that's the best thing you could do."

These words pierced Stephan to the quick and made him resolve not to give his parents' anxiety another thought. About ninety boys stole sacks, barrows, baskets, all they could find. At ten in the evening, when the campfires were all extinguished, they crept in twos and threes past the sentries and over the barrier. In long lines they raced down the mountain and had reached the outlying orchards within three quarters of an hour. Till one in the morning, by the soft light of a sickle moon, they picked like mad—apricots, oranges, figs. Here was a chance for Stephan to show his strength, though he had never done such work before. Haik the leader had managed to untether three donkeys and bring them along. They were loaded up at furious speed. And each of the boys had a heavy burden. But they managed to be back in camp by close on sunrise.

These vagrants, who had risked their lives for a trifle, without really knowing the danger, were received with scoldings, even blows, and yet with pride. Stephan darted away from the rest before they got to the Town Enclosure, and slipped into the sheikh's tent, which he shared with Gonzague Maris. Gabriel and Juliette never heard of this escapade. Its results were scarcely worth mentioning in a population of five thousand. All the same it gave Pastor Aram Tomasian the notion of going down, three evenings later, with a hundred reservists, guarded by decads, to make a similar attempt. Unluckily the yield was small. Mohammedan peasants in the neighbourhood had meanwhile raided all the orchards, stripping away the good fruit harvest, and leaving only unripe and rotting windfalls.

GABRIEL had made the most of the grace allowed him by the Turks. By now his defence-works could really be described as completed. The men of the decads, the workers of the reserve, had had to sweat as hard during this week as even before August 4. By now these trenches had all been lengthened and

351

deepened down, and the foreground areas strengthened with encumbrances. Connecting trenches linked up with the second line, as well as with the advanced sniping-points, which were well camouflaged with branches, to enable the hardiest defenders to snipe an attack in the rear, or shoot down stragglers. Gabriel was for ever racking his brains to invent new methods of defence, snares, entanglements, and feints. He wanted to make the issue of an attack depend less and less on the human factor. His casual training in the officers' school at Istanbul, his experience in the artillery battles at Bulair, helped him less than an old infantry manual, issued by the French War Office, bought, in sheer, idle curiosity, at a second-hand stall along the Paris quays. The sight of this book, now so unexpectedly a treasure, produced a strange philosophical sensation in Gabriel. It was too vague to be called a thought.

"I bought this book without ever knowing I should use it, simply because I liked the look of the title-page, or because the unknown subject vaguely attracted me, though in those days military science didn't attract me in the least. And yet, at the instant in which I bought it, quite independently of my will, my fate was predetermining itself. Really one would almost think that my kismet is mapped out from A to Z. Since in 1910 it made me stop at that second-hand stall on the Quai Voltaire simply because it needed this book for its future purposes."

This was the first meditation to which Gabriel had succumbed for many weeks. He shook it off as an encumbrance. Even in Yoghonoluk, at the time when he was preparing his defence, he had noticed how his sense of reality dimmed, the instant he let himself give way to his natural, meditative bent. He came to the instant conclusion that the true man of action (which he was not) must, of necessity, be mindless. As to this technical handbook, it furnished him with numerous warnings, hints, diagrams, calculations, which he could use on a small scale in any circumstances. Chaush Nurhan (they had named him "Elleon," the Lion, as a reward for his feats on August 4) drilled the decads to exhaustion-point all day. Gabriel set innumerable tactical exercises, so that every man might know the ground by inches, and be fully armed against all possible methods of assault. The alarm signals, too, had been perfected to the uttermost. In just an hour, notwithstanding the considerable distances, each point could now be occupied and surrounded, and the movements of troops, on their largest scale, be carried through.

THE camp itself was not merely divided into communes, its huts were arranged in lines of "streets," all leading towards the big Altar Square. This Town Enclosure was built over rocky, uneven ground, but these settlement streets were so disposed that the ups and downs had been fairly mitigated. The Altar Square, the central point of this primitive but crowded encampment, made an almost magnificent impression. When the mukhtar, Thomas Kebussyan, succeeded in getting his special wooden "town hall," his six colleagues, no less in dignity, would not be pacified till they too had obtained the right to have similar huts around the altar. But Father Tomasian's masterpiece was, and remained, the big government building, which had not only real doors and windows but a shingle roof, supplied from his stock. That solid structure stood as a kind of symbol for the bold hopes inspiring these defenders. It had three rooms; a big centre room, the session-room, and two little cabins at the sides. The right side-room was separated off from the session-room by a thick wall. This large-sized kennel was intended as the communal jail, in case there should be serious crime to deal with. Ter Haigasun was convinced it would never be used. The left-hand kennel had been assigned to Krikor, who meanwhile, between himself and politics, had erected a solid wall of books, behind which stood his bed. He passed in and out through a narrow gap in it. His decorative jars, retorts, and vases had been set up on shelves against the wall, while, to his deep personal satisfaction, petroleum tins, bales of tobacco, and ironmongery had all been impounded by the commune. So that the government barrack had not only the character of a Ministry and parliament house, but also of a court of justice and even a university and state library. For here Krikor received his disciples, the teachers.

This tiny sample of humanity, the five thousand souls encamped on Musa Dagh, had therefore caught up again, in one bound, with civilization. A small store of petrol, a few candles, only the most essential tools—such was their entire cultural heritage. The first hailstorm had almost ruined their wretched provision of mats, covers, bedding, the only remaining comforts they possessed. And yet, not the lowest human necessity had sufficed to extinguish in their souls those higher needs, for religion and order, for reason and intellectual growth. Ter Haigasun said mass as usual on Sundays and feast-days. School was taught on the school slope. The seventy-year-old Bedros Altouni, and Mairik Antaram, had succeeded in setting up a model hospital, and bickered with all the other leaders for the best food to give their patients. Compared to what was usual in the valley, the general standards had even risen. These worn, pale faces even expressed a certain peace.

The long August days were not long enough to get through all the work that had to be done. It began at four in the morning, when the milkmaids gathered in the square, where the shepherds had already herded the ewes and she-goats of the flock. Then the milk was carried in big tubs down to the northern side of the Town Enclosure, where already Mairik Antaram awaited it, to dole it out to the mukhtars, the hospital, the cheese-makers. At the same time a long line of women and girls were on their way to the nearby streams to fill their tall clay pitchers with fresh spring water, which remained cold as ice in these receptacles, even in the grilling midday sun. The many springs of clear icy water on Musa Dagh were one

354

of its greatest natural benefits. The seven mukhtars, as the lines of water-bearers returned, were already on their way to the pasturage, to pick out the beasts for the next day's killing from among the flocks. As to the supply it was now evident that the position would soon have become threatening. A fat sheep in these parts, in spite of its almost double weight when alive, gave less than thirty-six pounds of eatable meat. But since five thousand people, many of whom had the hardest manual labour to perform, had to live almost exclusively on this meat, it was necessary to kill about sixty-five sheep a day, if the decads and the reserve were to be fed properly. How long would life be possible on the mountain if the stock diminished at this appalling rate? Everyone could do the sum for himself. Ter Haigasun and Pastor Aram Tomasian, on the very first Sunday, gave stringent orders that no part of the sheep, not even the entrails, was to be wasted. At the same time the daily number of victims was reduced to twenty-five sheep and twelve goats. And none of this did anything to mitigate the many dangers besetting the herds. Much pasturage had been used up in the Town Enclosure and the camp-buildings surrounding it, not least by the various entrenchments. In the very first days on Musa Dagh these flocks were already beginning to lose weight, yet no one dared to send out the herdsmen into the meadows, beyond the North Saddle. The stockyard was near a little wood, a good distance away from the Town Enclosure. This did not prevent terrified bleatings from sounding every morning through the camp. At first the slaughtermen suspended their disembowelled wethers on the trees, to hang for two days. But this was the hottest time of year, and the meat was very quickly spoiled. Therefore, after the first unpleasant experience, they buried it, since it kept in the earth, and was better seasoned. As, in the earliest morning, one detachment of slaughtermen finished its work, to march straight back into the decads, the next began to get busy. On long tables, fashioned of tree-trunks slung together, the meat was chopped into equal parts. From there the women on duty as cooks carried it away to the campfires. There, on ten bricked open hearths, the huge logs and brushwood crackled already. Gargantuan pots were swinging on tall tripods above the flames. But the meat was roasted on long spits, or poles, at the open fire. Food was distributed once a day, by each mukhtar, to his commune under the supervision of Pastor Aram. The portions assigned to the separate villages were again set out on the long log-tables, where each family's share was divided up. So that a hundred and twelve housewives came marching, single file, to their village table, and each, from the hands of her mukhtar, received her exactly proportioned share. An official person, usually the village priest or teacher, checked the number of recipients from his list, and ticked off each meal as it was distributed. Naturally all this took time, and seldom happened without recriminations. Nature had, alas, not designed her sheep, or indeed her goats, with sufficient accuracy. The claims of absolute justice were never satisfied. The more morose among the women saw in the injustice of fate the evil machinations of hostile men, meanly directed against themselves. It needed all Aram Tomasian's tact to appease and convince these chiding matrons that, though Madame Yeranik or Madame Kohar had been scurvily treated by fate today, yesterday she had been fortune's favourite. Usually Madame Yeranik and Madame Kohar were quite incapable of such logic.

Before this distribution to civilians, the army had already received the best, carried down into its trenches by the young orderlies. But the whole camp had to be satisfied with a meal a day, since in the evenings only water boiled in the big cauldrons on the square. Some kind of roots had been thrown into it and the net result christened "tea," for the sake of calling it something.

Pastor Aram had also organized a police force. Twelve armed men kept order in the Town Enclosure. They went on their rounds day and night with the threatening tread of a constabulary. As they walked down the lines of huts, they made the inhabitants feel that this was war-time and everyone must be on his best behaviour. They were responsible for the sanitary measures on which Bagradian, Bedros Altouni, Shatakhian, and other "European fanatics" had insisted as a major problem. Much that had been usual in the villages was forbidden on Musa Dagh. No leavings to be thrown outside the tents, no dirty water emptied into the "street"; above all the dictates of nature to be obeyed only in the places designed for obedience to them. One of Bagradian's first measures had been the digging out of big latrines. Anyone caught infringing this law of hygiene was punished with a day's fast; his daily ration was not served out to him.

THAT, in its broadest outlines, is the life this people led on Musa Dagh for the first fortnight of its encampment. The germs of everything which makes up the general life of humanity were already there. This people dwelt in a wilderness, exposed to every peril of the void. Death so inescapably surrounded them that only the most sentimental optimist could still hope to avoid it altogether. The commune's short history worked itself out according to the law of least resistance. This law had imposed communal forms, to which it submitted with as good or ill a grace as it could muster, though all would far rather have felt free to fend for themselves, just as they chose. But the rich especially, the owners of expropriated herds, deeply resented this nationalization of private property. Their clear perception that, in a convoy, they would by now most probably have lost not only their property, but their lives, did not in the least assuage the bitterness of having been "pauperized." Even now, when what was left to them of life seemed likely to be a matter of days, they did all they could to distinguish themselves from plebeians by at least "keeping up appearances."

In the centre of the camp rose the altar. When, at about the hour of the last night-watch, one hour before the greying of the skies, the Milky Way, grown fainter, moved on above it, as though it were the centre and heart of all things, Ter Haigasun, the priest, would sometimes kneel on the highest step, leaning his head on his open missal. Ter Haigasun knew the world and was a sceptic. For that very reason he strove so passionately to draw into himself the strength of prayer. When everyone else had ceased to believe in any rescue, he, the last of them all, would have to be permeated with the sure sense of impending miracle. Certainly that they were not to be lost, the faith that can move mountains, raise from the dead! Ter Haigasun's soul struggled, in shy, solitary petition, after this mountain-removing faith in a paradox, which his mind refused when confronted with surrounding realities.

JULIETTE had pulled herself together. She was leading an entirely different life. Now she would be up just after sunrise, and dressed so quickly that she managed to help Mairik Antaram with her morning distribution of milk. From there, as fast as possible to the hospital. After all, it was the only thing she could do. Gabriel had been perfectly right. No one can go on living indefinitely as a "distinguished foreigner"—in a void.

A superficial observer would find Juliette easy enough to criticize. What did this snob really expect? What had she, who resisted her husband's world after fifteen years of married life, really got of her own to be so proud of? Were there not in Turkey, at that very minute, many other European women heroically engaged in efforts to help the slaughtered, outraged Armenian people? Was there not Karen Jeppe in Urfa, who hid refugees and kept back the saptiehs, with her arms spread out across her door, till they took themselves off, since after all they dared not kill a Danish woman? Had not German and American missionaries found their way with considerable hardship as far even as Deir ez-Zor, and into the desert, bringing such help as they could muster to the lost and famished children and widows of murdered men? None of these had married an Armenian, none had borne an Armenian son. Such strictures might sound extremely just, and yet they would be unjust to Juliette. She alone on Musa Dagh suffered with far more than the general suffering; she suffered worst of all from herself. Juliette was too miserable to be snobbish. Being French, she had a certain natural rigidity. Latins, for all their surface pliancy, are set and rigid within themselves. Their form is a perfection. They have perfected it. Northerners may still have something of the vagueness and infinite plasticity of cloud-shapes; the French as a rule hate nothing so much as to have to leave their country, get out of their skin. Juliette shared in a high degree this set quality of her race. She lacked that power of intuitive sympathy which usually goes with formless uncertainties. Had Gabriel, from the first days of their marriage, been firmly resolved to guide her gently in the direction of his own people, perhaps it would all have worked out differently. But Gabriel himself had been "parisien"—one of that race of assimilators who, when they thought of Armenia, thought of her as a classical exemplar, but as not quite real. What little he had managed to see of Armenians, the excited political contacts he had made in the year of the Turkish revolution, his engagement of Avakian to teach Stephan—none of all that had been enough to give Juliette the right perspective, far less to bring her over to his side. For fifteen years she had really only been aware that she had married an Ottoman subject. What it really means to be Armenian, the duties and destiny it entails, she had had to discover a few weeks previously, with appalling suddenness. So that really Gabriel himself was largely to blame for Juliette's attitude.

In these days she felt indescribably alone. She, the glittering, the dominant, the eternally vivid, who had never once failed to be admired, was now merely put up with—worse still, not even noticed! She was sure she was getting uglier every day, surrounded by such general disapprobation. And out of all this was born a fresh agony—France! Whatever war-news had managed to find its way to Musa Dagh had its source only in Turkish newspapers. It was weeks—months—out of date. Juliette knew only of French defeats, knew that foreign armies were on French soil. She, who had never troubled her head with politics, to whom the general fate had been a bore, whose own affairs had appeared supreme to her, was now suddenly overwhelmed with devouring fears for "la patrie." Her mother, with whom she did not get on, her sisters, with whom she had almost quarrelled, came infinitely close to her in her dreams. School friends appeared, who cut Juliette, although she kept going down on her knees to them. Now and again she encountered her dead father—*fin,* frock-coated, and distinguished, with the little red ribbon in his buttonhole. He stared in some amazement at Juliette, and kept repeating his pet expression: *"Ces choses ne se font pas."*

But, though her nights got worse and worse, Juliette was always punctual on duty. She had no desire to be "human," in the way Gabriel had advised. All she wanted was to overcome her solitude, her lost dismay. She served with the greatest devotion. Conquering her olfactory sense, Juliette would kneel down beside the patients, those half-unconscious old people, on the rough mats; strip their feverish bodies, wash off the dirt, bathe their crumpled faces in toilet water, whatever was left of it. In those days she sacrificed much. She gave up most of her own underwear, let them use her sheets to make cradles for suckling babes, hammocks for the sick. For herself she only kept "the strictly necessary." But, no matter how Juliette might exert herself, there was no gratitude in the dull fish-eyes of the fever patients, the hostile eyes of those in health; they would acknowledge nothing from her—the foreigner. Even Gabriel had not a word of praise, he who ten days ago had seemed so chivalrous. Was she a dead encumbrance even to him?

And Gabriel and Stephan, the only beings close to her in the world, were near, and yet as far away from her as though an ocean lay between. They scarcely bothered even to think of her. They eyed her with thinly veiled animosity. Neither could manage to seem affectionate. They did not love her.

And all the rest? The people hated her. Juliette felt the hate in their staring faces, their sudden silence, the instant she was seen in camp. The women's dislike of her scorched her back as she went along past the staring groups.

Here, forsaken of all, she would have to die; more alone and wretched than the wretchedest person on Musa Dagh.

At such welling moments of self-pity Juliette was careful not to admit to herself that perhaps she was not really so alone. Gonzague never left her side, having perceived the misery in her eyes. When and wherever he could, he redoubled his attentive services. Now more than ever he had become to Juliette the son of a French mother, a "civilized being," akin to her, almost her relation. But for the last few days something had seemed to imperil their good understanding—something not only from him, but from her as well. He had not overstepped one limit. But for the first time, without shedding an atom of his respect, he had made her perceive in him a desire. This feeling of being on the brink, this close proximity without contact, brought fresh confusion on Juliette. She had to think often of Gonzague. Added to which, in spite of his French mother, he still "made her feel queer." People who are always in perfect control of themselves, who can wait for ever, are uncanny. Gonzague was one of those who in anger turn white, but never crimson.

This change in Gonzague had begun by his losing every day a little more of the reticence which she had never understood. He began telling her things about his life.

361

EVERY morning Juliette spent three or four hours in the hospital-hut, usually till the patients had got their dinners. As a rule, at about that time, Gonzague Maris came in to fetch her. If she was still not ready, he waited. His watchful eyes followed her movements. She felt herself assaulted by those eyes, as indeed she was. For when, not without some vague intention, she lingered over hospital tasks, he would come straight up to her, and whisper: "That's enough! Leave it for now, Juliette. You're far too good for work of this sort."

Then, with soft resolution, he would force her away from the hospital-hut. She was glad he did so. Since Gonzague had no dutites in camp, and had not applied for any to the Council, he had spent his time in the discovery of some very charming natural paths, places in which to rest and look out to sea, along the coast side of the Damlayik. They were every bit as beautiful, he declared, as the views along the Riviera.

Now Juliette and Gonzague sat every day side by side, at odd hours, in cool nooks or sheltered clearings or on the closely wooded promontories, of this "Riviera," which, cut off from the plateau by a wide belt of myrtle, rhododendron, or arbutus bushes, extends in a long up and down line, on the edge of those gigantic walls which drop sheer into the sea. They both felt profoundly isolated. Who would ever miss them —the two foreigners?

On that day, August 14, the fifteenth day on Musa Dagh, Gonzague seemed entirely changed. Juliette had never yet seen him so sad, so boyishly sad, so incomprehensibly overshadowed. His eyes—in which there were no distances, even when they looked at a horizon—stared out, Juliette felt, into infinity. In reality he stared at a definite point, though to be sure, a jutting bend of the mountain hid it from view. His thoughts were on the plain at the mouth of the Orontes, where a big alcohol factory glittered in sunlight. Juliette's question, which expressed her sensations, not his, was therefore quite beside the point: "Are you homesick, Gonzague?"

He laughed shortly, and she, ashamed, perceived how painfully empty her question was. She thought of the life which Gonzague had related bit by bit, lightly discounting it, as ironical as though it half concerned him, were in fact the least important part of himself.

His father, a banker in Athens, had seduced his mother, a French governess. When the child was still not four, there had come a crash. Papa had vanished to America, leaving Maman with her baby, but nothing else. But she had been fond enough of her deserter to contrive, with the uttermost difficulty, to cross the Atlantic in pursuit of him, taking little Gonzague with her. There, though she never succeeded in getting on the tracks of the right man, she had, in the course of pursuit, found another. He was an elderly umbrella manufacturer from Detroit, who had married Maman and adopted Gonzague.

"So you see," Gonzague had said, "I've a perfect right to use two names. But, with my kind of appearance, I feel that it'd be all wrong to call myself Gonzague MacWaverly, so I stick to Maris."

He had given her very serious reasons for this. Gonzague's unfortunate mother had not been happy with her umbrella-maker. They separated. She had to leave the house in Detroit, and Gonzague wandered from boarding-school to boarding-school, till the age of fifteen. At about that time, by chance, he had learned the name of his real father, who meanwhile had managed to recoup himself. The old man was becoming conscience-stricken, since Gonzague's mother had died in the pauper ward of a New York hospital. He had sent the boy, with a little money, back to Athens, to some relations. Of the following years Gonzague had spoken very shortly. They had been neither good nor bad, and certainly not in the least interesting. Not till very late, after a wretched childhood and seedy youth, had he managed, in Paris, to find his bent—that is to say he had discovered that he possessed a few mediocre and very ordinary abilities, useful enough at least to enable him to push his way through the world. For some years he had lived in Turkey, since the help of his father's Athens relatives had taken him to Istanbul and Smyrna. In Istanbul he had acted as correspondent for American papers, which he supplied both with news and articles, describing life in the interior. This he had supplemented, whenever things were at their seediest, by rehearsing the choruses of fifth-rate Italian and Viennese touring companies. In the end he had managed to get attached to a cabaret manager from Pera, as accompanist, to tour through darkest Turkey with a troupe of very tawdry dancers and singers.

All this sounded perfectly genuine. What, after all, could have been left out, or embellished, in such sordid and likely little incidents? These meagre excerpts from his life had been given as carelessly, by Gonzague, as though they were beneath his notice—the base preliminaries to a real life, of which his eyes spoke as they rested on Juliette. She believed he was telling her the truth, yet his truth seemed to cancel itself out. For a second she suspected that Gonzague had another, equally colourless life in reserve for every woman he met.

"How many women," she investigated, "were there in that concert party which you toured with as far as Alexandretta?"

The thought of his troupe seemed so to annoy him that he almost answered her with a growl. "About eighteen to twenty, I imagine."

"Well, there are sure to have been some young and pretty ones. Didn't you care for any of them, Gonzague?"

He shook off such a suggestion in amazement. "Actresses have a very thin and difficult time. And professionals take love as part of their job, and refuse to do overtime."

Juliette's curiosity was not so easily dispelled. "But you lived some months in Alexandretta. A filthy little port. . . ."

"Alexandretta isn't nearly so bad as you seem to think, Juliette. There are a number of quite civilized Armenian families living there, with delightful houses and big gardens."

"Oh, I see. So it was one of those families made you stay so long."

Gonzague did not deny that a certain young lady in Alexandretta had caused him to break his contract with the cabaret manager. His vague descriptions oddly suggested Iskuhi to Juliette—a painted, bedizened Iskuhi, hung with cheap jewellery, which, however, seemed out of keeping with her image. Gonzague refrained from any further description of his experience, declared the whole thing to have been a mistake—wiped out and forgotten. It had only had this about it, that it had brought him, via Beilan, to Yoghonoluk, and shown him the way to Villa Bagradian.

Juliette reflected on Gonzague's position in the world and began to feel less cruelly lonely. Could there be a more ultimate method of belonging nowhere than his? He had resolved to take a reticent share in Juliette's fate, in her probable death, without winking an eyelash, for no thanks, as though it were not worth mentioning, as though it were being done out of sheer politeness! And besides Gonzague had a hundred thousand time less to gain here than Juliette. The word *"nostalgie"* which she had uttered a little while ago—how it troubled her now! Those eyes had only emptiness to look out on. Now Juliette saw that this young man, who boasted a microscopic memory, seemed to have no memories to fall back on, or only such as cancelled out. This young man who, with tense reserve, had shown her such devoted consideration, had never himself received any love. He sat like a boy beside her, on a smooth rock, almost against her, from shoulder to knee. But he did not touch her, still left the suggestion of empty space between them. This blade-like space, composed of virtue and self-conquest, scorched her almost. Gonzague said nothing. In Juliette's heart a very perilous, delicious pity was welling up.

"Gonzague?" she asked, and was startled by her own sing-song voice. Slowly he turned to her. It was like a sunbeam. Softly she took his hand. Only to stroke it. Then—there was nothing else to be done!—her face, her mouth advanced a little. And Gonzague's eyes flickered and died. The last expectant alertness was extinguished in them. He let Juliette come close, before, with a sudden jerk, pulling her to him. She whimpered softly under his kiss. Her youth had slipped away from this faithful wife, without her ever once having discovered of what vagrant desire she could be capable. Yet instantly she grew conscious of a pain, which seemed as though it would split her head. It was the same, almost hypnotic, headache which she had felt in the reception-room of the villa, that night Gonzague had played the piano so morosely. She thrust the man away, to collect her whole force of resistance. A thought shot up in her: "He didn't take my hand. It was I who took his." And, behind that thought, a second towered: "For weeks he's been deliberately leading me on, so that *I* might begin it, and not he." In the next instant, since Gonzague tightly clasped and kissed her again, her powers of resistance seemed all to melt. The pain was an intolerable ecstasy. A crimson darkness with, far down in her, a last, thin glint of terror: "I'm lost!"

For only now, in these, his kisses, did this so reticent young man, this tenderly gallant escort, become the real Gonzague. No longer the adroit child of nothing, but a force, of which she had had no inkling, which might make her either supremely happy or miserable. His mouth, entrancing and revengeful, drew out of her secrets she had not known.

He only let her go when a terrific din suddenly startled them. They leapt away from one another. Juliette's heart beat so, she could scarcely breathe. "My hair's all rumpled," she thought, and found it as hard to lift her hands as though they had been heavy implements. What is it? The Greek supported her. They sought out the infernal din. In a few steps he knew what it was.

366

"It's the camp donkeys. They've all gone mad!"

And, indeed, as they came to the nearby tethering-ground, a kind of nightmare met their eyes. These honest donkeys seemed transmogrified into a set of wildly fabulous beasts. They tugged at halters, reared, danced on hind-legs, lashed out on all sides. Foam dribbled out of their soft lips, their eyes looked glassy with fright. The long sounds that came shivering out of them sounded more like trilling neighs than the harmless up and down of a donkey's speech. Some crazing phantom seemed to have started up before them. It was not a phantom. Their animal, premonitory instinct had sensed a reality, in the very second before it happened. Far away, beyond the North Saddle, a broad rumbling—almost in the same instant the sound seemed to have come a little closer. There followed a short, sharp crash and, south of the Town Enclosure, fairly high up, a snowy smoke-cloud. Suddenly the donkeys ceased their din. Soft brayings and flutings melted gently into silence. People were running out of their huts. Very few realized what was happening, or that the dainty cloudlet above the mountain was a shrapnel-burst.

Ir had also roused Gabriel in the camp. He was tired, having scarcely slept on the night before. Disquieting messages kept coming in from the forward positions. There could be no doubt that Turkish spies had been around the trenches these last two nights, trying to slip in past the sentries. For tonight, therefore, Gabriel had sounded the great alarm, and placed standing patrols. As, towards midday, he sat on the bench at his headquarters, trying to snatch a few minutes' rest, he was set upon by an agonized day-dream. Juliette lay dead, on the wide bed of their Paris bedroom. She lay across it. She was worse than dead, she was frozen stiff, one single block of faintly flesh-coloured ice. He would have to lie beside her, to melt her corpse. . . .

Heavily, he shook off this nightmare. It was clear; he was

behaving badly to Juliette. Cowardice had been making him avoid her, the Lord knew how long. Even though his present life and duties left him without a second to spare, that was no reason to satisfy his conscience. He decided therefore, until tonight, to hand over the command to Nurhan and spend that afternoon with Juliette.

She was not in the tent. Iskuhi was just coming out of hers. Brother Aram was with Hovsannah. She did not want to disturb that married pair. Gabriel begged Iskuhi to stay with him, till Juliette should have come home. They sat down together, on the short-cropped grass of Three-Tent Square. Gabriel made an effort to discover what it was had changed Iskuhi so remarkably. Yes, of course—today she was not wearing one of the dresses Juliette had given her, but a wide flowered gown, made of some flowing, flimsy material, high at the neck, and with puffed sleeves. It made her look very old-fashioned, and yet it was unlike Armenian dress. Iskuhi's fragile shape had often seemed to him meagre and wasted-looking. But this scolloped, bunched robe lent her a gentle, hovering fullness, and hid her lame arm. Never before had her serious little face been so well framed, so Gabriel thought, as it was by the wide silk shawl, which she had flung over her head, to keep the sun off. He noted, in surprise, that Iskuhi's lips were full and sensuous. "She ought to be wearing a red veil," it occurred to him. And, since this was his hour of fatigue and drowsiness, pictures from his remotest days of life came up in his mind:

Yoghonoluk, grandfather's house. A wide, damask cloth, laid out for breakfast, on the soft turf of the lawn. Everyone in respectful attendance on the arrival of old Avetis Bagradian, to this ceremonious first meal of the day. The silver kettle steams on a tripod. Baskets piled up with apricots and grapes, melons on their flat dishes. Wooden platters, with new-laid eggs, honey, and "apricot leather." Thin cakes of bread, waiting under a spotless napkin to be broken by the master of the house, after prayers. Gabriel is eight, and wearing the same kind of entari-kilt that Stephan wears today. If only they'd hurry up with breakfast! Then he could sally forth, on to Musa Dagh, to hunt out great secrets. Meanwhile he looks down shyly at the damask-folds. Perhaps a big snake is hiding under them! A golden rustle announces Grandfather's approach. And, strangely, his grandfather is himself no more than this—this golden sound; he gives it forth, he never emerges from it. His gold lorgnon on its ribbon, his white pointed beard, his black and yellow morning-robe, his red Russia-leather shoes, never come into sight; his image remains hidden, though forcefully present. On the other hand, Gabriel could clearly see all the women slowly lifting their veils above their heads, reverently turning their backs on the master, as custom ordains. Had this been a real memory, or only a dream made up of fragments pieced wrongly together? Gabriel could not be sure. But in any case, for no apparent reason, Iskuhi had managed to weave herself into this carpet of his childhood. She sat facing him on the grass. He, lost in the study of her face, took a long time to remember that he must say something.

"I suppose you're fonder of your brother than you are of anyone else in the world?" He made it almost sound as though he were blaming her.

The first Turkish shell dropped a hundred feet south of the Town Enclosure, under the foremost, jutting point of the Damlayik. He hurried there, in long, swift strides. On the way he met Dr. Altouni, riding a donkey. The old man had to get down. Bagradian thrashed and kicked this beast till it brought him to North Saddle, at a most unusual gallop.

THIS time the Turks had prepared their stroke. The bimbashi-commandant of Antioch, that comfortable, boyishly rosy gentleman, with the little, elderly, sleepy eyes, led the onset in person. Strangely enough, his adjutant, the hatchet-faced and

369

resolute yüs-bashi, had taken short leave at about this juncture, and gone to Aleppo, to be quite clear of responsibility. Since the bimbashi's wise and peaceable suggestions had not prevailed in council against the Kaimakam, nothing now remained but to sally forth, in all possible haste, against Musa Dagh. His annoyance and rancour against his enemies lent the comfortable gentleman energy and unexpected *élan*. He spent nearly the whole of one day in the telegraph office at Antakiya. Its Morse apparatus was set in motion in three directions, Alexandretta, Aleppo, and Eskereh, to muster up all the small local garrisons and gendarmerie posts situated within the district frontiers. In four days the portly colonel had drummed together a fair contingent—about a thousand rifles—to back his artillery. It was composed of the two companies of regulars, detached, in the Antakiya barracks; two platoons of the same regiment, from smaller towns; a big posse of saptiehs; and lastly a number of sharpshooters, chetteh irregulars from the mountains around Hammam. He made use of the half-battery which had recently trundled into the garrison.

Meanwhile scouts had investigated the trenches on the Damlayik, if not reliably and completely, at least in part. The superstition was still unbroken that there were twenty thousand armed Armenians. So the bimbashi had enough arms and saptiehs at his disposal to make the smoking-out of this rebels' nest a possible matter of hours. His tactic would consist in a fully covered advance and sudden attack. That was essential. And both covered advance and sudden attack were well contrived. Every observer on Musa Dagh had been deceived. The colonel had split up his forces into approximately equal divisions, which were to operate independently of each other. The first marched on the night of August 13 with every possible precaution into Suedia and encamped, neatly disposed and concealed, in the ruins of Seleucia, under the South Bastion. The other corps, comprising the commander and

370

his artillery, came along a stretch of the highroad, Antakiya-Beilan, and turned off it up wretched mule tracks into the mountains. But here the bimbashi's strategic plan failed to "click." It proved very difficult to get the two big howitzers uphill, even though two men were kept continually shoving at the spokes of either wheel, while others had to toil with the heavy barrels of unlimbered guns for fifteen miles on the arduous hillside. The sumpter mules, used as team, had proved themselves almost useless for gun-dragging. It meant a delay of ten hours. This force, which had begun its march half a day earlier than the other, only reached those heights of Musa Dagh which extend northwards of the Saddle, towards midday on August 14, instead of in the night of the previous day. So that the double attack, timed for the first hour after sunrise, was not delivered. The captain in charge of the southern corps, who had not dared to let them show their faces outside their hiding-holes in the scorching ruins, till they got the pre-arranged signal (the first shell), was already fagged out by their long vigil in the pitiless sun. A fifteen-hour march up mountain tracks, without having rested the night before, only interrupted by three short halts, lay behind it. The colonel should have said to himself: "I'll give them a rest for today, and send word to the captain at Suedia to put off the attack till early tomorrow." And, considering how easygoing he was, anyone might have betted a hundred to one that this would be the old gentleman's decision. Yet exactly the opposite happened. Easygoing people are often also the impatient ones. If they find themselves entangled in something they dislike having to do, they get it over as quickly as possible. This bimbashi ordered the artillery mülasim to bring his guns at once into position, had a very hasty meal served out to the men, and, an hour later, led his companies, in long, thin skirmishing order, against the Armenian Saddle trenches, where first they kept a very respectful distance, as quiet as mice, in the gullies, behind rocks and trees.

The bimbashi cursed the Kaimakam, the yüs-bashi, the general in charge of transport, who, instead of proper mountain artillery, had sent him these huge, unwieldy howitzers—above all did he curse His Excellency Jemal Pasha, for a "sour-faced, humpbacked swindler." In his opinion all these political officers of Ittihad were nothing but a set of jumped-up traitors and scum. It was they who had conspired against the old Sultan, and were keeping the new one prisoner in his palace. Ridiculous subordinate officers, who promoted themselves generals, Excellencies, pashas! Once fellows of that description wouldn't have got as far as yüs-bashi! And all this disgraceful pother with the Armenians was simply due to Ittihad swine. In Abdul Hamid's golden days there might, of course, have been an occasional set on the Armenians, but never the sort of thing that such a highly placed officer as he, the bimbashi, would be asked to command. The tired and irritable old gentleman waited with his staff for the first shell. He had ordered the lieutenant in charge of the howitzers to begin by dropping a couple into the living-quarters of the Armenians. Not even the so-called war-office "maps" of these Ittihad swindlers were accurate, and the shells had to be aimed at the Damlayik by the distances marked on these. The bimbashi reckoned that shells in the camp would cause panic among the women and children, and so diminish the men's morale.

This calculation was shrewd enough. The howitzers, however, succeeded more by accident than aim. Out of twelve shots, three fell into the Town Enclosure. These shells not only damaged some of the huts but wounded three women, an old man, and two children, luckily not very seriously. But the direct hit of a shell destroyed the grain depot, set fire to, and burned up, all that was left of the cereals, together with what remained of tobacco, sugar, and rice. The depot crackled and blazed; it was a miracle that the flames did not spread to the huts, a little way off. And the people's confusion was even worse than this disaster. On the decads also the fire worked a ten-fold alarm. All who were off duty rushed to their posts. Nurhan, "the Lion," within ten minutes had the trenches entirely on the defensive. The orderlies and spies of the cohort of youth were soon assembled behind the lines. When Gabriel came galloping on his donkey, he found all parts of his machine in full working order. A few minutes later the first scout came running in with reports from the South Bastion. So that this Turkish raid had not quite succeeded. It encountered surprised, but resolute, defenders.

This was the day of Sarkis Kilikian's triumph, and of that of the South Bastion. In this region the enemy was still without experience. Turkish spies had not dared to advance too far into the wide, bare half-circle of this declivity, with its stony slopes and terraces of boulders. The captain in charge did not even know whether, behind the jagged blocks of these dominant rock-towers, there was a garrison. The Mohammedan population of the thickly peopled plain of the Orontes, the inhabitants of the market-towns of Suedia, El Eskel, and Yedidje, excited by this war on the mountain, affirmed that, for many days, nothing had stirred among these rocks, that no fire was seen at night there. But the company leader was cautious, and assumed Armenian entrenchments, at any rate on the southern edge of the Damlayik, even though appearances might suggest none. He had long since divided his men into frontal attackers and a surrounding-party. The first was to be composed of regular troops, the second of chettehs and saptiehs. While the ones climbed straight up the slope, the others, directly opposite, where the half-circle of mountain verged on the sea, above the hill-nest Habaste, were to descend on the rear of what they supposed the Armenian positions. The Turkish captain did not spread out his men in skirmishing order, but disposed them in long single file, to present as narrow a surface for fire as possible. Since the temple ruins of Seleucia, which had given cover to the troops, stood on a wide ridge, about two hundred feet above sea-level, the attackers had only a bare heap of stones, of about the same height, to get across, to come to the edge of the strong slope crowned by the South Bastion. This slope was not unassailably steep, afforded firing-cover on every inch of it, and was therefore, in the opinion of the bimbashi, far better designed for attack than any of the wooded sides of the Damlayik, which behind each tree-stem gave firing-cover to the Armenians. And besides, from the village street, visible at every point of the mountain, the advance up the hill could not have been camouflaged.

In the South Bastion the command was still very unstable, a grave defect in Bagradian's general scheme of defence. In his view, because of the steep, barren ground below it, this part was far less menaced by attack than either the North Saddle or the ilex gully. Therefore its fairly numerous garrison contained the undependable underworld of the Damlayik, those deserters and pseudo-deserters whom he wanted to keep as far as possible from the people. The section leader was an ex-regular from Kheder Beg. A slow, phlegmatic peasant, unable to assert his authority against these quick-tempered recalcitrants. Teacher Oskanian, the general superintendent appointed by the war committee, had made himself ridiculous on the first day by his pedagogic ruthlessness and pomposity. The exacting dwarf was quite unable to inspire in these hard-bitten men, with whom life itself had dealt so drastically, the respect he considered his due. It is therefore obvious that the strongest personality of this sector, Sarkis Kilikian, should gradually have gained the upper hand.

His humiliation by Bagradian seemed to have worked a change in the Russian. He no longer played at being a guest without obligations, consenting to live in camp for the time being, but submitted without a murmur to its discipline. More, he busied himself in his sector as a very inventive fortress

374

engineer. He strengthened and raised the loosely piled up blocks of limestone, which served as the parapet of their trench, though the work took several days of restless industry. He had also contrived a primitive but effective machine, which increased to annihilation-point their power of repelling an attack. Behind each of the three walls facing the hillside, at a fair distance from one another, he had constructed rectangular, gallows-like erections, made of oak stems. To the cross-beam of each of these gallows there hung level, fastened by strong ropes, a thick battering-ram, with at the end a kind of gigantic table-top, or iron-studded shield. The ropes which worked this mechanism could be lengthened or shortened, so that the point of impact of the battering-ram might be thrust full against the wall. When the very heavy shield-plate came hurtling, from a certain distance, pendulum-wise, against the stone-heaps, it gained a driving force that no human strength could have achieved.

At the moment when the howitzers opened fire and scouts ran in to report that Turkish rifles were beginning to clamber up the slope from above the temple ruins of Seleucia, the commandant appointed by Bagradian lost his head completely. He crouched down before a chink in his wall of stones, and stared at the slope, but could not manage to give an order. The doughty little Hrand Oskanian turned white as paper. His hands shook, so that he could not manage to pull back the lock of his carbine, to insert the first cartridge. His stomach turned, and the giddy Oskanian nearly toppled. Ten minutes ago a threatening Mars, the sombre teacher had no strength left, even to get out of the way. His voice failed. He followed Sarkis Kilikian like a puppy. So that the leader, with chattering teeth, stood begging orders of his subordinate. The Russian's agate eyes were as dead as ever. Deserters, and the rest of these decads, gathered round him at once, as their natural head. No one paid any further attention to the slow-witted peasant from Kheder Beg. Kilikian said almost nothing. He strode into the midst of this knot of defenders and pointed out those amongst them whom he designed to man the rock-towers, stone parapet, and supports. Platforms on high heaps of stone had been set up behind the battering-rams. Two men climbed each of these, to let the rams hurtle against the walls at a sign of command. The Russian followed the same tactic as Bagradian on August 4. He waited for the crucial second. But his dead, patient impassivity was a hundred times steadier than Gabriel's. As, at last, the advance-guard of the Turks appeared on the edge of the stone-slope, he took out his primitive tinder-box, to try to light a cigarette. Oskanian beside him twitched and panted: "Now, Kilikian—now! Right away." Having striven in vain to set light to his strip of tow, Kilikian's free hand gripped the teacher, to prevent his jumping up too early, to give the sign. The Turks, lulled into security by their safe clamber, and the utter quiet of the mountainside, had begun to get slack. They came into line, gossiped, and formed wide groups. Not till they were midway up the slope did Kilikian let out a long whistle. The battering-rams with their huge shield-plates came thundering down on the loosely built-up walls. The lighter stones of the uppermost layers, spurting up in a cloud of dust, whizzed down like cannonballs, while the heavy limestone blocks of the upper structure toppled slowly over, and crashed after them, in great, wild leaps, among the Turks. Even these first effects were terrible. But now the Armenian mountain itself took a hand, to complete the decimation, so cruelly that this natural landslide will not be forgotten by future generations along the Syrian coast. The defence walls had been built between jagged pyramids of rock. The force of the rams shook even the natural limestone crown to its foundations, and tore huge sections of jagged rock down into the valley. The force of this indescribable, stony assault was too much for the many loose boulders which strewed the face of the incline. With all the terrific hissings and cracklings of some never before experienced surge of breakers, they began to slide, tearing down, in a monstrous deluge of lime and chalkstone, all who were still alive among the Turks. It was more than a ghastly avalanche of rock. The Damlayik itself seemed to have broken loose from its anchor, and to be sliding down. This hailstorm spattered on over the ruins of the upper town of Seleucia, overturning columns, crushing in ivy-covered walls. For ten whole minutes it still looked as though the mountain itself were seized with an impulse to advance on Suedia—to the very mouth of the Orontes. The western group of the Turkish corps was grazed by this avalanche, just above the village of Habaste. Half the men were lucky enough to get clear. The other half were killed or maimed, the village itself in part destroyed. In fifteen minutes a silence, as of death, lay over everything. The avalanche stood peacefully and slyly in the glare. Dull, crackling thuds from the howitzers came from the direction of the Saddle. When every pebble had come to rest, Kilikian blew his whistle a second time. The amazed deserters and their comrades began to advance. The whole garrison of the South Bastion, led by the Russian, strolled down the slope and, without haste, slaughtered the Turkish wounded and stripped them bare. It was done with the most nonchalant thoroughness, without a thought for the fierce battle which their comrades in the north had to sustain. Sarkis Kilikian changed his rags. He put on a brand-new Turkish infantry uniform and, in this new kit, in spite of the smears of blood on the dead man's tunic, postured as though he felt himself reborn. But Hrand Oskanian, who had climbed the highest point in the line of rocks, was firing in the air like a lunatic, to establish his personal share in this victory. It surprised him more and more, as he let off this imposing clatter, to consider what a trifle bravery is—to a brave man.

NEITHER Gabriel nor the bimbashi were yet aware of the disastrous end of the south division. In the clatter of rifles around them they had both only heard the long rumble of the landslide as a faint thunder in the distance. Here, on the North Saddle, the fight was by no means such an easy one, and was going against the Armenians. Whether these howitzers were skilfully manned or merely lucky, the fact remained that in one hour of slow bombardment, four direct hits had blown away part of the chief communication trench, and that several mortally wounded men were lying about. Gabriel had several times been nearly killed by flying splinters. His skin felt as rigid as damp leather. He could clearly perceive that this was not one of his good days. Ideas and decisions did not come automatically as they usually did. He might—the thought seared him—have avoided these losses. He had delayed too long in giving Chaush Nurhan orders to retreat. But at least he had had the intelligence to carry out that retreat on the rocky side. The Turks had managed to set up an observation post, in a high tree, from which they could overlook part of the trench, and correct the aim of their artillery. But the stone barricades to the right were beyond their survey. Remembering their defeat on August 4, they still feared the steep and pitiless cliffs of Musa Dagh, and no longer dared to attempt envelopment. The defenders left their trench one by one, and went ducking, with their heads well down, past the boulders and jutting rocks of the labyrinth, till they came to their second line of entrenchments, also dug along an indentation. This second trench was today unoccupied, since Gabriel had not dared to withdraw so much as a decad from defence positions, along the edges of the mountain. He was fairly certain that the Turk would try to attack at a third point. His blood froze as he remembered that, if this reserve trench, too, should be lost, there would be nothing left to prevent the best-thought-out slow death of five thousand men and women the world had known. The Turkish observer did not seem to have noticed their retreat. Shells kept crashing down into the first trench at one-minute intervals. Since now nothing seemed to stir in it, the bimbashi considered it ripe for assault. There was an endless pause before, in the thick woods of the counter-slope, there arose a wild drumming and blare of bugle-calls. Bellowing non-coms and officers urged forward the extended lines. Their shouts mingled with the not entirely fearless shouts of the men. Most of them were recruits, snatched away from their Anatolian ploughs, who, after a few weeks of hasty training, were under fire for the first time. As, however, they saw that their attack seemed to be encountering no resistance, their courage rose to the point of valour; the wildest of all herd-emotions invaded them. They came racketing up the shrub-grown slope, strewn with impediments, and stormed the big main trench with rollicking shouts. The colonel saw that things seemed well under way and, knowing that this youthful impulse to victory must not be allowed to cool off, he left this trench in the hands of the second line of saptiehs, and drove these intoxicated storm-troops forward again, in clustered lines. But he did not venture to shift his howitzer-fire any farther forward, since he did not want to imperil himself and his men.

Not only Gabriel, every Armenian fighter in the second trench, knew what they risked. The mind, the life, the body of each one of them was a dark night, centred round one unendurably burning focus—to aim straight. Here leader and led no longer existed, only the petrifying consciousness: behind me the open camp, the women, the children, my people. And it was so. . . . They waited, as usual, till not one bullet could miss its mark. Gabriel, too, and Aram Tomasian, fired for the first time with complete concentration on their purpose, as though in a dream. What happened then happened independently of them all, or of Chaush Nurhan—that is to say their will was fused into the general will. They did not reload when they had fired their round of five cartridges. As though obeying one collective impulse, the Armenians swung out over the top. It was all quite different from what it had been on August

4. No blood-lust, not one shout, could force its way through tight-set lips. Heavy, benumbed, four hundred men of all ages fell upon their terrified Turkish assailants, who suddenly woke from their dream of victory. A bitter hand-to-hand encounter, man against man, swung this way and that. What use were the long bayonets on the Mauser rifles? Soon they strewed the earth of that strip of ground. Bony Armenian fingers blindly sought the gullets of their enemies; strong teeth fastened themselves like the fangs of beasts of prey, unconsciously, in Turkish throats, to suck the blood of vengeance out of them. Step by step, the lines of the company retreated. But the saptiehs, whom the old bimbashi—no longer rosy, but now apoplectically violet in the face—wanted to throw into battle, let him down. The gendarmerie was not, their chief declared, a fighting unit. It was there to keep order, and nothing more. It was not obliged to take part in assaults against a fully armed enemy. Also it was subject to civil, not military, law. This naturally so good-tempered bimbashi shouted, like a man bereft, that he would have the police chief shot by his policemen. Who was responsible for the whole filthy Armenian business in the first place? Officials, and their stinking curs of saptiehs, so useful against helpless women and children, otherwise good for nothing except to loot. But not all his anger helped the poor old man. The outraged saptiehs vacated the trench, and withdrew to the counter-slope. Yet even so, had not help come at just this minute, it is hard to say how this grappling fight might not have ended.

When news reached the Town Enclosure of the miraculous landslide and total destruction of the south division, the whole people went mad with the lust to kill. Not Ter Haigasun nor the Council could keep them back. Their souls, in blasphemous presumption, became certain that God was on their side. Meanwhile the orderlies came in, to tell them of the northern retreat. The reserve caught up its iron bars, mattocks, and pick-axes. Men and women shouted at Ter Haigasun: "To the

North Saddle." Today they'd show these Turkish hounds! There was nothing left for the priest but to place himself at the head of this bellowing horde. The freed decads also came streaming northwards. These superior, although undisciplined, numbers brought the decision within a few minutes. The Turks were hurled back, past the conquered trench, as far as their original position. Bagradian shouted to Ter Haigasun to get the reserve immediately back into camp. If once the howitzers started shelling them, they might do unpredictable damage, in these dense crowds. The priest succeeded with great difficulty in driving back his stampeding flock. Meanwhile, dripping with sweat and blood, the defenders feverishly began to block up gaps in their main trench. Gabriel's rasped nerves expected the first shell at any minute. There was still more than an hour to twilight.

The shrapnel, whose thin howl Bagradian fancied he kept hearing, still did not come, except in his mind. But another, quite unexpected thing happened. A long bugle-call. A lively stir along the wooded edge of the counter-slope, and very soon the scouts came in, to report that the Turks were in quick retreat, by the shortest way, into the valley. There was still enough light to watch them encamp on the church square at Bitias, and see their colonel riding with his staff, at a sharp canter, towards Suedia, via Yoghonoluk and the southern villages. This day had been more victorious, above all, more blest, than August 4, and yet, that night, there was no festivity, not even any warm jubilation, in either the entrenchments or the Town Enclosure.

THEY had brought in the dead. Now they lay in a row, covered over, on the flat square of meadowland which Ter Haigasun, because of the depths of its soil, had chosen for their mountain burial ground. Since the day of encampment on Musa Dagh, only three old people had so far died, whose recent graves were marked with the roughest limestone blocks, painted with three black crosses. These fresh graves must suddenly be increased to sixteen, since eight had been killed in the hand-to-hand fighting or by shellfire, and five others had in the last hours died of wounds. The relatives squatted beside each body. There were only low whimperings, no loud cries. All round the hospital-hut lay wounded, with crumpled faces and sunken, questioning eyes. Inside, there was only room for a few. The old doctor's hands were full of work, to which he felt himself quite unequal, either by his strength or science. Besides Mairik Antaram, he had Iskuhi, Gonzague, and Juliette to help him. Juliette, on that day especially, worked with an almost frantic self-abandonment, as though, by serving its wounded, she could atone for her lack of love for this people. She had brought out her well-stocked medicine-chest, filled, before they left Paris, under the supervision of the Bagradian family doctor. Her lips were white. She kept stumbling as if she might collapse. Then her eyes would seek out Gonzague. She did not see in him a lover, but a pitiless monitor, forcing her to put out more strength than she had. Apothecary Krikor had also, as behoved him, brought supplies. He had only two remedies for wounds—a few bandages and three large bottles of tincture of iodine. These were at least useful, because the iodine helped to keep from festering those wounds over which old Bedros Altouni was forced to growl, and leave them to nature, to heal or not to heal. Krikor dealt out his panacea with a miserly hand and, as the solution kept diminishing, diluted his iodine with water.

Stephan, who with Haik and his gang, was straying about over the battlefields, in the graveyard, and round the hospital-hut, watched all this piteous confusion. It was his first sight of death and dying, of maimed, and of screaming or groaning wounded. These horrors made him older by years, but calmer. His ardent, immature face clouded with a new kind of hostility. Now, as he stared out in front of him, he had taken on the look of Haik, his rival, yet with a dash of strained, overwrought excitement. When it was dark, he reported, as his duty was, to his father, in the north trench. The Leaders sat in a ring round Gabriel. He had the fuses of a grenade and a shrapnel in his hand, and was explaining the method of setting them off. On the grenade the ring was notched with the letter P, that is to say the shell was designed for a percussion fuse. The notching on the shrapnel fuse showed the figure 3, denoting a three-thousand-metre range, the distance between the mouth of the gun and the aiming-point. This fuse had been picked up about half a mile behind the front-line trench. So that one might, without being too far out, calculate the howitzer emplacement as about two thousand metres beyond the Saddle. Gabriel passed round the map of Musa Dagh. He had marked the possible point. The guns, if one thought it out, could have been set up only in the treeless gully which, even towards the north, precipitously skirted Musa Dagh. Only that narrow, but open, strip would offer a good field of fire to artillery. Everywhere else there were high trees impeding it, which would have required an impossible elevation for the gun barrels. Stephan, Haik, and the other boys had squatted down behind the men, and were listening breathlessly. Nurhan "the Lion" suggested the possibility of attacking the battery. Gabriel rejected it at once. Either, he said, the Turks would give up the attempt, and remove these howitzers to the valley, or they had a new plan of attack, and would shift the emplacement in the night. In either case, to attack the guns would be unnecessary, and highly dangerous, since a strong protecting force, perhaps even a whole infantry platoon, with plenty of cover, could practically wipe out the attackers. The Turks had shown what it meant to attack in the open. But he, Bagradian, refused to risk another Armenian life. Nurhan still stubbornly clung to his idea. It lead to a vehement dispute, this way and that, till Bagradian sharply closed the discussion:

"Chaush Nurhan, you're fagged out, and so are we all, and

no good for anything. That's enough! Let's get some sleep. In a few hours we'll see what else we can do."

But the boys were not fagged out; they were ready for anything. Stephan got leave to spend the night in the trenches. His father, who had already spread out his rugs, gave one to him. Gabriel had lost all desire for a bed and enclosed space in which to sleep. Tonight it was too stuffy to breathe freely even in the open. The exhausted men slept like the dead. One of them trod out the fires before they lay down. The double guard of sentries went to their posts, to keep a sharp look-out on every inlet to the Saddle. The boys, like a noiseless flight of birds, sped away among the rock-barricades. A bright August moon was already well in its second quarter. They stood in its sharp light in a close ring, among chalky boulders, chirruped and whispered. At first it was mere aimless, pointless chattering, in the bright, sharp light. But they, too, in the depths of their adventurous souls, were restless with the same itching purpose that filled young Stephan. It began in mere childish curiosity—"to have a look at the guns." Haik's band comprised a few of the brightest of the scouts' group. Couldn't one go on a reconnoitring expedition, without having expressly been given orders by Hapeth Shatakhian or Avakian? Stephan threw out the enticing question. His first mad sally into the orchards had raised his prestige to the height of Haik's. Haik, with the ironical indulgence of the invincibly strong, had begun to tolerate the rise of the Bagradian brat. Sometimes, in his mocking protection, there was even a faint suggestion of amiability. Haik signed to the rest to wait for him without getting excited. He wanted first to see what was on, up there. He, whose clear affinity with nature was far stronger than that of any among them, quietly dismissed would-be companions. He vanished soundlessly, to appear again suddenly in the swarm, not half an hour later, with the news that you could see the guns as clear as if it were daylight. His eyes glinted as he said it. They were big, beautifully golden-looking things, with a distance of about six paces between them. He had not counted more than twenty gunners, all asleep, and not one officer. There was only one sentry post.

Haik had counted accurately. And the fate of these howitzers was the reason why the poor, rosy-cheeked bimbashi was obliged to consider himself lucky that he could end his days as a paymaster's official, attached to the Anatolian railway, instead of as a General-Pasha. He swore a hundred oaths before the court martial, by Allah's mercy, that he had posted all the usual guards, as set down in the Sultan's regulations; that criminal saptiehs and Chettehs had gone lounging off without his leave. This truth could be proved, but it did not help the poor old gentleman in the least. Had it not been his duty to post a platoon of regulars round his guns? But the bimbashi's bad luck had not been confined to this single blunder. The artillery lieutenant, in direct contradiction of orders, without having left one decently trustworthy non-commissioned officer, had followed the infantryman, and gone down to the valley to fetch up next day's *ordre de bataille*. In addition to which, the donkeymen, pressed into service as gun-draggers, had all wandered back to their villages, having drawn the very logical conclusion that nobody could want them during the night. Such discipline in the field, not to mention its unheard-of results, made the sentence an unusually mild one. Strangely and fortunately enough, Jemal Pasha, "the sour-faced, humpbacked swindler," who as a rule insisted on having everything explained to him in detail, refrained from investigating personally. This may have been due to that general's preoccupation with Suez—or to some other reason, connected with the ugly Jemal's attitude towards Enver, the popular idol of Istanbul.

Haik and his two best scouts crept on cats'-feet along the narrow shelf of rock on the farther side of the Saddle. Stephan followed them, rather more clumsily. The one-legged Hagop had naturally had to stay behind. This time it had been

Stephan, his friend, who sharply told that ambitious cripple to stop pestering. That night no Sato hung around the edge of the pack. She had something better to do. Stephan and Haik carried guns and cartridges, borrowed from the piled-up arms and cartridge-belts of the decads. This day was to decide their chronic rivalry, a dispute which had gone on some time. Whenever Stephan, insisting on his excellent mark-manship, had boasted that at fifty paces he could shoot the face out of a playing-card, Haik had displayed the coldest scorn: "Can't ever stop bragging, can you?" Here was a chance to show the cocksure Haik that Stephan might have bragged vainly of much else, but at least not of being a good shot. And of this Stephan gave gruesome proof.

Haik guided the town-bred Stephan through rhododendron thickets to the very edge of the battery emplacement. Ten paces off them snored the sleepers. Sentries gazed vacantly up at the night sky, starless in the bright moonlight. Time and space extended infinitely, without misgivings, and full of patience. First Stephan tried several branches, to get a really comfortable rest for his barrel. He aimed very long, and without excitement, as though the flesh-and-blood figures over there had been wooden dummies in the shooting-booth of a country fair. This child of European culture was impelled by only one sensation—the desire to get the human, white, moon-lit forehead of a guard before his barrel, well between the sights. He pulled the trigger without a qualm, calmly heard the report, felt the kick and, delighted with himself, saw the man sink down. As the sleepers stumbled to their feet, not yet quite knowing what had happened, he aimed more quickly, but not a jot less steadily, pulling the trigger twice, three times, four times, tugging at the breech with a quick, strong jerk. These fifteen Turks were redifs, elderly men, who scarcely knew the meaning of the campaign. They ran about in confusion. Five already lay in pools of blood. No visible enemy. These staid, respectable peasants, forced into the

386

army, did not seek cover—they rushed, in the wildest pell-mell, into the wood—far, far, never to return! Haik wildly shot off his whole five bullets after them. Not one hit—as Master Stephan could note contemptuously. The howitzers, the limber, the dragging-cart, the shell-locker, the rifles, the mules, were all abandoned. Thus did one fourteen-year-old schoolboy, with five cartridges, avenge the million-fold decimation of his race upon harmless peasants forced into arms—upon the wrong people, as is always the case in war revenge.

WHEN the outpost sentries heard shots crackle through the quiet of this moony night, they aroused their chief. But the schoolboys, huddled among the rocks, awaiting Haik and Stephan, became panic-stricken. They felt responsible. With loud cries and waving arms, they came rushing out. But only Hagop, with all his frenzied, stubborn nimbleness, came hopping to Gabriel, who had started up, still dazed with alarm. The cripple pointed wildly at the counter-slope, with repeated cries: "Haik and Stephan—over there." Gabriel did not grasp what had happened. He knew Stephan was in danger. He rushed off like a madman, where Hagop pointed. A hundred men caught up their rifles and followed their chief. The "Lion," Chaush Nurhan, was naturally one of them. But when, arrived at the emplacement, Bagradian saw the dead, and Stephan unharmed, he jerked his son so roughly to him that he might have been intending to shoot him too. All the rest were dazed. No one so much as noticed the two young heroes, those capturers of guns who, with such huge, new bronze toys to amuse them, had forgotten all the reality around, how little time they had to waste, and even the weltering death under their feet. For an instant the Armenian men stood breathless. This incredible thing was too huge to grasp, this booty too absurdly unattainable, for any among them to find time to ask how the fight had come about. Quick—get hold of the guns before the Turks come! Two hundred arms got to work on it. The teams, the limbers, the munition box were rushed up the slope, the howitzers slung to the limbers. Every man of them pushed or tugged at the ropes, or put his shoulder to the wheels. The guns went jolting on, up the fissured, pathless earth of the mountain. But night melted jutting rocks and bushes, the hard resistance of every obstacle, into soft flexibility. For a while it seemed as though the howitzers, borne on this mad strength of gripping hands, were hovering along above the earth.

It was not two hours before the guns, in spite of the incredibly difficult terrain, had been set up where Gabriel wanted them. He had been given a short account of Stephan's deed. But the fear still thudding in his heart would not let him speak of it. He could not praise his son. This scatter-brained daring, the escapade of a half-grown schoolboy, was, he felt, a dangerous example not only to the other boys, but to the decads as well. If everyone now began to want to be heroic, that would be the end, on the Damlayik, of the only power—unified discipline—which might, at least for a time, guarantee the survival of the camp. Deeper still was his anxiety for Stephan. So far his luck had been incredible. Really the boy must be off his head! And you couldn't lock him up, on Three-Tent Square. . . . But Gabriel did not follow out these thoughts, since now his whole mind was set on the howitzers. Their type was familiar to him; the battery he had served in the Balkan war had had guns of the same calibre. They were Austro-Hungarian 10 cm. howitzers, of the 1899 pattern, delivered to Turkey by the Skoda factory. The lockers in the gun-cart of the second still contained thirty shells. Gabriel found all he needed, and tried to remember exactly how to use it—the aiming-apparatus for firing from behind cover, a box of firing-instructions, and schedule, in the trail-box. He began to remember all he had learned, reckoned out the distance to Bitias, strove to get the exact position of the

Turkish encampment, screwed at the rear-sights to determine
the given field of direction, took stock of the elevation of his
enplacement, raised the barrels, with the little wheel, to centre
the bubble, and only then pulled out the breech, set the fuses
of two shells with the key-ring, shoved the round projectiles
into the bore, and pressed in the cartridges after them. His
unpractised hand took very long to do all this, and Chaush
Nurhan could do next to nothing to help him. As the sun
came up, Bagradian, having retested all these aiming factors,
knelt with Nurhan, as regulations directed, one on either side
of the gun-carriage, watch in hand. Two short, terrific cracks,
bang upon bang, rent the air to shreds. The gun kicked, em-
bedding itself deep in the ground. These shells had been
badly aimed; they dropped far wide of Bagradian's target,
somewhere in the valley. But this mere gesture was enough to
apprise the whole Mohammedan countryside of the new victory of the Christians, the loss of Turkish artillery, the impregnability of the Damlayik, and the fact, now public property, that the Armenian swine had entered into a compact with
the jinn, known of old as the evil spirits of Musa Dagh. The
Chettehs had all vanished in the night, and a section of saptiehs, not attached to this nahiyeh, along with them. Now the
few survivors of the companies were convinced that even a
full division would be routed, if it assailed this devil's mountain. The bimbashi could not have ordered a fresh attack
without risking a mutiny from his young troops. Nor did he
even consider such foolhardiness, occupied with a far more
modest problem: how to get the long line of carts, full of dead
and wounded, back to Antioch, unperceived, as he had given
strict orders they should be. The old man's cheeks had no more
colour in them. It was all he could do to sit his horse, after
two sleepless nights and the strain of battle. His fate was
sealed. The bimbashi's very limited powers of reflection, which,
even in peaceable times, were far too desultory, could conceive no method of pulling down to destruction along with

389

him the cursed Kaimakam and his set of rascally, foxy civil servants who were really responsible for it all.

The two thunderclaps, almost in their ears, seemed to those within the Town Enclosure like the menacing signs of divine assistance. The toughest, dourest among these peasants embraced, with tears in their eyes. "Perhaps Christ really means to save us, after all." Never before had their sunrise greetings sounded so heart-felt. As to the Bagradians, their kingly rank, doubly proved, seemed for ever established. Some of the peasants came to Gabriel, begging his permission to confer on Stephan the title "Elleon"—"Lion." Gabriel rather sharply refused. His son was still only a child, without any real notion of danger. He didn't want him to get conceited, or stuff his head with a lot of foolery, which might only end in disaster. So that Stephan, through his father's severity, was balked of public recognition, and had to content himself with the flatteries which, for a few days, surrounded him on all sides. In after-years those Armenian chroniclers who described the battle on the Damlayik wrote only of "the heroic action of a young sharpshooter" without naming him. But of what use would even the most explicit praises have been then, to Bagradian's son?

Gabriel had long been a different man, and Stephan too had changed completely. The gently nurtured cannot do butcher's work unpunished, though right may be a thousand times on their side. On this boy's delicate forehead some savage god of Musa Dagh was already setting his dark seal.

THIS great night of August 14 witnessed yet another, though far less memorable, event. Sato had gone creeping down through the twilight, to her friends in the valley. They must hear the whole tale of battle, learn how sixteen corpses lay covered on the bare earth, how the shrieks of the wounded rose and rose—loudest of all when the stupid hekim, Altouni, dabbled brown water on their wounds. Sato, that walking newspaper, alike of mountain- and of grave-dwellers, could, tonight, revel in sensationalism, earning her social keep for days ahead. When Sato could satisfy her clients, and feel herself a beloved child, her eyes seemed to change into slits of flickering light, and her throaty jargon proclaimed sensation with joyous zest. The churchyard folk rejoiced along with her—old Manushak, old Wartuk, and Nunik, the oldest of them all, or so she said. They wagged knowing heads. Deep self-importance possessed them. No longer superfluous outcasts, they had an office to perform, incontestably theirs, through all human memory. The dead had need of them. Sixteen dead awaited them on the Damlayik. And, once they came about their business, their arch-enemy, Hekim Altouni, would have lost his power. No "enlightener" dared molest keening-women.

So Nunik, Wartuk, Manushak, and a score of other beggar-women besides, set forth, with the slow, dignified tread of functionaries, for their dens, dug in the earth-mounds of the graveyard. They dragged forth the crammed and filthy sacks upon which they laid their beggar-women's heads. What it was that rotted in these sacks, in dense and permanent corruption, passes description. The miscellaneous rubbish of fifty years' picking up off the ground. The collector's itch of all old, poor women in every land, the itch to save up moth-eaten remnants, scrape together mildewed garbage—this usual, jealously guarded treasure-trove of rags and rottenness, had taken on the dimensions of a veritable orgy of stinking uselessness. Yet behold, these old women's sacks seemed, besides their tatters, their cloth patches, empty boxes, stony crusts and cheese-rinds, to contain the professional equipment of Nunik, Wartuk, Manushak. Each of them plunged in her hand, to draw the same out of her luckybag—a long, grey veil, a pot of greasy salve. They squatted down, and began to smear their faces, like mimes. It was a dark purple face-stain, which they worked into their deep-cut wrinkles, changing their incredibly

391

ancient faces into timeless and imposing masks. Nunik especially, with the lupous nose and strong white teeth gleaming out of her dark, lipless visage, quite justified her romantic reputation as the "eternally wandering" medicine-woman. It took her a long time to make up. Suddenly they broke off their preparations and puffed out their stump of candle-end, the wick-flame, in the rancid oil cup set up before them. Hoofs and voices came scurrying past. This was the instant when the bimbashi and his staff rode away to Suedia. When the sounds had petered out in Habibli, the wood village, the women rose, enveloped their grey, matted heads in the veils, took each a long stick in her hand, and their broken, clappering shoes set out. Their stringy, old women's legs seemed to manage surprisingly long strides. Sato came after, scared at their majesty. As, plying their staves, they went on in silence under the moon, these keening-women had almost the look of the masked leaders of a Greek chorus.

What stored-up, inexhaustible vitality, what stout hearts, the Armenian women possessed! Not one, as they emerged from the steep ilex gully on to the burying-ground of the encampment, breathed a jot more quickly. These purple-faced wailers had all the strength they needed to set to work. Nunik, Wartuk, Manushak, and the others crouched round the dead. Their dirty claws uncovered the already stiffened faces. And their song, older perhaps than the oldest song of all humanity, rose to the skies. Its text was no more than the ever-repeated names of these fresh corpses. Names, keened over and over, without a break, till the last stars faded in greenish ether. Poor though its text, the more richly varied was its melody. Sometimes it was a long groaning monotone, sometimes a chain of howling coloratura, sometimes the empty, drooping repetition, maimed with its grief, of the same two notes; sometimes it was a shrill, greedy demand—yet none of this in free obedience to an impulse, but strictly conventionalized and handed down by a long tradition. Not all the singers had Nunik's voice or inherited technique. There were mediocre, and so vain, artists among them, whose thoughts as they worked were occupied with fees and inheritance. What use were all his pounds and piastres to the richest man, up here? Let him give lavish offerings to the beggar-folk, and he would do not only a deed pleasing to God, but a useful work. The keening-women, the blind, the outcasts, were able to lay out chinking piastres, even in Mohammedan villages, without risk. So that Armenian money would not be wasted on them, but be of use to poor Armenian bodies, and the benefactors thus acquire celestial merit at bargain prices. Between the chants, her colleagues admonished Nunik, with all their might, to insist on this common-sense standpoint, and raise the usual fee for a corpse-watching. Through the grey light came the relatives, bringing their long, fine-woven shrouds. These had been stored up by every family, and had to be taken with every house-moving. The shift in which a man stands up from the dead, his most festal garment, is a gift given by the members of each household to one another, on the most solemn occasions in their lives. The task of weaving such a shroud is accounted a particular honour. Only the worthiest women may perform it.

These women's howls had died into a low, almost soundless, windy sigh. It went with the corpse-washing, the enshrouding, like cold comfort. Then the long shifts were tied under the feet in double knots. This was to keep the limbs from dispersal, so that the last storm, which shall drive all bones together, to be judged, might not find it hard to fit the right ones. Towards midday the graves stood open, and all men ready for the burials. On sixteen biers, made of strong branches lashed together, the fallen were carried twice round the altar, while Ter Haigasun chanted his funeral dirge. Afterwards, on the burial-ground, he addressed the people:

"These, our dear brethren, have been snatched away by bloody death. And yet we must devoutly thank the Blessed Trinity that they have died in battle, in freedom, and are to rest here in this earth, among their own. Yes, we have still the grace of a free death, of our own choosing. And, therefore, to see aright the grace in which God lets us live, we must think again and again of the thousands from whom such grace had been withdrawn; of those who have died in the worst bondage, who lie out unburied on the plains, in ditches along the highroads, and are being devoured by vultures and hyenas. If we climb that knoll to our left, and look out eastwards, we shall see stretching away before us the endless fields of our dead, where there is no consecrated ground, no priest, no burial, and only the hope of the Last Judgment. So let us then, in this hour in which we lower these happy ones into earth, remember what real misfortune is, and that it is not here, but out yonder."

This short sermon drew deep groans from the villagers encamped on Musa Dagh, who had all assembled. Ter Haigasun went to the tubs which contained their consecrated earth. Sixteen times he put in his hand, to open it over the head of a dead fighter. It moved with the slowest deliberation. They could see how sparing he was of that precious soil.

3

The Procession of Fire

Nunik, Wartuk, Manushak—today they were in luck professionally. Before they so much as found time to wipe their faces clean with lettuce leaves, another engagement presented itself. It was one of an exactly opposite kind. If the woman's labour was prolonged, as they had every reason to hope it might be, they could count on three full meals at least. And, in the very just supposition that any human event may occur at any time in a population of five thousand, they had brought all the essentials of their craft, wrapped in the crumpled folds of their garments—sevsamith, the black fennel seed, a little swallow dung, the tail hair of a chestnut horse, and other similar medicaments.

Even before the earth of the Damlayik had closed over the last of the dead, Hovsannah's labour had begun. Only Iskuhi was with her in the tent, everyone else had gone to the burial. Iskuhi's lame arm prevented her being of much use to her sister-in-law. There was no seat with a back to it against which the labouring mother could bear down. Cushions gave her no leverage, and the bed had only a low iron frame. Iskuhi sat with her back to Hovsannah, so that the tortured woman might press firmly against her body. But Iskuhi was too frail to hold out against Hovsannah's heavy thrusts; cling as fast as she might to the bed-frame, she always slipped. Hovsannah let out a short scream. It came as a signal to Nunik. That wailer's alert instinct had drawn her away from the burial.

These mourners' work was done, their surprisingly high fees had been clawed together.

Iskuhi was about to leave the tent in search of Mairik Antaram when the three fates, unbidden, thrust into the tent. Their rigid purple faces shone in the gloom. The two Tomasian women were speechless; not that the mourners themselves alarmed them—who did not know them in Yoghonoluk?— but at the sight of their funeral trappings, which they still wore. Nunik, who divined at once the superstitious reason of these fears, calmed them: "Little daughter, it's good we should come like this. It keeps death behind us."

Nunik began her obstetric treatment by drawing the sis out of her garments, the thin iron poker to stir up the tonir fire. She began tracing out big crosses along the inner wall of the tent.

"Why are you drawing crosses?" asked Iskuhi, spellbound.

Nunik explained as she worked. All the powers of the air assemble round the beds of labouring women, the evil more numerous than the good. When the child pushes into the world, in the very instant when his head pushes into life, these evil spirits hurl themselves upon it, to possess and permeate. Every human born must, of necessity, take something of them. It is because of this that madness lies asleep at the bottom of all our hearts. So that the devil has his share of all men, and only Christ Saviour was never devil-ridden. In Nunik's view the highest art of the midwife lies in her knowledge of how to cut down the devil's share. These crosses served as prohibiting signals, as mystic quarantine. Iskuhi remembered her dream of the convoy, night after night. The face of kaleidoscopic evil, Satan and all his works, still hovered above her. And she, too, with her free hand, had tried to ban him by tracing a great cross in the air. Oh, for how much earthly terror must Christ Saviour at every instant not be in readiness! This was by no means the end of Nunik's wisdom. She explained to the startled women how all our entrails—the

396

lungs, the liver, the heart especially—are in sympathy with a different devil, who will strive to get entire possession of them all. The whole act of birth is no more than a wrestling-match of good and evil, for the full ownership of the child. So that a wise mother would use the old, well-tried feints and aid which Nunik gave her. If she did, her child was certain to get past its first, dangerous days.

When sudden panic had abated, the presence of these three bedizened midwives was remarkably soothing—lulling—in its effect. Hovsannah even dozed, and seemed not to notice how Wartuk tied up her wrists and ankles with thin, silk cords. But Nunik came close to the bed, and counselled her: "The longer your body remains closed, the longer your strength remains shut in. The later you open your body, the more strength will enter, and issue out of you."

Meanwhile the little, sturdy Manushak had lighted a twig fire in front of the tent. Two smooth stones, like flat loaves, were put to heat in it. This was a far less occult remedy, since these warm stones, wrapped into cloths, would serve to warm the exhausted body of the mother. Even Bedros Hekim might have approved of this more practical part of magic obstetrics, and of the fennel-water, which Manushak heated over her fire. None the less his remaining hairs bristled with rage when he found his three arch-enemies with the patient. He swung his stick and, with all the nimbleness of youth, drove off the keeners. His sharp little voice pursued them with insults. "Carrion-crows" was perhaps the mildest.

We see, therefore, that Dr. Bedros Altouni was a very ardent champion indeed of western science. Had not old Avetis Bagradian sent him to get his education and supported him a whole five years at the University of Vienna, that he might hold aloft the torch of enlightenment above the darkness of this people? But how were things with him in reality? What reward had fate given the hekim for having kept his promise to his old patron? In all the long years through which, astride his patient ass, the doctor had gone jogging round the villages, and indeed been in constant request by Moslems, up and down the whole district, he had had to admit the oddest experiences. His whole scientific heart might rebel, but his eyes had had to see many cures obtained by the lousiest quacks, the filthiest nostrums, in flat defiance of all antiseptic or hygiene. In eighty percent of these cures "evil eye" had been the diagnosis. For this the specifics were spittle, sheep's piss, burnt horsehair, birds' dung, and even more attractive medicaments. And yet, more than once it had happened that a patient, given up by Dr. Altouni, got a lightning cure from having swallowed a strip of paper scribbled with a verse from Bible or Koran. Altouni was not the man to credit the magic of swallowed strips, not, at least, to the point where doubts assailed him. But what use was scepticism? A cure was a cure! In Armenian villages the news of such miraculous therapy would get about from time to time, so that Altouni's patients all forsook him, to seek out the Arab hekim in the neighbourhood, or even consult Nunik and her worthy sisters, the other fates. And frequently there would be confirmed "enlighteners"—this or that schoolteacher, for instance—who deserted the doctor for the quack. It certainly did not improve his temper.

There was another reason for Dr. Altouni's bitter wrath. Perhaps it was the really valid one. Science! Enlightenment! Progress! All well and good. But to diffuse the light of scientific advancement one must oneself be scientifically advanced. And who, cut off from all knowledge of recent discoveries, medical books, or medical journals, could advance in the shadow of Musa Dagh? Krikor's library contained the works of many years on every conceivable subject except medicine, although, or perhaps because, he was a chemist. Bedros Altouni had only a German *Handbook of Medicine* published in 1875. It was a solid work; it contained the essentials. But it had one grave defect. For devouring time had not only affected the vade mecum, but also the doctor's memory of German. The Handbook had, as it were, been struck dumb. So now Dr. Altouni never opened it, nor even used it as amulet and fetish. All that, decades ago, he had learned theoretically, had melted into an inconsiderable something. For the doctor there were ten to twenty diseases that could be named. Though he had seen innumerable pictures of human suffering, he crammed them all under the few headings he possessed. In the depths of his sad and simple heart Altouni felt every bit as ignorant as the hekims, quacks, and keening-wives of the district, whose gruesome cures so damnably often succeeded, with a little help from patient Nature. It was just this utter lack of conceit which, without his ever being aware of it, made of Altouni a great doctor. On the other hand it provoked these frenzied outbursts at the sight of Nunik, Wartuk, Manushak. But today these midwives did not let themselves be dismissed. They lingered on the edge of Three-Tent Square, eyeing the enemy with derision.

Hovsannah, the pastor's wife, was the first woman among the people to lie in childbed on the Damlayik. Even in the everyday valley a birth was a kind of public event, to which all assembled, near and distant relatives, not excepting the men. How much more solemn, therefore, and public an occasion, up here in camp—since now, in perhaps the most perilous situation in which that people had yet been placed, the first Armenian child was to be brought forth. Even the resplendent spoils of war, the two golden howitzers, shed their glory on it. The crowds which had that morning surrounded those trophies now jammed into Three-Tent Square, the most "select" place in this poor camp. The curtains of poor Hovsannah's tent were lifted and she was mercilessly exposed to the sun. Her birthpangs were her own, but she was the people's. The inquisitive came in and out. Altouni, having soon realized himself superfluous, had made way, with a grunt, for his wife, who as a rule replaced him at a child-bed. He walked away, taking no notice of the deep salaams of the keening-women, towards the hospital-hut to visit his wounded.

Mairik Antaram stayed with Hovsannah. With sharp words, even with fists, she cleared the tent of its intruders. Decisively she set about the duties which for many decades she had performed. Yet, old as Mairik was, she could still, even today, not help at a childbirth without some thoughts of the two miscarriages which dated back to her earliest youth. Iskuhi stroked her sister's forehead with hands as cool as ice, in spite of the heat. She kept eyeing Mairik with shy anxiety, afraid of missing some direction. All the energy of the doctor's wife could not keep people out of the hut; they kept on returning, to give advice, encourage, ask how things were getting on. Gabriel too came in for news. Iskuhi, in the midst of all this bustle, was still struck by the haggard paleness of his bearded face. Also she felt surprised that Juliette should remain scarcely half an hour with Hovsannah—they had lived together so long, in a single family. Aram, the husband, was in and out every twenty minutes. But he always went again. He was, he kept saying, more needed than ever; after yesterday's victory over the Turks he must keep an eye on the general discipline. Really his own excitement, and worry about his wife, drove him round in circles.

The women of the people were shaking their heads over the fact that Hovsannah Tomasian did not scream as she lay in labour. They sensed some pride behind it. It was perhaps the pride of shame. Nunik, Wartuk, Manushak, had long since come back into the foreground. Nunik herself squatted inside the tent, watching all Antaram's laborious efforts with reflectively professional eyes, much as a world-famous surgeon might watch the work of a village barber.

After more than eight hours' labour pains Hovsannah at last brought forth a son. This child, who in its mother's womb since Zeitun, had known much fear and suffering, was unconscious, and did not breathe. Antaram shook the tiny body, still

400

covered with blood and afterbirth, while Iskuhi had to breathe into its mouth. But Nunik and her colleagues, who knew better, seized like lightning on the afterbirth, to pierce it with seven needles, owned by seven different families. They cast the whole into their fire. The life which, to escape its fate on earth, had taken refuge in this dead matter, must be freed by fire. A few seconds later the child gurgled; he began to breathe, and then to whimper. Mairik Antaram rubbed him all over carefully with mutton fat. The crowd, grown silent, began applauding. The sun sank. Pastor Aram, with all the clumsy, rather absurd, pride of a young father, took up the little wrinkled thing, which should grow to a man, and held it out to the people. They all rejoiced and praised Tomasian, since this was a male. The broadest jokes went the rounds of the fighters. None of them could remember the real future. It remains uncertain which of them was the first to notice the little, round fiery birth-spot which this true son of Musa Dagh bore above his tiny heart. The women put their heads together to consult as to the meaning of this sign. But Nunik, Wartuk, Manushak, whose profession it was to decipher such omens, would say nothing, bound up their veils, took their staves, and so retraced their steps, well recompensed. Their old brown legs moved in long strides. Again they were like the mimes of an ancient chorus as, under the rising moon, they took their way down mountain slopes towards the graves of the past.

Nor more than three days and nights had passed, and scouts were already announcing incomprehensible movements in the villages. Gabriel climbed at once to his observation post. His field-glass certainly showed a most active scurry, in sharply differentiated forms. Long lines of ox-carts across the plain of the Orontes, along the highroad between the villages, on the paths and cart-tracks leading off it. Big crowds in these villages themselves, people in fez and turban, darting in and out, in obvious haste. Gabriel tested every strip of ground with his spy-glass, but could not make out one soldier's uniform, and not many saptiehs. On the other hand he noticed that this time it was not the familiar populace of Antakiya, or its suburbs, that invaded the empty streets. Today's incursions looked far more opulent, and seemed to have a definite object. Great stir on the church square of Yoghonoluk. Little turbaned shapes were clambering up the fire-escape of the church, and moving about in the empty bell-tower, to the side of the big cupola. The long-drawn, thread-like notes of a tiny voice grew audible, perceptible rather, sent out to the four quarters of the globe. It was the prayer-cryer of the Prophet, standing above the house of Christ, giving out of himself his plangent sing-song, which causes every Moslem heart to beat faster, and which seemed to be bringing in the faithful from every cluster of huts, village, market town, in the empty land. The fate of the Church of Ever-Increasing Angelic Powers, built by Avetis the elder, was therefore sealed. The mad desire to answer this desecration with a shell flashed into the grandson's mind. He checked his impulse. His basic principle— always to defend, never attack—must be broken least of all by himself. And the mountain, towering secretively over its enemies, as though shamming dead, threatened more effectively. Provocation could only weaken their defence, since it gave the Turks, the ruling people, their moral right to punish rebels.

As he watched all this mysterious stir in the valley, Bagradian asked himself how many more onslaughts they could drive back. In spite of the spoils of double victory, and Nurhan's workshop for making cartridges, the munition supply was very limited. It made his heart stand still to remember how the smallest slip, the most trifling failure, must lead to irretrievable disaster. There was no middle way for those on the Damlayik; it was either final victory, or the end. His tactical skill was merely useful to put off that end as long as he could. To achieve that object the capital sum of wholesome fear which, after two defeats, they obviously inspired in the Turks, must not be frittered away. The new population of the valley increased every minute. But this time it did not mean an attack, of that he was certain, after long and minute investigation. Perhaps they were only holding a demonstration, perhaps this was the solemn investiture of a Christian district by Islam. In front of the church door of Yoghonoluk he made out a small group of men in European dress. The müdir with his officials, presumed Bagradian, glad to see no officer among them, come to get the hang of the situation. All the same he ordered that the trenches were to keep on the sharpest alert, set a double guard at every observation post, and groups of scouts at all possible approaches to the Damlayik, as far down as the vines and orchards, so that no surprise attack at night should be possible.

Gabriel had judged correctly. It was the freckled müdir who stood in the church square of Yoghonoluk. But a greater than he, the dyspeptic Kaimakam in person, had come to have a look round for himself. There was excellent reason for it. This last, disastrous defeat of a force of regulars had made things happen in Antioch—things which entailed important consequences.

BETWEEN the Kaimakam and the poor, rosy-cheeked bimbashi a life-or-death struggle had started instantly. That forthright veteran of the simple barrack squares of former days was in no way up to the latest Ittihad finesse. Only now did he begin to get some inkling why his deputy, and keen competitor, the yüs-bashi, had chosen this moment to go on leave. By granting it he had walked into the trap. Very soon now the major would have ceased to deputize. It began by the Kaimakam's slyly contriving to stir up popular hatred against the bimbashi. In Antioch there was only one hospital, superintended by the civil authorities. Soldiers without much the matter with them were ill in barracks, but if hospital treatment became necessary the military command had to put in a request to the Kaimakam. The Kaimakam made skilful use of his red tape. But, in any case, he had finished the colonel. Yet the thing might have gone dragging on for weeks, with piles of reports and investigations, before they removed him from his command; and, to pursue his policy in the kazah, the Kaimakam needed dependable Ittihad collaborators, not indolent dug-outs, survivals of the days of Abdul Hamid. He and the major had judged the event with sufficient accuracy, and made their arrangements together. A few hours before the bimbashi got back to Antioch, the disconsolate herald of his own downfall, a long line of ox-carts with dead and wounded, the victims both of guns and avalanche, had come into the town, at the dead of night. No light shone in the windows of the Hükümet. When these carts halted outside the hospital, its superintendent categorically refused to admit their occupants. He had been expressly forbidden to take in soldiers without written permission from the Kaimakam. Curses and threats left him unmoved. The surgeon, by the light of an oil lamp, and of the moon, in the open air, put on the most necessary bandages. He, too, had neither space nor permission to admit two hundred extra patients into his wretched lazaret. In despair he sent off an assistant to the Kaimakam, to get his instructions. It took a very long time for the messenger to come back without any. The Kaimakam was so soundly asleep that nobody had succeeded in waking him. So that at last it had to be decided to take these scream-ing, or groaning, men to barracks, where at least they could have a roof over their heads. Meanwhile the sun was up, it was full daylight. An indescribable impression was made on the people of Antioch by these carts, slippery with blood. And when, at almost the same instant, the poor bimbashi, so tried by fate, rode with his staff across the Orontes bridge into the town, he was welcomed with stones, and could scarcely get back to his quarters, by devious lanes. Only now, with crowds thronging the market-place, did the Kaimakam, whose sleep was so deliciously long and tranquil, send necessary permission to the hospital. The long line of cart-loads of wretched men jolted slowly back there. The carts had been given careful orders to trundle through the Long Bazaar. This repeated sight of sallow, agonized faces, bandages stiff with blood, provoked an uproar. A furious crowd collected in front of the barracks, and broke all the poor bimbashi's windows—and windows, in these parts, were valuable luxuries. Not only that! What was left of the military arm had grown so timid, so subdued, so scared of the mob, that it closed its barrack-gates, like any terrified little shopkeeper. In every collection of massed humanity there slumbers a primitive hatred, easily roused, against its rulers. As it heard the deathly quiet behind barrack-gates, this mob grew aware that it had triumphed, and opened fresh fire. His officers kept imploring the bimbashi to let them turn out the guard with fixed bayonets, to clear the square. But the old man, stretched on his sofa, could heed no counsel. He could only whimper: "It isn't my fault," again and again. Utterly worn out by this strain and hardship, he sobbed except when he fell asleep, and slept whenever he was not sobbing. The garrison had to endure the further disgrace of requesting police and saptiehs to rid the square of its turbulent populace.

All this delighted the Kaimakam. He, with the manicured müdir from Salonika, had meanwhile repaired to the local telegraph office. This time these gentlemen between them composed a masterpiece of political acumen and tactful insight. A dispatch to His Excellency the Wali of Aleppo. This voluminous telegraphed document contained eleven hundred words, and covered ten closely written forms. A document as involved and subtle as the deed drawn up by a needy but ambitious solicitor, as glib as the most liberal newspaper editorial. It began, with colourful emphasis, by describing the recent disastrous efforts to "liquidate"—these heavy, yet so unnecessary, losses (with figures attached): stigmatized as the un-heard-of military delinquency that indeed it was, this sur-render of insufficiently guarded howitzers to a set of rascally mutineers. The Kaimakam then dismissed the unhappy busi-ness with a resigned suggestion that any attempt on his part to influence military decisions was almost bound to be misin-terpreted. On the other hand he felt it very urgent to insist on the highly uncertain state of public feeling in this matter, so outraged, for the moment at least, as to demand, even by street demonstrations, the instant removal from his command of the present bimbashi. And he, the Kaimakam, had not a suffi-ciently strong force of militia and saptiehs at his disposal to control any really serious outbreak. Therefore the popular out-cry would have to be conceded to without delay, and would His Excellency be so kind as to remove and punish by court martial the present responsible commandant? All this, the Kaimakam continued, was merely the indirect result of dual control, since the Syrian vilayets were subject both to their civil governors and the High Command of the Fourth Army. For so long as such dual control continued, he could guarantee neither peace in the kazah nor the so desirable completion of the enforcement of the edict of deportation against Armenians. He gave lucid legal demonstration that measures to ensure the migration of the Armenian millet were a process of the civil arm, in which even the most highly placed officers had no warrant to act independently. In their case military com-petence was fully comprised in the concept "auxiliary." But the use of such auxiliary troops depended, by the text of the edict, solely on such decisions as the civil authorities might arrive at. The present prevailing practice was therefore illegal, since the High Command frequently acted at its own discre-tion, in many cases withheld its auxiliary forces, acted in a manner hostile to district governors, and would even some-times commandeer the gendarmerie—a section of the civil arm —for its own objects. Such dangerous practices had resulted in stirring up the Armenian population to a resistance which, if it spread, might entail unpredictable consequences to the whole empire. The Kaimakam closed this very unusual service telegram on an almost threatening note. He could only undertake the liquidation of the armed camp on Musa Dagh on condition that he were given full control of all effectives. For that purpose he must have military auxiliaries, so armed and of such strength, at his disposal as to make possible the complete and thorough clearance of the whole mountain. Nor could it be a question of undertaking such punitive action with an officer unversed in the particular circumstances. He begged most urgently that the present deputy-major might be promoted military commandant of Antakiya, since this Armenian undertaking ought to be left entirely in his control. Otherwise—should these minimum requests not be considered possible of fulfilment—he, the Kaimakam, ventured most respectfully to suggest that the disaster above described had better be accepted as a *fait accompli,* without any further countermeasures, and the rebels left to their own devices on Musa Dagh.

The Kaimakam's report was a masterpiece of political insight. Should he obtain only a portion of his requests, he would be the most independent district governor in Syria. A well-trained official heart of the last generation would no doubt have fluttered in apprehension at the rather challenging tone of this huge dispatch. Not so the Young Turk. Such blunt decisiveness was attuned to the ears of the present authorities. They were on their knees before the progressive West, and so, in superstitious awe of such words as "initiative" and "energy," even though the voice that spoke them was somewhat harsh.

Simultaneously the ruined bimbashi, whose rosy cheeks had certainly faded out for ever, was scrawling a long dispatch to the base commandant, his immediate superior. It was verbose, full of prolix accusations against the Kaimakam, who had forced him to this disastrous undertaking, without having allowed him any time to make the necessary preparations. The bimbashi's tone was doleful, subdued, ceremonious, and consequently as wrong as it could be. The broken old man was removed within twenty-four hours and summoned to attend a court martial. He vanished through the night into obscurity, from the scene of many years' comfortable activity, the most innocent victim of Armenian success in war.

But His Excellency the Wali of Aleppo was so impressed with the suggestions of the Kaimakam of Antioch that he had them telegraphed on to Istanbul, with a strong personal recommendation, to the Ministry of the Interior. This subordinate had touched, with his finger-tips, a very sore spot in his superior. Ever since the great Jemal Pasha, with the unrestricted powers of a Roman proconsul, had been commanding in Syria, all walis and mutessarifs had shrunk to the stature of minor deities. Jemal Pasha treated these mighty ones as so many commissariat officials attached to his army. They were given curt orders to deliver at such and such a point so and so many thousand oka of grain, or, in a given time, to put this or that highroad in faultless repair. This general seemed to regard the whole civil population as an onerous set of unnecessary parasites, and civil government as a quite unnecessary evil. His Excellency of Aleppo was therefore delighted with the chance to rap this iron pasha over the knuckles, and apprise the Istanbul authorities of the wretched failure of arrogant fire-eaters.

Talaat Bey, however, read the Kaimakam's masterpiece with mixed feelings. It was his job to protect the civil arm against encroachments by the military. And to him these Armenian deportations were a matter of far greater urgency than the boring ambitions of discontented officers. He stroked his white piqué waistcoat with his great paws, several times, as his habit was. At last the nimble fingers of the telegraphist, attached to these mighty paws, clipped the sheets together, scribbled, and attached the slip: "Urgently request immediate settlement."

The dossier wandered without delay on to the desk of the

Minister of War. It was Enver Pasha's habit never to refuse a request of Talaat's. That evening, when they came together at the Endjumen, the smaller cabinet meeting, Enver came straight to his friend. The young war-god smiled demurely, and blinked long lashes. "I've sent Jemal an urgent wire about Musa Dagh. . . ." And without awaiting Talaat's thanks, with a daintily mischievous *moue:* "I'm sure you ought all of you to thank me for having sent that mad creature to Syria—well out of mischief!"

THERE was an Arab hotel before the Jaffa Gate in Jerusalem. Its windows looked out over the David citadel, with the towering minaret. In this hotel General Jemal Pasha, the general in command of this particular army, had set up his temporary headquarters. Here he read the dispatches from Enver, the Wali of Aleppo, and other functionaries, imploring him to provide for the instant quelling of this wretched Armenian revolt. (In those days it was the habit of all Young Turkish potentates to wire volumes to one another. It was more than a matter of mere urgency. It sprang from a barbaric joy in the use of talking electricity.) Jemal Pasha sat alone in the room. Neither Ali Fuad Bey nor the German, von Frankenstein, his two chiefs of staff, were with him. Only Osman, the head of the bodyguard, stood at the door, a valiant and romantic mountaineer, who gave the effect of a uniformed dummy in a war museum. Jemal's bodyguard served two objects. Their barbaric splendour was a concession to Asiatic love of display, which could not otherwise be indulged, in the mechanized drab of modern warfare. At the same time they served to allay a fear—one which all through the ages has distinguished dictators from their less successful fellow-men—of assassination. Osman had orders never to leave the general alone, especially not with any caller from Istanbul. For Jemal by no means felt it to be impossible that his brethren, Enver or Talaat, might send him some highly recommended expert—in the art of death. The general scanned the dispatches, especially Enver's, with close attention. Though really this seemed a trifling matter, it turned his sallow face sallower still; the lips, pouting out through the black beard, turned white with rage. The general sprang to his feet, began pacing up and down. He was as short as Enver, but stockily, not daintily, built. He hunched his left shoulder a little, so that people who did not know him well thought him deformed. Heavy red hands hung down limp, out of the gold-striped sleeves of his general's tunic. The mere sight of them was enough to explain the rumour that this was the grandson of a former Istanbul executioner. Enver was composed of the lightest substance, Jemal of the heaviest. If the one was all dreamy caprice, the other was all arid, passionate brooding. Jemal loathed the silken favourite of the gods, with all the detestation of physical underlings. He had had to sweat for everything which dropped into Enver's lap—martial celebrity, luck, women's favour. Jemal took up the dispatch again, and tried, through its official impersonality, to get the tones of Enver's coquettish voice. Throughout these minutes the fate of the seven communes on Musa Dagh was more in the balance than ever previously. A chit from Jemal would have sufficed to send two full battalions of infantry, machine-guns, a mountain battery, against the Damlayik. That would have settled matters in an hour, in spite of all Bagradian's valour. As Jemal read the dispatch a second time, his anger seemed to simmer up to boiling-point. He snapped at the disconcerted Osman to get out, and, on pain of death, not disturb him again. Then he went across to the window, but drew back at once, fearful of showing the world his naked soul. Oh, if he could only dispose of Enver! That society beauty of the war! That inflated little drawing-room pet! That climber, who never in all his life had done one really masculine act, who'd wangled his reputation as a general by retaking Adrianople with his cavalry—sidling into it, when the whole business was really settled. And a Jemal had to play

410

second fiddle to this vain, insignificant playboy of the Ottoman empire! That cunning sissy dared attempt to rid himself
of a Jemal, by fobbing him off with the Syrian command—
Jemal's rage against the Mars of Istanbul deepened by several
fathoms of the soul. An absurd trifle had released it. Enver's
telegram began with the words: "I beg you to take immediate
measures." No thought of addressing him as "Your Excellency," not even with the simplest "Pasha"! And Jemal was
a stickler for forms, especially when in contact with an Enver.
He would use the most pedantic ceremony, even in their intimate conversations. Feverishly touchy, he watched lest Enver
should fail in due respect or abate one jot of his martial dig-
nities. This wire, with its insolent beginning, was the last
drop in Jemal's cup of hate, which was running over. Enver,
for several months, had made monstrous demands on the general, who had always complied without a word. First Jemal
had been commanded to send back his third and tenth divisions to Istanbul, later even his twenty-fifth, and finally the
whole Thirteenth Army Corps, which had been moved to
Baghdad and Bitlis. At the moment the dictator of Syria commanded no more than sixteen to eighteen shabby battalions,
and this in a huge war area extending from the heights of
the Taurus to the Suez canal. All that was Enver Pasha's
work—the war situation was merely a pretext. Of that the
rabid Jemal was persuaded. The general-in-chief, with his
usual pickpocket methods, had disarmed him, drawn his
teeth, at the same time depriving him of any possibility of
a victory. A hundred scurvy, treacherous details, seen with the
full lucidity of hate, stood out in Jemal Pasha's mind, all so
many further proofs of the low-down way in which Enver
had always treated him. He and his clique had constantly
kept Jemal at arm's length, failed to inform him of their most
important resolutions, to invite him to intimate sittings. This
relationship, from the very first, had been a train of carefully
thought-out snubs and—worst, most disgraceful of all—Jemal

could not assert himself against Enver! The fellow's very presence and personality made him feel irretrievably second-rate, although he knew himself far superior, both as a leader and a general. Jemal Pasha, hunching his left shoulder, still wandered round and round the table. He felt quite powerless. Crazy juvenile schemes flashed into his mind: Move on Istanbul with a new army, take prisoner this insolent puppy, open the Bosporus to the Allies, make peace with the present enemy. For the third time he took up the dispatches, but at once slammed them down on the table again. What would be the most poisonous mischief he could do to Enver and his clique? Jemal knew that in the Armenian deportations they saw their most sacred patriotic mission. He himself had often referred to them as that. But he would never have endorsed that typical piece of Enver amateurishness which made of Syria the cloaca for Armenian corpses. The Minister of War had been careful not to ask him to sittings in which the deportation law was discussed. If he had, not a shred would have been left of darling little Enver's pretty schemes. Another reason in that, why the soapy swindler had moved him south-east, out of the way. Now, in his wild itch for revenge, he wondered whether to bar the eastern frontier, drive the convoys back to Antioch, and so bring to nothing the whole great work.

As he was thinking this, his German chief-of-staff, Colonel von Frankenstein, knocked at the door. Jemal at once put to flight the larvæ of his heated imagination. He was again the steadily reflective, almost scrupulous general known to his entourage. Pouting Asiatic lips retreated into the meshes of the black beard. He was always particularly careful to give this German general the impression of grumpy, very objective logic. Von Frankenstein met the most stonily casual of Jemal's commanding officer's stares. They sat down to the table. The German opened his portfolio, drew out notes, and began a report on the disposition of fresh troops in Syria. He noticed

412

the heap of dispatches. Enver Pasha's instructions lay on the top.

"Your Excellency has had an important courier?"

"Don't disturb yourself, Colonel," Jemal replied. "Nothing that really matters here depends on the Minister of War, but solely on me." One red hand gripped Enver's dispatch, which the other tore into minute shreds, and strewed them out of the window, as far as to the citadel of David. Gabriel Bagradian had found an involuntary ally. This touchy potentate neither answered, nor would he send one cannon, one machine-gun, to Antakiya, to smoke out Musa Dagh.

JEMAL PASHA's refusal to intervene had saved the mountain camp from sudden destruction, not from a slower, constricting process. The dictator of Syria and Palestine might himself refuse to take a hand. But there were other, subordinate commands, with powers to act independently. The keen, hatchet-faced major reigned in Antakiya in place of the poor cashiered bimbashi. He contrived to get the general in Aleppo to detach several companies from the garrison there. The Wali also wrote to the Kaimakam, to expect the arrival of a large reinforcement of saptiehs. So that the Kaimakam had had success from his move in the Aleppo quarter. And success stimulates ambition.

Bagradian, as he stood at his observation post, had often felt as though the Damlayik were a dead point in a wide vortex, a centre of absolute rigidity, in a swirling and very hostile world. And today, as ox-carts, loaded mules, and crowds came streaming into the valley, the movement round this one dead point began to take most visible form. What was the meaning of the flood? . . .

The Kaimakam, who saw the hour approach when outstanding political services should place him in the forefront of the party, had contrived to weave a new, strong thread of destruction into the mesh that bound the Armenian people. He had taken advantage of the Arab nationalist movement, which for some time past had kept Syrian officials with their hands full. Such widely extensive secret societies as El Ahd, "the Oath," and the "Arab Brotherhood" were disseminating fiery propaganda against Istanbul with the object of uniting all Arab tribes into one independent state. Here, as everywhere else in the world, nationalism had set to work to break up the rich, indeed profoundly religious concepts of the state into their paltry biological components. The Caliphate is a divine idea, but Turk, Kurd, Armenian, Arab denote only terrestrial accidents. The pashas of former days knew well enough that their concept of all-embracing spiritual unity—the Caliphate—was nobler than the uneasy itch of pushful entities for "progress." In the indolence and vice of the old empire, its *laisser-aller,* there lay concealed a cautious wisdom, a moderating, resigned governing principle, which entirely escaped short-sighted westerners striving after quick results. The old pashas knew with the subtlest instinct that a noble, even if ruined palace will not bear too much renovation. But the Young Turks managed to destroy the work of centuries in a breath. They did what they, the chiefs of a state comprising several races, never should have done. Their mad jingoism aroused that of subject peoples. Yet let us be just to the world's fools. It is a dull eye that can see no author behind the play. Men want what they must. The vast, supernatural ties of empire are loosened. It only means that God has swept the chessboard clear, and begun a new game against Himself.

In any case, Arab nationalism was on the march. From the south it spread through Turkey to the line Mosul-Mersina-Adana. In the Syrian vilayets it was very much a factor to be reckoned with, since already, on the rear of the Fourth Army, or on its flanks, that mutinous envy spread abroad which so endangers an army in the field. All the uproar against the poor bimbashi in Antioch had its secret source in this envious mood.

And the Kaimakam had the inspiration to win over this simmering Arab populace at the Armenians' expense. All Armenian property, by the text of the law of deportation, went to the state; that at least was how it stood on paper. In reality it was left to the discretion of provincial governors to make what use of it they pleased. On the very day after the last disaster on Musa Dagh, the Kaimakam had begun to send out officials into all districts with a numerous Arab population within possible reach of the seven villages. In each he had caused it to be proclaimed that the most fruitful land in the whole of Syria, between Suedia and Ras el-Khanzir, with vines and orchards, silkworm and bee farms, richly treed and watered, with houses and barns, was to be freely parcelled out among all those who should arrive forty-eight hours later to settle in the Armenian valley. The müdirs slyly suggested that industrious Arab cultivators were to be given the preference over Turks.

Hence this astonishing migration. The Kaimakam had come in person for an indefinite stay in Yoghonoluk, to supervise this parcelling out of land, and ingratiate himself with the Arab notables. He took up his quarters in Villa Bagradian. In forty-eight hours the villages looked as populous as ever. Arabs and Turks, grown rich, began to fraternize. Never had they seen such houses. Palaces! It seemed almost a pity to live in them. In a trice the church had become a mosque. Allah was praised in it that same night. The mullahs thanked Him for all these new and bounteous gifts—though it is true that a shadow still lay over them, since up there the insolent Christians were still alive. It was every believer's duty to help exterminate them. Only when that was accomplished, could they settle down to enjoy these blessings, as just men should. The men came out of the mosque with glittering eyes. They too were hotly eager to make quick work of those whose places they had taken so that a vague, nagging uneasiness in their honest peasant hearts might cease to trouble them.

The men above grimly watched their houses being occupied. But to them it was all the same.

What had happened to time? How many eternities did a day need to creep into night? And yet how quickly the day passed in comparison to night, the snail! Where was Juliette? Had she been living long in this tent? Had she ever lived in a house? Had she lived in Europe long ago? Certainly this could not be Juliette, who now lived captive among the mountain folk. Certainly it could not be Juliette who awoke each morning with the same start of horrible surprise. A tired, pale creature slipped out of bed, stood on the rug, pulled off a nightgown, sat on the camp chair, at the looking-glass, to examine a pale, yet sun-scarred, face. Could it be Juliette? Could the face, with its dull eyes and brittle hair, please any young man? Juliette, for the last few days, had dismissed her maid in the early morning. She had begun, with nervous hands, as though she were committing a crime, to attempt some kind of toilette, with what was left of her many essences. Then she had dressed, tied on a big white apron and, round her hair, a napkin, like a coif. It was all she ever wore, now she worked in the hospital. Coif and apron gave moral support. They felt like a uniform. Uniforms were *de rigueur* on Musa Dagh.

Before coming out of the tent Juliette would fall on her knees, and embrace her pillow, thrusting away daylight once again. At first, days (years?) ago she had merely felt bewildered and unhappy. But now she longed for such guiltless unhappiness. Never, since the world began, had any woman behaved so basely—she, a true, a self-respecting wife, in whose long marriage there had been not one single "affair." But would not a hundred affairs in Paris have been as nothing compared to this meanest, basest treachery, in the midst of a desperate struggle with certain death? Juliette knelt like a little girl, whispering, "I can't help it," into her pillow. What use was that? By magic, how she could not tell, here in this inexorable "foreignness" she had surrendered to what seemed most akin. In a very low voice, as though to summon some counter-force from herself, she cried out, "Gabriel!" But Gabriel had vanished as much as Juliette. Less and less could she discover his true image in that album of faded photographs, her memory. And the unknown, bearded, brown Armenian who, now and then, came in to sit with her—what had he to do with Gabriel? Juliette felt scared of her own tears, wiped her eyes carefully, and waited until they looked a little less red and hideous.

Bedros Altouni had had all those patients who were not feverish dismissed and carried back to their huts. Though he gave no definite reasons for having done it, he had somewhat ticklish ones. The news of the Armenian victory of August 14 had spread like wildfire through plain and mountains. It had appealed especially to deserters in hiding in the surrounding hills. On the very next day twenty-two of them had come to the outposts and asked to be taken into camp. Gabriel, who had to be on his guard against spies and traitors, had closely cross-questioned them. But, since losses had to be made up, since they all appeared to be Armenians, and since each had a rifle and cartridges, he took them all in. Among them was a very young man who looked bewildered, and seemed uneasy. He declared that only a few days before he had escaped from barracks at Aleppo, and that the long tramp had worn him out. But that same evening, deathly pale, the young man had come into the hospital-hut where, having mumbled something unintelligible, he had collapsed. Altouni had stripped him at once. The poor lad chattered and shook with fever. His chest was a mass of red spots, which increased considerably in the night. Bedros consulted his Handbook, a thing he had not done for a long time. Its hieroglyphics were unreadable. He asked the Frenchwoman's advice:

417

"My dear, just have a look at this one, will you? What do you think?"

Juliette was not the kind of woman who gets used to the horrors of disease. Each time she entered this nightmare hut she had to make an effort not to be sick. She did her best, her share of everything, and yet her shudders of nausea increased, the longer she stayed, instead of diminishing. Yet now incomprehensible ecstasy filled her. It was as though she could atone for her guilty betrayal—here and now. This scrubby, sour-smelling creature at her feet, with spittle dribbling from his mouth, twisting and turning unconsciously in delirium, was Stephan and Gabriel in one. Juliette knelt beside him and leaned her head—as though she herself were slowly fainting —with closed eyes, on his shrunken chest.

Gonzague's voice startled her awake: "What on earth are you doing, Juliette? You must be crazy."

And the old doctor seemed as conscience-stricken as Madame Bagradian herself: "It'd really be better, my dear, if you came here less, and didn't work so hard."

Gonzague caught her eye secretively. She followed, obedient. In his case, too, Juliette had lost her sense of time. It was all confused. How had it happened? In which of her pasts? Since when had she followed defenceless, whenever he called? How dense and heavy this silence and complicity, even now. But he had not changed. The same impenetrable alertness of eyes and thoughts, and never an unguarded second. Camp life had done nothing to his appearance; his hair was as neatly brushed as ever, his coat as spotless, his body as clean, his skin as clear, his breath untainted. Was she in love with him? No; it was something far more horrible. Since unhappy love, if only in a dream, can devise some path, some way of escape. This sensation was pitiless. Often Gonzague seemed as remote as Gabriel. He, at first the trusted, the familiar, the pleasantly "lost" child, who aroused comradeship and pity, had changed into a cruel inevitability, from which there could be no escape. When he touched her, she felt what she had never felt. But each touch made her loathe her treachery more. Many of the embowered and wooded solitudes along these cliffs had become accomplices. Her ebbing pride cried out in Juliette: "I—here on the ground—I? . . ." Yet each time Gonzague seemed to contrive to efface all ugliness. Perhaps he had a genius for the moment, just as there are gamblers, huntsmen, collectors, who have trained one faculty to its uttermost. At least he shared such people's inexhaustible patience. *She* had lured Gonzague on to the Damlayik; modest yet assured, he had bided his time. His concentration evoked in Juliette its opposite, inattention, and lamed her will. Often she was devoured by absent-mindedness. They sat down to rest in a quiet place, which they called "the Riviera" between themselves.

Gonzague broke a cigarette, and lit one half carefully. "I've still got fifty." Then, as though to give a more cheerful turn to this sad thought of tobacco running out: "Well, we shan't be here so much longer."

She stared at him without seeing he was there.

"I suggest we get out of this, you and I. It's about time."

She still seemed not to hear what he was saying. He explained his plan with the driest precision. Only the first two hours might be a bit difficult. A day's excursion, south, along the mountain-ridge—that was all it was. One might have to do a little climbing to get down on the right from the tiny village of Habaste to the Orontes plain and the road to Suedia. He'd used last night to get the lie of all that ground, and, quite easily, without having met a soul, got within a square mile of the alcohol factory and into the manager's house, who, as Juliette knew, was a Greek, and a most influential person. It was amazing how simply it could be done.

"The manager's entirely at our disposal. On August 26 the little factory steamer sails with a cargo for Beirut. She'll stop there on her way to Latakia and Tripoli, and, according to schedule, she ought to touch Beirut on the twenty-ninth. She sails under the American flag. You see, it's an American firm. The manager's certain there won't be the slightest danger, because at that time the Cyprus fleet is putting out again. You'll have your own cabin, Juliette! When we're in Beirut, you'll have won. All the rest is just a question of money. And that you've got . . ."

Her eyes looked blank. "And Stephan and Gabriel?"

Gonzague was blowing ash off his coat. "Stephan and Gabriel? They'd be taken anywhere for Armenians. But I asked the manager about them. He says he can't do anything for Armenians. He's so well in with the Turkish government he can't afford to take any risks. He said so definitely. So, unluckily, Gabriel and Stephan can't be rescued."

Juliette drew away from him. "And I'm to let myself be rescued. . . . By you?"

Gonzague jerked his head almost imperceptibly, unable, it appeared, to feel any sympathy with the woman's exaggerated scruples. "Well, you know how he himself wanted to send you! And with me, what's more."

She pressed both fists into her temples. "Yes, he wanted to send me and Stephan. . . . And I've done this to him. . . . And I lie to him! . . ."

"You shan't go on lying, Juliette. I'd be the last to want that of you. On the contrary! You must tell him the whole thing. Better do it today."

Juliette sprang up. Her face looked very red and bloated. "What? You want me to kill him? He has the lives of five thousand people in his hands. And, at a time like this, I'm to kill him!"

"You distort everything by exaggerating," said Gonzague, still seated and very serious. "Usually it's strangers we kill. One sees that every day. But sometimes we're forced to choose between our own lives and those of what we call our 'nearest and dearest.' Is Gabriel really your nearest and dearest? And will it really kill him if you escape, Juliette?"

Such calm words, his self-assured eyes, brought her back to his side. Gonzague seized Juliette's hand and lucidly expounded his philosophy. Each of us has only one life. His only duty is towards this single, never to be repeated, life; towards nothing and nobody else! And what is the truest essence of life? What does life consist in? It consists in one long chain of desires and appetites. Though often we may only imagine we want a thing, the essential is that we want it intensely. Our duty is ruthlessly to satisfy our desires and appetites. That is the one and only "meaning" of life. That is why we expose ourselves to danger, even death, for something we want, since, outside this urge to satisfaction, there can be no life. Gonzague gave himself as an instance of the only logical, straightforward way of behaving. He had not hesitated a second to accept discomfort and danger for something he loved. He concluded disdainfully: "But all that you, Juliette, mistake for love and self-sacrifice is no more than convenient anxiety."

Her head dropped heavily on his shoulder. She was steeped again in tormenting absent-mindedness. "You're so tidy, Gonzague. Don't be so horribly clear and orderly, Gonzague. I can't stand it! Why aren't you the same as you used to be?"

His light hand, a miracle of tender awakenings, passed stroking down the length of her arm, over her breast, down to her hips. She broke into babbling sobs. Gonzague comforted her: "You've still got time, yet, to make up your mind. Seven long days. And, after all, who knows what may happen in the meantime . . ."

TER HAIGASUN after a long interval had summoned the entire Council of Leaders. They sat on the long bench in the council-room of the government-hut. Only Apothecary Krikor, as his habit was, heard the discussion from his sleeping-apartment, without himself saying a word. The sage, it appeared, had, with the object of perfecting his inner life, almost entirely renounced human contacts. He spoke to scarcely anyone now but himself, though in the depth of night his soliloquies went on and on. Nobody hearing them would have been in the least the wiser. For Krikor merely ranged long lines of imposing encyclopædic concepts in, so to speak, dreamy single file. As for instance: "Burning core of the earth—celestial axis —swarm of the Pleiades—fructification of blossom . . ." Such high-sounding concepts seemed to raise Krikor's soul above itself, bringing it nearer the underlying cause of all things. He tossed them in the air. They hovered in swarms above his head. Out of them he fashioned a dome, set with the glimmering mosaics of Science, under which he lay with the enigmatic smile of a Buddhist priest. There exists a degree of ascetic perfection too elevated to permit of its being shared, since everything exalted is also asocial. Krikor had perhaps attained it, he no longer taught. The Leaders, his former disciples, never came near him now, or even inquired for him. The days were done when, on nightly walks with Oskanian, Shatakhian, Asayan, and other dust-devouring mortals, Krikor had named the stars and numbered them, out of his own mind. Now these giant stars, these giant worlds, circled in silence within his brain, and the sage had ceased to feel any pricking urge to give of them enthusiastic tidings. Krikor scarcely got an hour's sleep. A fierce pain, worse every day, cramped his joints and tendons. When, noticing he was ill, his old friend Bedros Altouni asked medical questions, he received a triumphant Latin answer: "*Rheumatismus articulorum et musculorum.*" Not a word of complaint passed Krikor's lips. He had been sent this illness to preserve the supremacy of the spirit. It had no other consequence. Everything around him drifted away. Reality grew buzzingly remote. So that, as, for instance today, the men sat discussing, he heard their words with the staring eyes, the uncomprehending, muttering lips, of a deaf-mute. It was as though the words which expressed such earthly necessity had almost ceased to have a meaning.

This time they talked for hours. Avakian and the parish

clerk of Yoghonoluk sat apart, taking notes of their chief resolutions, to be shaped into minutes. The camp guard had been posted outside the government-hut—a personal edict of Ter Haigasun. Since their priest was not given to formal gestures, it must be supposed that he had some good and far-sighted reason for taking this protective measure. Today the guard had only the duty of shielding the Council from interruption, keeping unauthorized persons out of the hut. Later, more dangerous sittings might have to be held, on days when the Council needed protection. Ter Haigasun presided with half-shut eyes, as frostily weary-looking as ever. Pastor Aram Tomasian, as chief supervisor of the domestic economy of the camp, read out his report on the state of food supplies, which the priest had set down as the first item on the agenda. He gave an exact picture. Following on the first, disastrous hailstorm, the direct hit of the shrapnel had not only destroyed their remaining flour, but all their other precious stores: all oil, all wine, sugar, honey, and—apart from unnecessary things like tobacco and coffee—that first of all necessities, salt. There was only enough salt left to cure their meat for three more days. And the meat itself, which every stomach already rebelled against, was diminishing at a really alarming extent. The mukhtars, who were present, had arranged a count of remaining cattle, and reckoned that, since they had lived on Musa Dagh, the collective herds had shrunk by a third. Such economy could no longer continue, as supplies would very soon be exhausted. The pastor asked the mukhtar, Thomas Kebussyan, as an expert breeder, to explain the state of the herds. Kebussyan stood up, wagged his head. His squinting peasant's eyes stared at all and nobody. He launched out on a string of moving complaints over the loss of his own beautiful sheep, which it had taken him so many years of industrious breeding to rear. In the golden days before the migration, a full-grown wether had weighed anything from forty-five to fifty okas. Now it scarcely weighed half that. The mukhtar attributed this to two special reasons.

The first of these was sentimental. This cursed communal ownership—not that he did not admit that it was necessary—was bad for the sheep. He knew his sheep. They were getting thin because they belonged to nobody, because they couldn't feel any master worrying about them, their good or bad health. His second reason was less political, more enlightening. All the best pasture in the enclosure, which had not only to feed the sheep, but goats and donkeys into the bargain, was almost cropped down. The sheep were being badly foddered; how could they be expected to put on fat, or tender flesh even? And it wasn't any better with the milk. You couldn't so much as think of butter or cheese any longer, Kebussyan concluded in a whine; some other pasturage was essential if they wanted to improve the condition of the stock.

Gabriel opposed this very decisively. These weren't the piping times of peace; at best this was life in a Noah's Ark, on a deluge of blood. There could be no question of allowing people or herds to stray as they pleased. Turkish spies were all round the camp enclosure. To let the herds graze outside that enclosure, especially on the northerly heights, would be more of a risk than anyone dare take on himself. Damn it! There must surely be some other pasturage, within the camp. Couldn't they drive the herds up the steeps?

"The grass up there is short and all burnt out," interrupted the Mukhtar of Habibli; "even camels couldn't manage it."

Gabriel refused to be led astray. "Better that we should have less meat than none at all!"

Ter Haigasun endorsed Bagradian's warning and asked the pastor to finish his report. Aram went on to the lack of bread, and the consequences of unmixed meat-eating. There were a hundred reasons, besides this diminishing of the herds, for trying to find some other food besides meat. Forays into the valley were out of the question, now that all the villages were reoccupied. On the other hand Bedros Altouni would agree with him that the people's health would be bound to suffer in the end, unless some other food could be found. They could see for themselves how much sallower and thinner people were looking. They must all have felt it. So that a change of diet would have to be made possible at all costs.

And Pastor Tomasian had a scheme. So far they had all neglected the sea. At certain points along the cliffs it was possible to climb down to it in half an hour. He himself had discovered a disused mule-track which could easily be built up and made fit to use. What was the good of having skilled road-menders both among the villagers and deserters? Two days' work, and there would be a very easy road down to the beach. They must form a group of young people, the strongest women and biggest lads of the cohort of youth, to lay out a salting-ground down in the hollow under the cliffs. A raft, knocked together out of tree trunks and a few oars, would be enough to put out to a calmer place, a few hundred yards out to sea. The women could set to work that very day making draw-nets. There was plenty of twine in the camp. And another thing! He, Aram, remembered that as a boy he had always been out stoning birds. The boys of Yoghonoluk must be much the same nowadays. Well, let them all bring out their catapults! Instead of hanging about and getting under people's feet, the lads ought all to be out bird-killing.

The pastor's suggestions were applauded and discussed in detail. The Council empowered him to organize these projects for food supplies. Then Bedros Altouni gave his health report. Of the twenty-four wounded in the last battle all, thank God, except four, who were still feverish, were out of danger. Twenty-eight he had already sent back home, to be looked after by their families. They would soon all be ready for the line again. But what gave the doctor cause for far worse uneasiness was the strange new illness brought into camp by a young deserter from Aleppo. Since last night the boy had been on the point of death, and was probably dead by this time. But worse still, the other hospital patients had begun to show signs of being infected by him; cases of sudden vomiting and high fever and choking fits. So it must be a case of that epidemic of which he now remembered seeing accounts, in the last few months, in Aleppo newspapers. But one epidemic of this description was as dangerous to the camp as were the Turks. Early that morning therefore he had made arrangements for the strictest isolation of all these cases. Far from the Town Enclosure, as everyone knew, there was a small, shady box-wood, with a stream between two high mounds. It was well out of the way of both the decads and workers. He suggested that the Council form a group of hospital attendants, out of all the least useful people in camp, who must also be kept apart from everyone else. Bedros gave Kevork, the sunflower-dancer, as an instance of the kind of person he meant. He obviously would be ideal as a nurse. He turned to Gabriel.

"My friend, I must ask you particularly to beg Juliette Hanum not to come back to the hospital-tent. I shall be losing a very good assistant. But frankly her health is more important to me than her help. Even apart from any danger of infection, I'm worried about your wife, my son! We others are hardy sort of people, and scarcely a mile away from our homes. But your wife has changed a good deal since we've been on the Damlayik. She sometimes gives me very queer answers, and she seems not only to suffer physically. She isn't strong enough for this life. How could she possibly be? I advise you to look after her more. The best thing for her would be to stay in bed all day, and read novels, and get her mind far away from here. Luckily Krikor could supply a whole townful of ladies with enough French novels to make them forget their troubles."

Altouni's warning startled Gabriel into a sense of guilt. He remembered that it was almost two days since he had last spoken to Juliette.

Hapeth Shatakhian now began a vehement complaint at the undisciplined state of the boys. Impossible to make them come

to school. Ever since Stephan Bagradian and Haik had captured the howitzers, the whole cohort of youth had got out
of hand. They felt themselves full-grown fighters, and were
constantly cheeky to the grown-ups.

The mukhtars fully endorsed the teacher's complaint.
"Where are the days," yammered he of Bitias, "when boys
weren't even allowed to speak to men, but had to use humble
signs in addressing them?"

But Ter Haigasun did not feel the problem of sufficient immediate urgency to discuss. Suddenly he asked Bagradian:
"How does our defence really stand? What's the longest you'll
be able to hold out against the Turks?"

"I can't answer that, Ter Haigasun. Defence always depends
on attack."

Ter Haigasun turned shyly resolute eyes, the eyes of a
priest, directly on Gabriel. "Gabriel Bagradian, tell us what
you really think."

"I have no reason to want to spare the Council, Ter Haigasun. I'm perfectly sure our position is desperate."

Then Gabriel made an important suggestion. Absurd as the
hope of rescue might appear, the Council must not allow itself
to await inevitable destruction in effortless indolence. To be
sure the sea looked as horribly empty as though ships had never
been invented. But no stone must be left unturned. And after
all, God knew whether, against all probability, there might
not be an Allied torpedo boat outside the Gulf of Alexandretta.

"It's our duty to suppose there is, and it's our duty to act on
the supposition, and not miss a possible chance. And then
what about Mr. Jackson, the American Chief Consul in
Aleppo? Has he heard of these Christian fighters in need, on
Musa Dagh? It's our duty to let him know about us and
demand protection from the American government."

So Gabriel explained his plan: two groups of messengers
would have to be sent out, one to Alexandretta, the other to

Aleppo—the best swimmers to Alexandretta, the best runners to Aleppo. The swimmers' task would be easier, since the Gulf of Alexandretta was only thirty-five English miles to the north, and they could find their way across the summits of almost deserted mountains. Their real object would be to swim out to any warship in the gulf. It would need the greatest strength and determination. The runners to Aleppo would not need to be so determined, but they would have an eighty-five-mile road to cover and would be able to walk only at night, never using the highroad, and in constant danger of being shot. If these couriers managed to reach Jackson's house, the camp might be as good as saved.

Gabriel's suggestion, which after all afforded some vague hope of rescue, and served in any case to alleviate the impending certainty of death, was most eagerly and generally discussed. It was decided to send out two swimmers. One young man might be enough to send to Aleppo. There was no sense in uselessly exposing lives. Two people can hide better than three, and one person finds it easier to slip past saptiehs and customs officials than two. On Ter Haigasun's suggestion, the swimmers and the runner were to be chosen from among the volunteers. The runners (either one or both, it was still not decided) would be given a letter to take to the American consul; the swimmers, another addressed to the supposititious naval commander. To prevent these letters from falling into Turkish hands, should either of the messengers get arrested, the leather belts which the couriers wore were to be split open and the letters sewn up inside them.

Ter Haigasun appointed a day and hour at which to demand volunteers, and arranged the method of the announcement. The münadirs should be instructed to drum it that same evening around the camp. Gabriel offered to write the letter to Jackson. Aram Tomasian undertook the other, to the ship. He at once went apart from the rest and drafted the text to give to the swimmers, in spite of all the noise of a new point under discussion. From time to time he seemed carried away by his composition, would suddenly spring up and read out a passage, with the majestic intonation of a parson learning his sermon by heart. It did not take him long to finish it. It has been preserved as a document of the forty days:

To any English, American, French, Russian, or Italian admiral, captain, or other commander whom this may reach:

Sir! We beseech you in the name of God and human brother-hood—we, the population of seven Armenian villages, in all about five thousand souls, who have taken refuge on that mountain plateau of Musa Dagh, known as the Damlayik, and three leagues north-west of Suedia above the coastline.

We have taken refuge here from barbarous Turkish persecutions. We have taken up arms to preserve the honour of our women.

Sir! You no doubt have heard of the Young Turkish policy which seeks to annihilate our people. Under the false appearance of a migration-law, on the lying pretext of some non-existent movement for revolution, they are turning us out of our houses, robbing us of our farms, orchards, vineyards, and all our movable and immovable goods and chattels. This, to our personal knowledge, has already been done in the town of Zeitun and its thirty-three dependent villages.

Pastor Aram went on to describe his experiences on the convoy between Zeitun and Marash. He told of the edict of banishment issued against the seven villages, and gave vehement descriptions of the desperate plight of the villagers in camp on the Damlayik. His appeal ended as follows:

Sir, we beg you in the name of Christ!
Bring us, we implore you, either to Cyprus or any other free territory. Our people are not idlers. We want to earn our bread with the hardest possible work in so far as we are given a chance to do it. But if this is too much for you to grant us, then at least take our women, take our children, take our old people. At least supply those of us able to bear arms with guns, munitions, and

enough food to defend ourselves to the last breath in our bodies against our enemies.

We implore you, sir, not to delay until it is too late!

In the name of all the Christians up here

Your most obedient servant,
PASTOR A.T.

This manifesto was drafted in two languages—on one side of the sheet in French, on the other in English. The two texts were carefully revised under the ægis of Hapeth Shatakhian, that accomplished linguist and stylist. But the task of copying them out, in minute and beautifully shaped letters, was, strangely enough, not entrusted to teacher Oskanian, famed far and wide as possessor of the best calligraphy, in every alphabet, but to Avakian, a far less expert artist. Hrand Oskanian leapt out of his seat and glowered at Ter Haigasun as though he were going to challenge him to a duel in front of the assembled Council. This new humiliation bereft him of words, his lips moved but could form no sounds. But the priest, his mortal enemy, only smiled blandly at him.

"Sit down and be quiet, Teacher Oskanian, you write far too beautiful a hand for this job. Nobody who saw all your squiggles and flourishes could ever believe our position was desperate."

The black-haired dwarf advanced on Ter Haigasun with his head high. "Priest! You've mistaken your man. God knows I am not anxious to do your scribbling!" He shook his fists in Ter Haigasun's face as he added in a voice unsteady with rage: "There's no calligraphy left in these hands, Priest! These hands have given proof of something very different, much as it riles you!"

Apart from which absurd little incident the sitting had been held in perfect amity. Even the sceptical Ter Haigasun could hope that, whatever happened in the near future, peace at least would reign unbroken among the elect.

430

Again after that day's council Gabriel went to look for his wife, both in her tent and the place where she received her visitors. Here, too, Oskanian and Shatakhian had come in vain, as they had so often in these last days, to pay their respects to Madame. Hrand Oskanian especially had been extremely disappointed at not being able to display himself to Juliette as the Lion of the South Bastion. He could only set his teeth and admit that a tailor's dummy like Gonzague was more welcome than a powder-blackened hero. But mistrustful and silent as he was, he never got as far as suspicion. Madame Bagradian was too supremely far above him to allow of one such unseemly thought. When Gabriel caught sight of the teachers, he turned away quickly. He wandered indecisively on from Three-Tent Square towards the "Riviera." Where, he wondered, would Juliette be at about this time? He had turned towards the Town Enclosure when Stephan ran across his path. The boy was as usual surrounded by the whole Haik gang. The dour Haik himself walked on a few paces ahead, as if to set a distance, proclaim his leadership, his own doughty independence. But the poor crippled Hagop kept obstinately beside Stephan while the others swarmed noisily round them. Sato lurked as usual in the rear. The boys paid no heed at all to the presence of the commander-in-chief; they tried to swarm past him without saluting, without even noticing he was there. Gabriel called sharply after his son. That conqueror of the guns detached himself, came slouching out from among his fellows, and approached his father with the solemn pomposity of an ape, which he had managed to learn from his new comrades. His tousled hair hung over his forehead. His face was scarlet and damp with sweat. His eyes looked filmed over with the very intoxication of conceit. Even his kilt was stained and torn with peculiar heroism.

Gabriel sternly inquired: "Well, what are you messing about here for?"

431

Stephan gurgled and looked round vaguely. "We're running—having a game . . . we're off duty."

"Having a game? Big chaps like you? What are you playing?"

"Oh, nothing special—only . . . playing, Dad!"

As he gave this disconnected information, Stephan eyed his father rather strangely. He seemed to look up at him and say: Dad, why are you trying to keep me down out of the position I've had such trouble to get, among all these chaps? If you snub me now, they'll all begin ragging me. Gabriel did not understand the look.

"You don't look like a human being, Stephan. Do you really dare to let your mother see you in that state?"

The boy did not answer, he only stared at the ground in anguish. So far at least his father had been speaking French. But the order that followed came in Armenian; it was spoken so that the whole camp heard: "Off you go now, straight to the tent and wash, and change your clothes! And report to me tonight when you're fit to be seen!"

Then, when Gabriel had gone a few angry steps further south, he suddenly stopped. Had the boy disobeyed him? He was almost certain that he had, and indeed when, after a while, he went back to the sheikh-tent, he found no Stephan.

Gabriel tried to think of a punishment. This was not merely a case of a boy's disobeying his father, it was a breach of camp discipline. But it would not be easy to punish Stephan. Gabriel went across to his trunk, which was kept in his tent, and pulled out a book. Dr. Altouni's advice that Juliette should read, and so get her mind off gruesome reality, had given him the same inclination. Perhaps, for the next few, slack hours, he could manage to forget reality, both outside and inescapably within him. For today, nothing need be feared. The day wore on. Scouts from the various outposts came in every hour with their reports. Nothing new in the valley. A patrol had ventured nearly as far as Yoghonoluk and re-

432

turned to report that it had not met a single saptieh. Gabriel glanced at the title of his French novel. It was by Charles Louis Philippe, a book he had enjoyed, though he only half remembered it. But it was sure to be full of little cafés, with tables and chairs, out on the pavement. Wide sunbeams on dusty faubourg boulevards. A tiny court with an acacia and a moss-green, closed-in fountain in the middle. And this poor court had more of the spring in it than all the glamorous myrtles and rhododendrons, anemones and wild narcissi, of Musa Dagh on a March day. Old dark wooden stairs, worn smooth as sea-shells. Invisible footsteps clattering up them.

As Gabriel opened the book, a little three-cornered note fell out of it. The child Stephan had written it a few years previously. That, too, had been in August. Gabriel had attended the big conference assembled in Paris between the Young Turks and Dashnakzagan. Juliette and the child had been staying in Montreux. At that famous "congress of fraternization" it had been resolved that the liberty-loving youth of both peoples should act side by side to build up a new fatherland. Gabriel had, as we know, tried to keep his promise by having himself, with other idealists, inscribed as a reservist officer on the lists of the Istanbul training-school when war-clouds gathered over Turkey. Stephan's little letter had lain since then, innocent of any gruesome future, within pages describing the Paris of Charles Louis Philippe. It had been written with immense pain, in stiff, French, copy-book letters:

"Mon cher papa! How are you? Will you stay a long time in Paris? When are you coming to see us? Maman and I miss you very much. Here it is very pretty. Lots of kisses from
Your loving and grateful son,
STEPHAN.

Gabriel, seated on the bed in which Gonzague Maris slept, examined the shaky childish handwriting. How could that

433

prettily dressed little boy sitting in a sunny room at Montreux, scrawling on Juliette's thick linen notepaper (which retained its scent), be one with the young scamp of an hour ago? Gabriel, as he sat there thinking of Stephan's restless animal-eyes, of the throaty chatter of the herd, did not know in the least that he himself had been transformed as much as his son. A hundred details of that far-off day in August came back to life in him, darting into his mind from that simple letter. No massacre, no gruesome brutality, seemed more poignant than this withered leaf, shed from a life that might never have been.

After attempting the first five pages of Charles Louis Philippe, Gabriel shut the book. He did not think that now, as long as he lived, he would ever be able again to fix his thoughts on one. It would be just as impossible for a navvy to turn his hands to minute carving. With a sigh he stood up off Gonzague's bed, and smoothed down the coverlet. He noticed then how, across the bed-end, Maris had laid out his clean clothes, carefully washed. Thread, scissors, mending-wool, lay beside them; for the Greek did all his own darning and mending. Gabriel could not tell why the sight of this washing warned him of some approaching departure. He went back to his trunk and threw in the novel. But he pocketed the child Stephan's letter. He came out of the tent thinking of the station at Montreux. Juliette and little Stephan had awaited him. Juliette had carried a red sunshade.

GABRIEL stood outside Hovsannah's tent. He asked through the chink in the door if he might come in to see the new mother. Mairik Antaram asked him inside. In spite of all Mairik's efforts the baby seemed determined not to flourish. Its tiny face was still a brownish colour, and as wrinkled as immediately after birth. Its wide-open eyes stared without seeing.

Mairik Antaram's voice sounded impatient.

"Cheer up, Hovsannah, and be glad that your baby has a birth-mark on his breast, not on his face. What do you expect?"

Hovsannah closed weary eyes, as though she were tired of continually asserting her better nature in face of empty consolations.

"Why doesn't he take his milk? And why doesn't he cry?"

Mairik Antaram began to busy herself warming swaddling-clothes round a hot stone. She cried out, without looking up from her work: "Wait another two days, till after the christening. Lots of children won't begin to cry till they're baptized."

Hovsannah grimaced this away. "Provided we can make him live till then."

The doctor's wife got very angry. "You're a wet blanket, Madame Tomasian. You depress everybody! Who can say, up here on the Damlayik, what'll have happened in two days, to anyone! Christening or death? Not even Bagradian Effendi could tell you for certain whether we'll be alive in two days."

"Well, if we are alive," said Gabriel, smiling, "we must all have a christening feast, here outside the tents. I've talked to the pastor about it. Madame Tomasian, you must say whom you want invited."

Hovsannah lay on, indifferent. "I don't belong to Yoghonoluk. I know nobody here."

Iskuhi, sitting on her bed, had listened to all this without saying a word. Gabriel eyed her. "Iskuhi Tomasian, would you care to come for a walk? My wife's disappeared. I want to look for her."

Iskuhi's face questioned Hovsannah, who with a plaintively exaggerated voice urged her to go with Gabriel. "Of course you must go, Iskuhi! I shan't need you. It'll do you good. You can't help with the swaddling."

Iskuhi hesitated, she could feel some hidden spite in Hovsannah's words. But Mairik Antaram insisted: "You go along,

435

Sirelis, my pretty! And don't let me see you again till tonight. What sort of a life is this for you!"

Gabriel and Iskuhi went towards the Town Enclosure, though there was not much chance of finding Juliette there. They walked between the narrow lines of huts. People were sitting out in front of them. The air up here was cooler and pleasanter than it had been down in the valley. The sea sighed mildly, in long cool breaths. All were at work. The women were patching clothes and washing. The old men of the reserve were plying their trades, soling shoes, planing wood, curing lamb and goatskins. Nurhan's munitions works appeared to be working overtime.

They left the camp. They could only exchange monosyllables. The most trivial questions and replies. They went westwards along the highest peak. Here it was barren. They had come out of the wild plateau landscape. They were on the verge of a desert without birds' voices, only stirred by a little breeze, which blew across them, carrying their words to one another.

Gabriel did not look at Iskuhi; it was so good to feel her invisibly beside him. Only when they came to steep declines, did he watch with delight her hesitant feet which seemed to grow so charmingly embarrassed. Then all talk between them ceased. What was there to say? Gabriel took Iskuhi's hand. (Her lame arm made her walk on the right of him.) As they walked she surrendered to him in silence, keeping nothing back, insisting on nothing. They did not speak of this emotion which unfolded so swiftly. They never kissed. They went on, belonging to one another. Iskuhi went with Gabriel as far as the edge of the northern trench. When she had said goodbye, he stood there a long time looking after her. No wish, no scruple, came to life in him, no vague anxiety, thought of the future. Future? Absurd! He was light with joy from head to foot. Iskuhi's being withdrew so delicately that not one thought of her disturbed him as he worked out his new plan

436

of defence. Later, when Stephan came to report, he forgot to punish the boy for his disobedience.

THE new life on Musa Dagh had also its religious consequences. In the last few decades it had been a sort of fashion among Armenians to change one's creed. Protestantism especially, thanks to the efforts of its German and American missionaries, had gained much ground since the middle of the previous century. It is enough to remember those admirable mission fathers of Marash, whose indefatigable efforts—educational, charitable, architectural—had been of such service to Cilician and Syrian Armenians, including those of the seven communes round Musa Dagh. But it was certainly a most fortunate circumstance that religious differences had caused no essential rift in the national unity. Christianity itself had so hard a struggle against the Turks as to preclude petty spite and religious intolerance. Pastor Harutiun Nokhudian of Bitias had been quite free in the seven villages to preach his doctrine and theology. In all major questions of conduct he had submitted himself to Ter Haigasun. Up here on the Damlayik Pastor Aram, his successor, took over the old pastor's duty of ministering to such Protestants as remained, though he too submitted to the priest. Ter Haigasun let him have the use of his altar every Sunday after Mass to deliver his sermon, which usually not only Protestants but the whole population came to hear. Differences of ritual had ceased to matter. Ter Haigasun was the uncontested high priest of this mountain, and administered to people's souls as the superior both of Pastor Aram and the smaller married village clergy. Therefore it went without saying that Tomasian should ask him to baptize his new-born son.

The christening had been fixed for the following Sunday, the fourth in August, their twenty-third day in camp. But Mass and other duties prevented Ter Haigasun undertaking it till late in the afternoon of that day. Since Hovsannah was still feeling too weak to manage to get as far as the altar, Aram had asked the priest to baptize the child on Three-Tent Square, so that the mother might be present at the ceremony.

Gabriel kept his promise to Hovsannah and sent out about thirty-five invitations, to notables and the most important section leaders. The reception into Christ's communion of this first-born on Musa Dagh was a good way of maintaining cordial relations with the chief personalities of the people. He had still nine ten-litre jars of the heavy local vintage. Kristaphor was ordered to bring out two of them and a few bottles of mulberry brandy. He could not, to be sure, offer his guests more solid refreshment; the food supplies on Three-Tent Square were already alarmingly reduced.

The guests assembled, at four, outside the tents. A few chairs had been brought along for the older people. The sacristan had stood a little tin bathtub on a low table. The very ancient and beautiful font in the church had had to be left behind in Yoghonoluk. Ter Haigasun robed in the sheikh-tent. Gabriel, by Aram's wish, had consented to stand gin-kahair, godfather.

The church choir, led by the diminutive Asayan, had taken up its position around the table, with its crucifix and the tin font. The lukewarm christening water had already been borne before the altar. Now, to the singing of the choir, one of Ter Haigasun's subordinate priests dropped three drops of the sacred christening oil into the tub.

Gabriel, the ginkahair, gingerly took the child from Mairik Antaram. The women, in honour of the occasion, had laid that sallow, brownish, puckered object, which showed no strength, on a special cushion—a magnificent cushion in view of the general circumstances. The child's eyes stared without seeing at the world, into whose cruel life he had come so guiltless. Nor did his voice yet find it worth its while to whimper one assent to the light of God, which lights up this cruelty so

438

magnificently. Gabriel held out the wretched bundle, which seemed in its estrangement to resent being captured by religion, with all its consequences, in front of the priest, as the service prescribed. Ter Haigasun's eyes, so humble, yet so coldly sacerdotal, did not seem to know that this was Gabriel. Or at least they did not see the man, only the officiating person, with a ritual duty to discharge. It was always the same whenever Ter Haigasun stood at the altar or wore his vestments. Every human memory and relationship faded out of his eyes, to give way to the stern equanimity of his office. He asked the ritual question of the godfather. "What does this child ask?" And Gabriel, who felt very clumsy, had to answer: "Faith and hope and love." This was repeated three times. Only then the question: "And what shall this child be called?"

He was to be called after his grandfather Master Mikael Tomasian. At this point of the ceremony that ancient was comically inspired to stand up and make a little bow, as though he were being cited to share in the future of his descendant. Opinions differed among the lookers-on as to what that future might prove to be. Even if by some miracle they were saved, the sickly, apathetic little body would scarcely have the strength to hold on to life. Mairik Antaram, Iskuhi, and Aram Tomasian had come over to Gabriel. The child was unwound from its swaddling-clothes. Iskuhi's and Gabriel's hands touched more than once. A morose hopeless mood was on the spectators. Hovsannah stared with a pinched puritanical face at the group round the font. Something seemed to impel her very soul to the bitterest desolation, hostility. It may have been the thought of that deep bond between Aram and Iskuhi, brother and sister, from which at this instant she felt shut out.

Ter Haigasun took up the child with inimitable, dexterous certainty. His hands, which had christened a thousand children, worked with the almost super-terrestrial grace and elegance which all born priests display in even the manual part of their office. For a second he held out the child to the people. Everyone could see the large red birth-mark on its chest. Then he dipped it quickly, three times, in water, making the sign of the cross each time with its body. "I baptize thee in the name of the Father, of the Son, of the Holy Ghost." Hovsannah had pulled herself up from her seat. She bent forward with a convulsive grimace. This was the decisive moment. Would her child, as it touched the baptismal water, break out at last, as Mairik Antaram had promised her, in a long wail? Ter Haigasun reached the suckling back to his ginkahair. It was not Gabriel, however, but Antaram who took him and dried his sickly body, gently, with a soft cloth. The child had not cried. But Hovsannah, its mother, shrieked aloud. Two long hysterical screams. The chair fell down behind her back. She hid her face and stumbled into the tent. Juliette, sitting at her side, had plainly heard her cry form, and repeat, a word: "Sin! Sin!"

ARAM TOMASIAN remained some time in the tent. He came back looking pale and laughed uneasily. "You must forgive her, Ter Haigasun. She's never really managed to get over the shock of Zeitun, though she hasn't shown it up to now."

He signed to Iskuhi to go in and look after Hovsannah. The girl glanced desperately at Gabriel, and seemed to hesitate. He said to the pastor: "Couldn't you leave your sister with us, Tomasian? Mairik Antaram's in the tent, you know."

Tomasian pulled back a chink in the canvas door. "My wife has been asking for her so urgently! Later, perhaps, when Hovsannah's asleep . . ."

Iskuhi had already disappeared. Gabriel could feel that the pastor's wife could not brook the fact that, while she herself suffered unspeakably, her young sister-in-law should not be chained to the same suffering.

Nor in the ensuing jollifications could the guests shake off the weight of this christening. Gabriel had had another long table set end to end with the one at which Juliette "received." They all sat down along the benches. This arrangement, in the eyes of these socially hyper-sensitive people, seemed to indicate a dual treatment, which wounded a number of snobbish souls. The "best people" were all at Juliette's table. Ter Haigasun, the Bagradians, Pastor Tomasian, Krikor, Gonzague Maris and—shamelessly—Sarkis Kilikian. Gabriel, who had invited that ragged outsider, now even asked him to sit beside him. Madame Kebussyan, on the other hand, in spite of the eagerest manœuvrings, had found no seat among the notables. She had been forced to take her place with the other mayoresses, though her husband's wealth, notwithstanding the fact that she had lost it, should really have set her high above them. Gabriel, however, talked almost exclusively to Kilikian. He kept beckoning to Missak and Kristaphor to fill up the Russian's tin mug, since Kilikian would only drink out of that, and had thrust away the glass set out for him. Was it mere stubbornness? Or a deep mistrust in the heart of the continually persecuted? Gabriel could not be certain. He tried very hard, but quite unsuccessfully, to get on friendly terms with his neighbour. That impassive death's-head with agate eyes, brooding on nothing, would only give monosyllabic answers.

Gabriel's feelings towards Kilikian were complex. Here was a man of some education (three years in the Ejmiadzin Seminary). Hence, something more than the ordinary Asiatic proletarian. And again, his life had been so astounding that this young man's features looked as ravaged by it, his eyes as dead, as though he were old. Set against the relentlessness of this fate, the common Armenian woe became as a shadow. Yet the man had mastered it, or at least he had not succumbed, and that, to Gabriel, was enough to prove an unusual personality—which compelled respect. Yet vague mistrustful feelings of equal strength counterbalanced this positive attraction. There could be no doubt that Kilikian looked, and had often

441

behaved, like a dangerous criminal. His vicissitudes could not always have been unmerited; somehow they were too much in keeping with his personality as a whole. Impossible to say whether prison had made him a criminal or some inborn criminal tendency led him there by way of politics. Nor did anything about the Russian in the least suggest the socialist or anarchist. He seemed not to have the slightest feeling for ideas and general social objectives. Nor was he altogether malicious, though a good many women in the camp called him "the devil," from his appearance. This did not mean that at any minute he might not have been ready to do a murder in cold blood. His secret lay in his being nothing at all explicit, in his seeming to belong nowhere, to be living at some zero-point of incomprehensible neutrality. Of all the people on the Damlayik he and Apothecary Krikor were certainly the most unsocial beings. The Russian, though he attracted him profoundly, depressed Bagradian.

"I am glad I wasn't wrong about you, Sarkis Kilikian. We have you, as much as anyone, to thank for our success on the fourteenth. Those machines of yours were a very good invention. I suppose you remembered something you'd learned at the Seminary? The Roman siege-methods, was that it?"

"Haven't an idea, don't know anything about it," Kilikian grinned.

"If the Turks don't venture another attack on the south, that'll be your work, Kilikian."

This seemed to make some slight impression, but not a pleasant one. The Russian glanced with dead eyes at Gabriel. "We might have made those things far better."

Gabriel felt how inexorably the Russian was rejecting him. He began to be annoyed at his own weakness, which had nothing to oppose to this. "I suppose you got some experience of engineering in the boring-turrets of the Baku oil fields?"

The Russian smirked at him mockingly. "Wasn't even semi-skilled. I was nothing but an ordinary hand."

Gabriel pushed some cigarettes across to him. "I've asked you here, Kilikian, to tell you some intentions of mine with regard to you. It's to be hoped we'll be getting a few days' peace; but sooner or later they're bound to start a fresh attack that will make all the others seem like child's play. Now listen, my son, I intend to give you an extremely responsible post——"

Kilikian emptied his tin mug to the very last drop, set it down reflectively. "That's your look-out! You're the commandant."

Meanwhile, the long "churls' table" had begun to get extremely noisy. These people had become unused to alcohol, and it soon went to their heads. And Juliette had given orders for a third jar to be unsealed. There were two very argumentative factions—optimists and pessimists. Mukhtar Kebussyan had climbed up on the bench, where he stood swaying and rolling his bald head. He eyed them all with immense and vacant satisfaction. He was slyly mysterious:

"We ought to negotiate. I've been mayor of Yoghonoluk for twelve years. . . . I've negotiated with the Turks, with the Kaimakam and the müdir . . . the Kaimakam was always most cordial . . . I was punctual to the minute in paying in the communal bedel . . . and I used to be taken into his office —they all know me—the whole lot of them—Kaimakam, Mutessarif, Wali, Vizir, Sultan—they all knew I was Thomas Kebussyan! If I go along to negotiate, they won't do anything to me, they know I'm a taxpayer . . . you aren't taxpayers, there's no comparison . . ."

The smaller taxpayers, the village mayors and headmen of minor villages, were annoyed; they pulled Kebussyan down off his perch. Chaush Nurhan shouted that he wouldn't stand any more useless people in camp, eating up the supplies— he'd make the whole lot of them toe the line, whether they were seventy years old or not. Laughter. The tipsy row looked as though it might end in blows. But luckily Gabriel gave

443

orders that no more of his wine was to be distributed before quickly leaving the table with Samuel Avakian, who had come to him to whisper some announcement.

Almost all the notables had retired. Ter Haigasun had stayed just half an hour. Aram Tomasian had soon followed him and gone back to his wife in the tent. Gonzague and Juliette sat together. Hrand Oskanian was still in attendance on Juliette. He sat on the grass at her feet, and refused to take a place that had been vacated. But suddenly the silent little schoolmaster scrambled up, with the aid of his musket, as though a snake had bitten him. He stared in horror at Juliette, then he turned and left them stiffly. Oskanian had not had much to drink. And yet, before he had gone a few yards, he was telling himself that what he supposed he had just seen must have been an illusion, brought on by wine. It was not to be thought, it was something altogether impossible, that a fair-haired pale-skinned goddess should sit rubbing an amorous knee against that of a shady adventurer, her subject, of whose origins no one knew anything. Yet for all his conclusive reasoning Oskanian's heart was still beating hard, as he crossed the square before the altar. Juliette, grown suddenly restless, stood up to say that she must go in to see Hovsannah, neglected by her culpably all this time.

The noisy quarrelling and spiteful laughter at the plebeian table was getting more and more malicious, although all the men had long been drunk. Several uninvited people, most of them young, had come crowding in, and they heaped fuel on the flames. The sun sank. It had grown late. This excited christening-party cast wildly contending shadows across the grass. No doubt a brawl would have begun, had the sound of a long roll of drums, outside the Town Enclosure, not put a stop to it. Sudden quiet. "The münadirs," said somebody, and someone else cried out: "Alarm!" The young men and the old were suddenly startled out of their quarrelsome forgetfulness of realities. They all went rushing off excitedly, to take

444

their places in the sections. Pastor Aram was seen rushing in wild haste towards the Town Enclosure. Within a few minutes Three-Tent Square was entirely empty. "Alarm!" repeated Gonzague thoughtfully, and small gold points glinted in the quiet brown depths of his eyes. This Turkish attack was just what he wanted. This time it would probably end badly. Oughtn't they to use tonight?

Krikor could not manage to get up from table without help. Gonzague aided him. The old man's agonized legs would not obey him. He would have collapsed, had not Maris carefully steered him home. Krikor, however, seemed scarcely to notice that he was in pain. It was nothing more than an unfortunate contretemps of nature. It took a very long time to get him to the government-hut.

"Alarm?" he asked as indifferently as though he had scarcely noticed such a trifle, and so forgotten it again.

"*Alarm!*" Gonzague impressed it on his mind. "And this time it's not going to be a joke."

The apothecary stopped. His breath failed at every fifth step. "What does it matter to me?" he breathlessly asked. "Do I belong to them? Of course not! I belong to myself." And his shaky hand traced a circle round him, to indicate the exclusive majesty of his ego-world.

"If I don't believe in evil, there isn't any evil in the world . . . there isn't any death unless I believe in it. . . . Let them kill me, I shan't even notice it. . . . Anyone who can get to that point reshapes the world out of his mind."

He tried to raise his hands above his head. But in this he failed. Gonzague, whose whole nature continually prompted him rather to see a misfortune before it had happened than to let it happen before he saw it, had understood nothing of all this. And yet he politely asked, to please the apothecary: "Which of the ancient philosophers were you quoting then?"

The mandarin's mask stared indifferently out through gathering dusk. The white goatee twitched up and down. The

445

high hollow voice announced contemptuously: "That was said by a philosopher whom no one but myself has ever quoted, or ever will quote—Krikor of Yoghonoluk."

GABRIEL had ordered the great alarm without having been quite sure of immediate danger. This time it needed the dark to show him what a force the Turks had massed—just how large it was still impossible to determine—in the Armenian valley and across the Orontes plain. The combined regulars and sharpshooters seemed too numerous to be quartered in villages and so had to camp in the open. The wide half-circle of their campfires extended from the ruins of Seleucia, almost as far as the farthest Armenian village, and northwards as far as Kebussiye. By degrees the spying patrols came in with astounding news. Turkish soldiers had sprung up suddenly out of nowhere: and not only soldiers but saptiehs and Chettehs, Moslems from all over the countryside, suddenly armed with bayonets and Mauser rifles. Their officers were forming them into detachments. The number of armed men could not be estimated. Fantastic figures went from mouth to mouth. Yet, as Gabriel watched the huge half-circle of camp-fires and considered it, these figures seemed not so fantastic after all. Two things were certain. First, the Turkish commander had a strong enough force to besiege the Damlayik or storm it from South Bastion to North Saddle. Secondly, they must feel so vastly superior as to have no need to protect their advance and attack suddenly. This open advance, intended (as indeed it did) to fill the Armenians with consternation, pointed to a definite "case," which Bagradian had already provided against under the heading "general attack." He had worked it out and used a defence manœuvre. Gabriel felt much calmer than he had before the two previous attacks, though this time things looked hopeless for the mountain-folk. After the first alarm he sent his runners out to the various points of defence, to collect all the leaders and the free decads at his headquarters. They were quite sober now, and all looked terrified. Gabriel, as he was empowered constitutionally to do, took over full control of the camp for the period of battle. He gave orders that all freshly killed meat was to be got ready during the night. Two hours before daybreak the trenches must be fully provisioned. Further, whatever wine or brandy was still available in the camp must be shared out among the fighters. He placed all the remaining ten-litre jars on Three-Tent Square at their disposal. (This gift was later to cause the myth of Bagradian's inexhaustible store of supplies.)

When decads, group leaders, and the people of the reserve had all assembled, Gabriel made a short speech. He explained the kind of battle they must expect, and kept nothing back. He said: "By all human reckonings we have only the choice between two deaths, between easy death in battle, or a mean and terrible death by massacre. If we realize this quite clearly —if we are men enough to make up our minds quite coolly to choose the first, decent death in the field, then perhaps there'll be a miracle, and we shan't have to die. . . . But only then, brothers!"

A new division for the case of a general attack was formed. Chaush Nurhan, the Lion, was given command of the North Saddle. A further change of command was that Gabriel entrusted Kilikian, as he had promised to do a few hours previously, with the important sector above the ilex gully. Two entirely new fighting groups were constituted, a mobile guard and a band of komitajis. For the last Nurhan and Bagradian, remembering the guerrilla troops in the Balkan war, picked out about a hundred of the most determined men among the decads, the best shots and most expert climbers. They were to disperse over the whole valley side of the Damlayik and form ambuscades along the slopes, in tree-tops, behind rocks and bushes, in hollows and folds of the ground. They were to let the attacking Turkish columns come on undisturbed, then suddenly open fire on them from behind, if possible from

447

several points at once, without sparing munitions. Each komitaji was served out with twelve magazines, that is to say sixty cartridges, a lavish ration under the circumstances. But this time Bagradian did not propose to stint munitions, since the coming battle would doubtless bring the final decision, and he saw no reason for trying to economize bullets. Only a few remnants of the original cartridges, and those they had plundered, or else refilled, still remained in the stores. In his simple, logical way he explained their duties to the sharp-shooters, so that each of these youngsters understood exactly what was wanted. The chief rule was still "a dead man for every bullet." When the komitajis had been formed, the mobile guard was picked out from among the decads. Gabriel reduced the garrison in the South Bastion, whose strong defence works made it an almost impregnable position, to only the most neces-sary fighters. The reservists filled in the gaps. This released about one hundred and fifty rifles for his mobile guard, which he led in person, and with which he would attack in any place where the lines seemed menaced. Most of these storm troops were mounted on the camp donkeys. Donkeys in these parts are not as slow-footed and obstinate as elsewhere, but will take any pace. The two groups of the cohort of youth, the orderlies and the section of scouts, had always to keep at the heels of the guard, so that widely extended communications between all sections and the command might never be broken.

Such were the main outlines of this *ordre de bataille,* already worked out by Gabriel to meet the case of general attack. He had prepared it all with the greatest calm, during the first two hours of the night. Lastly he summoned the whole re-serve. It was ordered to vacate the Town Enclosure by sun-rise. One half of it was destined to stand by for action in the various sectors, the other took up its position on the long reaches of the high plateau. These strips of ground, which in many places, as for instance before the ilex gully sector, were only about a thousand feet wide, formed a very dangerous zone. Here only a few redoubts, or rather a few loosely piled up stones, defended the Town Enclosure from assault. When Gabriel had also addressed the reserve, and made them realize themselves as the final barrier against the worst horrors of rape and child-slaughter, Nurhan the Lion sounded the bugle-call. Its fierce stutter managed to shape out a few notes of the Turkish "lights out." This was the order to get to sleep.

Gabriel went to look at the howitzers. He intended to spend the night adjusting them. With Nurhan's help he had managed to train a few of the more intelligent men for artillery duty. The last two scouts were in before midnight. They reported nothing not known already. The only fresh details they could give was that the half-moon flag had been hoisted over Villa Bagradian, that many horses were tethered in a line along the courtyard, and that officers kept coming in and out. It was therefore clear that the Turks had made the villa their headquarters. Gabriel waited for the late rising of the moon. Then, with compasses, he carefully began to mark out distances on his map, and to draw calculations. A big, inflated-looking full moon gave enough light to enable him to sight an auxiliary mark and adjust his guns by it. The men of the battery were instructed to drag the lockers close up to each gun. There were still five shrapnel and twenty-three grenades in the boxes. Gabriel had half these shells placed in a row behind the guns. He went from one to the other and set the fuse with his clamping-key, by the light of his electric torch. Iskuhi appeared as he was doing it. At first he did not notice she was there. She called to him softly. He took her hand, and led her far away from the gun, till they were alone. They sat down under an arbutus bush; it was covered all over with red berries, which, in the moonlight, had the dead look of drops of sealing-wax.

Iskuhi's voice came subdued and hesitant: "I only wanted to ask you whether it would disturb you too much if tomorrow I stayed somewhere near you."

449

"There's nothing in the world that does me so much good as to have you near me, Iskuhi."

Gabriel bent close over Iskuhi to look far down into her eyes, which met his ardently. An odd thought sped across his mind. This feeling which drew them together might not be love, at least not love in the ordinary meaning of the word, not the kind of love which had bound him to Juliette, but something very much greater, yet less than love. It heightened all his faculties immeasurably, made him celestially happy, without any desire diverting that happiness. It may have been the unknown love of the same blood, which quickened him like a mystic spring, welling up in Iskuhi's eyes; not the wish to be joined in future, but the utter certainty of having been so in the past. His eyes smiled into hers.

"I have no sense of death, Iskuhi. It's mad, but I simply can't make myself think that this time tomorrow I mayn't still be alive. Perhaps it isn't a bad omen. What do you feel?"

"Death's sure to come anyway, Gabriel. There isn't any other way out for us, is there?"

He did not extract their double meaning from her words. An incredibly light assurance sprang up within him. "One oughtn't to look too far ahead, Iskuhi. I won't think anything but tomorrow. I don't even think of tomorrow night. Do you know I'm looking forward to the morning!"

Iskuhi stood up to go back to her tent. "I only wanted to ask you to promise me something, Gabriel. Something quite obvious. If things get so that there's no more hope, please shoot me and then yourself. It's the best solution. I can't live without you. And I shouldn't like you to go on living without me—not a second! So may I still stay somewhere near you tomorrow, please?"

No! She must give him her word not to leave her tent during the fighting. But, in exchange, he promised that if things got desperate he would either fetch or have her sent for, and kill them both. He smiled as he was promising this, since in-

deed nothing in his heart felt the slightest prescience of an
end. Therefore he did not fear in the least for Stephan, or
Juliette. Yet, as he again took up his work on the guns, he
found himself surprised at his own assurance, which the
fiercest reality all round him, in a threatening half-moon of
fire, seemed so contemptuously to disprove.

THE Kaimakam, the yüs-bashi from Antakiya, the red-haired
müdir, the battalion commandant of the four companies sent
from Aleppo, and two other officers sat that evening in the
selamlik of Villa Bagradian, holding a council of war. That
reception-room was as brilliant with candlelight as it had
been when Juliette received notables. Orderlies cleared away
the meal, which these officers had eaten in her salon. Bugle-
calls sounded outside the windows, and all the pother of resting and victualling soldiers. Since with these Armenian devils
you never knew, the Kaimakam had ordered a guard for headquarters. It was now engaged in setting up its camp, laying
waste the park, orchard, and vegetable garden in the process.
   This council had lasted a fairly long time without showing
signs of complete agreement. They were discussing an important matter. Would it, or would it not, be really advisable
to begin operations against the Damlayik tomorrow at sunrise, as arranged? The Kaimakam with the misanthropic
complexion, the dark-brown pouches under his eyes, was the
hesitant, dilatory member of this discussion. He defended
his lack of resolution by insisting that, though at the Wali's
request the general in Aleppo had sent them a full infantry
battalion, he had failed in his promise of mountain artillery
and machine-guns. The Kolagasi (staff captain) from Aleppo
explained this by informing them that such arms had all been
cleared out of Syria, with the transferred divisions to which
they belonged, and that in all Aleppo there was not so much
as a single machine-gun. Would it not, demanded the
Kaimakam, be better not to attack for the next few days and

send an urgent telegram to His Excellency Jemal Pasha, begging him to assign them the weapons they needed? The officers considered this impossible. Such direct appeals were likely to irritate the incalculable Jemal, and might even move him to counter-measures.

The yüs-bashi from Antakiya pushed back his chair and took out a sheet of paper. His fingers shook, less from excitement than because he was a chain-smoker. "Effendiler!" His voice was thin and morose. "If we're going to wait about for machine-guns and mountain-artillery, the best thing we can do is to winter here. The army in the field has so few of them that our request would simply be ridiculous. May I again remind the Kaimakam of the exact strength of our attacking force?"

Tonelessly he read out his figures: "Four companies from Aleppo: say a thousand men. Two companies from Alexandretta: five hundred men. The strengthened garrison from Antakiya: four hundred and fifty men. That means nearly two thousand rifles of trained infantry. Why, regiments at the front can't be nearly as strong! Further—the second line: four hundred saptiehs from Aleppo, three hundred saptiehs from our own kazah, four hundred chettehs from the north—that's another eleven hundred men. And, besides all that, there's our third line, of two thousand Moslems from the villages, whom we've armed. So that altogether we shall attack with a force of about five thousand rifles. . . ."

Here the yüs-bashi stopped to gulp down a small cup of coffee and light a fresh cigarette. Somebody used the pause to interrupt him:

"Don't forget the Armenians have two howitzers."

The major's hatchet face looked almost animated; his yellowish forehead began to glisten. "That artillery is completely useless. First, they have no ammunition. Second, nobody knows how to use the things. Third, we shall get hold of them very quickly again."

The Kaimakam, who, bored or weary, had sunk far back in his chair, raised heavy eyes. "Don't underrate this Bagradian fellow, Yüs-Bashi. I've only seen the man once, in a bath. But he behaved with unusual insolence."

The young freckled müdir with the carefully manicured nails interposed reproachfully: "It was a great mistake on the part of the military authorities not to have called him up. He's in the reserve. I know for a fact that Bagradian volunteered several times. Without him the coast would be perfectly quiet and normal."

The major cut short these reflections: "Bagradian this! Bagradian that! Such civilians aren't so very important. I went up yesterday and reconnoitred the Damlayik just to see for myself what the position was. They're a ragged-looking crew. Their trenches seemed to me to be quite primitive. At a generous estimate they've got between four and five hundred rifles. We should have to spit in our own faces if we hadn't cleared them out by midday."

"We certainly should, Yüs-Bashi," agreed the Kaimakam. "But any animal, even the smallest, gets ferocious when it's fighting for its life."

The Kolagasi from Aleppo most explicitly endorsed the major's view. He fully hoped that within two days he would be out of this primitive neighbourhood and back in the pleasant town of Aleppo.

Since the officers all seemed so confident, the Kaimakam dismissed the sitting with a yawn: "Well, then—you guarantee success, Yüs-Bashi?"

That draconian officer poured swaths of smoke out of his nostrils. "One can guarantee nothing in any military enterprise. I must reject the word guarantee. I can only say that I don't want to go on living if the Armenian camp isn't liquidated by this time tomorrow."

Upon which the lolling Kaimakam heavily rose. "Well, let's get to bed."

453

But that night the potentate's sleep was not of the soundest. He had taken up his quarters in Juliette's room. It was still saturated with perfume from the many flasks of scent that had been broken in it. They enmeshed the slumbering dyspeptic in such cloying and irritating nightmares that his rest was broken by several sleepless hours.

His awakening was no better than his sleep had been. Scarcely had the light begun to break when he started up to the sound of a terrific explosion. He rushed, half-dressed, outside the house. The destruction was great. The shell had dropped sheer in front of the steps. The fragments of every window in the whole house strewed the ground. The gust of the shell had torn a wing of the front door off its hinges and flung it back into the hallway. Three deep breaches gaped in the brickwork, and iron shards stuck up everywhere out of the ground. But worst of all was the sight of the Aleppo staff officer. That unfortunate had been designed by fate to be making his way out of the house at the very instant of the explosion. Now he sat huddled against the wall. His blue eyes looked vacantly childish. He breathed heavily, seemed lost in some dreamy past. A splinter had skimmed all the flesh off his right shoulder, another wounded his left hip. The yüs-bashi was assisting him. It looked as though he were telling him rather sharply not to give way so comfortably to his wound. But the Kolagasi was insubordinate. He paid no attention whatever and lurched over, slowly, on to his side. The yüs-bashi turned away angrily and bellowed at the frightened men not to stand about there with their mouths open, but go along and fetch the doctor and an ambulance. It was not so easy. The surgeon was attached to the third company in Bitias. The major had the wounded Kolagasi carried upstairs into Stephan's bedroom and deposited on Stephan's bed. He returned to consciousness, but only to implore the major not to leave him until his wound had been dressed. The Kaimakam, by nature a confirmed civilian, to whom bloodshed was as repugnant in practice as it frequently seemed desirable in theory, crept into the cellar as though by accident—down the dark cool stairs. Gabriel's bombardment continued. Another shell had just come crashing into the orchard.

It was more than ironic fate which had directed the trajectory of the first straight to Bagradian's own front door, checkmating the battalion commander. Perhaps it was not mere accident, but a living witness to the fact that God is not invariably on the side of the biggest battalion. In any case this laming of the command delayed the attack by over an hour. The Turks, in the orchards and vineyards, who had already disposed themselves in extended order to advance, were kept back. The Armenian swine seemed to have known what to aim at, and have expert gunners! And, though the next eight shells were not quite so lucky, the valley was at least wide enough to ensure that, wherever they might drop, shrapnel and grenades caused panic. Three houses in Bitias, Aziz, and Yoghonoluk were set alight. A detachment of encamped saptiehs, drinking morning coffee out of tin mugs, sustained heavy losses from a grenade. Leaving three dead and many wounded, these upholders of law and order retired for ever from the engagement, without having fired a single shot.

This howitzer bombardment at least gave the results envisaged by Gabriel, though he got no clear perception of his success. It disorganized the Turkish plan of attack. The morale of the new civil population was so disastrously affected by it that shoals of Turkish women had begun already to take flight in the direction of the Orontes plain. Not least was the paralysis of the leadership, which lasted a considerable time. Not till long after the howitzers had ceased their fire, did lines of riflemen summon enough courage to advance and disappear into the woods on the lowest slopes of Musa Dagh. For an instant Bagradian reproached himself with not having possessed enough audacity to post at least the four hundred men of his first defence, the half of his decads and komitajis, here and there along these lines of advance, and so molest the attack before it had time to develop properly. But in any case the hundred komitajis already enrolled had disposed themselves halfway up the height so skilfully, and were fired with such mad, clear-headed audacity, that they wrought more damage and confusion among the groups which came panting past them than any open attack could have achieved. Twice, three times, their invisible cross-fire hurled these companies, engaged in toiling their way through thickets, wildly apart, and fully dispersed them. Cut off from their leaders, and expecting death at any instant, these groups went rushing down the slopes. It was not cowardice. Defence was impossible. After which unsuccessful attempt there was nothing left for the major but to rally his companies on the line of the lowest slope, order a short rest, and serve out rations. Meanwhile the komitajis were undisturbed as they gathered up the rifles and cartridge-belts from dead or wounded, and carried them off behind their lines.

The Kaimakam, who had come out to see the command, caustically inquired of the yüs-bashi: "Are you going to repeat your tactic? If you do, it doesn't look as if we'd ever get up the mountain."

That irate major's face turned coffee-coloured. He began to bellow at the Kaimakam: "Take over the command yourself if you like! It's your responsibility far more than mine."

The Kaimakam perceived that one must be careful in dealing with this touchy officer. This was not the moment at which to quarrel. He shrugged, in his usual sleepy way. "You're quite right. It's my responsibility. But don't forget, Major, that you'll be responsible to me. If there's another fiasco we shall both of us have to take the consequences, you just as much as I."

This was so true that the major had nothing more to say. Since the highest quarters, the Wali, the Minister of War, had

had their attention drawn to Musa Dagh, a third failure would mean a court martial for the major. It would probably handle him even worse than it had his rosy-cheeked predecessor. He and the Kaimakam were linked together for good or ill. He must be kept in with. He grunted a pacific remark and set to work again. The companies in the north were ordered to advance immediately against the Armenian trenches along the Saddle. The South Bastion along the steeper ridge was not to be meddled with, since neither the major nor his effectives were anxious for another avalanche. The major called his officers together and ordered them to tell their platoons that any man who turned back in the next advance would be shot down without mercy. A long line of saptiehs and chettehs, detailed especially for this executioner's work, were posted along the hollows of the fore-slope. They received stringent orders to open fire on retreating infantry. Neither saptiehs nor sharpshooters had any objection to the duty. At the same time the major advanced a third, very long line of armed villagers (they even included a few women) into the region of apricot orchards and vines. The companies' terror of the major's drastic orders had its effects. The men, driven on by panic, came rushing up the steep slopes. They did not so much as dare to get second wind. They shut their eyes and stormed through the komitajis' fire. The afternoon was well over by the time the three platoons, under gruelling bullets from above, managed to set foot on the upper slopes, and dig themselves in, as best they might, with their infantry spades, under the Armenian positions, or else take cover behind rocks, heaps of rubble, or folds in the ground. By this heroic advance between two fires, the major's troops had obtained their first outstanding success. That officer, drunk with the lust of battle, waving his sword, led on fresh lines to the assault. These, too, succeeded in implanting themselves below the Armenian trenches, and so extending the line of attack. Such successes inspired the Turkish soul. They opened wild fire

457

along the new line, on every attacking point. At first it mattered nothing to the major whether his bullets found a mark. For two whole hours the ears and hearts of these Armenians were to be so basted into terror that the dregs of their courage should ebb away. They were also to be shown that the Turkish state had enough bullets at its disposal to keep the fire as hot as ever for the next three days. The defenders crouched back, paralysed, in their trenches, letting this dense hailstorm of bullets patter and spin above their heads. The worst of it was that the infantry nearest the Town Enclosure sent unlimited shot among the log huts, so that from time to time both dum-dum and ordinary rifle-bullets caused terrible wounds among the inhabitants. Ter Haigasun therefore gave orders for the whole enclosure to be vacated, and for noncombatants to retire towards the sea and among the rocks.

During this long frenzy of munition wasting, the major advanced one after another, his company reserves, his saptiehs, and last of all his armed peasants, all led by officers, so that overwhelmingly superior numbers, when at last he stormed, might have their effect in ever-increasing lines of men. The second, third, fourth lines of attack were stationed at fairly wide intervals behind the front. When these shaken and excited troops, emerging from the komitajis' cross-fire, had come on bellowing up the slopes, the major ordered his first line to attack. The Armenians, seasoned by now in the art of repelling such wide advances, fired down from their, as a rule higher, positions and calmly dispersed the attacking waves. Quickly as these lines, one after another, were advanced, they broke each time, severely handicapped by the roughness of this mountain terrain, far from the Armenian trenches. In spite of superior numbers and unlimited supplies of ammunition the Moslems could not manage till almost nighfall to advance one pace on any point of attack. The Armenians still found it comparatively easy to repel them without too many losses, owing to the fact that their defences had been so skilfully contrived. Here and there their trenches formed sharp angles, so that the oncoming Turks had to take both front and flank fire. Added to which the komitajis, who suddenly on this or that part of the line spattered the reserves with a quick and deadly rain of bullets, disconcerted these regulars. The compulsory valour of these attacks, all equally vain, had already cost the major as many men as the last defeat of the poor bimbashi, whose losses had brought him such dire disgrace. But the yüs-bashi was made of sterner stuff. He would not retire. Again and again he put himself at the head of his men, avoiding death a hundred times, by virtue of that miraculous law which seems to protect all real valour in leadership. He usually stayed with the ilex-gully sector, since gradually it had grown apparent that this was the weakest part of the defence. Gabriel, thanks to his mobile guard, had still control of all the threads. "Three hours more," he thought, "and it'll be dark." The guard had again and again come galloping up to reinforce a threatened sector, hold unsteady trenches, fill up the menaced gap between two divisions, and relieve an exhausted decad. Now, however, Gabriel lay fagged out, white, breathless as a corpse, he could not tell where, and finding it hard to regain his strength. Avakian sat beside him, and about twelve orderlies of the cohort of youth awaited his orders. Haik was one of them. Not Stephan. Messages came in every minute. Mostly they came from the North Saddle, which till now had been having an easy day. But at about this time the Turks seemed to change their intention and prepare a big coup against the north. Chaush Nurhan's messages were more and more anxiously framed. Not only the major but the whole staff of other officers had come up from behind cover on to the counter-slope. He had recognized them quite plainly through his field-glass. Bagradian intended to use the guard, his last defence, as sparingly as he possibly could, and not let himself be imposed upon by the inexperience of individual section leaders. This north section was by far the best defended posi-

459

tion, and he could see no reason for sending up reinforcements into this particular system of his defence, before the real fight had even begun. It seemed far more important to Gabriel to stay continually in the vicinity of the ilex-gully sector, by far the most menaced, and do his best to avert disaster there. So there he lay, with his eyes shut, and seemed not to heed the continual messages from the north ridge. "Only two and a half hours more of it," his thoughts kept whispering. A lull had set in. The firing died down. Gabriel let exhaustion overwhelm him. It may have been this mental and physical enfeeblement which caused him to fall into the major's trap.

SHARP echoes of the fight sounded all along the "Riviera." Some acoustic trick made the ping and clatter of the bullets seem to whip the ground all round Gonzague and Juliette. They got the sensation of sitting in the very midst of a battle, although really it was a good way off. Juliette kept tight hold of Gonzague's hand. He listened. The whole of him seemed to be listening. He sat very excited, and very still.

"I think it's coming nearer all round. At least, that's what it sounds like."

Juliette said nothing. The hissing din was so fantastically strange that she seemed not to understand and, so far, scarcely to have heard it. Gonzague only bent slightly forward, to get a better view of the surf as it leapt round the rocks many feet below. The sea today was unusually rough: its distant anger mingled with the din of the rifles. Maris pointed south, along the coast. "We ought to have made up our minds sooner, Juliette. By now you should have been sitting quite peacefully in the manager's house, beside the alcohol factory."

She shivered. Her lips opened to speak, but she took a long time to find any voice; she seemed to have lost it. "The ship leaves on the twenty-sixth. This is only the twenty-third. I've still got three days."

460

"Well, yes"—he calmed her down with the tenderest forbearance—"you've got three days. . . . I won't deprive you of one of them . . . if others don't."

"Oh, Gonzague, I feel so strange, so incomprehensible . . ." Her voice died halfway through the sentence. There seemed no object in trying to describe a state of mind which was so entirely unfamiliar. It was like drawing something soft and very vulnerable out of its protective chrysalis by the very part that felt most coldly exposed. All her limbs had a cold life of their own, scarcely in touch with her general consciousness. She could, she felt, regretfully take off her arms and legs at any minute and lock them up in a trunk. Ages ago, when she inhabited her bright and reasoned world, Juliette would not have remained inactive. "I must have something the matter with me" would have been her instantaneous reaction, and so she would, no doubt, have taken her temperature. Now she could only sit and wonder how it was that her appalling situation should at the same time feel so right, so comfortable. As she thought this, she twice repeated: "Incomprehensible . . ."

"Poor Juliette. I understand exactly. You've lost yourself—first for fifteen years, and now for the last twenty-four days. Now you can't find either the sham Juliette or the real one. You see, I don't belong anywhere. I'm not Armenian or French or Greek, or even American; I'm really and truly nothing, so I'm free. You'll find me very easy to be with. But you must cut loose."

She stared, not understanding a word he said to her. The rifle-fire was nearing the climax of its excitement. Impossible to sit quietly in one place. Gonzague helped her to her feet. She stumbled about as though she were dazed.

He seemed to get restless. "We must think what to do, Juliette. That doesn't sound very reassuring. What are your plans?"

She half completed the gesture of putting her hands up to her ears. "I'm tired. I want to lie down."

461

"That's quite impossible, Juliette. Just listen. They may break through at any minute. I suggest we move away from here, and wait farther down, to see what's happened."

She shook her head stubbornly. "No. I'd rather go back to the tent."

He clasped her hips, and gently tried to draw her his way. "Don't be annoyed, Juliette. But you know it's really absolutely necessary to get this thing straight in your mind. In the next half-hour the Turks may be in the Town Enclosure. And Gabriel Bagradian? How do you know he's still alive?"

The howling and crackling all round them seemed to reinforce Gonzague's fears. But Juliette suddenly started out of her torpor to all her old energy and decisiveness.

"I want to see Stephan. I want Stephan here, with me!" she cried out with almost angry vehemence.

Her child's name rent a horrible fog of unreality which had crept upon her from every side. Her maternity had become a well-built house—its walls impenetrable, strong enough to keep out the world. She seized Gonzague with both hands and pushed him impatiently. "Go and bring Stephan to me at once, you hear. . . . Please don't lose any time. Find him. I'll wait! I'll wait!"

For a second he thought it over. Gallantly he suppressed every objection, and bent his head. "All right, Juliette. I'll do whatever I can to hunt up the boy. And as fast as I can. I won't keep you waiting long."

And actually, within half an hour, Gonzague Maris had come back with a savage and perspiring Stephan, who came reluctantly at his heels. Juliette threw herself on her son and hugged him, shaken with dry sobs. He was so tired that, the minute they all sat down, he slept.

GABRIEL the scholar, the *bel esprit,* had fully proved that he had the ability to lead men. The threat of death had forced it to the surface. Acknowledged and professional generals have

462

often made the mistake that he now was guilty of—they have allowed their subjective preference for a certain, closely studied part of their plan unduly to influence their decisions. So that Gabriel, prejudiced in favour of the main achievement of his great scheme of defence, let himself delay too long before at last he heeded Chaush Nurhan's messages, which had ended as desperate cries for help. Since the Turks neither renewed their attack in the ilex gully, nor at any other of the whole circle of possible attacking-points round the mountain, since rifle-fire died down on all sides, to begin again with unexpected ferocity in the north, it began to look as if the enemy would attempt a break-through on the Saddle, with the whole strength of his far more numerous effectives. For that reason Gabriel drew together his decads, dispersed over the whole length of the mountain-slope, and led them northwards, to await the onslaught of the Turks in the second-line trench, among the rock barricades. Gabriel expected it any minute, since the fire kept growing in intensity and dusk by now had already gathered. (No one but himself could man the howitzers, so they had to be left to stand unused.)

Sarkis Kilikian, a section leader above the ilex gully, had behaved most gallantly all that day and beaten back five attacks. For a time it looked as though the extended lines of Turks, notwithstanding all their losses at that one point, would not try to force their break-through at any other, since this, after all, was the key position, which led straight into the heart of the camp. Since in the first few hours of today's fighting Gabriel still had not been certain that the Russian would manage to hold out, he had spent a good deal of the day in and around the ilex-gully sections, and several times had attacked with the decads, falling on the flanks of the Turks. Sarkis Kilikian's task had been anything but easy. The main trench extended only the length of a fairly long strip of ground; the trenches of the flank defence were not very favourably placed, and were moreover several hundred paces away from the next sector. And these gaps were not filled up, as were those between most of the other attacking-points, by steep descents, walls of rock, or such thick undergrowth as made them impossible to negotiate. The Russian commanded a comparatively small force of eight decads, and it was set fairly wide apart, considering the character of the terrain. Yet he had got through the day without too many losses; only two dead and six wounded. Something of Kilikian's personality, his cadaverous peace, his indifference, seemed to have gone over into his men. Whenever the Turks began to attack, these defenders aimed with a deliberation for which "bored" seems the only word. They felt, it seemed, equally at home in life or death, so that really it made very little difference which of these two places of sojourn they inhabited in the immediate future. As Kilikian levelled his gun, he was careful not to let go out one of the excellent cigarettes of which Bagradian had made him the present of a box. Now, after so many blood-smeared hours, he stood resting his shrunken body against the parapet, and stared down the slope below the trench, strewn about with tree trunks and branches, shrubs and dwarf-pines, that fell sheer in a steep declivity to the actual mouth of the ilex gully, which the enemy occupied. Gabriel had, of course, in the first few days caused the edge of the camp to be cleared of tall trees. Kilikian's youthful death's-head never moved. His impressive agate eyes betrayed the supreme faculty of reducing life to a minimum of action. In his looted uniform the Russian, with his sloping shoulders and figure slender as a girl's, accentuated still further by a very tightly drawn belt, looked like a dapper officer. He said nothing at all to the men beside him, who were equally silent. Their eyes kept straying towards the shadows of trees and shrubs, which from second to second lengthened and narrowed out, became golden, secretively alive. Every Armenian on the Damlayik, except perhaps Krikor and Kilikian, had his mind full of one thought only, of the same thought as Gabriel Bagradian: "Only two more hours, and then the sun

464

will be down." From the north came a burst of rifle-fire. Down here, wood and mountain might have been in the deepest peace. Many of these exhausted men were closing their eyes. They had the strange sensation that stolen sleep would somehow drive time on more quickly into the arms of rescuing darkness. There were more and more sleepers. Till at last scarcely one man of those who held these trenches was still awake. Only the dead, polished eyes of Sarkis Kilikian, their leader, stared fixedly at the dark wooded edge of the ilex gully. What happened in the next few minutes must be classed as one of those enigmas which no explanation explains or motivates. The streak of incomprehensible lethargy in Kilikian, that trait in him which the boy of eleven, lying under his mother while she bled to death, had already begun to build up in himself as protection against too great an intensity of suffering, might at a pinch be made responsible. In any case he never moved, nor did his eyes change their expression, when single attacking infantrymen, followed little by little by whole swarms of them, began to emerge at the edge of the wood. Not a shot announced the attack. The Turks seemed too timid to want to detach themselves from the jagged edge of the ilex gully. They waited uneasily for the defenders to let off their rifles. Since that did not happen, they thrust forward—there were at least three hundred of them—ran on and again waited, ducking down behind every obstacle, for the Armenian fire. Some of the men in the trench were still asleep. Others seized their guns and blinked at the noiseless, stealthy picture beneath them. At this instant the liquid glow of sunset intensified, and burst into a thousand gold sequins and splinters. The half-moons on the officers' kepis glittered. Strangely enough they did not wear trench caps in this campaign. The Armenians, dazed with sunset brilliance, lifted their rifles and stared at Kilikian, awaiting his orders. Then came the inexplicable. Instead of, as he had before, quietly signing to them to aim, deciding how near the Turks were to come, and then setting his whistle to his lips, the Russian, reflective and deliberate, climbed out of the trench. This looked so like an order that, half in bewildered exhaustion, half in blind trust in the unknown intention of their leader, one after another swung over the parapet. The Turks, who had stalked their way forward to within fifty paces, started, and flung themselves down. Their hearts stood still.

They were expecting a fierce attack. But Sarkis Kilikian quietly stood in front of the centre trench, not going either on or back, not shouting any word of command. Three hundred Mauser rifles opened a gruelling quick fire on the rigid human targets above them, who stood out black against the glittering sunset. In a few seconds a third of the garrison of this sector were crouching, with groans and howls of pain on the blood-soaked earth of Musa Dagh. Sarkis Kilikian stood on, in thoughtful surprise, his hands in his pockets. The Turkish bullets seemed to avoid him, as though fate considered that to put an end to this unique destiny by a simple death in the field would be far too banal a proceeding. When at last he raised his hand and shouted something to his riflemen, it was much too late. He was swept along in the general flight of what still remained of the garrison, a flight which only turned and collected itself half-way to the stone barricades. These were four fairly oblong heaps of piled-up stones, almost outside the Town Enclosure. Before the fugitives reached their cover, they left twenty-three dead and wounded behind them. The Turkish infantry, shouting indescribable war-cries, took possession of the vacated trenches. Their reserve crowded in after them, the saptiehs, the chettehs, and last the armed villagers. A fair number of bellicose Moslem women had followed their men. When these women, hidden behind the trees of the ilex gully, saw the success of the Turkish advance, they broke forth, like frenzied mænads, from the wood, took each other's hands, formed a chain, while from their throats came a long, shrill sound unlike any other, the zilgith, the ancient battle-cry of the women of Islam. This raking scream let loose the devil in the men. They, as their bold creed instructs them, had ceased to care for life or death; they dashed in a mad gallop against the wretched heaps of stone, without firing another shot, with fixed bayonets.

In this disaster several bits of isolated luck came to the aid of the Armenians. As they saw the Turks bayonet their wounded and tread them into the ground with their army boots, the whole watchful, frigid alertness of their unavoidable destiny came upon them again. They lay stiffly behind their cover and aimed quietly, with all their accustomed deadly certainty. The Turks had the last, dazzling sun in their faces, the Armenians at their backs. Another advantage in misfortune was the confusion arising from the circumstance that attackers before the neighbouring sectors, running past their own officers, left their posts and, drunk with victory, swarmed towards the breach. Therefore defenders also left their trenches and crowded, left and right, towards the danger-spot. The consequence was a confused hand-to-hand struggle, in which friend and foe (many Armenians were wearing plundered Turkish uniform) got mixed in together unrecognizably. It was a long time, and many men had to lose their lives, before the enemies sorted themselves out, and superior numbers succeeded in driving back the Armenians towards the Town Enclosure. Bagradian arrived with his mobile guard at the very last second to avert the worst for the camp itself. The Turks were driven back, but only as far as their captured trenches, which they held stubbornly.

Luckiest of all, it was now night, and a cloudy moonless night into the bargain. It had gathered quickly, unperceived. The major could no longer venture on another decisive thrust. In the dark the Armenians, who knew the Damlayik like their own bodies, had still, in spite of their many wounds, the advantage over a whole division. The Kaimakam, disturbed profoundly by the immense losses they had sustained, did not quite know what to do with this unused victory. The major swore by all his gods that by three tomorrow he would have the whole business cleared up. He developed his next plan of action. The Turks, all except a few camouflaged protecting garrisons, were to be noiselessly withdrawn from the defence sector. The whole force should encamp for the night in the wide ilex gully and be ready, a few hours before daybreak, to thrust forward, like a great battering-ram, through this last, inconsiderable obstacle.

But that did not prevent the new Moslems in the villages, since now they were all householders, from preferring a night indoors to one in the open, and leaving the troops.

Towards six o'clock Pastor Aram Tomasian, bathed in sweat and broken with fatigue, came into the women's tent, gulped down two glasses of water, and gasped: "Iskuhi, Hovsannah. Get ready. Things aren't going well. I'll fetch you in time. We must find somewhere to hide, down among the rocks. I'm going out now to look for Father."

Tomasian had vanished again at once without properly getting his breath. Iskuhi, who had kept her promise, and not left the tent all day, helped the complaining Hovsannah to get dressed as well as she could, gave the child its bottle of watered milk, and with her left arm drew out from under the bed what little baggage they possessed. But suddenly she stopped her unfinished work and left Hovsannah without a word.

An hour after sunset. The big square, with its trampled grass before the altar in the Town Enclosure. The leaders had not retired into their hut, but were sitting on the grass by the altar steps. The people squatted close around them in heavy silence. The huts were abandoned. From time to time the screams of badly wounded men came across from the "hospital." Some of the recent dead had been rescued from the last attack. They lay in rows, incompletely hidden by sheets and sacking. No light. No fire. The Council had forbidden any

468

voice to be raised above a whisper. The crowd was so heavily silent that all could easily distinguish the whispering voices of representatives.

Ter Haigasun seemed the only one there who could still keep his presence of mind. His voice sounded quiet and circumspect. "We have only one night, that is to say eight hours' darkness."

He was misunderstood. Even Aram Tomasian, whose heart was torn by the thought of Hovsannah, Iskuhi, and the child, proposed all kinds of hasty plans. He suggested in all seriousness that perhaps it would be better to clear the camp and seek shelter in clefts among the rocks, in the limestone caves and grottoes of the cliffs. But his suggestion found no partisans. It was evident that these men, without any reason for it, had begun to love their habitation and would defend it to the very last. They began to argue. These few hours of darkness threatened to crumble away, minute by minute, without results. Here and there out of the crouching people, a woman's suppressed shriek and convulsive sobbing from time to time. This day had brought death to over a hundred families, reckoning those whose wounded had fallen into Turkish hands. Nor did anyone know how many seriously wounded were still lying out before the positions, whom no one so far had managed to bring back to camp. The heavy night pressed like a low ceiling on Musa Dagh.

As their whisperings grew wilder and more pointless, Ter Haigasun assailed Gabriel sharply: "We've only one night, Bagradian Effendi. Oughtn't we to use these eight hours?"

Gabriel had stretched himself out full length, his arms under his head, and was staring up at the dark above. He could scarcely defend himself against sleep. Everything sank away. Meaningless words came splashing round his ears. At this instant he had not even the energy to answer the priest. To himself he mumbled something incomprehensible. It was then he felt the little, ice-cold hand touching his face. It was too dark

469

to recognize Iskuhi. After long straying about from post to post, she had found him at last. Now she sat down, as though it were the most natural thing for her, at his side, in the circle of the leaders. She did not seem even ashamed before her brother. This was their last and only night.

Iskuhi's cool hand roused and quickened Gabriel like fresh water. His torpor began to melt away, his mind to germinate. He sat up and took her hand, not heeding whether anyone saw his tenderness in the dark. Iskuhi's hand seemed to lead him back to himself through the stubborn confusion of his fatigue. His muscles became taut. That physical well-being filled him which a thirsty man feels who has drunk his fill. Suddenly the Council held its breath. Voices came nearer. They all sprang up. Turks? Some lanterns swung into view. It was a komitaji detachment returning to camp. It wanted its orders for tomorrow. The komitajis reported that only one of their number had been killed, and two taken prisoners by the Turks, and that they had kept their positions as before. At the same time they announced that the Turkish companies were vacating most of the sectors on the height, to collect again in the ilex gully. Communication between the captured trenches and the command was being maintained by chains of patrols. Their intentions were clear as daylight.

"We'll use tonight, Ter Haigasun!"

Gabriel said it so loud that the crowd could hear him. Simultaneously the other leaders seemed to have conquered their paralysis. The same thought flashed through all their minds before Bagradian said a word. Only a strong surprise attack on the Turkish camp could avert disaster. But for such an attack the exhausted fighters of this day of blood had no strength left in them. The whole people, women and children, must in some way or other take part and give it the added physical weight of thousands. Now they were all talking at once. Every mukhtar and teacher had his suggestions, till Gabriel sharply commanded silence. They must not discuss this question aloud. It was not impossible that Turkish spies had slipped into camp. Gabriel sent Chaush the Lion back to his sector to pick a hundred and fifty fighters, out of the twenty decads by which it was manned, who had suffered comparatively little. He was to bring them quietly. Those left behind could and must suffice to hold their particular trenches and rock barricades against a counter-attack. The South Bastion and the sectors on the edge of the mountain, twenty decads in all, were to furnish the same, and did in fact, in the course of the next few hours, silently assemble on the altar square. With his komitajis and mobile guard Bagradian rallied a force of over five hundred. All these movements took a long time, since they had to be done in absolute quiet, and no commands, but only the most necessary directions, briefly whispered, could be given. It was very hard, in the thick darkness, to classify. Only his knowledge of each individual among them enabled Bagradian to divide into two groups these wearily torpid men. The first, the larger, was in charge of the captain of the komitajis. When they had eaten a few rations and received their supply of cartridges—which again in the dark proved very difficult and laborious—they were moved some way towards the south, to creep down by remote tracks, noiseless as shadows, with endless precautions, through woods and thickets, across clearings and open spaces, nearer and nearer the Turkish camp. They had more to help them than their own instinctive knowledge of the ground; they had the campfires of the companies, which the yüs-bashi had allowed to be lit on the edge of the ilex gully. These fires were built up on barren or rocky places, since otherwise, though the great gully itself was heavy with damp, the dryness of the undergrowth beyond might easily have caused a heath fire. But, in spite of these campfires, komitaji leaders managed to surround the whole elliptical valley. Armenians sat motionless in the trees; they lay hidden behind the thick arbutus bushes; here and there they curled themselves, without proper cover, round

471

knotted roots. With never-shifting eyes they watched the camp, which gradually quietened into silence. They kept their rifles trained, although it must still be more than an hour before sudden firing up on the mountain gave them the signal.

Bagradian had ordered Chaush Nurhan to lead the attack against the captured sector with the other group of a hundred and fifty rifles. Nurhan advanced his men from behind stone barricades, towards the chief trench, with its flank supports. More than the dark—a soughing beneficent wind muffled this crouching, rustling movement so perfectly that the Armenians managed to get some little way past the trenches, on either side, and so have them surrounded. One thing was especially in their favour. The Turkish trench garrison, one of the strong companies left behind, had stupidly lit a couple of acetylene lamps, which sharply lit up the soldiers' heads and plunged all else in densest obscurity. Here, too, endlessly calm and set on their object, the Armenians sighted the garishly outlined targets. It was as though nobody breathed. Not a limb stirred. Every life seemed buried in the shaftless coal mine of this night.

The Kaimakam and the major were standing together at the place where, between ruined walls, the track first leaves the lower slope, to continue upwards through the wide conduit of the ilex gully. They were on the lower edge of the camp. Some men with lanterns and torches stood in a group to light them.

The yüs-bashi glanced at his ultra-modern wristwatch, with its luminous face. "Plenty of time. I'm going to have them waked an hour before sunrise."

The Kaimakam seemed concerned for the major's physical well-being. "Hadn't you better sleep in your quarters, Yüs-Bashi? You've a heavy day behind you. Bed will be good for you."

"No! No! I don't want any sleep."

The Kaimakam said good-night, went a few paces followed by his lantern-bearers, came uphill again. "Don't misunderstand my question, Major. But can I be quite certain that nothing unexpected will happen in the next few hours?"

The major, who had not come down to meet him, but stayed where he was, with his head half averted, repressed an angry reply. This civilian meddling was insufferable. He growled: "Naturally I've taken all the usual precautionary measures. Although my poor fellows need their rest, I've set very strong outpost lines. You needn't have bothered to come back, Kaimakam. I've also made up my mind to send out patrols to beat up the country all round our camp."

And as the major said, so it was done. But these patrols, exhausted corporals and men, went stumbling half asleep past the rigid Armenians, whose eyes shone feline out of the leaves. They were soon back to report to the officer in charge that the country all round was clear and in order.

BAGRADIAN threw down the flaming matchstick with which he had just lit a cigarette. Little flames darted along the grass, and set fire to a tuft of it. Iskuhi, still at his side, trod out the greedy flames.

"How dry everything is," she said.

It was this match that inspired the impossible thought in Bagradian. He stood there, lost in it. The notion was double-edged. It might do his own people as much damage as the enemy. Bagradian held out his handkerchief, to test the direction of this strong wind. West wind, sea wind, driving branches downwards towards the valley. Neither he alone nor the Council could make the decision. Ter Haigasun, the supreme head of the people, must say yes or no.

After an instant's silence Ter Haigasun said: "Yes."

Meanwhile the whole armed force had vacated the altar square and Town Enclosure. Both storming-parties breathlessly awaited the signal. Between the surrounded trench and the rock barricades the whole mass of reservist villagers. But that was not all. It must unfortunately be recorded that Stephan,

473

long since escaped from his mother, was very elated and pleased with life, in spite of imminent catastrophe. This creeping and whispering in the dark, this close proximity of so many bodies on the alert, these sudden gleamings and extinguishings of hooded lanterns, and a hundred more such adventurous uncertainties, keyed up young Stephan's excited nerves to the sensation of having been transported into the midst of a pleasantly thrilling world of dreams. All this was enhanced by the very unusual order just issued to the cohort of youth, and their pride in being allowed, as the last defence of the encampment, to share in plans still not divulged. It is therefore easily understood that, even from their present exhausted state, Stephan and his comrades had been roused to irrepressible excitement.

This strange order concerned the stores of oil. All the oil casks on the Damlayik, including those of the Bagradian family, were being rolled without further explanation on to the altar square, as well as whatever branches, sticks, and cudgels could be got together from the sites of the extinguished fires. First Stephan and his comrades, then the women, and all children of nine and over, were ordered from these piles of brushwood to pick out as strong and thick a brand as possible. The teachers and Samuel Avakian, who supervised this distribution, had all they could do to prevent noisy quarrelling. They struck with their fists and whispered: "Quiet, you silly devils." It was the same round the oil casks. The branches must be dipped to the middle in the thick liquid, and twirled round in it. There were at least three thousand of them. It took a very long time. The people were still crowding round the casks when a whistle-blast gave the signal and the hidden attackers opened fire on those trenches taken by the Turks. Its sounds were echoed at once a hundredfold by hollow din out of the gully, interspersed with drowsy long-drawn cries of alarm, so hoarse as hardly to be human.

Gabriel Bagradian stood on a little summit of rock entanglements. During the sudden, crackling tumult of battle, a sound entirely different from that of any previous attack, the leader, in a kind of dream-like expectancy, had said nothing at all to the people waiting behind. Several minutes went by. The crackle of small arms sounded thinner. Gabriel could scarcely realize that the first act of his surprise-attack had succeeded so quickly. But Chaush Nurhan was already giving the signal —a few vehement flourishes with his lantern. The trench was back in the hands of its first defenders, who overflowed it, rushing down the slope after the enemy. Some of the Turkish infantrymen got lost in the dark and fell into the hands of pursuing decads. Some of them ran, stumbled, leapt downhill, towards the shouting gully and were bayoneted, or felled by their pursuers' rifle-butts. Gabriel sent Avakian back to the reserve. "Ready and forwards." He waited till the whispering shoals approached the rock on which he stood; then he ran forward and headed them. Slowly they crowded onwards down the slopes, through the thick shrubs, past the dead, down towards the din-filled grove.

There it was like a hunt in full cry. The bravest among the officers, onbashis, and soldiers might try, again and again, to come up close to the brushwood conflagrations around their camp and douse them—they extinguished their own lives. The ring of komitaji rifles drove them back into the centre of the gully. Officers yelled contradictory orders. No one heard. Infantrymen and saptiehs ran about bellowing to find their rifles; yet, when they had them, they found them impossible to use. Every shot they fired might have killed a brother or a comrade. Many flung away their arms, which impeded them, as they ran or leapt through this thorny pathlessness. The very inner life of Musa Dagh seemed to do its share in this gruesome destruction. The revengeful thicket grew rankly luxuriant. Trees became treacherously taller. Whipping twigs and plants twined like lashes round the sons of the Prophet and brought them low. Those who fell, lay on. The indiffer-

475

ence to death which marks their race descended on them. They buried their heads in thorny nests. The yüs-bashi, by dint of his own cool energy and many strokes with the flat of his sword, had collected round him a little knot of utterly flabbergasted infantrymen. When sergeants, corporals, and old soldiers grew aware of their officer, in a feeble glimmer of dying campfire, they joined the rest. The major, thrusting his sword towards the heights, yelled: "Forward!" and: "After me!" With an odd excitement he noticed his phosphorescent wristwatch. Suddenly he remembered the words which he had said last night to the Kaimakam: "I don't want to go on living if tomorrow that Armenian camp still isn't cleared." And truly at that moment, he did not want to live. "After me!" he yelled again and again. He could feel the whole force of his own will-power, able by its single strength to transfer this rout into a break-through. His example had its effect. And even their longing to be out of this inferno of a wood urged the soldiers on. They roused themselves to leave the cover of their own apathy and, bellowing, followed their commander. They came scatheless to the upper end of the gully. With thudding hearts, utterly exhausted, having lost all consciousness of reality, they went on, lurching up the mountainside, into the light of lanterns, the fire of decads, which received them. They were flung back like so many lifeless dummies. The yüs-bashi did not at first perceive his wound. He felt very surprised at suddenly finding himself so isolated. Then his right arm felt heavy. To feel the blood and pain pleased, almost delighted, him. His shame, his loss, had become far less. He dragged himself back, with his eyes shut. . . . "Fall down somewhere," he hoped, "and forget it all."

When, from recaptured trenches the din of battle retreated downhill, that was the sign for the Town Enclosure. A tongue of fire shot up. One of the oil-soaked torches began to crackle into flame and, within a few minutes, had passed it on to a thousand more. Most of the villagers had followed the example of Haik, Stephan, and the other boys, who then, with a torch in each hand, moved off in a long, extended line. Earth had never seen such a torchlight procession. Each one who bore these spluttering candles at arm's length was startled by this incomprehensible clarity, which seemed to light up his very soul. The light was not, as single flames are, an intensification of endless dark, but, like the light that fires a whole people, it shot a glorious breach in the dark of space. The long, far-flung lines and groups moved onwards slowly, ceremoniously, as if they were on their way, not to a battlefield, but to a place of prayer.

Down in the villages, in Yoghonoluk, Bitias, in Habibli, Azir, in Wakef and Kheder Beg—yes, in the north, in Kebussiye even, the honey village, not one new tenant could get to sleep. When the wild clatter of the surprise attack reached these villages, their armed inhabitants snatched up rifles, set out, and now garrisoned the low ridges, though they did not venture too near the gully. But their women stood in the gardens, or on the roofs, avidly and fearfully listening to the furious yelping of the bullets. Suddenly, at one in the morning, they saw the sun come up behind the Damlayik. Its black ridge stood sharply outlined; behind it spread a tender, rosy glow. This unearthly vision, this never-to-be-equalled sign and wonder, worked on these credulous women's spirits like the trump of doom. And when, a short while later, the whole edge of the mountain burst into flames, it was too late for natural explanations. Jesus Christ, the prophet of unbelievers, had let the sun of His might rise behind the mountain; the Armenian jinn of Musa Dagh, in alliance with Peter, Paul, Thomas, and the other worthies of the Evangel, were protecting this people. The ancient myth of supernatural powers behind the Armenians had found its completest confirmation. More than these simple women became imbued with it. The mullahs, too, watching the miracle from the round gallery encircling the church dome of Yoghonoluk, took flight out of

477

this mosque that had been the Church of Ever-Increasing Angelic Powers.

Less magically, but far more terribly, were those Turkish soldiers still on the mountain-slope appalled by this irresistible line of lights. It gave the impression of vastly superior numbers, sprung up out of nowhere, as though the whole Armeian nation, all the convoys dispersed over Turkey, were gathered at that time and in this place to avenge, with torches and balls of fire, on a mere handful of their oppressors, the monstrous wrongs they had endured. The little garrisons of Turks before each defence-sector raced back down the slopes. No officer could manage to hold them. All still alive in the cursed region of the ilex gully had fought their way, heedless now of bullets, through thickets, and come out on the lower slopes. The Armenians were not numerous enough to box-barrage the mouth of the gully. A few valiant officers and men, missing their bashi from among them, had once again forced their way out, to snatch up that wounded, unconscious officer just as he was about to be taken prisoner. They carried him down to Villa Bagradian headquarters. During which painful journey he came to himself. He knew now that everything was over, that the Christians had scattered his whole power, that for him there could be no return, no reinstatement. From the depths of his soul he cursed the bullet which had only shattered his right arm, and not done its business more efficiently. He only longed to faint again. That prayer, however, remained unanswered. The clearest, coldest perception of precisely what this would mean worked on and on in him.

The procession of fire had no more enemies left to face. Slowly the long lines of incendiaries approached the ilex gully, the woods around it. About half-way down the slope Ter Haigasun halted the long lines and gave the order (passed from one to the other) to cast flaming stumps into the undergrowth. The flames sank down in the smoking shrubs. From all sides, in a few minutes, there came an endless crackling, as of pistol shots, as if the whole Damlayik would explode. Flames shot high in many places. The woods were on fire. Woe, if the wind should veer in the next few hours. The Town Enclosure, which lay nearest the edge of the mountain, would have been the prey of flying sparks and tongues of flame, borne down the wind. It was fortunate that Gabriel Bagradian should have cleared a glacis before these sectors. This forest fire ate its way so quickly, so instantaneously, up the sun-dried flanks of the Damlayik, that what stood here in a roaring mass of flame looked like no earthly fire, no earthly fuel. There was scarcely time for komitajis and decads lower down the slope to rescue the spoils of the attack; more than two hundred Mauser rifles, abundant munitions, two field-kitchens, five sumpter mules with their fodder, bivvy sheets, rugs, lanterns, and much besides.

WHEN the real sun came up, a stony sleep lay on the Damlayik. The fighters slept where they had fallen. Only a very few had had the strength to drag back into cover. The boys slept, coiled in heaps on the bare earth. Women in the Town Enclosure had sunk down lifeless on their mats, unwashed, tousled, without a thought of their tiny children who whimpered hungrily. Bagradian slept; so did all the leaders. Even Ter Haigasun had not the strength to complete his Mass of thanksgiving. Towards the end of it, overcome with exhaustion, he had sunk down like a drunkard before the altar. The mukhtars slept, without having picked the day's sheep for killing. The butchers slept and the milkmaids. No one went to work. No fires were lit in the kitchen square, nor water carried from the wellsprings. No one could attend to the many wounded still lying in agony in their trenches, nor to those who in the course of hours had managed to drag their way to the hospital-hut. All who are summarized so impersonally in that one colourless word "wounded" lay strewn about in horrible reality: faces without eyes or noses, chins mushed into bleeding pulp, bodies smashed by dum-dum bullets, yelping men with stomach wounds, dying of thirst. Only death, not Bedros Hekim, could help these wretched. But till he bent compassionately over them, they too were helped through dragging hours by some narcotic, feverish half-sleep.

Down in the valley slept the infantry, the saptiehs, chettehs, as many as came clear of the slaughter. The officers slept in their rooms at Villa Bagradian. Yesterday's first victim, the Kolagasi from Aleppo, had been taken back in an ambulance to Antakiya many hours ago. Now another wounded officer had replaced him on Stephan's bed. The Kaimakam, too, in Juliette's bedroom, had been overcome by sleep. He had been engaged on a report to the Wali of Aleppo when it became no longer possible to sit upright.

But his mind and conscience worked in the depths of sleep with more cruel truth than ever in the meshes of consciousness. He had just encountered the worst set-back in his career. Yet every failure contains the elements of grace in it, since failure, with a grin, reveals the ineptitude of human estimates of worth. This Kaimakam, this high official, this member of Ittihad, he of whom the party thought so highly, this Osmanli, steeped to the marrow in all the pride of his warrior race—what had he just been forced to experience? That the weak were strong, the strong in reality impotent. Yes, impotent even in those heroic activities which made the weak appear so despicable. But in his sleep the Kaimakam's perceptions went deeper still. So far he had never one instant doubted that Enver Pasha and Talaat Bey were in the right; more, that against the Armenian millet they had acted with consummate statecraft. Yet now furious doubts of Enver Pasha and Talaat Bey reared up within the Kaimakam, since failure is also the stern parent of truth. Had men the right to work out skilful plans by which this or that people should be stamped out? Was there even, as he had asserted a thousand times there was, enough practical basis for such a scheme? Who is to say

480

that one people is worse or better than another? Certainly men cannot say it. And God, that day on the Damlayik, had given a most unmistakable answer. The Kaimakam saw himself placed in certain contingencies which made him feel not a little concerned for his skin. He was sending in a written resignation to His Excellency the Wali of Aleppo, destroying, of his own free will, the whole structure of his career. He offered the Armenians, in the person of Gabriel Bagradian, wrapped in a bathgown, freedom and friendship. In the central committee of Ittihad he urged the immediate recall of all Armenian convoys and passed a compensatory tax to indemnify them. But the Kaimakam's soul only haunted such ethical summits in deepest sleep. The thinner wore the fabric of his slumbers, the nearer he returned to everyday consciousness, the more utterly did his surface mind reject any such foolhardy suggestions. At last, in far smoother, more peaceful repose, he hit on a convenient way out. Why not simply omit any superfluous, uneasy report to the central authorities? The Kaimakam slept on till midday.

The dead slept, the Christians and the Mussulmans, strewn here and there in the bushes above the ilex gully, the thickets of the northern side. The licking flames of this huge mountain conflagration crept nearer with overweening playfulness. These flames seemed to rouse the sleepers; they raised them up from underneath, so that the dead, with a stiff jerk of terror, sat bolt upright, before their bodies started crackling, and they sank back into the cleansing holocaust. From hour to hour the fire increased, spreading far and wide across the Damlayik, to north and south. It halted only at the barren stone slopes of that incline which falls sheer from the South Bastion, while a rocky inlet protected the North Saddle against it. The green slopes of this mountain blessed with many springs, this miracle of the Syrian coast, triumphed once again with flaming banners, till at last nothing was left to devour but a strong obstacle field of glowing embers. Thus did Musa Dagh armour with

481

fire, with red-glittering debris, her weary sons, lost in their gulf of sleep, unaware that for some time now they need fear no more from their pursuers. None realized how a friendly wind kept danger helpfully off the Town Enclosure, driving sparks and tongues of flame downhill. The villagers and the decads slumbered on till late afternoon—only then did the Council meet to resolve that every imperilled point must be fully cleared of wood and undergrowth. This was a new and exhausting task.

They had slept all through the day, all but one of them. She in her tent sat on the bed and never moved. But it served her little to make herself feel smaller and smaller within the buzzing cocoon of her inexpressible alienation, her inescapable guilt.

4

Sato's Ways

Although the lucky wind still kept its direction, this forest, or rather mountain fire had a deeply depressing effect on all these people. There was no more darkness. The red-eyed nights squinted and blinked at them. Crazy shadows leapt up to dance. Unendurable heat, at midnight just as at midday, without a breath of cooling air. Biting fumes strangled every breath. They ate into the membrane of nose and throat. A unique and curious form of cold in the head spread savagely through the whole camp, making tempers more and more uncertain.

Instead of pride in victory, jubilant thanksgiving, the first signs of demoralization began to show themselves, those signs of a sinister inward process, which threatened to destroy all discipline in sudden bursts of wild ill-temper. This, in great measure, was the cause of the ugly brawl with Sarkis Kilikian, which took place, unluckily, on the very night of this day's repose. It is one of the reasons why neither Ter Haigasun nor Gabriel would let themselves be influenced by the fact that now, by God's mercy, a long truce might be expected. To be sure, this mad idea of setting a mountain on fire had, with the vast new loot of rifles, much improved the prospects of the defence. Even the hope that the Turks might renounce all further attempts was by no means so insane as it had been. And yet—only the breast of the Damlayik was in flames; its hips, the stone slopes above Suedia and the North Saddle, were as liable as ever to be attacked. In no circumstances therefore must the stringent routine of the trenches be relaxed. The leaders' authority must be kept as implacable as ever.

It was just as essential to re-establish the morale of the Town Enclosure. What Ter Haigasun called "normality" must be re-affirmed against all destructive evil powers. So that, when it met that night, on the evening of the twenty-fourth, the Council of Leaders, to avoid any mass excitement, decided against ceremonial burial of the dead.

In this late afternoon, detachments, sent to bring in the dead, came back with sixty-seven corpses, out of the hundred and thirteen missing men. There were also a good many mortally wounded, who died that night, since they had no proper medical aid. Dr. Bedros Altouni had much to say to the Council on this point. In his sharp little voice, which certainly was not suited to solemn talk of corpses, he informed them that, since the summer heat was unbearably intensified by this fire, it was essential to bury at once. Every minute's delay was a danger to the whole camp. He, Dr. Altouni, disliked having to say such a thing to mourners, but by now, surely, everyone's nose must have convinced him of the absolute necessity for funerals. Not a second to lose! Let every bereaved family set to work and dig its grave at the place appointed. The Council, in Altouni's opinion, would have been far wiser to leave all the dead to the mercy of the great fire. It had not been able to make up its mind to do so.

So the dead were wound into their shrouds, for the comfort of orphans and widows. A heap of his own earth was granted to each.

This order did not, as some had feared it might, cause much ill-feeling among the people. They feared too much for their own health. And corruption had already become apparent. Three hours after midnight, it was finished. This exhausting work had stifled pain. Only a very few surviving relatives remained standing by the graves, with the candles they had been keeping so long. Reflections from the mountain fire swallowed these poor corpses into their shadow. Nunik and her colleagues had stayed in the valley. They dared no longer leave their holes, since the Turks had caught two old beggarmen in the maize-fields, and thrashed them to death.

On the following morning, August 25, two very important public events were due. The first concerned the selection of volunteers for Alexandretta and Aleppo. Swimmers and runners must leave at once. The other event was the trial of Sarkis Kilikian. The case stood as follows: There could be no doubt that Sarkis had to answer to the people for heavy losses, and yet Gabriel had not thought of calling him to account for criminal negligence, since in all previous attacks the Russian had behaved with the coolest gallantry. Gabriel had a certain insight into human incalculabilities, and knew besides that it is impossible to reconstruct with any reality a determined instant in any battle. But other leaders disagreed. There had been a brawl on the altar square. Sarkis had stood surrounded by an angry mob of his comrades. . . . Let him explain— answer their questions—justify himself! He neither justified nor explained. He stood, with his bleached face, his incurious eyes, his mouth shut before the frenzied accusations that spattered around him. This silence may not have been as insolent, malicious, self-assertive, as it seemed. Perhaps Kilikian himself could not understand his sudden negligence, and disdained all such easy excuses as "fatigue" or "misunderstood intentions." He was shoved this way and that; fists kept dancing under his nose. Probably any jury would have found that he acted in self-defence, had it not been that he struck the first blow. . . . And had not that blow been so terrible!

For a while, apathetic as ever, he let them shove and push him as they pleased, seemed indeed scarcely to notice what was happening. Suddenly, then, he snatched his bony fist out of a pocket, and dashed it in his youngest tormentor's face, so horribly that the lad collapsed, streaming with blood from a broken nose, having lost an eye. It was done with incredible

485

swiftness. For a half-second Kilikian had straightened up out of his slouch, his eyes had seemed to flare—then they went as dead again as ever. No one would have thought him the aggressor, and, at first, luckily for him, most did not know how it had happened, and retreated a step. But when, with shouts of anger, they closed in on him, it would have gone very badly with him indeed, had the police of the Town Enclosure not saved him by taking him in charge.

During the morning of his trial by the Council, he admitted indifferently that it was he who had struck the first blow; that he had known just what its effects would be. Nor would he attempt to prove self-defence. He seemed too detached, too bored, too slack, to speak. The circumstances in which he must live or die may have been, to such a man as Kilikian, a matter of more profound indifference than other people could ever realize. Gabriel heard the case without saying a word. He neither defended nor accused. The exasperated people demanded punishment.

Ter Haigasun, having heard the last witness, sighed: "What am I to do with you, Sarkis Kilikian? One only needs to look at you to see that you don't fit into any order established by God! I ought to have you turned out of camp."

He did not, but instead sentenced Kilikian to five days' imprisonment in irons, intensified by three days' fasting. This punishment was worse than it may appear. For a brawl, in which he had not really been the aggressor, Kilikian found himself degraded from his rank as a respected leader and thrust back into the criminal underworld. It was the harshest degradation. But no indication on his part suggested that he had any honour left to degrade. After the trial they bound him hand and foot with ropes and placed him in the lock-up which formed the third room of the government-hut. Now Kilikian looked as he had so many times in the course of his inexplicable life, in which punishment had come so swift on the heels of the vaguest misdoing, or of none at all. To these

penalties also he submitted, with indifferent eyes, as to yet
another, familiar, inescapable incident, in a life so subtly
contrived. But this prison-house differed at least from all
other, similar, institutions in his wide experience by the fact
that he had to share it with so august a spirit as Krikor. Right
and left, two kennels, with plank beds, as alike as cells. The
one, a shameful lock-up; the other—the universe entire.

GABRIEL could feel in every nerve the advent of an incalculable
event which would nullify the results of their recent victory.
He had therefore urgently insisted that the messages must go
out that day. Something must be made to happen quickly.
And, even if the attempt proved vain, it would at least engender hope and expectation. The volunteers assembled, as
the leaders had ordained, on the altar square. The whole
camp was astir, since this choice of messengers, freely come to
offer their lives, concerned the whole people.

Gabriel came from a short inspection of the decads. In view
of the dangerous slackness and irritation, which threatened to
spread all through the camp, he had ordered fresh drill and
fighting-exercises for that same afternoon. His whole first
defence had now been adequately armed with the two hundred freshly captured Mauser rifles. The best of his reserve
had been sent to fill in the gaps, left by the recent, heavy fighting. Already Chaush Nurhan's jerky bugle-calls could be
heard, drilling these recruits. Iskuhi had come half-way to
meet Gabriel. Since the first, sudden emotion sprang up between them, she had sought him out with the frankness of a
little girl. They were walking side by side, without a word, the
rest of the way to the altar square. Gabriel, whenever he had
her with him, would be filled with the same strange, restful
security. Always it was the same sensation, that what he felt for
her was the most intimate thing he had ever known. Her
warmth, as of a clear fire, seemed to reach far back, beyond
any frontiers of conscious memory. Nor did she leave his side

in the place of assembly, although she was the only woman, standing here without excuse in the midst of these debating men. Had she no fear that they all might comment on her behaviour? That even her brother, Aram, might suspect?

About thirty young men waited as volunteers for the Council of Leaders to choose among them. Five of them were still in their teens. The eldest among the cohort of youth had been allowed to give in their names. Gabriel, with a start of fear and anger, saw his son Stephan beside Haik. After a brief consultation with the other members of the Council, Ter Haigasun announced his choice. It was he who always gave the final decision in any estimate of the people's capacities and strength.

The swimmers had been easy enough to pick out. In Wakef, the southernmost village, on the edge of the Orontes plain, and hence nearly on the coast, there were two famous divers and swimmers, one nineteen, the other twenty. Ter Haigasun handed out the leather belt, with its appeal, sewn up inside, to the possible commander of any English, American, French, Russian, or Italian gunboat. The swimmers were to set out that night after sunset, over the North Saddle, having spent their last afternoon with their families.

The question of the runners to Aleppo took a few minutes longer to settle. They had decided that only one young man should go out on that dangerous mission. But no Armenian adult, Pastor Aram Tomasian was convinced, would have the same chance as would a boy of getting to Aleppo alive. Armenian boys wore almost the same dress as Turkish. A boy would have twice the chance of slipping through. The justice of this was admitted. And one name occurred to them all: "Haik." That dour, resolute lad, with the fabulous swiftness, his body as hard as polished stone, was the right messenger, or nobody. Not another peasant in all that countryside had Haik's sightless adaptability to the earth over which he moved, that omniscient eye, as of some great bird, that setter's nose,

488

the ears of a rat, the slippery nimbleness of an otter. If anyone here could succeed in evading death on the road to Aleppo, it must be Haik, and only he.

But, when Ter Haigasun gave out Haik's name from the altar steps, there was a most unseemly protest from Stephan. Gabriel's face twitched with anger as he saw his son come impudently forth from his place in the line of volunteers and plant himself there under his nose. Never before had the crude precocity, the mental and physical untidiness, of his own son seemed so apparent.

Stephan bared his teeth, like an angry dog. "Why only Haik? I want to go to Aleppo, too, Father."

His mutinous voice shrilled out over the whole square. Such words, from a son to a father, were never heard among Armenians. Not even the unusual circumstance, this zeal in their defence, could excuse them.

Ter Haigasun looked up impatiently. "Tell your son to behave himself, Gabriel Bagradian."

Pastor Aram Tomasian, used at Zeitun to dealing with difficult boys, tried to pacify Stephan. "The Council of Leaders has decided that only one is to go to Aleppo. A big, intelligent fellow like you ought to know what the Council's orders mean to all of us. Absolute obedience—isn't that it?"

But the conqueror of Turkish howitzers was not to be fobbed off with legalities. Having no distinct notion of this duty, nor of how unfit he was to perform it, he could only feel he was being snubbed, set below the great competitor. The presence of so many assembled worthies did not deter in the least his touchy impudence. He still glared boldly at his father. "Haik's only about three months older than me! He can't even speak French. Mr. Jackson won't understand him. And what Haik can do, I can——"

Now Gabriel lost his temper. He came one quick step nearer Stephan. "Do? You can't do anything. You're a soft European —that's all you are. A spoilt city child! Why, they'd snap you

489

up like a blind cat. Get out! Go to your mother. If you stay another minute, I'll——"

Such harshness was most unwise. It hit Stephan's most tender susceptibilities. He was being publicly kicked down from the place he had found it so hard to win. Now all his deeds had been done in vain: his fruit-stealing, his heroic capture of the guns, which had nearly earned him the title "Lion." In a flash Stephan grasped the fact that no deed is done once and for all, that we always have to begin again at the beginning. He became suddenly very quiet. His sunburnt skin flushed darker than ever. He stared at Iskuhi with big eyes as though he were only just discovering her. It seemed to him that she answered his look severely, in a frigid stare. Iskuhi as the hostile witness of his defeat! It was too much! Suddenly Stephan began to bellow, not like an almost grown-up hero, a crack shot, the captor of enemy artillery, but like an unjustly punished schoolboy. Yet these childish sobs evoked no sympathy in the others, rather a kind of unholy glee. It was a fairly complex state of mind that invaded not only Stephan's comrades, but the grown-ups, and concerned not only the son but, for some obscure reason, Gabriel. "You don't belong here." It needed only a pretext for that sensation, and there it was! Stephan at once suppressed his howling grief. But its brief display had been quite enough to arouse contempt, not only among his comrades, but in all the other groups of the cohort of youth. Only Haik stood lost in serious thought. All this had nothing to do with him. . . .

Now the only thing left to Stephan was to slink away, with suspiciously heaving shoulders. Gabriel watched him go, in silence. He had ceased to be angry, having remembered the little boy in Montreux—Stephan, charmingly dressed, his head bent sideways over the notepaper, forming big, round letters. He thought: "Stephan's getting a big boy. He'll be fourteen in November." . . . And this "he'll be" . . . "in November" . . . what idiotically Utopian thought was this? A chill presentiment stole over him. . . . Something that can no longer be prevented! . . . Gabriel went to Three-Tent Square for another talk with his son.

But neither Stephan nor Juliette were to be found there. In the sheikh's tent he changed his underclothes. As he did so, he missed one of the coins given him by the Agha Rifaat Bereket. It was the gold coin, with the head in sharp half-relief of the great Armenian king, Aschod Bagrathuni. He turned out the pockets of every suit. The gold coin was nowhere to be found.

It was most unlucky that this new incursion of Turks and Arabs should have put an end to Sato's vagrant double life. And her status among the children was lower than ever. Ter Haigasun, a few days ago, in spite of all the teachers' recalcitrance, had insisted that school must be properly kept. But now, not even that martinet, Hrand Oskanian, could enforce discipline in class if Sato were sitting among the rest. "Stinker! Stinker!" chirruped the whole merciless flock, the instant that vagrant entered the school enclosure. Even up here, in this last refuge of the persecuted, Sato, that lousy orphan, supplied these children with a welcome pretext for feeling distinguished and nobly born. During one such class, taken by Iskuhi, their derision howled so loud that even the teacher, without concealing her own repugnance, drove the hated Sato out of class. "Go away, Sato; and don't let me see you again, ever!"

So far, in stolid indifference, ignorant alike of honour and shame, Sato had managed to hold her own. But now that her admired Iskuhi, her küchük hanum, had joined the enemy, thrusting her forth, Sato had to obey. In her short European frock with the butterfly sleeves, which, ragged and caked with mud, made her look grotesque, she went trailing off. But only as far as the nearest bush, under which she lay down quietly, like a jackal watching a caravan-camp with ravenous eyes.

491

Sato was not so poor as she seemed. She, too, had a world. For instance, she could understand the animals which strayed across her vagrant way. Iskuhi and all the others would no doubt have said without hesitation that Sato was a cruel little beast to them. Everything about her suggested it. But—on the contrary! This bastard waif vented none of her spite on beasts, which she handled with a protective, whispering sympathy. Her insensitive hands would pick up a hedgehog, and she would whisper so long that at last the ball began to unroll, the pointed snout darted forth, the alert, businesslike eyes of a small bazaar-shopkeeper sized her up quickly. Sato, who could only speak to grown-ups as though she had a gag in her mouth, was expert in every shade of bird-cry. Such gifts, which would no doubt have commanded respect, she diligently hid, fearing they might do her social damage. And, as with beasts, so could she talk with the old madwomen, crouching in their holes round the Yoghonoluk churchyard. Sato never noticed that these breathless, disconnected gabblers used their tongues in any way differently from other, sanely gossiping matrons. In any case it was very pleasant to take one's share in such friendly talks, which made no fatiguing demands on one's choice of expression. The smaller beasts, these female half-wits, and sometimes even a blind beggar, formed a realm apart, in which Sato found herself respected, as every human being must needs feel respected, in order to live. Though, to be sure, with Nunik, Wartuk, Manushak, Sato was still a respectful underling.

But now this communion was shattered. It was dull. There was really no point in straying about within camp bounds. Little by little, this idle restlessness got diverted into channels of its own: spying on grown-ups. With the sharp instinct which mocked all that unintelligible book-learning, Sato perceived whatever was animal in these grown-ups, all that might have escaped their control, all cravings, their mad self-seekings. Of those emotions of whose dangerous existence in the world she was scarcely consciously aware, she could nonetheless hear the grass grow. The avid little spy, like a magnet, drew all that was not in order towards herself.

It is therefore not in the least surprising that Sato soon realized how things were between Gonzague and Juliette. The pricking, ominous sense of a major catastrophe invaded her. All disinherited people know this delightful prescience of catastrophe, the delicious hope that the world is about to crash, which forms one of the strongest impulses both to minor scandals and revolution. Sato kept close behind these two. Next to Bagradian himself, Juliette and Monsieur Gonzague were the most resplendent apparitions in Sato's world. She did not hate them in the least, in the way bad servants hate their masters. She felt a primitive's curiosity for something which seems almost superhuman.

She had soon spied out their hiding-place, the secret place of myrtle and rhododendron. With delight trickling down her spine, she forced her muzzle slowly through the thicket. Her glittering eyes were avid for this sight sent by the gods. The august, resplendent hanum, from France, the giantess, the ever-perfumed . . . now her hair hung in wisps over a face which advanced its almost lifeless surfaces, its wide, dolorous mouth, towards the steady features of the man who, with drooping lids, still seemed acutely on the alert as, first, he savoured the gift, before drawing it close. Sato, shaking with excitement, watched the play of Gonzague's long, narrow hands, like the knowing hands of a blind tar-player, come and go across the hanum's white shoulders, and cup her breasts.

Sato saw all there was to see. Also, what was not to be seen. The schoolteachers had given her up long ago. Not even "twice two's four," not even the alphabet, could be hammered into this creature's stuttering mind, occupied with its own aimless images. Sato could make no progress, since her over-developed sense of tracks and clues engulfed all mental possibilities. Hidden among myrtle and rhododendron, she could taste the delicious ardours of this interlude, and yet, all the time, be well aware how lost and bewildered Juliette was, how resolved, Gonzague. Her mind was nothing, her instinct everything. Sato would have had no reason to curtail the raptures of the *voyeuse*, had there not been a certain complication, wounding to her most vulnerable emotion. Another couple had not long escaped her setter's nose. They offered no spectacle, had found no refuge for their desire. These two did not steal away together into labyrinthine bushes along the coast; they preferred the barren knolls and empty reaches of the high plateau. It was hard to spy them out without being seen. But Sato, luckily, or unluckily, had the faculty for making herself invisible. At this she was even better than Master Haik. This second pair kept drawing her off the scent of her sweet absorbing espionage on the first. True, she scarcely managed to see them kiss. But, between Iskuhi and Gabriel, this never-kissing passion burned far deeper, into Sato's heart, than all the embraces between Gonzague and Juliette. These two had only to touch hands, and glance briefly at each other; then, as though shattered, avert their eyes, to assure Sato that their union was far more maddeningly complete than all the close proximity of the others. Above all the communion between Iskuhi and Gabriel was detestable, and made Sato sad.

Her memory had imagined a golden age. Had the orphanage teacher in Zeitun not always been good and gentle with Sato? Had she not often expressly said: "My Sato"? Had she not even allowed her Sato to squat on the grass at her feet, and pat these feet, and stroke them even? Who but the effendi was to blame for the fact that this happy relationship, this mutual esteem, and their caresses, had ended harshly? Who but the effendi was responsible for the fact that, when Iskuhi's Sato approached her, with a loving and open heart, she only snapped: "Go away, Sato, and don't let me see you again, ever"? Sadly the waif sought out a place to think in. But planning and reflection were never her strong points. Either she evoked transient images, or would start at the sudden flash of a perception. These perceptions and images had no need at all of the assistance of anything like conscious understanding. They worked blindly towards an aim: just as they could join up threads, let them drop, take them up again, and so spread a web of planned revenge, of which their mistress was almost unaware.

JULIETTE was on her way to Gabriel.

Gabriel was on his way to Juliette.

They met between Three-Tent Square and the North Saddle.

"I was on my way to look for you, Gabriel," she said. He said the same. That absent-minded "running to seed," which for so long had infected the "foreigner" had done its work. Where was Juliette's "sparkling step"? She walked like someone who has been sent somewhere on an errand. As indeed she had. Gonzague had sent her to tell the truth at last, and announce her wishes, since this was the time of separation. . . . "Am I getting short-sighted," she thought, "I see so badly?" She was surprised at the November twilight of this hot midsummer afternoon. Was it the swaths of smoke all over the Damlayik? Was it that other, confusing vapour, thickening daily, which seemed to have clouded her mind? She was surprised that, as she stood facing Gabriel, Gonzague should have become so absurdly unreal. She was surprised that this Gonzague let her encumber him. Everything seemed so far away, and so surprising. . . . Her garter had slipped, and her stocking was falling below her knee, a sensation she loathed. Yet she never stirred. "I've suddenly lost the strength even to bend," so it crossed her mind. "And yet, this evening, I shall have to climb down all those rocks, to Suedia."

The husband and wife began a really remarkable conversation, which ended in nothing. Juliette started it: "I blame myself terribly for not having been with you these last few days. You've had a great deal to go through, and you've done magnificently. And you're always in danger. Oh, *mon ami,* I've behaved disgracefully to you!"

Such an admission, a few weeks previously, would have moved him. Now his reply was almost formal: "I, too, have you on my conscience, Juliette. I ought to have been considering you more. But, believe me, especially recently, I just haven't been able to manage it."

Very true, although he gave it a double meaning. His truth should have given her courage to speak hers. She only hastened to agree: "Of course you haven't. I can quite see you've had very different things to think of, Gabriel."

He proceeded along this dangerous road: "I've naturally always known, and been very glad to think, you weren't entirely deserted."

This got them both to the point in their tepid dialogue, at which it was as though they had both shammed dead, although the vistas around them were free on all sides. It could have been Juliette's chance, had she seized it quickly enough. She could have spoken her mind:

"I'm a stranger here, Gabriel. The Armenian fate has been stronger than our marriage. Now I've got my very last chance of avoiding that fate. You yourself have suggested I should, a hundred times, and were always making plans to save me. I'd hoped I had the strength to hold out to the end. I haven't. I can't ever have, since this fight isn't my fight. Let me go."

None of these very simple and natural words passed Juliette's lips. Filled as she still was with the vain delusion that she, in their marriage, had been the donor, the superior, she was sure that, if she said it, he would break down. Could she suppose that perhaps he might only answer her good-naturedly:

"I quite understand, *chérie.* Even if I must perish because of it, I still haven't the right to hold you back. I'll do all that's

496

still in my power to help you. I'll even let Stephan go, for your sake, since I know how much you want to save him."

Frankness, in these few minutes, might have made as clean a job of it as that, had not things been really too complex to disentangle. Juliette knew as little of Gabriel as he of her. Nor did she know if she really was in love with Gonzague. Gabriel was equally unaware how much he was in love with Iskuhi, and of what kind of love it was that linked them. Juliette's religious and bourgeois past made her recoil at the thought of sinful happiness. She had many reasons for mistrusting the transparently impenetrable Gonzague, and not least that he was three years younger than she. In Paris there would have been a traditional form for all of this. On these fantastic reaches of the Damlayik the sense of sin oppressed her heavily.

But these were only minor complications. For several minutes at a time she was perfectly ready to nurse the thought that she would fly the mountain with Gonzague and await the steamer in the little house beside the alcohol factory. Then, in the very next instant, it all seemed too fantastically impossible. It would need the most resolute courage to risk so final an adventure, even if she avoided death in the process. Would it not really perhaps be better to wait and see what happened on Musa Dagh than to find oneself suddenly left in Beirut? The thought of the long climb in the night, of the dangerous business of crossing the Turkish plain of the Orontes, of the sea-voyage among the casks of alcohol, the threat of submarines—the prospect of all these dangers and fatigues entangled itself into what, in the circumstances, was a merely ridiculous feeling of propriety: *"Ça ne se fait pas."*

But what was all that, compared to the pain of losing Stephan? She kept clear of him nowadays. She had ceased to make sure he washed and was properly fed. She no longer, even at night, according to the sacred custom of mothers, came to his bed in the sheikh tent, to see that he was settling down properly. All these omissions, these neglects, were summed up in a prudishly guilty feeling, which weighed most heavily on her for Stephan's sake. And, laden with all this guilt, she had come to Gabriel, to be frank, to say good-bye.

They eyed one another, the wife and husband. The husband, as it seemed to him, saw a face which looked at once elderly and dissipated. He fancied he caught a shimmer of white upon the temples. All the less, therefore, could he understand these sparkling eyes, this mouth, which seemed to be so much bigger, with chapped, swollen-looking lips. "She's going to bits, with this life," he thought. "What else could one expect?" And though, not so very long before, he had had the impulse to tell Juliette about Iskuhi, he abandoned it now. What good would it be? How many days have we still before us?

The wife saw a lined, distorted face, every feature different, framed in one of the round, untidy beards which she couldn't abide. Each time she saw it, she had to ask herself: "Can this oriental bandit really be Gabriel?" And yet the voice was still Gabriel's voice. Might she not surely have been faithful to it?

Thoughts buzzed through her head: "I'll stay, I'll go, stay, go." But her heart was moaning: "Oh, if it were only all over!"

Their talk swerved neatly off its dangerous track. Gabriel described the favourable prospects of the near future. Most probably they'd a long rest to look forward to. He emphatically repeated Altouni's very good advice: "Lie in bed and read, read, read." A swath of smoke from the great blaze drifted heavily across her vision. They had to pass through resinous, sharply fragrant wood-smoke.

Gabriel stopped. "How one smells the resin! This fire's been a good thing, for several reasons. Even the smoke. It disinfects. Unluckily we've already twenty people lying in the isolation-wood, infected by that blasted deserter from Aleppo."

He could manage to talk of nothing but public events. So he was too indifferent to feel anything of what her silence had tried to express to him! . . . "I'm going, I'm going, I'm going"—it kept sounding in her ears, like a roaring seashell. Then, in the very midst of a smoke-swath, Juliette turned pale and lurched, so that he was forced to hold her up. His touch, a thousand times familiar, pulsed through her body like an anguish. She could just manage to turn her face to him.

"Forgive me, Gabriel, but I think I'm . . . I'm going to be ill. . . . Or I am already."

Gonzague Maris was already waiting for Juliette, at the place on "the Riviera" which they had arranged. He waited, observant and self-possessed, smoking his half-cigarette to the very end. Being an extremely thrifty soul, he had still twenty-five whole cigarettes. He never threw away the ends, but saved them up to use in his pipe. Like most people reared in shabby gentility, in a series of cheap little boarding-schools, people with definite pretensions, who have never owned more than two suits at a time, Gonzague was a fanatic for economy. He used what he had to the last thread, the last bite or drop.

When Juliette came towards him, in a curious, lurching stride, he sprang to his feet. His gallantry towards his mistress had not changed in the least since she became one, and the clear attentiveness in his eyes, under the closely slanting eyebrows, still remained, even though a glint of firm criticism intensified it.

He at once noticed her defeat. "So again you've not spoken."

She sat down beside him without answering. What could be the matter with her eyes? Everything, even the closest surroundings, was being tossed on a noiseless storm, or veiled in rain. As the fog cleared, palms began growing out of the sea. Camels, with disapproving, averted faces, walked in procession across the waves. Never before had the surf below beaten so noisily or seemed so near. You simply couldn't hear yourself speak. And Gonzague's voice came from far away.

"All this is no good, Juliette. You've had days to do it in! The steamer won't wait for us, and the manager won't help us a second time. We must leave tonight. Do try and be reasonable."

She hid her breasts with her clenched fists, and leaned forward, as though to master a stubborn pain. "Why are you so cold with me, Gonzague? Why won't you ever look at me? Do look!"

He did just the opposite: he looked far out to sea, to let her feel he was annoyed. "I always used to imagine, Juliette, that you were a plucky, determined kind of woman, and not sentimental."

"I? I'm not what I was. I'm already dead. Leave me here. Go by yourself."

She expected a protest. But he said nothing. These silences, which renounced her so easily, were more than Juliette could bear. She whispered, in a very subdued voice: "I'll come with you—tonight."

Only then did he lightly caress her knee. "You must pull yourself together, Juliette, and get over all these scruples and hindrances. You've got to cut loose. It's the only way. Let's get it all clear, and not deceive ourselves. There's nothing else to be done. You'll have, somehow, to tell Bagradian. I'm not suggesting in the least that you'll need to make a general confession. This is our chance, and we shan't get another. That explains the whole thing. You can't just—vanish. Quite apart from the fact that it would be so incredibly mean, how would you live? Have you thought of that?"

And so, with all the steadiness and certainty of his voice and manner, he kept persuading her that Bagradian would be bound to make what arrangements he could, to assure her immediate well-being. There was not a hint of vulgar adventure in what he said, though he frankly reckoned on Gabriel's, and perhaps Stephan's, imminent death. (As Juliette saw, he was perfectly willing, if she insisted, even to encumber himself with

Stephan, though it would certainly complicate their escape.)

As he came to the end, he grew impatient, since their last, precious hours were now on the wane. And how many times had he not had it all to say before? Had Juliette been able to think, she would have had to admit the justice of every word. But, for the last few days, the most casually heard, or thought, words or expressions had clung like leeches to her brain, obstinately refusing to be pulled off. Now she heard the words: "How would you live?" The loud "live" blared in her mind incessantly, as the needle on a worn-out phonograph record sticks and repeats the same maddening notes. Incredible mists kept rising out of the earth, as though they had been sitting beside a swamp. She herself had become a worn-out phonograph record, and the needle stuck.

"How should I live, how should I live, how should I live, in Beirut, Beirut. . . . What for?"

Gonzague took pity on Juliette, whom, as he imagined, her conscience tormented. He wished to help her. "You shouldn't take it so badly, Juliette. Only think what it means! You'll be saved! If you like, I'll be with you—but not if you don't."

As he was saying that, she could see the sick boy from Aleppo, the deserter, over whose mangy, red-spotted chest she had bent a few days ago in such an exalted wave of despairing emotion. She must really go and see her mother. Maman was living in a hotel. A long corridor, with hundreds and hundreds of doors. And Juliette had forgotten the number. . . .

Now Gonzague's voice was tender and charming. It was doing her good. "I shall be with you."

"Will you? Are you with me now, Gonzague?"

Amiably, he became matter-of-fact. "Now, listen carefully, Juliette. Tonight I shall wait about for you here. You must be ready by about ten. If you need me sooner—let's suppose Bagradian wants to speak to me—send someone along. I'll help you. You can easily bring your big suitcase. I shall manage to carry it. . . . Be careful how you choose your things. But you'll be able to buy anything in Beirut."

She had really been doing her best to understand him. She began repeating it, like a child: "Tonight, about ten. . . . I'm to bring a suitcase. . . . I can get anything in Beirut. . . . And you? . . . How long will you stay with me?"

These vague mutterings, at so decisive an hour, exhausted his patience. "Juliette, I loathe the words 'for ever' and 'always' . . ."

She gazed devoutly at him. Her cheeks flamed. Her half-open lips pouted out. It was as though she had just opened the right door. Gonzague was sitting at the piano, strumming the *matchiche* he had played the night the saptiehs came. He'd said to her: "There are only moments."

It filled her with profound hilarity. "No, don't say 'always' or 'for ever.' Just think of the moment!"

Now she could understand, with an indescribable super-clarity, that there are only moments—that, tonight, the steamer, the suitcase, Beirut, her decision, had really not the slightest meaning for her; that impenetrable solitude was awaiting her, into which neither Gonzague nor Gabriel would find a way, a solitude full to the brim of home-comings, in which it would all be settled and cancelled out. The happiness of it came rushing in on her, filled her with strength. The amazed Gonzague had no longer a shattered woman to deal with, a woman driven into a corner—he had the *châtelaine* of Yoghonoluk, more beautiful than ever before. He took Juliette in his arms. It might have been for the first time.

Her head toppled strangely from shoulder to shoulder. But he paid no heed. And the meaningless words which she seemed to mutter in dreamy esctasy passed his ears unheard.

UNTIL the men came where she could look at them, Sato still did not know what was going to happen. She was on guard a few yards away from the adultery, but was feeling too empty,

too morose, to crawl in through the bushes and view the pair.
. . . Yes, if she could only have worked it up a bit! How
pleased old Nunik would have been with her; what thanks
and pence she might have earned! But Sato was caught! Sato
was no longer allowed to take profitable messages to the valley, and bring them back from the valley to the mountain.
All the more corrosive, therefore, her jealousy, the one cogent
emotion she still possessed. To get Iskuhi away from the
effendi! To pay the effendi back! She lay, with her knees
drawn up under her, staring at the smoky sky.

Then came the men. They came on slowly. Sato perceived
the Leaders of the Council—Ter Haigasun, Bagradian Effendi,
Pastor Aram. After these, the mukhtar Thomas Kebussyan,
Teacher Oskanian, and some village elders of Bitias. The elect
had only just finished a short, but very serious conversation,
and seemed depressed. They had every reason to be so. The
food situation was very grave. The herds had not diminished
"according to plan," but by the unknown law of some wild
progression of ever-diminishing returns. Rations were being
cut down every day. Yet that did nothing to check the dwin-
dling supplies, for which bad fodder seemed responsible. In
spite of all Tomasian's efforts, his fishery made no headway.
And this new, contagious fever in camp was beginning to
take alarming forms. Only yesterday four fever patients in
the isolation-wood had died. Dr. Bedros Altouni could scarcely
move on his weak little legs, crooked with age. Over fifty
wounded lay in and around the hospital-hut, and at least as
many in the log huts, all without drugs or proper bandages,
left to their own devices, or God's. Worst of all, this growing
exasperation, an unforeseen result of victory, which had taken
such a hold on all men. No doubt the cruel heat of the burning
countryside, this itching cold in the head produced by pine-
smoke, the over-fatigue, had all contributed—and the eternal
meat. Its deepest cause was the fact that life up here was in-
supportable. In the last few days, apart from the Kilikian in-

cident, there had been many brawls, and knives had been used.

Today all this impelled the leaders to give more attention than they had to the seacoast side of the Damlayik. Up on the "Dish Terrace," which stood far removed from all these happenings, there fluttered the great signal: "Christians in Need." Two scouts of the cohort of youth were continually on duty beneath it, scanning the sea for passing ships. It seemed likely that some undependable lad had overlooked one ship, or several, since not even a fishing-smack had been sighted, and this in August, at a time when, as a rule, the Bay of Suedia is covered with this kind of petty craft. Did God really intend to let the sea become a desert, merely to take from his Christians on Musa Dagh what slight hope they still had of survival? The Council had decided to strengthen this look-out, and recondition it. The watch on the "Dish Terrace" was henceforth to be kept by grown-up men. At some jutting point, farther south, a second would have to be established. The leaders had come out today to settle on the likeliest promontory.

At first the soft crop-grass of this highland muffled, even for Sato, the men's approach. When she twisted round on her side, they were fairly near her. She was up in a flash—something sprang to life inside her—and waving wild arms in their direction. At first they paid no attention. Whenever Sato made her presence known, in any group, it was the same. All eyes would seem not to have noticed her, all heads would be slightly averted, in a kind of severe, shamefaced discomfort. Sato was an "untouchable"; all who encountered her felt the same, though, to the Christian, all God's creatures are, by birthright, equal in His eyes. Today these serious men, full of care and business, saw, without having seen, this waving half-wit, and went calmly on. But the last of them, Thomas Kebussyan, suddenly stopped and turned round to Sato. Her conquest had so definite an effect on all the others that they, too, halted, as by a spell, and eyed the sign-giver. So much at least, her strength had achieved. The leaders stood as if bewitched, eyeing the repulsive little creature, since now she pranced about like an evil thing under unclean influence. Sato's eyes sparkled, her spindle-legs, beneath that once so maidenly little frock, twitched with excitement. The contorted mouth, such a mouth as only deaf-mutes usually show, was doing its best to jabber words; the waving arms kept pointing again and again, into the myrtle bushes. The suggestion given by all this gradually disarmed these men's resistance. They came almost up to Sato, and Ter Haigasun grumpily inquired what she was doing here and what she had to tell them. Her sallow gipsy-face grimaced and twitched. She blinked in tortured desperation as though it were impossible to reply. All the more eagerly she continued her urgent pointings, towards the sea. The men looked at one another. The same questioning thought was in all their minds: "A warship?" Little as they cared to have to do with this misbegotten ape of sinfulness, everyone on the Damlayik was aware what a keen pair of eyes Sato had. Perhaps those repulsive lynx-eyes had discovered a tiny thread of smoke, away on the farthest horizon, where no one else could have managed to see it.

Ter Haigasun gave her a little prod with his stick and told her curtly: "Go on! Lead the way! Show us what you've seen."

She went hopping proudly, started to run, stopped from time to time to beckon the men. Sometimes she put her hand to her mouth, imploring them not to talk, or even make a noise with their feet. And now, full of a strange excitement, they all obeyed her and held their tongues. All walked cautiously, on tiptoe, suddenly fallen under the influence of this little guide and their own deep curiosity. On, past box and arbutus, they came into the mass of thick-leaved shrubbery which, in a broad belt, forms the frontier of the coastside of Musa Dagh. There were many gaps through the dark, cool undergrowth, corridors, intertwining lanes. A stream ran in and out among it, to fall in cascading swaths over the cliff.

Here and there a pine or rock wrapped round in creeper sprang up out of the confusion. Nothing else suggested a wild mountain summit. In many cases it almost gave the impression of an artificial maze in some southern garden. On his many strategic excursions in those early, preparatory weeks, Gabriel had scarcely visited this paradisial belt of the Damlayik. Yet, cool and refreshing as it was, he followed now, at the tail of the group, with a sensation of heavy discomfort, on legs which seemed to resist every step he took.

Sato had picked so artful a way through the undergrowth that the men all suddenly found they had emerged on the clearing most favoured by these lovers, a little open space fronting the sea. Sheer amazement, like a blade of descending lightning, bewildered Juliette and Gonzague, who had fancied themselves more hidden than ever before. One of those eternal uneasy moments began, whose acute discomfort anyone who has had, as a victim, to experience it will remember to the end of his days, with only the burning wish he had not been there. Gabriel arrived in the nick of time to see Maris spring up and swiftly put his clothes in order. Juliette sat on motionless, with bare shoulders and hanging hair, her fingers, right and left, digging into the ground. She stared like a blind woman at Gabriel, seeing him, not with her eyes, but with all her senses. The event passed in complete silence. Gonzague, who had retreated a few steps, followed these proceedings with the victorious and precise smile of a fencer. The strangers, Ter Haigasun first of all, having turned their backs on the woman, stood rigidly staring, as though they were finding it impossible to bear their own shame another instant. The Armenian people, between the Caucasus and Lebanon, are implacably chaste. Hot-blooded people are always inclined towards severity, only the tepid are easy-going. These people esteemed no sacrament so highly as marriage, and looked down disdainfully on the lax polygamy of Islam. The men who now turned their backs in shame would probably not have hindered Bagradian, had he ended the business once and for all with a revolver bullet. Certainly Ter Haigasun would not, nor the Pastor, though he had lived three years in Switzerland. But Hrand Oskanian stood leaning forwards over his rifle, not moving an inch. It looked as though that gipsy-faced teacher were about to thrust the barrel into his mouth, as though his eyes only sought the right minute to pull the trigger. He had good reason for this symbolic posture. The madonna of his only prayer had degraded herself for ever in his eyes.

The unapproachable backs of the men were expectant. But nothing happened. No shot from Bagradian's army-revolver. When, after a while, they could turn their faces back to this reality, they saw Gabriel take the cowering woman's hands and help her up. Juliette tried to walk, but her feet refused. Bagradian supported her under the elbows and led her away between the myrtle bushes, as one leads a child.

The men, with unforgiving eyes, watched this incredible proceeding. Ter Haigasun growled a few short words at them and, slowly, each by himself, they left the place. Sato scampered around the priest, as though that supreme head of the people owed her a reward for her useful services.

Not another look was cast at the stranger, who stayed on alone.

No people can manage to live without admiration, and just as little without having something to hate. Hate had long been brewing in the encampment. All it had needed had been an object. Hate against the Turks and government? That was too vast a target to appease; it was only there as space or time are ever-present in human consciousness, as the first condition of all living. Hate against one's immediate neighbours? Whom could such daily jars and bickerings satisfy? Not even the chiding women themselves. So that the flood which, in spite of bloody slaughter and many rigorous privations, had collected in the hearts of these people had to find another channel for itself.

Before the men vacated that painful ground, Ter Haigasun had shouted a few curt words to them. These words contained the admonition to keep what had happened a close secret, since the priest all too clearly foresaw the repulsive sequel, should this scandal reach the ears of the Town Enclosure. Ter Haigasun had warned men, but not husbands. Mukhtar Thomas Kebussyan, in spite of all his inflated dignity in public, was both uxorious and henpecked. An organic necessity to supply his stronger-minded mate with as much gossip as he could find for her was so compelling a part of his nature that he ran straight home, to lay this jewel, with many imploring admonitions to silence, at his wife's feet. Madame Kebussyan had scarcely heard him out before, with a scarlet face, she flung a shawl about her shoulders and ran forth from the mayoral residence to seek the huts of the other mukhtars' wives, those ladies "of the best society" whom she, within certain limits, patronized.

Sato took charge of all the rest. It was her threefold triumph. First, she had done something to the effendi, from which he would not easily recover. Second, having stirred this hell-broth, she had now a perfect right to regard herself as the highly considered and useful member of a virtuous, order-loving community. Third, she had first-hand information. It was the least deceptive of her assets.

She began by enticing a few over-developed schoolgirls with her racy suggestions of "knowing a thing or two." They were joined by others. Sato was a born journalist. She eked out her "story" to its limits, and soon had the never-experienced thrill of finding herself the centre of attraction. Finally, in the coarsest words, used to form the ugliest pictures, Stephan heard of his mother's shame. At first he could not realize what it all meant. Maman stood far too high for Sato and her mob even

508

to mean her when they used her name. Maman (as recently Iskuhi) was a veiled goddess in Stephan's eyes. Stephan grew more and more bewildered as the rabble surrounded him with its gibes and Sato kept jabbering out fresh nuances. Suddenly she had lost her throaty stutter and was talking with the fluency of an expert. Just as failure benefits the soul, so is success good for the body, so that these few minutes of heightened consciousness triumphed over Sato's speech defect. Stephan's big eyes widened. He had nothing to say.

But then it needed only a second for him to throw himself straight on the spy and punch her head, so hard that blood streamed out of her mouth and nose. He had done her no serious harm; for a while her nose bled. But Sato, like all primitives, could get far more woefully panicked by blood, was more terrified of it, than the developed. She let out long, terrific howls, as though she were at least being massacred. And now the tables were turned. A cynic would have rejoiced to see it. Sato, the jackal, the waif on the edge, the "stinker," the pariah cur, had in a trice become the object of universal sympathy and concern. Hypocritical voices were being raised: "He's hit a girl." And so a long suppressed dislike of foreigners, of stuck-up outsiders, could be released. That kingly rank, silently accorded the Bagradians for a few hours after every repelled attack, was forgotten. All that remained was the deeper hatred of people who "don't belong." The boys, with murderous, twisted faces, all set upon Stephan, and there followed a fight that was half a chase, from the Town Enclosure to the altar square. Hagop kept pluckily with Stephan. He hopped in, with wide, angry leaps, again and again, between his friend and his pursuers. Haik was not there to prove how he really felt towards the Bagradians. That Aleppo runner was spending his last hours on the Damlayik, alone with his mother, the widow Shushik. Stephan, though he fled before the pack, was stronger and bigger than most. When two of them hung on his arms, he shook them off, as a

509

bear shakes hounds. A terrible pain seemed about to choke him. . . . "I can never go home again."

This children's brawl only ended what the mukhtars' wives, headed by Madame Kebussyan, had begun. Before sundown the communes knew everything. They "knew everything" with a number of embellishments, designed to make them more virtuously indignant. It was the hour at which, for some atmospheric reason, smoke from the mountain fire rose thickest. In black layers it swathed the Town Enclosure, giving forth a sharp, acrid resin, exacerbating throats and mucous membranes. Sneezings, snufflings, hawkings, became an agony. . . . What? Was it really possible? Could these people, just two days clear of death, these people, almost certain, sooner or later, not to escape death's clutches a second time—could they, in their present desperate plight, be so concerned with a piece of scandal, and one in which the protagonists were foreigners?

There is only one answer. They were *foreigners*. Gabriel's leadership had changed everything. The queen, the king's consort in a monarchy, is, as a foreigner, doubly blamed and called to account with double severity. Juliette had not sinned merely against her husband, but against the whole of his race.

So that, two days after the fiercest of these battles, which had bereaved over a hundred families, groups of outraged people stood round the altar, as though, for them, huddled on their raft in waves of blood, there could be no more important topic than the shame and scandal of the Bagradians. It was not the very old women who set the tone of this indignation, nor the very young. It was women of the matronly sort, between the ages of thirty-five and fifty-five, who in the East seem far older than they are, and whose sole remaining pleasure in life is the contemplation of others' joys and the acrid discussion of them. The young women kept fairly quiet and listened reflectively to the virtuous scoldings of these elect.

These young women were all very pale. It was on them that life on the Damlayik weighed heaviest. Their faces, under caps or head-shawls, were drawn and anæmic-looking. Armenian women, even of the lowest class, are in their youth frail and delicate-limbed. Grief, anxiety, and privations had moulded these youngest women on the Damlayik to an even more fragile, delicate form. They nodded sagely to the matrons' chiding disapprobation, and only now and again put in a word. At the moment they could not feel too indignant at the thought of an adulterous woman, knowing as they did what was in store for them and all their sisters. Not merely death, but death by rape, unless one had the extraordinary good luck to be bought by a rich Turk from the saptiehs, for his harem, where one would have to reckon on being slowly vexed to death, with petty persecutions, by the elder women.

Madame Kebussyan had control of every thread of out-raged wrath. Now was her time to pay back the *châtelaine* of Yoghonoluk (who, to be sure, had shown her unfailing kindness) for all those unpleasant inferiority-feelings experi-enced at evening receptions. And more—here was the mayoress's chance to re-establish her position as social leader of the district. She was far too wide-awake a lady to restrict her observations to adultery merely. Soon there was an even better, more nutritious subject for virtuous censure. She, the mayor's wife, had seen the inside of that luxurious sheikh-pavilion, to which she had been invited again and again till she was sick of going there. More than once, with amazed, scandalized eyes, had she watched "that woman" display her stores; her cupboards, her trunks, her chests, bursting with supplies. Nobody had any idea! Vast stores of rice, coffee, raisin-cakes, tinned meat, smoked herrings, sardines. All the choicest European dainties, heaped up in that tent. No end to the sweets, the jams, the chocolate, the crystallized fruits and —above all—the loaves of finest flour, biscuits, and cakes!

It cannot be denied that such graphic descriptions had their effect on the nagging bellies of the males. Otherwise they directed their indignation against Gonzague Maris, rather than Juliette. Against the *foreigner,* the interloper. It would not have needed very much more to make a few young men get together and agree to shoot the adulterer out of hand.

When Ter Haigasun came into the square, Madame Kebussyan planted herself in front of him. "Priest, you'll have to punish them!"

He tried to thrust her aside. "Mind your own business."

But, more and more shameless, she blocked his way. "This *is* my business, Priest. Haven't I got two married daughters, and two daughters-in-law? You know that yourself! And aren't men's eyes greedier than the eyes of wild dogs? And women's hearts slyer still? Everyone lives and sleeps in a heap, in the huts. How can mothers be expected to keep order and discipline, with such an example?"

Ter Haigasun gave her a little shove. "I haven't the time to hear your foolishness. Get out of my way!"

But this queen of tongue-waggers, usually a most ordinary little woman, with nimble mouse-eyes, drew herself up, red as a peony with Juliette's sin, to her full, solemn height. "And the sin, Priest? Christ the Saviour has kept death away from us so far. He's fought on our side—He and the Holy Mother of God. But now they've been insulted, by mortal sin. Won't they deliver us over to the Turks, unless there's penance done?"

Madame Kebussyan felt she had played her trump card. She glanced round victoriously. Her husband, Thomas, kept close beside the priest; his little squinting eyes saw all and nobody. He seemed anxious not to be drawn into all the fuss. Ter Haigasun did not answer the malicious woman directly, but the crowd, which was pressing in on all sides:

"Yes, it's true. Christ Saviour has preserved us, so far. And do you know how? By working the miracle, when we needed one, of sending us Gabriel Bagradian, a gallant officer, who knows and understands war. Otherwise we'd have been finished long ago. Those still alive have his brain and courage to thank. You'd better think of that, and of nothing else."

A FEW leaders had collected in Ter Haigasun's hut. This was a private and very difficult case. Half-conscious delicacy had caused them to assemble here, instead of in the government barrack. Since this was a purely moral difficulty, and Ter Haigasun was invested with supreme authority in such matters, they entrusted to him without further discussion the business of deciding what to do. He named two messengers, Krikor and Bedros Altouni. The one was to go to Gonzague Maris, who had lived in his house, and whom he had, so to speak, brought to Yoghonoluk, the other—the doctor—to Gabriel, as his oldest friend, and the protégé of his family.

Krikor was still crippled with rheumatism. But his brief excitement at the christening had done him more good than any of the drugs he still possessed. In the last few days he had managed to move about more freely, though with very slow, hobbling steps. Ter Haigasun had him routed out of his kennel, and curtly explained to him his errand. He was to find this foreign guest of his at once. Two orderlies of the cohort of youth would do their best to help him discover the Greek. When he was found, Krikor must inform him plainly that it would be as much as his life was worth to come near the camp. He was to disappear as fast as possible. Krikor raised vehement objections. He was, he insisted, a chemist by earthly occupation, and not the porter of an inn—not a bouncer. Ter Haigasun gave only the laconic answer: "You brought him; now you must rid us of him."

So there was nothing else for it. Krikor, after many protests, set forth on his unpleasant errand. As he hobbled, bent over his stick, he rehearsed, in a series of tragic soliloquies, the most tactful words in which to discharge it. Bedros Hekim's task was a much easier one. He was to warn Gabriel of the over-excited state of the public mind, adding an elaborate request that Juliette Hanum should keep her tent for the present.

Whereas the others had listened silently to Ter Haigasun's instructions to Krikor and Bedros, one of the Council, as a rule obstinately taciturn, raised his voice in an excited speech. So far, the sombre Hrand Oskanian had been generally thought of as ridiculous. His malicious vanity had been tolerated because he was known as a competent schoolteacher. He revealed himself now as a fiery fanatic. Such a wild strength was in his words that they all stared at him in amazement. Oskanian urged dire vengeance on Gonzague. They must first take away the blackguard's American passport and teskeré, and then strip him. They must tie his hands and feet and get some plucky fellows to carry him down to the valley, that night, so that the Turks might mistake him for an Armenian and kill him by inches!

This crazy outburst was received in uncomfortable silence. But the teacher was not so easily put off. He began, in all seriousness, to give reasons why the punishment he suggested was strictly necessary.

Ter Haigasun heard his prolix utterances, not, as he usually did, with half-shut eyes, but with eyes fast closed. His hands took frosty refuge in his sleeves, always a clear sign of his displeasure. "Well, Teacher, is that all?"

"No, it isn't. And I'm not going to stop till you see the truth as plainly as I do."

Ter Haigasun jerked his head uneasily, as though to scare away a humming gnat. "I think we've said all we need say in the matter."

Oskanian foamed. "Does the Council of Leaders intend to let this blackguard go with its blessing? So that tomorrow he may betray us to the Turks?"

Ter Haigasun stared up wearily at the leafy roof of the hut, which the wind rustled. "Even if he wants to betray us, what can he tell them?"

"What can he tell them? Everything! The position of the

514

Town Enclosure. The pasture grounds. The trenches. The bad state of our supplies. The infection——"

Ter Haigasun cut him short, wearily: "None of that will be any use to the Turks. Do you really imagine they're so stupid that they don't know all that by this time? . . . And besides, that young man isn't a traitor."

The others all agreed with the priest. But Hrand Oskanian shot out his fist, as though to hold an escaping victim. "I've made a suggestion," he cackled, "and I demand that you put it to the vote, in the usual way."

The priest's waxen face took on some colour. "Any gossiping fool can make suggestions. But it rests simply and solely with me to have them put to the vote. I don't put unnecessary suggestions to the vote. Remember that, Teacher! And there's nobody here who wouldn't consider this mad and debased. Let anyone who doesn't hold up his hand."

Not a hand moved. The priest nodded his dismissal. "So that's enough, once and for all. Do you understand me?"

The defeated teacher stood up in all the dwarfish pride of his inches. He pointed in the direction of the camp. "Our people out there takes a different view of it."

If Oskanian's behaviour had so far merely disgusted the priest, this demagogic remark made him suddenly furious. His eyes glinted to sudden flame. But he controlled himself. "The Council's duty is to guide popular feeling, not be led by it."

Hrand Oskanian nodded with all the resignation of a Cassandra. "You'll live to remember what I say."

Ter Haigasun's lids dropped over his eyes again. His voice was very quiet indeed. "I most urgently recommend you, Teacher Oskanian, not to warn us, but to warn yourself."

In this highly uneasy atmosphere they awaited the return of their messengers. It was a very long time before they came. The crippled chemist was back earlier than the doctor. He was half dead with pain, and had to lie down on Ter Haigasun's couch. He groaned, and only when the priest had made him take two deep swigs out of his raki flask, had he strength to report. Gonzague Maris had forestalled his mission and intended to leave the mountain that same night. He would only wait till a certain hour, to give his mistress her chance of escaping with him. The chemist had been most impressed by his former guest's gentlemanly attitude. Gonzague had behaved with distinction. He had not only made Krikor a present of every scrap of print he possessed, but assured him that, whenever he got the chance, he would do his best for the persecuted people on Musa Dagh. Ter Haigasun waved aside the sinner's promise, with a little gesture of dismissal. It was already dark by the time the other messenger returned. Bedros Altouni, too, looked exhausted as he came into the presbytery-hut. He, too, sank down, and began to rub his crooked little legs. The old man stared and at first said nothing, and Ter Haigasun had some trouble in making him speak. What he said was not reassuring, and he growled so low that his sharp little voice could scarcely be heard: "Poor woman——"

These words amazed the mukhtar Kebussyan. His bald, shiny head rocked to and fro as he thought of his censorious spouse: "What do you mean, poor woman? She's rich——"

Bedros Hekim's eyes scorched the mukhtar. "What do I mean? I mean that, for at least three days, she's been in high fever. I mean she's delirious. I mean she'll most probably die. I mean that she's been infected in the hospital-hut. I mean I'm sorry for her. . . . Damn it all, I mean—I mean it wasn't her fault; it was simply her illness. I mean . . ."

GABRIEL had half guided, half carried Juliette most of the way back to the hut. There, she fell over the bed, unconscious, with turned-up eyes. He tried to bring her round. All that was left of scent on her little dressing-table he sprinkled on her forehead and lips. He shook her, he chafed her temples. Her happy soul hid, far away from him, in the farthest regions of its oblivion. Fever had cooked for days in Juliette's blood. But, in these last hours, it must have shot up like a tropical plant. Her skin looked raw and inflamed. Like parched earth, it sucked in every drop of moisture. Her breath came quicker and quicker. This life seemed to be rushing towards its end.

Since he could not rouse her, Gabriel bent over Juliette and, hoping that, free of her clothes, she would come to herself, began to undress her. He tore her frock and her shift. He sat down on the end of the bed and took her feet upon his knee. They were heavy and swollen, so that he found it hard to free them of shoes and stockings. He never even noticed the absence in him of any of those painful emotions which, it is said, such an experience should engender. No pain of outraged susceptibilities, no distressing thought that these feverish limbs had been another man's pleasure an hour ago. Not even the frigid, hopeless consciousness that the troth of a lifetime had been broken. He felt benumbed, but only with pity for Juliette.

Gabriel felt no surprise. It seemed as though this fate were his own contriving. Incredible as that might sound, it was precisely Juliette's infidelity, followed by her collapse, which brought them together again after they had been so long apart. Only now that this pitiful body had strayed so far in its hostility that it gave itself to another man, did he, wistfully, remember. Full of the most anxious tenderness, his clumsy fingers tugged and nestled among these clothes, which resisted so stubbornly. He stood looking down at the white body while a hundred thoughts and sensibilities sprang up, half formed, to vanish in nothing.

What had happened? In the corner of the tent he noticed the bucket of spring water which always stood there. He dipped in handkerchiefs, to lay compresses. It was not easy. Her rigid body was hard to lift. Gabriel thought of calling one of her maids, who now, since their mistress had grown so vague, and had, moreover, almost ceased to reward them,

517

only came on duty now and then. But shame prevented him. He must be alone, now.

When the old doctor came, he found Bagradian staring vaguely at the unconscious Juliette. Bedros, at a first glance, doubted if she really were unconscious, or half pretending. His second showed him how feverish she was. The usual clinical picture of this epidemic. Sudden rise of temperature, and unconsciousness, which usually came at the end of a fairly long period of scarcely noticed ill-health. He lifted the patient upright. She showed immediate signs of vomiting and difficult breathing. It was obvious. But, when he examined the skin of her breast and loins, where usually there were most signs of infection, he found only three or four small red spots.

The doctor would have asked Gabriel to leave the tent and not come back. He said nothing. He had noticed Gabriel's eyes, shadowed and shrunk far back into their sockets. Nor did he deliver himself of his message, or dwell on the moral unrest of the Town Enclosure. On the other hand, he asked to be shown the medicine-chest, which Juliette had had prepared before their departure for the East. It was a big chest, but now three-quarters empty. Most of its contents she had sent to the hospital. The old man pressed a tiny flask into Gabriel's hand, who was still quite dazed. This, in case the pulse should begin to get faint. His wife would be in to-morrow and help to nurse. Gabriel wasn't to worry about Juliette's unconsciousness or delirium. It was the natural result of her temperature. And, as things were, it was a blessing. She had an even chance of life or death. The greatest danger would only come when she'd got the poison out of her system. Then the fever dropped with a sudden rush, and, in many cases, took the heart along with it. Bedros dipped a glass in a bucket, looked about for a spoon, and tried, with an expert hand, to force a few drops between Juliette's lips. This one practised gesture was quite enough to confound the lying self-mistrust which made him call himself "a shaky incompetent."

"You must keep on making her drink," he instructed Gabriel, "even if she doesn't come to herself."

Juliette's husband only nodded.

The doctor peered about, round the narrow tent. "Somebody'll have to stay up with her."

Since by now it was fairly dark, he lit the oil-lamp. Then he took Bagradian's hand. "Well, it'd be something, wouldn't it, if the Turks attacked again tonight?"

Gabriel did his best to smile. "We've set Musa Dagh on fire. They won't."

"No." Altouni's sharp little voice had a note in it of profound disappointment. "Pity!"

He went, bowed with years and inhuman labours, without one word of direct sympathy to this man whom he had helped bring into the world. All words, the good and the bad, had long seemed worn out and useless. Gabriel meant to go some of the way with him, to get fresh air. But he turned back at the curtain of the tent. Had the Turks chosen that minute to begin an attack on all his trenches, Gabriel could scarcely have managed to force himself to come out of the dark. He lay down, opposite Juliette's bed, on the divan. Never, he supposed, in all his life had he been tired until today. These three battles, with all their bloodshed, all the sleepless nights, the eternal backwards and forwards, from observation post to trench—each of these monstrous days on Musa Dagh hung on him, like a gnome with a clay face, stupidly heavier, heavier, every second. It was the tiredness which feels too tired to care about the horror of reality. A dull, unrefreshing sleep invited him to fall into its pit. Gabriel grew aware of Iskuhi's presence as he lay there, deep within this hollow. He tugged himself out of it with great difficulty, and sprang to his feet.

"You can't stay here, Iskuhi! Not one second. We can't see each other any more."

Her eyes were wide and angry. "And if you get ill—am I not to be ill, too?"

"But what about Hovsannah and the baby?"

She went to the bed and laid the palms of her hands on Juliette's shoulders. In this position she turned to Gabriel. "There! Now I can't go back into our tent. I can't touch Hovsannah again, or the baby either."

He tried to draw her away. "What will Aram Tomasian say to that? No! I can't answer to him for it, Iskuhi. Go along, Iskuhi, for your brother's sake."

She bent over the patient's unconscious face. It was becoming more restless every instant. "Why do you send me away? If it's to happen, it has already! My brother? None of that matters to me now."

He stole up, uncertainly, behind her. "You oughtn't to have done that, Iskuhi."

Her face seemed, almost avidly, to mock. "I? Who am I? You're the leader. If you get ill, that's the end of all of us."

She wiped the patient's lips with her handkerchief. "When we first came from Zeitun, Juliette was so kind, so wonderful to me. I have a duty towards her, if I'm able to do it. Can't you see that?"

He buried his lips in her hair. But she caught him to her, with all her strength. "It'll all soon be over. And I'm not going to lose you; I want to have been with you!"

It was the first open expression of Iskuhi's love. They held each other as close as though a corpse had lain beside them, who knew no more. But the corpse was not dead. She was breathing heavily. Sometimes a little moan forced its way out of her swollen throat. Was her voice seeking someone for ever lost to her? Iskuhi let go of Gabriel. But his hands seemed still to be crying out for her. They had begun to talk the briefest commonplaces, for the sake of the unconscious Juliette.

During the night Juliette had a spell of consciousness. She babbled wildly, and tried to sit up. What a long way she had had to come back! Even so, she had not managed to reach the Damlayik, only the flat in the Avenue Kléber. "Suzanne

. . . What is it? . . . Am I ill? . . . I'm ill. . . . I can't get up. . . . Why aren't you helping me?"

She was demanding a service of her maid. Gabriel and Iskuhi helped the invalid, still in her Parisian bedroom. Juliette shivered all over. She moaned: *"C'est bien*. . . . Now perhaps I shall get to sleep. . . . It's my angina again, Suzanne. . . . I don't think it'll be very much. . . . When my husband comes back, wake . . ."

This mention of the former Bagradian, living so secure in Juliette's world, had its shattering effect on the present one. He dipped another cloth in water and renewed the compress round Juliette's throat. He covered her up with the greatest care, whispering: "Yes, you must try to go to sleep, Juliette."

She answered something unintelligible. It sounded like the tiredest thanks, the most childish promise to be good, and get to sleep. Gabriel and Iskuhi sat in silence, hand in hand, very close, on the divan. But he never took his eyes off the patient. Life had developed a curious pattern. The unfaithful husband served his faithless wife—while he deceived her. Now Juliette seemed really asleep.

Time was up. Gonzague Maris had made up his mind to wait no longer. He shook himself. The past's the past! And yet it was not so easy as he had imagined to slip clear of this, the strangest week in his life. He was forced, in astonishment, to admit that a definite longing kept him back in it. Did he love Juliette more than he thought? Was it some guilty sensation clouding his freedom? In the last few days the woman had behaved unaccountably. Again and again her agony had stirred his pity, roused a wish to help and protect her. And besides, it had ended so disastrously. As he thought of that ghastly minute, he set his teeth, his controlled face became distorted. Must he, like any other seedy adventurer, submit to this end—this horrible breaking off? More than once he had left his hiding-place and come in the direction of Three-Tent Square—to see Bagradian, to fight for Juliette. And yet, each time, he had turned back. Not because he had been a coward, but rather, unaccountably uneasy. It was a feeling he had never experienced.

"I've ceased to belong here." Some strong, although invisible rampart had, since those devastating minutes, built itself up between Gonzague and the whole world of Musa Dagh. It was scarcely possible any longer to force a way through the aerial ramparts that protected the Armenian mountain. And Juliette was on the other side. Added to which came the exquisitely phrased suggestions of Apothecary Krikor, his former host. Krikor had not once directly alluded to the painful subject of his mission. He had congratulated Gonzague on having an American passport; expressed regret at the fact that every earthly sojourn should be, of necessity, so transient. Declared it to be the privilege of youth to keep on setting out with a light heart. Life does not become really depressing, till only one good-bye remains to be said. Maris had listened, with due attention, to the old gentleman's practical philosophy, having grasped the casually hinted fact that every further minute spent on the Damlayik contained its perils for Krikor's guest. And this consciousness of lurking danger intensified as the night wore on. The waning crescent moon stood directly over him. He had waited a full hour past the time arranged. He had lost Juliette. He went back again a few steps in the direction of the camp. He turned, his mind made up.

Perhaps it was better this way. Slowly, with lingering care, he drew on his gloves. This finicking gesture, in the midst of a dark, oriental wilderness, might have struck a superior watcher as somewhat grotesque. But Gonzague only put on his gloves to protect his hands as he climbed down. He buckled his small suitcase on his back. As his habit was, whenever he left a house, he drew out a pocket-comb and arranged his hair. The consciousness of having forgotten nothing, of not having left one unnoticed fragment of himself—his fresh and pleasant sensation of being "all right"—began to invade him, in spite of all. Slowly he sauntered on, among rhododendrons, myrtles, and wild magnolia, into the moonlight, as though not a wilderness lay before him, but a charming promenade. He remembered having said to Juliette: "I've got a good memory because I find it so easy to forget." And indeed, with every fresh step southwards, his memories became fainter, his heart more free. He was already quickening his pace, inquisitively turning towards a future which his passport and temperament made secure. The chalk cliffs along the coast, hollowed out with incredibly black shadows, glittered like sharp snow-fields in the moon. The surf beat dully below him. As his path became harder to negotiate, Gonzague's feet relished each step. He enjoyed the controlled play of his muscles. . . . How incomprehensible people were! All this pain and slaughter, merely because they refused to let the impartial light have power in them, preferring their stupid, untidy obscurity. So simple, so easily mastered—these black-and-white regions of the moon. To feel oneself nothing; in the void. It was simply that! Gonzague frowned. He felt some vague sympathy for Krikor. Krikor of Yoghonoluk, whom no one had ever quoted, or ever would quote! He had to clamber along the edge of a bare surface of rock, to surmount two crevices. Already he had in view the jutting ledge, behind which his descent would begin. He stopped to rest. The unfathomable gulf lay open beneath him. "Shall I get to Suedia? It's all the same. Lose my foothold? It's all the same. First you fall hard," it occurred to him, "then you fall soft." How far behind he had left Juliette, even now! . . . As Gonzague thrust his way on, among shrubs and bushes, four shots rang out in quick succession, and spattered past him. He threw himself down, pulled back the catch of his revolver. His heart thumped. Krikor's warning! . . . It was not, after all, a matter of such indifference whether or not he got to Suedia. The erring feet of avengers pattered by, but Gonzague jumped up, seized a big stone, and hurled it down, at a wide tangent. A noisy scurry below. The pursuers thought they had tracked their victim, and sent several bullets pinging after him, while Gonzague sped away from them, almost on wings, to the point where the mountain slopes to the village of Habaste.

He stopped, panting for breath. Better this way! These Armenian bullets had tidied out of his mind whatever sense of guilt still clouded it. He smiled. His eyes, under the short, slanting brows, moved alertly, scanning the way in front of him.

At this minute Juliette still hovered uneasily between half-consciousness and oblivion. Hadn't someone said: "Yes, sleep. Get to sleep, Juliette"? And whose voice? Well? Had they kept on saying it? Or just said it . . . ? "Yes, sleep. Get to sleep, Juliette."

She opened her eyes. In thirty seconds, she knew that this was the tent . . . and Gabriel and Iskuhi. It was very hard to move her tongue. Her gums, her mouth, had no sensation in them. These people were encroaching on her solitude. Why wouldn't they leave her in peace? She turned her head, heavy as a mountain, on one side. "What do you leave the lamp burning for? . . . Do put it out! . . . The oil's smelling—so unpleasant."

Juliette's eyes saw nothing. She had been looking for what wasn't there to find. But something really terrible became clear to her. She seemed to have got back all her strength, to be well again. She flung off the blanket. She swung both legs out of bed. She shrieked: "Stephan! Where's Stephan? Stephan's to come to me!"

Iskuhi and Gabriel forced Juliette, who struggled hard, back into bed. Gabriel stroked and pacified; he talked to her: "You're ill, Juliette. Stephan mustn't see you. It'd be dangerous for him. . . . Be reasonable."

But her whole life, hearing, comprehension, were centred in the screams which kept coming out of her: "Stephan? Stephan? Where?"

524

This super-conscious terror which shrieked in the patient communicated itself suddenly to Gabriel. He pulled back the canvas door and rushed out, into bright moonlight, to the sheikh-tent, where Stephan slept. It was empty. Bagradian struck a light. Dead lay the couch of Monsieur Gonzague. Its occupant had left it painfully tidy. It looked as smooth and undisturbed as though it had not been slept in for weeks. Not so Stephan's, over which there writhed a wild, disordered vitality. The sheets hung down. On the mattress stood the boy's open suitcase, out of which underclothes, suits, pairs of socks, welled, in many-coloured profusion. The food-chest in the corner had been forced open and plundered carelessly. Stephan's rucksack, acquired in Switzerland, had gone. And, of Gabriel's things, the thermos flask, which only yesterday he remembered having placed on that little table, was not to be found. Having looked again carefully, all round the tent, in search of clues, he went slowly out into the night again, stood outside, with his head bent slightly, and thought it out. What did it mean? "Probably up to some new idiotic trick, which those damned boys have hatched out among them." But everything hopeful and good in this explanation was contradicted by some sardonic, deeper knowledge. He was very calm, as he always was at decisive moments. In the servants' sleeping-quarters he found only Kristaphor, whom he roused. "Get up, Kristaphor, quick! We must wake Avakian. He may know something. Stephan's missing."

These words were said without excitement. The worried steward wondered how his master could be so calm, after all that had happened. They went towards the North Saddle to find Avakian. For a second Gabriel turned back indecisively to Juliette's tent. There, it was all quiet again. He went on so quickly that Kristaphor could scarcely keep beside him.

BOOK THREE

DISASTER, RESCUE, THE END

"To him that overcometh will I give to eat of the hidden manna, and will give him a white stone, and in the stone a new name written, which no man knoweth saving he that receiveth it."

REVELATION ii, 17

1

Interlude of the Gods

"HERE, my dear Dr. Lepsius, you have only a very small part of our dossier on the Armenian question."

And so this affable privy councillor laid his white, nobly veined hand on the dusty heap which towered so high above the desk that his equine, aristocratic features kept disappearing behind the pile. The tall windows of the noticeably empty little room stood open wide. A lazy breath of summer found its way in from the Foreign Office garden. Johannes Lepsius sat a little stiff on the visitor's chair, his hat on his knees. Scarcely more than a month had passed since his memorable talk with Enver Pasha, yet the pastor looked alarmingly changed. His hair seemed sparser, his beard looked greyer than it had, his nose seemed to have shrunk and become more pointed. His eyes no longer beamed. The dreamy distances had gone out of him, replaced by an expectant, mocking suspiciousness. Could the sickness in his blood have made ominous progress in these few weeks? Or was it the curse on all Armenians which, in secret affinity, was devouring him, the German? Was it the unheard-of amount of work he had managed to do in so short a time? A new campaign against death and the devil was fully organized. There was even money to hand; the most influential people had been won over. And now all that remained was to force an answer from the sphinx-like countenance of the State. The pastor's eyes, from behind their twinkling glasses, scornfully viewed these piles of documents. The affable privy councillor raised his eyebrows, not from surprise, but to let his gold-rimmed monocle fall.

"Believe me, not a day passes without some instructions going out from here to the Embassy in Constantinople. And there isn't an hour at which our ambassador isn't doing his best to influence Talaat and Enver in the dreadful Armenian business. In spite of the most pressing cares of state, the Chancellor himself is most emphatically behind us, in all this. You know him—a man like Marcus Aurelius. Oh, and by the by, Dr. Lepsius, Herr Bethmann-Hollweg asks me to apologize. It was unluckily quite impossible for him to see you today."

Lepsius leaned far back. Even his sonorous voice had become uneasier and sharper. "And what successes have our diplomats to report, Herr Geheimrat?"

The white marmoreal hand fished at documents. "Look here, all this is from Scheubner-Richter in Erzerum. All these are from Hoffmann in Alexandretta, and Rössler, the chief consul in Aleppo. Why, they do nothing else but send reports! They're working themselves to the bone for the Armenians. Heaven knows how many of these poor people Rössler alone hasn't managed to save. And what thanks does he get for all their humanity? The English press describes him as a bloodhound who stirred up the Turks to massacre in Marash. What's one to do?"

Lepsius was now doing his best to meet and fix the affable eyes which came and went behind paper clouds, like a somewhat capricious moon. "I know what I'd do, Herr Geheimrat. Rössler and the others are very fine men, I know them—Rössler especially is a very fine fellow indeed. But what can a poor, unimportant consul manage, if he isn't properly supported?"

"Really, Herr Pastor, I don't understand. Not properly supported? That's more than unjust."

A slight nervous gesture from Dr. Lepsius implied that this

530

matter was far too serious, and time too short, to beat about the official bush. "I know perfectly well, Herr Geheimrat, that all kinds of things are being attempted. I know all about the daily interventions and démarches of our ambassador. But we aren't dealing with statesmen who've grown up in the diplomatic game, we're dealing with people like Enver and Talaat. Every conceivable démarche is far too mild for people of that kind, and not even the unheard-of would be enough. The extermination of Armenians is the keystone of their whole national policy. I've convinced myself of that in a long talk with Enver Pasha himself. A whole barrage of German démarches would at best only be a nuisance to them—a strain on their hypocritical politeness."

The privy councillor folded his arms. His long face took on an expectant look. "And do you, Dr. Lepsius, know another method of intervening in the domestic policy of a friendly, an allied power?"

Johannes Lepsius looked as intently into his hat as though he had stored a sheet of notes in it. But, God! no notes would have been necessary. Ten thousand notes, day and night, kept singing in that poor tired mind, so that now he could scarcely ever sleep. He made an effort to collect himself, to broach the thing shortly and methodically.

"We ought above all to be perfectly clear as to what is happening, has already happened, in Turkey. An anti-Christian persecution of such dimensions that former persecutions under Nero or Diocletian bear no comparison. And more—the worst crime in recorded history so far—that in itself means something, I think you'll admit . . ."

Vague curiosity lit up the pale eyes of the privy councillor. He was silent as, with careful words, Lepsius felt his way, further and further. No doubt, since his defeat by Enver Pasha, he knew a little more than he had, about how to deal with politicians.

"We mustn't see the Armenians as some kind of half-savage,

531

eastern tribe. . . . They're educated, cultivated people, with a nervous sensibility which, frankly, I say one doesn't often find in Europe."

No twitch in the narrow, equine face gave any reason to suppose that perhaps, in its view, this classification of the Armenian "mercantile race" was slightly exaggerated.

And Dr. Lepsius continued. "This isn't by any means a mere matter of domestic policy, for the Turks to settle as they think fit. Not even the complete extermination of a tribe of pygmies can be considered as entirely a matter between exterminators and victims. All the less can we Germans afford to take refuge in deploring, or despairing, neutrality. Our enemies abroad hold us responsible."

The privy councillor pushed away the documents with a shove, as though he needed air. "It's part of the deepest tragedy of Germany's position as a combatant that we, no matter how clear our consciences may be, should be loaded with the blood-guilt of other races."

"Everything in this world is primarily a matter of morals, and only very much later one of politics."

The privy councillor nodded approbation. "Excellent, Herr Pastor! I quite agree. In every political decision one ought first to calculate the moral effect."

Lepsius sensed a victory. He must make the most of his advantage. "I'm not here as a mere powerless individual, Herr Geheimrat. I don't think it's too much to say that I'm here in the name of the whole of German Christendom, both Protestant and Catholic. I'm acting and speaking on behalf of such influential men as Harnack, Deissmann, Dibelius . . ."

The privy councillor glanced appreciatively, his eyes gave due weight to each of the names. But Johannes Lepsius was now in his old, and dangerous, full spate: "The German Christian refuses to look on any longer with folded arms at a crime against the whole of Christianity. Our consciences will no longer permit us to be its lukewarm accomplices. The empire's hope of victory is dependent on the satisfaction of German Christians. I personally am sick with shame that the enemy press should be printing columns on these Armenian deportations, whereas the German people gets fobbed off with Enver's lying communiqués and otherwise isn't told a word. Haven't we earned our right to know the truth about the fate of our co-religionists? This shameful state of affairs must be ended."

The privy councillor, rather astonished at the hortatory voice, set finger-tips together, remarking innocently: "But the censorship? The censors would never allow a thing like that! You really have no idea how involved such matters are, Herr Lepsius."

"Not to be tricked in the simplest right of the German people."

The privy councillor smiled indulgently. "What would be the results of such a press-campaign? A heavy strain both on German nerves and the Turkish alliance."

"That alliance must not be allowed to make us accomplices in the eyes of history. So we want our government to act as quickly as possible. Why don't you demand, with the uttermost insistence, in Istanbul, that a neutral commission of inquiry of Americans, Swiss, Dutch, and Scandinavians be admitted to Anatolia and Syria?"

"You know the Young Turkish potentates well enough yourself, Herr Lepsius, to be able to judge the sort of answer we should be likely to get to such a demand."

"Then Germany must use the most drastic methods."

"And those would be, in your opinion . . . ?"

"The threat to withdraw all support from Turkey, recall the German military mission, and retire German officers and troops from the fronts."

The repose, the winning affability, on the privy councillor's steady features, melted into genuine kindliness. "You know,

Herr Lepsius, you've been described to me just as you are—so . . . innocent."

Slim, he arose. His grey summer suit sat less stiffly on him than they do usually on his kind. His slight negligence of manner inspired instant sympathy and trust. He turned to the big map, Europe and Asia Minor, hung on the wall. His blue-veined hand approximately covered the Near East.

"The Dardanelles, the Caucasus, Palestine, and Mesopotamia are German fronts today, Herr Lepsius, more even than Turkish. If they collapse, the whole war structure collapses with them. We really can't threaten Turkey with our own suicide unless we want to make ourselves ridiculous. I don't think I even need remind you of the tremendous significance which His Majesty the Kaiser attaches to our power in the East. But aren't you even aware that the Turks by no means feel indebted to us—on the contrary, they consider themselves our creditors. I don't see why you shouldn't be told that a very powerful group on the Committee would be perfectly ready at any minute to change horses, and negotiate with the Allies. You might easily live to see France and England, who today raise such a howl over Armenian atrocities, shut both eyes to the same atrocities tomorrow. You speak of truth, Herr Lepsius. The truth is that the Turks hold trumps in this particular game, that we have to mind out p's and q's and keep well within the limits of the possible."

Johannes Lepsius listened quietly. He had heard them all, again and again, these "truths" which the children of this world utter with their sharp logic. They led to incontestable conclusions. Whoso admitted a single link in the chain was for ever lost. But the pastor was far beyond the point of admitting anything. In these few weeks his mind had grown a shell, which rendered it impervious to such processes. He would not let himself be drawn out of it. Stubbornly he remained on his own ground.

"I'm not a politician. It's not my business to find possible ways by which, even now, a part of the Armenian nation can be saved. But it *is* my duty as the representative of a great number of German Christians, who think as I do, to voice the urgent petition that such ways and means may be discovered, and discovered before it's too late."

"No matter how we may turn the thing and twist it, Herr Lepsius, it may be possible here and there to ameliorate the lot of these Armenians, but unluckily we shan't be able to change it."

"Neither my friends nor I can accept that unchristian standpoint."

"Please realize that, in this Armenian destiny, certain historical forces, too vast for us to control, may be working themselves out."

"I only realize that Enver and Talaat have taken advantage, with devilish cunning, of the best possible moment at which to cast themselves for the role of historical forces."

The privy councillor smiled rather mincingly, as though it were his turn now, to display a sample of his religious views. "Doesn't Nietzsche say: 'What totters, ought it not to be thrust down?'"

But Nietzsche was not the man to disconcert such a child of God as Johannes Lepsius. Rather annoyed at the generalities in which the conversation kept petering out, he answered shortly: "Which of us knows whether he's falling, or pushing down?"

The privy councillor, back at his desk again, took another brief glance at the map on the wall. "The Armenians are going under because of their geographical position. It's the fate of the weak, of the hated minority."

"Every man and every nation at one time or another becomes 'the weak.' That's why nobody should tolerate persecution, let alone extermination, as a precedent."

535

"Have you never, Herr Lepsius, asked yourself whether national minorities may not cause unnecessary trouble—whether it mayn't be better that they should vanish?"

Lepsius took off his glasses and polished them hard. His eyes peered and blinked wearily. Their myopic look seemed to give his whole body something courageous.

"Herr Geheimrat, are not we Germans in a minority?"

"What do you mean by that? I don't understand you."

"In the midst of a Europe united against us, we're a damnably imperilled minority. It only needs one bad breakthrough. And we've not chosen our geography so brilliantly either."

The privy councillor's face had ceased to be kindly, it looked sharp and pale. A whiff of dusty midday heat beat in through the window.

"Quite right, Herr Pastor. And therefore it's the duty of every German to be concerned for the fate of his own people, and to think of the rivers of blood which, what you prefer to call the German minority, is shedding. That is the only standpoint from which a German can view the Armenian question."

"We Christians depend on the grace of God and our obedience to the Gospels. I tell you quite frankly, Herr Geheimrat, that I reject any other standpoint. For weeks now I've been seeing more clearly every day that power will have to be taken out of the hands of the children of this world, the politicians, if ever communion in the Lord, the Corpus Christi, is to become a reality in our poor little world."

"Render unto Cæsar——"

"But what *is* Cæsar's—apart from a worn-out penny piece? Christ was too wise to tell us that. No! No! the peoples are the slaves of their racial differences. And their flatterers, who want to live off them, intensify such things and stimulate their vanity. As though there were any special merit in being born a dog or a cat, a turnip or a potato. Jesus Christ, Who gives us the eternal example of the divine man, only put on human form in order to conquer it. So that on earth only the true sons of God should rule, from the very fact that they have conquered their race, their earthly conditioning. That is my political creed, Herr Geheimrat."

The Prussian aristocrat's face showed not the slightest suggestion of irony. "You talk like a confirmed Catholic, Herr Pastor."

"More Catholic than any Catholic—since the Church of my trust does not share her power with any lay authority."

The privy councillor screwed in his monocle again; this conveyed the suggestion that the time for debate had come to an end. "But till we can re-establish the Holy Inquisition, we poor children of this world have got to take the responsibility."

Johannes Lepsius, who perhaps had gone a little too far, drew back into his shell. His voice sounded calm, almost offhand: "Let me still be quite frank with you, Herr Geheimrat. Till a few days ago I was hopeful, and I still believed that Herr Bethmann-Hollweg would support me in this fight with more drastic measures than he has, so far. You have let me see quite finally that our government's hands are tied in its dealings with Turkey, and that we must confine ourselves to the usual interviews and démarches. But no reasons of state tie mine. And now the Armenian question in Germany rests solely on me. I'm not inclined to make concessions and give in. I, in conjunction with my friends, intend to enlighten our own people. Since only when men know the truth will it be possible to establish our work of Christian assistance on a broad basis. I therefore request that my hands may not be tied in these activities."

The privy councillor had been deep in the study of his wristwatch; he glanced up from it, pleased. "One frankness is worth another, Herr Pastor. You mustn't therefore misunderstand me if I tell you that for some time now, we've been keeping an eye on you. Your stay in Constantinople was the subject of a great many complaints. I repeat, you have no idea how complex the situation is. I'm sorry. I have the greatest respect for your humane activities. And yet, in the political sense, such activities are—well, not desirable. I would advise you, my dear Herr Lepsius, to keep them within very definite bounds, and make them as unobtrusive as possible."

The pastor's reply came more like a growl than a solemnity: "A call has come to me. No power on earth can prevent my following that voice."

"Oh, you mustn't say that, Herr Doctor Lepsius." The startled privy councillor's face looked almost flurried in its kindliness. "A few powers of this world are already doing their very best to prevent you effectively."

The pastor patted the whole left side of his coat before he stood up. "I'm extremely grateful, Herr Geheimrat, for all your frankness and your advice."

The tall, slim councillor faced Herr Lepsius, in a kind of self-satisfied embarrassment which sat him perfectly. "I'm so glad we've managed to come to such a quick understanding, Herr Pastor. You're looking as though you needed a rest. Wouldn't it be better for you to slack off a bit—just go on living from day to day. Don't you live in Potsdam?"

Johannes Lepsius regretted having taken up so much official time. But the privy councillor showed him out with a positively ingratiating smile.

"My dear Herr Pastor! It's a long time since I've spent such an interesting hour."

Down in the stuffy, midday Wilhelmstrasse, Johannes Lepsius stood and asked himself whether, as his Lord instructed him, he had been as meek as a dove, as wise as a serpent. He was instantly forced to the admission that both dove and serpent had failed to come off. But luckily he had been sufficiently prudent to obtain, some time ago, all the necessary passports, identification descriptions, travelling permits, and permissions to export currency. That was why, a few minutes ago, he had tapped the left side of his coat so carefully, to assure himself of these sacred objects. He turned sharply round. Suppose even now a detective were tracking him! His mind was made up. The express for Basel left at 3:40. He had still more than three hours in which to telephone Potsdam for his luggage and make all his other arrangements for setting out. Even tomorrow the frontiers might be closed to him. But he must get back to Istanbul! That was his place, even though he had still no clear idea what to do there. In Germany, in any case, his work would go forward without him. The organization had been built up, the office opened, patrons, friends, collaborators, won over. His place was not in far-off safety, but on the very coasts of the sea of blood.

The scurry and din of the Potsdamer Platz deafened him. The short-sighted Lepsius waited a long time for his chance to get across it safely. The thunder, rattle, clatter, and grating of cars, motor-buses, trams, surged round his ears, like a single tone. Like the bells of some great barbaric cathedral. A little rhyme came up in his mind; he had taken it down many years ago, on the deck of a little dancing steamer, as it bore him across to the rocky island of Patmos-Patino, the holy apocalyptic isle of St. John. Its refrain sang in him:

A and O
A and O
Ring the bells of Patino.

And that little rhyme seemed to link two such different places as Patmos and Potsdamer Platz.

THE life of a shy night animal in Istanbul.

Johannes Lepsius knew himself spied upon and tracked. Usually, therefore, he left the Hotel Tokatlyan only at night. On the day after his arrival he had paid his duty-call at the German Embassy. Instead of the Minister, Embassy secretary, or press attaché, a very minor official indeed had received him, with the plain, unvarnished inquiry what object brought him

539

back to Constantinople. Lepsius answered that he was there without a definite object, merely to rest in this city of which he was extremely fond. That he had no definite object was true enough. The pastor had still no clear idea of what he could manage to undertake. He was out of favour with the Turks, and now even with the Germans. That splendid naval commander attached to the Embassy, for instance, who had been so helpful in getting him the interview with Enver, met him now with the cut direct in the Grande Rue de Péra. God alone could say what dirty lies weren't being told about him everywhere. Often a cold shudder ran down his spine at the thought that he was alone in the Turkish capital, that his country's Embassy had not only ceased to afford support, but was almost hostile. Should Ittihad be inspired with the notion of getting him neatly out of the way, not much diplomatic fuss would be likely to be made over his corpse. At faint-hearted moments he thought of going back to Germany. He was only wasting his time. This was already the third week in August. Suffocating heat struck up from the Bosporus. "What am I after here?" he kept asking himself. And so compared himself to an unskilled burglar, trying to pick the lock of an iron door with his bare hand, without even a jemmy, or skeleton key, and obliged moreover to work under the eyes of the police. But so much was clear. The lock of that door into the interior would have to be picked, for there ever to be a chance of real help. Funds sent by official channels melted away, with nothing to show for them.

Johannes Lepsius was so daring as to visit the Armenian patriarch, Monsignor Saven. Since they last met, what little there was left of life in it seemed to have ebbed out of that priest's dead face. This holy man abstractedly eyed his visitor. When he recognized him, he could not hold back the tears.

"It'll do you no good, my son," he whispered, "if they know you've been coming here to see me."

Now Dr. Lepsius heard the full horror of the truth, as it

had developed in the weeks he had been away. The patriarch told it curtly, dryly, as though not in words. Any further attempt to help was worse than useless, it was superfluous, since the deportation law had already taken full effect. Most of the clergy, all the political leaders, had been slaughtered. This people now was composed of famished women and children. Any neutral or German help given to these Armenian women provoked Enver and Talaat to further savagery.

"The best thing is not to try to do anything, but to keep still, and die."

Had Lepsius not noticed how this house, the patriarchate, was surrounded with police spies? Every word they were saying would be reported next morning to Talaat Bey. And so, with terror in his eyes, Monsignor Saven asked his visitor to put his head close against his lips. In this way did Lepsius get news of the Armenian revolt on Musa Dagh, the defeat of Turkish regulars, that the mountain had so far proved impregnable. The patriarch's whisper became unsteady: "Isn't it terrible? They say the army has lost over a hundred men."

Johannes Lepsius did not consider it terrible by any means. His blue eyes shone like a boy's behind sharp-rimmed glasses. "Terrible? Magnificent! If there'd been three Musa Daghs, we should have heard a very different story. Oh, Monsignor, I only wish I were up on the Musa Dagh."

The pastor had said it far too loud. The patriarch's hand lay, stiff with fear, upon his mouth. As he took leave, Lepsius handed over some of the funds collected in Germany. The priest crammed the banknotes, as swiftly as though they were red-hot coals, into the patent safe in his office. Not much hope of their ever reaching their destination, Deir ez-Zor. The monsignor was whispering again, sharply, in the German's ear, something which at first was unintelligible.

"It isn't we of the patriarchate, nor you, nor any other German, nor any neutral, who can help us. We should have to find Turks as intermediaries, you understand. Turks!"

541

"Turks?" Dr. Lepsius murmured, recapturing a glimpse of Enver Pasha's face. "What a mad idea."

WHAT a mad idea, and yet already, independently of Dr. Lepsius, it was on its way to being realized. The pastor, in his hotel dining-room, had made the acquaintance of a Turk, a doctor of about forty. Professor Nezimi Bey was very well dressed and westernized. He lived in the Tokatlyan, but had his consulting-room in one of the best streets in Péra. At first Lepsius mistook him for one of the least uncongenial incarnations of the spirit which infused the Young Turkish world. But, in spite of his European science, of clothes admirably cut, appearances proved to be deceptive. They often got into conversation. Three or four times they arranged to have their meal at the same table. Lepsius was extremely cautious. He was forced to be so. The Turkish doctor was anything but cautious or reserved. The German started, and held his tongue, as the doctor began to vent his hatred of the policy of the people in control, his utter detestation of Enver and Talaat. Had they sent an agent provocateur? But, as he eyed Nezimi's pleasant features, considered his position, his way of expressing himself, his really surprising powers as a linguist, such suspicion seemed to be too absurd. Impossible that Enver should dispose of agents of this calibre. Yet Lepsius was still wary enough not to let himself be led into talking freely. He did not deny that he was doing his best, as a Christian priest, to mitigate the lot of his co-religionists. But he would not criticize, and confined himself to the role of attentive listener.

Though Nezimi seemed not explicitly pro-Armenian he raged against the Committee's deportation policy. "Those fields of Armenian corpses will mean the end of Turkey."

Lespius still looked stolid. "The vast majority of the nation is behind Enver and Talaat."

"What?" Nezimi glared up at him. "The vast majority of the nation! You foreigners haven't any idea how insignificant

542

that party really is. Above all, how morally insignificant! Why, it's composed of the shabbiest parvenu scum. When people of that sort insist on their Osmanian race, it's the worst insolence! These pure-bred Osmans mostly come out of the Macedonian stew-pot in which the racial ragout of the whole Balkans floats."

"That's an old story, Professor. Usually the people who dwell on their race are the ones who have most need of something of that kind."

Nezimi gazed sadly at Lepsius. "It's a pity that a man of your kind, who has made so close a study of our conditions, should still have no idea of the real Turkey. Do you know that all true Turks detest these Armenian convoys, even worse than you do?"

Lepsius pricked up his ears. "And who are these true Turks, if you don't mind my asking, Professor?"

"All those who haven't lost their religion."

But Nezimi would say no more than that. That same evening he knocked at the pastor's door. He gave an impression of strange excitement.

"If you like, tomorrow I'll take you into the tekkeh of the Sheikh Achmed. It's the greatest honour I could pay you. And there, besides, you'll be able to speak your mind about the Armenians, and perhaps find out some way of helping them." And he repeated: "I shall be doing you the greatest honour."

So that, immediately after luncheon next day, Nezimi escorted Dr. Lepsius, as they had arranged. Most of the way was done on foot. That day a cool breeze off the Sea of Marmora tempered the sweltering midday sun. Flocks of herons and storks sped across the vivid afternoon sky of Istanbul, to their nests on the opposite side. The doctor conducted Dr. Lepsius along past Enver Pasha's Seraskeriat and the mosque of the Sultan Bayazid into the endless streets of Ak Serai. They walked interminably westwards. They had penetrated the ruined confusion of the innermost town. Pavements had ceased

543

to be. Herds of sheep and goats flocked round them. The ancient Byzantine city wall, above a chaos of wooden houses, frowned on them with its crenellated turrets. But the pastor was by no means in the mood to rejoice his æsthetic sense at the spectacle of a highly picturesque, even if intensely squalid, neighbourhood. Nor did that innermost heart of Islamic piety, which today was to open itself for his benefit, interest him as a new experience. Like all minds in the throes of some obsessing, tormenting struggle for an end, he saw it all solely in its relationship to Armenian woes. So that, anything but receptive to new experiences, he was already turning over suggestions and projects. It was these and not curiosity which inspired him to question his guide. "I suppose we're on our way to the Mevlevi dervishes."

Lepsius, in spite of long sojourns in Palestine and Asia Minor, knew next to nothing about Islam. To him it was merely the fanatical enemy of Christendom.

But since it is one of our saddest human weaknesses that we always know least of the very person whose mind we should penetrate to the core—of the enemy—the pastor had the vaguest notions of the world of true Moslem belief. He had only said "Mevlevi dervishes" because their very well-known name was familiar to him.

Dr. Nezimi waved off the suggestion: "No! No! Sheikh Achmed, our master, is the head of an order, called by our people 'the thieves of hearts.' "

"What a strange title for an order. Why 'the thieves of hearts'?"

"You'll see that for yourself."

Still, even on their way, the guide condescended to explanations. He informed the German that the flood of Mohammedan religion divides itself into two main powerful streams, the Shaariat and the Tarikaat. Let the Shaariat stand approximately for the concept of the Catholic secular priesthood, the idea of the Tarikaat would be falsified by comparisons with

western monasticism. To be a dervish does not mean to renounce the world and withdraw for one's whole life into a
tekkeh. Anyone might become a dervish, provided he fulfilled certain conditions, and he need not therefore renounce
his profession or family. The grand vizir was equally eligible
with the tailor, coppersmith, bank-clerk, or officer. So that thus
the most diverse brotherhood was scattered up and down the
whole country, and brothers knew one another everywhere,
"by instinct," without further recognition.

Johannes Lepsius asked, reflectively purposeful: "So that
numerically these dervish orders constitute a considerable
power?"

"Not only numerically, Herr Doctor, believe me."

"And in what does their religious life consist?"

"You, I believe, would call it 'spiritual exercises.' But probably that's another misleading expression. We meet from time
to time. We exercise our spiritual faculty. We pray. It's called
'zikr.' And everyone, once or twice in his life, has to serve the
tekkeh, and live there some time. But the chief thing is, we
obey our teacher and superior, out of the fullness of our hearts,
from love."

"Your teacher and superior is the Sheikh Achmed, Professor?"

Though Lepsius had not directly asked who Sheikh Achmed exactly was, Nezimi supplied the answer:

"He is a weli. You would say 'holy man'—and that again
would be a complete mistranslation. His life, which is a higher
life than other men's, has enabled him to develop powers in
himself. You know the French expression—*initiation*. And as
you'll see, the most splendid thing about him is that he's just
an ordinary man."

They stopped at a high wall. Fig trees, and the tops of
cypresses, goldenrain and wistaria, betrayed a garden. Nezimi
Bey tapped with his stick on the worm-eaten door, let into the
wall. They were kept a long time waiting. Then an old man,

heavily built, with mild, kind eyes, came and opened to them. The dark miracle of the garden disclosed itself. A cedar, many centuries old, stood predominant. The two rusty halves of a heavy chain dangled from the strong branches of the tree. Long ago, Nezimi told the pastor, the cedar had been chained in its youth, till its sap, rising in strength, forced the chain asunder. A symbol of the dervish's life. In this peace, strangely cut off from the din of streets, splashed a fountain. That too seemed fully emblematic of the Turkish reverence for water. A strange dark house bounded the garden to the right, to the left a bright one, in good repair. They entered the bright, wood house, having left their shoes. Nezimi led the German up dark close stairs to a kind of loggia, built over the big apartment of the tekkeh, which, with its slim wood pilasters and walls cut in filigree at the top, had the look of a vast pavilion. In its east wall, turned to Mecca, there was a throne-niche, built in, with a raised mat. A few men squatted on either side of this raised divan. The doctor described them as "caliphs," as deputies or trusted followers of the sheikh, the men nearest his heart. They all wore the white turban, even the infantry captain, who oddly was one of them. Lepsius also noticed a little, spare old man, who must be suffering from a nervous complaint, since his thin, goat-bearded face kept twitching. One remarkably handsome man with a soft brown beard, wearing a long, shirt-like cowl, Nezimi called "the son of the sheikh." Beside this youthful-looking man, whose robe seemed to glint with a sheen of silver, there squatted a fifteen-year-old boy, the son of the son, as whitely clad as his father. But Lepsius's eyes were especially turned on one of these men, something in whose bearing and attitude showed him to be the master of them all, the strongest personality in the room.

Thus did the pastor picture to himself the great caliphs, Bayazid, Mahmud the Second, perhaps the Prophet himself. A face tense with fanaticism, a blue-black beard forcing its way up the face almost to the sockets of the eyes. The staring look which rested on nothing, had no mercy in it, either for enemy or for friend even. "That is the Türbedar of Brussa," Lepsius heard, and he learned further that this title described a very exalted symbolic office, the guardian of the tombs of sultans and holy men. The man was also a great scholar, not only in the learning of the Koran but in several modern sciences also. The little old gentleman, sitting there facing him so quietly—yes, that one there, with the white hands, twisting amber beads—also fulfilled a high symbolic function, "Supervisor of the genealogical table of the Prophet."

"Do these men always live in the tekkeh?"

"No, it's a great and very fortunate coincidence that you should be visiting the sheikh today. The old gentleman over there, the supervisor, comes from a long way off, from Syria, Antioch, I think. He's the Sheikh's oldest friend, you know. His name is Agha Rifaat Bereket."

"Agha Rifaat Bereket." Lapsius repeated it absent-mindedly, as though the name were not entirely unknown to him. But he had no eyes, either for the Agha, or for the thirty-five other people whose murmuring voices filled the apartment, but only for the proud Türbedar. Therefore he did not notice the arrival of the Sheikh Achmed until the instant when he took his place on the divan. Nezimi Bey had been right. Outwardly the head of this ghostly order, which must control the lives of a hundred thousand faithful, showed little of his dignity and powers. He was a corpulent greybeard, whose features expressed staid good-nature, and did not fail to suggest a practical shrewdness in their estimate of the things of this world.

They had all sprung up, and were crowding eagerly, avidly round the old sheikh, to kiss his hand. Not until all the others had stilled their love and reverence to the uttermost, by means of this gesture, did the Türbedar bend down over the soft, fat right hand of Achmed.

The zikr ecstasy he now witnessed left Dr. Lepsius not only

547

cold, but full of a dark, surging uneasiness. The ceremony began as follows: the Sheikh's handsome son stood in a line of young men, all clad in the same long, white cowl, against the west wall of the apartment. The little boy, his small face preternaturally solemn, ended the right wing of this line. There arose from nowhere the nasal, monotonous note of a shawm-pipe. A man, standing with his eyes shut in front of a gold-carved Koran lectern, intoned a sura, in humming, disturbing falsetto. The old sheikh waved his hand in a scarcely perceptible little gesture. The shawm and litany stopped together. The son flung back his head, listening, as if he were trying to catch the lightest drizzle of rain upon his face. Out of his throat came strangled sounds; the happiness seemed too great, of being permitted to speak the syllables of that verse which concentrates in itself the whole strength of the revealed Book: "La—ilah—ila—'llah." "There is no God but God." Now all the others threw their heads back, and the six syllables of their creed fused into a crooning, murmurous hum. This, like the opening notes of a composition, defined the theme that now was developed. Now the son's body was swaying in a light, angular rhythm. As the "La—ilah—ila—'llah" defined its cadence, he swayed from the waist towards the four corners of the hemisphere, forwards, back, to right, to left. The fourfold beat passed into the others. But there was none of the symmetry of drill or ballet in the surge. Each obeyed his own law. Each individual in this brotherhood seemed to be alone with himself, in ecstatic invocation of his God. And this gave birth to a new rhythm, a far more manifold, higher symmetry than drilled, imposed unity can effect; the symmetry of storm-swept woods, of lashing waves. There must be full freedom and solitude of the ego before his God, to make possible a higher community. The old sheikh, his caliphs, and the others took part in these zikr exercises with slight accompanying movements. The boy of the young sheikh bent his little body about, on all sides, with desperate seriousness. Sometimes his poignant baby-voice could be heard shrilling out of the general surge of the "La—ilah." After about ten minutes the dervishes were bending at right angles, their cries had risen into hoarse, unmodulated bellowings. Another slight sign from the old sheikh. The ceremony stopped, suddenly. But now, superabundant joy, a most intimate, happy satisfaction, seemed to have stolen into the hearts of both participants and onlookers. Exhausted smiles lit up these faces. The men embraced. Johannes Lepsius had to think of the early Christian agape. But . . . ? The love-celebration here below him did not come out of the mind, the spirit, but out of these wild contortions of the body. He could not understand. Meanwhile two more men had come into the room, through a little side-door. They carried water-pitchers, dishes with food, even garments, before Sheikh Achmed, who kept breathing over them. Now they had received healing-power. After a pause the zikr began again, on a level of still greater intensity. The holy number, four, was in the ascendant. Therefore there ensued four ecstasies, each broken into by a pause. The power and tempo of the last was of such almost unbearable wildness that sometimes Lepsius shut his eyes with a feeling of seasickness. As the last zikr rose to near its height, the little, thin, dried-up old man with the twitching face suddenly leapt from the dais down into the room, and began spinning, like a whirligig, to collapse in epileptic writhings. The pastor turned to the doctor, sitting behind him. Surely Nezimi would hurry down to the help of the epileptic. But this well-dressed man, this man who had studied at the Sorbonne, seemed himself no longer to know where he was. He twirled the upper half of his body. His eyes were sightless. And between his lips, from under the little clipped moustache, he too now babbled the long withheld "La—ilah—ila—'llah." The pastor had never felt so uncomfortable. But his feeling was not only one of dislike for the sight which seemed so foreign and barbarous—it was one of uneasy embarrassment at the fact that he, with his western

549

soul, should not feel sufficiently developed to enter into the God-intoxication of the twirlers in the room below.

THIS deep uneasiness still possessed him as he came into the innermost recesses of this so madly foreign world—into the audience-chamber of the sheikh. He had not perhaps been more uneasy on the day when he had been faced with Enver Pasha. Yet Sheikh Achmed received him cordially. He advanced a few steps to meet Lepsius and Nezimi Bey. In the big room there were also, of the sheikh's caliphs, the Türbedar from Brussa, the Agha Rifaat Bereket, the young sheikh, and the infantry captain. There was nothing here on which to sit save low divans against the wall. Sheikh Achmed indicated that Lepsius should take the seat close beside his. Lepsius had to squat on his crossed legs, like all the others. The old sheikh's eyes, which, besides their shrewd, keen knowledge of the world, had in them an inexplicable quiet, as of windless places, turned to the guest.

"We know who you are, and what brings you to us. I have no doubt you will understand us, as we hope to understand you. Perhaps our brother Nezimi has told you that, here, we depend less on words than on the contact of heart to heart. Well, then, let us try how it is, with our two hearts."

The German's coat was buttoned up. Sheikh Achmed, with his own white hand, unbuttoned it. He smiled a kind of apology. "You see, we want to get nearer each other."

Dr. Lepsius spoke and could understand Turkish very well; his Arabic was also good. But Sheikh Achmed used a difficult mixture of these two languages, so that, when he became too idiomatic, he used Nezimi as his interpreter. The doctor translated:

"There are two hearts. There is the heart of flesh, and the secret, heavenly heart, which surrounds the other, just as its scent surrounds a rose. This second heart unites us with God and other men. Open it, please."

550

The heavy body of the old man, of possibly eighty years, bent forward attentively towards the pastor. A little gesture indicated that he was to shut his eyes, as his host did. A sure peace descended on Johannes Lepsius. The parching thirst, which only a moment ago had worried him, disappeared. He used this time to collect his thoughts, behind closed lids, and prepare the reasoning with which he intended to strive for the Armenians. God had led him here, in wondrous fashion, where perhaps he might find entirely unexpected allies. Monsignor Saven's wish that, not Germans or neutrals, but Turks themselves might be intermediaries—that absurd wish—had begun to seem feasible. When Lepsius opened his eyes again, the old sheikh's face seemed bathed in warm sunlight. But the sheikh said nothing of the results of this trial of hearts; he only asked the pastor to tell him what service he felt he could possibly render. The important conversation began.

JOHANNES LEPSIUS (at first the Turkish words came stiffly and slowly; he often turned to Nezimi to supply him with the right expression): "Through the great goodness of Sheikh Achmed Effendi I have come here, into this honourable tekkeh, as a Christian and stranger. . . . You have even allowed me to be present at your religious exercises. The fervour and devotion with which I saw you strive after God has filled my heart with delight. Even if I, as an ignorant foreigner, cannot understand the innermost meaning of your holy customs, at least I was able to feel your great piety. . . . But, in view of this piety of yours, this religious feeling, the things that happen, are allowed to happen, in your country, seem to me all the more terrible."

THE YOUNG SHEIKH (obtains with an upward glance, his father's permission to speak): "We know how for many years you have been a warm friend of the ermeni millet. . . ."

JOHANNES LEPSIUS: "More than simply their friend. I have devoted my whole life and strength to the ermeni millet."

551

THE YOUNG SHEIKH: "And now you want to accuse us of what has been done to them?"

JOHANNES LEPSIUS: "I am a foreigner. A foreigner has never any right to make accusations. I am here, not to accuse, but only to complain, about these things, and to beg your help and your advice."

THE YOUNG SHEIKH (with an obvious stubbornness, not to be softened by pleasant words): "And yet you hold us Turks, in general, responsible for all that has happened?"

JOHANNES LEPSIUS: "A people is made up of many parts: of the government and its executives, of those classes that stand behind the government, and of the opposition."

THE YOUNG SHEIKH: "And which of these do you hold responsible?"

JOHANNES LEPSIUS: "For twenty years I have known your conditions well. Even in the interior. I have negotiated with the heads of your government. God help me—I must say it! To them alone attaches the full guilt of this wiping out of an innocent people."

THE TÜRBEDAR (raises his thin, fanatic's head, with its pitiless eyes; his voice and being dominate the room immediately): "But who was responsible for our government?"

JOHANNES LEPSIUS: "I don't understand your question."

THE TÜRBEDAR: "Well, let me ask you another. Have Osmans and Armenians always lived together uneasily? Or was there not a time in which they lived at peace, side by side? You know our country, so I suppose you also know our past."

JOHANNES LEPSIUS: "As far as I know, the big massacres did not begin before the last century—after the Berlin Congress . . ."

THE TÜRBEDAR: "That answers my first question. At that Congress you Europeans began to meddle in the domestic affairs of the empire. You urged reforms. You wanted to buy Allah and our religion of us, for shabby sums. The Armenians were your commercial travellers."

JOHANNES LEPSIUS: "Did not that age, with its general development, demand those reforms more urgently even than Europe? And, after all, it was very natural that the Armenians, as the weaker, busier people, should have wanted them most."

THE TÜRBEDAR (flares up; his just wrath fills the whole room): "But we don't want your reforms, your 'progress,' your business activity. We want to live in God, and to develop in ourselves those powers which belong to Allah. Don't you know that all that which you call activity, advancement, is of the devil? Shall I prove it to you? You have made a few superficial investigations into the essence of the chemical elements. And what happens, then—when you act from your imperfect knowledge? You manufacture the poison gases, with which you wage your currish, cowardly wars. And is it any different with your flying-machines? You will only use them to bomb whole cities to the ground. Meanwhile they only serve to nourish usurers and profit-makers, and enable them to plunder the poor as fast as possible. Your whole devilish restlessness shows us plainly that there is no 'progressive activity' not founded in destruction and ruin. We would willingly have dispensed with all your reforms and progress, all the blessings of your scientific culture, to have been allowed to go on living in our old poverty and reverence."

THE OLD SHEIKH ACHMED (attempts to bring a more conciliatory note into their talk): "God has poured his draughts into many glasses, and each glass has its own form."

THE TÜRBEDAR (can still not manage to calm down, since he feels that here he has found the right adversary on whom to vent his profoundest bitterness): "You tell us our government is guilty of all this bloody injustice. But, in truth, it is not our government, but yours. It went to school to you. You supported it in its criminal struggle against our most sacred treasures. Now it carries out your instructions, in your spirit. Therefore you yourself must admit that, not we Osmans, but Europe, and Europe's hangers-on, are in truth responsible for the fate of this people whom you champion. And the Armenians are justly served, since it was they who wanted to bring back these criminal traitors into our country. It was they who cherished them, and acclaimed them, in order that now they should be devoured. Can't you yourself see the justice of God in these events? Wherever you and your disciples may go, you bring corruption along with you. You may do hypocritical lip-service to the religion of the prophet Jesus Christ, but in the depths of your hearts you believe in nothing but the blind forces of matter, and eternal death. Your hearts are so dull that they know nothing of the powers of Allah, which wither within them, unused. Yes, your religion is death, and all Europe is the harlot of death!"

THE OLD SHEIKH (with a stern glance commands the Türbedar to control himself; then he strokes the pastor's hand, as though to comfort and propitiate): "Everything lies within God's purpose."

THE YOUNG SHEIKH: "It's true, Effendi, you can't deny it. The nationalism which dominates us today is a foreign poison, which comes from Europe. Only a few decades ago our whole people lived faithfully under the banners of the prophet— Turks, Arabs, Kurds, Lasas, and many more. The spirit of the Koran nullifies earthly differences of blood. But today even the Arabs, who really had nothing to complain about, have become nationalists, and our enemies."

THE OLD SHEIKH: "Nationalism fills up the burning void which Allah leaves in the hearts of men when they drive Him out of them. And yet! Men cannot drive Him forth against His will."

JOHANNES LEPSIUS (sits with his legs crossed under him, as the personification of Europe accused; he does not however forget his object; therefore, he has listened amiably to the curses of the imposing Türbedar from Brussa; they hurt him far less than his squatting legs): "None of what you have said to me is new. I myself have often said much the same to my fellow-countrymen. I am a Christian—in fact a Christian priest—and in spite of this I gladly admit to you that many of the Christians whom I meet are no more than lukewarm, indifferent lip-servers . . ."

THE TÜRBEDAR (still obstinately righteous, in spite of Sheikh Achmed's silent reproof): "So you see that not we Turks but your Christians are the real guilty."

JOHANNES LEPSIUS: "My religion commands me to see all guilt as the unavoidable heritage of Adam. Men and whole peoples cast this human guilt at one another, like a ball. It is impossible to assign its limits in time, or trace it back to any one event. Where should we begin, and where leave off? I am not here to speak even a word of reproach against the Turkish people. It would be a very great mistake. I am here to beg reconciliation."

THE TÜRBEDAR: "You come, asking to be reconciled, after having aroused the malice."

JOHANNES LEPSIUS: "I am no chauvinist. Every human being, whether he lives it or not, belongs to a national community, and remains a part of it. That is an obvious fact of nature. As a Christian, I believe that our Father in heaven created these differences between us, to teach us love. Since no love is possible without diversity and tension. I too, by nature, am very different from the Armenians. And yet I have learned to love and understand them."

THE TÜRBEDAR: "Have you ever cared to reflect how much the Armenians love and understand us? It was they who, like an electric wire, conducted your devil's restlessness into the midst of our peace. And do you take them for innocent lambs? I tell you that, whenever they get a chance, they coldly slaughter any Turk who happens to be at their mercy. Perhaps you may not be aware that even your Christian priests are delighted to do their share in that kind of murder."

JOHANNES LEPSIUS (it is the first time that he has had to check himself from answering sharply): "If you say so, Ef-

555

fendi, I can only believe that such crimes have been committed, here and there. But don't forget what your hojas, mullahs, and ulemas have done to stir up your people. And besides, you are the strong, the Armenians powerless."

THE TÜRBEDAR (who, besides being learned, is skilled in polemic; he knows the art of retreating at once from the realms of the dangerously particular, into the fortified region of generalities): "You have strewn calumnies through the whole world against our religion. The most malicious is that of its intolerance. Do you really suppose that, if we had been so intolerant, there would be one Christian left alive in the empire governed for centuries by the Caliph? What did the great Sultan who conquered Istanbul do in the first year of his reign? Did he banish Christians from his territory? Did he? No, he set up the Greek and Armenian patriarchates, investing them with power, splendour, freedom. But what did you Christians do in Spain? You drove the Moslems, who had made their homes there, into the sea, by thousands, and burned them alive. Do we send you missionaries, as you us? You only send out the cross before you so that the Baghdad railway and the oil trusts may pay better dividends."

THE OLD SHEIKH: "The sun is arrogant and aggressive, the moon mild and full of peace. The Türbedar speaks harsh words, but not to you, who are our guest. You must understand that our people also are embittered at the misrepresentation of our religion. Do you know which word most frequently beautifies the Koran, after the name of God? The word. Peace! And do you know how it stands in the tenth sura: 'Once men were a single brotherhood. Then division came between them. But had God not sent forth His commandment, their division would have called down judgment upon them.' But we too strive, just as the Christians do, after a kingdom of unity and love. We too do not hate our enemies. How is it possible to hate if the heart has opened itself to God? To bring peace is one of the chief duties of our brotherhood. Listen;

even this Türbedar, who speaks so harshly, is one of our most zealous peace-makers. Long before your name became known to us, he was working on behalf of the exiles. And not only he! We have our peace-makers even among soldiers." (He beckons to the infantry captain who, presumably as the youngest and least initiated brother of the order, is sitting on the mat farthest away from him.)

THE CAPTAIN (comes shyly to take his place next the old sheikh; he has big, gentle eyes and a sensitive face; only his carefully trained moustache helps him to the severity of an officer).

THE OLD SHEIKH: "You visited the Armenian concentration camps in the east, on our behalf?"

THE CAPTAIN (turns to Johannes Lepsius): "I am staff-captain in one of the regiments attached to the headquarters of your great countryman, Marshal Goltz Pasha. The pasha's heart is also full of grief and pity for his Christian co-religionists. But he can do very little to help them against the will of the Minister of War. I reported to him, and was given leave for my task. . . ."

THE OLD SHEIKH: "And which places did you visit on your journey?"

THE CAPTAIN: "Most of the concentration camps for exiles are on the banks of the Euphrates, between Deir ez-Zor and Meskene. I stayed several days in each of the largest."

THE OLD SHEIKH: "And will you tell us what you saw there?"

THE CAPTAIN (an agonized glance at Lepsius): "I would much prefer not to tell you in front of this stranger. . . ."

THE OLD SHEIKH: "The stranger must learn to see that the infamy is that of our own enemies. Speak!"

THE CAPTAIN (stares at the floor, seeking for words; he is unable to describe the indescribable; his negative, hesitant words convey none of the stench of a reality at which he still shudders with disgust): "Battlefields are horrible. . . . But

557

the worst battlefield is nothing compared to Deir ez-Zor. . . . Nobody could ever imagine it."

THE OLD SHEIKH: "And what was worst?"

THE CAPTAIN: "They're no longer human. . . . Ghosts. . . . But not the ghosts of human beings . . . the ghosts of apes. It takes them a long time to die, because they chew grass, and can sometimes get hold of a piece of bread. . . . But the worst thing is that they're all too weak to bury their tens of thousands of corpses. . . . Deir ez-Zor is a horrible cloaca of death. . . ."

THE OLD SHEIKH (after a long pause): "And how can they be helped?"

THE CAPTAIN: "Helped? The best anyone could do for them would be to kill them all off in one day. . . . I've sent a letter to all our brethren. . . . We've managed to find homes for over a thousand of the orphans in Turkish or Arab families. . . . But that's scarcely anything."

THE TÜRBEDAR: "And what will the consequence be, if we take in these children, and care for them lovingly in our houses? The Europeans will only insist that we stole them, to sully and mishandle."

THE OLD SHEIKH: "That is true, but beside the point." (To the Captain): "Did these Armenians see in you, a Turk, only an enemy, or could you manage to gain their confidence?"

THE CAPTAIN: "Their dehumanized misery is so great that they have ceased to be able to distinguish between friend and enemy. . . . Whenever I came into a camp, they came round me in swarms. . . . Usually there were only women and old men, all half naked. . . . They roared with hunger. . . . The women scraped up my horse's dung to pick out the undigested oat-grains. . . . Then later they almost tore me to bits with their prayers. . . . I'm loaded up with petitions, and messages, which I can't deliver. . . . Here, for instance, this letter . . ."

(He finds a filthy slip in his pocket and shows it to Johannes Lepsius.)

558

"This was written by one of your Christian priests, of your persuasion. He was squatting beside his wife's unburied corpse . . . she'd lain there three days. . . . A very small, thin man, there was scarcely anything left of him. His name was Harutiun Nokhudian, his home was somewhere on the Syrian coast. Most of the people in his neighbourhood took refuge on the top of a mountain. I promised to have the letter delivered to them. But how?"

JOHANNES LEPSIUS (petrified by the horror of all this, has long since ceased to feel his cramped legs under him; on the letter which he takes from the captain he can read only the inscription, written in big Armenian letters, "To the priest of Yoghonoluk, Ter Haigasun") : "So even this request will have to go unfulfilled, like all the others."

AGHA RIFAAT BEREKET (his amber rosary has vanished into his sleeves; this frail old gentleman from Antakiya bows several times in little, swaying movements to the sheikh) : "No, this request shall be granted. . . . I myself will take Nokhudian's letter to his friends. In the next few days I shall be on the Syrian coast."

THE OLD SHEIKH (turns with a little smile to Lepsius) : "What an instance of God's power! Two brothers, strangers to one another, meet here, in this great city, so that the prayer of a wretched man may be granted. . . . But now you probably know us better. This is my friend, the Agha from Antakiya. . . . He's not in the prime of life, as you are; he has seventy years on his shoulders. And yet, for months, he has worked and travelled on behalf of the ermeni millet—good Turk as he is. Why, he's even obtained audiences with the Sultan and the Sheikh ül Islam on their behalf."

AGHA RIFAAT BEREKET: "He who guides my heart knows its purposes. But unluckily the others are very strong, and we very weak."

THE OLD SHEIKH: "We are weak because these lackeys of Europe have stolen religion from our people. It is as the Türbe-

559

dar said it, though in harsh words. Now you know the truth. But the weak are not afraid. I cannot tell whether your efforts for the Armenians are dangerous to you. But they can be very dangerous indeed both to the Agha and the captain. If a traitor or a government spy denounces them, they may disappear into jail for ever."

JOHANNES LEPSIUS (bends over Sheikh Achmed's hand, but the kiss remains uncompleted, since the pastor finds that he cannot conquer his shame and reserve): "I bless this hour, and I bless your brother Nezimi, who brought me here. I had given up hope. But now I can hope again, that, in spite of all convoys and concentration camps, some part of the Armenian nation may still be saved, with your help."

THE OLD SHEIKH: "That rests with God alone. . . . You must arrange a meeting with the Agha."

JOHANNES LEPSIUS: "Is there any chance of saving these men on Musa Dagh?"

THE TÜRBEDAR (angry again, this sympathy with rebels is too much for his Osmanic heart): "The Prophet says: 'He who goes to the judge to plead for a traitor is himself a traitor. Since, wittingly or unwittingly, he stirs up disorders.'"

THE OLD SHEIKH (for the first time he has lost his dry shrewdness of manner; his eyes look a long way out, his words are indecipherably ambiguous): "Perhaps those who are lost are already in safety, and those in safety already lost."

Then the sheikh's servant and the thick-set porter with the kind eyes brought coffee and lokum, Turkish sweetmeats. Sheikh Achmed with his own hands presented the coffee cup to his guest. Johannes Lepsius would have liked, before saying good-bye, to turn back their conversation to the Armenians. But he could not succeed. The old sheikh impassively refused all further discussion. But the Agha Rifaat Bereket promised the pastor to visit him that same night in his hotel. In three days he would have to leave Istanbul.

At the Seraskeriat, Dr. Nezimi Bey took leave of Lepsius. They had walked the whole long way almost in silence. The Turk imagined that what he had just seen so impressed the pastor that his thoughts were too eagerly occupied to enable him to say a word. That was true, but in a different sense. A man set on one object has his head full to bursting of new ideas. The pastor was not so much thinking of this mysterious new world in which he had just been spending a few hours. He was thinking of the breach into the interior, which such miraculous hazard had suddenly opened. He kept squeezing Nezimi's hand, to express his thanks, without saying a word. And such words as Nezimi said passed almost unheeded. The Turk was advising him to pay great attention, in the next few days, to all the minor incidents of his life. Any man honoured by Sheikh Achmed with "the test of the heart" would be sure to encounter many incidents which, if seen in their true light, would be full of meaning. Alone, outside the Seraskeriat, Lepsius stared up at the windows of Enver's citadel. They glittered in the late afternoon sunlight. He rushed for a cab. "To the Armenian patriarchate!" Now all the spies in the world meant nothing to him. He burst in on the cadaverous patriarch. Monsignor Saven's thought was miraculously on its way to being realized. Old-Turkish circles were helping the Armenians, though nobody had known it so far. The best among the Turks were enflamed with inextinguishable hate against their atheistic leaders. This fire must be used for their special purposes. . . . Monsignor Saven put his fingers to his lips imploringly. Not so loud—for Christ's sake! The pastor's quick mind was organizing a vast new scheme of assistance. The patriarchate was to get into secret touch with the great orders of dervishes, and so lay the foundations of a manifold and extensive work of assistance, which should grow till it became a definite rescue-work. The religious strata among the Turks must be strengthened in their fight by a new, strong impulşe, and powerful opposition to Enver and Talaat developed in the people itself. Monsignor Saven was far less optimistic than Dr. Lepsius. None of all this was unknown to him, he whispered, in a scarcely audible voice. Not all orders of dervishes were of this kind. The greatest, most influential, for instance, the Mevlevi and Rufai, were blind haters of the Armenians. Though they detested Enver, Talaat, and the other members of the Committee, they had nothing against the extermination. Lepsius refused to let his confidence be shaken. They must grasp any hands held out to them. He suggested that the patriarch himself should go in secret to see Sheikh Achmed. Nezimi Bey would arrange a meeting. But Monsignor Saven was so horrified at this daring suggestion that he seemed relieved when the temperamental pastor left his room.

Lepsius dismissed his araba at the farther side of the bridge. He would walk the short way back to the Tokatlyan. After months of heavy depression, he felt today as marvellously light-hearted as though he had some great success to look back on. Yet really he had done nothing at all, only glimpsed a faint chink of light, from behind the iron door. His mind was so full of projects that he walked on further and further, past his hotel, along the Grande Rue de Péra. A deliciously cool evening had descended. A clear green sky shimmered above the tree-tops of a park-like boulevard. This was one of the best parts of the town. Here there were even street-lamps, which now began to light up, one by one. A car, at a moderate pace, came on towards him. It was lit up within. An officer and a fat civilian sat talking excitedly. Sudden vague terror parched Lepsius's throat. He had recognized Enver Pasha—the glittering youth with the fresh complexion and long, girlish eyelashes. And his neighbour, with his fez on one side and his white waistcoat, was no doubt Taiaat Bey, as that minister appeared in many photographs. So now Lepsius was again facing the great enemy. In his heart, strangely enough, he had always wanted to. He stood enthralled, looking after the car. It had not gone on a hundred and fifty yards before two shots rang out, one after another. A jarring of brakes. Indistinct figures sprang out of the shadows. Sharp voices began to brawl. Were they calling for help? The pastor shivered in every limb. An attempt to assassinate! Had fate overtaken Enver and Talaat? And would he be called as a witness? He was drawn irresistibly to the scene. He did not want to see, yet could do no other. But he came reluctantly nearer the shouting group. Someone had lit a garish acetylene lamp, around which idlers gaped, giving loud advice. The chauffeur lay, cursing and grunting, under the car. But Enver and Talaat Bey stood peacefully side by side, puffing cigarette smoke. It was merely a puncture. The front tires had met some sharp obstacle on the road and burst; the machine was damaged. But the really ridiculous thing was that Enver had ceased to be Enver, Talaat, Talaat. The one had become a very ordinary-looking officer, the other a still more insignificant business man or civil servant. The white piqué waistcoat was the one reality that remained. Lepsius cursed his fervid imagination, which could raise such spooks. "I'm crazy," he grunted to himself.

But when, an hour later, Agha Rifaat Bereket sat in his room, he had quite forgotten the incident of the car. The Agha, in his turban and long blue cloak, was most out of place in this European hotel bedroom. Certainly he had nothing in common with the hard wooden chair on which he sat, the harsh, cold light of electric globes. Lepsius could see that this old gentleman, the Syrian caliph of the Sheikh of the Thieves of Hearts, was making a considerable sacrifice. Lepsius begged him to take five hundred pounds of his German relief fund, and use them, if he possibly could, on behalf of the men on Musa Dagh. Yet, in this, the pastor did not act as rashly as many might suppose. Those little twinkling hands, he could see for himself, would be a safer deposit for his money, and probably would put it to better use. than all the powerless consulates and missions. Perhaps, at last, it could really be spent as they intended. Rifaat Bereket wrote out a very formal receipt, in elaborate calligraphy. It covered an entire page. He handed it ceremoniously to the German.

"I will send you a letter with particulars of all my purchases."

"But—should you not succeed in getting your supplies on to the mountain?"

"I have very good documents. . . . Don't be afraid. Whatever I have left over I will share out among the concentration camps. And you shall receive particulars."

Lepsius asked him to address his letter to Nezimi Bey. That would be safer. He must, by Allah's mercy, be prudent! They could not risk this new way being blocked.

"So, after all, I haven't come back to Istanbul for nothing." Dr. Lepsius, back in his room, having conducted the Agha to the street, was convinced of that. His pious visitor had left something of himself behind in the little bedroom, a deeper peace than heretofore. In the certain knowledge that today his work had advanced, the pastor got into bed. But now the men in the tekkeh came to life again, their strength, their eyes and faces, came crowding in on him. Till now he had not realized so clearly how much more forceful, larger than life, were these personalities, which today it had been granted him to meet: Sheikh Achmed, his son, the Türbedar. His thoughts strayed off into long disputations with them, which brought him sleep. But sleep did not last. Dull thunder woke him in the night. His windowpanes were rattling very oddly. This clatter was a familiar sound. The guns of the French and English fleets knocked for admission. He sat up in bed. His hand fumbled for the switch. But he could not find it. It was like a sharp stab in the heart. Had not Nezimi warned him to scrutinize every little incident? Anything might have its special significance. That "attempt" on Enver's and Talaat's lives. It had been a facet of truth, no empty delusion, but in deep organic

564

relationship with Sheikh Achmed's power. Lepsius longed to close his eyes against some glimpse of a God-forsaken pit which gaped beneath him. A deep awe invaded his spirit. Had he been granted a glimpse into the future, or only surrendered to some obscurely murderous thought in himself? The guns growled. The panes rattled. Absurd! Absurd! he tried to tell himself. But his feverish heart already knew that God had re-established His justice, before the scales had broken under their load.

2

Stephan Sets Out and Returns

HAIK and the swimmers set forth under the eyes of the whole people, gathered at twilight round the North Saddle to see them go. It was the first time Gabriel had been absent from a public occasion of such magnitude. Yet nobody seemed to miss the leader, the man who had beaten back the Turks in three great battles, the general whom these folk of the seven villages had to thank for the few remaining thousand breaths they might still be permitted by fate to draw.

But Stephan had lost most prestige. What a day of disasters! First, he had not been allowed to volunteer. He, the conqueror of the howitzers, had been considered too inferior to go with Haik! And not even that was enough! His father had rated him in public, degraded him in front of Iskuhi, in front of all the other fellows, whom he had scarcely won over to his side, to the rank of weakling. It was very natural indeed that the ambitious Stephan, wounded in his honour as he was, should not have realized the anxiety concealed in a few harsh words, and only felt contempt and dislike in them.

And yet, even so, it might all have come right again, had Maman, that very afternoon, not completed his father's cruel work. In spite of the coarse and hideous words, whose meaning Stephan could only half understand, he had still no real conception of the incident, so pregnant in consequences. Or rather, whenever he tried to visualize it, his thoughts became confused, his grief intolerable, as it struggled nearer and nearer the truth. Then, like a runner, he clenched both fists in front

of his chest, astounded that a heart should have room in it for
so much burning agony. All ambition and vanity had been
silenced. Only this burning grief remained. Stephan had quarrelled with his father. He had lost his mother, in some obscure fashion more grievous than death. As the hours dragged
on, it grew clearer and clearer to him that he could go back
neither to one nor the other. In a curious way he felt cut off
from them. They had become enemies. For that very reason
he must not go back to them, no matter how much all the
child in him might cry out with longing to do so. Even before he took his great decision, he had made up his mind to
avoid Three-Tent Square. It was out of the question to meet
Monsieur Gonzague again and share his sleeping-quarters,
now that in the eyes of all the boys the Greek had become a
mean scoundrel. As evening approached, Stephan had made
up his mind. He cut the knot of all these problems. He had
crept into the sheikh-tent and hastily stuffed all that seemed to
be necessary into his Swiss rucksack. Whatever else might
suffer, he would never again eat at Maman's table, or sleep
in his bed. He would live on his own, apart from everyone—
though how, it was still impossible to decide. Then, later, he
stood a few minutes outside the doors of Juliette's tent. It was
laced up tight from inside. Not a word, or sound, from within.
Only the faint light of an oil lamp through the chinks. His
hand was already reaching up for the drumstick of the little
gong, which hung over the door. But he conquered his weakness and went striding off, with his rucksack on his shoulders,
no longer stifling sobs. On the North Saddle he had come into
the midst of the gathered crowds, waiting for the departure of
Haik and the swimmers. No one would speak to him, the
fallen hero! They all stared at him oddly and turned their
heads. Often he heard such laughter behind him as froze his
heart. At last Stephan lay down behind one of the defence-
works, where he could stay unscathed and watch it all without
being noticed.

First the two swimmers were sent with a blessing on their way. Since they were Protestants, it was Aram Tomasian who addressed them. But Ter Haigasun made the sign of the cross over their foreheads. Then pastor and priest led the young swimmers past the first trenches and over the bend of the Saddle, to the point where the shrub-grass slope rose northwards. Thin smoke-streams from the distant forest fire impregnated this air—it almost imperceptibly veiled the moon, causing its metallic light to tremble, in vibrant haze. It really looked as though these swimmers and their escort were setting out into some beyond, steeped in light, but from which there could be no returning. The crowd would have liked to come surging after them. But the armed guards had formed a cordon and would only let relations come past it. Pastor Aram had arranged it so, in order that these last good-byes might not be encroached upon by strangers. The first farewells were said by distant relatives and the boys' godfathers. Each of these had some small gift to bestow—a few remnants of tobacco, some precious sugar, or even only a holy picture or a medal. The priests took care that these first proceedings should not be too long drawn out, and scarcely had the more distant relatives bestowed their gifts when they departed, with Ter Haigasun and Tomasian. Only their nearest and dearest were left for a short while with the swimmers. A short, strangled embrace! The boys kissed their fathers' hands. The mothers turned away sobbing. They waved disconsolately. Then, even their parents had left them alone.

This, and what happened after it, filled the lonely Stephan's heart with a bitter-sweet grief. The swimmers were still not alone. Suddenly two girls were standing beside them. They were as like the boys as their two sisters. The crowd even was put to silence by the sight of these four young people, who disappeared together up the slope, hand in hand, into the vague, moonlit smoke-haze. But it was not long till the girls were back again, slowly coming downhill, each apart from the other.

Meanwhile Ter Haigasun had said a few words of admonishment to the Aleppo runner, blessed him, and crossed his forehead. This farewell was far quicker and more casual. The widow Shushik had neither any relatives in these parts, nor had she managed to make one friend. Strangers are always suspect. Nor had Widow Shushik herself so far made any attempt to consort with her neighbours. Her huge peasant hands had always fended for themselves. Therefore only Aram Tomasian and Ter Haigasun could accompany her, as now she offered up her sole remaining treasure, her Haik.

Ter Haigasun, replacing his dead father, embraced and kissed the young Aleppo runner, and held out his hand for the boy to kiss. He and Aram had a sum of money to give to Haik, so that he might, if need arose, buy his life with bribes. They left the mother and son alone. But Shushik did no more than stroke Haik's forehead in quick embarrassment, before she turned to follow the two priests. Yet Stephan noticed that she did not go back among the people, already streaming off towards their huts, but wandered indecisively away, in the direction of the rock barricades.

It was the first time that Gabriel Bagradian had not spent a whole night in the north trench. For tonight the Council had given the command to Chaush Nurhan the Lion. Luckily no attack seemed possible. The scouts announced no threatening movement in the valley, only peaceful troops going about their normal soldiers' routine along the village roads between Wakef and Kebussiye.

This sense of security possessed not only the garrison but Nurhan, who played cards with the elder men. They all were relaxed. The South Bastion was an almost undisciplined nest of deserters. Sentries kept leaving their posts to gossip with comrades. The commandant, who as a rule was not to be joked with, even allowed his men to infringe one of the strict-est prohibitions and light several twig-fires.

These freshly kindled bonfires and shouting voices enabled Stephan to make a quick dash over the crest, on the opposite side, without being seen or hailed from the camp. He was in a hurry, since Haik must by now be well ahead. Stephan ran as hard as he could. The rucksack on his back was by no means heavy: five boxes of sardines, a few bars of chocolate, a couple of biscuits, a few underclothes. The thermos flask which his father had forgotten in the tent he had asked Kristaphor to fill with wine for him. These, and a rug, formed his whole accoutrement, apart from his kodak. Stephan could not bring himself to part with that Christmas present, the last in Paris, though he had used up every roll of film. It was sheer childishness. And, since Haik carried no weapon, he had also abandoned his intention of stealing a gun from one of the stands of arms. In a few minutes he had come to the counter-slope. There a long, wide clearing stretched in front of him, upon which, in ebbing moonlight, unsullied here by any smoke-swaths, the Caucasian giantess Shushik sat erect. Her long, rigid legs, under spreading skirts, and the shadows cast by them, fantastically lengthened by the moon, covered a whole stretch of Musa Dagh. But Haik her son, bony and tall as he was, had nestled up to his mother like a suckling. He sat half in her lap, and kept his head buried in her breasts. It looked, in this marble light, as though the woman had bared them, to let her almost grown-up child drink from her blood again. Haik, the dour, tough Armenian boy—the disdainful Haik—seemed to long to creep back for ever into his mother. His breath came short, with little sobs. Her own stifled grief kept forcing its way out of the giantess, as she stroked her sacrificed child. Stephan stood rigid in his hiding-place—ashamed at having to look at this, and yet not able to see enough of it. When Haik suddenly sprang up and helped his mother to her feet, Stephan felt as though his body were cut in two. The widow's son only said a few curt, admonishing words, and then at last: "Now you must go."

The uncouth Shushik at once obeyed, without inflicting the pain of another embrace upon her boy. She left him in a busy haste to end it quickly. Haik stood motionless, looking after her. His face twitched as she turned, but he did not raise his hand to greet her. When Shushik's great shadow had disappeared, he sighed with relief and set out slowly. Stephan waited, in his hiding-place, to give Haik a little leeway. His companion must have time to forget these farewells before he ran after him. But young Bagradian had not reckoned with Hagop. That yellow-haired cripple, the "book-reader," a sensitive boy, had not managed all day long to get young Stephan off his conscience. He too had scoffed at his friend. True that Hagop had done his best to atone for treachery when the crowd began to chase Stephan. But cripples, like all other despised people, find it hard to repress a feeling of triumph when any superior, even their own friend, is degraded. So it was not enough. Hagop not only felt guilty, but very anxious. He was full of presentiments. For hours he had been looking about for Stephan, hopping with wild nimbleness round the enclosure and all the other places where boys assembled. He had even dared to spy into Juliette's tent, through a chink in the canvas door. He could not rid his mind of what he had seen: the tall, white woman stretched out like a corpse on the bed, and the leader, standing and staring down at her, as though he were dreaming where he stood. Then, when the one-legged Hagop had caught sight of Stephan with his rucksack in the crowd that had come to say good-bye to the messengers, his vague fears had become certainties. Now, panting with the exertion, he held on to Stephan.

"You mustn't do that. No! You've got to stay here!"

Stephan with a brutal shove sent Hagop spinning to the ground. "You're a dirty dog. I don't want anything more to do with you."

571

Gabriel's son was not of the kind who forgive easily. But Hagop caught him by the leg. "You aren't to go. I won't let you. You're to stay here."

"Let me go, or I'll give you a kick in the face."

The cripple hauled himself up by Stephan; he hissed despairingly: "You've got to stay. Your mother's ill! You don't know yet . . ."

Even this did not lure. Stephan only hesitated a second. Then he drew down the corners of his mouth. "I can't do anything for her. . . ."

Hagop hopped a few steps backwards. "Don't you know you'll never come back here—that you won't ever see her again?"

Stephan stood for a while and stared at the ground; but then he turned and began to run after Haik.

Hagop still panted after him. "I'm going to shout—I'll wake them. . . . They'll lock you up. . . . I'll shout, I tell you!" And indeed he began. But his thin voice could only carry far enough to stop Haik, who was still not two hundred yards away from them. The Aleppo runner turned and stood still. Stephan rushed to meet him, with Hagop following, scarcely a hand's breadth after his two-legged friend.

To prevent Hagop's voice from cutting across him Stephan shouted as he ran: "Haik, I'm coming along with you."

The "people's messenger" let the two come along before he answered. He scrutinized Stephan, half closing his serious eyes. "Why are you keeping me back? I can't afford to lose a second."

Stephan clenched resolute fists. "I mean to come with you to Aleppo."

Haik had cut himself a stick. He held it out like a weapon, as though to impede the unauthorized intruder. "I'm sent by the Council of Leaders, and Ter Haigasun has blessed me. You haven't been either sent or blessed. . . ."

Hagop, whom Haik's presence always made timid and

572

rather fawning, repeated this with malicious zeal. "You haven't been sent or blessed. To you it's forbidden."

Stephan gripped the end of Haik's stick, which he pressed like a hand. "There's enough room for you and me."

"It isn't a question of you and me. It's a question of the letter which I've got to deliver to Jackson."

Stephan slapped his pocket in triumph. "I copied out the letter to Jackson. Two are better than one."

Haik planted his stick on the ground, firmly, to put an end to it. "Always trying to be cleverer than anyone."

This, too, Hagop faithfully echoed. But Stephan gave not an inch of ground. "You do as you like! There's enough room. You can't stop me going to Aleppo."

"But you can stop the letter from reaching there."

"I'm no worse a runner than you."

That scornful note crept into Haik's voice, which so often before had made Stephan wild. "Can't ever stop bragging. . . ."

After all today's intolerable wounds, this was too much for Stephan. He sat on the ground and hid his face. But Haik let him feel all his disdain.

"Crying already—and *that* says it wants to go to Aleppo!"

Stephan could only sob: "I can't go back— Oh, Jesus Christ —I—can't go back. . . ."

Now perhaps Haik got an inkling of what was happening in Stephan. He may perhaps have thought of Shushik, his mother. Perhaps he even felt he would like a companion on the long, dangerous way. Who can say what he thought? But at least his manner became far more conciliatory as now he remembered Stephan's words. "You're quite right. There's plenty of room for you, too. No one can stop you."

But Hagop summoned up all his courage for one desperate objection. "What? I can stop him. Christ Saviour—I'll go and tell the leaders."

This was the stupidest thing he could have said. It was these few words brought the decision, since they put Haik in a rage. Serious and tall as he was, Haik, in the depths of his heart, still obeyed the moral code of schoolboys—that one fundamental law of their being, which all the world over is the same: no squealing! It made no difference what you squealed for, or when. To squeal remained the one unforgivable crime. So Haik, with his brutal frankness, turned on the cripple: "Tell the leaders, will you? Before you do, I'll knock your one leg so lame that you won't be able to crawl back home on it."

Hagop hopped back, a good long way, in sheer alarm. He knew Haik, whose habit it was to carry out his threats with two iron fists. Haik could not abide the fair-haired Hagop. This opposition had provoked all his natural tyranny. It turned the scale in Stephan's favour. Now came his matter-of-fact question: "Have you got enough to eat for five days? It'll take as long as that—if we get there, that is."

Stephan thumped his knapsack magnificently; he might have had supplies for a long expedition in it. And Haik made no further inquiries. He ordered curtly: "Well, quick march! You've made me waste too much time as it is!"

He had not said which way Stephan was to march—back to the camp, or on to Aleppo with him. He went striding on, and concerned himself no further with the others. Stephan kept close on his heels. So that Haik had not taken Stephan with him, but only allowed him to come along. Certainly there was "plenty of room" in the trackless mountains.

Hagop stood undecided, watching the people's messenger and the runaway till they disappeared over the top of the next moonlit slope. It took him nearly an hour to hop back to the Town Enclosure. Stephan's senseless flight weighed like a rock on him. What ought he to do? In his family's hut they were all asleep. His father growled a few sleepy words of reproof at him for being so late. Hagop, without undressing, flung himself down on his mat and stared up at the roof of branches, through which faint moonshine was filtered, as through a close sieve. He had still not managed to get to sleep when Avakian, long after midnight, came in to wake the whole family. Poor Hagop confessed at once, and led Gabriel, Kristaphor, Avakian, and the other men whom Gabriel had summoned to help him to the place where he had left Stephan and Haik. Search parties were sent out at once. It was sunrise before Gabriel got back, having searched in vain, with Kevork the dancer. The boys had got much too far ahead. Nor had Haik followed the route set by the Council, but let his own sure instinct guide him.

WHILE the swimmers, skirting the Cape Ras el-Khanzir, were directing their steps with certainly towards Arsus, the village on the coast, the boys walked on all night long, by difficult up-and-down paths through the mountains. Haik had been warned to remain as long as he possibly could on the safe mountain ridges till he came to the southern end of the valley of Beilan. Then, having come down on to the plain via Kyrk-Khan, he was to keep along near the big highroad which leads to Aleppo by way of Hammam. These moonlit August nights would make it easy for him to push on over reaped maize-fields and burnt-up plains, where he would find enough cover if he were threatened. But as he came nearer the big town, he must venture out on to the highroad and jump into one of the peasants' carts loaded with maize or liquorice-root. With God's help he could hide in it and get past the military barriers into the outskirts of the town. But, whatever happened, the letter to Mr. Jackson must not be found on him. Haik explained all this precisely to Stephan, giving gruesome pictures of dangers and obstacles which they would meet, the instant they touched the plain. Here in the empty mountains it was still child's play. After about an hour's walk the goats' path, which Haik, without seeing it, sensed with his feet, dipped into the valley.

The people's messenger stopped and admonished Stephan:

575

"Now's your time, if you want to turn back. You can't get lost. Think it over! Later you won't be able to do it."

Stephan made an angry movement. But his heart was full of doubts. His reasons for running away from home seemed suddenly not quite so valid as they had been.

Haik pointed to the Damlayik, where a far, red shimmer still showed the woods to be on fire. "You'll never get back there, and see them again——"

Young Bagradian still could not manage to find out what he really wanted. He would rather have died than let Haik think that he was soft. Shamefaced, he pulled out the map of this neighbourhood which had once hung in Uncle Avetis's study. He pretended, with a solemn face, to be doing his best to get his bearings in the clear moonlight. But Haik, annoyed by such "stuck-up twaddle," struck the map out of Stephan's hand and wasted no further good advice. This brought out all Stephan's resolution. He'd show him! Why, he could march much better than Haik! He began to walk on, at a crazy pace, straining every muscle to tire the other. But Haik did not so much as think of allowing Stephan to force him to an idiotic speed. He kept an even pace, almost a slow one. Stephan's heart stood still. He was alone! Instead of "showing" Haik, he had only managed to lose his way and—he could feel —without help from the other, would never manage to find it in this wilderness. His heart thumped, but he dared not call. When, after one eternal minute, Haik came out through some bushes into the moonlight, not troubling even to notice the independent one, Stephan submitted in silence to the stronger, though he pretended not to have had this shameful experience. That settled their long struggle once and for all. Haik was supreme. They soon came into the narrow valley. On their right was the long, straggling village of Sanderan. Thank God, not a light was burning in it! Only one nasal human voice could be heard, raised in a subdued hum. It was a hair-raising sensation to go creeping past inhabited houses, with death in all of them. But the wild dogs of Sanderan could not be tricked; they picked up the trail of the young Armenians, and followed them a long way past the village. Haik, with his incredible certainty, found another goat-track, leading north-west, back into the mountains. As once again they walked through a sparse wood, drenched in moonlight, a sense of wild adventure crept into Stephan. The air was so fresh! He forgot everything. He would have liked to shout and sing. Was there such a thing as being tired? By sunrise, in spite of several halts, they had covered a distance of nearly ten miles, and reached the place where the mountains slope down northwards in wide terraces of woodland. Stephan, map and all, would have been quite lost.

Haik sharply pointed their direction. "We've got to go that way. Beilan!"

He could sense it all, though he had only been to Beilan once in his life, with his mother, that is to say, riding on donkey-back, and even so by quite a different way, along the coast. Now he was pleased, and said they had better hunt out a sleeping-place and rest till midday. That short sleep would have to be enough; otherwise it wasn't to be managed. Haik did not need to nose round for long before finding a shady place, with good turf to sleep on, and even a stream; though that was, perhaps, not such a miracle in these watered surroundings of Musa Dagh. For Haik, whose very skin made him aware of the hidden peculiarities of every strip of ground, the least alteration of temperature, any difference in vegetation or of animals near him, it was nothing at all to pick out water. The boys set up their camp beside the stream, which here, even, formed just the kind of pool they had been looking for. They slaked their thirst. And then, to Haik's amazement, this child of the West pulled a cake of soap out of his rucksack and began to wash himself. Haik watched these superfluous proceedings with serious, sarcastic eyes. When Stephan had done, he dipped his feet deliciously into the cold pool, since feet were what mattered. Then they swapped food with all the pleasure of youth. Shushik had given her son three big sausages stuffed with finely chopped mutton, fat, and onions and a loaf as hard as stone—though Heaven knows how she had got hold of it. It was the worst crime on the Damlayik to hide bread or flour or corn of any kind, punished by several days' fasting. Yet such secret treasures kept appearing in the huts, and their origin still remained a mystery. It is always the same old story. No legal rationing, not even the most drastically controlled, can quite dam up the creative torrent of life, which always succeeds in producing the incredible, out of nothing.

It was almost symbolic that Stephan should have offered French sardines and Swiss chocolate in exchange for mutton sausage and stale bread. Haik scarcely knew the names of such foreign dainties. The boys did not control their appetites, but made big inroads into their supplies without even thinking of tomorrow.

Suddenly Haik remembered, packed his away, and advised Stephan: "Better drink water and save the food."

So it was done. They drank great gulps of spring water out of the aluminum top of the thermos flask, and Stephan mixed in some of his wine. He felt as well as though this were a holiday excursion, and not the expedition of two Armenians menaced on all sides, on their way into the pitiless town—an expedition which he had neither the right nor ability to take part in. All his grief seemed left behind, once and for all, on the Damlayik. How deliciously exciting it seemed to be resting here, having walked all night, in the harmless, pleasant, morning sunshine. Stephan folded up his rug for a pillow. The sunshine warmed him more and more. He sat up again to ask like a child: "Do you think there'll be any wild animals?"

The self-important Haik pulled out his clasp-knife and laid it beside him. "You needn't worry. Even when I'm asleep, I see everything."

Stephan was not worrying in the least. What a good watcher, even when asleep, Haik was! Never before had he felt more nestling trust in a human being than he did in this rough boy, for whose admiration he had striven so hard. He surrendered utterly to his leadership. He fell asleep. His hand fumbled to seek his friend.

"Now we must make tarbushes," explained Haik, "so that we won't be noticed if we meet people." He unfolded his aghil sash and wound it adroitly round his felt cap. Stephan did his so badly that Haik had to help him. While adjusting the headgear of the prophet he instructed the inexperienced one: "If necessary you'll have to copy me. Do everything exactly the way I do it. And don't ever talk."

It was late afternoon. Between the top branches of oaks and beeches a golden sky, full of swarming carrion birds. The boys had been nearly six hours on the road. But the word "road" is euphemistic. Far and wide, there was not so much as a goat-path. They had forced their way along the dried-up beds of streams which would be sure to lead them into the valley. Literally they had "forced their way," impeded at every step by masses of resistant undergrowth, clinging creepers, and walls of shrubs, as hard and elastic as rubber, but barbed all over with long prickles. Incredible how many terraces and rocky steeps they had already had to clamber down. The mountain seemed always to have nothing more to say, and never to come to the end of what it was saying. Stephan had ceased to feel his body. His hands, his knees, his legs were covered with scratches and wounds. For hours he had said nothing. But not complained. Now they were sitting together on a bare rock, overlooking the chalk-white highroad from Beilan. It looked brand-new. Stone heaps all along it indicated the work of human hands. And indeed this by-road, which linked up the harbour of Alexandretta with the plains of Aleppo, and so the Mediterranean with all Asia, was a tribute to the unleashed energy, the power, of Jemal Pasha, the Syrian dictator. That iron-willed general had ordained that within a month the wretched, broken track should have become an impeccable highway, smooth and properly underpinned—and lo! it was done. The Turks were amazed at the energy they found they possessed. At this point, under Stephan's and Haik's eyes, the road took a bend eastwards. They could look down on only a small section of it: not a man or vehicle, no mule or horse, came into sight, only here and there a hare or squirrel flitted across the white chalk ribbon. Stephan gazed down with longing eyes at its smooth possibilities. But even Haik seemed to be yielding to temptation. Without having said a word to Stephan to warn him how imprudent it was to do so, he jumped up and ran down the slope. When they felt the smooth road under their feet, it was like a drink when one is thirsty. All Stephan's ambition and energy were renewed. He kept pace with Haik. Right and left, steep banks began to rise. The road had become almost a tunnel, a narrow pass between two cliffs. This oddly enough increased their sense of security, and with it their carelessness. Then the cliffs widened out a little, the road took a steep downward incline. Another bend and the plain would surely open out! This road carried irresistibly onwards; they were borne, so to speak, along its current. Straight to disaster! Since when they came round the bend, they found, not the plain in front of them, but a Turkish guard-house, over which waved the half-moon flag. Four horrible-looking saptiehs lounged in front of it. A detachment of inshaat taburi were working away along the edge with spades, mattocks, and hammers. The travellers had been too exhausted to catch the sounds of their picks and shovels, the hoarse, dreary song of these labourers. They were so terror-stricken that even Haik took a full minute before he moved. But then he snatched Stephan's hand and tugged him away. They went galloping off round the bend, up among the trees. Unluckily the place was bare of rocks or shrubs to hide in.

There were only the slender stems of young beeches, which gave no cover. The slope ascended gently. Where did it lead? Haik's inner eye had a vision of the head saptieh bending forward, shading his eyes, growling out an order, and giving chase, with his whole corps. It was worse than a nightmare. Voices! The leaves began to rustle with Turkish steps. Stephan shut his eyes and kept close to Haik, who flung his left arm round his body. Haik's right hand gripped his open claspknife. They prepared for death. But the sharp whisper they heard was not in Turkish.

"Boys! Boys! Who are you? Don't be afraid!"

These Armenian words came sepulchrally. When Stephan opened his eyes, it was to see a ragged Armenian soldier emerge breathless between the tree-stems. A scrubby skull, with eager eyes in it. Even to the eyes, the man was not unlike Kilikian. Haik controlled himself, put away his knife. The roadmender's voice shook with excitement.

"Aren't you the son of the big widow Shushik, who has her house on the road to Yoghonoluk? Don't you know me?"

Haik approached the skeleton incredulously; loose rags enveloped its bones, its feet were bare. He eyed it sharply.

"Vahan Melikentz, from Azir?" He sounded as hesitant as though he were trying to pick up a name at random. The labourer-private nodded an eager head; tears had begun to trickle into his bristles, so moved he was at meeting his two young countrymen. Haik had only guessed at his name. What had this ragged scarecrow to do with Melikentz, the dignified, gossiping bee-keeper he had met almost every day?

Melikentz raised despairing hands. "Are you crazy? What do you want to come here for? Thank Christ Saviour, the onbashi didn't catch sight of you. Yesterday, down there by the bend, they shot five Armenians, a family trying to get to Alexandretta."

Haik, once again in full self-possession, gave the ex-beekeeper a dignified account of his mission.

Melikentz was horrified. "The road's full of inshaat taburi, as far as Hammam. And yesterday two companies came into Hammam. They're to be sent against the Damlayik. All you can do is to walk at night along by the Ak Denis swamp. But then you'll fall in."

"We won't fall in, Melikentz," Haik declared, with laconic certainty. And he asked his countryman to show him the nearest way to the plain.

Vahan Melikentz mourned: "If they miss me, or I'm late falling in, I'll get the third-degree bastinado. Perhaps they may shoot me. . . . I wish they would! You lads have no idea how little I care. Oh, if only I'd gone along with your lot, and not with Nokhudian the pastor! You were the clever ones! Christ help you! He hasn't helped us!"

And Melikentz was in fact risking death to show them their way. Yet they had only to go on by a short, fairly easy stretch of woodland. The poor bee-keeper talked continually; he seemed to want to recover a whole lost harvest of unused words, if only to scatter it, before his last breath. The fate of those on Musa Dagh seemed to interest him less than describing his own. So that Stephan and Haik learned something of what had been done to Nokhudian's followers. All the able-bodied men among them had been told off from the rest in Antakiya, and sent to Hammam for road-building. Their women, children, the old and sick, had been driven on towards the Euphrates. Pastor Nokhudian had managed to get nothing from the Kaimakam—nothing at all! But the Armenian inshaat taburi were being used in a very special way. To each detachment was assigned a particular stretch of road, which had to be finished off at double-quick time. When the onbashi reported the task as completed, the detachment was drummed together, herded into the nearest wood, and there neatly dispatched, with a quick volley, by a special firing-party, expert by now at this routine.

"Our bit of road," said Melikentz dryly, "goes as far as Top

Boghazi; that's about another four thousand paces. It'll be about six or seven days, at most, if we're clever. Then it's our turn. So if they shoot me today I'll only have lost six, or at most, seven days."

Yet, in spite of his simple calculation, Melikentz left them in breathless haste, having brought them where he could point out their way. Six days of horrible living were, after all, six days more of life. As he said good-bye, he gave Haik a lump of Turkish honey, given him by a compassionate Mussulman woman.

A rusty sunset was in the sky when they found themselves standing on the last, the lowest, of the mountain slopes. Flat land spread before them to the horizon. They were looking over a wide lake, in whose milky flatness the insipid sunset palely glistened. It was the Lake of Antioch, of which distant glimpses were to be had even from certain points of the Damlayik. But here Ak Denis, the "white sea," looked so near, you could almost touch it. The northern ridge of the lake was girdled with a broad belt of reeds, alive with plungings and cawings. Clumsy-winged herons, silver and purple, flapped out of these reeds, to circle low above the lake, drawing ornate legs slowly after them that cut the surface of the water. Then they sank slowly down to brood. A wedge of wild ducks clattered with the swiftness of torpedoes through the milky flood, to land among the reeds on an island. From where they stood the boys could hear the bickerings of reed-thrushes, the human, almost political disputation of ten thousand inflated, gigantic frogs. This reedy fringe of Ak Denis ebbed away gradually into the plain. Far out there were still thick clusters, but also there were stagnant pools, blind eyes, the whites of which looked tremulous. In contrast to the empty steppes this belt of urgent life along the lake seemed almost an exaggeration. It extended like the corpse of a fabulous dragon, being gnawed at by ornate birds of prey.

Whereas Stephan saw only the lake, Haik's sharp eyes had

at once spied out the nomad tents strewn here and there along the east, the few horses, browsing with hanging heads in the smoky void. He pointed, certain of their direction. "That's our way. Between the road and the swamp. We'll get on, as soon as the moon rises. Here, give us your flask! I'll go for some water. Here, the water's still good to drink. We must drink a lot. Meantime, you can get some sleep."

But Stephan did not sleep. He only waited till his mate got back with two brimming flasks. Obediently he drank as much as he could. Neither thought of eating. Haik spread his rug to wrap himself into it. But Stephan crept up to him. It was no longer enough to sleep as they had that morning, in cool proximity. Now he could not hide his fearful need of friendship and love. And lo! Haik understood. Haik was no longer dour and reserved; Haik did not keep him at arm's length. Indeed he almost seemed to welcome the confiding closeness of young Bagradian. Like an elder brother, he drew him close and covered him. The two boys slept in each other's arms.

HAIK and Stephan were in the plains. But now, against all expectation, they found that the rough, uneven Musa Dagh, full of clefts and gullies, had been far easier to walk on than this flat expanse, called El Amk, the "sinking ground." This sly, uncertain soil, covered with a greenish scurf, was already hostile, no longer Christian earth.

It was characteristic of Haik, with his sharp senses and almost superhuman sureness of nerve, to have chosen this way —at night especially. El Amk was really nothing but a göl, a swamp, about twelve miles long, the hair-thin edge of which would have to be kept to. There were not many shepherds, peasants, or nomads with courage enough to use this short-cut, to save themselves the long journey by road to the Kara-Su bridge. But it was the only way the boys could have chosen, since Vahan Melikentz had warned them of soldiers, saptiehs, and inshaat taburi along the whole length of the highroad. Haik had taken off his shoes, to be able to "get the feel" of the ground with his bare feet. Stephan did likewise. He had, as we know, long ceased to vie with his companion. They walked on the very thin, warm crust of a loaf, with the dough beneath them. This crust was cracked all over, and through the cracks rose dense, sulphurous vapours. Stephan proved intelligent enough to follow close on Haik's tracks, who, like a dancer, stepped out gingerly, with close attention, as though each step had been prescribed.

During this dance confused thoughts kept invading Stephan, they rasped and cackled in him. "Everyone goes along a road. Why can't we go along a road? . . . Oh, why are we Armenians?"

Haik shut him up, enraged: "Don't talk such rot! Better look out where you're going. Don't step where it's green. Understand?"

So then Stephan did his best to relapse into the mental coma which helps us most to put up with bodily discomfort. He curvetted faithfully after Haik, engaged in picking out a way full of the oddest curves on this perilous crust. Thus they continued an hour—two hours—during which the moon at times lighted their way benevolently, only to vanish in evil caprice. Yet in spite of all the long way they had come, Stephan's exhaustion seemed rather to diminish as the night wore on. Dregs—half thought, half emotion—began to collect, like sediment, in his mind. It could not be controlled. He had to say it, no matter how afraid he might be of Haik: "I say, is it true that we aren't going to see our people" (he avoided any more intimate designation) "ever again?"

Haik did not stop his figured progress. It was some time before, on firmer ground again, he gave any answer. What he said, in spite of its Christian certitude, was said with clenched fists, rather than with folded hands. "I shall certainly see mother again."

It was the first piece of intimate self-revelation that Stephan had had from Haik's lips. But, since Stephan, the *lycéen*, had not the certain faith of a race of tough Armenian mountaineers, he became subdued, and replied uncertainly: "But we can't ever get back on to the Damlayik."

It was obvious from Haik's savage growl, ready to spring, how much this talk went against the grain.

"The Damlayik's behind us. If Christ wills, we shall get to Aleppo. There Jackson will hide us in the consulate. That's what it says in the letter." And, spitefully: "Of course, there's nothing about *you* in it."

But by now Stephan's thoughts were not in the least concerned with himself, only with his father and mother, from whom he had so stupidly run away. Why? He himself no longer knew. All life had strangely shifted its perspective. The Damlayik had become the wildest nightmare, everything that had happened before it, reality. The sole reality. Well-ordered, clean, just as it should be. Jackson would put an end to all this nonsense. After all, it simply couldn't happen that a Stephan Bagradian should find himself in such a position that he would never see his parents again. His thoughts were in a sense becoming Jackson's—full of helpful schemes.

"Jackson'll cable. You *cable* to America, you know. Do you think the Americans'll send ships to fetch our people?"

"How should I know that, you sheep?"

Haik's increasing pace betrayed his wrath. The awed Stephan was forced to swallow down his need, and hurry to keep up with his leader. Though there was no wind, he felt as though a gale were swirling against him, preventing him from going a step further. Try as he might, he could not manage to get all this straight in his mind. His head swam. A stark beam of moonlight filled the whole world. An emerald-green streak of it streamed in upon him. For a second he forgot their danger.

The scream pulled Haik up short. He knew instantly what

had happened. A shadowy Stephan struggled for life. He had already sunk in up to the knees.

Haik hissed at him: "Quiet! Don't kick up such a row!"

But uncontrollable panic forced scream upon scream out of Stephan. He could not prevent them. He believed himself fallen between the jaws of a slimy whale; the monster sucked him slowly in, turning him over on its tongue. Already the pulpy, tumid mass was above his knees. Yet, in spite of it all, the seconds in which he did not struggle were oddly peaceful, and did him good.

Haik commanded: "One foot first. The right! Your right foot!"

Stephan, letting out little screams of terror, made useless movements. His legs had no strength left in them. Now came another, sharp command:

"Lie over on your belly!"

He bent forward obediently, so that he could just touch dry land with his finger-tips. When Haik saw that Stephan had not the strength to fend for himself, he wriggled flat on his face to the marshy place. But even the stick, gripped by the struggling Stephan, was not enough to give him sufficient strength. Then Haik undid his turban-cloth and threw it out to Stephan to knot round his chest. He held on like iron to the further end of it. It served as a kind of life-line. After endless efforts Stephan could at last free his right leg, which had not sunk in so very deep. Half an hour had passed before Haik drew him up like a drowning man on to firm ground. Another half-hour elapsed before Stephan had recovered enough strength to stumble on, along the dangerous way, with Haik keeping hold of his hand. He was covered in slime, well up to his chest. In the air, it dried quickly, and under its thick crust the skin of his arms and legs contracted. It was indeed lucky that Stephan had put his shoes in his rucksack and thrown the rucksack far away from him on to dry ground while he was struggling.

Haik firmly led his half-swooning friend. He did not reprimand him for his carelessness, but repeated several times, like an incantation: "We've got to be over the bridge before it gets light. There may be saptiehs there."

All that was left of pride and ambition in young Bagradian came into play again. "Yes, I can walk . . . all right again . . . now."

As they turned northward, the ground became firmer. It was less like walking on a mattress. Stephan let go of Haik and pretended he could step out briskly. A distant glitter, a breath of coolness. Haik sensed the Kara-Su river. Soon they were clambering up the dam on to the road, which lit up the night like a broad beam. The sentry-box on the bridge was empty. The boys—as though the devil were chasing them—raced past this, the greatest of all dangers, which, luckily, had ceased to be perilous. But this time the smooth, easy highroad no longer seemed to comfort Stephan as it had that afternoon. That smoothed-out path of civilization took the last strength out of his legs. Beyond the bridge, he stumbled more and more. He began to walk in zigzags, and suddenly lay down on the roadway.

Haik stood, staring down at him. Only then, he expressed despair: "I'm wasting time."

ALMOST an hour beyond the bridge, the road, built over a long, high stone embankment, passes the outskirts of the big swamp, El Amk. The embankment is called Jisir Murad Pasha, and is the real beginning of the wide steppe country which stretches on for many hundreds of miles, away past Aleppo and the Euphrates, as far as Mesopotamia. But not so very far beyond this embankment there lies, on the northern side of the road, the most charming strip of hilly country, like a last green consolation before rigid death. At the foot of this little cluster of hills is a big Turkoman village, Ain el

Beda, the "clear fount." But long before clusters of huts thicken to become this village, the road meets single houses, white farmsteads of wood or stone that catch the eye. Here, fifty years ago, Abdul Hamid's government had ordered a tribe of Turkoman nomads to settle down. No people make better or more hard-working peasants than do such converted nomads. It was proved by the well-built, well-roofed houses of this green and gentle strip of country.

The first of these farms stood on the road-edge. An hour after sunrise its owner came to the door of his house, to sniff the wind, test the weather, look in all four quarters of the sky, and so spread out his little praying-mat that, turned to Mecca, he might perform the earliest of his five daily devotions. This pious man had been unaware of the two boys. He saw them out of the corner of his eye, squatting together, close beside his house, on their rugs, and going through the same prescribed praying motions. The sight of such early morning fervour in two young men pleased the Turkoman. But, as a peaceable Moslem, he had no thought of interrupting his own lengthy devotions with profane inquiries. Haik, by allowing him many halts, had managed to drag Stephan past the Jisir Murad Pasha embankment as far as to the verge of these little hills. The sight of peasant homesteads had caused him again to warn young Stephan to imitate his every movement and, above all, say as little as possible. Stephan could speak only a few words of Turkish, in an accent that would have betrayed him instantly. As to the Moslem prayer, said Haik, it would not be a sin if one kept on whispering fervent "Our Fathers." But this Stephan could not manage. As stiff and lifeless as a doll, it was the very utmost he could do to effect a wooden copy of Haik's fervent duckings. When it was over, he sank down at once on his praying-mat, to stare up at the fresh dawn sky through glassy eyes.

The Turkoman peasant, a man well past the prime of life,

came waddling over towards the suspects. "Well, you rascals! Out on the road so early, eh! What are you after? What are you looking for?"

Luckily he himself spoke patois, so that Haik's Armenian accent did not strike him as particularly strange. And into Syria, that great stock-pot of the races, all languages are tossed together. So that the Turkoman's ear was not mistrustful.

"Sabahlar hajr olsun!" (Good morning, Father!) "We come from Antakiya. Lost our parents on the road! They went on with their cart, to Hammam. We wanted to run about a bit and got lost. The lad here, Hüssein, was nearly drowned. In the marshes. Now he's ill. Just look at him! Couldn't you give us somewhere we could sleep?"

With the motions of wisdom, the Turkoman stroked his grey beard. Then, taking the boys' part, he said, very justly: 'What sort of parents can these be, who go losing their children in a swamp, and then go on again? . . . Is this lad your brother?"

"No, but a kinsman, from Antakiya. My name is Essad. . . ."

"Well, this Hüssein of yours really does seem ill. Has he been drinking marsh-water?"

Haik only answered this with a pious proverb. He hung his head. "Give us food and somewhere to sleep, Father!"

None of all this deception was really necessary, since the Turkoman's heart was full of benevolence. For months now, convoys of Armenian exiles had come past his house. He had often helped Armenian sick, Armenian pregnant women, with food and drink, with shoes and clothing, beneficent, according to his means, quietly beneficent, without even thinking too much of the reward that he was laying up in the hereafter. But these works of mercy had to be done with circumspection, on account of the saptiehs. The crime of pitying an Armenian merited, by the new laws, the bastinado, prison perhaps, or, in very flagrant cases, death. Hundreds of good-hearted Turks all over the country, their hearts wrung

by the sight of miserable deportees, had had strange experiences. The peasant looked well at the two tramps. Those
thousands of Armenian eyes which had begged his charity on
the highroad came into his mind. The results of his comparison were fairly easy to deduce, especially in the case of the one
who was sick. Yet it was just this so-called Hüssein who
aroused pity in the Turkoman, rather than the so-called Essad
who, first, was not ill and, second, seemed smart enough for
anything.

So the master of the house called sharply, and two women
at once came forth to him, an old and a young, who, quickly,
seeing these strangers, let down their veils. They were given
a gruff order and disappeared again with busy haste. The
Turkoman led Stephan and Haik into his house. Next its
smoke-filled parlour, in which it was almost impossible to
breathe, there was a small, empty room, a kind of storeroom,
lit only by an opening in the roof. Meanwhile the women
had come with mats and coverlets. They spread two couches
on the dry floor. When they saw Stephan's arms and legs, still
masked over with a thick crust of slime, they brought in a
flat tub of hot water and monstrous scrubbing brushes and
began, with resolute, motherly strength, to rub down his
arms and legs; in the course of which arduous work the elder
even lifted her veil, since these were only half-grown children.
Under the scourings of these peasant women the rigid crust
not only flaked off Stephan's body, but off his spirit. Homesickness, long repressed, flooded his mind like boiling water.
He bit his lips, his eyes blinked treacherously. Moved by this
childish grief, the Turkoman women raised their voices in
strange, melodious consolations—not a word of which he
could understand. Then the old woman brought them a dish
of barley-groats in goat's milk, a flat loaf, and two wooden
spoons. As the boys ate, a numerous family of Turkomans
made its appearance, grinning with delight at its own hospitality, some in the doorway, some in the storeroom itself,

pressing the boys to eat their fill. But, in spite of their friendly words and the warm food, Stephan could scarcely swallow two mouthfuls, so sore and swollen was his throat. Haik finished up the whole portion, with the serious thoughtfulness of a worker in a heavy industry.

The inquisitive family departed. Stephan slept at once, but the canny Haik first made a few quick plans for tomorrow's route. He hoped that by evening Stephan would be feeling all right again, so that they might set out as the moon rose. Hammam could be easily reached in the night. If the road were clear, so much the better. If it were not, they could keep a little to one side of it, along the foot of the hills. And these hills would certainly be the best place in which to sleep tomorrow night, when they came past Hammam to the point where they would have to take their short-cut, avoiding the wide bend of the highway. Notwithstanding these many contretemps, Haik was, so far, satisfied. The greatest dangers lay ahead, but the troublesome part of their route was over. Unluckily he had not reckoned with Stephan. Whimpers and groans roused him from the sleep of exhaustion to which, in this safe room, he had let himself surrender without scruple. Stephan, twisted with pain, sat cramped on his mat. Fearful colic seemed to cut his body in two, the results of his adventure in the swamp, El Amk. And now he was clean, Haik saw that his whole body was covered with mosquito-bumps. Impossible now to get any sleep! The people of the house were as kind as ever. The women heated up round stones to lay on the sick boy's belly, and brewed a tea that may have been beneficial but which was certainly nauseating, for he could not hold it down.

The peasant had given "Essad" and "Hüssein" leave to sleep on his roof. They, who had lived weeks in the fresh air, could not hold out in this stuffy den, smoky, verminous, rancid with the stench of frying fat. Now they were sitting on their mats, between pyramids of corn-cobs, piled up bundles of reeds, stacks of liquorice-roots. Stephan, shivering with fever, wrapped in a rug, never took his eyes off the west. At this, the hour before evening, the mountains over along the coast looked huge, even taller than they were, ridge upon ridge of them, tinted in the richest hues, from deepest sapphire to silver, faint as a breath. And they looked incredibly near. Had Haik and Stephan really had to walk for the whole night, and half a day, to get no farther? That last ridge, which broke off sharply over towards the south, must be the Damlayik. It stood like a petrified wild beast with the hunt in full cry after it. Its long back trailed away northwards. Its head ducked down, among the nearer heights. But its claws struck out wildly behind it, where the wide gap of the Orontes gave a suggestion of the sea. Stephan saw only the Damlayik. He thought he could distinguish the South Bastion, the knolls, the indentation of the ilex gully, the North Saddle, from which such ages ago he had taken leave without saying good-bye. What had made him do it, exactly? He strove to remember, but in vain. The Damlayik seemed to be breathing hard, it seemed to hover nearer and nearer, across the Aleppo road, above this peasant's house amid Turkoman hills, straight to Stephan Bagradian.

Haik understood. The kindness of those who are really strong, which surrenders itself so easily to the fallen, invaded him. "Don't be afraid. We'll stay on here till you're able to run again."

The feverish Stephan still gazed in ecstasy at the mountains. "They're quite near—quite near. . . . I mean the hills are."

But then he sat up with a jerk, as though it was high time to get along. Haik's menacing words assailed him sharply. He repeated them with chattering teeth: "It isn't a question of you or me; it's a question of the letter to Jackson. . . ."

Haik nodded, but not reproachfully. "It'd have been better if Hagop had squealed on you . . ."

Stephan's shrunken little face was not angry now. It tried

to smile. "That doesn't matter. . . . I won't make you lose any time. . . . I shall go back . . . tomorrow."

Haik suddenly ducked his head, signed urgently to Stephan to do the same. Down the near roadway, which had not, all that day, been much frequented, came a curious procession, with babbling cries, with cries of anguish. It was only a few saptiehs, herding on a small Armenian convoy towards Hammam. Convoy was an absurd misnomer. These were only the sweepings of old people and tiny children, raked together from some God-forsaken village. The saptiehs, whose business it was to have reached Hammam before midnight, cursed and pummelled the wretched crew till, like ghosts, they vanished round the bend.

This significant interlude seemed to cause Haik to make up his mind. "Yes. You'd far better go back. But how? You can't get through the swamp without me. . . ."

Stephan, to whom the mountain looked so near, had lost all sense of possible measurements. "Why not? It's not so far . . ."

But Haik shook his head decisively. "No, no, you can't get through the swamp by yourself. You'd better go back by way of Antakiya. Over there—see? It'll be far easier. . . . But, even that way, they'll cop you on the road. You don't speak Turkish. You can't pray like they do, and anyway, as you look now, the sight of you would be enough to make them wild. . . ."

Stephan sank back dreamily on his mat. "I shall only walk at night. . . . Perhaps they won't cop me, if I do that . . ."

"Oh—you!" Haik growled this in scornful pity. He began to think how far back he could go with Stephan without wasting more than a day of his great mission. But young Bagradian, whose shivering, comfortable fever made everything seem so easy of achievement, lay there babbling: "Perhaps Christ Saviour'll help me."

And, as things were, this really seemed, to Haik, Stephan's

one chance. Apart from celestial aid there was not much prospect of his safe return to Musa Dagh. But, for the moment, it really began to look as though Heaven were on Stephan's side. For now the Turkoman peasant came climbing up a ladder on to his roof, and began to throw down bundles of reeds and liquorice-root. Haik sprang up at once and zealously helped him with the work.

When the roof was clear, the peasant had a surprising inspiration. His eyes twinkled. He said to Stephan: "Where do you lads want to make for? Early tomorrow I'm going in to market, to Antakiya. Since you two come from Antakiya, I don't mind giving you a lift and taking you home. We'll be there by evening. . . ."

And, proudly, he jerked his thumb towards the big stable behind the house. "I don't drive an ox-cart, you know. I've got my little pony, and a wagon with real wheels."

Haik pushed his imitation turban slightly askew, to scratch his reflective head, which his mother, Shushik, had clipped to the bone before he set out. "Father—would you mind taking my cousin, Hüssein, here, to Antakiya with you? That's where his folk live. Mine don't. They're in Hammam. Pity you aren't going to Hammam with your horse. I'll have to walk it."

The Turkoman studied the cunning one attentively. "So your folk live in Hammam, do they? Allah kerim, God is good, young man! I suppose I know everyone in Hammam. What sort of a business do they do there?"

Haik answered this with a look of pained indulgence: "But, Father, didn't I tell you, they've only been there since yesterday? They live in Khan Omar Agha. . . ."

"Yanasyje! May they be happy there! But Khan Omar Agha is full of military—the ones they're sending against the traitor ermeni on Musa Dagh."

"What's that you're saying, Father? Military? My folk knew nothing about that. Well, perhaps by now the soldiers'll have left again. After all, Hammam is big and they'll probably be able to find a shake-down."

There was really nothing to say against that. The Turkoman, not having managed to unmask Essad, thought hard for a while, moved his lips without any sound, and finally left them alone again.

Already, long before midnight, Haik got ready to leave. But, before he went, he did all he could for Stephan. He stuffed one of his sausages in the rucksack. God knew whether he mightn't lose himself and come to the end of his supplies. But Haik himself had no fear of finding as much food as he wanted anywhere in the plains of Aleppo. He filled Stephan's thermos flask at the stream which ran beside the house and brushed the caked mud off Stephan's clothes. As he did all this, with almost angry care, he kept repeating precise instructions as to how Stephan was to behave.

"He'll be carrying in these goods of his to market. The best thing you can do is not to say anything. You're ill—see? As soon as ever you see the town, jump out, but very, very quietly, mind—understand? And then you'd better lie down in a field—find some sort of hole—a ditch. And there you can wait till it gets dark. . . . Do you see?"

Stephan sat huddled up on his mat. He dreaded the colic, which was returning. Even more did he dread being left alone. The night was not cloudy, like last night, but stainlessly clear. The vast Milky Way, dense and sparkling, overarched the Turkoman's roof. For an instant Stephan felt Haik's hand in his. That was all. And he could hear his voice, as gruffly disdainful as of yore: "Listen—mind you don't forget to tear up your letter to Jackson!"

Haik's foot was already on the ladder, but he turned back once again to Stephan. Quickly, without a word, he made the sign of the cross on his forehead and on his chest. It was done shyly.

Where there is danger of death, any Armenian is the priest

and father of any other. So Ter Haigasun had instructed him, when he taught him their religion in Yoghonoluk, at a time when not one of them had known that death was already near.

JUST outside the village Ain el Beda the cart-track turned into the plain. The Turkoman lashed his little horse into a trot, through the fresh, empty morning. The laden cart rattled, with agonizing jolts, over the deep, stiff ruts. But Stephan scarcely noticed these painful joltings. He lay on his rug among bundles of reeds in a feverish doze. The fever was merciful. It deadened his sense of time and space. It surrounded him with vague but most pleasant pictures, so that he did not bother to think where he would be taken, nor what the future might produce. And again this fever, which tanned his brown skin to a deeper shade, helped him to play his part. Each time the peasant rested his horse, climbed off his seat, and came round to have a look at his passenger, Stephan would moan, and shut his eyes. So that none of the good Turkoman's many attempts to get into conversation really succeeded. All he got were monosyllabic groans with, now and again, a whining prayer to continue their journey. Haik had taught him what to say: "Ben bir az hasta im"— "I'm not very well." The reckless Stephan kept repeating it, on every occasion. It got him out of all his religious exercises, since Islam dispenses the sick and ailing from the performance of religious duties, which make demands on the body. When they had crossed the little river Afrin, by a wooden bridge, the peasant thought it time for their midday halt. He took his horse out of the shafts and strung on its nosebag. Stephan too had to get down, and sit with the old man by the roadside, on the dry steppe. This cart-track was scarcely frequented. All that morning they had only met two ox-carts, coming in the opposite direction. Most of the peasants in these parts used the great highroad, which leads from Hammam to Antakiya.

597

The Turkoman unpacked a flat loaf and goat's cheese, and pushed some over to Stephan. "Go on, boy, eat! Eating kills pain."

Stephan did not want to wound his host, and did his best to swallow some cheese. He chewed and chewed at the first mouthful but could not manage to get it down.

The friendly Turkoman watched with troubled eyes. "Perhaps you'll want more strength than you have, little son!"

Stephan could not understand the guttural, but knew that he must look as though he did. So he bowed, laid his hand on his heart, repeated his slogan, hoping for the best: "Ben bir az hasta im. . . ."

The Turkoman kept silence for some time. Then he began to work his huge jaws and, gripping his knife, made a mighty gesture, as though he were cutting something in two. Stephan froze to the marrow. He listened to Armenian words: "Your name's not Hüssein! Stop your tales! Do you really want to go to Antakiya? I don't believe it."

Stephan was almost unconscious. For all his fever, cold sweat stood out on his forehead.

The Turkoman's little deep-set eyes had a very sad look in them. "Don't be afraid, whatever your real name is—and trust in God! As long as you stay with me, nothing shall happen to you."

Stephan gathered all his wits about him and tried to stammer something in Turkish. But the old peasant waved him to silence, his hand still brandishing its knife. He needed no more words. He was thinking of the droves of wretched people, driven day and night past his house by saptiehs.

"Where do you come from, boy? From the north? Did you get away—escape from the convoy? Was that it?"

Stephan could only confide. No denials would have been any use, now. He whispered, in quick, staccato Armenian, so that only his host might hear what he said, and not the listening, hostile world: "I come from round here. From Musa

Dagh. From Yoghonoluk. I want to get back home. To my father and mother."

"Home?" The old, horny peasant hand stroked at the grey beard, with the gesture of wisdom. "So you're one of those who went up on to the mountain and are fighting our soldiers?" The good man's voice had become a growl. Now, Stephan thought, it'll be all over. He sank on his side, surrendered to fate, buried his face in the brown, dry grass. The Turkoman still held his big knife. He had only to stab. When would he do it? But the old man's growl was all that assailed him: "And what's the name of the other—your cousin Essad? He was a sly one. He'd not be so easy to catch as you, boy."

Stephan did not answer. He waited, ready for death. But soon he found himself being lifted, by hands as hard as stones, but gentle.

"You can't help your parents' sin. May God return you to them. But it won't help you, or them either. Now, come on! We'll see what's best to be done."

So Stephan was put back into the wagon, among bundles of reeds. But now the Turkoman seemed to have grown impatient, and thrashed at his little horse, though the beast had covered so many miles, and his rough brown coat glistened with sweat. They went at a sharp trot, at times they galloped, while the peasant talked oddly to himself—or cursed his horse. Yet, no matter how much Stephan was jolted, he felt himself more and more safely in God's hand. He thought, with an effort, of Maman. Was she really so ill? She couldn't be. But, strangely, Maman became Iskuhi. It was hard to get the two to separate. Stephan could do nothing to keep them apart, though their double image was strangely painful to him. Then Haik's voice began to warn. He mustn't waste time! This was the daylight! He ought to be sleeping, getting up his strength to walk in the night. He obeyed his friend and shut his eyes. Fever refused to let him sleep.

The peasant drew up and told his feverish passenger to get down. Stephan, with an effort, came to himself and crept out of the cart. Not far off he saw a bare little hill, surrounded with walls of fortifications, and white, domino houses at the foot of it.

The Turkoman thrust at this picture with his whip. "Habib en Nedjhar, the citadel. Antakiya! You must hide yourself better now, boy!"

And in fact, two hundred paces further, the jolting track opened out on to the district highroad of Hammam, also reconditioned by Jemal Pasha. The new road was full of unexpected traffic.

The Turkoman pushed apart his bundles of reeds; this left a deep cavity in the cart. "You crawl in there, son! I'll take you on through the town, and then a bit further along, past the iron bridge. But no further than that! There now, get in and lie still!"

Stephan stretched himself out. The peasant covered him very skilfully, so that he got enough air, and was not too burdened with the load. There, in this grave, all thoughts were obliterated. He lay, no more than a lump of indifferent heaviness, bereft of courage, without fear. They were trundling now, on the broad highway, pleasant and smooth. Noisy voices all round them. Stephan in his coffin heard them indifferently. They trundled on, jolting, it appeared, over cobblestones. Suddenly with a startling jerk, they stopped. Men were approaching, standing round the cart. Saptiehs, no doubt—police or soldiers. Their voices reached Stephan vaguely, and yet loud, as though through a speaking trumpet.

"Where are you going, peasant?"

"In to the town. To market. Where else should I go?"

"Got your papers all right? Hand over! What are you carrying?"

"Goods for market. Reeds for the binders, and a couple of okas of liquorice . . ."

"No contraband? You know the new law? Grain, maize, potatoes, rice, oil, to be given up to the authorities."

"I've already delivered my maize in Hammam."

Hands were already hastily turning over the top layers. Stephan could feel them doing it—bereft of courage, and of fear. Now the tired little horse was going on again. They drove through a tunnel of noisy voices, at walking pace. Less and less light seeped through to Stephan. It was dark when they got held up the second time. But the Turkoman did not stop. A high, chiding voice pursued them.

"What new habits are these? Next time you'll drive by daylight. Understand? Will you clodhoppers never realize we're at war?"

The hoofs were rattling over the wide, square paving-stones of the Crusaders' bridge, called "the iron bridge" for some forgotten reason. Beyond the bridge the Turkoman took the load off his feverish passenger. Now Stephan could again lie wrapped in his blanket, upon bundles of reeds.

The old man was delighted. "Cheer up, son! The worst's behind you! Allah means well by you. So I'll take you on, a little way further, as far as Mengulye, where I can stable and spend the night with a friend of mine."

Though Stephan's hold on life was now so relaxed, his relief at this was still sufficient to plunge him at once into leaden sleep. Again the Turkoman urged his poor jade to a trotting pace, to arrive as soon as possible with his protégé in the village of Mengulye—from which, however, a good ten-mile walk lay ahead of Stephan to get him back to the place where the road branches into the valley of seven villages. But the simple mind of this Turkoman peasant was not endowed with nearly enough prescience to foresee the intricate ways of Armenian fate. Stephan was roused by the glare of acetylene lamps, hooded lanterns, bobbing up and down above his face. Uniforms were bending over him, moustaches, lambskin kepis. The cart was in the midst of a camp of one of the companies sent by the Wali from the town of Killis to the Kaimakam of Antakiya as reinforcement. The soldiers' tents stood in two lines along the road. Only the officers had taken up their quarters in Mengulye. The Turkoman stood peaceably by his cart. He was striking at his little horse, perhaps to cover his own fears.

One of the onbashis cross-questioned: "Where are you going? Who's the boy here? Is he your son?"

The peasant shook his head reflectively. "No! No! He's no son of mine."

He tried to gain time to form a good thought. The onbashi bellowed at him not to stand there, saying nothing!

Luckily, having attended its various markets, the old man knew the names of most of the villages in the district. So now he sighed, rolling his head about: "We're going to Seris, to Seris, over there at the foot of the mountain . . ."

He sang it like an innocent litany. The onbashi turned a sharp beam on Stephan.

The Turkoman's voice began to whine: "Yes, you take a look at the child. I've got to get him back to Seris, to his own folk."

Meanwhile corporals and privates had begun to swarm around the cart. But the old man seemed suddenly full of excitement. "Oh, don't go too near! Don't go too near! Be careful!"

And indeed this warning startled the onbashi. He stared at the peasant, whose finger pointed at Stephan's face.

"Can't you see for yourself the child's got a fever on him, and doesn't know where he is? Keep off, you over there, if you don't want the sickness to get you, too. The hekim has sent the lad away from Antakiya. . . ." And now this worthy Turkoman appalled even the onbashi with his use of the words "spotted typhus." In these days, in Syria, not even the words "plague" and "cholera" had such power-evoking terror as "spotted typhus." The soldiers darted off at once, and even the grim, resolute onbashi stepped back. But now this excellent man from Ain el Beda pulled out his papers, demanding scrutiny, waving them close under the very nose of this sergeant, who, with a curse, renounced his office.

In ten seconds the road was clear again in front of them. The Turkoman, beside himself with pride and satisfaction at his own success, left his exhausted pony to its devices and walked, chuckling, beside Stephan. "You see, my boy, how well Allah means by you. Didn't he mean well by sending you to me? Be thankful you found me. Be thankful! For now I shall have to go half an hour further with you, to sleep somewhere else."

Stephan's last terror had so paralysed him that he scarcely heard what his friend was saying. And when later the Turkoman waked him, he could not stir. The old man took him up in his arms, like a child, and set him down on the road which leads along the bed of the Orontes, into Suedia.

"There's not a soul about here, boy. If you hurry, you can be back in the mountain before it's light. Allah does more for you than he does for most of us."

The peasant gave Stephan some more of his cheese, a flat loaf, and his water-flask, which he had had refilled in Antakiya. Then he seemed also to be giving him counsel and advice, some heartening words, as he bade God-speed. It ended with the wish of peace, "Selam alek." But Stephan could hear none of all this, since a loud roaring was in his ears, and his head was swimming. He could only see how the light turban and whitish beard moved rhythmically, and how both turban and beard permeated the darkness, with ever more beneficent light. How Stephan Bagradian longed for that mild sheen, the source of all light and consolation, as the stumbling clatter of hoofs became remote. The vanishing cart hung out no lantern. The moon had not yet risen from over the steep gullies of the Amanus.

TER HAIGASUN had sent down a message—probably his first, since he had held jurisdiction over these parishes—to the graveyard dwellers in all the villages. Nunik and her sisters were to set out through the country round Musa Dagh, after news of the lost Stephan Bagradian. Should they succeed in getting any important information, or even, perhaps, bringing back the fugitive, a great reward was to be theirs. They would be given their own camp beside the Town Enclosure. It was a stroke of genius in Ter Haigasun to have offered such a high reward. Gabriel Bagradian was the most important man on the Damlayik. The whole future would depend on the state of mind and body of the leader. All that could be done must be attempted to prevent Gabriel's inward strength—Juliette had delivered the first blow against it—from sustaining irreparable damage from Stephan's fate. This reward seemed immense to these dregs of the villages. And yet Nunik had scarcely a hope that they would gain it. Since the last great Armenian victory, things had been getting cruelly difficult for the people left behind in the valley. The müdir had issued an order, posted up in all the villages, by which it was the duty of every Mussulman to arrest any Armenian he encountered—no matter who. Blind, sick, mad, crippled, an old man or a child, it was all the same. This significant order was designed to render impossible all espionage on behalf of the mountain camp. It had not been pasted up two days on the walls of the church, and already the graveyard population, which originally, in the seven villages, might have been reckoned at close on seventy people, had shrunk to forty. Those who had survived were therefore forced, if they wanted to go on living a little longer, to find some really close and effective hiding-place. And, Christ be praised, they had found it! Only the bravest and strongest, like Nunik, the eternally wandering, ventured forth between midnight and daybreak, in search of food—at the risk of destruction—to poach a lamb or a she-goat. Stephan's way home led past this sanctuary.

About a mile outside the village Ain Yerab, the ruins of ancient Antioch cluster together into what becomes a veritable town. This town is surmounted by the pilasters and vast broken arches of a Roman viaduct. The road, which, so far, has been an easy one, here narrows down to a vague track, which leads on, along the bed of the river, deeply channelled into the rocks, through the stony waste, which once was a human habitation. At places the way is strewn with square-hewn stones, fragments of columns, fallen capitals, which almost block it. Stephan, dazed with fever as he was, went stumbling on, tripping up again and again on blocks of stone, getting himself entangled in creepers, skinning his knees, falling flat, dragging himself up, stumbling forwards. From his right, concealed in the farthest ruins, firelight kept flickering faintly from time to time. Had Stephan been Haik, he would have sensed, even without the firelight, from miles off, the presence of these miserable beggars, whose very misery made them his allies. His sure feet would have carried him straight to them. But where might Haik be at this hour? Thirty paces off the side of the path he followed there was safety waiting for Stephan, with even a lighted bonfire to help him look for it. Nunik, Wartuk, Manushak, would have been able to hide Stephan safely, nursed him for a day and a night, and then, by the sure ways of their experience, brought him back to the Damlayik, to claim the great reward. But this town-boy was afraid of fire. He felt himself being pursued as he rushed on up the steepening road. He came to the top, and drank a swig of flat, lukewarm water out of his flask. Musa Dagh was before him. Here in the moonlight the thick, black smoke-swaths which eddied up off the centre of the mountain could plainly be seen. The flames seemed to have died down, since now there was no longer a wind to fan them. Now and again a burning coal would glow and vanish.

Even then fate gave young Bagradian one more chance. Nunik had sensed something. Leaving her little fire, she had caught a glimpse of a scurrying shape, which could not have been the shadow of a man. There were a few waifs and strays among the beggar-folk. One of those children, a little boy of not more than eight, was sent out to find who the shadow was. But when Stephan heard a patter and scurry behind him, he did not turn round, but went racing onwards, like a mad horse. He used every ounce of his strength in his desperate run. Noises kept hammering in his ears. Was his father calling him? Was it Haik hissing: "Quick march"? He ran, not as though a child were after him, but the whole infantry company whose clutches he had escaped that night. Here these aqueduct ruins ceased abruptly, the road broadened out. The first dark ridges towered over the road. Stephan ran for dear life. A malicious panic drove him down the first side valley, which he mistook for his own, of the seven villages. His flight was giving him such wings that it felt as though he were actually hovering high over the stone-strewn heath as he ran. Stephan turned into the valley, without knowing that he was yelling with all his might. But he did not get far. He tripped over the first real obstacle, a tree-trunk flung across his way; and then lay still.

WHEN he came to himself, the day was upon him in misty twilight. Stephan firmly believed that it was still the day before yesterday, the very same hour at which he had come out of the swamp El Amk—he and Haik—into pleasant hill-country, to the Turkoman's house. He had forgotten all that had happened since, or could only remember it as a dream. His diseased sense of time was reinforced by the fact that there was a house in front of him, though to be sure not a white limestone house, but a wrinkled clay hut, an ugly one at that, without any windows. But out of this house, too, there came a man, in a turban, with a grey beard, perhaps not the Turkoman guardian angel, but at least an old man. And lo! —this old man too snuffled the wind, looked up at the sky, turned to the four quarters of the hemisphere, spread out a little carpet, squatted, and began to pray, with many bobbings and duckings.

Like a flash Haik's warning came back to Stephan. Imitate everything! And so, in the place where he had fallen, he began to copy. He could not manage more than a few feeble swayings and moans. But this man also saw him at once.

Yet, not so pious, it seemed, as the Turkoman peasant, he stopped in the middle of his prayer, stood up, and came across to Stephan. "Who are you? Where do you come from? What do you want?"

Stephan made himself kneel up; he bowed and put his hand to his heart. "Ben bir az hasta im, Effendi."

Having said it pat, he made a sign that he was thirsty. At first the greybeard seemed to hesitate. Then he went to the well, dipped a pitcher, and brought it back. Stephan drank avidly, though the water seemed to cut him as he was drinking it. Meanwhile someone else had come out of the house; not, as Stephan fully expected, helpful women, but another, scowling, man with a black beard, who repeated the greybeard's questions, word for word: "Who are you? Where do you come from? What do you want?"

The lost Stephan made two vague motions in different directions. They might mean either Suedia or Antakiya.

The scowling blackbeard became angry. "Can't you speak? Are you dumb?"

Stephan smiled with big, vague eyes at him, as helpless as a child of three. He was still on his knees before them. The greybeard walked round him twice, like a craftsman sizing up a finished job. He took Stephan under the chin and twisted his head towards the light. It was a test. The blackbeard also seemed very interested. They went a few steps aside and began to talk in quarrelsome voices, but still keeping an eye on Stephan. When they had finished, their faces had the solemn look of men charged with a difficult public duty.

The blackbeard began the interrogation: "Young man, are you circumcised or uncircumcised?"

Stephan did not understand. Only then did his confiding smile become a look of anxious questioning. His silence roused the Moslems to wrath. Hard, chiding words beat down like hailstones. Stephan, for all their shouts and flourishes, knew less and less what they were after. The blackbeard's patience gave out. He grasped the kneeling Stephan under the armpits and jerked him up. It was the greybeard who undid his clothes and investigated. Now their worst suspicions were confirmed. This sly Armenian, trying to pretend he was deaf and dumb, was an insolent spy, sent out by the camp on Musa Dagh. No time to lose! They shoved the tottering Stephan on before them, down the narrow valley-path from Ain Yerab, to the big highroad. They then held up the first ox-cart come from the neighbourhood of Antakiya, in the Suedia direction. The driver had at once to change his direction, in the name of commonweal and public service. The bailiffs lifted their prisoner into the cart. Next him squatted the blackbeard; the greybeard walked excitedly with the owner, explaining this danger, now averted.

Stephan's fate was sealed. But now some merciful power had made him cease to know where he was. His head sank down across the knees of the blackbeard, his mortal enemy. And behold! that grim-faced avenger did not thrust away his victim. He sat as rigid as though he were doing his best to ease the young man. That hectic face in his lap, with its open eyes, staring up into his, and yet not seeing them, this feverish breath, those red, dry lips, this whole surrendered childishness, leaning against him, roused in the blackbeard's narrow mind the wildest bitterness. That was what the world was like. You had to dash your fist in its face!

But Stephan had even forgotten Musa Dagh. He had even forgotten his captured howitzers; he had forgotten those five sleepy peasants whom he, the crack shot, had picked out so neatly. Haik was scarcely even a name. Iskuhi was as faint as a breath. Stephan was wearing his own European clothes again, his Norfolk jacket and laced shoes. They felt very safe and comfortable, his feet marvellously clean. He was walking with Maman down splendid boulevards, and then along the lakeside at Montreux. He and Maman were living in the Palace Hotel. He sat with her before white tablecloths, played in gravel beds, sat in white-washed classrooms with other, all equally well looked after, boys. He was sometimes smaller, and sometimes bigger, but always he was safe and at peace. Maman carried her red sunshade. It cast such a vivid red shadow that at times her face was hard to recognize.

All this was perhaps uneventful, but so quietly pleasant that Stephan did not notice the saptieh guardhouse on the edge of Wakef. One of its two gendarmes reinforced the blackbeard in the cart and held Stephan's ankles. And in Wakef itself they were joined by a whole detachment of saptiehs. The more the commotion, the further they came into the valley. This escort drew a small crowd after it, men, women, children.

It reached the church square in Yoghonoluk long before midday. And by then there were about a thousand people, including many old soldiers and recruits, at present garrisoned in the villages. Quickly the red-haired müdir was sent for, out of Villa Bagradian. The saptiehs pushed Stephan out of the cart. The müdir ordered him to strip; there might be some writing, hidden on his naked body. Stephan did it so quietly and indifferently that the crowd mistook his peace for sullenness; it enraged the onlookers.

Even before he was quite naked, someone had punched the back of his head. But this blow was merciful. It left Stephan not quite stunned, but well back in that delightful world in which he had been beginning to feel so at home, and from which he might otherwise have emerged again.

Meanwhile the saptiehs had emptied his rucksack. In it

they found Stephan's kodak, and his copy of the letter to Jackson.

The müdir held Stephan's Christmas present up to the crowd, most of whom had never seen a camera. "This is an instrument by which you can always tell a spy."

He deciphered, and read out to the people, with loud bursts of triumph in his voice, that highly treacherous letter to the consul. When he had done, the whole square bellowed with hate.

The müdir came close up to Stephan. His beautifully manicured hand chucked him under the chin, as if to encourage. "Now, my boy, tell us your name."

Stephan smiled and said nothing. The sea of reality was remote. He could just hear its waves break in the distance.

But the müdir remembered the photograph of a boy which he had seen in the selamlik of the villa. He turned back solemnly to the crowd. "If he won't tell you, I will. This is the son of Bagradian."

The first knife was thrust into Stephan's back. But he could not feel it. Because he and Maman were just on their way to fetch Dad, who was due in Switzerland from Paris. Maman still had her red sunshade. Dad was coming out of a very high door, all by himself. He was dressed in a snow-white suit, without any hat. Maman beckoned to him. But, when he saw his small son waiting, Gabriel opened his arms, in a movement of unfathomable gentleness. And since Stephan was really such a little boy, Dad could lift him close to his radiant face, and then high above his head—higher and higher.

Nunik found his body that night. It was a very mangled but not disfigured corpse. Saptiehs had flung it naked into the churchyard. Nunik came only just in time to get it away from the wild dogs. She sent off one of her waifs to their camp in the ruins, to call all the other beggar-folk. Today they must put off fear, since a mighty thing had come to pass. The line of Avetis Bagradian, the founder, was now for ever extinguished. This was the hour at which to do Ter Haigasun's bidding, and carry Bagradian's son back to the mountain. The reward could not be withheld. A life of safety was in prospect.

The shy beggar-folk came to the graveyard in little groups. The corpse-washers set to work immediately. They cleaned the blood and dirt off the scarred, beautiful body of the boy. And the generous Nunik did even more for the last Bagradian. Out of her incredible sack she drew a white shift, in which to wrap him. As she was doing this ultimate service a blind beggar raised his sing-song voice:

"The lamb's blood flowed towards their house."

When it was done, Nunik, Wartuk, Manushak, and the other keening-women among the beggar-folk took up their heavy sacks. They walked, bent double, under the load. In the second hour of this new day the procession, noiseless, almost invisible, in spite of a crescent moon, crept up the Damlayik, to reach the Town Enclosure by secret paths, unscathed by the mountain conflagration. Nunik, with her long staff, led them. When they were safe in the woods, they lit two torches to carry one on either side of the bier, so that the corpse might not return unlit, unhonoured.

3

Pain

GABRIEL was again spending his nights in his usual place in the north trenches. Ter Haigasun had become alarmed at the slackness he noticed among the men, the obvious relaxation of their discipline. It was at his most urgent request that Gabriel, even on the night after Stephan's disappearance from the Damlayik, consented to resume his command. To do so was a clearer proof of his own steadiness and discipline than all three battles. For, in these days, his hands kept trembling, he could not swallow a bite, nor sleep a wink. Uncertainty as to Stephan's fate was not his worst, most terrible suffering. The real anguish lay in its being impossible to do anything to find him, rescue him. Could he perhaps recondition his mobile guard and carry out a sortie with them, even as far as the streets of Aleppo? Perhaps such a night-expedition, spreading its terrors all through the countryside, might end by overtaking Stephan and Haik. Naturally he checked this romantic fantasy. What right had he to risk the lives of a hundred people in a wild attempt to save his son? Stephan, after all, had done on his own impulse what Haik did as the messenger of the people. There was no general reason whatsoever for moving heaven and earth to bring him back.

So Gabriel, as though gasping for air, flung himself back into his work. Chaush Nurhan was given orders to put the decads through daily fighting-manœuvres. It was like the very first days. No one, not even in the rest hours, was to leave his post. Leave for the Town Enclosure was granted only in urgent cases. Hard tasks were imposed on the reserve. Against the next great Turkish attack the trenches were not only to be improved, but, to trick the enemy, partly shifted, and what was left of the old ones rendered impregnable by high stone parapets. No one dared oppose Bagradian's desperate activity. But his restless demands did not, strangely enough, make people irritable or arouse their hate. They rather invigorated and electrified, filling the camp with fresh desire to do battle. Life, after a short relaxation, had again its object and its content.

Gabriel felt no personal hostility, merely a growing sense of isolation. It is true that, even before, there had never been any real cordiality, either between him and the leaders, or between him and the rank-and-file. Friendship was out of the question. They simply obeyed him, as their leader. They respected him. They were even grateful. But he and the people of Musa Dagh were two different sorts of human being.

Now, however, they actually shunned him; even Aram Tomasian, who until now had seized on every chance of a talk. He noticed how, right and left of his sleeping-place, in the north trench, his neighbours moved their rugs farther away. Their superficial reason for doing it was that Gabriel, who every day spent an hour or more by Juliette's bed, might be infectious. But far more complex feelings lay behind. Gabriel Bagradian was a man struck by misfortune, a man for whom, they could feel instinctively, even worse misfortune lay in store. It is a human instinct to shun the unlucky.

The camp epidemic had still not spread. This was mostly due to the weather, and to a certain small extent to Bedros Hekim. Out of a hundred and three cases of fever, only twenty-four had so far died. If any member of the camp felt in the least feverish or unwell, he must pack up his rugs and pillows at once and go straight along to the isolation-wood, the fever hospital of the Damlayik. This shady wood was pleasant enough. The patients did not mind having to be there.

But a shower would certainly have altered its conditions much for the worse.

Twice a day, riding on his donkey, Bedros Altouni came to see Juliette. He was puzzled at the fact that, in her case, the fever seemed not to be taking its normal course. The crisis seemed to take a long time coming. After the first attack her temperature had fallen slightly, but without the patient regaining consciousness. And Juliette, unlike the other patients, was neither quite unconscious, nor delirious; she was in a kind of deep, leaden sleep. Yet, in this sleep, without waking out of it, she could turn her head, open her mouth, and swallow the milk which Iskuhi gave her. Sometimes she stammered a few words from another life.

In the first days Iskuhi scarcely left her side. She had had her bed moved into Juliette's tent. She saw nothing more of Hovsannah and the baby. It had become impossible.

Juliette's maids were nowhere to be found. They were afraid of infection and much disliked having to touch either the patient or her belongings. What, after all, had they to do with this foreigner, who was in such bad odour all round? So that, for the present, the whole burden lay on Iskuhi.

But when the doctor's wife came to relieve her, she had literally to force her out of the tent for a few hours' rest, and even then Iskuhi refused to sleep. She sat on the ground not far off and never stirred. If she heard any voice or caught any footfall, she started in panic and tried to hide herself. The thought of meeting her brother or father appalled her. Her best hour was the last before sunrise, when she sat, as now she was sitting, in front of the tent, to wait for Gabriel. He usually came to her then, at this, the stillest of all hours, since as a rule a whole night in the trenches proved more than he could manage to endure. Gabriel, followed by Iskuhi, went in, to Juliette's bedside. The oil lamp on the little dressing-table cast its light full on to the patient's face. Altouni had asked that Juliette might never be left unwatched. She might come to herself, or her heart might begin to fail. Gabriel bent over his wife and forced back her eyelids. He might have been trying to force her spirit back into the light. Juliette became rather restless; she moved a little and breathed heavily, but she did not wake. Iskuhi's voice began relating the day's incidents. Inside the tent their talk was always matter of fact. But, even outside it, their love was not safe. Recently, as they walked at about this hour in Three-Tent Square, Iskuhi had caught sight of Hovsannah's tent curtain moving, and she felt Hovsannah's eyes watching them. So that now they crept out of the tent on tiptoe and went to the "garden"—that bank dotted about with myrtle bushes where Juliette once had received admirers. Tonight at least they were concealed. Yet, for all the utter loneliness of the place, they spoke in a half-whisper and never touched.

"You know, Iskuhi, I thought at first I might go mad. But the moment I felt you near me, the horror passed. I'm free of it now. Quiet! It's beautiful here. We haven't much longer."

He leaned far back like a man in pain who at last has managed to find a painless attitude, and wants to keep it. "I used to love Juliette, and perhaps I do still. At least as a memory. But this between you and me, what is it, Iskuhi? I was fated to find you now, at the end of my life, just as I was fated to come here—not by chance, but . . . well, how shall I put it? All my life I'd only sought for what was foreign to me. I loved the exotic. It enticed me, but it never made me happy. And I attracted it, too, but I couldn't make it happy either. One lives with a woman, Iskuhi, and then meets you, the only sister one can ever have in the world, and it's too late."

Iskuhi looked away past him, at bushes, faintly stirred by the night wind. "But suppose we'd met somewhere out in the world—would you still have noticed I was your sister?"

"God only knows. Perhaps not."

She showed no trace of disappointment. "And I could see at

615

once what you are to me, that time in the church, when we came from Zeitun . . ."

"That time? I never used to believe one could turn into another person. I used to think one goes on adding to oneself, developing. The truth's just the other way. One melts in a fire. What's happening now to you and me, and our whole people, is a smelting process. That's a stupid way of putting it. But I can feel how molten I am. Every bit of dross, every unnecessary part of me, has gone. Soon I shall only be a piece of metal, I feel. And that's the real reason why Stephan's done for. . . ."

Iskuhi caught his hand. "Why are you saying that? Why should Stephan be done for? He's a strong boy. And Haik's certain to get to Aleppo. Why not he?"

"He won't get to Aleppo. . . . Just think what's happened. And he has all that on him."

"You oughtn't to say things like that, Gabriel. You'll be doing him harm, with them. I have every hope for Stephan."

Suddenly Iskuhi turned her head to watch the sick-tent. Gabriel thought, without knowing why: She wants Juliette to be dead, she must want it.

Iskuhi had jumped to her feet. "Can't you hear something? I think Juliette's calling."

He had heard nothing, but followed Iskuhi. She rushed to the tent. Juliette was writhing on the bed, like a bound woman, trying to free herself. She was neither awake nor quite unconscious. Whitish scurf covered her bitten lips. From her glowing cheeks it was obvious that fever, in the last few minutes, had touched the limit of the possible. She seemed to recognize Gabriel. Her hand strayed and caught his jacket.

He scarcely understood her muttering question: "Is it true? —Is all this true?"

Between her question and his reply came a little pause full of icy stillness. But then, bending down over her, he stressed each syllable, like a hypnotist: "No, Juliette, that's all not true . . . it's not true."

A shuddering sigh: "Thank God. . . . It's not true."

Her body relaxed. She drew up her knees, as though to creep back happily, innocently, into her womb of fever. Gabriel felt her pulse. A wild, yet scarcely perceptible little beat. It seemed doubtful if she'd get through next day. Quick —that stimulant from the medicine chest. Iskuhi thrust the spoon with the strophanthus mixture between Juliette's teeth.

Juliette came to herself, tried to sit up, and moaned: "And— Stephan's milk too . . . don't forget!"

For Pastor Aram there began an annoying day. He had buckled a lantern on to his belt and gone out before it was light to climb down the rocks to the sea and test the first result of his fishery. The raft was ready, and they had ventured out on this windless night, with draw-nets and little lanterns, to fish, in the ordinary way, off the coast. The idea of it obsessed Tomasian. It seemed not only to hold the possibility of a necessary change of diet and abundant supplementary supplies. It was more than that even. It was their only real salvation from the ever-increasing threat of famine. Surely, if they worked hard enough, it ought to be possible to make the sea yield up its daily ration of two to three hundred okas of fish. No matter how strictly they might economize, in six weeks the last sheep would have been killed— and that by the most optimistic reckoning. But if he, Aram Tomasian, could only get his fishery to flourish, new courage, new endurance, new strength to resist, would come from the sea. The very thought of the sea, as the inexhaustible source of all life, would work a miracle.

And so, in the greenish light of early morning, the young pastor climbed down to the beach, along a path rebuilt by order of the Council. Yet, as he climbed, he was thinking neither of sheep nor milk, nor even of his own fishery. His little son was just sixteen days old—his eyes as big as the eyes of all Armenians. But they saw nothing. And still this baby had not cried. The only sound it ever managed to bring out was a toneless whisper. Every day the truth seemed more cruelly plain. His son was born blind and deaf.

Yet the fiery birthmark on his body was spreading—that mysterious sign which Musa Dagh seemed herself, with some invisible seal, to have burned into the flesh of the pastor's child. Since no ordinary medical aid seemed of use, Hovsannah had nearly got to the point of consulting Nunik, if she could find her. But now, since the Turks had invaded the valley, the old women of birth and death were seen no more on the Damlayik.

The child had suffered much in Hovsannah's womb, on the way from Zeitun to Yoghonoluk. That was the logical explanation. It did not satisfy Hovsannah. She felt herself punished by God. It was not for nothing that Hovsannah had been reared a Protestant. A child should be God's blessing. This child was God's punishment. God sends His punishment for sin. And Hovsannah was unaware of having committed any. Yet, since sin undoubtedly there was, it must be in others, and clearly in those who were most about her. Aram had certainly not sinned. Hovsannah was an avidly faithful wife, whose marriage, as he knew, was spotless. Where, then, was this sin, this taint, which branded her sinless child? There was always, first and foremost, that prime mover of God's wrath, Juliette Bagradian. In her, the adulteress, the fashion-maniac, the godless woman, the foreigner, Hovsannah perceived the epitome of all sinfulness, whose taint infects like a disease. Yet they lived shamelessly in proximity to her, in her very tent, slept in her bed, ate off her plates. . . . And Hovsannah's thoughts did not end there! Slowly the truth had forced its way into her heart and, once perceived, she embraced it greedily: Iskuhi! It was not to be doubted! Hovsannah knew how it stood with her young sister-in-law. She too was an adulteress

618

in her heart, without control, without belief, desperately resolved to be a sinner. Had she not always, even in Zeitun,
been stubborn, preoccupied with herself, crazy for pleasure—
even in the days when Aram demanded of his wife the bitter
sacrifice of sharing her house with such a woman. But Aram
had always refused to look at the truth; it had always been a
sheer impossibility to say one frank word about Iskuhi, his
dear little sister. In the moment when Hovsannah Tomasian
had run weeping from the christening of her child, she had
seen the hidden connexion of all these things, in an indistinct
and poignant vision, without really knowing anything. But
now she knew all! She knew that her child was accursed of
God. She no longer wept. With clenched fists she measured
out the length of her tent—five paces—up and down, like a
madwoman in her cell. And last night she had refused to go
on keeping silence and demanded of Aram that he take her
to Father Tomasian's hut. In the stench of sin surrounding
the Bagradians, her child would never be free of God's punishment.

The pastor, who suffered much at his wife's dementia, gaped
at her, unable to understand. "What's it to do with us and our
child that Juliette Bagradian is a sinner?"

Hovsannah had plucked the child away from her breast.
She had felt her rising anger poison the milk in her. "So even
you want to be blind, Pastor?"

He had done his best to clarify her senseless rage. Then at
last he had lost his temper with her and reproved her sharply.
Iskuhi was risking her life, he had said, for the sake of a
stranger. And all the thanks she got for her Christian goodness and pure charity was to be slandered so vulgarly—and by
her—by her own sister-in-law! He, Aram, understood Hovsannah's present condition; he was willing to forget what she had
just said, and forgive her for saying it.

But Hovsannah laughed scornfully. "You can convince
yourself, Pastor, of the way in which your tender-hearted

Iskuhi nurses the sick. Just stick your head inside the tent one night. You'll find them together. Sometimes they go out shamelessly for walks in the middle of the night . . ."

Hovsannah's laugh, and her words, kept sounding in the pastor's ears all the way down the cliffs to his fishery. He could think of nothing else. The cold truth became more apparent with every step. God had punished him in this child for his own great sin in Marash, his betrayal of the orphan children. He himself was the guilty one, and not Iskuhi. Down on the shore, among the rocks, Aram, to make bad worse, learned that his great idea had so far only produced the most meagre results. In spite of the calm sea, the raft had come to bits as they put out, and three young fishermen had almost been drowned. In view of such dangers the results were extremely unsatisfactory: two small baskets of tiny silver sprats and jellyfish. The catch would just have been enough for one big soup-tureen. Tomasian mocked them savagely, and gave fresh orders. The salting-ground had been more successful than the fishery. A good haul of salt could be carried up to the Town Enclosure.

Aram scarcely remained there fifteen minutes. His uneasy heart drove him back. He had no clear idea what he could do to save Iskuhi. Had he not, even in her childhood, always respected and been reserved with her? And besides—it was the only way with Iskuhi. Her personality, in spite of all her quiet, friendly submissions, had something as hard and unyielding as a crystal in it. It would not be encroached on.

In Zeitun and on Musa Dagh, the pastor had given proof enough of his courage. But now, as he reached the shrubs which fenced off these rocks, he was undecided and faint of heart. Perhaps the straightest solution would be to go straight to Bagradian and have it out with him. But—no! How could he ever dare to bring out such an evil suspicion to a man of Bagradian's rank, who compelled respect. A man whom fate had just struck so cruelly, driven as he was to desperation for the life of his only son! Tomasian saw no way out of it. He had almost made up his mind to leave it alone, at least for the present. Yet, before turning into the Town Enclosure to speak to his father, he resolved to take a last, quick look at Hovsannah. He encountered a very different person. Iskuhi sat before Juliette's tent, gazing out with unseeing eyes in the direction in which Gabriel had just disappeared. She did not notice her brother till he was close to her.

Aram sat down, facing her, on the ground and strove uncomfortably to find words: "It's a long time since we've had a talk with each other, Iskuhi."

This she dismissed with a gesture, as though no human memory could suffice to measure the gulf between past and present.

Aram felt his way slowly: "Hovsannah misses you very much. She's always been so used to having you help her. . . . And now there's this poor little child, and so much work to do."

Iskuhi interrupted impatiently: "But surely, Aram, you must know that just because of the child this is about the last time I ought to go in to see Hovsannah . . ."

"I know you've undertaken to nurse here. That's very good of you. . . . But perhaps now, your own family needs you even more."

Iskuhi seemed very surprised. "The hanum in there hasn't got anyone. . . . But Hovsannah's up out of bed and has all the people she wants to look after her."

Pastor Aram swallowed hard several times, as though he had a pain in his throat. "You know me, Iskuhi, how I hate beating about the bush. Will you be perfectly frank with me? Placed as we are, anything else would be ridiculous . . ."

She let her eyes rest with vague hostility on her brother. "I am being quite frank with you."

Now he began to get uncomfortable and strove to build a bridge above her innocence. If it were only a question of a companion, a friend, someone with whom she sympathized—of anything not desperately serious. He felt hotly anxious that she should tell him so, sternly reprove, and inform him sharply that her sister-in-law's suspicions were all a lie.

"Hovsannah's very worried about you, Iskuhi. She keeps saying she's been noticing certain things. We quarrelled half the night about it. That's why I ask you, so please forgive me. Is there anything between you and Gabriel Bagradian?"

Iskuhi did not blush, nor did she display the least embarrassment. Her voice was quiet and steady: "Nothing has happened yet between me and Gabriel. . . . But I love him, and I mean to stay with him to the end."

Aram Tomasian sprang up, horrified. He was a jealous brother. Any news that she was in love would have been unwelcome. This blow, so calmly delivered, hurt all the more. "And you dare say that so calmly, to me—to my face!"

"You asked for it, Aram."

"Are you like that, Iskuhi, you? I just can't realize. And what about your honour, your family? Don't you, in Jesus Christ's name, remember he's a married man?"

She raised her head suddenly to look at him. The conviction in her face was irremovable. "I'm nineteen—and shall never be twenty."

Pastor Aram blazed out at her indignantly: "In God you'll grow older, since in Him your soul is immortal and responsible."

The louder Aram became, the softer Iskusi: "I'm not afraid of God."

The pastor struck his palm against his forehead. I'm not afraid of God! He mistook for the most hardened defiance words that had really expressed the deepest certainty.

"Do you know what it is you're doing? Can't you feel the stench in which you live? In there, there's that woman lying unconscious, sick to death. A shameless adulteress! But you're betraying her a thousand times worse than she ever betrayed.

You're leading a worse, more brutish life than the lowest Moslem women. . . . No, I'm doing the Moslems an injustice . . ."

Iskuhi clutched at the rope with her right hand and held it tight. Her eyes grew bigger and bigger. Tomasian thought his words were taking effect. God be praised, he had still some influence over his sister.

He began to moderate his just wrath: "Let's be reasonable, Iskuhi. Think of the consequences—not only to you and me, but to Bagradian and the whole camp. You must rectify this terrible disorder. You must finish at once—make a clean sweep. At once. Father shall come along and take you home."

A deep breath forced its way out of Iskuhi. She leaned far back. Only now did the pastor perceive that her dolorous movement was not the result of his objurgations, but that something which had happened behind his back was filling Iskuhi with horror. When he turned, it was to see Samuel Avakian, breathlessly in search of Bagradian. The student could scarcely stand upright. His face had become a twitching mask, tears were streaming down it. Iskuhi pointed feebly towards the North Saddle. He would find Bagradian there. Then, without noticing Aram, she hid her face. She knew everything.

It was one of Sato's peculiarities never to sleep two nights in the same place. She was entirely lacking in that sense which most of us have, that we can always go back to the same place to sleep in, a secure shelter in a community, even for the half of life we spend in the dark. Not only did she refuse to sleep two nights on the same ground, but would often change her bed in the course of one.

She slept curled up, without rugs or pillow. Her dreams, though they were like superimposed photographic images, were not always merely illusory. Now and again they kept pointing like stubborn fingers, informing Sato of events in

623

her immediate neighbourhood or beyond it. That happened tonight. Sato had gone to sleep among those clumps of arbutus and myrtle from which she had watched Gonzague and Juliette. Something told her Nunik was near, and indeed at the head of a long procession.

So Sato jumped up and went racing off to find Nunik, guided by the instinct of her dream. It was still dark when, leaving behind her the many-folded plateau of the Damlayik, she struck off south of the burning woods and crossed the mountain-ridge. At this place, apart from many red-berried shrubs and clumps of isolated trees, the ground becomes more barren and stonier. The flames had darted so far on spread wings. Charred trees and single islands of glittering shrubs bore witness to the great conflagration. But the fire itself had withdrawn its outposts. The springs and streams which ran to the valley, though not dried up, had begun to force new channels for themselves and bubbled up like medicinal springs, steaming on the frontiers of the kingdom of flames.

Sato encountered Stephan's funeral train in a little, treed-in gully which led on upwards to the last defence posts on the south side. More than this fire, and the consequent necessity to come by the longest way round, had forced Nunik and her train to ascend so slowly. The real hindrance lay in the age and decrepitude of her followers themselves. Nor did the fact that four blind beggars, with wild, prophetic heads, carried the bier, increase the speed of the cortège. Nunik had appointed them coffin-bearers, since they were the only men available whose arms and legs still had some vestiges of strength. She strode on ahead of them. Wartuk and Manushak guided them, past bushes, tree-trunks, and blocks of stone, as one guides a team of slowly nodding buffaloes. Stephan's white-shrouded body had been laid out on one of the ancient, richly carved biers, half a dozen of which still stood unlooted in a corner of the churchyard of Yoghonoluk.

Sato darted across the train like a puppy, scampering on

ahead, not caring how many times she did the journey. She came back again and again to the bier as, with the tappings and lurchings of the blind, it swayed along.

Her pitiless, greedy eyes took in every detail of this young body, lying under its sheet. She would have given anything to have lifted the cloth off its face, to have seen how Stephan looked, now he was dead. Then, when they were almost at the top, she left them and ran on into camp. She wanted to be the first to wake Kristaphor and Avakian and herald young Bagradian's death. Shortly before sunrise the dead arrived in the big square, followed by the tapping, limping cortège. The bier was set down before the altar. The keening-wives with their rabble squatted around it. Nunik uncovered the boy's face. She had done Ter Haigasun's bidding as well as she could. The reward was earned, and could not be contested. Already there arose, scarcely audible, the tremulous hum of the dirge.

Stephan had now become completely that Persian prince whom his mother had been so startled to perceive, the first time he had worn Armenian dress. Though Nunik had counted forty wounds, knife-thrusts, bruises, contusions, all over the body, though his back was broken, and his throat gaped with a horrible slit in it—they had not touched his face. Stephan, behind closed lids, could still see the father for whom he longed, coming through the high door of the station at Montreux. Not forty murderers had managed to efface his smile of delight that Dad should be lifting him in his arms again. He had died without being present at his own death. This bestial martyrdom had, by God's grace, only assailed him as a far-off odour might. Now he seemed at perfect peace with himself, the dreamy prince.

The first to come into the altar square, to step back appalled from the bier and the crowd surrounding the altar, was Krikor of Yoghonoluk.

TER HAIGASUN on the previous evening had come in person to release Kilikian from bondage and send him back to his trench in the South Bastion. Krikor had been sorry to lose this Russian, whose disgrace had kept him there a few days and nights. Now he was sick, nobody came to see the apothecary. The teachers, his disciples, had all abandoned him, not only because their war-service left them no spare time, but because, since now they were men of action, they rather scorned their wordy past. And gone, too, was Gonzague Maris, whose talk Krikor had enjoyed.

His loneliness was twice as long as a normal loneliness, since, out of the whole twenty-four hours, Krikor scarcely slept more than one or two, always towards midday. Night, on the other hand, as it is with many eager and great minds, was the time of Krikor's clearest perceptions, when life beat in him at its highest. For the first two nights of Kilikian's imprisonment Krikor had felt the presence of a human being in the other kennel as an unbearable encroachment on his peace. On the third his irritation at being disturbed changed into a curious need to see the prisoner and converse with him. Only scruples about undermining the Council's authority, since Krikor was himself a leader, had prevented him from yielding to this impulse. In the fourth night it became so overpowering in his solitude, that Krikor could control it no more. Gasping with pain, he managed to haul himself out of bed and drag to the door which led into the lock-up, take down the key from the niche, and laboriously, with his knotted, swollen hand, unlock it. Sarkis Kilikian was lying on his mat with open eyes. The apothecary had not waked him, nor was he in the least surprised at this visit. Kilikian's hands and feet were tied, but so mercifully that he could move with ease. Krikor put his oil lamp down on the floor and sat beside him. Kilikian's bonds shamed Krikor's soul. To put them on an equal footing, he held out his own poor hands.

"We're both manacled, Sarkis Kilikian. But my bonds hurt

626

me worse than yours do, and tomorrow I shall still be wearing them—so don't complain."

"I'm not complaining."

"But perhaps it might be better if you did."

Krikor passed his raki flask to the Russian, who took a long, reflective swig. The old man drank with equal care. Then he looked at Kilikian. "I know you're an educated man. . . . Perhaps, in the last few days, you'd have liked a book to read."

"You've come too late with that, Apothecary."

"Which languages can you read in, Kilikian?"

"French and Russian, if I must."

Krikor's smooth mandarin's head, with the jumping goatee, nodded disconsolately. "Well—you see what a man you are, Kilikian!"

The deserter slowly gurgled out a laugh, that long, slow laugh of his, for no reason, that laugh which had so startled Bagradian, on the night they tried out the tents.

But Krikor would not let himself be put off. "You've had an unhappy life, I know. . . . But why? Didn't you live at Ejmiadzin, next door to the finest library in the world? I was only there a day, but I should have liked to stay on to the end of my life, among all those books. . . . And you ran away . . ."

Sarkis propped himself half up. "I say, Apothecary, you used to smoke. . . . I haven't had a whiff for five days."

The groaning Krikor dragged himself off again, to bring this prisoner back his chibuk, with the last box of his tobacco.

"Take this, Kilikian. I've had to give up that pleasure, since I can't manage to hold a pipe."

Sarkis Kilikian enveloped himself at once in a smoke-cloud. Krikor held up the lamp, to give him a light.

"And yet, Kilikian, you brought your misfortunes on yourself. . . . I can see from your face that you're a monk; I don't mean anything parsonic, I mean the kind of man who possesses the whole world in his cell. And that's why things have gone so badly with you. Why did you run away? What did you think you'd find in the world?"

Sarkis Kilikian gave himself up so exclusively to smoking that it was still not certain whether he heard Krikor and understood him.

"I'll tell you something, my friend Sarkis. . . . There are two sorts of men. That is to say there are the human animals, billions of them! . . . The others, the human angels, count by the thousand, or, at most, by the ten thousand. Among the human animals also belong the world's great men—the kings, the politicians, the ministers, the generals, the pashas—just as much as the peasants, the craftsmen, and labourers. Take Mukhtar Kebussyan, for instance. And, as he is, so are they all. Under thousands of different forms, they all have only one activity—the fabrication of dung. Since politics, industry, agriculture, military science—what is all that but the fabrication of dung, even though perhaps the dung may be necessary. If you take his dung away from a human animal, what remains in his soul is the worst possible agony, boredom! He can't stand himself. And that boredom produces everything bad in the world, political hatred, mass murder! But delight lives in the hearts of the human angels. Aren't you, for instance, delighted, Kilikian, when you see the stars? The human angel's delight is what the real angel's song of praise is, of which the great Agathangelos declares that it is the highest activity in the universe. . . . But where was I—ah, yes, I was going to say, that there are human angels who betray themselves, who fall away from themselves. And for them there can be no mercy and no grace. Every hour revenges itself on them . . ."

Here that master of words, Krikor of Yoghonoluk, lost his thread and was silent. Sarkis Kilikian seemed to have understood nothing of all this. But suddenly he put aside the chibuk. "There are all kinds of souls," he said; "some get snuffed out

628

in their childhood, and nobody asks what kind of souls they were."

With his fettered hands he found a razor in his pocket and took it out. "Look here, Apothecary! Do you suppose I couldn't cut these ropes with that? Do you think I couldn't smash up this whole shack with a few kicks, if I wanted to? And yet I don't."

Krikor's voice came hollow and indifferent, as of yore: "We all have such a knife, Kilikian. But what use is it to you? Even if you got out of here, you wouldn't get past the camp bounds. All we can do is break the prison within ourselves."

The deserter said nothing, and he lay still. But Krikor fetched a book from his kennel, and, with his metal-rimmed glasses on his nose, began to read from it in a lulling voice. Kilikian, with unmoved agate eyes, lay listening to long-drawn periods, which confusedly told of the being and influence of the stars. It was the last time that Apothecary Krikor ever shared his treasure with a young man. It seemed to him for some unknown reason to be worth taking the greatest trouble to get a new disciple, in the person of this escaped seminarist. Vain labour! The next night, the one just ending, the fisher of men was as lonely—lonelier—than ever.

KRIKOR, on two sticks, drew slowly nearer the dead Stephan. His yellow face remained bent over the dead face of the young Bagradian. Soundlessly, then for minutes together, he shook his bald, domed, pointed head. But these were more than the usual dithering head-shakes which came whenever he was ill. These jerks and tremblings of his denoted his utter inability to make any sense out of a world in which beings born to the Spirit spend their time in fanatical throat-slitting, not in the many delights of definitions, formulas, and couplets. How few human angels walked the earth! And even these few betrayed their angelhood, fell below themselves. Krikor searched his unique treasures of quotations for a saying which might furnish support. But now his heart had too much grief in it to find the right one. Bent double, he limped back to the hut.

Among his tinctures the apothecary still kept a tiny, thin glass phial, sealed with a drop of wax. Decades ago, by the receipt of a medieval Persian mystic, he had tried to distill the authentic attar of roses, long lost to the world. Here, in this tiny pellet of glass, he kept his one drop of this essence, gained with the labours of many days. Krikor dragged his way back to the bier and crushed the thin glass ball over Stephan's dead forehead. A heady perfume darted up; it spread strong wings and remained hovering above the forehead of the victim. This perfume was in effect that of the genius whose invisible body, in the words of Krikor's authority, is composed of the essential being of three and thirty thousand roses.

Meanwhile Ter Haigasun and Bedros Hekim came into the square. At the head of the bier the priest stood rigid, his frosty hands hiding in the sleeves of his robe. The bony, searching fingers of the old doctor uncovered, only for an instant, the stiffened body of the boy. Then mildly and soothingly he smoothed down the coverlet again. The light grew brighter. From the streets of huts, the nearest trenches, people came crowding in, and pressed round the altar.

Only the widow Shushik tore at the quiet, with long, ugly screams. Haik's mother roared like a wild animal, even before she had seen Stephan's body. For, to her, Haik's fate and Stephan's were one and the same. It made no difference at all that her son was not lying on this bier. If one had been caught and slain, how should the other not have been slaughtered? But Nunik, Wartuk, Manushak, had left her son's carcass to the wild dogs, since he was only a poor peasant lad, about whom no one cared to trouble. Shushik did not sound like a mother. She sounded like a dying beast, which shatters its own life with monstrous bellowings. A few women came towards her, she who, even up here, lived by herself, apart from all, refusing as obstinately as ever to have truck with any of her neighbours. But now they came whispering round her. She must keep up her courage. What had happened could only mean one thing—that Haik had managed to get away and would be safe in Jackson's protection within a few days. Surely if they'd killed him too, he'd be lying here! Young Bagradian had not the strength or slippery cleverness which, by Christ's help, would bring Haik safe to Aleppo.

Shushik heard nothing of it all. She stood crouched forwards, pressing her hands against her breasts, and bellowed dully at the earth. They called Nunik to witness. That ancient threw back her veil from her lupous face. She had still, in spite of their present dangerous life, secret sources, in the valley, of information, which had not dried up. She took her oath that young Bagradian had been caught alone, without a companion, in the neighbourhood of the village, Ain Yerab, by two of the newly installed inhabitants, who had taken him to Yoghonoluk, to the müdir. But the truth did nothing for Shushik. She did not believe it. The others scarcely dared approach the giantess, whose huge limbs struck fabulous terror into them all. Then suddenly the widow Shushik allowed them to do with her what they would. The women redoubled their whispering comfort. And, indeed, Haik's mother seemed to be pacified, seemed to take hope, the further away she came from the corpse. A great longing for human warmth expressed itself in her narrow head, which fell, powerless, on to her right shoulder—in her huge body, which bent low down, to the daintily frail Armenian women. She put her arms round the shoulders of two of these women, and let them lead her where they would.

But when, with the sobbing Avakian after him, Gabriel Bagradian reached the altar square, not a soul came near him. Indeed the crowd drew off a fairly long way, so that between him and the altar there was a space. Even the beggars and the keening-women scrambled up and vanished among the people. Only Ter Haigasun and Bedros Altouni stayed where they were. But Gabriel did not hurry his steps; he slowed them. Here it was! He had thought of it for five days and nights, in every gruesome facet of possibility. He had no strength left to taste the reality. He dawdled on, step by step, across the space leading him to his son, as though, by walking very slowly, to put off the last shock a few seconds longer. His whole body seemed to dry up. It began with his eyes. They burned with that dryness that no winking lids can mitigate. Then came the inside of his mouth. Like a strip of dried, crinkling leather, his tongue lay between raw gums. Gabriel tried to swallow up some saliva, and spit it out of him. All he could do was to gulp at repulsive air-bubbles, bursting in his fiery throat. The most horrible thing was that every effort at self-control ended convulsively in nothing. Every power in him ebbed away from his grief, which gaped like an empty hole, in the midst of his being. And he himself was unaware that this hole, this nothing, this void within him, was pain's reality. Slyly he tested himself. How does this happen? Why can't I suffer now? Why don't I shout? Why don't I feel any tears? Even his grudge against Stephan was not quite dead. And here lay the child he had loved! But Gabriel had not the power to keep a clear sight of this dead face. His dry eyes saw only a long white streak, and a little yellow one. He wanted to keep his thoughts on quite definite things, on the guilt that burdened him. He had neglected the boy, driven him to flight with scornful words. That he had come to perceive in the last few days. But his thoughts did not manage to get far; images, useless details, most of which had nothing to do with Stephan, kept rising out of the empty hole to break in on them. At the same time, out of the same void, there came a craving which, he thought, he had fully conquered, weeks ago —for a cigarette! If he had had any left, who knows that, to the horror of all the people, he might not have put it between his lips. He fingered unconsciously in his pockets. In this

632

second he suffered for his child because, even now, he would have to part from him. Why was he so far away from Stephan that he could not even manage to see his face? Once, in the villa at Yoghonoluk—on the table Stephan's clumsy sketch of the Damlayik—he had sat by Stephan's bed and watched him asleep. Now surely, now for the last time, he must get very close indeed to his son who was taking away, for good and all, everything that had been himself. Gabriel knelt by the body, that his blinded eyes might seize the tarrying image of that small face before it left him.

Ter Haigasun, Altouni, and the others watched the leader of their defence come slowly up, swaying a little, to the bier. They saw how then he stood forsaken, opened his lips, for snapping breaths, as though too little air were available; and how his hands kept moving in irresolute gestures. They saw how impossible it seemed to him to keep on looking at his son, so that now he stood with his head averted. When at last he crouched on his knees in silence, an æon had run its course in the hearts of the thousand silent people. But now Gabriel's face lay on Stephan's face. He might have fallen asleep or, on his knees, himself have died there. No tears had forced a way out of his shut eyes.

Yet all the women round him, and many of the men, were shedding them. Stephan's death seemed to bring the stranger near his people again. When another age had fulfilled itself in the hearts of the crowd, Ter Haigasun and Bedros Hekim took the kneeling man under his arms and raised him. They led him away, without a word to him, and he, obedient, gave himself over to them.

Not till they were far from the Town Enclosure, till already the three tents were in sight, did Ter Haigasun, on Gabriel's right hand, speak the brief words: "Gabriel Bagradian, my son, think that he's only gone one or two empty days ahead of you."

But Bedros Hekim, on the left, in a bitter, weary little voice, straight out of his heart, spoke the contradiction: "Gabriel Bagradian, my child, think that these next few days won't be empty, but full of devils, and bless the night."

Bagradian stopped, not answering either, and spread his arms, barring the way. They understood, turned, and left him.

Juliette's fever had not diminished. Her swoon seemed to lie more heavily on her than ever. She was lying now, stretched stiffly, not stirring a muscle, occupied only with her breath, which came, short and shallow, over scurfy lips. Was it the crisis of this fever, which killed or ebbed within a few days?

Iskuhi paid no heed to Juliette. Let her live or die as she might decide. Iskuhi no longer thought of the ominous threatenings of her brother Aram, who had told her he would cast her off if by midday she had still not left the Bagradians. Gabriel was standing in the tent, so upright that his head almost touched the canvas. But he seemed further away than the feverish Juliette, and not to know that she was beside him. She had crept across to him and pressed her head against his knees. Stephan's death moved her less than Gabriel's patience. Only she could tell how shy and needy his spirit was.

And yet Gabriel had decided to take on his shoulders a burning world, the whole Damlayik. His own had cut his tendons; first Juliette, and now his dead son. And still Gabriel stood upright. What was she, what was Aram, what were all the others compared to him? Insignificant insects! Uncouth, filthy peasants, without a thought in their heads, without a feeling in their hearts, unable even to see who it was had stepped down to them. Iskuhi felt bowed down by her own weakness, her own worthlessness. What could she do or offer to make herself worthy of Gabriel? Nothing! She put forth her open hand. Like a beggar. She was begging for a tiny mite of his pain, of the load that was on him. Her face glowed with devotion and agonized longing to serve, as she grovelled

634

there before the man who still gave no signs of perceiving her presence. She began to whisper, ardent, disconnected nonsense, which startled and shamed her as she spoke. How poor she was, how horribly poor, that she had no power in her to help him with. At last, out of her despair, she became maternal, almost unconsciously: It's not good to stand up when you're in such trouble. In trouble you ought to lie down. Sleep. . . . He must get to sleep. Only sleep would help him—not Iskuhi. She undid his leggings, fumbled with the laces of his shoes, forced him to lie down on her bed. She even managed, superhumanly, to use her lame arm to do it more quickly. It was a difficult job but, since Gabriel began himself to undress mechanically, it was done at last. As she covered him up, she gasped with exhaustion. She felt a quick, expressionless glance, pass over her.

"I'm lying soft." That was all Gabriel was thinking. For weeks he had only slept on the hard earth on the north trenches. His teeth began chattering. This shivering ague was half a pain and half a comfort. Iskuhi curled herself up small, in a corner, so that he might not know she was there until he wanted her. She prayed that a heavy sleep might overcome him. Yet the sound he made was not the heavy breathing of a sleeper, but a faint hum, a long and even moaning, like the women's dirge. Gabriel was still looking for Stephan in the empty horror of his grief. And could not find him.

Yet this droning sound seemed to ease his heart, since it never ceased until the minute at which, as a rule, the August sun pierced the chink in the door with a long ray.

This ray darted through the tent, and Juliette's face lay flaming under it. Then Iskuhi saw that the sick woman's state had suddenly changed. Beads of sweat stood on her forehead. Her eyes, wide-open, stared; her head was raised, listening. Something had roused Juliette's deepest enthusiasm. But she was finding it very hard to express this emotion. Her sick tongue made what she said scarcely intelligible.

635

"Bells. . . . Gabriel. . . . Listen! . . . Bells. . . . Hundreds of bells. . . . You hear?"

The dirge on the couch broke off, suddenly. Juliette, full of excitement, tried to sit up. She strained her weak voice to a cry of triumph: "Now the whole world's French!"

And what she said was true enough in its way—though her ear was deafened to its truth by the carillons of her patriotic dream. With Stephan's spilt blood, with the death of this only son, whom she had given the Armenian people, the whole world had indeed become French for her.

4

Decline and Temptation

STEPHAN was buried on the thirty-first day of Musa Dagh.
On the thirty-second came the great catastrophe.

Whose fault was it? That was never really cleared up. The
mukhtars blamed one another. It remained, however, undeniable that one of the first, most important orders of the
Council had been contravened with criminal negligence, with
catastrophic results to the whole community. And not only
had the responsible mukhtars failed to put a stop to this "new
custom," they had winked benevolently—let them say what
they liked, accuse one another, keep on insisting that the
pasturage in the Town Enclosure was all used up. Perfectly
true. The sheep needed fresh fodder. And this new grazing-
ground was close under the North Saddle, well ensconced
among rocks in the barren region of Musa Dagh, as good as
unknown to strangers and inaccessible. That was no excuse
for trusting the shepherds, who here as everywhere else in
the world were dreamy old men, with a few little boys to
help them. This sleepy fraternity, whose very nature inclined to the sheep it tended, still fancied that these were
piping times of peace. Never should the flocks, the most
precious of all the people's possessions, have been left without
an armed guard—not even in the camp grazing-ground. But
the mukhtars had trusted in God, in the closed-in pasturage, in
the natural indolence of the Turks, and had, as usual, neither
among themselves nor with other leaders, discussed these
secret infringements behind their backs. So that the Turks,

637

thanks to excellent spies, had an easy job and very profitable.

Two infantry platoons and a saptieh detachment were given orders to turn out at night and quietly climb Musa Dagh, behind the pass, by Bitias. Neither men nor officers needed reminding that quiet was necessary. The half-company, carrying muffled lanterns, stalked its way to the sleepy shepherds and their sheep. To the very last minute the mülasim in command did not believe that they could ever get there without a struggle. All the greater, therefore, the soldiers' astonishment at finding only a few old men in white sheepskins, who quietly, without any fuss, let themselves be killed. Before sunrise, at double-quick time, as though their booty might still be torn from them, they drove the herds safely back to the valley.

This cut the nerve of those on the Damlayik. Every sheep, wether, lamb, of the community, most of the goats, and all the donkeys—these used from time to time as carriers and riding-animals—had disappeared. By the widest calculation of all the animals of any kind still left in camp, they might manage with the greatest economy to last out another three or four days. After that, stark famine.

Early that morning, when Ter Haigasun heard this appalling news, he summoned the Council immediately. He knew exactly the effect that this would have on the people's minds. Since the outburst of hatred against Juliette, a causeless, purposeless embitterment had been growing hourly in the enclosure. It only needed a spark to fire the mine.

Only one leader besides Bagradian did not take part in this critical sitting, although he was present at it. Apothecary Krikor had been unable, since the previous morning, to leave his bed. Neither warmth nor medicine availed him. The one thing he longed for was peace, relief from pain. But, since he lived in the government-hut, almost in the house of parliament itself, peace was precisely the thing most unobtainable. He had put up a thick wall of books between his bed of pain and the cares of the world. He lay unable to move a limb. But once again it was apparent that no wall of the spirit, no poetry, science, no philosophy, is impenetrable enough to keep away the vulgar din of political strife. Today the din, even from the first, was alarming. The mukhtars especially raised their voices. Each, and as a body, they did their best, by shouting, to stifle their own conscience.

Ter Haigasun at last came out into the middle of the room and commanded them all to sit down. He found it hard to control his voice.

"Any army in the field," he began, "punishes such a crime as this with instant shooting. But we aren't a mere military battalion, but a whole, suffering people. And we're waging war, not against an equal force, but a force a hundred thousand times stronger. Now realize what your lying carelessness means! I ought not to shoot you, you miserable mukhtars—I ought to have you tore slowly limb from limb. And I swear to you I'd do it with pleasure, without the slightest fear of God's punishment, if it would be of the least use to any of us. But I'm forced to keep the appearance of unity in this Council to save our authority as a body. I'm forced to leave you treacherously careless mukhtars to your office, because every change of membership might be a danger to public order. I'm forced to take the blame of this on myself, and, with lame reasons and base excuses, defend the Council against the just wrath of the whole people. What Wali, Kaimakam, bimbashi, yüs-bashi, could not succeed in doing, you, the responsible leaders, have managed brilliantly. This is the end of us!"

The subdued village mayors sank into their seats. Ter Haigasun's eyes commanded Tomasian to speak. Aram was feeling very uncomfortable. Though he had nothing directly to do with the herds, he was the chief superintendent of the enclosure and held responsible for everything connected with food supplies. The pastor's narrow face looked extremely pale. His long, pointed fingers were playing with his black moustache, which he seemed to hate. The air at that moment was electric with a still antipathy between Gregorian priest and Protestant pastor, which usually never came to the surface.

Aram Tomasian stood up. "In my opinion it would be better to say nothing more about who's to blame. Since what's the use? What's done's done. Ter Haigasun himself tells us that we've got to show unity. We can't look back, we must look ahead, and rack our brains to find alternative supplies."

This sounded reasonable enough. But the pastor's speech had been unsteady.

Ter Haigasun's fist crashed down, dismissing it: "There are no alternative supplies."

But suddenly in a quiet corner an ally rose to support the mukhtars. Hrand Oskanian, who once, for Juliette's sake, had shaved every day, which, without soap, was in itself a quietly heroic proceeding, now looked like a wild man of the woods. His huge black beard fuzzed out round his nostrils; uncombed, wildly bristling hair crowned his low forehead. This sombre schoolteacher, pigeon-breasted, with long, swinging arms, really did look not unlike a dressed-up ape. Perhaps this usually silent little man meant what he said. Perhaps he was only seizing his chance to revenge himself on Juliette and Gabriel, or on Ter Haigasun, or on all his other superiors. In any case the same old story came out of him, in a fierce rush of exploding syllables:

"Do you still refuse to see the truth? I've been preaching it for the last week; I've been shouting my lungs out to convince you. Now at last you've your proof! Yet Ter Haigasun wants to shoot our own people! I ask him now, what reasons has he for wanting to hide the truth from the Council? Why does he keep on saying we've been betrayed? Who's he trying to shield? If there'd been no traitor in the camp, would the Turks ever have known of this new pasturage? Never! Never!

These meadows are completely hidden; shut in among rocks. No one, unless he knew the ground, could ever have found them. But Gonzague Maris nosed about all over the place. And this is only the beginning. Next thing will be, we shall have the Turks in the middle of the camp. That Greek will lead them up the steep paths, on the rock side, which he knows every inch of—where the mountain isn't even defended. . . ."

The mukhtars did not need to hear that twice. This new interpretation of events, though they did not in the least believe in it, restored all their former prestige. Thomas Kebussyan was delighted.

Anyone with a fixed idea has the chance of infecting other people with it, even big crowds. That is the secret of successful political propaganda, which obtains its effects by the simplest means: a limited, but telling, vocabulary, a demoniacally penetrating voice. The mukhtars and several of the others readily surrendered to the excitement induced by Oskanian's loud persuasiveness—on their behalf. Teacher Hapeth Shatakhian could scarcely manage to make himself heard. He glowered with wrath against his old rival, whom he had had to put up with by his side for eight long years.

"Oskanian," he shouted, "I know you. You're nothing but a swindling charlatan. You always have been—at every hour of your insolent life. You're trying to throw mud at innocent people. You spit at Gonzague Maris because he's an educated man, almost a Frenchman, not like you and me, born in a dirty village and forced to spend our whole lives in it. I, at least, by the kindness of Bagradian's brother, had the chance of studying some time in Switzerland—but you weren't good enough, so you've never stuck your nose farther than Marash. I won't have foul-mouthed apes saying this against the Bagradian family, whom we've all got so much to thank for. And, as for you, Oskanian, you're not only slandering the Greek, but Madame Juliette, because she thought you so ridiculous, with the pompous way you used to sit, saying nothing, you silly dwarf—you and your poems—your calligraphy . . ."

This was unjust. Oskanian had never dared lift his eyes to Juliette. Now he stopped jabbering and, with quiet dignity, replied: "I don't need your Frenchwoman's good opinion. It's far more she who needs mine. We've had to see with our own eyes what sort of people they are, by God!"

And now with accomplished demagogy the dwarf turned to the mukhtars. "I bless our mothers, our wives, our girls, before whom that stuck-up slut of a European ought to go on her knees."

The slogan was dexterously aimed. Applause!

Hrand Oskanian hurled himself full on his opponent. "I tell you, Shatakhian, you fool, that you've made yourself look silly a hundred times, with your *'accent,'* your *'causeries,'* and your *'conversation,'* your affected . . ."

He began to mimic Shatakhian's self-satisfied French to perfection—with its lack of individual quality, its nasal vowels, and sonorous consonants. Their discussion how to avoid certain famine had degenerated into a farce. It was a proof of the ineradicable childishness in human beings that some of the Council went off into fits of laughter at Oskanian's parody.

Bedros Altouni growled, leaning over his stick: "I thought Ter Haigasun called us here to discuss a catastrophe. I'm in no mood to see you perform, Oskanian. I've got more to do than you teachers, who I've noticed for some time have been playing truant from your own school—and so have your children. As for you, Oskanian, I don't mind giving you the benefit of thinking you're merely a little wrong in the head. That young man came among us in March. He had a letter of recommendation to the apothecary. At that time not even the Wali of Aleppo knew anything about the deportations. Did the Greek come here then, fully intending to betray the new grazing-meadows on Musa Dagh to the Turks? One sees

642

what logical heads they produce at the teachers' training-college in Marash!"

Hrand Oskanian, like the budding politician he had shown himself, knew well enough that no illogicalities would damage him. It needs an effort to think things out, and nobody likes having to make one. But if once you can make the other man look small, that in itself is enough to get the meeting on your side, since people enjoy it, and to rouse such feelings is all that matters. So he answered sharply:

"It may be, Doctor, that fifty or sixty years ago you managed to pick up a little bit of medicine. Who can prove that nowadays? Sometimes you seem to be able to find something in that old book you carry about with you. You've got that much in common with the apothecary, who for years did nothing else but harp on his library. I wouldn't mind betting that half those books of his are blank paper, neatly bound. But you old men are all alike when it comes to life. Otherwise you'd have known that, since war broke out, the government has been sending spies into Armenian districts—and Christian spies, what's more, so that they mightn't be noticed."

And he played his trump card to the mukhtars: "It all comes from the fact that these old jossers are as thick as thieves with the Bagradians—who send poor little fools like Shatakhian here to Europe, with the money they've managed to sweat out of us. Aren't these rich families the cause of all the troubles in the first place? These Levantines have nothing to do with us! The whole Armenian people has to be slaughtered to pay for their swindling business deals."

This touched an important chord in the peasant souls. Thomas Kebussyan squinted before him, lost in memories: "Even old Avetis was that way. Nothing but business all the time—in Aleppo, in Istanbul, in Europe. He was never here two months in the year. I've never cared to leave Yoghonoluk. Not that I mightn't have if I'd liked—my old woman worried me enough . . ."

Something began to move behind the books. Into the narrow gap between the walls of them came a groaning, hunched-up shape in a long white nightshirt. Krikor of Yoghonoluk, the celibate, had been wearing his shroud since the previous day. Since he did not want a Nunik or grave-digger to clothe him in the robes of renunciation, he had donned them himself, hard as it was to do so, knowing well that he would not survive to see the Damlayik taken by the Turks. His yellow cheeks had now such hollows in them that a five-piastre piece would have fitted in each. His shoulders were hunched up to his ears, his arms and legs swollen to disjointed clubs. When at last he managed to steady himself, between the two piled-up walls of his library, he did his best to bring into his voice the old, hollow, indifferent note of the sage. But that had ceased to be possible. His words came out tremulous, disconnected:

"This teacher here. . . . I've worked and worked at him . . . for years. . . . I've pumped the blood of scholars and poets into him. ·. . . I used to think . . . because he was intelligent . . . that he had the makings of a human angel in him. . . . But I was wrong. . . . No one, who isn't, can ever become it. . . . I used to say: 'He doesn't always think of dung.' . . . But this teacher is far, far below the poor people who only think of dung. . . . That's enough of him. . . . As to my guest, Maris. . . . I haven't told anyone, so far . . . he promised me to do all he could for us in Beirut . . . with the consuls. . . ."

Krikor was too weak to go on speaking. Oskanian pounced on him.

"And where did he get his passports? You believe any empty talk, but not the plainest facts."

The mukhtars seemed at last to have seen the light. Yes, where did he get his passports?

Pastor Aram sprang to his feet: "That's enough, Oskanian! Stop this intolerable fooling! We've wasted our time, and no-

644

body's said one sensible word. And in three days we shan't have anything more to eat."

The sombre schoolteacher was swept away in his aimless malice. It was as though, in this one hour, he were being forced to throw up all the bile which suppressed rage and slights had for years accumulated. He even came out with the kind of gossip which the most daring matrons ventured to whisper only with their heads together: "Aha! even the pastor? Well, of course he can't do anything else, since his sister has been living so close to Bagradian . . ."

Aram wanted to fling himself on Oskanian, but was pulled back by strong arms. Old Tomasian, red as a turkeycock, shouted and brandished his stick.

But Ter Haigasun was quicker than the two Tomasians. He gripped the teacher's collarless shirt. "I've given you time, Oskanian, to prove what needs proving. Now we all know who spreads the poison which I've felt for a long time in people's minds. They chose you as a leader because you happen to be a schoolmaster. Well, now I send you back to them, and I mean to let them know the truth about you. And, listen to me! I exclude you from all further sittings."

Hrand Oskanian howled that that meant nothing to him. He'd come there that morning fully intending to clear out of this collection of gossiping old men, whom the people itself would send packing today or tomorrow, as they deserved. But, for all his quick splutter of words, the once so silent teacher did not get to the end of what he was saying, since it was not a full minute before Ter Haigasun had sent him spinning, with a powerful kick behind, and locked the door on him. A sly quiet remained. The mukhtars winked at one another. There was a certain danger in the dictatorial methods of Ter Haigasun, who at any minute might do the same to one or another of them. But a chosen leader ought only to be deposed by the whole assembly, and not by any of its members, not even the highest. And, while the spectre of hopeless famine came in giant strides nearer and nearer the Town Enclosure with every minute, Thomas Kebussyan cleared his throat, wagged his hairless head, and raised what might have been described as a constitutional protest against the mishandling of an elected member of the Council. For the first time a clear opposition began to form. Apart from the mukhtars, it was composed of some of the younger teachers and one of the village priests who disliked Ter Haigasun. The two Tomasians, still hot with anger and embarrassment, remained undecided. But all the rest, beginning with Ter Haigasun, had, without knowing or wanting to do so, become the Bagradian party. Already the day's discussion had centred round Gabriel instead of round the great catastrophe. When Ter Haigasun gruffly closed all further discussion of him, to come at last to the question of how to obtain supplies, it was already too late. The sinister noise outside, on the altar square, demanded the Council's immediate intervention.

HRAND OSKANIAN was only a weak man. In any western community he would simply have been described as an "intellectual"; that is to say, a mediocre, book-learned individual, who does not feed himself by manual labour, and whose soul vacillates, since, finding no place in the raw conflict of powers, it devours itself, avid for power and acknowledgment. So that, in other circumstances, Hrand Oskanian's case might, for all its grotesque absurdity, have been harmless. Here on the Damlayik it had to be reckoned with. Hrand Oskanian stood entirely alone. And yet he was in touch with a certain world, an obscure, unexplored world, which today, for the first time, was destined to attract attention. The teacher had in a sense been appointed government commissar over this world. In that role his very status as "intellectual" was enough in itself to make him fail. His failure was not only due to Kilikian. The Russian, though the uncrowned king of the deserters, was silent and walked by himself. He might always be at

646

the centre of an event; but he himself was as inanimate as a saint on the top of a column, took as little interest as a ghost. But apart from Kilikian, in these twenty-three days on Musa Dagh more than eighty other deserters had by degres collected on the Damlayik, and the word "deserter," it was well known, covered in many cases a murkier origin.

Hrand Oskanian, therefore, was the one representative of authority on the South Bastion. He aped Bagradian, in that he slept with these deserters, and strove to share their whole life. It was by no means easy for him to do it. The dwarf's puny body had to keep stretching itself continually to try to come even with these toughs. He was forced, day in day out, to pretend to be "a devil of a fellow," live always beyond his real courage and strength. Next to the wound inflicted by Juliette Bagradian, this company, which now he kept, was perhaps the second deciding reason for the little teacher's strange development, of which his "revolutionary" behaviour in the Council had been no more than a sample. He was very proud indeed of having had the quarrel. He had begun to describe himself as "revolutionary."

The South Bastion was distant and solitary: as far removed as the sun from the altar square, and therewith from the spirit of order and leadership. The people showed a distinct dislike of having to go there. Whereas, for instance, between the North Saddle and the Town Enclosure there was always a vivacious coming and going, at most one or two inquisitive people ever strayed to the rocks of the South Bastion. This was not fully explained by the long way, or the fact that these deserters had no families in camp. Now and then Bagradian would send a surprise inspection. To his relief, it had never much to report. It was clear enough: these deserters might consider themselves lucky to have been allowed into the camp, where they were fed, instead of having to live like dogs. But nobody either knew, or cared to ask, how loyal they really felt to this people, or willing to sacrifice on behalf of it. The South

Bastion was a world in itself. It lived a life into which nobody inquired. It undertook, in payment for regular food, to defend that sector; and that was all. Yet the deserters, too, in keeping their unspecified contract, had so far scarcely troubled about the camp—the enclosure, the altar square, the Council—and very seldom let themselves be seen in the places where most people congregated. This, the morning of the catastrophe, was perhaps the first time they had invaded it in any considerable numbers. They had come quite aimlessly. The instinct "there's something up" had driven them there, the eternal instinct of their kind towards confusion, the breakdown of social order; towards a void, which at the same time seems a novelty.

There had often before been crowds on the altar square, meetings in which some daily occurrence had been discussed with great excitement. But today it presented a different picture from the most excited of previous gatherings. And now the beggars mingled their drabness with all the rest. Even the schoolboys, run wild since the last battle, as noisy as a flock of famished sparrows, as wild as any pack of young wolves, swarmed in, lifting up shrill voices.

In the general confusion and alarm it was not the poorest class which set the tone. Not the poor peasants, the farmhands, the day labourers, but a certain middling sort of "small proprietor." These "small men" behaved like lunatics, flung up their caps, tore at their hair, flourished wild arms and danced about in sheer desperation. This despair was less that of approaching famine; it was for what they considered their personal loss. They kept screaming that "their" property had been filched—their last! Anyone listening to their grief would have got the impression that the Turks had looted hundreds of thousands of sheep. Each of these small proprietors worked out his loss at fantastic figures. It was the same symptom of decline as Oskanian's spy-fever. Ever-increasing unreason was taking insidious hold of these people's minds.

648

At first the very poor, dazed by the shock, kept heavy silence. And they asked anxiously what the leaders thought. It was small proprietors who spread the excitement among the crowd. It was with these the mukhtars had to contend, whom Ter Haigasun had sent out to eat this broth of theirs. They, as the Council's executives, were in closest touch with the mass of the people.

But they scarcely managed to swallow the first spoonful of it. Almost before they could say anything, they were being shoved and punched, this way and that, all over the square. All their attempts to excuse themselves were lost in angry shouts of "You're the only responsible ones! You're responsible!" A pious lie might perhaps have eased the situation—the hint, for instance, that still, in spite of this misfortune, there were enough secret stores to hand—might have re-established the old insouciance, since on Musa Dagh a few days seemed an eternity. None of the elders was inspired with the saving thought of holding up this unhoped-for "something" to the crowd, to pacify it, at least for the time being. But Thomas Kebussyan, usually a canny man, who only now lost his head, used, under Oskanian's influence, the worst, most damaging method of attempting to turn off popular wrath. He threw the word "betrayal" among the people. In normally prosperous times the people has a sound enough instinct to judge the truth, and a very healthy fund of scepticism. Nor had most of these ever taken Oskanian very seriously. But now the mukhtars set his foot on the ladder of politics. His career was launched. The mass, which, in normal times, displays such devastating scepticism at any suggestion of rhetoric, becomes its prey at moments of catastrophe. And then the vaguest words, expressing the least concrete notions, take the strangest effect. The word "betrayal" was one of these. In only very few of the villagers did it evoke any clear concept of an actual happening. But it served to release every hostile instinct and give it direction, although not, to be sure, the direction the mukhtars would have liked. The leaders, all these notables and "bosses," had quietly arranged to sacrifice "the people," and that merely to save themselves. And it was their fault that the communes had moved on to Musa Dagh, and so exposed themselves to massacre. Pastor Harutiun Nokhudian had been the only real "friend of the people." He and his flock, now that the convoy had arrived there, were living in the east, in poor but quite peaceful circumstances. Shouts of derision and hatred of the Council bespattered the government-hut like a hailstorm, and kept increasing. The men of the South Bastion elbowed their way all over the crowds, and seemed to view all this confusion as a kind of bear-fight which, though it amused, in no way concerned them. But, wherever they might be, effervescence rose, like an aerated bubble in a drink.

Those attempts to mollify, undertaken now by Aram Tomasian, also miscarried. That miserable attempt to catch fish, which had yielded so little, was the pastor's set idea, his mania. Everyone knew what results it had yielded so far. Tomasian's attempts to hearten earned, first, laughter, and then, malicious scorn, and, since he refused to stop talking, they silenced him. Everyone knew what had come of all that, so far! Someone in the crowd must have given the impulse. It had been divided up into aimlessly clustered knots, but now it formed into a mass and crowded on to the government-hut. Soon not only fists, but spades and crowbars, were being brandished. The men who guarded it turned pale and pointed their rifles indecisively—with a captured Turkish bayonet fixed on each.

Inside the hut, apart from the sick apothecary, there remained only Bedros Hekim, Chaush Nurhan, and the priest. Ter Haigasun was aware that, now, after the mukhtars' and Tomasian's defeat, it would be the end of all authority unless he could manage to re-establish it. He did not doubt for an instant that he could do so. His eyes, which as a rule expressed so strange a mixture of observant shyness and cold decision, became tinged with black. He crossed the threshold, thrust aside the men of the guard, and went straight into the middle of the crowd, as though he could not see them, as though they were air. Nor had his attitude anything in the least constrained or anxious in it. He moved, as his habit was, with his head bent a little forwards, his secluded, rather chilly hands hidden in his cassock-sleeves. Every step the silent Ter Haigasun took was left free before him. Sheer curiosity—what's he after? what's he going to do? dispelled any other feelings. So, at a measured pace, he reached the altar, on the lowest step of which he turned, not vehemently, but almost as though he were settling down. This forced the crowd—all God-fearing Armenian men and women—to turn their eyes towards the holy table, from which sparkled the great silver crucifix, the tabernacle, chalice, and many lamps. Sunbeams fingered their way through the screen of beech leaves set up behind it. Nor did Ter Haigasun need to raise his voice, since sudden curiosity created deep quiet around him.

"A great misfortune has occurred"—he said it without any pained solemnity, almost indifferently—"and you inveigh against it, and want to be told who are guilty of it, as though that were any use at all. Before we set up this camp, you chose men to lead you, who now, for thirty-one days, have sacrificed themselves on your behalf without having slept the whole of one night. You know as well as I do that no other men among you are as well qualified to be your leaders. I quite understand that you should be dissatisfied with our present life. I am myself! But you chose perfectly freely to come up here and live on the Damlayik, instead of going, for instance, on the convoy, with Pastor Nokhudian. If you regret that now—listen carefully, please—you can change your decision as freely as you took it in the first place. There's a way . . ."

The speaker paused for half a second, but his dry tone remained as before; he continued: "We have an alternative. You, as you stand here now, form a majority. But I'll also send for the men from the trenches. . . . Let's surrender to the Turks! I'm perfectly willing, if you'll give me the power to do so, to go down straight away, to Yoghonoluk, in your name. Hands up, at once—anyone who wants me to do so."

In disdainful silence Ter Haigasun let two full minutes elapse. The quiet remained as dense as ever, not a hand stirred. Then he climbed to the top step of the altar, and now his angry voice beat across the square.

"I see that not one of you wants to surrender. . . . Well then, in that case, you must realize that order and discipline must be kept. There must be perfect quiet! Quiet, you hear, even if we've no more to eat than our fingernails. There's only one form of treachery here, and its name is disorder—undisciplined behaviour! Whoever betrays us in that way will be punished as a traitor, be sure of that! Well, now, it's high time you went back to work! We'll do our best for you. Meanwhile, everything as usual."

It was the method used with unruly children; at this moment it proved the only right one. Not a word of protest, no heckling, not another reproach, though Ter Haigasun's speech had not changed anything. Even the brawlers and agitators held their tongues; they were disconcerted. This alternative—discipline or surrender—worked like a cold douche on these roused emotions.

Since Ter Haigasun's speech had dissipated the great revolt, it was easy enough now to clear the altar square. The people, in noisy groups, went back to work, and everyday life seemed to begin again in spite of this horror. The guard blocked the mouths of the "streets," so that no further demonstrations might trouble the counsels of the leaders, who at last would have to leave their strife and face the merciless reality.

Ter Haigasun still stood looking down, across the empty square, from the altar steps. Might it not be as well to form a very strong police force, strong enough to quell, with blood-shed, the slightest unrest? But the priest dismissed the thought with a weary gesture. What good did it do to spread terror? With every day of real famine, order would vanish of itself. The Turks had no need to attack again, to make an end.

Yet that same day saw a most surprising event, which, in all their torturing up and down of hope and despair, raised their courage again for a short while. This incident might, not un-justly, have been called a miracle, even though the miracle proved ineffective.

IMMEDIATELY after Stephan's death the doctor had released his wife from all her other nursing duties and sent her off to look after Juliette. It was a great sacrifice on the part of Bedros Hekim, since the indefatigable Antaram had had sole charge of the hospital-hut and the isolation-wood. But it was for Iskuhi's sake that the good Altouni had so decided. Iskuhi was worn out by long sick-nursing; she had become the shadow of a shade. What a force of resistance she must have had in her, not to have taken infection from her patient, in spite of constant, close proximity—or at least not so far! The new nurse lived in the sick-hut, whereas Iskuhi moved to the one Hovsannah had relinquished.

Juliette was one of the patients with strong enough hearts to resist the fever-epidemic. As Gabriel began to be certain that, little by little, his wife was turning the corner, he pitied her deeply. After the critical time she had lapsed again into un-consciousness, or rather into the weakest lethargy. Juliette, when her temperature was highest, had always been able to take nourishment; now she refused it; that is to say her stiff, lifeless body refused. Antaram did her best to wake Juliette up. It was very slow work. Not till today had Juliette quietly opened her eyes, which seemed again to look at the real world. She asked for nothing, wanted nothing. Presumably she was trying to get back to those deep-sea regions of unconsciousness she had left so unwillingly. Nor did her expression change as Gabriel came up beside her, though for the first time her face showed quite clearly that she was awake. But what, now that the vivid rouge of fever had died out of it, had become of Juliette's good looks? Her dry hair hung as dead as ashes. Impossible to decide whether it had bleached or turned grey. Her temples were two deep hollows, at the sides of her jutting forehead. Her cheekbones traced the lines of a pitiful skull; her shapeless nose, skinned red, stood out repulsively. Gabriel held her shrivelled hand. Not real bone, it seemed, but brittle fishbones, composed its skeleton. Could it be Juliette's hand— her big, warm, firm hand? This stranger, suddenly here, embarrassed him.

"Well, so now you've got over it, chérie; another few days and you'll be about again . . ."

Words which appalled him. She looked at him and answered nothing. This thin, hideous patient had nothing of Juliette. Everything she had been was extirpated, with cruel thoroughness. He did his best to smile encouragement.

"It won't be easy, but I think we can still manage to feed you properly."

Her eyes had still their alert, clear emptiness. But behind this emptiness was her fear that he might break the crust of coma which still protected her against the encroachments of the world. Juliette seemed not to have heard. He left her. Most of his time Gabriel now spent in the sheikh-tent. He could not stand the sight of human beings and so neglected the duties of his command. Only Avakian came three times a day with reports of the general situation, which he heard in silence, without the slightest sign of interest. Gabriel scarcely ever emerged from his tent. He could only bear his existence in a closed space, in the dark, or at least the twilight. He walked half the day up and down the sheikh-tent or lay, without getting an hour's sleep, on Stephan's bed. For as long as his boy's corpse was still above ground, Gabriel had striven, with the pains of the damned, and unsuccessfully, to recall his image. But now that Stephan had been lying a day and a night under the thin crust of earth on the Damlayik, he came unbidden, at all hours. His father, lying still on his back, received him. Stephan, in his present phase of eternity, was by no means radiant and transfigured. Each time he brought his body, dripping with wounds. He had no thoughts of comforting his father, or even of letting him know that he had died in his arms, without suffering much. No, he pointed to each of his forty wounds, to the gaping knife- and bayonet-thrusts in his back, to the blow, with the butt of a gun, which had broken his neck for him, and, worst of all, to the gaping slit in his throat. Gabriel had to feel these forty wounds, one after another. When he forgot one, he hated himself. Now he was at home in his grief, as a blind man settles into a house, till he knows the feel of every corner and angle. At these times, when Stephan came to see him, he could not bear even Iskuhi. But, when the dead kept off, it eased him to have her sit by his side and lay her hand on his naked body, over his heart. Then he could even sleep for a few minutes. He kept his eyes shut. But Iskuhi felt how the dull thudding under her hand grew shy.

His voice came from a long way off. "Iskuhi, what have you ever done to deserve it? There are so many who've got away and can live in Paris or somewhere."

He looked at her, at her white face with very deep shadows under the eyes, no more now than the shadow of a face. But her lips seemed redder than ever. He shut his eyes again. Everything threatened to melt into Stephan's face.

Iskuhi slowly drew back her hand. "What's going to happen? . . . Do you mean to tell her? And when?"

"That depends on how much strength I have."

Gabriel very soon got the chance to display this strength of his. Mairik Antaram called him and Iskuhi. Juliette had tried to sit up for the first time and had asked for a comb. When the patient recognized Gabriel, fear came into her eyes. Her raised hand both sought and put him off. And the voice in her swollen throat would still not obey her.

"We've lived a long time with each other—Gabriel—very long time . . ."

He stroked her head, uncertainly. She spoke almost in a whisper, as though afraid of waking truth: "And Stephan—where's Stephan?"

"Hush, Juliette!"

"Shan't I be able to see him soon?"

"I hope you'll soon be able to see him."

"And why . . . mayn't I see him now—just through the curtain . . ."

"You can't see him yet, Juliette. . . . It isn't time yet."

"Not time? And when are we going all to be together again —and away from here?"

"Perhaps in the next few days. . . . You must wait just a little longer, Juliette."

She slid down and turned on her side. For a second it looked as though she might weep. Two long shivers passed down her body. Then the empty peace, with which Juliette had waked that morning to life, came back to her eyes.

Outside the tent it looked as though the strong sunlight was blinding Gabriel, whose walk was unsteady. Iskuhi used her unlamed arm to support him. But he caught his foot on a rough place in the ground, and, as he fell, pulled her down along with him. He lay silent, as though there were nothing in the world still worth the trouble of getting up for. Neither did Iskuhi rise, till she heard the steps which came nearer quickly. They scared her to death. Was this her brother? Her father? Gabriel knew nothing of her struggles, which she had kept from him. At any hour now, she expected her family to invade her, though she had sent Bedros Hekim to her father, to say that Mairik Antaram still needed her help. Iskuhi's fears had been unfounded. Not the Tomasians were

656

approaching, but two breathless messengers, from the north trenches. Sweat glistened on their faces, since they had run hard, the whole long way. They were so excited, they interrupted each other.

"Gabriel Bagradian—Turks—Turks are there—six or seven —they have a white flag and a green one with them. . . . They want to parley. . . . Not soldiers. . . . An old man's the leader. . . . They've shouted across that they'll only speak to Bagradian Effendi, and to nobody else. . . ."

MORE than a week had passed since the Turks encountered their great defeat. The wounded yüs-bashi, his arm in a sling, was already on duty again. There were more regular troops and saptiehs encamped round Musa Dagh than ever. And yet nothing happened. Nor was there any sign that anything would. The men on the Damlayik watched the indolent comings and goings in the valley and could not explain why, in spite of these threatening and ever-increasing forces, they should be left in peace. Nor could they know the reason. The Kaimakam of Antakiya had gone on a journey. Jemal Pasha had summoned all the walis, mutessarifs, and kaimakams in the Syrian vilayet round him, at his headquarters in Jerusalem. A series of unforeseen natural events demanded instant measures to cope with them, or the conduct of the war, indeed the whole life of Syria, the most important war-area, would be paralysed.

Two plagues of Egypt, accompanied by sub-plagues and assistant-plagues of all descriptions, had invaded the land from the north and east. The eastern plague, spotted typhus, forcing its way as a localized epidemic via Aleppo to Antioch, Alexandretta, the mountains along the coast, was an appalling proof of cosmic justice. The drastic horror of this illness distinguished it from the milder epidemic on the Damlayik, which, thanks to fresh air, good water, severe isolation of all the infected, and indeed to other, unknown causes, still kept within bounds. But the death-rate of Mesopotamian spotted typhus often stood at eighty percent. It had descended from the cloud of disease which hovered above the steppes of the Euphrates. Ever since May and June hundreds of thousands of dead Armenians had been rotting, on that very unconsecrated earth, in that godless common grave. Even wild beasts fled the stench. Only the poor troops had to force their way through that unspeakable mass of putrescent humanity. Columns of Macedonian, Anatolian, Arab infantry, with endless baggage and lines of camels, were herded on in daily route-marches to Baghdad. The bedouin cavalry clattered among them. The worldly wisdom of Talaat Bey, in the Serail Palace of the ministry, might well have been confounded by the perception of what strange results may emerge from any attempt to exterminate a whole people. But neither he nor Enver let it perturb them. Power and the dullest insensitivity have gone together ever since there has been a world. The second, northerly plague had certainly less of super-terrestrial consistency than the other, but its actual effects were perhaps more formidable. It, too, seemed an actual repetition of Biblical punishment. This plague of locusts swept down from the Taurus into the plain of Antioch, and so over the whole of Syria. The gullies, slopes, and ravines of that great mountain were no doubt the birthplace of these tough nomads, who irresistibly swarmed far and wide. Huge locusts, hard, shrivelled-looking insects, brownish, like withered leaves, clearing obstacles in one wide leap, as though horse and rider had grown together. They came on in different huge detachments, army-corps, covering the earth of hundreds of square miles of the sanjak, so that scarcely a strip of earth remained visible. This planned advance, the purposeful concentration of their descent, fully suggested that more than mere blind instinct guided their wrath, that they had a plan, and leadership. They seemed in fact to represent the big collective idea of essential locusthood. It was really terrifying to watch the descent of one of those swarms on a garden—on elms, plane trees, yews, even on the hardened sycamores. Each tree, in a few seconds, would be wrapped in a kind of furniture-cover, a rain-proof sheet of rough, dark serge. Every vestige of green shrivelled up and vanished under the watcher's eyes, as though eaten by invisible flame. Even the trunk was enveloped in whirling puttees of insects. Nothing suggested that individuals made up the unity of the swarm. A single locust, caught in the palm of a man's hand, betrayed the same pitiful fear as other insects, and strove to escape. Back in the swarm, he realized his own true nature, feeling his own pushful greed as the service of a great cause.

In August, east of the Syrian coastal area, as far as the valley of the Euphrates, there was no longer one green tree. But with trees Jemal Pasha did not concern himself. Harvesting, in northern Syria, never begins before the middle of July and lasts several weeks, since rye, wheat, and barley are not threshed at the same time as maize. The Moslem lets his sheaves lie out for weeks, having little to fear from rain. When the locusts descended in July, they found half the grain still standing, the other half in loose sheaves in the fields. So that, within a few days, in their fashion, they had gathered the whole Syrian harvest, and by the middle of the month there was not a stalk left to be harvested in fields stripped bare. On this Syrian harvest Jemal Pasha had impatiently reckoned.

The locusts had made short work of the whole commissariat plan of the current war-year. The price of bread shot up. In spite of the most stringent counter-measures, the inflated Turkish pound dropped well below its nominal value. These August days, in which Musa Dagh defended herself so gloriously, also saw the first deaths from famine in the Lebanon district.

Such was the state of affairs when Jemal Pasha summoned the meeting of Syrian governors at his headquarters. That powerful gathering was almost as perturbed as the Council

659

of Leaders on Musa Dagh. The walis and mutessarifs were no more able to stamp trainloads of grain out of the earth, than the mukhtars, ewes and sheep. But the potentate's speech was short and not conciliatory. By this or that day the Aleppo vilayet was to deliver so and so much corn to the commissariat. The officials turned pale with fury, not only at these outrageous demands, but even more at the pasha's tone in making them. Only one among them was all zeal and humility, and to be sure, in view of the disastrous business of Musa Dagh, he had very good reason for being so. The puffy, brownish face of the Kaimakam of Antakiya listened with intense enthusiasm to every word that fell from Jemal's lips. All the other governors haggled and bemoaned, but he promised to do the impossible. Even if he could get no rye or wheat, at least he would send maize, as much as was needed. But might he, please, be given the necessary transport? Jemal, in the course of one of these sessions, even got to the point of holding up the Kaimakam of Antakiya as a shining example to all the rest. The Kaimakam seized this chance for which he had striven with so much wisdom, and begged for a short interview after the sitting. This was a direct infringement of the laws of official hierarchy, but the Kaimakam hoped, by direct intervention, to win over the imperious chief of staff to his side. In Jemal's room, besides the Kaimakam, there was only Osman, the barbaric head of the picturesque bodyguard. The district governor of Antakiya obsequiously accepted a cigarette.

"I'm addressing myself directly to Your Excellency because I know Your Excellency's generosity. Your Excellency will no doubt have guessed my petition."

The small, stockily built Jemal, with his hunched shoulder, faced the Kaimakam, fair and square, whose loose, heavy bulk towered over him. The general's thick, Asiatic lips pouted spitefully through black surrounding meshes of beard.

"It's a disgrace," he hissed, "a filthy disgrace."

With bowed head the Kaimakam registered tribulation.

"I venture to agree entirely with Your Excellency. It's a disgrace. But it's not my fault, it's my misfortune, that this disgrace should have happened in my Kazah."

"Not your fault? It'll be the fault of all you civilians, if we lose the war because of this infamous nonsense with the Armenians and perhaps go utterly to bits."

The Kaimakam seemed deeply shaken by this prophecy. "It's such a misfortune that Your Excellency should not be guiding our policy in Istanbul."

"It *is* a misfortune, you can be sure of that."

"But I, after all, am no more than a minor official, who obediently must receive the government's orders."

"Receive? Carry them out, my good sir, carry them out! How many weeks has this scandal lasted already? You can't manage even to dispose of a few ragged, half-starved peasants. . . . What a success for His Excellency the War Minister, ha, ha! and His Excellency the Minister of the Interior!"

And the short, sturdy Jemal went across to the gigantic Osman, to smack him on the chest with the palm of his hand, so that every accoutrement hung on this waxwork jingled.

"My people'd have done it in half an hour."

Osman grinned. The Kaimakam too smiled, bitter-sweet. "Your Excellency's advance on the Suez canal was one of the greatest campaigns in our whole history. You must forgive me, a civilian, for presuming to seem to give an opinion. . . . But to me it always seems that perhaps the greatest feature of the campaign was that it should have cost Your Excellency so few men."

Jemal emitted a little laugh. "Right, Kaimakam. I'm not so magnificent as Enver."

And now the Kaimakam gave its most adroit turn to the interview: "The mutineers of the seven villages are extremely well armed. I'm not a soldier, Your Excellency, but I shrink from sacrificing another life against them. Your Excellency, as our greatest general, must know, even better than I, that a mountain fortress can't possibly be cleared without mountain artillery and machine-guns. Let those cursed Armenians be victorious! I've done all I could!"

Jemal Pasha, whose savage temper it was his constant effort to control, still could not force any calm into his voice.

"Apply to the War Minister!" he shouted. "I haven't any mountain artillery, or machine-guns either. People talk of my power—I'm the poorest commander in the empire. These gentlemen in Istanbul have robbed me of my last cartridge. And anyway—it's none of my business!"

The Kaimakam became very grave and crossed his arms, as if in salaam, upon his breast. "Your Excellency must forgive my daring to contradict you. But this matter does, perhaps, concern you a little . . . since not only civil servants are being made to look ridiculous in the eyes of the whole world by this defeat, but even the troops of the Fourth Army, which bears the famous name of Your Excellency."

"What do you take me for?" scoffed Jemal. "You don't get *me* to bite so easily."

So, to all appearances crushed to earth, and yet, inside himself, not quite so hopeless, the Kaimakam retired from the presence, past the highly decorative Osman. Nor did hope deceive him. This same Osman came after midnight to his quarters, to rouse and lead him at once to Jemal. The Syrian dictator was often pleased to prove, to himself his power, to others his originality, by such surprise invitations at all hours. He did not receive his late visitor in uniform, but wrapped in a fantastic burnous, which gave his by no means irreproachable figure the aspect of a picturesque bedouin sheikh.

"Kaimakam, I've thought over that whole business of yours, and I've reached some decisions . . ."

He struck the table with the flat of his red, plebeian hand. "The empire is being sacrificed to crazy and incompetent careerists."

The Kaimakam waited, in mournful confirmation, for what

would come. Osman paraded his splendours in the doorway. "When does that fellow get a chance to sleep?" the governor of Antioch reflected.

Jemal paced up and down the room. "You're right, Kaimakam, this disgrace of yours affects me also. It must be wiped out, it ought never to have been, you understand me?"

Still the Kaimakam waited, saying nothing. The little general's spitefully bearded face glanced up at him. "You have ten days, after which the whole thing must be wiped out and forgotten. . . . I shall send you one of my most efficient officers and everything necessary. . . . But you answer to me, mind! . . . I want to know nothing more about it."

The Kaimakam was clever enough not to say a word in reply.

The general took two steps back. Now he really did look like a hunchback. "I want to hear no more of this whole business! If I have to hear any more of it, if it is not all got smoothly out of the way, I shall have all those responsible shot . . . and you too, Kaimakam, will go to the devil."

The freckled müdir, installed in Villa Bagradian, was roused twice that day from his kef-siesta. The first time to receive a letter from the Kaimakam, apprising him of his immediate arrival. But when the sergeant of the saptiehs appeared a second time to drag him out of the cool villa into grilling midday heat, he showered wild curses on the head of that unfortunate disturber and longed to thrash him. And yet, once in the church square of Yoghonoluk, the müdir quickened his pace, since a really unusual sight awaited him. In front of the church stood a yayli, not drawn by horses even, but by mules. Nor was it even a proper yayli; it was an old-fashioned coach of some kind, with high wheels. Inside the coach sat an old gentleman whose garb and being suited it to perfection. A dark blue robe of silk reached down to his feet, clothed in the softest goatskin slippers. Around his fez, this very distinguished-looking old gentleman wore the tarbush-cloth of the pious. The ancient's soft, almost spinsterish fingers kept counting the beads of an amber rosary. The müdir perceived at once, in this old gentleman, an Old-Turkish patrician, a partisan of the opposite camp, which, in spite of the revolution, still retained vestiges of its power. Then he remembered having met the old gentleman before, on two or three occasions in Antakiya, where people had saluted and done him reverence.

The yayli did not stand there alone. A line of sumpter mules, heavily laden, stood behind it, scraping and clattering with their hoofs. Besides their drivers, the müdir saw two other elderly Turks, with mild, almost transfigured-looking faces, and a thin figure, leaning against the carriage door, whose face was thickly veiled. The young man from Salonika put his hand politely to his forehead to greet the ancient. Agha Rifaat Bereket beckoned him over. The disciple of Ittihad, enemy as he was of all tradition, came straight up to the carriage to hear what the old man had to say.

"We are on our way to the Armenian camp. Give us guides, Müdir."

It was made to sound like an order from above. The müdir stiffened. "To the Armenian camp? Are you wrong in the head?"

Rifaat Bereket took no notice at all of this jovial question. On the back seat of the coach lay an ultra-modern-looking, yellow pigskin attaché-case, in glaring, bristling contrast to the rest of that roomy, comfortable equipage. The soft white fingers pressed back the catch.

"I have a mission to the Armenians."

The Agha handed his teskeré to the red-haired müdir, who began to investigate it. When he could still not manage to find what he wanted, Bereket patiently commanded him: "Read the inscription above the seal."

And indeed the müdir obeyed with such alacrity that he

664

even read it aloud: "'The holder of this passport to be given free admission to all Armenian deportation camps, such admission not to be refused by any political or military official whatsoever.'"

The young man passed back the document into the coach, in his beautifully manicured fingers. "This isn't a case of a deportation camp, but of a nest of rebels, dangerous traitors, who've mutinied and shed Turkish blood."

"My mission is to all Armenians," the Agha mildly replied, stowed away his teskeré very carefully in his brand-new, business-like attaché-case, and, out of it, drew yet another document, the outward appearance of which was obviously, in itself, enough to conjure with. It was a big, intricately folded sheet, sealed with a complicated seal. The müdir's eye had first to get accustomed to the flourishes of Arabic calligraphy before he could decipher the name, Sheikh ül Islam, together with the demand, which that spiritual Supreme Head of Turkey had addressed to every orthodox Moslem, that they should assist to whatever he might require of him, no matter what such demands might seem to entail, the orthodox bearer of the document. "What influence that world of moths still possesses!" it occurred to the müdir. The Sheikh ül Islam, in spite of Enver and Talaat, was still one of the most powerful officers of state. This medieval screed was therefore an official order, which it might cost him dear to disobey. He eyed the sumpter mules, heavily laden with sacks of grain.

"And where do you intend to take these sacks?"

Rifaat Bereket, as his custom was, made his answer dignified but discreet. "They have the same destination as I have."

The müdir answered ceremoniously, though it annoyed him that the old Agha should remain quietly seated before him, the government representative, as though he were merely concerned with an official of the ancien régime.

"I don't know, Effendi, whether you've got this matter clear in your mind. The Armenians in this district have risen in

665

arms against the government and set up a rebel camp on Musa Dagh. They've dared to defy the Turkish army, arm themselves, and kill Turkish soldiers. Now we're starving them out. And you come here, Agha, with sacks of grain."

Rifaat Bereket heard all this with his head wearily inclined. Not till the müdir had finished, did the old man's rather prominent, wrinkled eyes look him up and down. "Were you yourselves not once in arms against your Padishah? Did not *you* oppose his soldiers, sword in hand, as attackers even? Revolutionaries should never appeal to lawfully constituted authority."

And for the third time, as he was saying it, the Agha felt in his magic attaché-case. It was almost like an incident in a fairy-tale to see him draw forth his mightiest charm: a parchment scroll headed with the Sultan's turban, decked with gems as signet. The supreme lord and Caliph, Mohammed the Fifth, commanded, in this irade, all his subjects, and in particular the civil and military authorities, that they should aid in all his undertakings the Agha Rifaat Bereket of Antakiya, and set no obstacle in his way.

The red-haired müdir stared at it uneasily. The "old gang" seemed to have turned up in full force, he must say! Hastily, and without enthusiasm, he set the Padishah's name to heart, mouth, forehead. Certainly the gesture did not in the least consort with the young man's light "summer suiting," bright red tie, canary-coloured gloves. Well, what ought he to do? Impossible to let rebels be provisioned. Equally impossible to impede any man under such obvious special protection from His Majesty the Sultan. But the slick young müdir from Salonika was wily enough to hit on a compromise, which at last, much against the grain, after many silent curses, he proposed. The Agha himself should be allowed past the Turkish outposts round Musa Dagh. But his train of mules with their provisions must be left behind in the valley. And in this the Agha Rifaat Bereket could not obtain the least concession.

666

There was a grain famine all over Syria. The Kaimakam of Antakiya must decide the destination of these supplies. On the other hand, there were a few smaller sacks of coffee and sugar, and some bales of tobacco. These luxury articles could proceed. To that at last the müdir consented, after much persuasion. Finally he made inquiries about the companions of the Agha.

"They are my servants and assistants. Here are their passports. Examine them, please. You'll find them in order!"

"And this man here. Why is he veiled, like a woman?"

"He has an ugly skin disease on his face and must not expose it to the air. Shall he lift his veil?"

The müdir grimaced and shook his head. More than an hour had passed before the yayli could proceed in the direction of Bitias. An infantry platoon, commanded by a mülasim, marched beside it. Two sumpter mules, with coffee, tobacco, sugar, and three others, for the Agha and his two assistants to ride, brought up the rear of the procession. When their way was clear before them, Rifaat Bereket left his coach and asked the mülasim to halt his men, to avoid misunderstandings with Armenians, who might open fire. The officer welcomed this suggestion and encamped, in regulation style, in the wood with his soldiers. The three old men rode on, sitting sideways across their donkeys, while the two sumpter mules were driven after them. The veiled man walked beside. In his right hand he carried the green banner of the prophet, in his left, the white flag of peace.

THEY sat facing each other in the tent. The Agha had demanded this talk without witnesses. Now the Agha's companions squatted outside, beside the sumpter mules, whose muleteers had unloaded their sacks and bales. The crowd round this group increased every minute. The Agha was as composed and dignified, he waited there as ceremoniously, as though he had been sitting at home in the mild afternoon twilight of his selamlik. The amber beads slipped through his fingers as uninterruptedly as time itself.

"I have come to you, Gabriel Bagradian, as the friend of your grandfather, the friend of your father, the friend of your brother Avetis; and I have come as the friend of the ermeni millet. You know that I have worked in the cause of peace, now destroyed for ever, between our two peoples. . . ."

Here he interrupted his litany. His pitying eyes examined the face of this once so prosperous-looking young European. Never would the Agha have recognized that shrunken, wildly bearded face. He thought for a moment before he continued: "There is guilt on your side and on ours. . . . This I only say so that your judgment may not err, in spite of all that has happened, nor your heart be hardened. . . ."

Gabriel's face looked graver and smaller still. "He who has come as far as I have come knows no more of guilt. No guilt can trouble me now, no right, no revenge."

Rifaat's hands lay still. "You have lost your son."

Bagradian's hand had happened to stray into his pocket. There it closed round the Greek coin, which he still kept with him as an amulet. "To the inexplicable, in us and above us." He held it up. "Your gift has brought me little good fortune, Agha. The coin with the king's head I lost on the day I lost my son. And the other——"

"You still do not know your last day."

"It is very close. And yet it seems to come far too slowly. I often long to rush down into the midst of your people, so that at last—at last!—it may all be over."

The Agha glanced at his shimmering hands. "You will not debase your life, but raise it. You, Bagradian, have more strength than most men. Yet God decides all."

The yellow attaché-case lay beside Rifaat's crossed legs. On it, ready to be delivered, Pastor Harutiun Nokhudian's letter to Ter Haigasun.

"As you know, Bagradian, for months I have travelled on

668

your behalf. I have renounced the peace of my old age. And, with God's help, I shall still get as far as Deir ez-Zor. But my first journey in Syria was to you. You have friends both abroad and here in Turkey. A German pastor has collected a large sum of money for you, and I keep in touch with him. I had managed to get together fifty sacks of grain to give you. It was not easy. They would not let them through. I felt they would not. But the Kaimakam will not succeed in confiscating them. They shall go to your brothers in the camps. Yet these sacks of grain were not my reason for climbing to the top of Musa Dagh. . . ."

He handed over Nokhudian's letter. "This letter will tell you what, otherwise, you would never have heard, the fate of your countrymen. But at the same time you must remember that our people is not all composed of Ittihad, of Talaat, Enver, and their servants. Many others, besides myself, have left their dwellings and gone eastwards to help the famished. . . ."

To be sure the Agha Rifaat Bereket was a very fine man indeed. He deserved that Gabriel should kneel to him, in the people's name. But these long, detailed descriptions of acts of benevolence and self-sacrifice did nothing to assuage Gabriel's bitterness. Real as these sacrifices were, their enumeration made him impatient. "You may help the exiles, but not me."

The old man kept all his equanimity. "I could help you, my son. That is my most important reason for sitting here in your tent."

And now, in the same even monotone, the Agha explained his plan for saving Gabriel, whose heart stood still as he listened. Bagradian, so began the Agha, must have noticed the five men of his escort. The two greybeards were members of a pious confraternity, engaged on the same duty as himself; the two muleteers were old servants, members for many years of his household in Antakiya. But the fifth man was a case apart. He had the deaths of many Armenians on his conscience, and, in Istanbul, the Sheikh of the Thieves of Hearts had converted him. Now he repented. He had taken an oath to do penance for these deeds done by the baser powers of his soul and make amends to the Armenians for the wrongs which his hatred had inflicted on them. This man, then, was ready to change clothes with Gabriel Bagradian and disappear. Down on the church square, the müdir had closely inspected all their passports and made a list of their names. It was almost a foregone conclusion that, when they returned, no one would ask for their teskerés a second time. But if, against all expectation, the müdir began to make things difficult, Gabriel need only show his double's passport. Nor would the mülasim and his soldiers, who had counted six people in the camp, and would take six people back to the village, be likely to suspect in the least that all the six were not the same. He, the Agha, as an honourable man, disliked such attempts to defraud the police; but here it was a question of bringing the last of the Bagradian family into the shelter of his house in Antakiya. This he must do for the repose of the soul, and in memory of, the blessed Avetis, of whose friendship he had received a hundred proofs; he, a Turk and a young man, from the old Armenian.

Gabriel felt stifled. A wind of life blew so mightily through him that he stumbled out of the tent to breathe. He saw the escort squatting in silence. He saw the man of the oath, who had long since taken off his veil. A dull and ordinary-looking face, on which neither the murder of Armenians nor the oath to expiate had left any perceptible traces. He saw the villagers crowding round them, all of whom seemed shaken with wild excitement. He saw Iskuhi, standing outside the sick-tent. And she, too, was as unreal and remote as everything else. Nothing was real, save the thought of living: A dark room in Rifaat's house. The wooden shutters of the window, outside which is the inner court with its fountain, are closed. And there, forgetting all, knowing of nothing, to lie, awaiting a second birth.

When, after several minutes, he had calmed down, Gabriel

went back into the tent. He kissed the old man's hand. "Why didn't you come to me before, Father, when everything was still easy, when we lived down there in the villa . . . ?"

"I hoped for a very long time that this fate of yours could be averted. And, from you, it can still be averted."

"No, by me, too, it must be embraced."

"Are you afraid? . . . We can wait till it's dark. There won't be the slightest danger in it."

"Day or night! It's not that, Agha." An embarrassed little pause. "My wife has nearly died, and today she's beginning to recover."

"Your wife? You'll find other wives."

"My child is buried up here."

"It's your duty to beget another, to carry on your line."

The old man's heavy eyes still looked impassive.

Gabriel answered him so softly that, no doubt, he did not understand: "No one who stands where I stand can begin again from the beginning."

The Agha cupped his small, nimble hands, as if to catch the rain of time in them. "Why do you think of the future? Think of the next few hours!"

The late afternoon light was filling the tent, the light of leave-taking. Gabriel stood up, unceremoniously. "It was I who first gave the seven villages the idea of this camp on Musa Dagh. I organized the whole resistance. I was leader in the battles against your soldiers, thanks to which we still remain. I am, and shall be, guilty—responsible—if, in a few more days, your people torture us all to death, even our sick and little children. What do you say, Agha? Can I simply leave them in the lurch?"

To which Agha Rifaat Bereket made no answer.

GABRIEL had the Agha's gifts carried at once to the altar square, so that the Council might set about distributing them. Mainly it was only a question of sugar, coffee, a little tobacco. But

671

the muleteers had also managed to smuggle in two sacks of rice. Since these gifts had to be shared out to two thousand families, it can be imagined how microscopic each ration was. What did that matter! To be able to drink hot coffee again, in little sips! To be able to draw tobacco smoke far down, into the very pit of one's stomach, let it out slowly, through nose and mouth, stare vacantly at the floating cloud, without any care, any tomorrow. The actual value of these gifts was far less than the revived morale engendered by them, and this on a day of general disaster. And the Turks left them all their mules, the two sumpter mules and those they had ridden. Only the old Agha still kept his, to ride into the valley.

Thus, then, the benefactor and his five followers went back with unbandaged eyes to the North Saddle. The man of the oath went on ahead with the green and white flags. He seemed neither put out nor relieved at having been deprived of his good work. As guard of honour, besides Gabriel, Ter Haigasun, Bedros Hekim, and two mukhtars followed the strangers. Around them eddied a crowd of bewitched villagers. This talk in the sheikh's tent, since no one knew what had passed there, had become a source of fantastic hopes. The Agha walked through a fog of blessings, tearful petitions, hopeful questionings. He could scarcely go forwards. Never, not even in the banishment camps, had the Agha Rifaat Bereket seen such faces as here on the Damlayik. The savage, feverish masks of men grimaced round him avidly. Waving arms, as thin as twigs, thrust out of tattered sleeves, held children close up to his face, as the women begged. Nearly all these children had swollen heads, on the thinnest necks, and their huge, staring eyes had a knowledge in them forbidden the children of humankind. The Agha perceived that not even the most brutal convoy could, in its effects, be more dehumanizing than this isolation, this cutting off. He believed that now he could understand by how much this draining off of the spirit exceeds in cruelty even the massacre of the body. The most horrible thing that had been done was, not that a whole people had been exterminated, but that a whole people, God's children, had been dehumanized. The sword of Enver, striking these Armenians, had struck Allah. Since in them, as in all other men, even unbelievers, Allah dwells. And whoso degrades His dignity in the creature, degrades the Creator in his victim. This, then, is God-murder, the sin which, to the end of time, is never forgiven.

To the old man, it felt as though he were walking through clouds of ashes, the thick death-cloud of the whole burnt-up Armenian race rising between time and eternity.

The Agha walked bent over his stick, growing older and older, more deeply bowed. Now he kept his eyes on the earth, which had brought forth all this and bore it. His little feet in their soft shoes tripped eagerly, unused to walking. Pressing his white beard close against his chest, he hurried on like a fugitive whose strength may fail. He had ceased to hear the sounds of these petitioners, see their arms imploring him. Away out of this! But Rifaat's strength took him only as far as the trenches along the North Saddle. There at the sight of the gaping decads, a violent giddiness forced him to earth. His two servants, the muleteers, came hurrying anxiously. The Agha was a sick man. The French hekim in Istanbul had warned him against overexertion. The more staid of these two servants drew out of the green velvet bag which he always carried for his master the smelling-salts and the little case of liquorice which stimulates the heart.

When the Agha had quickly recovered, he smiled up at Ter Haigasun and Gabriel, who were bending over him. "It's nothing. . . . I'm old . . . walked too fast. . . . And then . . . you give me too much to carry. . . ."

As he rose with the help of his two companions, he was conscious that his task would never be finished, that he never would get to Deir ez-Zor.

It was nearly midnight before his yayli reached the house in

Antakiya. He was lamed with exhaustion. Nevertheless, he wrote off at once, in intricate and elaborate calligraphy, a letter directed to Nezimi Bey, but intended for the Christian pastor Lepsius, to whom he gave precise account of all he had so far achieved.

AND, at about the same time as the Agha Rifaat Bereket wrote this letter to Dr. Lepsius, the soul of Krikor of Yoghonoluk freed itself from his agonized body. That night, before he went to sleep, the teacher Hapeth Shatakhian had been bitten with remorse on Krikor's account. And so, at two o'clock in the morning, this negligent chief-disciple of the philosopher tiptoed into the government-hut, came softly over to Krikor's bed, faintly lit, peeped over the wall of books, and whispered gently, so as not to wake the sick man, if he were asleep: "Apothecary—hullo, how are you?"

Krikor lay on his back. His breath came strangled. But his wide-open eyes were very calm. He chid the teacher because of the stupidity of his question.

Shatakhian edged his way round the rampart of books. He felt Krikor's pulse. "Have you much pain?"

Krikor gave his answer a double meaning: "I have when you touch me."

The teacher squatted down beside the sick man. "I'll stop with you tonight. It'll be better. . . . You might need something."

Krikor did not answer. He was far too occupied with his breath.

But the teacher became soulful; he mourned: "I'm thinking of the good old days, Apothecary; our walks together, and all your sayings."

Krikor's yellow mandarin face lay there immobile. He answered in a breathless, nasal head-voice. His goatee never stirred. "None of that was worth very much."

These defensive words were enough to release all Shatakhian's sentimentality: "It was worth a great deal. . . . For you, and for us. . . . You know I've lived in Europe, Apothecary. I can say that French culture has become a part of my flesh and blood. . . . Over there, one sees and hears and learns thousands of things: lectures, concerts, theatres, pictures, the cinema. . . . And you see, you were all those things for us, in Yoghonoluk—and more. . . . You brought us the whole world and explained it to us. . . . Oh, Apothecary, what might you not have become in Europe!"

These encomiums visibly worried Krikor. He answered in a haughty breath: "I'm quite satisfied . . . as it is. . . ."

Nearly half an hour more elapsed before that strange, falsetto voice resumed: "Teacher! Instead of talking nonsense, could you manage to do something intelligent? . . . Go over there to the shelf with the medicine on it. . . . You see that round black bottle? There's a glass beside it. . . . Fill it up."

Shatakhian, pleased to be of some real use, obeyed and brought back the brimming glass, which gave out a strong scent of mulberry brandy. "Well, you've prescribed yourself the best medicine, Apothecary!"

He put his arm under Krikor's head, propped him up, and set the glass to his lips. The sage of Yoghonoluk emptied it in long draughts, as though it were water. After a while his face had colour in it, a mocking glint had come into his eyes.

"That's it . . . best medicine . . . against pain . . . but now I must be alone. . . . Go to bed, Shatakhian."

Krikor's new expression and his more vivacious tone made the teacher uneasy. "I'll come in to see you tomorrow, Apothecary—the first thing . . ."

"Yes, come tomorrow—as early as ever you like. . . . But now you might just put out that lamp . . . it's the last oil . . . over there, my little candle . . . light it, please . . . put it up on the books . . . that's it. . . . That's all . . . go and sleep, Shatakhian."

When the teacher was again beyond the rampart, he turned

675

and looked back, over the books, at his master. "If I were you, Apothecary, I shouldn't worry about Oskanian; we've always known what he was like. . . ."

This last piece of advice was entirely superfluous, since now the apothecary inhabited an entirely peaceful world, in which such absurd puppets as Oskanian had ceased to figure. He stared fixedly out, without moving his eyes, and rejoiced in the luxury of painlessness. His heart was jubilant. He counted his internal assets. How light his baggage, how happy he felt! He would lose nobody, nobody would have lost him. All these human things seemed so remote, far away behind him: probably they had never existed. Krikor had most certainly always been Krikor, a man made differently from his kind. The people pity those who have to be alone at such a minute. This Krikor could not understand. Was there anything more glorious than such solitude? A delightful warmth stole up through his body. Krikor felt his limbs become supple again, his joints lose their stiffness. With a jerk, which did not hurt him in the least, he turned towards the light. Small white moths and huge dark ones circled the flame. Krikor thought: If it goes on like this, I shall get well. Not that he cared. He reflected upon this dance of insects. Myriads of stars in the form of butterflies, whose delicate bodies have been composed of the ashes of burnt-out worlds, as the Arab astronomer Ibn Saadi had already demonstrated. His mind became clouded, and he slept. But to wake was horrible. The kennel had shrunk mysteriously. Krikor could scarcely see. The moths had increased by thousands till they almost obscured the flame of the badly made candle.

No breath would come to the sick man. Desperate, gurgling sounds forced their way out of him; he jerked himself up and forwards, without noticing the pain. Viewed from without, it was a choking fit, but its inner reality was far worse. It was the monstrous sensation of not being able to hold out, and not in any temporal, passing sense, but a "not being able to hold

676

out" which would go on and on; through all eternity. It was the major punishment of any hell that may exist. And this eternal "not being able to hold out" had its definite counterpart in the mind. Knowledge that one knows nothing, an ignorance that yet knows all, are a pale description of this ocean of half and half, of perceptions just begun, thoughts rapidly fused into one another, teachings misunderstood, errors devoured. The most trivial things never really grasped! Oh, gruesome impotence of the spirit, which every blade of grass confounds. In this sea of nauseating rubbish Krikor was drowning. He struggled to save himself, escape. With a rattle in his throat he crawled out of bed and clung to his rampart of books. When, in his weakness, he lost his hold on it and fell on his back over the bed, he pulled down the top layers after him, and with them the extinguished candle. The books came thudding down round Krikor's body, as though to embrace him and hold him fast. For a very long while Krikor lay as he had fallen, relieved that he could breathe again, that his stifling fit of complete ignorance had released him. His pain came back on him in waves. Every finger burned as though he had just pulled it out of the fire.

And then the apothecary's books rendered him a last unique service—the read, the unread, the skimmed-through, the beloved. He stuck his burning hands into the leaves. Their pages were as cool as water. And more than that. A thin, icy peace came streaming into him from the intellectual life-blood of these books. Even with numb fingers, in the dark, Krikor could distinguish one from another. A final impulse: "Alas for this pleasure!" Then the burning died, throb by throb. The soft release from pain stole higher and higher. A shimmer of leaden daylight gleamed in through chinks in the log hut. This Krikor did not even notice, since now he experienced the supreme. It began with a great awareness of quiet, as if each thud of his ebbing pulse were saying: "I am the first person, I am the first person." And then that thing

677

began to grow which was—Krikor of Yoghonoluk. This is already a misstatement. Words, meant for time and space, cannot say it. Perhaps it was not so much a growing of the thing which *was* Krikor of Yoghonoluk, as a shrinking together, shrivelling up, of the thing which *had been* the world. Yes, the world crumpled with giddy speed: the hut, the Town Enclosure, Musa Dagh, the house down in the valley, and all that surrounded it. It could not have been any other way. It had no volume, since it was made of the ashes of burnt-out stars. At last only Krikor of Yoghonoluk was left, standing alone. He was the All, he was more than the All, since around his head moth-worlds danced, without his observing it.

5

The Altar Flame

TER HAIGASUN, after a long talk with Pastor Aram and Altouni, had decided that what was left of their provisions need not be economized. Would it not be altogether senseless to eke out life, and its pain along with it? Already—before real hunger had set in—there were enough enfeebled people on the Damlayik, old men and women, women and children, who sank to the ground and could not get up again. This slow grinding process had proved itself the worst kind of destruction. And the priest was willing to let the process be curtailed. So that, in the first September days, Bagradian's two cows were slaughtered, with all the remaining goats and kids; the milk of the she-goats was by now too thin, and came too sparsely, to be worth thinking about. Then came the sumpter and riding-mules, whose leather flesh it was almost impossible to boil or roast. Yet with tail, skin, hoofs, and tripe, these animals yielded great heaps of food, which both disgusted and satisfied. Added to these, there were Rifaat Bereket's coffee and sugar, about a quarter of a pound to each household. But the dregs were cooked up, again and again, so that coffee-pots became like the widow's cruse. This drink inspired, if not cheer and comfort, at least a pleasant surrender to the moment. Tobacco was almost as effective. Ter Haigasun, in spite of protesting mukhtars, had wisely ordained that by far the greater share of it, four whole bales, should be divided among the men of the South Bastion—among ne'er do wells and unreliables. Now they could wallow in smoke as never before at the best times in their lives. It was done to keep their minds off mischievous thoughts. Even Sarkis Kilikian, stretched on his back, and full of the joy of drifting tobacco-smoke, seemed to have nothing against the prevailing order. To be sure, Hrand Oskanian was a non-smoker.

On the thirty-fourth day of exile, twenty-four hours after Krikor's death, there were about two hundred sick people in the fever-wood, and more than a hundred others in and around the hospital-hut. Mostly, apart from the seriously wounded, they were cases of sheer enfeeblement, people who had broken down at work or about the camp. In a population of five thousand this was not an alarming proportion of sick, including, as it did, wounded men. But on that day, for no obvious reason, the curve of mortality shot upwards wildly. By evening forty-three lives were extinguished, and it looked as though, in the course of the next few hours, many others would follow them. The graveyard had long been too small to take in all these new inhabitants.

Ter Haigasun therefore introduced a new kind of burial, without first having described it to the people. Late in the moonless night they collected the bodies and carried them up to the Dish Terrace, which jutted out to sea like the long prow of a ship. Everyone had to take a hand, hospital attendants, the churchyard folk, and anyone else whose work in the camp was done at night. The ground had to be covered two or three times, before all these dead, tied into their shrouds, had been laid out in rows on the bare rock.

Since the new moon the weather had changed. There was no rain yet, but wind, in angry rebellious gusts, swept across the hillocks of Musa Dagh; sometimes a strangling wind from the steppes, sometimes a foamy sirocco from the sea, which veered and veered, as though to fool the staider elements, water and earth. Had Gabriel not placed his Town Enclosure so skilfully in a hollow of the ground, not a single hut would have been left standing. Here, on the exposed Dish Terrace, the wind seemed to have built its eyrie. When it leapt in sudden gusts upon these rocks, people found it hard to keep on their feet. The torches and church tapers held by the mourners were blown out by its first assault. Only the silver thurible still glowed faintly as the deacon held up to the priest. Ter Haigasun passed, blessing, in tiny steps, from corpse to corpse. This method of burial scandalized Nunik, Wartuk, Manushak, but, since they were on the Damlayik only by sufferance, they did not criticize. Two men lifted the first corpse by its feet and shoulders and bore it along to the narrow part of the ledge. There stood a giant with his legs straddled, unshaken by these buffeting gusts, with hands like two big, outspread lettuces, lifted in readiness. It was Kevork, the sunflower dancer, the half-wit. It had not been easy to make him understand his office. At last he had realized what was wanted and nodded with a broad grin. "Oh, yes—just what they do on ships!" So that then they learned, for the first time, that as a boy Kevork had sailed on a coaler in the Black Sea. The half-wit was by nature full of zeal, and nothing gave him greater satisfaction than a chance to make himself useful.

Kevork would not allow anyone else to rob him of even the smallest part of his dignity. He received the corpse, and, with a shove of his elbows, edged away the two other men who wanted to help him. The sea seemed still to keep some star-trace of former nights of perfect calm. Its white crests presented a reflected semblance of light, enough to outline the dancer as he worked. A few lanterns marked the threatening rock-edge. But, in spite of them, it was cruelly dangerous work for Kevork. For the Dish Terrace stood on what was known as the "High Wall," which fell sheer for over twelve hundred feet into the sea. The sea had eaten its way so deep into the foot of the High Wall, that this rock-plateau really looked like a dish, held out in space on a hand, and, from above, the surf could not be seen. A false step on this gigantic prow would have been the quickest, surest death. Yet now, when night was at its darkest, the dancer showed no trace of fear, no giddiness, though all the others drew quickly back. He, on this narrow, faintly illuminated ledge, was really dancing, rocking himself and the dead, like a powerful nurse. The corpses sank noiseless and invisible, into night. Kevork, in spite of the pitiful rations he had now been drawing for many days, had not lost any of his strength. When, after about an hour, rhythmically, on straddling legs, he had lightly heaved his forty-third body into eternity, he seemed downcast at the sight of his empty hands. He would have liked to cradle four hundred, a thousand, the whole people, and rock them asleep. An outsider might have been astonished to see how little horror there was in this burial, how much of beauty, indeed, there was in it.

UNEXPECTEDLY the swimmers got back from Aleppo. Early one morning these two young men turned up in the north trenches, having slipped in safely past the extended lines of saptiehs and soldiers, which for the last few days had surrounded all the heights of Musa Dagh from Kebussiye to the coast village Arsus in the north. The physical condition of these swimmers in no sense suggested the toils and perils of their ten days' adventure. They were thin as skeletons, but wiry, swaggering skeletons, tanned with sun and the salt air. Strangest of all were their clothes. One was wearing a shabby but one-time elegant gentleman's dressing-gown made of brown wool; the other, white flannel trousers, and with them the wreck of a dinner jacket from the dim antiquity of that garment's style. They both had heavy sacks full of hard army biscuits on their shoulders, an act of heroism on the people's behalf when one remembers the thirty-five miles of mountain country between Alexandretta and the Damlayik.

Their return caused jubilation among the villagers, but the news they brought was such as to extinguish all hope. They had stayed six days in Alexandretta without seeing the sign

682

of any warship in the outer harbour. A few battered Turkish tin-tubs were riding at anchor there, and coal-barges, fishing-smacks, and a Russian merchantman interned by the war. But the whole vast bay, which forms the deep snug angle between Asia Minor and Asia, lay empty, as empty as the coastline behind Musa Dagh.

For many months no one in Alexandretta had seen even the shadow of a warship far out at sea.

All this they related confusedly. Each jealously strove not to let the other go on speaking. They described their whole excursion day by day, every detail of it. If one forgot some trifle, the other at once became impatient. But the crowd, forgetting its own situation, could never have enough minute description.

In the first day after they had set out, they had kept to the summit of the mountains, skirted Ras el-Khanzir, and so come unperceived to the road that leads along the coast from Arsus to the port. Then they had spent a whole day on a hill close to Alexandretta, where, safely hidden in myrtle thickets, they kept a sharp look-out on the front harbour. At about four that afternoon, a narrow grey streak, far out at sea, turned coastwards, with a line of foam in its wake. The swimmers, forgetting all precautions, had dashed down to the sea, plunged in and swum out, past the wooden jetty, into the open harbour. As their orders instructed them, they swam on closer and closer, in wide circles, in the direction of this supposed French or English torpedo-boat, which quickly grew plainer before their eyes, till soon, to their horror, they had perceived that the half-moon flag flew on its deck. But the men on deck had sighted the swimmers. Piercing shouts! And, when these remained unanswered, the crew of this customs-inspection vessel, as now the slip turned out to be, commanded by the Turkish harbourmaster of Alexandretta, had peppered them with a dozen small shot.

They dived and swam on under water, experts as they were,

a very long way. Later they hid among the cyclopean rocks on which the jetty itself is built. Luckily it was already evening and the harbour deserted. Nevertheless, high over their heads, they could hear the heavy thud of sentries' feet on the rotten planks of the bridge. There they had sat, naked and wet. Their clothes, their supplies, were lost. To make it worse, some near, intermittent light kept picking them out, at about half-minute intervals. They made themselves as small as they could. Not till well after midnight did they manage, giving the long port-road a very wide berth, to get back to land. There seemed now no choice, save between perishing wretchedly in the hills and venturing boldly on into the town. But they found a third way. On a parklike hill, just outside it, planted with eucalyptus to keep off malaria, stood several big and opulent villas. The swimmers, judging by all they had heard of Alexandretta, felt convinced that one of these villas must surely be owned by an Armenian. And the name-plate on the first garden gate (they could read its inscription by moonlight) confirmed their hope.

· But the house was dead: no light, and the shutters nailed. The swimmers were not to be put off. They would have broken in to get shelter. They found a spade and a hoe left leaning against the garden wall. With desperate strokes they began to try to force the door without thinking that the din they made might equally well arouse an enemy. In a few minutes a chain rattled inside. The door was pulled open. A shaky light and a trembling man. "Who?"—"Armenians. For Christ's sake give us something to eat and hide us. We've come from the sea. We're naked." The circle of light from the trembling man's electric torch eddied across their shivering bodies. "Merciful God! I can't let you come in here. We should all be done for. But wait!" Minutes dragged by. Then, through the half-open door, two shirts and two rugs were handed out to them. In addition to which they were given copious bread and cold meat and two pound-notes each. But their panicked

684

compatriot still kept whispering: "In the Saviour's name don't stay here. They may have seen you, even now. Go to the German vice-consul. *He's* the only one who can help you. His name is Herr Hoffmann. I'll send an old woman to show you the way, a Turk. Follow her. But not too close! And don't talk!"

Luckily Herr Hoffmann lived in the same parklike neighbourhood. This German vice-consul turned out to be very well disposed. He had done already more than he strictly should have done, or could do, to help the Armenians in this district. Hoffmann had most kindly taken them in, fed them, given them a room, with two splendid beds in it, and fabulous meals, three times a day. He had offered to let them stay on in this magic sanctuary till things were normal again. Yet, on the third day of this life of ease, the swimmers had told him that they felt it was time to hurry back to Musa Dagh, to their own people. It so happened, by a curious stroke of fate, that Rössler, the consul-general, had come on a visit to Aleppo on the very day they informed the kind Herr Hoffmann of their decision. Rössler had advised the two young swimmers to be thankful they had managed to save their skins, warning them on no account to leave this safety and protection. These thoughts of a rescuing gunboat were the mere crazy fantasies of people whose troubles had unhinged their minds. First, there were no French warships of any description in the North-East Mediterranean. True, there was an English fleet stationed in Cyprus harbour, but, since its business was to guard the Suez canal and Egypt, it never strayed into the north. Why should it? There was no chance of landing troops on the coasts of Syria. Secondly, Herr Rössler had pointed out to them, it was a piece of most exceptional good luck for Armenian refugees to be taken into a consul's house. And real help was out of the question. Neither he, Rössler, nor his American colleague in Aleppo, Mr. Jackson, were able to offer it. But, he added, with obvious satisfaction, a few days ago

Jackson had managed to shelter a young Armenian, who also came from the camp on Musa Dagh. The swimmers had rejoiced that Haik was safe.

They had thanked Herr Rössler and Herr Hoffmann, but would answer further suggestions, indeed prayers, only with the curt embarrassment with which young men express such emotions. "We have our fathers and mothers up there . . . and our girls as well. . . . We couldn't stand it . . . if anything were to happen up there and we were here . . . alive . . . in this beautiful house."

So on September 2 Vice-Consul Hoffmann had let them go again. They had told him of the lack of bread on the Damlayik, and·he, though not by strictly official methods, had obtained two sacks of army biscuits from the Imperial Ottoman Commissariat, which he gave them as a parting gift. But the best thing he did was to take them in his consular yayli. The swimmers were put to sit on either side of him. On the box beside the coachman in his lambskin kepi, sat a resplendently uniformed khavass, who kept slowly waving a small German flag. Proudly they drove on past saptieh guardhouses. The gendarmes jerked to attention, with respectful salutes for the representative of Germany, his flag, and his two doubtful protégés. Herr Hoffmann had even taken them further, past the second guardhouse outside Arsus. There the two swimmers had got out and, weeping in spite of all their efforts, said good-bye to their warm-hearted protector.

Someone had fetched the widow Shushik from her hut. She was told that Haik was safe. First she seemed quite unable to grasp the fact. She crouched on the ground, bending forwards, dully. Since Stephan's death she had scarcely once raised her eyes. She looked more bony than ever. But now her hard, male fists hung limp at her sides. Now she only went from time to time to draw her ration at the distributing-tables. If anyone ventured to say a word to her, Shushik replied more brusquely than ever before. She was full of hate.

Now, as she sat hunched up, she could hear them whispering behind her.

"Shushik! Listen, can't you! Haik's alive. . . . Haik's alive."

It took a very long time before their whispers reached her mind, before her hunched and angry back relaxed gradually, became feminine. One of the swimmers completed this softening process: he embroidered his tale—a successful traveller.

"Rössler and Jackson see each other every day. The German himself told me how he'd seen Haik. He said he was looking fine!"

Then, at last, certainty could penetrate the remotest corner of Shushik's mind. Two long breaths, like groans. She stumbled a few steps nearer the rest. And these steps led Haik's mother out of a solitude which had lasted fifteen years, into the wide circle gathered round the swimmers and their families. One more tottering step and she lay full length, but at once propped herself up on to her knees. Into the colourless, ageless face of this giantess there came, like an astonishing revelation, like sudden sunlight, an inexpressible love of humankind. The standoffish Shushik, she who had kept herself to herself, raised heavy arms in the weakest supplication. Shushik's arms besought: Take me in, let me share this with you! Because I belong to you now. . . .

She had still not been thrust out of her shadow. As a rule she could only see moving blurs. If she made an effort, they came together and formed shapes. But she was far too clever to make efforts. Words and sounds beat in her ears, as hollow as though she lay in a padded room. So that, really, there she was, in the telephone-box at the lower end of the Champs Elysées, calling up the Armenian Club for Gabriel, because there was a new comedy at the Trocadéro, which she wanted to see. But, when these cool incertainties grew less vague, when they even threatened to take on solid form, she grew nervous and escaped at once. The one sense she could still trust and

687

enjoy was not only normal, but highly developed: her sense of smell. She sniffed whole worlds into herself. Worlds which committed her to nothing. Banks of violets, early scents of spring in little villa gardens in Northern France, where coloured glass balls mirror the roadway. Only, in Heaven's name, no roses! She could sniff that peculiar odour composed of sun-dust, of midday bustle, gasolene, stale incense, and cellar-damp, which assails our nostrils as we open the little wooden side-doors which will lead us on inside the cathedral. To confess oneself again—and receive holy communion! But is it really necessary to confess oneself, of something one has never really committed, something which was probably part of one's illness? Then again—that horrible, all-pervasive scent of myrtle bushes. At least not that, *Jésus! Marie!* The myrtle bushes can be effaced by a very strong counter-irritant—washing one's hair. So then she sat *chez Fauchardière,* Rue Madame 12, in the close, steamy warmth of her compartment, wrapped all in white, leaning well back in the swivel-chair. . . . Not scent this time, only the clean and rustic smell of camomile. (Peasant women, going to mass on Sunday.) Juliette's head was foaming with a cloud of camomile. And her hair was quite smooth now, skimpy, plaited, like a leggy schoolgirl's. But already the warm, foamy camomile surged up all over this juvenile blond head and ruffled it out into a woman's. Sensitive fingers began to work on it. A white coolness laid itself on Juliette's forehead, on her cheeks and chin. Soon she'd be twenty-four; at certain hours the skin round her eyes and mouth had a tired look. It ought to be evening all day long, and the sun turned into electric light. Oh, how nice to be able to be in love with oneself again! Not to live for others! To be really absorbed in one's own perfectly cared-for body, full of delight in its charms, armed by it against all self-mistrust, as though there were no such things as men. . . .

Yet, in spite of her wandering mind, Juliette could still keep a sharp eye on much that occurred in the present. (Even in her deepest unconsciousness, she had never lost her physical shame and cleanliness.) Now she could see plainly all the trouble Mairik Antaram was taking to get her well again. She heard how the doctor's wife and Iskuhi discussed the food which must be prepared for her. In spite of the dimness of her thoughts she still felt surprised that searching hands should always manage to find in the store chest a handful of fine ground rice, a packet of Quaker Oats, a bar of chocolate. Surely all that had been used up long ago! She tried to count all the people who lived on it. Stephan. Yes, and because of Stephan they ought to be very careful indeed. Then Gabriel, Avakian, Iskuhi, the Tomasians, Kristaphor, Missak, Hovsannah, and—and . . . She couldn't at first think of the name. Her brain became muzzy again at once, her head swam and sang. Nor could she count, and her sense of time was all out of gear. Before, after, the things that had just been happening —those that had happened long ago; it was all a jumble.

She lay alone. Mairik Antaram had had to leave her for a couple of hours to go to the hospital-hut. Then Iskuhi came into the tent and sat down opposite the bed in her usual seat, hiding her lame arm, as her habit was, with her shawl. Juliette, through eyelids grown transparent, saw that Iskuhi fully believed her to be asleep and so had ceased to control her thoughts and expression. But she knew even more. Gabriel had just left Iskuhi, and that, Juliette knew, was why this girl had come into her tent. And here Iskuhi would sit till he came back! Also she could see how Iskuhi's face, although it was no more than a hovering light, reproached her bitterly. Bitter reproaches for having let slip her chance to die. And this spiteful, this hatefully pretty, thing was really quite right. Since how much longer would Juliette be permitted to stay on, in her irresponsible border-kingdom? How much longer would they let her sleep and say nothing whenever Gabriel was about? Juliette felt—like strong rays beating on her face —this reproach, this blame, the enmity, in Iskuhi.

Juliette had always imagined herself hard, and the Asiatic soft and yielding. Yet the hard had been dissolved by the soft. As she lay there, seeming to be asleep, she was overtaken by sharp perceptions. How was this? Not she, Juliette, had first claim on Gabriel. Iskuhi had an older, prior claim, and no one had any right to contest it if she took her own back. A great self-pity shook Juliette. Had she not done everything in her power to win the love of this Asiatic, she who stood so immeasurably above her? Had she not formed that ignorant chit of a girl, dressed her up in all her own things, taught her how to care for her face and hands? (Oh, yes, and when she's stripped, that young woman, in spite of her pretty little breasts, has a grey-brown skin, and not even God could alter that for her. And a crippled right arm. Surely—such a fastidious man as Gabriel . . . ?) Juliette was astonished to consider how, ever since she remembered life again, this arch-enemy, in spite of her continued vomiting, had kept coming back solicitously to the bed with a spoon and a cup. Why, she might have poisoned the cup—she *ought* to have poisoned it; it had been her plain duty, so to do. Juliette blinked her thin eyelids. *Et, voilà!* Iskuhi had stood up; had, as she always did, stuck in the thermos under her left armpit; was unscrewing the top. This she put down on the little dressing-table, carefully filled it, came towards the patient. So it had been more than empty suspicion, then! The murderess was coming with her poison! Juliette pressed together her eyes and lips. And heard how the murderess, in the act, could still manage to sing, in her glassy voice, or at least hum softly. She sang like one of the mosquitoes which kept settling on Juliette's face. She listened intently.

Iskuhi bent down over her. "You've had nothing to drink for five hours, Juliette. This tea is still quite warm."

The patient opened glowering eyes. Iskuhi noticed nothing. She had put down her poison-bowl again and thrust an extra cushion under Juliette's head, to prop her up. Only then did she set her draught to Juliette's lips. Juliette waited, to disarm her arch-enemy's suspicions, pretending that she really was going to drink. Suddenly, with well-calculated cunning, she knocked the cup out of Iskuhi's hand. The tea spilt over the rugs.

But Juliette had sat up in bed and was panting: "Go! Get out, you! Go away! . . ."

She had far worse to encounter early that evening, when Gabriel came beside her bed. Now it was a case of escaping quickly, diving back swiftly into the labyrinth. But suddenly those dark paths were blocked, and the whole area of the borderland had become most absurdly constricted. Gabriel, as usual, took up her hand inquiringly. A fully conscious thud of her heart: Will he speak? Shall I have to be told everything today, and *know?* Mayn't I hide any more? She tried to breathe heavily, evenly. But she could feel at once that this time her sleep would not be limpid and just, but troubled by the will. Gabriel, too, said not a word. In a little while he lit the candles on the dressing-table—oil was no longer being used—and went away. Juliette breathed freely again. But in two minutes he was back with that big photograph of Stephan which he placed on her bed. It was the photograph done last year, which usually he kept on his writing-desk in Paris; also in Yoghonoluk.

But that isn't Stephan's photo at all, Juliette thought, it's something else, a letter perhaps, and, when I'm well, I can read it. But now I mustn't expose myself any longer to life. So bad for me! I really have still got a perfect right to vanish. She nestled down, and, with ice-cold hands, drew up the rugs to her mouth. But that threw the cardboard off the bed, with its picture side uppermost. The photo looked straight up at Juliette, whose head bent out over the bed. The candlelight, reflected in the glass, shone on the centre of that flat image. Now it was done. Now there was no more going back for Juliette. But Stephan's visit was not any result of the photograph. The boy's essential reality was standing behind Juliette's bed. It was as if he had dashed in, out of breath, from among all the others, the Haik gang, or from orderly duty, or a game, bursting in quickly, much against his will, to gulp down milk.

"Maman, were you looking for me?"

"Don't come yet, not today, Stephan!" implored Juliette. "Not today, please. I'm not strong enough. Come tomorrow! Let me be ill just another day! You'd better go along to your father——"

"I'm always with him——"

"I know you don't love me, Stephan . . ."

"And you, Maman?"

"When you're a good boy, I love you. You must wear your blue suit again. Because, otherwise, you're *so* Armenian. . . ."

Stephan was very annoyed by this. He seemed not in the least to want to go back to his other clothes. His silence showed her he was defiant. But Juliette kept on begging in an ever stormier voice: "Please, not today, Stephan! Come early tomorrow! Leave me this one night . . ."

"Early tomorrow?"

It was an empty question, not a promise, impatient, absent, hasty, with Stephan's head half turned back, towards his mother. Yet, even as Juliette felt her petition granted, she sprang out of bed. Her voice rasped and came out strangled: "Stephan! Stay here—don't run away—here! Stay! Stephan! . . ."

Mairik Antaram was on her way to Three-Tent Square to settle down her patient for the night. Shushik had joined her. For, since she heard her Haik was still alive, the widow had been shyly eager for company, and people to help. And who better than Antaram, the helper, could show her a way to this? These two women found the hanum lying out about two hundred paces in front of her tent. She cowered there in her night-dress, by the side of a bush, her shrivelled legs drawn up to her chin. Sweat still stood out on her forehead, but her open eyes were again vacantly remote.

Axes could be heard on the North Saddle from the distant, northern heights of Musa Dagh. The Turks were felling the ilexes of the mountain. Were they building gun-emplacements? Or setting up a fortified camp to have a point of retreat for their next attack; not, as previously, to be forced to leave the heights when it was dark, or else be exposed to sudden onslaughts. Scouts were sent out to investigate these crests of hill beyond the Saddle; four of the quickest boys in the scouts' group. They never came back.

Profound commotion! Sato, the master-spy, was sent forth. No harm came to her. And she came back. But nothing useful could be got out of her. "Many thousands of soldiers." Sato's notion of figures had always been most vague; either they were the lowest or the highest. As to what these "thousands" were doing, she could only give the mistiest report. "They're rolling wood," or "They're cooking." The duty seemed not to have interested her.

This happened on the thirty-sixth day in camp, the fourth of September. That morning every family had been served with its exact portion of donkey-flesh. No one knew that the ration might not be the last. At the same time all the observers sent in reports that the villages and the whole of the valley were stirring as never before.

And not only were there crowds of new soldiers and saptiehs, but swarms of inquisitive rabble had collected again from the Moslem villages. The cause of this tumult was soon apparent. When, armed with Gabriel's field-glass, Samuel Avakian climbed the high knoll to clear up the position, scouts came dashing in to him excitedly. Something entirely new had arrived. Most of the villagers had seen nothing like it before in their lives. It had just halted on the highroad from Antakiya to Suedia, at the entrance to the hamlet Yedidje, where a small detachment of cavalry were awaiting it. Avakian through his field-glass recognized a tiny, grey, military car, which must have risked its life in crossing the passes at Ain el Yerab. Three officers climbed out of the car and mounted horses, held there ready for them. This miniature cavalcade turned straight into the valley of the villages. The officers cantered on ahead; behind them, the cavalrymen; a few minutes more and they'd be in Wakef. The officer riding in the centre kept almost half a length ahead of the other two. The others wore the usual astrakhan kepi; he had on a field-grey service cap. Avakian could plainly observe the general's red stripe on his riding-breeches. The riders cantered all through the villages without one halt.

It took them scarcely an hour to reach Yoghonoluk. There, on the church square, some civilians were already awaiting them; no doubt the Kaimakam of Antakiya who, with the müdir and other civil servants, escorted the general pasha and his suite into Villa Bagradian. These very significant events were at once reported to the commander. Samuel Avakian sounded the major alarm on his own responsibility. Gabriel later endorsed this measure. He reinforced it, indeed, by giving orders that from now on the camp was to consider itself as being in a perpetual state of alarm, whether anything happened or not. But to Avakian he confided his opinion that the Turks were not ready yet by a long chalk, that neither today nor tomorrow would anything happen, and probably not in the next few days. He seemed to be right. Having spent two hours in the villa, these new officers remounted and cantered to Yedidje, even more sharply than they had come. They had not been half a day on the scene of action when the little, cheaply rattling car drove off again towards Antakiya. The Kaimakam accompanied these military gentlemen back to his provincial capital.

That same day Gabriel roused himself and shook off his pain. The soldier aroused in him by the banishment laws got

694

the upper hand again. From hour to hour he managed to extinguish his inner life. Pain was still there, but only in the form of some dim consciousness, like a wounded limb deadened with injections. He flung himself on his work with wild eagerness. Sudden resolution seemed to have worked a complete cure, so that now he stood more firmly erect than ever. Only now did he become fully aware what invaluable help he got from Avakian, his adjutant, or better, his chief-of-staff. That indefatigable tutor, that strangely impersonal ego, who never once—though in knowledge and intelligence he stood head and shoulders above most of the leaders—had appeared to lay any claims to leadership, had put forth iron strength. When Avakian appeared in the trenches, he spread that feeling of almost joyous zeal, that precious "morale," which is really complete trust in the leadership. It was because, even when there was no commander, the adjutant could reflect Bagradian's qualities, like light. And Avakian, too, since Stephan's death, had had little sleep. He had lived four years with the Bagradians and had loved Stephan like his young brother. Why, on that horrible day, had he not guessed what was going on in Stephan's mind? He would never forgive himself. Never? Alas, it was his only comfort that this "never" was only a matter of a few days, and that so everything—everything—weighed lighter. Avakian set himself to serve Gabriel. Among other things he had drawn up a new roster of the decads. From it Bagradian found that his fighters had diminished to seven hundred or so. But this great gap left by death did not connote any essential weakening of their fighting strength. The best reservists could be armed with the rifles of these dead. And then, thanks to the forest fire, the area of defence had shrunk to a few sections. The ilex gully was still an oven of glowing coals. Their heat could be felt in the Town Enclosure as much as ever, where, usually towards evening, it spoilt people's tempers. So that the weakest part of the line was now protected for ever against attack. And not only in this great sector of the Damlayik, but far around, on the lower slopes, ridges, and hillocks, caved-in tree-trunks still glowed. Here a compassionate hand had turned it all in favour of the Armenians. Gabriel finally disbanded the garrisons of sections, grown superfluous, and in place of them formed a strong chain of outposts, to protect the mountain from surprise attacks and Turkish spies. Judging by present signs and possibilities, the Turks were intending a massed assault in the north, probably supported by artillery, with a force that should ten times outnumber and wipe out the exhausted Armenians. Their axes rang all day on the Damlayik. But, in spite of these apparent preparations, Gabriel was far-sighted enough to send out spies in the southern areas. These brave young men ventured out at night as far as Suedia. They reported that only very few soldiers, and scarcely any saptiehs, were in the Orontes plain. All the troops were concentrated in the villages. The rock bastion with all its possibilities of an avalanche, seemed still, in spite of this new general, to inspire the Turks with insurmountable respect. None the less Gabriel decided to inspect the South Bastion next morning.

That evening he sat in his sleeping-place and stared up the slope of the Saddle across to the group of trees on the crest, between which Stephan had gone his way without his being able to prevent it. His neighbours in the trench still kept their distance. When he arrived, their talk suddenly stopped; they stood up and greeted him as the leader. And that was all. Not one of them said a word to him of Stephan. They may not have dared. They all eyed him so strangely—inquiring, disconsolate. For twenty-four hours he had seen neither Juliette nor Iskuhi. It was better not to. All ties were loosening. He must not let himself be cast back into weakness. He must be cold and free for the last fight. And, indeed, for all his immeasurable grief, he did feel cold and free. Here on this mountain summit even September evenings were chilly. Nor had the veering wind died down, though here and there it paused in its dance. Where were those peaceful moony nights when the forty wounds in Stephan's body had still not seared his father's mind? Gabriel stared on, out at the black wall opposite. Sometimes the wind mourned in the trees above. How timid their enemies were! On a night like this they could easily have dug themselves in along that slope without being prevented. Ah, well, they had no need of such arts, since they had artillery. That, in a hand's turn, would bring the end. Perhaps one ought not to be waiting for it, one ought to anticipate the attack, get a fresh idea. Had not he, Bagradian, always had the saving idea, so that here they still remained, unbroken? First, it had been the whole defence system, the completed plan of these entrenchments, then the komitajis, the mobile guard, the forest-fire, to save them again. . . . Anticipate! A new inspiration! But what? How? His mind was a blank.

NEXT day Gabriel visited the South Bastion as he had intended. But first he stopped to examine the howitzers. Their barrels were trained in opposite directions, the one on to the northern heights, the other on Suedia. Gabriel, in the days before Stephan's death, had set their direction by his map. It would at least be possible to hold up and disturb the Turks' advance. In the lockers there were still four shrapnel and fifteen grenades. The guns had a guard of eight men round them, trained by Nurhan, under his directions.

Nurhan, Avakian, and several decad commanders accompanied Gabriel on his surprise inspection. Their first impressions on reaching the South Bastion were not such as to arouse instant suspicion. Sarkis Kilikian, on release, had even consented to improve still further the machinery of his battering-rams. The powerful battering-shields had been enlarged by oar-shaped slats jutting over the wheel-edge. So that now the impact of the shield could take in a much wider surface of the loose-heaped stones. The shields themselves had been doubly

697

strengthened and clamped together with many strong iron
hoops. Judging by the look of them, these squat catapults
would be capable of hurling tons of stone down the slope as
far as the ruins of Seleucia. Kilikian seemed interested in
nothing else but these sinister toys. It was a boyish trait, this
sudden fit of obstinate concentration, with which he kept on
working at "wall-breakers." This zeal was in signal contrast
to the usual bleak emptiness of the man. But, from the first
instant he set eyes on him, Gabriel had sensed some eager,
subterranean well-spring in this victim of relentless fate. His
relationship with Kilikian was full of inexplicable tensions.
Something in the prosperous "Parisien," the cultivated bourgeois, was afraid of the radical denials, the void, within this
deserter. They had only once been directly in conflict, when
Kilikian was routed with ignominy. Yet, even on that occasion,
Gabriel, the victor, had felt uneasy, and today he could still
not feel entirely assured. Kilikian was the one man on Musa
Dagh with whom the chief never could manage to strike the
right note. Either he spoke to him too negligently, or made
him too much of an equal. But the Russian could always find
a method of keeping Bagradian at arm's length. That, for
instance, he should still lie quietly on his back while the chief
for the second titme praised his catapults—it was not only
insolent, it was subversive insubordination, and ought to have
brought down instant punishment. Gabriel did not punish; he
turned away to look about for Teacher Oskanian. But when
Gabriel had been seen approaching, Oskanian, in hysterical
panic, had made himself scarce. He was unaware that neither
Ter Haigasun, Bedros Hekim, nor Shatakhian had told
Gabriel of that sorry Council meeting, at which the teacher
had spat out so much venom against Bagradian's family. To
have been turned off the Council of Leaders had put an edge
on Oskanian's vanity. Apparently he was now intriguing to
found an "Oskanian party." For days he had blown off steam
to all and sundry, to simple-minded folk who did not belong

to the South Bastion but came there to visit him. "The idea," as he called it, took clearer and clearer shape in his mind. But this idea was not an original inspiration; it dated from a luminous dissertation of Krikor's, who years ago, on one of their philosophical walks, had discussed the thesis "the duty of living" and "the right to die," supported with sundry quotations from a number of high-sounding authorities, whose opinions he set one against the other.

In the trenches of the South Bastion the inspecting party discovered no flagrant infringements. The duty-routine as laid down for the decads was being followed, the posts had sentries, the advance-pickets were placed at the edge of the wide stone slope. Rifles left nothing to be desired. And yet, for all its surface order, these men's manner had in it something indefinite, slack, suspicious, which roused all Nurhan's ire. This garrison was made up of eleven decads. About eighty-five of the men were deserters. Not all of these fellows were doubtful quantities; on the contrary, the majority were quite harmless fugitives from barracks, who had escaped from a bullying sergeant, the bastinado, or enrolment in a labour battalion. But, whoever was at fault in the matter, whether it were due to want, depravity, or bad example—they had one and all taken on Kilikian's intractable apathy, as though that were the only way of approaching life for such men as they. They lounged, they loitered, they lay about insolently on their backs, they stretched and lolled, they growled and whistled provocatively, in a way which boded no good for the coming battle. These men might not have been a fighting garrison, not even indeed an authentic gang of brigands, but a mere horde of dissipated, disgruntled tramps clustered together in the wilderness. But Gabriel did not seem to take their behaviour too seriously. Most of these men had proved themselves fighters. Everything else was beside the point. They must be more carefully handled than the *élite*.

But one piece of carelessness was too much for him. The

bonfire! On the west flanks of the South Bastion, where the Damlayik curves off seawards, three high redoubts had been thrown up as flank-protection. These redoubts dominated the whole steep descent at that side of the mountain which ebbed away in wooded terraces towards Habaste and thus made every outflanking manœuvre impossible. And here, twenty paces below these redoubts (also crowned by protecting walls), a big, cosy bonfire was flaming on the open foreground-area— in friendly invitation to the Turks! It was one of the most stringent regulations that no open fires should be lit in the trenches unless they had been sanctioned by the leaders. Yet even this was not enough! Round this fire there squatted not only a ragged crew of the least desirable deserters, but two trollops who had moved from the Town Enclosure to this society. And these women were turning the tenderest goat's flesh on long spits before the flames. Chaush Nurhan and the others hurled themselves in a frenzy on the group. Bagradian came slowly after them. Nurhan gripped one of the deserters by his ragged shirt and jerked him up. He was a long-haired lout with a brownish face and small, quick eyes, eyes which did not look in the least Armenian.

Nurhan's long grey sergeant's moustache twitched with fury at him. "You louse! Where did you get that goat from?"

The long-haired deserter tried to free himself. He pretended not to know who Chaush Nurhan was. "What's it to do with you? Who are you anyway?"

"That's who I am!"

One crack on the jaw sent the fellow spinning, nearly into the fire. He picked himself up and began to whine: "What did you hit me for? What harm have I ever done *you?* We went out at night to Habaste after this goat."

"To Habaste, you filthy pig! You found that goat in the camp, you poor crook. You stole their last bite from starving people. . . . Now we've our explanation. . . ."

The long-haired thief turned shifty eyes on Gabriel, who

700

stood aside, leaving his subordinates to deal with this very uninspiring business.

"Effendi," the deserter whined, "aren't we human beings? Do we feel less hunger than anyone else? And yet you ask us to work; we've got to be on duty all day and night, worse than in any barracks . . ."

To this Bagradian answered nothing, but signed sharply to his people to tread out the fire and impound the goat's flesh.

Chaush Nurhan menaced, waving a roasted goat's leg: "You'll get hungrier yet before you've done. Better start eating each other up."

The long-haired culprit approached Bagradian, with humble arms crossed on his breast. "Effendi! Give us munitions! We've only got a cartridge-belt each. You've taken all the rest away from us. Then we could go out hunting and shoot ourselves a hare or a fox. It's all wrong that we haven't a few more cartridges. The Turks might come along any night."

Gabriel turned his back on him. On their way back into camp, Nurhan the Lion declared, still very excited: "We ought to clear out that whole South Bastion. Best thing would be to turn twenty of the worst of them out of camp!"

But Gabriel's thoughts had long been occupied with more important things than this very unpleasant little incident.

"That's impossible," he said absently. "We can't send our Armenian fellow-countrymen out to certain death."

"Armenian fellow-countrymen?" Chaush Nurhan spat far and scornfully.

The face of the long-haired man came to Gabriel's mind. "There must be scum, among five thousand. It's the same everywhere."

Chaush glanced suspiciously at Gabriel. "It's bad to let a crime of this sort pass."

Bagradian stood still; he took hold of the old sergeant's Mauser rifle and stamped the butt of it hard on the ground. "We've only got one punishment, Chaush Nurhan—and this

701

is it. All the rest is absurd. Wasn't it too ridiculous to shut Kilikian up in the government-hut, where he had poor Krikor to keep him company? To punish these fellows round the fire, we should have to shoot the lot of them."

"Well, that's what we ought to have done. . . . But now we ought to put them into separate units, Effendi——"

Gabriel stopped again. "We'll have separate units, Chaush Nurhan, something entirely new . . ."

He said no more. He himself was still not sure what this new thing was.

WHEN, on the morning of September 6, the women came to the distributing-tables to receive the day's ration for their families, some of them were given only bones, with a few stray morsels of donkey's flesh still clinging to them. In desperation the mothers besieged the mukhtars, who as usual superintended the distribution, each at the table assigned to his village. These headmen stepped back before the flood, grey and green in the face, like their own bad consciences. By Council's orders, the best meat had gone to the trenches, they stammered; the fighters had to get up their strength for the coming attack. And as for the very last she-goats and donkeys, it had been decided not to slaughter them; the goats for their milk, which went to the smallest children; the four last donkeys because they would be needed in the fight. Nothing, therefore, remained but that mothers of families should begin to look about for their own provender. They must try to concoct some kind of herb-broth, of arbutus berries, acorns, Indian fig, wild berries, roots, and leaves, which at least should serve to deaden hunger. The mukhtars, as they gave this disconsolate counsel, kept bobbing and putting their hands in front of their faces, fully expecting that these women would strangle and tear them in pieces in their rage. They did no such thing. They hung their heads and stared at the earth. The feverish restlessness in their eyes changed into that dazed expression which they had worn that day in the church of Yoghonoluk, when the government decree had flashed down like lightning on them. The mukhtars began to breathe again. They had nothing to fear. The shoals of women began to separate. Slowly they turned their backs on the empty distributing-tables.

Then, in a little while, these women dispersed in all directions, in long, star-shaped lines about the mountain-plateau, went here and there among the rocks on the coastside, and even ventured down into such green spaces over the valley as fire had skirted. Their children ran with them, some not older than three or four, getting under their mothers' feet and hindering them. If only they could have crossed the North Saddle as formerly, there might still have been hope of nutritious finds. But the area within camp-bounds had been cleared as bare as the plundered bone of a wild dog. Some of these women strayed for the hundredth time in and out among the arbutus and bilberry bushes to glean what still remained unpicked. Others among the rocks tried to climb down to those rare places where grew Indian figs, whose big soft fruit was esteemed a delicacy. What good was all that? Their bellies all cried aloud for flour, for fat, for a piece of goat's cheese. No blessing lay on Pastor Aram's fishery. Without the necessary assistance it was impossible to construct a raft which would hold in the rough seas, and the nets also had proved useless. Nor did better luck attend the bird-catchers, though their decoys and springs were properly made. But here there were no birds as yet; they were all still in the cool north. Quail, snipe, and woodcock would not fly into such childish traps.

DURING these desperate expeditions of women the Council of Leaders held a session. The leaders were still unaware that this was their last day in the government-hut. The wall of books set up by Krikor against the world still remained unaltered. Ter Haigasun's face was a waxen death-mask. The priest asked Pastor Aram to speak.

Today's counsels, and their very unfortunate sequel, were predetermined by the strained feeling already arisen between Aram Tomasian and Gabriel. Tomasian had still not questioned Bagradian. He loved Iskuhi. Now that he scarcely ever saw her, that Hovsannah kept slandering his sister in the wildest outbursts, he loved her as never before. Her words kept ringing in his ears: "I'm nineteen, and shall never be twenty." So that Tomasian tried not to bring things to a head.

But this first meeting with Gabriel, whom he had not seen since Stephan's death, filled Aram with a kind of bitter embarrassment. He could not manage to bring out a word of sympathy.

The sitting opened with his report:

"What we decided to do has been done. And now all the meat has been distributed. Only the very last portion was secretly kept back for the decads. At most it can last another two days. Today the women and children have their first complete fast day, unless we care to consider the rations of the last few days as a fast."

Mukhtar Thomas Kebussyan raised his hand, having first squinted round the room to make sure that all his partisans of the last sitting were in their places. "I can't see why the men in the trenches should be fed, and the women and children left to starve. Strong, well-set-up young fellows ought to be able to tighten their belts a bit."

Here Gabriel intervened at once: "That's very simple, Mukhtar Kebussyan. The fighters need their strength now, more than they ever did."

Ter Haigasun, to support their leader, switched the debate off food again: "Perhaps Gabriel Bagradian will give us his view of the real strength of the defence decads."

Gabriel pointed to Chaush Nurhan. "The morale of the

704

decads is really not much worse than it was before the last fight. It's surprising enough, but that's how it is, and Chaush Nurhan will bear me out in what I say. And our defence works are far stronger now than last time. The possible points for a Turkish attack are far more restricted. Roughly, there's only the north for them to attack in, and all their preparations prove what I say. In spite of this new general of theirs, they'll never dare attack the bastion; that's as good as certain. The garrison there, as we all know, does us no particular credit. But I intend sending Nurhan along there for a couple of days to keep them in order for a bit. This Turkish attack in the north will be worse than all the others put together. It'll all be a question of whether they have artillery and how much they have. Up to now we haven't managed to find out. It all depends on that. That is to say, unless we resort to some new method . . . but I'll talk of that later."

Ter Haigasun, who had sat as usual, with chilly hands and downcast eyes, could not suppress the essential question: "Good—but what then?"

Gabriel, consumed with longings for the end and its freedom, spoke far too resonantly for the little room: "Well, only think! At this minute all over the world millions of men are living in trenches, just as we do. They're fighting, or else they're waiting to fight, bleeding, dying, just like us. That's the only thought that pacifies and consoles me. When I think that, I feel I'm no worse, no less honourable, than any other man among those millions. And it's the same for us all! By fighting, we cease to be just manure, rotting somewhere round the Euphrates. By fighting we gain honour and dignity. Therefore, we should see nothing ahead, and think of nothing else, but how to fight."

A very small minority indeed seemed to share this heroic view of the situation. Ter Haigasun's "what then?" was going the rounds.

Gabriel looked round, surprised. "What then? I thought

we'd all agreed on that. What then? We'll hope nothing more."

Here was a chance for Asayan, the choir-singer, to do his friend Oskanian a service. He had promised that, in this sitting, he would let slip no chance to sow mistrust. He need only hint at the "treachery" of Gonzague Maris, at the Agha's mysterious visit to Gabriel.

He cleared his throat. "Effendi, a warrior's death is not always quite so heroic and single-minded. Personally I wish nothing better. Nor do I presume to express an opinion on your respected wife. Perhaps you made some arrangements on her behalf with the Turkish pasha who visited you a few days ago. We know nothing of that! But what, may I ask, is to happen to *our* wives, sisters, and daughters?"

It was in Gabriel's nature not to be prepared for such attacks. Arrows of malice and vulgarity were more than he could readily contend with, mainly because he always needed a certain time in which to become fully conscious of them. He stared at Asayan, not understanding him.

But Ter Haigasun, who knew Bagradian's nature from A to Z, took up the cudgels on his behalf: "Singer, keep a guard on your tongue! But if you really want to know why the Agha Rifaat Bereket from Antakiya came here to see the effendi, I'll tell you. Gabriel Bagradian could long since have been safe in the Agha's house in Antakiya, eating his bread and pilav in peace and quiet, since the Turk suggested that he should escape and offered him a very good chance to do so. But our Gabriel Bagradian preferred to keep faith with us and go on doing his duty to the last minute."

This declaration was a necessary breach of Gabriel's confidence. A long, rather uneasy silence followed it. Apart from Ter Haigasun, only Bedros Altouni had known the truth. The silence continued. But it would be a mistake to suppose that it expressed any general approval of Bagradian's act in refusing the Agha. The mukhtars, for instance, had no such

706

thoughts. Each of these worthy men "of the people" asked himself how *he* would have reacted to such a temptation. And they each quietly decided that this European grandson of old Avetis had simply behaved like a silly fool. Aram Tomasian was the first to ease the silence with his voice.

"Gabriel Bagradian," he began, but could not keep his eyes on his opponent, "feels everything as a militarist, as an officer. After all, no one can reproach me with having run away in these last fights. But I don't feel as a militarist. Things strike me differently. We all see things differently from Bagradian, there's no getting away from that. Is there any object, I ask myself, in spilling more blood in another unequal battle, merely in order to be left to starve quietly for three days longer at most? And even that would be an unheard-of bit of luck. What should we gain?"

Till that instant Aram's "way out" had still been the vaguest of half-digested notions, without proper reality. His bitter urge to contradict Bagradian suddenly gave shape to this nebulous project, made it seem to him like a well-thought-out suggestion. "Ter Haigasun and all the rest of you must admit that there's no point in our holding out up here on the Damlayik; that we should do better to shoot our wives, and then ourselves, than die slowly of hunger or fall into the hands of the Turks. I therefore suggest that we leave the mountain, tomorrow or the day after, as soon as possible. As to the best means of doing it, that must all be carefully discussed. I would suggest that we go northwards, though of course not on the heights, since those are barricaded by the Turks, but along the coast. We might take Ras el-Khanzir as our first objective. The little bay there is very sheltered and certainly has more fish in it than the coast here. We shan't need a raft, and I give you my word that the nets will be enough. . . ."

That sounded less fantastic than perhaps it was. Above all, Aram's speech suggested action, and the vague, but compelling prospect of being able before death to break through the mummification of the Damlayik. Heads, which up to then had never moved, began to sway as though a faint wind rippled them, faint colour came into the faces.

Only Gabriel Bagradian had not changed as now he raised his hand for permission to speak. "That's a very pretty dream of Pastor Aram's. I admit that I've had similar dreams myself. But we must test fantasies closely by the chances they have of becoming reality. I'll therefore—though, as responsible leader I have no right to—assume that we succeed during the night in getting past the Turks, and reaching Ras el-Khanzir. I'll even go much further than that; I'll frivolously suppose that saptiehs and soldiers fail to notice a long, straggling procession of four to five thousand people, moving—the moon's in her second quarter—all along the brightly illuminated chalk cliffs above the coast. Good! We reach the sloping rocks of the cape unhindered. There we should have to get round a long promontory, since the little bay only eats into the coast beyond the cape. . . . Don't interrupt me, Pastor, you can rely on what I say, I have every detail of the map in my head. I don't know whether these bays are just bare rocks or whether they offer any kind of inhabitable ground. But, even so, I'll give the pastor the benefit of the doubt. Well, therefore, we find sufficient camping-ground, and the Turks are struck so blind that they need six, or if you like eight, days to hunt us out. And now comes the really important question: What shall we have gained? Answer: We shall have exchanged the known for the unknown. We shall have exposed our worn-out, famished women and children to a long, scrambling march, over pitiless rocks, along the cliffs, which probably they could never manage. Instead of this camp, to which we're accustomed, we should have to build up another, without strength and without means. Surely everyone sees that! Since we no longer have any mules, we've naturally had to leave all our beds and rugs, all our cooking-utensils, our tools, behind on

708

the Damlayik. But without tools, even if we found ourselves in Paradise, with bread growing on every tree, we could never start a new life. The pastor won't deny that. We relinquish a strong and tested fortress, for which the Turks have the greatest respect. We exchange a dominant position, on a height, for an exposed, helpless position in a valley, where there is no cover. We should be slaughtered within half an hour, Tomasian! We should of course have one great advantage. Down there we should not have such a long way to fall into the sea as we shall up here, from the Dish Terrace. But, anyway, I'm afraid the fish may get more to eat off us, than we're ever likely to get off them."

Aram Tomasian had listened to this clear exposé with occasional excited interruptions. The voice of common sense, which even now warned him, at this decisive moment, not to let himself be driven by blind emotion, grew fainter and fainter. Nor, as he attacked Bagradian, so hotly that he could scarcely control his voice, did he once look him in the face. "Gabriel Bagradian is always so despotic in defending his own point of view. He won't allow us to have any intelligence of our own. We're nothing but a set of poor peasants. He's so far above us! Well, I don't deny that that's so. We're poor peasants and craftsmen, not his equals. But, since he's just asked us so many questions, may I ask *him* a few in exchange? He, a trained officer, has made the Damlayik into a good fortress. Admitted! But what use is all this fortification to us to-day on the Damlayik? None at all! On the contrary. It prevents our trying to find a last way of escape. If the Turks are intelligent, they won't let themselves in for another battle, since they can gain their object in a few days without losing a man. But whether or not there's another battle—where is there some idea, some new attempt to escape death? I know it's not nearly so much trouble to perish here, in our usual surroundings. At least one hasn't got to make any effort. Personally I consider it despicable simply to sit down lazily and rot. And the most important question of all: What suggestions has Gabriel Bagradian got to make, to keep off hunger? Is it enough for him to jeer at my attempt with the fishery? Unluckily it was, and remains, the only attempt. If I'd had support, if every able-bodied man hadn't been always drilling all day long, it might have been rather more successful."

And the pastor, who so far had at least kept an appearance of calm, sprang forward passionately and shouted: "Ter Haigasun, I'm making a very serious suggestion. That all the still available animals be slaughtered, cooked, and divided up. That we strike camp tomorrow night, or at the very latest the night after. Re-encampment in one of the bays, where fishing is easy!"

The quick, gruff method of this suggestion confused these peasants' heavy minds. The mukhtars shifted uneasily on their benches, rocking from side to side, like praying Moslems. Old Tomasian, Aram's father, blinked in alarm.

But Kebussyan wiped his perspiring baldness and uttered a piteous complaint: "Oh, if only we'd gone on the convoy! . . . Alive or dead . . . we'd have done far better!"

Here Ter Haigasun drew a crumpled filthy slip out of his cassock-sleeve. This was his chance, not only to stifle Kebussyan's sigh, but to defend the Damlayik against Aram. He read out his fateful slip in a fairly low voice, almost tonelessly:

" 'Harutiun Nokhudian, Pastor of Bitias, to the Chief Priest of the coastal district round Suedia, Ter Haigasun of Yoghonoluk.

" 'First, peace and long life to you, beloved brother in Christ, Ter Haigasun, and to all my beloved countrymen along with you, up on Musa Dagh, or wherever else this letter may find you, and, let me hope, still on the mountain. If God wills, this letter will reach you. I shall have given it to a well-disposed Turkish officer to deliver. Our trust in God has been put to a terrible test, and He, I am sure, would forgive us, had we lost it. I write you this beside the unburied earthly remains of my dear, saintly, angelically kind wife. She, as no doubt you will remember, always was concerned for my health and well-being, and would never permit me to exert myself, go out bareheaded, or take stimulants, to which my weak, sinful nature was over-inclined. But now everything is reversed. Her eager prayer has been heard. It is she who has gone on and left me alone, having died of hunger. Her last act was to force me, in the morning cold of these steppes, to take her neck-scarf and wrap it round me. God punishes me, like Job. I, the weak, the ailing, have a strength in me which refuses to be extinguished, and which I have cursed a thousand times. But she, who protected me on earth, has died, and I have to outlive her. All the young men of my parish were separated off from us in Antakiya, and we know nothing of what has happened to them. All the rest, except twenty-seven, of us are dead, and I fear I shall be the last, I who am not strong or worthy enough to die! Now we get a small daily ration of bread and bulgur, because commissions have been in the camp, but only enough to prolong our suffering. Perhaps today they will send us inshaat taburi to bury all the many, many corpses. When they come, they will take my dear one away from me, and yet I must be thankful that they do it. I have covered this sheet. God keep you, Ter Haigasun, when shall we ever meet again . . .' "

The priest had read even these last lines in a toneless, matter-of-fact voice. Yet every syllable hung like a counter-weight on the bearded faces of the men, weighing them down.

Bedros Altouni raised his voice, as rusty and sharp as an old knife-blade: "Well, I think that now Thomas Kebussyan will have ceased to long for the blessings of deportation. We've been living our own life here thirty-eight days now. It's not been easy, but it's been quite decent, in my opinion. Pity that later we shan't any of us get the chance to be proud of it.

I suggest that Ter Haigasun should publicly read Nokhudian's letter from the altar square."

This was most heartily agreed upon. For in the Town Enclosure Kebussyan's sigh, "Oh! if we'd gone on the convoy!" had long begun to go the rounds. But Gabriel had paid no heed to all this, having sat there lost in his own reflections. He had already heard the little pastor's letter. Now he was thinking of Aram's emotional display of hostility. He knew at once that Iskuhi was the cause. All the less, therefore, would he allow himself to be touched by Aram's insulting tone. He had a very great proposal. He strove, therefore, to make his words as conciliatory as possible:

"It's never occurred to me to gibe at Pastor Aram Tomasian's plans. From the very beginning I've considered his suggestion for the fishery a good one. If it's failed, that isn't the fault of the idea, but of the bad tools. As to his suggestion of a new camp, I was forced in duty to show that it's not only unpractical, but that it would hasten the end and make it crueller than ever. On the other hand, Pastor Aram was perfectly right to ask me what I propose to do about famine. Now listen, please, all of you! I'm going to answer all these questions at once. . . ."

In a sense Gabriel also was improvising, much as the pastor had. He, too, had turned the proposal, which now he developed in all its details, over in his mind in the night, as one among several possibilities, without taking it really seriously. But so it is. Once an idea, a project, is put into words, it is already in the first stage of reality, and has gained a solidity of its own. He turned to Nurhan the Lion, to Shatakhian, to those who, he hoped, would support him.

"There's an old method which the besieged have used from time immemorial. . . . The Turks have shifted their camp on Musa Dagh. Even if they have six or eight companies and Lord knows how many saptiehs, they'll need most of these troops to enclose the mountain. We need only reckon how big the distance is from Kebussiye to, say, Arsus. It's evident they want to starve us and that therefore they'll wait a few days longer before beginning their big attack. That's proved by this departure of their general who's going to lead it. You see how important they feel us! . . . I'm supposing that this general, with his officers, the Kaimakam, and perhaps even other highly placed personages will come back very soon and quarter themselves in my house. . . . So, therefore, I want to attempt a sortie, you understand, Ter Haigasun? As follows: We'll form an attacking party of picked decads. I don't know yet whether it'll be four or five hundred men. By tonight I shall have thought out the whole scheme in detail. There are plenty of ways, between gaps in the fire, of getting down into the valley. They'll have to be exactly reconnoitred. But I know for a fact that, down there, their command has only posted patrols, who skim the valley during the night. We should merely have to find out when they relieve each other, and get past when their backs are turned; it wouldn't be hard. And at, say, two or three in the morning we could attack. . . . What? . . . No, not Yoghonoluk, we certainly shouldn't get as far as that. . . . We could attack my house, with a fully superior strength. Naturally we should have found out the number of men they have on guard there. Apart from officers' orderlies, I reckon at most on a company of infantry or saptiehs. We'll kill off the sentries and take quick possession of the garden and stables. All the rest is really not for discussion here. It's my business and Chaush Nurhan's. With God's help we shall take prisoner the general, the Kaimakam, the müdir, the yüs-bashi, and the other officers. If the whole attack is successful, we can have those highly placed gentlemen back in the Town Enclosure within two hours, and perhaps even flour and provisions."

"Gabriel Bagradian's dreaming, now," crowed the choir-singer, Oskanian's little deputy.

But the gentle Shatakhian sprang up enthusiastically. "In

my opinion Bagradian's again made the only really bold suggestion. It's even more magnificent than the others were. If we really succeed in getting hold of the villa, and taking prisoner a general, a kaimakam, a yüs-bashi, there's no saying what mightn't come of it. . . ."

"It's perfectly obvious what would come of it," Aram Tomasian cut into this disdainfully. "If we capture one of their generals and a high official, the Turks will cease to consider us a joke. They'll send out regiments and brigades against us. And if Gabriel Bagradian imagines the army will negotiate for its martinets and make concessions, he's much mistaken. The death of a general or a kaimakam at the hands of Armenian rebels is just what they want. It puts them completely in the right in every foreign country; it's the fullest justification of their Armenian policy. They welcome anything of that kind. What do you people in Yoghonoluk know about it? I was in Zeitun——"

Shatakhian boiled with rage: "It's not Gabriel Bagradian who's 'much mistaken,' it's you, Pastor, in spite of all your Zeitun. I know Ittihad, I know the Young Turks, even if I've only lived in Yoghonoluk. They stick together. They never sacrifice one of their own. In no circumstances. *Point d'honneur!* And the shameful death of a general or a kaimakam would damage their whole prestige in the eyes of the people. They couldn't stand up to it! On the contrary they'd do all they possibly could to buy off their big bugs, with flour, and fat, and meat—with freedom even."

The teacher's too exuberant optimism moved all the doubters to scorn. Again there arose the empty, malicious strife of the last sitting, in which no opinion could fully assert itself. All that it lacked was the threatening crowd round the hut. Ter Haigasun, who, as usual, bore with the din for a certain time, tried to get peace by saying dryly that the usefulness of captured generals and kaimakams had better not be discussed until they'd been caught.

714

Meanwhile the suffering demon in Tomasian had taken full possession of the pastor. He was wild and senseless enough to attack, for no reason, the Orthodox priest: "Ter Haigasun! Aren't you the supreme, responsible head! I accuse you, here, of indecision. You let everything slide. You don't want anyone interfering with you. It's a sheer miracle that with your—what shall I call it?—your unconcern, we should still be alive today. . . ."

This scabrous attack on the highest authority—unique, unheard of as it was—so much annoyed Altouni, the agnostic, that he stridently defended the Orthodox Gregorian vicar against the Protestant's attack: "What have you to complain of here, young man? Nice state of things! You know nothing at all of us or of our life, since your father packed you off, as a boy, to Marash. Don't you get too big for your boots!"

Called to order like an impudent schoolboy, and already hot with shame at his own tactlessness, Aram's voice became shriller than ever: "I may be too much of a stranger to understand you, though the real strangers among you seem to understand you well enough. But I still keep to my first suggestion. More—I've decided to do what I think fit on behalf of myself and my family. When was it ever written that we must all keep together to the end? It'd be far wiser to break up the whole camp. Let each family save itself—as best it can. It's much easier to catch a whole shoal of us in one place. But, if we disperse all over the coast, then perhaps some at least of us will be left alive, in one way or another. I mean to pack up and get out with my whole family and find a way for myself. I said *my whole family*, Gabriel Bagradian."

Ter Haigasun had not once lost his temper through the whole of this very stormy session. When, exactly six days previously, he had kicked Oskanian out of the hut, it had been done regally, with just the necessary emphasis. Even now he showed no signs of excitement as he stood up, pale, almost ceremonious. "That's enough. Our sessions have no further object. The people elected us to lead them. I herewith, on the thirty-eighth day, declare this warrant to be cancelled, since this Council of Leaders has no longer the necessary strength and unity to make decisions. If it's possible for a man like Aram Tomasian, responsible for the civil law and order of this camp, to suggest its being broken up, it's obvious that we have no right to exact obedience and subordination from anyone else. So that, here and now, things become as they were again, before the Council was chosen by the villages. The mukhtars take over the sole charge of their communes, and I, as chief priest of the district, the guidance of the community as a whole. And in that capacity I request Gabriel Bagradian that he should continue to lead our defence. His command is independent. It rests with him whether he decides on a surprise attack or on any other method of armed resistance. Further, in my capacity as priest, I decree a solemn Mass of petition, the time for which shall be given out later. I have no right to reject any possible chance of a rescue. Consequently, Pastor Aram Tomasian, after this Mass, will get his opportunity of repeating his present suggestion to the whole people and giving his reasons. Then the majority can decide whether it would rather leave the mountain or continue to trust to the valour of our fighters and the plans of our military leader. But, once this decision has been taken, we must also pass a resolution that anyone who, by deed or word of mouth, sets himself up against the general will is to be shot instantly.— Well, now! Any further suggestions?"

In peaceful times it is very pleasant to be a leader, but when one is two paces away from destruction it seems more inviting to lose oneself in the anonymous herd. The mukhtars had become simple village mayors again, and nothing more. The Council of Leaders, chosen by the Great Assembly in the garden of Villa Bagradian, dispersed quietly, without protest. Ter Haigasun had made a wise move and at the same time a tremendous sacrifice. The leadership had been purged of all its cantankerous, independable elements. But now he alone, in this hour of finality, would have to guide his people through death, to God. They left the government-hut in silence.

But Aram hated Ter Haigasun; he hated Gabriel Bagradian, and himself even more than either. He took curt leave of his father, without answering his many despairing questions. The days of the Zeitun convoy came back to chide him. Had he not even then disgraced the Gospel and left his sheep, his children, on the third day? Bitterly the pastor admitted that it is always the same sin by which men are trapped. And how much more basely, shamefully, crazily, had he failed to with-stand today's temptation. Aram at first wandered about the Damlayik; then he clambered down the path to the beach, for another effort to solve the insoluble problems of his fishery.

It would be better, he felt, not to wait for the people's de-cision and set out at once with Hovsannah and the child. Kevork would be all the help they needed. He would of course have to leave his father, who would certainly refuse to fly. The swimmers had easily reached Alexandretta, via Arsus. Why should not he and his small family, in three night marches along the coast, be able to get as far as they? Herr Hoffmann, who had given them hospitality, was a Protestant, and would not shut his doors against a Protestant pastor. Naturally his priesthood was at an end, after today's disgrace-ful lapse into sin. Tomasian felt in his pocketbook. He had fifty pounds, a lot of money. Then, with a grimace of moral repugnance, he stared down at the surf around his feet. And Iskuhi?

It was written, however, that neither Aram's plan nor Ga-briel's should reach fulfilment, and that no plebiscite should be held. It is always the same: the dam has broken before the waves come surging over it, and usually in the least expected place.

In the area of the South Bastion there was a wide plateau,

717

facing seawards, overgrown with short, dry crop-grass. There Sarkis Kilikian and the circumspect commissar of the section, Hrand Oskanian, had set up their camp. Two deserters a few yards off played a game of shells with the long-haired thief of goat's flesh. These "deserters" might have been anything. The various fortunes of the game were being acclaimed with cries in every language spoken in Syria. The teacher was doing his best to impress the Russian with his grandiloquence. He talked so loud and so emphatically that even the tattered gamesters stopped to listen from time to time to his bold opinions. But Sarkis, stretched out full length, and with Krikor's cold chibuk between his teeth, was stubbornly silent under all the excited efforts of the dwarf.

"You're an educated man, a man who has studied, Kilikian," the fuzzy-haired teacher was insisting, "so you'll understand me. I've never said much, you know. I've valued my thoughts too much. I never even said it to the apothecary, who cribbed a lot of my opinions. You know what life is, Kilikian —it's knocked you about more than any of us. And me, too, if you'll believe me. I, Hrand Oskanian, have never been anything all my life but a measly teacher in a dirty village. What can you know about me? But all the same, I have my idea. Would you care to hear it?—'Finish the whole thing' is what I say. Since what's the good of anything else?"

Sarkis leaned up on his elbow to crumble a piece of the tobacco Krikor had given him. All the others mixed this pure, blond leaf with dried herbs. Sarkis smoked his unmixed, not seeming to worry about the fact that his ration was thus finished twice as quickly. The once silent Oskanian had found a master of silence in the Russian. Kilikian's silence would have withered the leaves off a tree. In the teacher's case it served to unloose a flood of boastful words, on the surface of which, undigested, dishonoured, swam stray shreds of Krikor's conversation.

"Well, then, Kilikian, you understand me, and I you. You

don't even need to tell me so. Like you, I don't believe there's a God. Why should there be such a piece of tomfoolery? The world is a lump of dung, spinning in space—mere chemistry and astronomy, that's all it is! I'll show you Krikor's book of stars—there you can see it all, in pictures. Nothing but nature. And, if anyone made it, the devil did. There's a pig hidden in it, an unclean swine. But it can't take the last thing off me, Kilikian, see what I mean? We can spit in its face, we can make it look small, show it who really is the stronger, stamp it out! You see?—Well, that's my idea! I, Hrand Oskanian, small as I am, can show nature and the devil, and God Almighty, what's what! I can annoy them, punish them. The gentlemen shall turn yellow with rage at Hrand Oskanian, against whom they're all so powerless, understand? I've found one or two people who see what I mean. I go along to the huts in the night sometimes. Ter Haigasun, ha, ha! can't stop me doing that. Have you ever watched that half-wit Kevork chucking out his corpses off the rock? They fly like white birds. Well, that's my idea! We'll all fly away, you and me and one or two more of us, before they force us, against our wills. One short step, and you don't know anything more till you touch the water. See? Then we shall all be dissolved in the waves. We shall have chosen that for ourselves, and so the devil and the Turks, and all the other gentry, will shout for rage, because we've beaten them, because it's really they who've been the weak ones. Do you see, Kilikian?"

Sarkis Kilikian had long since been stretched out on his back again. His death's skull stared up at scurrying clouds. Nothing about him suggested that he had even listened to Oskanian's panegyric of suicide.

But the long-haired thief stopped his game and glanced attentively at this cunning vanquisher of nature, as though he at least had grasped "the idea," and considered it really not so bad. He wriggled a little nearer. "How many store-chests are there in those three tents?"

The teacher stuttered and flushed. He had spoken shamefully into a void. And any mention of Three-Tent Square was still painful. On the other hand, here was a chance to show all these hard-bitten devils who he really was, a "notable," the educated member of a very different social class, one of the people's chosen representatives.

Oskanian's tone was something between bragging and disdain. "Only store-chests? Chests are about the least of what she has. Why, they've got huge great cupboards, boxes twice the size of wardrobes. And more women's clothes inside them than the richest pasha ever heard of. And all different. She not only wears a different dress every day, she changes three times a day . . ."

"What do I care about her clothes? What I want to know is how much food she has."

Oskanian threw back his head. It was now so hirsute with wiry beard and fuzzy hair that only a tiny patch of yellowish face still peeped from its midst. "Well, I can tell you that exactly. No one knows that better than I do, because down in the villa the hanum asked to see me when all the stuff was being chosen and packed up. Well, they've got whole towers of little silver boxes with fish in oil swimming in them. They've got sweet bread and chocolate and biscuits. They've got jars and jars of wine. They've got American smoked meat, and whole baskets of groats and oatmeal."

Oskanian stopped at the oatmeal. Beads of sweat stood out on his forehead. He slapped his knee mournfully. "Finish it! Finish it all!"

And Sarkis Kilikian answered, in a very monosyllabic growl: "We mean to . . . tomorrow evening."

The little teacher's hands turned cold as ice as he heard this sleepily casual remark. Nor did they become any warmer when Kilikian, in four curt, casual sentences, explained their intentions. Oskanian's round, pebble eyes stared as intently at the Russian as though his ears were not enough to listen with. Yet what he heard had for long been common talk among the men of the South Bastion. Sarkis Kilikian the deserter, and a few others under his influence, had had quite enough of the Damlayik. They intended to get away early before it was light, on the morning after the following day. The basest treachery to the commune! Perhaps only Kilikian had this feeling, to some slight degree. The others merely saw Musa Dagh, not as a fortified camp, in which they had pledged themselves to hold out, but as a temporary shelter, paid for at the very high rental of nearly forty days' fighting service. Now they were hungry. Famine had, in a sense, dissolved the contract. For several days no food had come down to them from their hosts save a few heaps of repulsive bones. Were they really to be asked to starve slowly, merely in order to fall into Turkish hands? What did they care for the people of the seven villages? Only a few of them had belonged to the Armenian valley. After all, before Ter Haigasun and Bagradian had come to take possession of the Damlayik, they had lived fairly well on the mountain. Not a man of them had the least intention of sharing the fate of the five thousand. Why should they? They could so easily save their own skins. It merely meant that they returned to the old life—the life before the forty days. Beyond the Orontes, to the south, there extended the barren heights of Jebel el Akra, ridge upon ridge, almost as far as Latakia. This Jebel el Akra was not well watered and green like Musa Dagh, but barren, trackless, ragged, and so the place for refugees. Quite a simple plan. In the night, about a hundred strong, they would descend on the Orontes plain, past Habaste and the ruins. Since all the troops in the valley were concentrated round the northern heights, there would probably be only a few pickets of saptiehs on night-duty guarding the edge of the mountain and the Orontes bridge at El Eskel. Not much fear of dangerous resistance! Whether or not they had to fight their way, the hundred could no doubt soon be across the narrow plain and have reached the mountains by sunrise. During their secret discussion a few of the more scrupulous among them had asked if it might perhaps not be permissible to warn the Council of their decision. This mere question had nearly led to their being thrashed. What would have been the results of such stupidity?

And this criminal element refused to be satisfied with mere disappearance into the night. It had serious reasons to back its policy. First, there was the question of munitions. On that would depend the future existence of any vagrant robber band. That was the real meaning of the demand made by the long-haired thief with such cringing insolence to Gabriel, on the day their forbidden bonfire had been extinguished. Chaush Nurhan issued cartridges very sparingly. Only when a fight had almost begun, were munitions brought into the trench, and even then someone in the confidence of the leaders would distribute as few of them as possible. These deserters at present had only about five shots to a rifle. An impossible state of affairs! But in the government-hut the lockers stood one above the other, there were troughs of cartridges. Nurhan's "factory" had worked on without a break, not only filling the used cases, but making fresh bullets for them to fire. The deserters felt it unavoidably necessary to supplement their present supplies from the camp armoury. With that object they must visit the government-hut; when and how still seemed undecided. And at the same time they could take a look round the enclosure, to see if this or that might not be worth carrying. A prolonged sojourn on the barren heights of Jebel el Akra would demand certain necessary implements, which the people here in camp, whose fate was sealed, could have no possible further use for. And, while they were looking round the enclosure, they could always keep their eyes open for certain unpopular public figures. Ter Haigasun, for instance. The priest had never pretended to like deserters. He had taken every possible chance of bringing the rigours of camp life home to them. You might reckon that the South Bastion as a whole had had five fast days to put up with. Nor had Ter Haigasun scrupled to sentence one or another of its garrison to a sharp dose of bastinado. It could do no possible harm to settle accounts.

Sarkis Kilikian still lay on his back, heeding neither Oskanian's conversation nor the dark hints of the long-haired thief. Had any mortal been able to look into his mind, he would have found nothing there except impatience. His impatience was that of the scurrying clouds above his head. The brain behind that extinguished mask was restless with longing to break out of one jail into the next.

The teacher had long since scrambled up on to his thin little legs. And he jutted his pigeon breast, as if to show that he, the panegyrist of suicide, would shrink from no deed, however bold. He stood there pursing his lips and wagging his head at them. He never stirred to warn the camp. Kilikian and the others must take this as a sign of admiration. The thought of giving the alarm fluttered behind the teacher's forehead like a caught bird. Against it his perpetual vain terror of being thought weak by Kilikian and the other "daredevils"—he a "daredevil" among the rest! So that then, against his better judgment, a piece of vague, but still profoundly treacherous information slipped out of him:

"Tomorrow in the late afternoon, Ter Haigasun has arranged a special Mass of petition. But the decads are to stay in the trenches."

One of the other "daredevils" answered Oskanian's self-abasement appropriately: "Well, then, you'll stay here with us till tomorrow, see! So that we can be sure you'll keep your mouth shut."

The deserters shoved their government commissar in front of them back to their trenches. They need not have troubled to do this, since he came as a voluntary prisoner, without thoughts of escape. And they never once let him out of their sight. He sat perched glumly on an observation post, staring down at the narrow ribbon of highroad, far below, which leads from Antakiya to Suedia. Hatred of Gabriel, Juliette, Ter Haigasun, suddenly seemed to have flickered out of his heart. Fear had replaced it. He prayed that the Turks might attack. But they seemed to have no intention at all of breaking their heads a second time against the rocks of this barren slope. There was peaceful traffic on the road through the Orontes plain. Ox-carts, sumpter mules, two camels even, took their slow way to market at Suedia, as though on Musa Dagh there were not so much as an Armenian. Only near Yedidje, at the foot of the outer slopes of the mountain, did a tiny dust-cloud suddenly rise. As it settled again, a small, grey army car could be distinguished.

It had dawned, the fortieth day on Musa Dagh, the eighth of September, the third of famine. Today the women had not troubled to go in search of unnutritious herbs from which to concoct a bitter tea. Spring water was just as filling. All still able to stand clustered round the various well-springs—old men, mothers, girls, children. It was a queer sight. Again and again, one after another, these exhausted faces bent down to the water-jets to drink without thirst, out of hollow hands, as though to drink were an urgent duty. Many lay down flat, breathing heavily, feeling that their bodies were like some porous clay that stiffened slowly in the air. Others dreamed happily. They felt certain that now they were growing wings, that as soon as ever they liked they could spread them for a short blissful flight. Over them all lay a veil of gentle slowness. The small children were all fast asleep; the bigger ones had ceased to be noisy. That morning three old people died, and two sucklings. The mothers kept their wretched creatures pressed against empty breasts until they stiffened and became cold.

In contrast to these in the Town Enclosure, the men out in the trenches had still life and energy enough in them. Though they, too, were anything but sated. The meat ration and the

724

remains of Gabriel's tinned food had not been even enough to take the first edge off their hunger. Yet these privations produced a strange mentality in the fighters. They inspired them with a crazy longing to do battle, get things settled once and for all. This new state of things had at least the advantage that Gabriel could arrange his proposed night-raid without having to trouble himself with the question whether or not the people would elect to leave the Damlayik. He was sure of his fighters. He had planned the attack for that same night.

So every detail of this raid into the valley was discussed. He had forgotten nothing. Every man had his place, and every minute had been considered. Nothing had been left to chance.

He had decided to keep the Turks occupied all that day, and alarm them, on the northern heights, with sudden bursts of firing and shows of attack, to get them to move as many troops as possible out of the valley. Unexpectedly they anticipated his wishes and performed this tactic of themselves. Their preparations plainly showed that, within the next twenty-four hours, everything was going to be decided. The heights beyond the Saddle were alive with the bustle of trench warfare before an attack. Over there, the Armenians could catch sight of lines of infantrymen, slowly and gingerly advancing, dragging thick tree-trunks, stripped of their branches, which they dropped with a clatter on the hillside. There could be no doubt that these smooth, strong stems were to be made to serve as moving cover, when the extended lines crawled on. Gabriel and Chaush Nurhan went from man to man in the front-line trench, levelling sights to get the distances. Whenever one of the Turks on the counter-slope ventured too far out from among the trees, they gave single orders to fire. By midday a few enemies were disposed of. The one deadly bullet was always answered by a wild, undisciplined volley, which either passed over the heads of defenders, or spent itself in the heaped-up stones of the parapets. The fighters perceived with crazy pride that their new defence works were so strong that it would need artillery to deal with them. But of that there was still no indication. The strange drunkenness of hunger produced bouts of madness in these men. They were eager to use any method of luring the Turks to attack. They climbed their trench and danced on the parapet; many ventured far out into the obstacle zone. The Turks refused to be enticed.

At about midday Ter Haigasun came to visit the trench. Gabriel asked him to say a prayer in their midst, since the decads would not be present that afternoon at the great service of petition. He prayed with them. Gabriel had also to tell the priest that these men's votes need not be taken at the plebiscite, since they had announced their decision through Chaush Nurhan of going wherever their leader might care to take them. Ter Haigasun was surprised at Gabriel's energy; tne leader glowed with the excitement of coming action. Only a few days back he had still believed that this soul had not the raw strength needed to recover from Stephan's horrible death. But on his way back to the enclosure Ter Haigasun knew that Bagradian's soul had withstood nothing but itself, and even that, perhaps, for no more than these last few hours of intensity.

GENERAL ALI RISA BEY was one of the youngest brigadier-generals of the Turkish army. He was not yet forty. But Ali, both in appearance and mentality, was the exact opposite of his chief, the picturesque dictator of Syria. He was, up to a point, representative of the very latest, most European type of soldier. It was only necessary to watch him walk up and down, as he did at present, in the selamlik of Villa Bagradian, where a subdued officers' council followed his steps with timid eyes, to perceive his mentality. And the whole difference became apparent when one compared this young general with, for instance, the wounded yüs-bashi, whose arm was still bandaged, and who waited, in the respectful posture prescribed, on some stray remark from his superior. This major, with his cigarette-stained fingers, his tired and dissipated face, had something forlorn and slightly soiled about him, when contrasted with Ali Risa Bey. And now, impatiently, the general pushed open the drawing-room windows to let out the clouds of smoke, with which the other officers filled the room. He neither smoked nor drank; he loved neither woman nor man; and it was said that, because of a weak stomach, he lived exclusively on raw goat's milk. A translucent ascetic of war. The onbashi came in to him with a report.

The general glanced at it; he compressed thin lips. "We've just had some losses from an Armenian attack in the north. . . . I intend to make company commanders strictly responsible for this sort of thing. . . . I hope you gentlemen will all take note of what I say: I've promised His Excellency that not a single man on our side shall be sacrificed in this whole action. . . . We're clearing out a camp of scoundrelly mutineers. . . . Anything else would be sheer disgrace. . . . Disgraceful enough to have let it get so far."

His glance sought out the adjutant. "Still no news of those two batteries?"

The adjutant answered a brief "No." For two days now they had been impatiently expecting the arrival of mountain artillery, sent to Aleppo. But, since this transport came, not via Aleppo, but by way of Beilan and the difficult route across the passes, it was delaying endlessly. So that now the general had been forced to put off his main attack till tomorrow.

He stopped again in front of one of the junior officers. "How many yards of telephone wire are there in the company stores?"

The young officer paled and began to mumble. Ali Risa Bey did not even listen. "Well, it's no business of mine. But by this evening, by one hour before sunset, mind, a telephone must have been installed in this house, connecting me up with the mountain, both northwards and southwards. How it's to be done is your look-out. I shall want telephonic reports of to-morrow's attack from the major. Now you can go."

The wretched junior, who had not the vaguest notion how many coils of wire the companies had, and considered this an impossible duty, shuffled off despairingly to attempt it.

And now the general added sharply: "Yüs-Bashi . . . If you please . . ."

That wounded hero pulled himself together. The two went into the empty anteroom. Ali Risa threw a frigid, hasty glance at the yüs-bashi's wounded arm. "Yüs-Bashi, I'm giving you your chance in these operations to redeem the gross blunder of which you've been guilty."

The yüs-bashi raised his wounded arm in suggestive protest; he had done more than his duty! "I myself, General, went close up to those support trenches of theirs, above Habaste, yesterday. They're perfectly empty. The crew is no longer manning its supports. It was an hour before sunset."

"Good! And your four companies?"

"I think that covered advance of theirs in the night has fully succeeded. Not so much as a lantern was shown. All day yesterday the men never moved out of Habaste. Now they're disposed under the rocks, in fully concealed positions. And the three machine-guns of my group."

"Tomorrow evening, when it's over, you'll telephone me, Yüs-Bashi. Once you're on the summit, I don't want you to go on any further."

With that the conversation came to an end. Ali Risa had already turned away.

But the yüs-bashi's voice halted him: "General, excuse me, please. I want to say something. It's just this. . . . These deserters—I've managed to find out that it isn't only a question of Armenians. . . . And yesterday an ex-Armenian came to see me, a lawyer, a Dr. Hekimian—he's been converted to the true belief. . . . Well, he's ready to treat with these fellows, and get them to vacate their trench voluntarily. . . . Perhaps

728

we might have to make a few concessions, but on the other hand we'd be certain of not having losses."

The general had listened quietly. Suddenly he interrupted: "Out of the question, Yüs-Bashi! We can't ever allow it to be said of us that we could clear out these Armenian devils only because some of them happened to be traitors. Just think what the foreign press would say! It would pour out venom over His Excellency and the whole Fourth Army."

Heavy steps came echoing over the tiles of the entrance-hall. The tall, sagging shape of the Kaimakam, followed by the freckled müdir, came into the room. The Kaimakam touched his fez carelessly. "At last, gentlemen! General, your batteries will reach Sanderan in three hours. Your people seem even less businesslike than mine . . ."

Ali Risa's clear, ascetic face always irritated the ultra-bilious Kaimakam. He decided to annoy this soldier. With his hand already on the door-handle, he turned before going out of the room, supercilious. "I hope our armed forces don't intend to disappoint us a fourth time."

SHUSHIK, Haik's mother, served Juliette clumsily, but with deep devotion. Juliette was really convalescent, although so wasted and enfeebled that she tottered with every step she took. Her face had a bluish, whitish tinge. Or rather her face was colourless, as if, after such an illness, it wanted to look as different as possible from the dark, sunburnt faces all round it. Now Juliette could sit up for an hour, two hours, every day. She would sink down in front of her looking-glass, put her head on her arms, and never move. And she would kneel, as she had before in her desperation, by the bedside, pressing her face into the small, lace-edged cushion, her last home. The worst sign of spiritual havoc was that now her two dominant instincts—to look beautiful and to keep clean—seemed to have died in her. The laundry basket stood open in the tent. But she neither felt in it nor asked for any clean things. Nor, in utter contradiction to the fantasies that obsessed her mind, did she reach out for the flask of *eau de printemps,* in which dregs still waited to be used, to attempt to freshen her dried-up skin. She did not even step into the slippers which stood ready beside her bed, but tottered barefoot the few steps she was able to manage.

Shushik saw in Juliette a mother driven mad by the horrible death of her only child. Haik was alive! And more than that! His life for all time was secure. Jackson protected him, and America! These words, to Shushik, connoted supernatural powers. Jackson! He was not a man, but presumably the head-archangel himself, brandishing a fiery sword. She had been more blessed than any other mother on Musa Dagh. Must she not day and night bestir herself to serve and thank, thank and serve! And who should she thank, who serve, if not this other mother, on whom the full curse had descended? This was a rich hanum, a distinguished lady, a foreigner. Shushik's voice had been loud and rough for years, and yet now she cooed like any sucking dove, almost singing her comfort. It was all so simple. This world is this world. But over there Lord Jesus, the Saviour, has arranged things so well that all shall be reunited. And first of all mothers will see their children again. Up there in heaven mothers see their children, not as those grown-up sons and daughters whom they have left behind them in the world, but as real little children, just as they were between two and five. And good mothers, up there in heaven, are allowed to carry their children in their arms.

Blissfully lost in such a prospect, the gigantic Shushik raised her arms up and cradled a tiny, invisible Haik. Shushik imagined that this foreigner did not understand her speech. She sat down on the ground beside the hanum, considering how she could comfort and be of use. She touched Juliette's frozen feet. With a soft little moan of pity she pressed these feet between her breasts, while her great, leathery peasant

730

hands first stroked, and then began to chafe them. Juliette shut her eyes and sank back. Shushik had no doubt that the unhappy woman was mad. And she fully understood this madness—how far along the way to it she herself had gone, before that blissful news called her back! She was far too rough and simple to suspect that this was not real madness at all, but a kind of burrow, in which the hanum crouched away from daylit consciousness. And Bedros Hekim shared Shushik's view, considering Juliette's present state of mind as an aberration, resulting from the spotted plague. A surprising incident, in the course of his visit to the patient on the morning of this fortieth day, seemed fully to justify his belief. The old man had sat on the edge of Juliette's bed, doing his best in such French as he could muster to bring hope and life to this frozen soul. Everything seemed to be going splendidly. The war would be certain to end within a few weeks, and so the world would be at peace again. Madame must have heard of the visit of the Agha Rifaat Bereket, from Antakiya. Well, this old, influential Turkish gentleman had clearly hinted that Gabriel Bagradian and Madame would be given permission to go back to France, almost at once. His kindness changed the grumpy old sceptic into a most inventive teller of children's tales. Even the edged scornfulness of his voice sounded protective. But, as he sat relating these pretty fables, Iskuhi had come suddenly into the doorway.

Juliette, who, with amiably absent eyes, had seemed all this while to be listening to the doctor's poetry, started at the sight of Iskuhi. She sat up in terror, drew up her knees, and began to scream: "Not her! Not her! Tell her to go! . . . I won't take anything from her! . . . She wants to kill me. . . ."

Strangest of all, Iskuhi stood listening to these frenzies and never moved, her own small face like a mask of madness, looking as though she too might scream her answer. Bedros Hekim, perturbed, stared from one to the other. Now he could sense some gruesome reality. Long after Iskuhi had

731

vanished, Juliette, whose enfeebled heart was thumping, would still not be pacified.

WHAT had happened to Iskuhi?

For five days she had not seen Gabriel. For two days she had had no food. But Iskuhi wanted to go hungry, and not only because she starved with her whole people. For five long days she had not seen Gabriel, but in exchange her brother Aram had twice come to the door of her tent. Then she crouched inside and refused to open. Each of these five days with all its hours, which lasted years, had crept intolerably. Why did not Gabriel come? Iskuhi waited for Gabriel every second of the day and night. Now, even if her exhausted body had had the strength to let her do it, she would not have gone out to him in the trench. Less every hour would she have gone! She was lying, breathing deeply on her bed, in what had been Hovsannah's tent, and could not manage to move a limb. A roaring in her ears, like surf on a beach, seemed to burst her skull. And yet this roaring was still not loud enough to overwhelm the truth in her mind. . . . How many minutes were there to waste on the Damlayik? And Gabriel wasted not only irreplaceable minutes, but whole eternal days of their short love. Wasted? Love? Implacably Iskuhi brought to mind all that she had experienced with Gabriel. Yes, Gabriel had been gentle with her. But his grief was for Stephan. And, when he opened his heart, it had been in compassion, sorrow, for his adulterous wife. Gabriel had at least been frank with her. Really his whole attitude seemed to say: "Little sister, I thank you, with my cold hands, my distant, brotherly kisses, for having tried so hard to bear my pain with me. But how could you, a poor little girl from Yoghonoluk, ever do it? In spite of all this, and for ever, I belong to the Frenchwoman, the stranger. I shall die, not with Iskuhi, but with Juliette. Juliette may have played me false, but I bow to her, I only bend over Iskuhi."

732

Would it have been any different, Iskuhi asked herself, if Juliette had, as in her heart she had longed she might a hundred times, died of her fever? And she perceived: No! If Juliette had died, Gabriel would have loved her, Iskuhi, far less, even. How that sick woman could spy out secrets! Iskuhi wanted never to go back into Juliette's tent, never see her again. Yet it was not Juliette's fault; hers less than anyone's. What made Iskuhi unworthy to be loved? She was not European, only a poor village girl from Yoghonoluk, the daughter of an Armenian village carpenter. Was it really that? Was Gabriel himself "European"? Did he not even come from the very same Armenian village? She had lived two years in Switzerland, and he, in Paris, twenty-three. That was all the difference. When he looked at her, he told her that she was beautiful. Stop! That was it! Why did he often look at her so oddly, with eyes that half saw? Something in her disturbed him and made him cold. Iskuhi conquered her enfeeblement and hurried to look in the little mirror, which stood on the table. She need not have looked in her glass. She knew without looking. She was crippled—a cripple now, though not born one. In these six months since the convoy from Zeitun, her left arm had got worse and worse. If she did not help it with a sling, it hung, withered and twisted, at her side. Gabriel had to watch her deformity, no matter how skilfully concealed.

She knew! Once he had lightly kissed her crippled arm. Now Iskuhi felt she could remember the compassionate effort this kiss had cost him. Iskuhi fell back on her bed. The roaring in her ears rose like a sea-storm. She kept making convulsive efforts to justify Gabriel's absence by the facts. No doubt, in these last hungry days, things had been disorganized in his trenches. He must have had to work out a whole new defence. And shots had begun again. None of these reasoned explanations gained the least influence on Iskuhi. But, like the ground-note of the storm roaring in her ears, she could hear her own voice, yet a stranger's. Her voice sang the *chanson d'amour* which she had sung at Juliette's behest one day in Villa Bagradian. Stephan had been there, and Gabriel came into the room. The first lines of that ancient folk-song kept up a ritournelle in her head, till their sound crazed her:

> "She came out of her garden,
> And held them close against her breasts,
> Two fruits of the pomegranate tree . . .
> She gave them me, I would not take."

The song stopped there. Instantly the horror overcame her, which had spared her so long. The face on the highroad to Marash, the kaleidoscopic, twisting grimace of that scrubby murderer, was upon her. Its gyrations ceased, as if something had gone wrong with the kaleidoscope. And now in some secret fashion the staring mask was turning into Gabriel's face, but far more hateful, murderous even. Iskuhi could not breathe for fear and misery. Dumbly she wept for help. Aram!

And, indeed, at about this minute Pastor Aram had almost reached his sister's tent. He was with Hovsannah, who carried her poor brat in her arms. No sound from within when Aram gruffly demanded entrance. He whipped out his knife and slit up the lacing of the door, knotted on the inside. The pastor had let the big sack he shouldered slip to the ground. The woman, with her almost lifeless bundle, her suckling, kept a few paces behind him.

At that moment, had Pastor Tomasian been himself—mild, evangelical, affectionate, the strong, cheery brother of Zeitun— Iskuhi might perhaps have no longer hesitated, but gone along with him. Why should she stay alone in this empty tent? She knew she had not the strength to walk very far. Somewhere it would all end gently, the roaring in her ears, Gabriel, she herself. But, instead of the cheery brother of Zeitun, some fierce, unknown bully stood in her tent. He brandished a stick.

"Get up! Get ready! You're coming with us!" ·

734

These hard words rolled like rocks upon Iskuhi. Rigid on her bed, she stared up at this unknown Aram. Now she could not have moved, even had she been inclined to obey.

Tomasian gripped his stick more tightly still. "Didn't you hear what I said? I order you to get up this instant and make ready. As your elder brother, as your spiritual father, I order you. You understand? I'll see if we can't snatch you from your sin."

Till the word "sin" it had all been a maze. She had lain there rigid. "Sin" struck out a hundred well-springs of angry recalcitrance from the rock. All Iskuhi's weakness fell away. She sprang up. Retreating behind the bed, she clenched her small right fist to defend herself.

A new enemy glowered into the tent, Hovsannah. "Leave her, Pastor! Give her up! She's a lost woman. I beg you not to go too near her, she may infect you. Leave her! If she comes with us, God will only punish us still more! There's no sense in it! Come, Pastor! I've always known the kind she was. You were always foolish about her. Even in the school in Zeitun she could never keep her eyes off the young teachers, the sinful piece! Leave her, I beg you, Pastor, and come!"

Iskuhi's eyes grew bigger and bigger with rage. Since Juliette's illness she had seen no more of Hovsannah and had no idea that this was a madly hysterical woman. The young pastor's wife looked horribly changed. To appease God's wrath with a sacrifice, she had cropped her pretty hair close to her skull. Now her face looked small and witchlike in its malice. Everything about her looked small and shrivelled, except her belly, which still protruded, a diseased consequence of her labour.

And now Hovsannah, in an indescribable gesture of accusation, thrust her swaddled suckling out in Iskuhi's face. She screeched: "Look there! You alone brought this ill-luck on us!"

It brought the first sounds from Iskuhi's lips: "Jesus Maria!"

735

Her head sunk forwards. She thought of Hovsannah's difficult labour, and how she had used her back as support. What did these crazy people want? Why couldn't they give her any peace, on the very last day of her life?

The pastor meanwhile had pulled out a clumsy silver watch. He dangled it. "I give you ten minutes to get ready in."

He turned to Hovsannah. "No. She's to come with us. I won't leave her. I have to answer for her, to God. . . ."

Iskuhi still remained behind the bed, without a movement. Aram did not wait his whole ten minutes, but after three of them left the tent. His clumsy watch still dangled from his fist. Out on Three-Tent Square it had meanwhile become strangely noisy.

The twenty-three had appeared noiselessly; they now moved on across the open space between the sheikh-tent and Juliette's. The long-haired thief, from the airs he gave himself, seemed to be their "leader." Sato, the twenty-fourth member of the band, equally seemed to feel herself their guide. She kept rubbing her nose with her sleeve, artlessly, as though to suggest that she, an innocent, had no notion what might have brought these armed deserters unheralded to Three-Tent Square. Some warrior duty no doubt! And to all appearances there was nothing to cause alarm about these deserters, unless perhaps that one or two of them had planted Turkish bayonets on their rifles. But platoons of armed fighters were often to be seen about the camp on their way back from the trenches, or marching to them to take over. Today especially, since firing continued in the north, there was nothing particularly surprising in the sight of a few armed men. When Aram came out of Iskuhi's tent, the business had already begun. Yet for a while he watched in complete indifference. His mind, sullen and stupefied by his own unpardonable behaviour, merely supposed some order of Bagradian's, which the warrior-band had come to fulfil. And what, since he was already cut off from the people, did the defence of the Damlayik matter to him?

But Shushik had sharper eyes. Her tall body filled the whole tent-door. She perceived at once what lurked in Sato's consequential behaviour, her eccentric pointings again and again to the hanum's tent. Shushik planted herself in the doorway. She spread her arms out, ready to keep off disaster with her body.

The long-haired thief came out of the clustered pack. "We've been sent to take away the food which you still keep."

"I know of no food."

"You must know of it. I mean the silver boxes with the fish, swimming in oil, the wine-jars, and the oatmeal."

"I know nothing of wine or oatmeal. Who sent you?"

"What business is that of yours? The commandant."

"The commandant had better come himself."

"Well, come on—out of the way! I warn you for the last time, you silly bitch! You're not going to be let squat here for ever with all that grub. It's ours now."

Shushik said nothing more. She followed, with the eyes and hands of a wrestler, the movements of the long-haired thief, who, having cast away his rifle, was looking for the best attacking-point. So that when he tried to bear down on the giantess from the left, she had already gripped him round the middle; her iron hands lifted the miserable creature up and hurled him back among his fellows so violently that he tore two of them to earth with him. The gigantic Shushik stood on as before, not even breathing a jot more quickly, her arms spread, waiting for the next. But before Shushik even knew she would die, she was dead. A sly attack, delivered sideways with a rifle-butt, smashed in her skull. She died in a flash, at the very summit of her happiness, since even in these combative moments her heart was still brimful of the one feeling: Haik's going to live. Her body, hurtling to the ground, blocked the way to Stephan's less happy mother.

And now Pastor Aram understood. With wild cries, brandishing his stick, he rushed on the pack, which at that instant, scared by the murder, was drawing apart. Now Tomasian should have thrown his whole influence into the scales. He was the pastor, and one of the chiefs. But Aram had long since ceased to control himself. He did exactly what he should not have done—ran blindly upon them, striking, with his ridiculous stick, on all sides. The answer was a bayonet thrust, in the back, just under his right shoulder.

What's that, he thought, and what have I really to do with all this rabble? I am a man of God, the Word is entrusted to me to preach, nothing more. Let's leave all these strangers to their devices. His stick had dropped out of his hand. But fully aware of his spiritual dignity, he squared his shoulders, turned away again, and went back stiffly. Ah, yes, the women there! Well? Had Iskuhi at last made up her mind? Had she decided to be obedient? But why was she dressed in white? Yes, they must live again in friendship with one another, just as in Zeitun. Hovsannah would see that for herself. The way to the third tent seemed uncommonly long. The pastor smiled encouragingly at his wife. But she seemed to look past him with terrified eyes. Just three paces from her Aram collapsed on the dry grass, staining it with his blood. Though his wound was nothing much, he fainted. Hovsannah cowered down over him, helpless, at a loss, her child in her arms. When Iskuhi saw the blood, she ran back screaming into the tent, brought clean linen and scissors, and knelt by her brother. Only now did Hovsannah pull herself together and put down her suckling on the grass. They slit Aram's coat. Iskuhi pressed the cloth with all her strength against his wound. Her right hand reddened with the blood of her brother, from whom she was for ever alienated.

The long-haired thief, Sato, and a few deserters crowded over Shushik's body into the hanum's tent. Juliette, half-aroused from a heavy sleep, had heard the dispute, the shouts, the scufflings. "The fever, thank God! The fever back again!" she thought astutely. And even when the tent filled with stinking people, her lethargy could make stand against any fear. "Either it's the fever, and then I'm delighted. But if it's the Turks, it's better it should come now, between sleep and sleep." Nobody even thought of harming the hanum. They did not so much as notice the invalid. Their one concern was to find those culinary treasures, of which envious fables had gone the rounds. They dragged the big wardrobe-trunk and the rest of the luggage outside the tent. There every box and chest in the sheikh-tent had already been piled. Only Sato and the long-haired thief stayed on for a moment with Juliette, the one because he hoped to find something useful on his own account, the other from malice and curiosity. Since nothing more cruel occurred to her, Sato suddenly stripped the bed-clothes off Juliette. The man should see the stranger's naked-ness! He meanwhile had picked up a big tortoise-shell comb, as a souvenir, no doubt to comb his own long, matted hair with it. Lost in his contemplation of this treasure, he whistled his way out of the tent without touching the woman. Outside, the pack had rummaged and rummaged in the contents of the many trunks. Juliette's clothes and linen lay defiled, just as they had been by saptiehs in Yoghonoluk. The loot was miserably inadequate: two boxes of sardines, a tin of con-densed milk, three bars of chocolate, a tin of broken biscuits. That couldn't be all! Quick, into the third tent! Sato gesticu-lated. But now the little cracked bell had begun to ring across from the altar square, summoning to the Mass of petition. This signal, prearranged with the other group, called the de-serters to the second half of their day's work. They would have to hurry to get there in time. Each of them snatched up something, not to have to go off empty-handed—spoons and knives, a dish, and even a pair of women's shoes.

Iskuhi and Hovsannah had stanched the wound with their clothes. The pastor came to himself. He looked most surprised.

739

He could not realize what a mad dog had just been killed in him. No stubborn defiance forced him now to commit afresh the grave sin of cutting himself off from his people. Blood had been spilt. This spilt blood was the grace that saved him from the test that had not yet taken place. He watched Hovsannah. She was cleaning her hands with grass tufts, so that her child's swaddling-clothes might not be stained. Aram Tomasian felt surprised that a whole heap of rugs and cushions should have been thrust in behind his back, so that now he was sitting almost upright. Iskuhi, with her right hand, was still pressing the compress against his wound, and so prevented his lying back. Her thin, wasted face looked taut with the effort. Aram turned his head away and said: "Iskuhi," and, five or six times, only sighed out: "Iskuhi." He spoke her name with the sound of a tender "Forgive!"

THE sacristan jerked at his little bell like a lunatic. It swung from a pole beside the altar. These urgent peals were quite unnecessary, since the congregation of old men, women, and children had long since collected for Mass. But still, jerked fanatically by the sacristan, the little bell pealed on and on, far and away across their heads, as though not only Turkish infantry, but land and sea, had been called to witness that this was the hour of death for a Christian people.

From a cord strung between poles right and left on the top step of the altar, the curtain strung on rings hung down, waiting to be drawn before the priest, as it is in the Armenian rite at the Consecration, when he is hidden from the eyes of the faithful. The heavy fabric of this curtain kept being blown against the altar. Between the gusts long, anxious stillness. Shots could be heard from the North Saddle.

Ter Haigasun, in his presbytery-hut, next door to the government-barrack, had long been vested for this Mass. The singers and deacons who were to serve it, had waited some time around the door for him. Yet a deep uneasiness still prevented his coming forth to ascend the altar. What was this? His heart, which as a rule was not perturbed, thumped against his priestly robes. Did he fear the unknown, which was now so close?

Did he doubt if he had acted rightly in deciding to call directly on the people at this moment of their crying need? Ter Haigasun's lids fell heavily over his eyes. He saw himself alone among the dead, in his stiff Mass robes. Horrible as it was, he had always known he would be the last of them. His heart had begun to beat more evenly. But in exchange he was filled with the indescribable sense of mortality, a surer expectation of death than he had known in the worst minutes of battle.

One of the two assistant priests kept poking his head round the door of the presbytery-hut to warn him. It was long past Mass time; there was danger that the following general assembly might have to be prolonged till after nightfall. Yet still Ter Haigasun could not manage to tear himself free. It was as if some inner power would not let him go, as it strove to prevent this Mass of petition. Giddiness and weakness threatened to force him full length on the bed. He was ill, famished. Should he cancel the Mass, or let another priest say it instead of him? Ter Haigasun perceived that this time it was not weakness, but his fear of being unequal to the task which today lay before him. And something else, something vague. He stood up at last and gave the sign. The acolyte took up the tall cross to carry it on ahead of the procession. Slowly, with joined hands and downcast eyes, Ter Haigasun followed deacons and singers. That sacerdotal, inward-turning glance, as he passed on his way through dividing crowds as indifferently as though he had walked between bushes, was still aware of it all, with the sharpest intensity. Ter Haigasun had not more than fifty paces to reach the altar. Yet, with each of these, the spiritual state of the people round him seemed to pierce him like a radiating agony. That morning's lethargy had dissolved, replaced by restlessness and excitement. Human nature, in this final hour, had drawn up out of itself some last reserve or show of energy. The smallest children especially were becoming most artfully unmanageable. They kept bellowing with all their strength, throwing themselves flat on the ground. It was perhaps the swollen pain in their small bellies. Their angry mothers shook and slapped, since that was the only way to quiet them. Some grown-ups were just as restless. These were old men—mostly the familiar "small owners" —who launched out into long, rambling speeches, not stopping respectfully, as they once had, when the priest came past them to the altar. Ter Haigasun perceived that demoralization had kept pace with hunger. "A good thing," he reflected, "that the decads won't be coming to this meeting. As long as they hold out, all is not lost." In the midst of which consoling reflection he raised his eyes and stood for an instant, rooted. What did it mean? Armed men in the congregation! Singly, to be sure, or in little groups, but in any case in the flattest contradiction to his and Bagradian's definite order. Who had sent these men out of their trenches? Since now the women had conquered that morning's lethargy well enough to put on their Sunday best for this Mass, the brown streaks these warriors made were lost in the brightness of the whole. Ter Haigasun saw with his next glance that these were not trusted men from the nearer sectors, but deserters from the South Bastion, those strangers to the valley of Yoghonoluk, always kept on the farthest edge of the people, who luckily scarcely ever came into camp, and never to Mass. Were they grown pious suddenly? Ter Haigasun turned his head sharply to the government-barrack on his right. Where was the guard? Oh, yes, of course. Bagradian had needed everyone, some reservists even, in the trenches. Turn back! it flashed into his mind. Make some excuse! Put off this Mass! Send for Bagradian! Call together the mukhtars! Take precautionary measures! But, in spite of these reflections, he still kept on, in silent, hesitant steps. There, close round the altar, stood the notables, the mukhtars and their wives and daughters, those lines of grey, respected heads, in the order in which they had always gathered, in church, in the valley.

As to Gabriel Bagradian, he had promised to be in time for this Mass, but something must have made him unpunctual. As the lines of village elders drew apart to make a lane for the procession, Ter Haigasun's soul got its second warning. Between an unknown deserter and Sarkis Kilikian, Hrand Oskanian stood, hemmed in like a man under arrest. Again Ter Haigasun had the feeling that he must stop and sharply turn on the exiled teacher. "What's all this? What have you to tell me, Teacher Oskanian?" And again Ter Haigasun went on, scarcely lifting his eyes, guided by some power, or powerlessness, which now, for the first time on the Damlayik, sapped his strong will.

His foot on the first altar step, he remembered that he had forgotten Nokhudian's letter, left it behind in the presbytery-hut. This wrought in him excessive confusion. The forgotten screed and these ill-omens shook him so that it lasted a sheer eternity before he climbed on up to the tabernacle. The people behind seemed to sense acutely the wandering thoughts and feebleness of their priest, since now children's howls, restless shufflings, importunate gossip, grew every instant more unabashed. And into such hollow hearts as these the fervent spirit must seek to force itself, which was to pray down God's miracle from the skies! Ter Haigasun turned in agony. As he did so, Gabriel Bagradian came hurrying breathless into the square and stood in the first row. For a second he felt relieved. Behind his back the choir had begun the anthem. It was a short respite; he closed his eyes. Tired, hollow voices rose to the sky:

"Thou Who extendest Thy creating arms to the stars,
  Give our arms strength,
  That they, held out, may reach unto Thee.

"By means of the crown of the brow, crown also the spirit,
Deck the senses with prayer,
With Aaron's blossoming, golden robe.

"We, as all the angels of God resplendent
Are panoplied, robed about in Love,
To serve the secret, the holiest."

The choir was silent. Ter Haigasun stared at the little silver ewer which the deacon held for him. He dipped his fingers and kept them so long in the water that at last the astonished deacon drew it away from him. Only then did he half turn to the faithful, to make the sign of the cross above them, three times. He turned back to the altar and raised his hands.

Ter Haigasun's being stood divided. One part of him, the celebrating priest, went through the prescribed and ancient ritual of this exceptional service of petition, scarcely delaying a response. The other part was in several layers; it was an exhausted struggler, putting out his last ounce of strength, so that the priest might still be able to do his office. First and foremost this second Ter Haigasun carried on the struggle against his body. It warned, with every word of the liturgy: "So far, no further! Haven't you noticed that I've not a drop of blood left in my head? Another minute, another two, and I may shame you, by collapsing here at the altar." With only his body to contend against, the fight could easily have been won. But far wilier enemies lurked behind it. One of these was a juggler, perpetually shifting the sacred vessels here and there, before the eyes of the priest. Suddenly the tall silver candlesticks had become fixed bayonets. From the finely printed page of the missal there leapt the names of the dead in the parish register, crossed off with huge red pencil crosses, drawn over everything. A gust of wind from time to time scampered through the leaves in the leaf-screen, behind the altar, and these dead leaves, eddying past, settled irreverently on the tabernacle, on the gospels stamped with the golden cross. Ter

744

Haigasun, the celebrant, reached the psalm. His entirely separated voice was intoning:

"Judge me, O God, and plead my cause . . ."

The deacon sighed the response: "Against an ungodly nation: O deliver me from the deceitful and unjust man."

"Why dost Thou cast me off? why go I mourning because of the oppression of the enemy?"

"Then will I go unto the altar of God, unto God my exceeding joy."

Whilst Ter Haigasun continued this long alternation of responses, impeccably to the end, with the deacon, his eyes showed the other Ter Haigasun intolerable sights. Those dead leaves, strewn over everything, were not dead leaves, but dirt, dung, some kind of indescribable filth, scattered about the altar by God's enemies, by criminals. No other explanation was possible, since dirt cannot rain down from heaven. Ter Haigasun stared at the missal to avoid this horrid sight of desecration. But had not the people seen it too? And here he made his first mistake in the text.

The deacon had sung: "My Almighty God, keep us, and forgive us our sins."

Now the priest should have given his response. But the priest was silent. The deacon turned wide-eyed to the choir. And, since still Ter Haigasun did not raise his voice, he came a step towards him and whispered sharply: "In the house of the most holy . . ."

The priest seemed to hear nothing. And now the deacon whispered in desperation, half aloud: "In the house of the most holy, and in the place . . ."

Ter Haigasun woke.

"In the house of the most holy and in the place of songs of praise; in this dwelling of angels, this place of repentance of men, we prostrate ourselves before the resplendent and glorious sign of this God, in reverence, and pray . . ."

Ter Haigasun drew a deep breath. Under his mitre sweat

745

streamed down his neck, stood out on his forehead. He dared not wipe it away. And behind him there ascended the nasal voice of Asayan, the chief chorister:

"In this consecrated place of sacrifice, in this temple, we are gathered together, for praise and prayer . . ."

Asayan's voice rasped Ter Haigasun as never before. Christ help me! Ter Haigasun stared in agony at the altar crucifix. The voice of one of the beings who composed him warned: "Don't look away from it." But this very warning made him look away, further out, to the high screen of beech-leaves which shut off the altar. Someone stood there leaning against the framework, with folded arms, smoking a cigarette. Unheard-of insolence! Ter Haigasun swallowed down this interjection. In the next instant this somebody had ceased to be Sarkis Kilikian, whom he loathed, whom he had put in irons; this somebody was, for the time being, nobody. The screen confronted him, empty. But then the Russian came back, to turn into all possible kinds of people—once he even seemed to be Krikor—till at last a priest in Mass vestments stood there. And at first it seemed ridiculous to Ter Haigasun that the robed priest should really be himself. Nor was it he, since *he* wore no soldier's lambskin kepi, but a mitre embroidered with gold.

"Blessing and praise to the Father, the Son, and the Holy Ghost——"

He could get no further. Between him and the shape against the leaf-screen, his own detached voice dinned in his ears: "Why do you stand about fooling in broad daylight? What good is this Mass of petition?"

Ter Haigasun watched the ascending cloud of incense. But his own voice, and the shape against the leaves, persisted: "What a devil this God of yours must be, to ordain a year like this for His pious Armenians."

Ter Haigasun had begun the ritual vesper: "Almighty God,

holy and eternal, have mercy on us. Keep us from temptation and all its arrows."

And now the answer seemed not to come from Kilikian, but solely out of his own heart: "You don't believe! You don't believe in any miracle! You know quite well that, this time tomorrow, four and a half thousand Armenian corpses will be lying all over the Damlayik."

The deacon gave Ter Haigasun the thurible, so that he might give incense to the people. Intense, causeless thirst assailed him. Now no one was leaning against the screen.

But the voice was as close as ever: "You'd like to kill me. Kill me, if you have the pluck to do it."

The thurible crashed out of the priest's hand. That second produced an entirely new Ter Haigasun. With barbarian shouts he snatched up one of the heavy silver candlesticks and brandished it high. But to fell his enemy he rushed, not on the shape before the leaf-screen, no, but into the midst of his congregation.

WITHOUT this attack of delirium, brought on by hunger, there would probably have been no "putsch." Even the deserters in the South Bastion were Armenians, full of respect and fear for the altar. But the long-haired thief had collected his troops round the government-hut, ready to storm. When the tumult rose, at the end of the altar square, he took that for the signal. Ten of his people, with a view to producing the necessary chaos, began firing in the air. The others bashed in the doors, found the munition supplies, and in a few seconds had dragged them out before the hut. What happened on the altar steps happened with such dreamy quickness that neither Gabriel nor the mukhtars were quite aware of the incident. Its dreamy quality was the essential thing, and not the quickness, since perhaps it took a good two minutes. When Ter Haigasun, brandishing his candlestick, had hurled himself into the midst

747

of his faithful, general confusion had set in. People had dashed in all directions. Gabriel caught a glimpse of the priest, struggling through the crowd to reach some deserters. He, too, had not known who it was had invited the pack to this Mass and assembly. Ter Haigasun seemed to be looking for a definite individual. In the next instant he was surrounded, hemmed in by armed men. They wrenched his candlestick away from him, pushed him about from one to another with loud cries, in the end tore him to the ground. Then shots clattered down on the rear of the crowd. People rushed apart with mad howls of terror. The yammering mukhtars tried to run into shelter with their wives. Gabriel, with drawn revolver, forced his way into the mêlée to free Ter Haigasun. A deserter, following close behind him, brought down his rifle-butt, with all his strength, on Gabriel's skull. Gabriel collapsed. Has this crack on the head smashed his sun-helmet, it would have been all over with him. But the rifle-butt did no more than drive the tough cork helmet far down on his face, and the savagery of the stroke was mitigated. Gabriel fell stunned, not really wounded. Others had meanwhile roped Ter Haigasun with strong hemp cords to one of the corner posts of the altar-frame, driven deep into the ground. The priest struggled with astonishing vigour, but in silence. If he had had the knife, which as a rule he carried in his cassock-pocket, he would have finished off one rascal at least. The mukhtars stood a long way off, quaking and moaning. They had not even the strength to run for safety. And their wives and daughters, with inhuman screechings, tugged them back. The crowd still understood nothing. Half-crazed now by the crackling rifle-fire, it stampeded forward to the altar. But since, as they came there, the front lines were trying to get back, there arose an unholy vortex of terrified bodies, yelping with fear and pain. Already some of the worst deserters, who for months past had not touched a woman, were darting in from the outer edge of it, like cuttlefish, to grip in their dirty claws here a woman and there a girl. Another more sober group stormed the hut to plunder the wretchedest poverty.

Meanwhile there were signs of resistance. Some determined people pressed forwards to free Ter Haigasun. Two minutes more, and perhaps the square might have run with blood since, threatened with superior numbers, the criminals were already loading their guns. But fate, run mad, again surpassed herself. The wind blew up in a sudden gust, as it had so often in these last days, a whirlwind sweeping round the square. Since no one any longer watched the altar, the wooden lights and a vase of flowers were blown down. Ter Haigasun still tugged silently at the thick cords which lashed him to the altar-frame. From time to time he stopped to get up fresh strength, and, with every jerk, the frame swayed. His bloodshot eyes looked round for the other priests, the singers, Asayan the sacristan. They had all run off, or else dared not venture too near their superior, who was being guarded by deserters, no doubt to give plunderers of munitions their chance to get away in peace. Among those deserters around the altar stood Sarkis Kilikian. He watched with interest Ter Haigasun's attempts to wriggle free, not, it seemed, personally concerned in any of these incidents and fortunes, but merely inquisitive. After a time he slouched away. His weary-looking back seemed to be saying: "I've had quite enough of this. And it's about time." But scarcely was Kilikian out of sight when the terrible thing began to happen. Later Ter Haigasun connected Kilikian with this fire, merely because his disappearance coincided so strikingly with its outbreak. But in reality the Russian merely passed along the altar steps, not even touching the screen of leaves, about three feet behind the altar-frame. The jet of flame which now leapt skywards was at least three times as high as the plaited leaf-screen. A puff of wind from the sea turned it inwards at once, and spread it wide, on the right. Winged tongues of fire and scattering sparks detached themselves, to leap on to the roof of the nearest hut. This hut was

749

Thomas Kebussyan's solid residence, with the inscription on the door "Town Hall." The fire at first seemed to set to work rather gingerly, as though it had a bad conscience to surmount. But when the twig-roof of the mayoral residence had begun in the next minute to crackle and flame, there was no more holding it. As a row of lamps lights up on a city boulevard, so did this conflagration dart round the square, flaring up out of nearly every hut simultaneously. The gang may have lit some of these fires, to hold people back and to cover their retreat. And now a banner of flame waved above the government-barrack. One thing only remained certain, that these criminals, as the fire began, had rid the Town Enclosure of their presence.

When, with alarming suddenness, the leaf-screen sprang into flame above the altar, the crowd had burst asunder like a shell. Everyone forgot the criminals, no one so much as thought of the altar, with its bound priest, and the many presumably dead. With queer, almost whimpering noises, the people rushed down their lines of huts. No hope! Nothing to put it out with! Only—let them save what was to be saved! The essentials of life. It seemed not to occur to anyone to ask: "Is it worth while?" But the mukhtars, the village notables, those doddering ancients so palsied with terror a minute ago, so lamed with fear as to be quite unable to help Ter Haigasun, had suddenly legs. Their money was burning! The lovely, well-smoothed-out pound notes which they had stored in corners of the huts, under their bedding, waited forlorn for rescuing hands. The old men, with their wives and daughters, went scurrying homewards.

One last, violent wrench, and then Ter Haigasun ceased to struggle. The rough cords, through the stiff silk of his vestments, had taken the skin off his arms and chest. Ice-cold sweat poured down his spine. Flakes of blazing wood kept falling over the altar, which had partly already begun to burn. Now and again, these flaming embers scorched the priest.

His hair and beard were already singed by them. The heavy altar curtain blazed in a sheet of flame. So be it! The square was empty. Screeching families pranced round their flaming huts. Why call for help? A priest who dies a martyr, lashed to his altar, has earned sure forgiveness of his sins. A jet of loose flame scourged past Ter Haigasun. If only the Turks had been his assassins! Why his own people! Armenians! Dogs! Wild dogs! Dogs! A bellowing rage, which threatened to burst his head, broke out of him. Wailings of despair from round the huts. But when Ter Haigasun's furious shout, "Dogs! Dogs!" went howling across the square, it startled the money-grubbers, who left their vanity, ran to the altar to untie their priest. Before the first of them had reached him, the loosened post gave way and the frame crashed down in a burst of fire. The priest fell forward. They picked him up. Quickly cut his bonds. Ter Haigasun could go a few steps, but was soon forced to lie on the ground.

Bedros Hekim came out at the right minute, just as a few old men and women were taking pity on Gabriel, still unconscious. The doctor saw at once, before he had even felt his pulse, that Gabriel was still alive. With many groans old Altouni sat and took Gabriel's head on his knees. Cautiously he loosened the cork helmet, which the rifle-butt had driven so far down as to cover the eyes. The instant they were free Gabriel opened them. He thought he had only been asleep. All this had happened in some unbelievably short time—in an interval "outside time," so to speak. First he gradually felt the burning weight of his own skull. The doctor lightly fingered over his scalp. No blood. Only a huge lump. But perhaps the stroke had done inner damage, burst a vein in the forehead. Bedros gently spoke Gabriel's name.

Gabriel stared incredulously and smiled. "What's been happening here?"

Bedros Hekim laughed shortly. "If only I knew that myself, my son."

Tenderly he took Gabriel's cheeks between his brown and shrivelled hands. "Anyway, nothing's happened to you, I know that now."

Gabriel sprang to his feet. He refused at first to use his memory. He just managed to say in a drunken voice: "What about that surprise attack? . . . Have we made it? Jesus Christ, the South Bastion. . . . Now we're done for. . . ."

But Ter Haigasun, too, was on his feet again. And his voice seemed to issue from another drunkenness, a clear, super-conscious intoxication: "Now, no more!"

Bagradian did not hear him. The crackling and roaring was too loud to hear oneself speak. The fire ate its way step by step from hut to hut. And groups of trees on the edge of the Town Enclosure were already bright with flames. More and more families, with their arms full of rescued goods and chattels, had collected on the altar square, awaiting an order, an objective. Some of the women had used their last ounce of strength to bring their sewing-machines into safety. All eyes sought the leaders. But there were none, since both Bagradian and Ter Haigasun were still absently staring out at nothing in a kind of coma. And Dr. Altouni didn't count. No mukhtar, no teacher, showed himself; they were all too busy saving their property.

In this desperate pause there came at least help from the North Saddle. It is some proof of the uncanny quickness of these proceedings, the interval from Ter Haigasun's outbreak to this instant, that Avakian with ten decads only now put in an appearance, when all was over. Chaush Nurhan had sent at once to fetch him, the instant the deserters began to fire.

Avakian came running in horror to Gabriel. "Are you wounded, Effendi? . . . Jesus Christ, what's the matter? . . . Your face! . . . Say something, please. . . ."

But Gabriel Bagradian said nothing. In a few quick steps past the flaming altar, he left the square, the Town Enclosure, broke into a run, and stopped at last on the summit of a little hill. Avakian followed without a word. Gabriel strained his head forward, listening sharply, trying to hear through the crackling flame. A long-drawn rattle of bullets in the south. Machine-guns? And now again! But perhaps it was only deception, since the pain in his head threatened to burst it.

6

The Script in the Fog

THE junior officer had managed to discharge his impossible duty. He had laid down a field-telephone, not of course as far as Villa Bagradian—there was probably not enough wire in the whole Fourth Army to do that!—but at least as far as the village of Habaste, about four hundred feet below the South Bastion. It was a meritorious piece of service, considering how badly his men were trained and the many difficulties presented by the rocky terrain. General Ali Risa Bey, disguised in mufti for the benefit of observers on the Damlayik, had come in person to Habaste. The sun had just set when the primitive telephone on the little field-table before him began to buzz. It lasted a very long time, and there was still much surmounting of technical difficulties before, at the other end of the wire, the voice of the yüs-bashi became audible.

"General, I have to report, we've taken the mountain."

Ali Risa Bey, he of the clear, unmuddied countenance, the non-smoker and teetotaler, leant back in his little folding-chair, holding up the earpiece: "The mountain, Yüs-Bashi? How do you mean? You mean the south end of the mountain?"

"Quite so, Effendi, the south end."

"Thanks. Any losses?"

"None at all, not a single man."

"And how many prisoners, Yüs-Bashi?"

A technical defect became apparent. The general glanced keenly at the telephone officer. But soon the yüs-bashi's voice could be heard again, though not quite so distinct.

"I've taken no prisoners. The enemy trenches were empty. We'd thought they might be. Nearly empty. Only about ten men, counting, that is, four boys among them."

"And what's been done with all these people?"

"Our fellows disposed of them."

"They defended themselves?"

"No, General."

"That considerably lessens your success, Yüs-Bashi. These prisoners might have saved us a lot of trouble."

Even in this clumsy earpiece the major's wrath was still perceptible.

"It wasn't I gave the order."

The general's fervid coolness remained unruffled. "And what's become of all those deserters?"

"We only found the dregs of them, nobody else."

"I see. Anything more to report, Yüs-Bashi?"

"The Armenians have set fire to their camp. It looks like a considerable blaze. . . ."

"And what does that mean, in your opinion, Yüs-Bashi? What reasons do you suppose they have for doing it?"

The yüs-bashi's voice, revengefully acrimonious: "It's not for me to judge that, General. You'll know all that better than I do. Fellows may be wanting to clear off the mountain, in the night. . . ."

For two seconds, with pale grey eyes, Ali Risa Bey stared silently at distances. He gave his opinion: "Possibly. . . . But there may be some feint at the back of it. . . . That ringleader of theirs has had the best of our officers several times. . . . They may have planned a sortie."

He turned to his surrounding officers. "All outpost lines in the valley to be thoroughly strengthened tonight."

The yüs-bashi's voice came somewhat impatiently: "Any further orders, please, General?"

"How far have your companies got?"

"The third company and two machine-gun groups are

holding the nearest mound, about five hundred paces away from my base."

"We've been hearing machine-gun fire down here. What's the meaning of that?"

"Only a little demonstration."

"That demonstration was highly deleterious and unnecessary. Your men are to remain where they are and take proper cover."

The voice at the other end had now become spitefully astute: "My men to remain where they are. May I have that, please, as a written order, Effendi? . . . And tomorrow?"

"Tomorrow, half an hour before sunrise, the artillery to open fire from the north. Set your watch exactly by mine, please, Yüs-Bashi. . . . Good. . . . I shall be up there with you just before sunrise and lead the business from the south. . . . Thank you."

As he banged down the receiver, the yüs-bashi bared his teeth. "So he'll come along up in time for the walk-over, the goat's-milk pasha! And then he'll be 'the victor of Musa Dagh'!"

GABRIEL turned back silently to the altar square. All the short way back he gripped Avakian's hand. The fire had eaten its way further and further along the streets. The sun had not long been down. But, in spite of surrounding flames—the leaf-screen of the altar was still blazing—the world kept darkening around Gabriel. Black, miserable shapes, voices of black desolation, eddied round the square in meaningless arabesques. The scales of Gabriel's whole life tottered. Had he not fully earned the right to let himself collapse a second time, this time for ever, and know no more? Stephan was dead. Why start all over again? And yet, second by second, his splitting head began to fill with ever more lucid, purposeful thoughts.

Ter Haigasun, too, had recovered and scrambled to his feet. His first thought had been to pile his vestments, his torn

756

alb, the stole, and all the rest in a careful heap. He covered his own nakedness with a rug which someone had lent him. A strand of Ter Haigasun's beard had been singed away, and a large red burn covered his cheek. His face looked entirely different. Those yellowish, hollow cheeks, the colour of cameos, were suffused with some dark flush of fever and rage. He struggled in vain for words at the sight of Gabriel.

The people had ceased to struggle against the blaze. What energy they still had was barely enough to impel their crazy eddyings round the square, and these, little by little, ceased. Nor could the decads, sent by Nurhan, save anything more for them. They stood idle, watching the flames, which seemed not only to leap from outside upon the huts, but to burst from within them. The crackling roofs of leaves and branches were lifted, while puffs of wind drove fiery scraps across the sky. Soon the whole camp was squatting close on the bare earth of the big square, women, children, old men. These famished people could move no more. Firelight flickered across their earthy faces; the eyes showed no sign that they were aware of it. Their attitudes expressed only one desire: that no leader should ask them to stir another inch, raise another hand, or show the least sign of fresh activity. Here they would squat, awaiting the end without further resistance. That state which might be described as the "peace of annihilation" had come upon them.

But these shrivelled souls, these wasted bodies, were to be roused again from this comfortable understanding with death. Behind closed eyelids Gabriel had collected his thoughts. It happened almost against his will. At first he even struggled to escape the very painful effort it needed to concentrate. Then, it was as though, in that echoing mine which was now his head, not he, Bagradian, was thinking, but, apart, independently of himself, the task he had assumed, long ago in the valley, the task of carrying on this defence to its last possibility. An unbribable, implacable power went on calculating.

757

Had the last possible hope been lost? No. The Turks had apparently occupied the South Bastion. They had brought up machine-guns. The camp was on fire. What was to happen? A new line of defence, which should block their way as well as might be. Above all, the people must be cleared off the heights, they must be moved down on to the shore. Then to the howitzers!

Avakian approached. Gabriel called to him: "What are you still doing here? Quick, go to Nurhan! He's not to move from where he is! All the decads I chose for the attack to come here at once. And half the scouts group and the orderlies. We've got to form another line, with at least head cover."

Avakian hesitated, tried to ask questions. Gabriel pushed him away and went into the midst of the somnolent multitude. "Why are you in despair, brothers and sisters? No need for that! We've still got seven hundred fighters and rifles, and our two big guns. You needn't worry! It'd be better for the defence if the communes would set up their camp down on the shore for tonight. The men of the reserve to stop with me."

By this time even the mukhtars had come to themselves. Ter Haigasun ordered them each to collect his village and lead it down the path to the shore. He himself would go on, and find the best camping-grounds. The priest, there could be no doubt, was in high fever, and had to make a tremendous effort to turn back to life and to his duty. His face with the singed beard looked shrunken and dark.

He turned to Gabriel. "To punish is the most important of all! You must shoot down the culprits, Bagradian!"

Gabriel stared at him in silence. "*I* won't find Kilikian," he thought. By degrees the comatose people had struggled up again. A drunken, lurching confusion had begun. The mukhtars, the village priests, two of the teachers, herded and shoved them into groups. No one resisted. Even the children no longer howled. Bedros Hekim stole away unobtrusively, to bring at least those patients in the two hospitals into safety who could still move. Disaster gave this falling wreck of an old man the strength of a giant.

Gabriel left it to Ter Haigasun to break up the camp. Not another second must be lost, since who could tell how far the Turks, even in the dark, might not dare to advance? The howitzers were in danger. And another danger was the pack of scoundrelly deserters. Forward! Now it was not a question of thinking things out from A to Z, but of simple, blindly resolute action. Gabriel mustered together all the armed and half-armed men around him, the young and the old. Even little boys had to come along. The wind had fallen, it was quiet. The sharp pungence of smoke enveloped them. With it mingled the stink of singeing cloth. They could scarcely breathe, and their eyes were streaming. Gabriel gave the signal to move off. He and Shatakhian, who meanwhile had been routed out, went on ahead of the widely extended lines. Exhausted men plodded after them, a hundred and fifty, a third of whom were sixty years old. And this wretched, famished troop were to turn back victoriously four infantry companies at war-strength, commanded by a major, four captains, eight first lieutenants? It was a good thing that Gabriel did not realize the enemy's strength.

On their way to the howitzers they passed the big new graveyard. The graveyard folk had followed their custom in the valley and taken up their quarters beside the dead. And now Nunik, Wartuk, Manushak, and all the others bestirred themselves to cram their tight sacks with mouldy gear. Sato assisted them. This fresh migration seemed to make little difference to these folk. The two newest graves were Stephan's and Krikor's. Krikor had asked that his grave should not be picked out by any inscription. A rough wooden cross had been planted on Stephan's mound. His father went stiffly past, without a glance at it. Now it was night. But the red glow of the blaze over-arched the Damlayik. It might have been a huge city on fire,

759

and not a few hundred huts of twisted branches, a few clumps of trees.

Midway, however, as the grassy knoll of the howitzer emplacement came into sight, something unexpected happened. Gabriel and Shatakhian stopped. The plodding men behind them flung themselves down. Down the slope ran a line of riflemen. Only their black silhouettes were visible as they waved rifles frantically at the oncomers. Turks? The men sought what cover they could in the dark. But the black shapes, outlined by a flickering red sky, were advancing timidly. About thirty of them. Gabriel noticed that they were pushing a bound man on in front of them. He went forward to meet them. They carried lanterns. Five paces off, he saw that Sarkis Kilikian was their prisoner. They were deserters. They flung themselves down flat on their faces and touched the ground with their foreheads, the most primitive of all gestures of self-abasement. What was there still to say or justify? Their way out was barred. These ropes with which they had bound Kilikian were their proof that they regretted their heinous deed, had brought a scapegoat, were ready to suffer any punishment. Some, with an almost childish eagerness, heaped up their plunder at Gabriel's feet—cartridges stolen from the armoury stores plundered from the tents. But Gabriel saw only Kilikian. They had forced him down to his knees, his head flung backwards. In this flickering twilight the features of his face were quite visible. Those indifferent eyes as little expressed the wish to live as the wish to die. Impassively they watched their judge. Bagradian bent a little nearer this gruesomely impassive face. Not even now could he rid his mind of the tinge of liking and respect which he felt whenever he saw the Russian. Was Kilikian, that spectral observer, the real culprit? What if he was! Gabriel clicked back the catch of the service-revolver in his pocket. He set it to the Russian's forehead swiftly. The first shot missed fire. Nor had Kilikian shut his eyes. His mouth and nostrils were twitching.

It was like a suppressed smile. But it felt to Gabriel as though he had turned the unspent bullet against himself. When he pressed the trigger again, he was so weak that he had to turn his head away. So died Sarkis Kilikian—after an incomprehensible life in many jails, having escaped Turkish massacre as a child, and, as a man, a Turkish firing-party, to end at last by the bullet of a fellow-countryman.

Gabriel signed quickly to the others to fall in with the men behind.

Two of these repentant scarecrows had zealously spied out the Turkish positions. What they had to report was an exaggeration of hard reality. Perhaps their own miserable fear of punishment may have caused them to distort the already formidable; perhaps they tried to diminish their own guilt by describing a gigantic enemy power. Since how, even without this monstrous crime of theirs, could the few South Bastion defenders ever have resisted the sly envelopment by the Turks? Gabriel looked past them in silence. He was aware that he himself was largely responsible for their crime. He had not taken Nurhan's warning to redistribute these rascals in other decads.

Samuel Avakian and the men of the surprise-attackers had joined Gabriel some time previously. It was an hour before these few straggling skirmishers, in two lines, disposed themselves diagonally across the mound and in the many hollows of the plateau to the zone of bushes, and in among the rocks. Even the best fighters of the north trenches had come to the end of their strength. What could one ask of elderly reservists? Each man lay like a log where he had been told to lie, half awake, half asleep. The order to pile up stones and earth as head-cover was scarcely obeyed. When Gabriel had passed from man to man, down the whole length of this utterly hopeless front, and posted a few stray pickets in advance of it, he went off to the howitzers. He had every square inch of the

Damlayik in his head, every distance, the lie of all its ground. For the area of the South Bastion he could check his ballistic elements by his notebook.

This was the first autumn night, after a day of grilling desert heat. It was suddenly cool. Gabriel sat alone beside the howitzers, having sent their men to get some sleep. Avakian spread out a rug for him. But he did not wrap himself into it, since his body was hot all over, and his head, grown far too light, was threatening to fly away from it. Gabriel stretched himself out, neither sleeping nor waking. He stared up at the red flat lake in the sky. That red mirror of conflagration seemed to deepen and broaden out as he lay and watched it. How long has the altar been on fire? The melodious question kept repeating itself. Then, for some long time, he must have known nothing more about himself, since something in his neighbourhood waked him up. It was not a hand nor a voice, only something near him. But this very sensation of being waked, this long, fabulous instant of deepest experience, was so materially soothing in its effect that he struggled against any fuller consciousness. His exhausted unity with this presence was so complete, in this one short instant, that Iskuhi's reality almost deceived. Since she, after all, brought back the inevitable. The sight of her made him think, with a start, of Juliette. It was an age since he had seen his wife or thought of her. His first scared inquiry was therefore this: "And Juliette? What's happened to Juliette?"

It had taken all Iskuhi's failing strength to drag so far. For her, all these recent happenings had fused into something indistinct. She was aware only of the one persistent, burning question: "Why doesn't he come? Why has he left me? Why hasn't he sent for me at the last?" And now those questions were coldly throttled by the inquiry about Juliette. She said nothing, and it took her a long time to collect her thoughts for a hesitant account of all that had taken place on Three-Tent Square: the raid, Shushik's death, Tomasian's wound. Bedros had tried in vain to persuade Juliette to let Kevork carry her down to the seashore. Juliette would have no such thing and had screamed that she wasn't going to leave her tent. The wounded Aram also lay on, in his. . . .

Gabriel stared up at the flat red sky. It had become no paler. "It's all right as it is. . . . Nothing will happen before morning. . . . Time enough. . . . A night in the open might kill Juliette. . . ."

Something in these words hurt Gabriel. He switched on his electric torch. But now the last used-up battery gave out scarcely as much light as a glow-worm. In spite of the tragic red above him, and flames still shooting up in the Town Enclosure, this night felt darker than all former ones. He could scarcely see Iskuhi beside him. Softly he felt about for her face, and started, so cold and thin were her cheeks and hands. Kindness moved him.

He took the rug and wrapped her into it. "How long is it since you ate anything, Iskuhi?"

"Mairik Antaram had brought us something before it happened," she lied. "I've had enough. . . ."

Gabriel pressed her close, seeking again the half-sleep of her presence. "It felt so good, just now, to wake up beside you. . . . What a long time since I had you with me, Iskuhi, little sister. . . . I'm very happy now that you're here. . . . Happy now, Iskuhi."

Her face sank slowly against his; she seemed too weak to carry her head on her shoulders. "You never came. . . . So I've come. . . . It's got as far as that, hasn't it?"

His was the drowsy voice of a sleeper: "Yes, I think it's got as far as that. . . ."

In Iskuhi's words there was an exhausted, yet defiant insistence on her rights: "Well, you know what we promised . . . what *you* promised *me* . . . Gabriel . . . ?"

He returned from distances. "There may still be a long day in front of us."

She echoed his words in a deep breath, making a gift of them: "Still a long day . . ." She clasped his arm with ever-increasing warmth.

"There's something I want you to do for me, Iskuhi. . . . We've often talked about it. . . . Juliette's far poorer and more unhappy than we are. . . ."

Her cheek bent away from his face. But Gabriel took her lame hand, he kept stroking and kissing it. "If you love me, Iskuhi! . . . Juliette's so inhumanly lonely . . . inhumanly lonely . . ."

"Juliette hates me. She can't bear the sight of me. I never want to see her again."

His hand could feel the tension shaking her body. "If you love me, Iskuhi, I ask you, please, to stay with Juliette. . . . You must leave the tents at sunrise. . . . I shall feel easier. . . . She's nearly mad, and you're well. . . . We shall see each other again . . . Iskuhi. . . ."

Her head sank forwards. She was crying without any sound. He whispered: "I love you, Iskuhi. We'll be together."

After a long while she tried to get up. "I'm going now."

He held her fast. "Not yet, Iskuhi. Stop with me a little while now. I need you. . . ."

Long silence. His tongue felt too heavy to move. The sharp, thudding headache increased. Gabriel's light, winged skull changed into a gigantic lead bullet. He sank back into himself as though another rifle-butt had felled him. Sarkis Kilikian's eyes stared at him with apathetic gravity. He shuddered. Where was the Russian lying? Had he given an order to move the body? The events of these last hours seemed completely alien; they had nothing to do with him: they were like some mad rumour. He relapsed into vague and heavy broodings, in which he himself was the centre-point of a headache which surged about him in waves. Then, when Gabriel started up in terror, Iskuhi was already on her feet.

He felt in horror for his watch. "What time is it? . . .

Jesus Christ! . . . No, time . . . time! Why have you given me the rug? . . . Why, you're shaking with cold. . . . You're right; better go now, Iskuhi. . . . Go to Juliette. You've still got five, six hours in front of you. . . . I'll send Avakian when it's time. . . . Good night, Iskuhi. . . . Please take the rug. . . . I don't need it. . . ."

He held her in his arms again. But it felt as though she were struggling to get loose, and had grown more disembodied and shadowy. So he promised again: "This isn't good-bye. We'll be together . . ."

Some time after Iskuhi had left him, as he was about to stretch himself out again, the sudden memory of her made his heart sick. She had scarcely been able to move for weakness. Her legs and arms had been stiff with cold. Her fragile body had scarcely seemed to be there at all. Was not she herself ill and declining? And yet he had sent her away to look after Juliette. Gabriel blamed himself. He had not even gone a stretch of the dark and difficult way with Iskuhi. He hurried half up the slope and called: "Iskuhi! Where are you? Wait for me!"

No answer. She was too far away to hear him.

Towards two that morning the fire had sunk down in the enclosure. At about that time Gabriel waked Avakian. The student had thrown himself down beside the howitzers and was so heavily asleep that Gabriel had to spend some time shaking him. The character of a man may be tested by the way in which he behaves when you wake him suddenly. Avakian, after a few movements of protest, raised his head in drowsy confusion. But as soon as he felt that this was Gabriel, he sprang to his feet and smiled a startled smile into the dark.

Gabriel handed him a flask, in which there were still some dregs of cognac. "Here, drink, Avakian. . . . Buck up! I need you now. We shan't have any more time to talk."

They sat with their backs to the Town Enclosure, where, indistinctly, they could watch the pickets of the new line. Some of these were now carrying hooded lanterns. This maze of lights wound slowly back and forth. The wind was as quiet as ever.

"I haven't slept—not a second," admitted Gabriel. "I've had too much to think about, in spite of this lump, which lets me know it's there, right enough."

"Pity. You ought to have slept, Effendi."

"Why? Tomorrow's the day we've managed to put off so long. Yes, I wanted to say to you, Avakian, that really we've largely got you to thank for the fact that things have gone on as long as they have. We've worked splendidly together. You're the most dependable person I know. Forgive my stupid way of putting it. Of course you're more than just that."

This embarrassed Avakian. But Gabriel set a hand on his knee. "After all, some time we had to speak frankly. . . . And what other time is there?"

"Those swine have destroyed everything," raged the student, mainly because he was feeling embarrassed, but Bagradian waved away the past.

"No need to worry about that now. It had to come some day. And usually, in this world, what you expect comes in the way you'd least expect it. But it wasn't that I wanted to talk to you about. Listen! You know, Avakian, before all this, I'd always the feeling that you were going to come through. Why, I myself couldn't tell you. Probably it's sheer moonshine, but somehow I have a vision of you, back in Paris, the devil only knows how you managed to get there, or rather how you're going to manage it."

The tutor's pale and sloping forehead could be seen shimmering in the dark. "That's pure nonsense, forgive me, Gabriel Bagradian. What happens to you is bound to happen to me; there can be nothing else."

"Why not? I agree that, if you go by reason, there can't be anything else. But let's be unreasonable for once, let's say that, somehow, you get away."

Gabriel stopped and stared intently into the dark, as though Avakian's happy future was already fairly easily distinguishable. He took out his pocketbook and put it down on the grass beside him. "I didn't want to keep you here, I wanted to send you back to the north trenches. I feel easier when you're with Nurhan. But all that really doesn't matter much. I've something more important I want you to do for me, Avakian! Stay with the women. I mean with my wife, and Mademoiselle Tomasian. It's part of the good presentiment I have about you. Perhaps you bring luck. Do what you can! But above all, see to it, please, that the tent gets cleared in time before the sun's up. And see that Madame is carried down as carefully as possible on to the shore. Find somebody else, not Kevork. I hate the thought of his hands. Take Kristaphor and Missak."

Samuel Avakian protested. Tomorrow, in the last battle, he would be more necessary than ever. They had still the most important questions to settle. And so the conscientious adjutant began giving lists of the duties awaiting him.

But his commandant impatiently refused to consider them. "No! No! We've made all the preparations we can. You leave all that to me. I don't need you here any longer. This ends your war service, Avakian. The other is a personal request."

He handed over a sealed letter. "Here, friend, this is my will. You're to keep it till Madame is well again, understand? I'm still, of course, going by my ridiculous feeling that you'll come through. You see? And then, here's a cheque on the Crédit Lyonnais. I've no idea how much salary I still owe you. . . . And, of course, you're perfectly right to consider me mad. Placed as we are, such calculations are too ridiculous. I'm being pedantic. It may be all the sheerest superstition. Let's say I'm making magic. See? Just a little magic."

Bagradian sprang up with a laugh. The impression he gave

was young and dependable. "If I survive you, that nullifies both the will and the cheque—so look out!"

But his laugh sounded strained. Avakian kept the papers at arm's length and began to protest again. And now Gabriel got impatient. "Go now, please. I shall feel easier."

The last hours before sunrise dragged unbearably. Gabriel set his teeth as he stared through the brightening dark. In the first twilight he trained his guns on to the South Bastion. The dense early morning mists of this windless day took long to clear. A red, angry sun burst into the sky. Gabriel knelt as prescribed on the right of the first howitzer, and tugged with fervour at the fuse-tape. The cracking din, the wild kick of the gun-carriage, fire and smoke, the howling in the air, the crystal-hard seconds before the distant impact of the shell, were like a deliverance. All the unbearable tension in Gabriel's mind released itself in this piece of gunnery. What reason had the prudent commander of the Damlayik for wasting irreplaceable shells before the slightest sign of a Turkish attack? Was he trying to wake, or scare, the enemy? Encourage his own? Did he hope his shell would so devastate Turkish companies as to rob them of all their courage to advance? None of all this! Gabriel had fired this first shot, not for any tactical reason, but simply because to wait any longer was too unbearable. It was a sheer cry, half for help, half of tragic jubilation, that the night was past. And not only he—all the exhausted men of the line of rifles, bent double with cold, felt just as he did. The outposts climbed the nearest hillock for a wider view. But as far as they could overlook the uneven ground of this mountain plateau, the Damlayik lay deserted. The Turks did not seem to have left their base yet, nor in the north. But the answer came. It took a little time coming, and in this breathing-space Bagradian had leisure to fire two more shots. Then the deep, the monstrous crack of a thunderbolt. No one knew what it was. High over him a hiss of iron, which seemed to fill the entire mountain, from Amanus to

El Akra. The impact crashed down far in the distance. Somewhere in the Orontes plain. This thunderbolt had risen off the sea.

THAT same night the communes had set up their unsheltered camp, pell-mell, among rocks, on the crags, without any definite plan. Ter Haigasun had given the mukhtars orders to bring Oskanian to him, dead or alive. The priest's whole soul was engrossed with the one fiery longing to avenge the outraged majesty of the law, this base betrayal of the community, on the guilty parties.

But Teacher Hrand Oskanian was in hiding, not far from the Dish Terrace. He was not alone. The neophytes of his cult of suicide had joined him. On Musa Dagh there had not so far been one case of suicide. Even tonight Oskanian only had four miserable converts. A man and three women. The man was fifty, but looked like an old man. He was one of the silk-weavers round Kheder Beg. Oskanian's teaching had found in Margoss Arzruni a willing disciple. Of the women the eldest was a matron whose whole family had died. The two others were still quite young. The child of one of them had perished in her arms on the day before. The other, unmarried, came of a well-to-do Yoghonoluk family and was known everywhere as a lugubrious, rather scatter-brained person.

Oskanian, while the putsch was still in progress, had escaped and in terror sought this refuge. But Margoss Arzruni, the prophet's apostle, had tracked him down, and now brought the teacher these three faithful women, all ready to make his words a reality. It is easier to kill oneself in company. And the silk-weaver was one of those implacable apostles who will not permit the prophet to go back one iota on his evangel. For many days, that these sayings might come to fruition in his mind, he had visited the Master in the South Bastion. The five sat close to one another, sheltered by one of the great boulders which block up the way to the Dish Terrace. They

769

were freezing, and so huddled together. The apostle of suicide was himself vaguely surprised that he, almost at the point of carrying out the most solemn resolution of which a human being is capable, should still be feeling a certain glow of pleasure at the nestling proximity of a female. It did not trouble him, however, as he let himself be catechized by the matron, who, full of trust, questioned her teacher (since no doubt he had examined this side of the question) as to possible results in the Beyond for those who begin eternity for themselves.

"It's a great sin, Teacher, I'm sure. I only ao it so as to see my folk again, quickly again! But perhaps I shan't be allowed to see them again. I may have to stay in hell for all eternity, because, you see, I know it's a great sin."

Oskanian raised his pointed nose, which glimmered through the dark. "You'll be giving back to nature what nature has given you."

This portentous saying seemed to afford Arzruni, the silk-weaver, a diabolical satisfaction. He rubbed his hands together, crowing in a weakly strident voice: "Well, old woman, hear what he says! Does that satisfy you? Of course, if it's only your folk you're wanting to see again, you can always wait for that till tomorrow. The Turks aren't likely to overlook *you*, you know. No one'll want you for his harem. But I'm not going to wait. I've had enough of it!"

She bent forward, crossing her hands over her breasts. "Jesus Christ will forgive me. . . . God knows all. . . ."

This gave the teacher his chance of a pungent saying.

"God knows all!" he screeched. "The one reason for forgiving Him for having made this world the way He has would be that He knows nothing—*nothing!*—about it. . . . He bothers His head with us about the same as though we were lice. See? He might have His hands full otherwise. . . ."

The apostle Arzruni echoed in an ecstasy of derision: "Yes, He might have His hands full otherwise. . . . Like lice . . ."

But the prophet, whose acumen had almost exhausted him, turned to this matron who hesitated to sin. "Why should He bother about you, since He's only a fool notion in your head?"

The silk-weaver blinked, getting the sense of it; this dawned on him, and he roared with satisfaction, slapping his thighs and swaying about like a praying Moslem. "Fool notion in your head—old woman—understand that? Only in your head. . . . Well, spit him out of it, spit him out!"

These blasphemies and Arzruni's laugh evoked wild sobs in the young mother. She remembered how, after a long struggle, someone had taken the small, stiff body out of her arms. This man, one of the hospital staff, had run off to fling her three-year-old son away with the others, somewhere. She had spent hours looking for his corpse. She only hoped they'd thrown him in the sea. This mother longed to be in the sea, with her baby. She sprang up with a piercing scream: "Oh, why do you sit here talking like this for hours? Do come along!"

But the Master reproved: "It's got to be done in the proper order."

It was well past midnight when they set about determining precedence. Arzruni proposed they should draw lots. But Oskanian was of the opinion that the women should be the first to go; it was more seemly. First the eldest, he said, then the younger, and last the youngest. He gave no further reasons for this arrangement, but, since the women raised no objections, they left it at that. Finally he declared himself willing to draw lots with his apostle. Fate went against or, if one prefers it, for him, since it gave him precedence of the silk-weaver. It was quiet, without a breath of wind. But a flurried sea still growled on the rocks far below. The darkness was thick enough to bite. The teacher crept, fumbling his way very gingerly indeed, to the rocks' edge, with the help of a lantern which he set down there. Its light, most curiously steady, marked the boundary line between Here and There. Then, as master of ceremonies of the Gulf, escort from here into eternity, he waved an inviting hand in its direction.

The matron knelt for a few minutes, crossing herself again and again. She came on, in little, tripping steps, and vanished without a cry. The young mother followed her at once. She went with a run. A short, sharp scream. . . . The lugubrious girl was far less eager. She begged the teacher to give her a shove over the brink. But Oskanian refused her this good office, protesting loudly. The lugubrious girl went down on her hands and knees, and so on all fours dragged on to the edge. There she seemed to think it over. Her hand went out for the lantern, which it upset. The lantern rolled to destruction. But, instead of keeping still, or crawling back, the girl stretched her hands out after it, bent forwards, and so lost her balance. A terrible, endless scream, since the wretched girl clung on, another full two minutes, to some jutting ledge, before she plunged down. . . . Oskanian and Arzruni stood in the dusk, without a word. A long, long pause. That scream still cut its way through the heavy consciousness of the teacher.

At last the apostle reminded his prophet: "Well, Teacher, now it's your turn."

Hrand Oskanian seemed to consider the whole position in all its bearings. He remarked, in a not too self-conscious voice: "The lantern's gone. I'm not going to do it in the dark. Let's wait for the twilight. It can't be so long now. . . ."

The silk-weaver observed with some show of reason: "Far easier in the dark, Teacher."

"For you, perhaps; not for me though." The Master sounded very reproachful indeed. "I need light."

With this lofty and inspiring remark Margoss Arzruni seemed fairly satisfied. But he kept close to Oskanian. If his teacher, who had sat beside him, made the smallest movement, the disciple would at once catch him by the lapel (Oskanian still had on the tattered wreck of that swallow-tail milord's morning-coat, ordered and selected to outrival Gonzague with Juliette). The grip with which Arzruni detained his prophet was loyal, nervous, and mistrustful. Hrand Oskanian had become the prisoner of his teachings. Once he jumped up. The silk-weaver sprang up by his side. There was no getting away from this disciple.

When, ages later, the edge of the rock outlined itself in misty twilight, Arzruni rose and took off his overall: "Teacher, it's not dark now!"

Oskanian was a long time stretching, yawning, as a man yawns after deep, refreshing sleep. He stood up portentously. He blew his nose several times with trumpet blasts before, followed by his guardian apostle, he would take the first inevitable steps. But he turned again, still some way from the sharp verge. "Better that you should go first, Weaver."

The shrivelled Arzruni, in dirty shirt-sleeves, craned his observant head in the teacher's face. "Why me, Teacher? Didn't we draw for it? You drew to go first, didn't you? And the three women have gone on in front of us. . . ."

Oskanian's hirsute face looked very white. "Why you, you say? Because I mean to be the last! Because I don't intend to have you run away and joke about me."

It looked at first as though the silk-weaver were giving his whole mind to this. But when the Master least expected it he found his apostle at his throat. Yet he had sensed an attack. He soon knew that, small as he was, he was stronger than the rickety Arzruni. And yet that fanatical weaver, whose deepest faith was suddenly shattered, threatened to be a dangerous customer. Oskanian felt himself thrust back, a good foot nearer the roaring deep. No doubt this madman was trying to pull them down to destruction together. The teacher suddenly flung himself on the ground, gripped a clump of a shrub with one hand, the weaver's right leg with the other, and so upset him. Still gripping hard to the steel-tough shrub, he kicked out wildly at the body and face of his sprawling disciple.

Exactly how it happened he did not know, but almost the next instant he found himself kicking into the void. The body of Arzruni the silk-weaver toppled over the edge into the fog. Oskanian sat up stiffly. Still sitting up, he worked his way backwards along the ledge, back, back. He felt himself saved. But that only lasted a few minutes. Then he knew that even this victory was in vain. Never again could he return into the company of the just and the respectable. Nor could he fly. The little teacher jumped to his feet and wandered, in little, hesitant steps. During their struggle the weaver had torn a swallow-tail off his coat. Oskanian puffed out his pigeon-breast, as he always did at the laboured moments when he felt he must assert his puny self. But then his chest crumpled together, as he hopped in the fog like a bird with a drooping wing. He strove to comfort and move himself to tears by means of a poetic phrase, on which his whole mind was suddenly focused: "In sunlight, not in the grey dawn."

In the course of these hoppings Oskanian stumbled over a flag-pole. It was their banner with the cry for help inscribed on it: "Christians in Need," which the wind had long since overturned and carried away. Both as a look-out station and burying-ground the Dish Terrace had for days been out of use. Hrand Oskanian picked up the heavy flag-pole and shouldered it without knowing what he did. Then, most grotesque of ensigns, he hopped about with it, in ever-increasing desperation. How he longed to forbid the sun to rise, over there, from behind the Amanus mountains! But here it already was, red and angry. One last, helplessly lived thought: "Off this cursed rock! Find somewhere to hide! Better starve slowly!" But for Oskanian there was no going back. He must make good his poetic word about the sunshine. The women and the weaver were expecting him. His banner held almost at arm's length, he lingered on around the edge. Mists cleared below him. Wide beams, swaths, banks of it, unwound themselves in coiling arabesques, leaving, here and there, a patch of sea as flat and dull as a dark-grey cloth. At one place on this cloth something was glittering. Hrand Oskanian shut his eyes. Now he must be really out of his mind, as he'd always feared he would be one day. He opened and shut his eyes again and again. The fog meanwhile dispersed and vanished. But not the glittering thing on the broad grey cloth; it might have been stuck to it. It no longer shimmered vaguely in and out, but was a long, blue-grey ship with four funnels, which, seen from above, looked rather small and not quite worth taking seriously. A few wisps of fog still hovered round it.

The teacher had very sharp eyes. The javelins of a young, impetuous sun, eager to do battle, made it easy to read the big, black letters along the bow: *Guichen*.

Oskanian let out a few yammering howls. *Guichen*. The miracle had been wrought. But not for him. They were all to be saved. Only not he. Suddenly he jerked his pendant banner: "Christians in Need." Faster and faster, like a lunatic, the teacher brandished the heavy pole, every minute, indefatigably. From the captain's bridge of this armoured cruiser a French signalling flag soon gave him his answer. Oskanian never noticed that. He had ceased to know that he was himself. He waved and waved the big white sheet in wild half-circles. He groaned with the effort. But, for as long as his strength continued, he still might live. Bagradian's howitzers cracked far off, above. Shorter, each time more unevenly, the half-circles of the Armenian flag still oscillated. Perhaps, Oskanian thought, I might manage to get on board and not be seen. And, as he thought it, stepped over the edge, drawn forward by the weight of his own flag-pole more than by any act of his own will, with a shriek of wild terror, into nothing.

At that minute the twelve-inch guns of the *Guichen* halted the Turks with a shell that crashed down into Suedia.

THE general, the Kaimakam, and the yüs-bashi were struck to the very soul by this order to halt. A few minutes before receiving it, they had come together, as arranged, in the yüs-bashi's headquarters. Even the thick, dyspeptic, lethargic Kaimakam, for whom early rising and climbing hills were a more than ordinary sacrifice, had come. His four company commanders stood round the yüs-bashi, waiting to take his personal order to advance. Their scouts had done excellent work in the night. They could bring in precise information of this new refuge along the seashore. It was also known that two enfeebled, badly protected lines barred the south entrance to the Damlayik. Therefore, by order of Ali Risa, only two companies with machine-guns need trouble to attack this rickety front. The attack was timed for the moment when, in the north, mountain artillery had begun to shatter Armenian trenches. But the Kaimakam and yüs-bashi were quite positive that, by about that time, resistance would have been effectually broken. This time they were done for! Bagradian's first howitzer shell had struck on the stone slope under the rocks, his second went even wider, his third came down rather close to this group of officers. Splinters and showers of stones whizzed round them. Two infantrymen lay yelping.

The yüs-bashi carefully lit a cigarette. "We've some losses, General!"

Ali Risa's transparent, youthful face flushed to the ears. His lips looked even thinner than usual.

"Yüs-Bashi, I order you to see to it that this Bagradian doesn't get killed and is brought to me personally."

Scarcely had these words been uttered, when the first forbidding thunderbolt was heard. The officers hurried up to their western redoubt, from which there was a good view out to sea. The grey-blue *Guichen* sat firmly, as if frozen into its leaden waves. A black stream of smoke rose from its funnels. Round the mouth of its gun the flash-smoke had already dispersed. Its commander seemed to have planted only one shell in the Orontes plain for demonstration purposes.

The first to find a voice was the Kaimakam. It shook with

excitement. "Let's understand each other, General! You're in command of the military assistance. But the final decision rests with me."

Ali Risa, without answering this, examined the *Guichen* through his field-glass. And on this occasion the Kaimakam, who usually seemed expectantly half-asleep at a moment of great decision, lost his temper. "I demand, General, that you start operations immediately. That ship over there can't hold us back."

Ali Risa lowered his field-glass and turned to his adjutant. "Telephone down to Habaste. My order to be sent on full speed to every gun-emplacement in the north: 'Artillery not to open fire.'"

"Artillery not to open fire," the adjutant repeated, and rushed away.

The Kaimakam straightened his loose, but mighty bulk. "What does this order mean? I demand an explanation, Effendi!"

The general did not seem to see him; his grey-blue eyes were turned on the yüs-bashi.

"Retire your advance companies. All troops to vacate the mountain and concentrate in the valley of Yoghonoluk. Get a move on!"

"I demand your explanation!" bellowed the Kaimakam; the pouches under his eyes had a deep blue look. "This is cowardice. I'm responsible to His Excellency. There's no reason for holding up operations."

A long, cold glance from the young general passed into him. "No reason? Do you want to give the Allied fleet its pretext for shooting the whole coastline to bits? Their long-range shells will carry to Antakiya. Do you suppose that cruiser out there is going to stay by itself, Kaimakam? Would you like the French and English to land and set up a new war front in the heart of undefended Syria? What's your opinion, Kaimakam?"

But the Kaimakam, yellowish-brown in the face, was spluttering now through foamy lips: "All that has nothing to do with me! I, as the responsible person, order you——"

He got no further. Since naturally the general's counterorder had not, in the few minutes, reached Turkish gunners, their first shots had begun to crackle from a notch in the North Saddle. And now the long, shapely barrels in the turret of the *Guichen* had begun to turn. There was scarcely time to draw three breaths before—crack after crack—the first shells fell among the domino houses of Suedia, El Eskel, Yedidje. At once the tall chimney of the alcohol factory ran up an American flag. Wooden Turkish houses already flamed.

Ali Risa yelled at the yüs-bashi: "Telephone cease fire, damn you! The saptiehs to evacuate all civilians. Everyone into the valley of the villages!"

The freckled müdir from Salonika, who so far had stood in respectful silence, was seized with frenzy in his turn. His hands flew up to his mouth; he bellowed as though, through all the noise of her guns, he were determined to be heard on board the *Guichen:* "This is a flagrant infringement of international law. . . . Open coastline. . . . Interference with domestic policy. . . ."

But Major-General Ali Risa picked his walking-stick up off the ground and turned to go. His officers crowded in round him. He stopped. "Why shout so, Müdir? You'd better thank Ittihad."

"I don't feel well," moaned the Kaimakam, who, considering the state of his general health, had already exerted himself too much that day. His heavy body sank down. He seemed to do his utmost not to faint. The same words over and over again came spluttering through his blackened lips: "This is the end. . . . This is the end. . . ."

The müdir had to fetch four saptiehs to carry his sick superior down to the valley.

It might well have been supposed that Gabriel, too, would sink to earth, the moment his consciousness of this miracle had fully permeated his spirit, under the sheer weight of such relief. But nothing of the kind! Gabriel was too numbed to feel. The most prudently and carefully chosen words could scarcely render with truth what he felt at that moment. No, not disillusionment. That would be too rough a way of putting it. Rather the need for unwelcome effort, which an organism fagged to death has got to make to readjust itself. Thus the human eye defends itself, coming out of the dark into bright light, against this all too startling change, even though the soul may have longed for it.

Bagradian's first reaction was the order, which he sent along the lines of his defence: "No one to move! Everyone to stop where he is!"

This was a highly important order. Since Gabriel did not know what the Turks intended, and then he, himself, with his own eyes, had not yet seen the flag this warship flew. Also it seemed highly improbable that this ship could or would pick up four and a half thousand people. No less surprising was the effect of this miracle on the defenders, who, after this eternity spent in the expectation of death, lay paralysed in their long, extended order. A boy, breathlessly waving, had brought the news. It did not release one cry; tense silence followed it. But suddenly the lines broke. Those who had heard of this miracle crowded up the hillock to the howitzer emplacement, to their commander. Not this was remarkable, but the change in the deep, gruff voices of these men. Suddenly they piped and whined. High falsetto tones surrounded Gabriel. It sounded almost like a tremulous kind of women's chiding, or the outburst of terrified lunatics. Their voices, before their souls well knew they were saved, ran up into their heads. They obeyed his order at once. They lay down again in extended lines, each with his rifle, as though nothing stupendous had come to pass. Only Teacher Hapeth Shatakhian implored the chief to send him out as envoy to the ship, since he, whose French was so perfect, so flawless his accent, was obviously the man to negotiate. The teacher smiled all over his face. Gabriel, who, by his own example, wanted to keep the decads together till the last danger of a Turkish attack should have passed, let Shatakhian go, with these instructions: Whatever happened, communication must be maintained between the encamped people down on the shore and their armed defenders on the mountain. Ter Haigasun and Bedros Altouni were to board the French ship with Shatakhian. Moreover: the captain of the *Guichen* must instantly be informed of the fact that a French lady, dangerously ill, was in their camp.

The artillery fire which opened against the North Saddle confirmed Bagradian's worst suspicions. The Turk had no thought of dropping his prey without further question. But, as soon as this artillery fire died down again, the big guns on board the *Guichen* dropped neatly crashing shells on to Ottoman villages. The whole Orontes plain might well have been roused for the Last Judgment. Even when Gabriel climbed his observation post, Suedia, El Eskel, Yedidje, and indeed even the distant Ain Yerab gave out smoke and flames. On horses, mules, in ox-carts, in streaming shoals, the people were rushing on for safety into the valley of Yoghonoluk. After a time Gabriel went back beside the howitzers. Already the shells, set to fuse, were standing there behind the carriages. He had intended to swivel his guns round to the north, and, when things had got so far, drop shells into the Turkish advance. He gave up this intention, though he by no means considered the danger past. Gabriel sat on the ground by the howitzers. He stared out, and at the same time, inwards.

"Now perhaps I'll be back in a few weeks in Paris. We shall live in the old flat in the Avenue Kléber, and start life again." But this thought—which an hour ago had been the fantasy of a lunatic—did nothing to fill up his astonishing emptiness. Not a trace of kneeling jubilation, that rush of warmest gratitude to God, warranted by the unthinkable miracle. Gabriel had no desire for Paris, for a flat, for cultivated people, for comfort; no, and not even for a bellyful, a bed and cleanliness. Whatever trace of emotion he managed to find in himself could be described as the nagging desire to be alone; it grew in him from minute to minute. But it would have to be such solitude as there is not. An unpeopled world. A planet without animal needs, or movement. A cosmic hermitage, and he the only person in it, gazing out at peace, without any past, present, and future.

THE new camping-grounds of the village communes were set fairly far apart. Yoghonoluk and Habibli were fairly high up, whereas Bitias, Azir, and Kebussiye had picked out places along the beach, where receding rocks left free a few uneven clearings, grown about with hard, dry shrub.

They had all still been asleep when Teacher Oskanian waved his flag. It was no longer a sleep of human beings, but of dead matter, as rocks or mounds sleep. The crack of doom from the ship's guns broke it. Almost four thousand women, children, greybeards, opened startled eyes to the light of this fourth day of panic. Those down on the beach saw an incredible mirage, born of enfeeblement; it rose quiet on the solid sea. Some stumbled to their feet, to shake off the phantom. Others lay on the hard rock, indifferent to it, chafed to the bone as they were, since their bones had no flesh on them. They did not so much as turn on the other side. But then, among these grown-ups, suddenly, there arose a short-breathed, wheezing whimper, like the weak protest of very sick children. It spread from one to the other of them. And now the feeblest wraiths hovered upright. Boys, who had still more strength in them than anyone, began to clamber up the rocks.

The big cruiser, the *Guichen,* had anchored about half a sea-

781

mile off the coast. A devastating sight awaited its officers and ratings. They saw hundreds of bare skeleton arms held out to them, begging collectively. The human forms of which those arms were a part, and indeed the faces, looked blurred even through a field-glass, like so many ghosts. Added to which a sharp entanglement of thin voices, as of chirruping insects, which had the effect of coming from much further off than it actually did. Then, down between the rocks, more and more of these human grasshoppers came hurrying to increase the number of begging arms. Before the commander of the *Guichen* could decide what to do for these persecuted, two diminutive shapes had dived from a rock, boys it seemed, and begun to struggle towards the ship. They got to within about a hundred yards of her, and then their strength seemed to fail. But a boat had been providentially sent out to them, which took them up. Another boat moved off shorewards. It was to bring back the envoys of these curious "Christians in Need." But it was soon apparent that, when God sends us a miracle, reality has always enough malice in it to make it seem, by a hundred artful tricks, less miraculous. This coast was so difficult to land on, the surf so heavy, that even the well-manned boat of the *Guichen* could scarcely manage to put ashore, and Aram's failure to make his fishery answer was justified. Almost an hour of unsuccessful efforts to land had passed before Ter Haigasun, Altouni, and Hapeth Shatakhian could come on board. This was the hour during which the *Guichen,* provoked thereto by the challenging gunfire on Musa Dagh, sent heavy shells crashing all over the Moslem plain.

When Captain Brisson received the delegation in the officers' mess, his guns had already ceased their fire. Brisson gave a little start of horror at the sight of these men—these three shrivelled bodies hung with rags, these wildly bearded faces with high foreheads and huge eyes. And Ter Haigasun looked the wildest. Half his beard had been singed away. The burn glowed on his right cheek. Since his everyday cassock had been burned in the presbytery-hut, he still wore the borrowed rug draped round his shoulders.

The captain held out his hand. "The priest? The teacher?" he asked.

But Shatakhian gave him no time for further inquiries; he gathered together his whole strength, bowed, and launched out on the long speech, rehearsed aloud on the path to the beach and, later even, in the boat. He began in somewhat inappropriately: *"Mon général . . ."*

When from these long-winded, eastern outpourings, Captain Brisson had managed to disentangle essentials from much that was beside the point, the orator, delighted with his own prowess, stood hoping that so august a hearer might deign a word of praise for his faultless accent and choice vocabulary. Captain Brisson only glanced from one to another of them and asked what was Madame Bagradian's maiden name. Hapeth Shatakhian was delighted to furnish even this, and to proclaim his familiarity with the names of the best French families. And then Ter Haigasun spoke. To the teacher's amazement, indeed disgust, he spoke fluent French, though he had never even troubled to say so, in all these years as school superintendent. He told at once of the hunger and enfeeblement of his people, begging for help without delay, since otherwise many women and children might scarcely get through the next few hours. As he was saying this, Dr. Bedros Altouni collapsed and almost fell off the chair he sat in. Brisson sent at once for café and cognac, and a plentiful meal for the three delegates. Yet neither the old doctor nor the others could manage to swallow more than a few mouthfuls. Meanwhile the ship's commander had summoned the quartermaster and given orders to send out boats immediately with whatever supplies might be available. The ship's doctor, hospital staff, and an armed detachment of marines were also ordered ashore.

Brisson then explained to the Armenians that the *Guichen* was not an independent unit, but the leader of a mixed English

783

and French squadron, under orders to sail north-west along the Anatolian coast. Yesterday evening, three hours before the main body of the fleet, she had put out from the Cyprus bay of Famagusta. The fleet commander, the rear-admiral, was on board the *Jeanne d'Arc,* the flag-ship and vessel of the line. They would have to await his decision. But an hour ago a wireless message had been sent out to the *Jeanne d'Arc.* The envoys need not be afraid; there was no danger that a French admiral would leave so valiant a commune of the persecuted Armenian Christian people to its fate without more ado. Ter Haigasun bent his head, with the singed beard.

"May I permit myself a question, Monsieur le Capitaine? You tell me that your ship is not independent, but under orders. How did it happen then that you came this way along the coast instead of sailing north-west?"

"Gentlemen, I'm sure it must be a long time since you smoked. May I offer you a packet of cigarettes?"

And Brisson handed the teacher a big packet. He turned his grey, naval head to Ter Haigasun, thoughtfully.

"Your question interests me, *mon père,* because in fact I went against my orders, and came a good way out of our course. Why? At about ten we passed the north cape of Cyprus. An hour after midnight I received reports of a big fire on the Syrian coast. It looked as though a fairly large town had been set on fire. A wide expanse of red sky. We were well out to sea, at least thirty miles off land. And now I hear that you'd only set fire to a few huts. Of course fog often acts as a magnifying-lens. Such things are conceivable. Half the sky was red! So, from curiosity—it must have been mere curiosity—I altered our course."

Ter Haigasun rose from his chair. It looked as though he had something very important to say to them. His lips moved. But suddenly, in a few uncertain steps, he went to the wall of the cabin and pressed his face against the glass pane of a porthole. Captain Brisson supposed that the priest, like the old

doctor, was on the verge of a collapse. The priestly face shimmered in rays of sunlight, as though cut in amber.

Ter Haigasun's eyes were sightless with ecstasy as he stammered in Armenian: "The evil only happend . . . to enable
God to show us His goodness."

He raised his hands lightly, as though all this suffering had
been surmounted by its meaning. The Frenchman could not
understand. Bedros Hekim sat asleep, with his head on the
table. But Hapeth Shatakhian was not thinking of the fire
in the Town Enclosure, which began with a sacrilegious altar
flame to end in redemption.

Two hours later the great *Jeanne d'Arc* was on the horizon,
with behind her the English and the French cruisers. The big
troop-ship did not arrive till close on midday. In a wide,
beautifully even line, these blue-grey turreted fighters approached the land, drawing long foam-trails in their wake.
The squadron commander had signalled back to Captain
Brisson that not only would he pick up these Armenian fugitives, and change his course in order to do so, but was himself most anxious to inspect this heroic encampment, where
the offshoots of a Christian people had held their own for forty
days against superior forces of barbarians. The rear-admiral
was a pious, indeed a celebrated Catholic, and this fight of
Armenians in defence of the religion of the Cross had really
moved him.

When the squadron had anchored in perfect symmetry,
there began a sparkling stir on the glassy sea. Bugle-signals
vied with one another. Chains and pulleys creaked. Slowly the
big boats hovered down. Meanwhile the sailors of the *Guichen*
had improvised a kind of landing-jetty at the most accessible
place along the shore, where Pastor Aram's raft came in unexpectedly useful. The rescued people lay, sat, squatted on narrow ledges and watched this sight through half-seeing eyes, as
though it were no concern of theirs. The head-surgeon of

the *Guichen,* with his assistants and medical staff, were busy with the sick and those exhausted with hunger. He praised Bedros Altouni highly, for the fact that yesterday, even when life seemed almost at an end, he had still arranged a separate camp for infected people and those suspected of being so.

Altouni admitted with a sigh that many of these poor people up on the Damlayik had died for want of proper care, though they might quite well have been saved with the usual nursing. The head-surgeon frowned. It was a great responsibility for him to take in these fever patients. But what was to be done? Christians could not simply be left to the mercies of the revengeful Turks. Since the head-surgeon was humane, he gave his Armenian colleague a hint: "Don't say too much about it." The troop-ship was almost empty, with big, well-arranged hospital cabins. The head-surgeon winked at the old doctor not to give it another thought.

Vast supplies of bread and tinned food had been divided up among the healthy, in so far as there were any "healthy" to eat. The ships' cooks had boiled big kettles of potato-soup, and the good-natured French sailors lent their own mess-tins. But the people received all this as though it were none of it real—dream-bread and dream-soup, which could never satisfy. Yet a new state of mind possessed the communes when everyone had gulped down his portion, unchewed, almost untasted. People felt almost lifeless, weary to death, and yet, having eaten, the forty days seemed as remote as some half-forgotten saga. Their bodies might protest against this unaccustomed food (oh, bread, bread, a thousand times desired) —to their souls all this seemed merely normal, as if nothing else had ever been, as if God's grace were no more than "normality."

The rear-admiral landed, with his numerous staff, by the rickety bridge. A swarm of craft shot in the wake of his motor-launch. Detachments of marines with machine-guns had been ordered ashore from every vessel, to protect the squadron commander. These troops landed and invested the narrow ledges of rock in such dense throngs that, hemmed in by innumerable French uniforms, the admiral scarcely managed to get a sight of this camp he was so curious to inspect. Then, as he came on closely through crowds of villagers, he asked for an exact account of the origin and course of this defence. And here Shatakhian got his second chance, a still better one, to air his French and charm an august French ear with his perfect accent and choicely extensive vocabulary. The rear-admiral was a small, dapper old gentleman with a soldierly face, austerely ornate. His cheeks had the brown tan of the sea. A little, snow-white moustache. His light-blue eyes were unrelenting, yet their look seemed mollified by distances. This old gentleman's dapper little body was not clothed in regulation naval uniform, but he wore a comfortable drill suit, to which only the narrow strip of decorations on his chest gave martial distinction. He asked several questions about the fighting strength of the Turks, and then, with his thin bamboo cane, pointed up the walls of rock and once more informed his suite of his decision to inspect the plateau and encampment. One of them ventured to observe that this would entail a climb of hundreds of metres, which perhaps might be too much for the chief. Nor would they be able to get back on board in time for lunch. This audacious officer got no answer. The rear-admiral gave the sign to proceed. His adjutant had to send off secret instructions to the marines to hurry on up the winding path at the double and reach the Damlayik plateau before the admiral. Such an incursion into enemy territory was a highly risky proceeding. The mountain seemed surrounded by Turkish troops and Turkish guns. It might lead to inconvenient surprises. But the chief's well-known obstinacy made any further objections hopeless. It was decided, therefore, to drop a few shells, in the course of this picnic, in villages along the coast, to warn the Turks to keep their distance.

The long-suffering adjutant had also to arrange for a special snack, since the effort entailed by such a climb might well prove a strain on an elderly naval officer. It was one of the admiral's pet foibles to show the younger men surrounding him how sound he was of wind and limb. He went blithely on, well ahead of the rest. Sato was his alpine guide. She darted on and back, and on again, as her habit was, like a young mongrel bitch, covering the ground at least three times. Never in all her life had the orphan of Zeitun beheld such resplendent shapes. Her greedy, magpie eyes devoured these uniforms with their rows of medals, their gold braid, while her paw scraped out the last fat in a bully-beef tin. Her body glowed with the brandy the sailors had given her. She wriggled it urgently, in the indescribable rags of what had once been her "butterfly frock," cajoling these dazzling gods. And she stretched out her dark brown paw to them while a sound indigenous to these regions came almost unbidden to her lips: "Bakshish."

The officers stopped several times, looked about, and began to admire the beauties of this treed and watered Musa Dagh. More than one was inspired to the same description as Gonzague Maris: "Riviera." Others again were charmed by its wildly virginal quality. The last to ascend were two young naval lieutenants. So far neither had said anything, nor had they even admired the view. The one, an Englishman, stood still, though he did not turn back to look at the sea, but stared straight at the wall of rock in front of him.

"I say, you know, those Armenians! I don't feel as though I'd been looking at people; nothing but eyes."

GABRIEL had not broken his lines. Though he had had reports that the Turkish forces were being withdrawn, both north and south, he seemed still to put no faith in this peace. It may merely have been a matter of war-morale, still no armed defender should quit his post till his people's fate has been fully determined. But perhaps there were deeper reasons for his austerity. The new Gabriel had advanced too far along unknown paths to be able to find his way back to the old so quickly. The forty days had worked in him a transformation which held him banned by a kind of magic. Many a rougher man had the same experience. No one in his line protested or groused against Bagradian's long resistance, least of all the conscience-stricken deserters, who could not do enough to display their servility. Gabriel had spoken to the decads. No one must fancy they were safe till their last women and children were on board. Their steadiness must show the French the worth of the Armenian nation. They must leave this camp and their old home as undefeated soldiers, rifles in hand, in the steadiest order. Nor would he consent to leave the howitzers shamefully undefended on the Damlayik, for the Turks to take back that night. He intended rather to present such magnificent trophies to the French nation.

The fact that Ter Haigasun had had ample supplies sent up to the Damlayik, bread, marmalade, wine, and tinned meat, was no doubt as persuasive as Gabriel's words. Also tobacco. The men lay about in a pleasant half-sleep, better pleased with their long rest than they would have been at having to move, no matter where.

Their rest ended when the marines appeared on the plateau to march straight to the howitzer emplacement in one long, extended line. Then the Armenians sprang up and with shouts of joy rushed to meet the French. These sailors, in smart, clean uniforms, were in glaring contrast to the scarecrows, ragged and famished, of Musa Dagh. The men at last were fully conscious of this marvellous triumph of their enterprise. Then came the group of officers, and Gabriel went slowly to meet it. His approach was casual, he would have been ashamed to make it seem too soldierly. He had left his rifle on the ground. He looked now like a huntsman or a mining-engineer. He took off his dented sun-helmet to confront the rear-admiral.

That old gentleman eyed him keenly for a second before holding out his hand. "You were the commander?"

Gabriel pointed at once to the howitzers. It seemed most important to show these rescuers that he did not come to them empty-handed:

"Monsieur l'Amiral, I give over to you and the French nation these two guns which we captured from the Turks."

The rear-admiral, who possessed a highly developed ceremoniousness, stood at the salute. All the other officers drew themselves up. "I thank you, Commander, in the name of the French nation, which receives these Armenian trophies of victory."

He held out his hand again to Bagradian. "Did you yourself capture these howitzers?"

"No, my young son, who was killed."

A long and general silence followed this. The rear-admiral pushed aside a stone with his bamboo cane. He turned to his escort. "Will it be possible to get these guns down, and on board?"

The expert of whom he asked it looked rather dubious. Given the necessary assistance, it would, with the greatest difficulty, be possible, if they could have a whole day at their disposal.

The admiral thought it over for a minute. He decided: "See to it these guns are rendered useless. Better blow them up, but carefully, please!"

So much the better, Gabriel thought; two pieces of artillery less in the world. And yet he was sorry. For Stephan's sake.

The admiral proffered consolation: "You have done the good cause most signal service, Monsieur le Commandant, even though these howitzers are destroyed."

This brought the transition from ceremony to practical matters. The rear-admiral asked for a complete account of Gabriel's battles and defences. As Gabriel briefly described them, he grew conscious of the deepest impatience. These kempt and soigné officers in their smart uniforms seemed as faintly, patronizingly interested in a reality which constricted the heart as they might have been in any indifferent piece of amateur soldiering. The three battles? They had been by no means the reality. What did these electro-plated bigwigs know of the Armenian destiny, of the gradual, slow undermining of every individual life up there? His impatience became tinged with disgust. Couldn't he simply turn his back on them and walk away? Now he was merely a civilian, and he should be looking after Juliette and Iskuhi, to make sure that they were properly bestowed. No—in Christ's name! The French, after all, were miraculous saviours; they had a right to eternal gratitude. At last the pertinacious rear-admiral expressed the wish to see their chief sector, the North Saddle. He had already whispered to his officers to take careful notes of all they heard. He no doubt intended a precise report to the French Admiralty. This rescue of seven Armenian villages was, after all, not merely significant; it was highly decorative. So that therefore there was nothing left for Gabriel but to satisfy the admiral's wish. He sent along word to Chaush Nurhan the Lion. At the same time, led by a few orderly-scouts, a detachment of marines with a machine-gun, to protect the admiral, went ahead. When half an hour later Gabriel and the officers climbed the Saddle, Chaush Nurhan had already disposed his men in exemplary lines, to receive the French as soldiers should.

Gabriel, not heeding the admiral, went straight up to his weatherbeaten sergeant, whom he embraced. "Chaush Nurhan! It's all over now! Thank you! And I thank every one of you!"

The bearded men broke their neat rank and surrounded Gabriel. Many of them snatched his hand to kiss. This eager acclamation of their leader had in it, too, a dash of mistrust and dislike of these very resplendent guests. But the officers seemed profoundly affected by this scene, so much too manly to be soldierly. When the rear-admiral had briefly examined the trenches and rock barricades, he considered it his obvious duty to express esteem for Gabriel Bagradian and the officers with him, in a speech. This speceh, although volubly Gallic, had in it the astringent severity of the admiral's profession and of his creed. "Monsieur le Commandant," he began, "today in every country, and on all seas, deeds are being done of the highest valour. But these are trained soldiers who confront each other. Here, on Musa Dagh, it was otherwise. You had no trained men at your disposal, only simple, peaceable peasants and craftsmen. And yet, under your leadership, this handful of insufficiently armed villagers not only held its own against an enemy many times as strong, but emerged victorious in the desperate struggle for bare life. This deed merits not to be forgotten. It was only possible with God's help. God helped you because you fought for more than yourselves, for His holy Cross. You, therefore, Monsieur, have given proof of the most exalted of all heroisms—Christian heroism, which defends something more precious than hearth and home. The French nation thanks you out of my mouth, and is proud to be able to assist you. I shall be delighted to bring you all, to the last man, to a place of safety, and herewith inform you that my squadron will convey you to an Egyptian port, to Port Said, or Alexandria. . . ."

As Gabriel bowed the deepest gratitude in answer to this sincerely felt little speech, cordially grasping the rear-admiral's small, thin hand, he casually thought: "Port Said? Alexandria? I? What should I do there? Live in a concentration camp? Why? . . ."

The clear, hard eyes of the little admiral had in them an almost fatherly look of sympathy. "Monsieur Bagradian, I ask you to be my guest for the voyage, on the *Jeanne d'Arc* . . ."

He awaited no thanks, but drew out a big, gold, bourgeois watch, from its chamois-leather case, and glanced uneasily at it. "And now may I have the honour of being presented to Madame Bagradian? I used to know her father very well."

In the night Juliette had made fast the entrance to her tent with every available strap and bit of string. For her lifeless hands it had been an exhausting task, and she could scarcely drag herself back to bed again. It was not any fear of plundering thieves which caused her to shut her tent so carefully. Strangely enough, the whole deserter episode, the grimacing mask of the long-haired thief, Sato's hands stripping off her sheets, had passed Juliette by like any other dream. She made fast her tent to prevent its ever being light again, to keep another day from ever beginning, so that she might be left alone in bed, with her beloved, lace-trimmed little cushion, off which her head should never again be lifted. She proposed a kind of walling-up for herself. And so, as familiar darkness enclosed the chrysalis of her being, she felt frostily at peace. Now she had never lived on Musa Dagh, never lost a son, never known that Turks were coming nearer and nearer to kill her. Magically, the inside of her tent had become the innermost refuge of Juliette, beyond which there was no longer anything but the vague sounds of a dangerous world. Her reason had long since been unseated, her being sat inconceivably secure.

Towards morning the little gong outside the curtain was loudly struck. Juliette never stirred. Nor did Avakian's begging, imploring voice, which she recognized, move her to reply. Then came the cracks of the howitzer-fire, and the terrifying shell from the *Guichen*. But for Juliette it was still dark night, and she crept even closer under her coverlets, so that nothing should worry her in the grave. Her fears for the darkness of her sepulchre were stronger than any instinctive panic. Her sick memory forgot each shell as it was fired. She crouched closer and closer into herself not to hear these voices. But they kept assailing her. And now even her tent walls heaved, being wildly shaken from without. Were the Turks there?

Kristaphor's voice chimed in with Avakian's: "Madame, please! Open! Open at once, please! Madame!"

The tent heaved more and more violently; Juliette raised her head once. And now she also recognized Mairik Antaram.

"Answer, my darling, please, for Christ's sake! A wonderful piece of good luck!"

Juliette turned over on her side. She knew what these Armenians called "good luck." Let Gabriel come, too, it makes no difference, I shall stay where I am, I won't be drawn out. Who, after all, is this Gabriel Bagradian? Is my name also Bagradian by any chance? Juliette Bagradian? At last somebody outside slit up the laces, impetuously broke open this insecure vault. But she turned her back on the intruders, to show that, whenever she chose, she could be alone, in her own world. Avakian, Antaram, Altouni, were yelling, in strange, little high-pitched voices, something about a French warship called the *Guichen*. Juliette pretended to be unconscious, but pricked up her ears, and decided, with the incredulous mistrust of all neurotics: a trap! Had not Dr. Altouni only last night tried to force her to leave her beloved tent, her own, her very own—to go off and live with all the others, those filthy animals, who made her feel sick and hated her. No doubt this clumsy trick was concocted by Gabriel and Iskuhi, this story of a *French* ship was to lure her out, put her at their mercy, with nowhere to hide. But Juliette was not to be got so easily. Her enemies should not manage to dislodge her from this motherly and beneficent encasement in which she need not know any reality. Juliette let Avakian, Antaram, and Kristaphor beg and whine, and lapsed into unconsciousness.

When at last all attempts proved useless, the old woman shrugged. "Let her be! There's plenty of time."

But Avakian and Kristaphor dragged the mishandled trunks outside the tent and loyally began to pack and tidy all that

794

had not been stolen or torn to shreds. Gabriel sent to fetch them before they had finished.

Then, still early that morning, the curtain was again drawn back, and there stood two men with Mairik Antaram. But these were two young men, in blue uniforms, with sparkling buttons and Red Cross bands round their left arms. Juliette, stiff on her back, saw two chubby, rosy, male faces, with clear, merry eyes. A delicious, startled commotion at the sight of the inexpressibly akin went shuddering through her. The shorter of the two young men saluted her stiffly; his brotherly voice spoke the sounds of a vanished world: "Sorry to disturb you, Madame. We're the hospital orderlies of the *Guichen*. We have orders from the head-surgeon to carry Madame down with all the rest. We'll be back later. Would Madame be so good as to be ready?"

And the little fellow drew himself up, his hand went up in salute to his sailor's cap, while the other, with clumping, embarrassed steps, came on into the tent to set down a thermos flask beside the looking-glass, a dish of butter, and two rolls of fine white bread. "Head-surgeon's orders, tea, bread, butter, for Madame, just to go on with . . ."

He announced it like the progress of a battle, clicking his heels and turning his snub-nosed, chubby profile towards the bed, without appearing to see the woman on it. A deliciously clumsy boy! But Juliette emitted a whispering sigh, whereupon the two hospital orderlies, feeling that perhaps they disturbed the patient, clumped out of the tent on noisy tiptoe. They followed Mairik Antaram to the hospital-hut, which the flames had spared. There the whole hospital staffs of the battleships had collected, with stretchers, to carry sick and wounded down to the coast.

Juliette stretched out two nostalgic arms towards her vanishing compatriots, and then flung off the sheet. She sat up on the edge of the bed. Her chrysalis sheath had split at last. Covering her face with both hands, she ran fingers through her wildly tousled hair. In horror, she whispered: "Frenchmen! Frenchmen! What do I look like! Frenchmen!"

And then it was as though, in this dried-up body, there shot to life a pillar of the old, flaming energy. She sat down before the glass. Her stiff, shaky fingers confused every *objet de toilette* that the dressing-table still displayed. She daubed on rouge, without having rubbed off the face cream, and so looked more sickly and withered than ever. She worked away at her head with a brush and comb, whispering: "What do I look like!" again and again. She was too weak to manage to put her hair up. Then she put her head down on her arms and began to sob quite uncontrollably. But self-pity as usual proved so soothing that its soft caress made her forget she had any hair, and she left it hanging. A new, sharp panic. "Frenchmen! Frenchmen! What have I got to put on!" She began to look about for her things, the wardrobe-trunk, all the other luggage—nothing! The tent was empty! Juliette rushed like a mad thing round and round those few square yards. It was the old nightmare. She was being forced to attend a soirée, the most brilliant soirée, in her nightgown, with bare feet. After long, vain searchings, she ventured to put her nose outside the tent. The clear, gold September sunlight nearly drove her into it again. But the next minute she was on her knees by the wardrobe-trunk. . . . Who'd played this dirty, common trick on her? Iskuhi? Everything was in ribbons, crumbled, turned inside out. Not one frock, of all those faded, last year's rags. Juliette had nothing to wear! And yet she must look her best, since these were Frenchmen!

Mairik Antaram found Juliette sitting on the ground, amid heaps of such slips, stockings, frocks, and shoes as the deserters had left her. She was too exhausted to move, but she clamoured obstinately: "The French are here! The French are here! What have I got to put on? . . ."

Mairik Antaram stared at the invalid, unable to believe her ears. Was it conceivable that this woman, who scarcely had managed to say a word ever since she had ceased to be delirious, the woman who had put forth all her strength to defend herself against the horror of knowledge—that now her mind could so run on clothes? But slowly Antaram understood. It was not vanity. Why, her brothers were coming! She was shy, she wanted to be worthy of them! Madame Altouni knelt beside Juliette and, in her turn, rummaged among gay heaps. But whatever she picked out made Juliette angry. After a long time, during which the invalid, in this curious fashion, defied her fate, and Mairik Antaram displayed celestial patience, a frock found acceptance at last. To be sure it was a stiff and formal frock, lace-trimmed at the opening round the throat. While the old woman, who really had little skill in such subtle arts, was with the greatest difficulty helping the almost inanimate Juliette to get into it, the patient moaned: "It's all wrong!"

But would any frock have been the right one in which to welcome rescuing brothers, since for broken lives there can be no rescuer?

GABRIEL hurried on ahead to prepare her for the rear-admiral's visit. She was sitting on the edge of her bed when he reached her. Mairik was holding a cup of tea and petting the refractory Juliette as though she were a spoilt child. "If you want to look your best for the Frenchmen, you must keep up your strength, dear, or all your clothes will be no use . . ."

Juliette stood up with formality as though a stranger had come in, whom she must follow. Mairik Antaram left the tent with a glance from one to the other of them. She took one of the rolls, since she herself was nearly dead with hunger. Gabriel saw his old life; it confronted him in a livid flash of perception, and he knew that the way back to it could not be bridged. This old life was wearing a stiff, taffeta frock, every movement of which rustled with memories. But the cheeks and limbs of the old life were shrunken and colourless; its form

797

could scarcely keep upright and aroused compassion in him. How close to him she had still been as an invalid! Only now, as he saw her in formal silks, could he measure the gulf of the forty days. He had to talk to her very guardedly: "Thank God, my dear, you're almost as you used to be . . ."

He asked if she felt she had the strength to come a few steps to meet the admiral of the French squadron. He was sure she would not want to receive him here, in this dark sick-tent. Juliette looked round the place which so recently she had chosen to be her sepulchre. Then she put out her hands in a queer little gesture of longing for her lace-edged pillow. Gabriel took her by the arm.

"You'll have all your things there with you tonight, Juliette. They shan't forget anything."

But Juliette, in spite of this appeasement, turned again at the door of her tent, like Eurydice, towards the dark.

The admiral came with only his adjutant and a young officer. He had been warned not to come too close to this convalescent. The infectious fever on Musa Dagh was apparently a very dangerous species. But the admiral was a valiant seaman, on whom warnings usually had the contrary effect. In his stiff little steps, which over-emphasized those of youth, he came to her and kissed her hand. "You too, Madame, as a Frenchwoman, a stranger, have played a considerable part in the sufferings and heroic deeds on this mountain. Permit me to wish you a speedy recovery."

"And France, Monsieur?"

"France is in the midst of terrible trials, Madame, and must hope that God will show her His mercy."

The sight of Juliette really seemed to perturb the old gentleman. He took her shrivelled hand between both his. "Do you know, *mon enfant,* that this must be the first time I've set eyes on you, since you grew up. . . . You must have been quite a little girl the last time, when I spent a whole day with your parents not long after they married. I was never a very intimate friend of your father's, but I think that, when we were young men, we frequented more or less the same world. . . ."

Juliette let out a little sob, but it brought no tears; only strange, disconnected chatter: "But naturally . . . the house was sold after Papa's death . . . and Maman . . . Maman lives now . . . Ah! I forget the street! . . . You know nothing of her, Monsieur? But probably you'll know my brother-in-law. . . . I mean the one in the Ministry of Marine . . . a high official . . . What *is* his name? . . . My head! Coulomb, of course, Jacques Coulomb. . . . You know him? I so seldom see my sister. . . . But when I get back to Paris, I shall see all my friends again, *n'est-ce pas?* . . . You *will* take me to Paris?"

Juliette tottered. The admiral lent her his support. Gabriel ran into the tent for a chair. The invalid sat. But weak as she was, she could still chatter. Presumably she felt herself obliged to make conversation. Her gabble became stiffer every minute, more like a parrot. She mentioned more and more people, mutual acquaintance, so she supposed. Her talk jumped disconnectedly from one to another of them.

The old seaman grew more and more uncomfortable. At last he called to one of his young men: *"Mon ami,* you'll see to everything and accompany Madame on board. The *Jeanne d'Arc* is a warship, so you mustn't expect to be too comfortable. We'll do everything we possibly can to render your voyage agreeable, my dear child."

Even when the admiral, accompanied some of the way by Gabriel, had departed, Juliette's parrot-voice still chattered on. The young officer, left by his chief to escort and protect, sat nervously eyeing those poor pale lips, out of which spluttered endless questions which he could not answer. And the shadows under Juliette's eyes grew deeper. The officer was very relieved when Bagradian came, and then in a few more minutes the marines, who carried a stretcher.

At first Juliette struggled against it. "I won't lie down on that. What a horror! I'd far rather walk."

"You can't, Juliette. Be reasonable now, and lie down. Believe me, I shouldn't mind being carried down in one myself."

The two pink and white faces smiled encouragement. "Don't be afraid, Madame, we'll carry you as though you were glass. You won't feel a thing!"

Juliette surrendered and, on the stretcher, lay perfectly still, as she had before. Gabriel brought out a rug, put her beloved cushion under her head, and gave her hand-bag to the officer. He stroked her hair. "Don't worry. . . . Nothing that matters will be left——"

He broke off suddenly. The officer glanced at him inquiringly. Gabriel nodded. The stretcher-bearers lifted her up, took the first steps. An excited Sato waited a little way off, to act as guide.

"I'll soon have caught up with you," shouted Gabriel.

Juliette shifted round so vehemently, that the stretcher-bearers stopped and put her down. A mad, twitching face turned back to Gabriel, and a voice screamed—a voice he had never heard her use: "I say! Stephan . . . Look after Stephan!"

In deliverance even, the cup of sorrow was not full. A loud voice kept calling from the Tomasian tent: "Gabriel Bagradian! Come along, man!"

Gabriel had supposed Iskuhi to be with her sick brother. She was nowhere about. He went into Aram's tent. Bygones had now become absurdly indifferent. He found the pastor excited and feverish.

"Where's Iskuhi, Gabriel Bagradian, for Christ's sake! Where have you left Iskuhi?"

"Iskuhi? She was with me for a time after midnight up on the howitzer emplacement. Then I asked her to go to my wife."

"That's just it!" shouted the pastor. "This morning I was still perfectly certain that Iskuhi was with you in the line. She hasn't come back—she's disappeared. . . . I've sent out to look for her. . . . They've been looking hours for her. . . . The French stretcher-bearers have been waiting a long time to carry me down. But I won't leave the mountain without Iskuhi. . . . If anything's happened to her . . . I won't leave the mountain at all."

He caught hold of Gabriel's arm and pulled himself up, in spite of his wound. "It's my fault, Bagradian—I can't explain to you now—but I'm the guilty one. It's only just that God should be punishing me personally in my child and sister, after He's saved us all. And my wife was also the instrument of His justice."

"Where is your wife?" asked Gabriel steadily.

"She's gone running down to the beach. With the child. They told her there was some milk down there. I couldn't keep her."

His excitement got the better of the wounded Tomasian. He tried to get up, but fell back at once. "Damnation! You see I can do nothing! I can't move. Do something, Gabriel Bagradian! It's partly your sin with Iskuhi. . . . Even you . . ."

"Wait, Pastor. . . . I'll go."

Gabriel said this in a weary voice. He moved off across Three-Tent Square and then some way further. He did not get far, but sat down somewhere to stare up at the sky. One thought trailed through his weary mind: So this is what it means to be saved! He tried to recall his talk with Iskuhi in the night. But his mind had kept no details, only a spectral breath of resignation. She had come to remind him of his promise to be with her at the very end. But he had turned her away, sent her to Juliette. Iskuhi must be somewhere safe. Had not that been his thought? But she had wanted something he could not give, a resolute, happy belief in their destruction. He had had to rob her of that courageous belief. Where was Iskuhi now? Gabriel could not have said what made him so certain that Iskuhi was no longer alive.

Gabriel was wrong. Iskuhi lived. Even as he set to his lips the whistle which should summon further help, Kevork the dancer had discovered her. Only just in time! The sole explanation was that Iskuhi must have lost her way in the dark on the stamped-out path, and so fallen into a little ravine, or rather a hollow, not very deep, overgrown with shrubs. Certainly this hollow was some way off any beaten track, on the very uneven ground which leads up to Dish Terrace. But what it was she had sought in that spectral region, between midnight and morning, no one could say. No harm had come to her, more than a few scratches on arms and legs; no wound, no broken bones, not even a shock, not even a sprain. Yet this fall in the dark had turned that state of deadly weakness, against which she had struggled for days, yet cherished, to final collapse. When Kevork carried her in, in arms which had certainly known very different burdens, she was fully conscious, had huge, almost merry eyes, but could not speak. Luckily among the hospital orderlies who had still the last patients to carry down, there was a young second surgeon of the *Guichen*. He gave Iskuhi a strong heart-stimulant, but insisted that it was urgently necessary to get her on board as soon as possible to avoid the worst. So without delay or many words both Iskuhi and Pastor Tomasian were strapped on the stretchers. Gabriel had scarcely time to give Kristaphor orders that, as soon as the luggage had been moved out, the three tents and everything in them were to be set on fire without delay.

GABRIEL kept close beside Iskuhi, as often as it was possible to do so. But the path was almost too narrow for one man, and in places where the bare rock-wall opened out on their right, the bearers had all they could do to get past, with their

loads. Just ahead of them swayed the wounded pastor. Iskuhi
came next, with the young doctor. But she was not the last
of the procession, since three men crippled with wounds from
the fight of August 23, and a woman in labour, brought up
the rear. Behind these again a swarm of stragglers, men from
the decads who had been to what was left of their family huts
to rake about in the ashes for anything the fire might have
spared. The bearers halted two or three times on the wider
ledges for a rest. Then Gabriel bent down over Iskuhi. But
he himself could scarcely speak. And two paces further lay
Pastor Aram. The doctor kept returning every minute to make
Iskuhi take a sip of milk, or feel her pulse.

Gabriel whispered disconnectedly: "Where were you trying
to get to, Iskuhi? . . . What were you after . . . out
there? . . ."

Her eyes answered: "Why are you asking me something I
don't know? . . . It was as though I hovered up off the
ground. . . . We've scarcely any time left, less than we had
in the night."

He knelt beside her and put his hand under her head, as
though this would make her speak. Yet his own words were
scarcely audible: "Any pain, Iskuhi?"

Her eyes understood him at once and answered: "No, I don't
feel my body. But what really hurts me is that this should have
happened as it has. Wouldn't it have been better without this
ship? This is a kind of end, but not ours, Gabriel. . . ."

Gabriel's eyes could neither speak nor perceive as Iskuhi's
could. And so, therefore, he said something entirely false:
"This is just a collapse, Iskuhi. . . . It's because you've had
nothing to eat." And, turning to the surgeon, he spoke French:
"Isn't it, Doctor? In three days, when we've got to Port Said,
you'll be feeling ever so much better. You're still so young,
so young, Iskuhi."

Her eyes darkened and answered sternly: "At a moment
like this you ought not to be saying such banal things to me,

Gabriel. I don't in the least mind whether I die or go on living. You're wrong if you think I want to die. Perhaps I shall live. But can't you see it'll all be different, once the ships have taken us on board; even for us it will. We can only really be together for as long as we've still the earth of Musa Dagh under our feet; you as my love, I as your sister."

Not all, but much of this, Gabriel seemed to have understood. His next whisper came out hesitant, like the mirrored echo of what her eyes said: "Yes, where will we be . . . you and I . . . sister?"

Her lips opened at last, to form two syllables, their passion contradicted all she had said: "With you . . ."

The stretchers were lifted again for the easy remainder of the way. Already many voices had arisen. Down on the beach, on the narrow ledges, there was a dangerous crowding and jostling, made still worse by the many sailors who, on various pretexts, had got shore-leave. Embarkation was already in full swing, a hundred times entangled confusion, and wild yelling. Gabriel was besieged on all sides with demands, requests, questions, petitions. The people, for no reason, had made of him the secret worker of this miracle by which they were saved. And now, as the kinsman of mighty France, the man sent by God, it would still be his business to go on helping his fellow-countrymen in their exile far from Musa Dagh. His former enemies on the Council, Thomas Kebussyan, and his lady, with the quick mouse-eyes, most urgent of all, could not now show him enough obsequious cringing. He had to fight his way on through a flood of excited demands for protection. So that when, at last, he came to the landing-stage, the boat with Aram and Iskuhi had put off, ahead of all the others, by order of the officer in charge of sick-transport. Juliette, too, had long been taken on board the *Jeanne d'Arc* in the admiral's motor-boat. The sunlight glared off the sea in unbearably dazzling splintered rays. Many boats were on their way to the ships, others were moving along the coast.

Iskuhi lay hidden in hers. Gabriel could make out only the rigid shape of Hovsannah, clutching to her breast her miserable bundle, the quiet first-born of Musa Dagh.

THE embarcation proceeded slowly. There were many difficulties to surmount. Though a good half of the villagers might easily have been taken aboard the troop-ship, the doctors unanimously opposed this easy solution of the room problem. It would be far too risky to herd together hundreds of people in close proximity to their sick. It must, on the contrary, be so managed, that only these sick, the enfeebled, the doubtful cases, the waifs and strays, were shipped on the transport steamer. They must be kept well apart from the crews and from healthy Armenians. The wretched troop-ship, therefore, in contrast to the warships—even more to the splendid *Jeanne d'Arc*—was a Gehenna, an abode of woe, of destitute flotsam and jetsam. A special medical commission, composed of doctors and naval officers, examined every single Armenian for lice and disease before he was classified. Its methods were very severe. Anyone in the least doubtful was banished at once to the transport. Ter Haigasun was the only one of the former leaders on Musa Dagh with a seat on this classification board. Bedros Altouni's strength had ebbed precariously in the course of the day. The head-surgeon had long since shipped him on the *Guichen*. The mukhtars, too, seemed to regard their term of office as at an end. They had retired into private life, as the fathers of families. Nor did the teachers, or any of the subordinate village priests, consider this a concern of theirs. They had ceased to worry.

So that only Ter Haigasun remained to defend the interests of the people, that is to say to persuade the officers and doctors not to separate families unnecessarily, and to see to it that even the troop-ship got the right passengers.

Gabriel approached the medical board, which functioned not far from the landing-jetty. He put his two hands on Ter

Haigasun's shoulders. Ter Haigasun turned. His face was as quietly waxen again as ever. Only his singed beard and the burn on his cheek told of the last events on the Damlayik. His shyly resolute eyes remained fixed on Gabriel. It had seldom happened in all these days: "Good that you've come, Gabriel Bagradian; I've something to ask you."

Ter Haigasun was speaking very quietly, though certainly the French would never have understood his Armenian. "The two worst scoundrels have disappeared, I mean Oskanian and Kilikian; and some others as well . . ."

"Kilikian's dead," said Gabriel, and the thought did not worry him in the least.

A brief glint in Ter Haigasun's eyes seemed to indicate that he understood. He pointed across to the flat rock, where a knot of Armenian men stood herded together. "Well, this is my question. Have those scoundrels over there any right to be saved? Oughtn't I to drive them back?"

Gabriel took a second or so to answer. "Had we any right to be saved? And who's doing the saving? Anyway, we, the saved, haven't the right to exclude anyone from safety."

Ter Haigasun's eyes were twinkling. "Good. I only wanted to make certain . . ."

The priest was now no longer the sorry sight he had been that morning. A ship's chaplain had supplied a coat. His old trick of hiding his hands in his sleeves forced them, with an unaccustomed movement, into his pockets. "I'm glad, Gabriel Bagradian, to find that we still agree about everything as we always did."

And now his smile had almost a look of embarrassed tenderness. Gabriel stood a long time to watch the commission. Since his thoughts were far from it, he saw only empty coming and going.

At last Ter Haigasun turned, in some surprise. "Still here, Gabriel Bagradian? The motor-launch for the *Jeanne d'Arc* has put out again. . . . Look! You shouldn't stop here helping me. Your duty's finished. Mine isn't, yet. So go with God's blessing and rest. I shall be on the *Guichen.*"

Something in Gabriel impeded any final leave-taking. "Perhaps I'll be back here later to look for you, Ter Haigasun."

He pushed his way back through the waiting crowds and went aimlessly a few paces up towards the mountain path. Avakian came down it to meet him. After him Kristaphor, Missak, Kevork, dragging the Bagradian trunks. The faithful Avakian had saved everything which human strength and ingenuity could manage to drag down this steep path. Only the bedding and the furniture had been left to burn in the tents.

Gabriel laughed. "Hullo, Avakian! Why all these exertions? This looks like a pleasure trip up the Nile."

Reproachfully, through nickel-rimmed glasses, the student gazed at his employer with the eyes of a poor man who knows the value of things better than the unsuspecting rich.

But Gabriel put his arm into the tutor's, and held him fast. "Avakian, there's something more I want you to do for me. I've been thinking all this time how we can manage it. I'm endlessly in need of rest. I must have it. And it's just what I shan't get in the next few days. The admiral has asked me to sit at his table. So that for hours on end I shall have to talk to indifferent strangers, tell them stories, brag, or pretend to be modest, all equally tiring. Anyway, another prison! And I won't do it! You understand, Avakian? I refuse! At least for these three days I'll be alone—entirely alone. And so I've decided not to go on the *Jeanne d'Arc,* but on the troop-ship. There there'll be only a few officers. They'll be bound to give me a berth to myself, and I shall rest."

Samuel Avakian seemed horrified. "But, Effendi, the troop-ship is certain to be kept in quarantine."

"Well, I'm not afraid of quarantine."

"But wouldn't it be another prison, which might last even longer than forty days?"

"If I really want it, they'll let me out."

Avakian sought hesitant objections. "Won't you be hurting the admiral, who, after all, is our good angel?"

"That's just it. And this is where I want you to help me, Avakian. You must go to him at once in my name, and apologize with some really convincing reason. Tell him the troop-ship has some of our most independable people on board, people without prospects. And say there's been no time to get the thing properly organized. Tell him there must be somebody there who can guarantee to keep people like that in order. Say I've undertaken it. . . ."

Avakian did not seem in the least convinced. But now Gabriel insisted: "It's really quite a good reason. You needn't worry. An old sailor like that will perfectly well understand a scruple of that kind. He just won't give it another thought, believe me. Well—do it, Avakian, please!"

The student still hesitated. "So we aren't going to meet for the next few days?"

These words sounded anxious. But Gabriel glanced across at the embarcation jetty. "Time to go, Avakian! The motor-launch of the *Jeanne d'Arc* mustn't have to make any more journeys. Stick to those papers of mine for the present."

The motor-launch was signalling impatiently. Avakian scarcely had time to shake Gabriel's hand. Gabriel watched him go, lost in thought. Then he asked one of the officers what time the last boat would leave for the troop-ship. Most patients were on board, he was told, the rest, those told off to travel on her, would be shipped last of all. That may go on for hours, thought Gabriel, watching the dense crowd which still pushed and shoved round the isolation commission on the landing-place. He felt rather pleased and rejoiced to know himself free of the admiral and life on board the *Jeanne d'Arc*. He lounged away towards the mountain path. Since he had so long to wait, it would be a relief to get far from these sounds of cackling women, the glare of this September sun, into shadows and quiet. Gabriel had to pass the place where the lousy herded, waiting, sent there to be out of the way of the more favoured. Many of them, especially the churchyard folk, had gone there at once to avoid the trouble of submitting themselves to inspection for lice. Bagradian watched his future fellow-passengers. Sato grinned, ran a bit of the way with him, and stuck out a begging paw. She had never done it in Yoghonoluk. A few contrite deserters sprang up eagerly. Nunik and the other keening-women sat on sacks whose mouldy treasures they intended to carry off to another continent. They held long staffs in their left hands, with the right they touched their breasts, lips, foreheads, to greet the master, Gabriel Bagradian, the last, the son of Mesrop, grandson of Avetis Bagradian, the great benefactor and founder of churches. But in him Nunik, the timeless, beheld the child at whose birth she secretly had worked a magic, carefully hidden away from Bedros Hekim, traced crosses on walls and lintel with her sis, to drive off devils. The blind, white-headed prophets crouched on the rock, gently singing to themselves. Thick clusters of flies were on their eyelids, and they did not trouble to drive them off. Unmoved by what had been, untroubled by what was to come, these prophets sang in their low voices. They scarcely cared to ask how all this had happened; having lost no homes, they followed only the rumours in their minds, and let Nunik, Wartuk, Manushak, the guides of the blind, lead them, wherever they might choose. Their frail hummings sounded pleasantly mournful, with rapturous, high-pitched, treble quaverings.

Yet this was the sound which made Gabriel's heart sink. It lured Stephan to his side. He climbed on and on up the path as far as he could get from the song of the blind. But in exchange he had soon to listen to Juliette's parrot-chatter all over again, and then to her scream: "Look after Stephan!" He went on, faster and faster, thinking too deeply to know his thoughts. At last he stopped in surprise; he had come so far up the mountain. But this seemed a pleasant enough spot. A natural rock-seat, shaded with myrtle and arbutus, with a mossy back to it. Here, in this pleasant place, he sank down. From here he could see everything below him, the swarm on the rocky beach, the five blue-grey, motionless ships, fast soldered to their thick waves. The troop-ship was the farthest out to sea. The *Guichen,* with Iskuhi, was the next. The pastor's fishing-raft had been roped in firmly to the rocks. Over it the marines had set a plank-bridge. The rescued multitude shuffled in single file, down the long plank, to reach the boats. Often the whole contraption began to sway, spray flew up, and the women screeched. This picture put everything else to flight. The swarm still looked as big as ever. "I've a long, long time," thought Gabriel. But that he ought never to have thought. Nor should he have sunk down in this pleasant place, any more than a half-frozen man should lie down in snow. The embarcation dimmed before his eyes. God spread a mighty sleep over Bagradian. This sleep was made up of all the strain, all the watchful nights, of the forty days. Against it there was no longer will nor strength.

A mother whose child can no longer keep its eyelids from shutting says of it: "He's dropping with sleep." Gabriel Bagradian was dropping with the sleep of the dead.

7

To the Inexplicable in Us and above Us!

FIVE ships' sirens hooted. Their entangled notes were various: short, threatening, hollow. Gabriel quietly opened his eyes. He looked down for the swarming ant-heap which he imagined he had seen a minute ago. Surf leapt more angrily than it had on an empty beach. The raft was beginning to come apart. The *Guichen* had already turned her course. Her bows, running south-west, cut a deep foam-cleft in the sea. The other ships of the squadron were ahead of her. Like heavy, yet gracefully purposeful dancers, they strove to execute a perfect figure. At its centre, the *Jeanne d'Arc* slowly manœuvred. Gabriel watched all this attentively. Only then did he think: And Ter Haigasun? Didn't he notice? No! He thinks I'm on the *Jeanne d'Arc*. Gabriel jumped up and began to shout, with signalling arms. But his voice would not carry, and the movements were not those of a desperate man. Just then the sun struck the jutting rocks of Ras el-Khanzir, and the high cliffs of Musa Dagh lay deep in shadow. All reason should have sent Bagradian flying out to the rocks, to climb the furthest of them, and use any means to get himself seen. The deck of the *Guichen* was thronged with Armenians, leaning over the rail, to watch their mountain out of sight, which seemed to lower darkly over them with the glumness of a murderer balked of his prey. Though the sea might be breathing loud, the screw throbbing, someone on deck, or in the observation-turret, would surely have seen Gabriel Bagradian. But the wretched Gabriel not only refused to leave his shadowy place, he even

811

stopped his cries and signallings, as though grown tired of such vain formality. A man placed as he was ought surely to have shouted for help like a madman; he ought to have hurled himself into the sea, swum after, been fished out, or drowned, if necessary. The ships seemed to move so slowly. There was still time.

Gabriel could not understand his own calm. Was he drowsy still? The flask which the Frenchman filled with café and cognac for him still lay on the pleasant rock where he had sat. He drank long gulps to make himself feel desperate. They had just the opposite effect. His blood quickened, his muscles began to feel more alive, but his peace remained, just as before. No cries. No deathly panic. He felt joyous, consoled. The earthy, the material Gabriel was ashamed. I'll climb to a higher point with a clearer outlook and wave my coat. But there was no sense in doing that. Gabriel was merely making excuses to hide his intentions from himself. He was impelled to climb, not to descend. And, naturally, he was still thinking: What shall I live on? He felt in his overcoat pockets. Three rolls and two bars of chocolate, that was all. No food at all in his jacket pockets, the map of the Damlayik, a few old letters and notes, an empty cigarette-case, and then, Agha Rifaat Bereket's coin, with the Greek inscription. He kept his hold of this golden object. Then he remembered that on the evening of the great exodus, he had turned back to the villa to get the coins. How much better to have left them. And it felt as though now, at the very last, he would throw the amulet away. He did not, but pocketed it again, and began to ponder the inscription. Not in the earliest day of the defence had Gabriel felt so strong and well. Every trace of fatigue had gone out of his legs, his knees felt supple, his heart was not beating a jot faster than usual, so that, before he knew how it had happened, he had come out on to a free ledge, high above the sea. Gabriel walked to the end of the jutting point, to wave his greatcoat in wide circles round his head. But scarcely had he even begun to do this when he let his arms drop to his sides again. And now in one clear flash, he realized—that *he did not want the ships to see him*. That his being here was no unlucky accident, but the deepest decision; not God's decision only, but his.

How was that? He could find no trace of warped emotion or sensibility in himself. His mind was as clear as his heart was peaceful. He even felt at last that a long, dense lethargy had fallen away. Everything in him longed for final settlement, with a consciousness of power he had never known.

He left his place overlooking the sea. His body, aware of its own lightness, bore him in long, active strides up the rough track, no more than a stamped-out zigzag, between walls of rock, in among crevices, along water-courses marked with stones and logs to show the way. But the clarity even of Gabriel's senses was so acute that it was not necessary to heed either the landmarks or these dangers. He knew that, with so heightened a consciousness, he could make no false step, fall down no precipice. His pulse and perceptions worked together. This bit of the way was a proud settlement of accounts. He could see now why, that morning, when the miracle thundered from off the sea, he had felt a kind of disappointment. Here was the reason why he had felt such mysterious discomfort when the admiral said that they would land the people of Musa Dagh, and him with them, in Alexandria or Port Said. That discomfort had in it the germ of this instant's super-resolution. In those first minutes of general safety he had sensed at once that for him such return to life would be impossible, merely because the real Bagradian, the Bagradian come to life in the forty days, would have had to be saved. Saved for Port Said or Alexandria? For some camp for Armenian refugees? Saved, to exchange Musa Dagh for a narrower and lower pen-fold. To climb down from this supremacy of decision, into serfdom, and wait for another miracle? Why? An old saying of Bedros Altouni came back to him.

To be an Armenian is an impossibility! Quite true! But Gabriel had done with impossibilities. The one thing possible filled him from top to toe with incredible certainty. He had shared in the destiny of his blood. He had led the struggle of his own villagers. But was not the new Gabriel more than part of a blood-stream? Was he not more than an Armenian? Once he had thought of himself as "abstract," as an "individual." He had had to pass through the pen-fold of a commune really to become so. That was it, that was way he could feel so incredibly free! A cosmic hermitage. The thing for which, that morning, he had so longed. Now he had found it, as no other mortal ever had! Every breath was an intoxication of freedom. The ships departed, and Gabriel stayed on this rocky slope of Musa Dagh, which rose sheer and empty, as though just created. Only God—and Gabriel Bagradian. And Gabriel was, by the grace of God, more real than all people or any nation.

Then, at the summit of his pride came a hint of weakness. Women! Where women are there is guilt in men. Gabriel had returned to that gentle slope where the stretchers halted to rest, and Iskuhi's eyes spoke farewells to him. Yet he saw no Iskuhi here, but Juliette, in her stiff taffeta edged with lace. What would become of her? Gabriel stood for a while looking out to sea. Those ships sailed so slowly. They had still not reached the central spaces midway to the high horizon. Perhaps men on the look-out might see him still if he waved his coat above his head. But another thought had come into his mind. Juliette would be free, and so could easily get back her French nationality. Once it was found that he was missing, the admiral and everyone about her would be kindness itself to Juliette. This clear reflection increased his liberty still more. Now he went on more carefully, bending his head a little forwards up the stone slope, to where the track opened out among trees and bushes. Gabriel had passed two further bends in it before his heart stood suddenly still. Was it possible! Had Iskuhi really hidden somewhere, at the last minute, to stay behind with him? This seemed for the next few seconds by no means the work of imagination. He could sense her even. And then Iskuhi's steps came after him. He could hear the sharp, clear tapping of her heels. Where shall we be, you and I, sister? She had kept her word. "With you." He did not look round, but went hurrying on a long way, then stopped. Iskuhi's light and equal steps came after. They were unmistakable. Clearer and clearer, a woman's steps coming up the slope. The path rustled with shifting stones, they went scurrying downwards. Gabriel waited. Iskuhi must have reached him by now. But her heels still tapped, they were neither nearer nor farther off. So that at last he guessed that Iskuhi's footsteps were not outside him, but within. His hand slipped down along his body, to find his watch. When he pulled it out, it ticked so loudly as no longer to sound like a woman's footsteps, but the sharp strokes of a fine hammer on rock. Solitude exaggerated the noise. Or was this Gabriel's own particular time, rising in intensity with his life?

He had still the watch in his hand as the shadows cleared for a final certainty. That sleep of his had been no ordinary sleep. That sleep had been preordained to assist his weakness, so that his fate might be fulfilled. Without it he would have sunk back into the world. But for him God intended otherwise. When had that been? Was it imagination, or had he really spoken the words: "For some time now, I've known with the stoniest conviction that God intends to use me in some way." Now he knew the whole depths of that intention. Now it was no longer merely freedom, comfort, and joy that filled his heart. No, something new, entirely new, burst into consciousness. The ecstasy of supernatural unity, the ghostly ray. My life is guided, and therefore safe. With his arms a little apart he wandered on again, on feet that could not feel they trod. The next clearing opened among rocks. The sea-line rose higher and higher. The squadron, in the triangular form of a stork's flight, receded gradually into distances. But Gabriel had ceased to spy out ships. He looked up into the afternoon sky; its blue deepened to gold every minute. In this last ascent the path was already lost.

He crossed the belt of myrtle and rhododendron bushes. Ought he not to have thought of the next few hours, the night, a safe place to hide in? Since what mortal man could hope to go on living as he lived now, once it was dark? Nothing asked this in him. His feet went along the accustomed ways. Three-Tent Square. The tents were not only water- but fireproof and had baffled the flames. Even inside, the fire had not done much to them. The beds were still standing. Gabriel passed without stopping by Juliette's tent. He halted at the edge of the Town Enclosure, still undecided. He wanted to go north, to the main defences, his work. But he took the opposite direction, towards the howitzer mound. Perhaps he was even a little curious to see how the marines had spiked these guns. Between the Town Enclosure and the mound stretched the wide graveyard. In this sparse earth there had still been room for a hundred graves. Those of the first days had unhewn limestone blocks or slabs with inscriptions daubed in black. Only a wooden cross marked off the last of them. Gabriel went to Stephan. The earth still looked fairly fresh. When was it they'd buried him? On the thirtieth day, and today was the forty-first. And how long is it since that day when he took me by surprise, as I lay here asleep? This time I'm taking him by surprise. And we two have Musa Dagh to ourselves again. Gabriel did not move from Stephan's grave, though he thought not only of Stephan but of a hundred incidents in those fights. Nothing disturbed his tremendous peace. He scarcely noticed there was a sunset.

Suddenly it was cold and dark. He shook off his thoughts. What was that? Five ships' sirens on differently entangled notes, threatening, long, but so far away. Gabriel picked up his overcoat off the ground. They've found out I'm not on

816

board. They're calling me. Quick, to the Dish Terrace! Light a fire there! Perhaps—perhaps. Life raged within him. He took one step, and started back. They were creeping in on him, in a half-circle. Were these wild dogs? No eyes gleamed through the dark. Gabriel pretended not to have noticed, looked up in the air, went back another step and ducked, behind Stephan's grave. But unexpected shots flashed out from the side; one, two, three volleys.

GABRIEL BAGRADIAN was lucky. The second Turkish bullet shattered his temple. He clung to the wood, tore it down along with him. His son's cross lay upon his heart.

LIST OF CHARACTERS

Sheikh Achmed—*head of Islamic order called "The Thieves of Hearts."*

Ali Fuad Bey—*chief of staff, Turkish Fourth Army.*

Ali Nassif—*Turkish gendarme of Yoghonoluk.*

Ali Risa Bey—*brigadier-general, Turkish army.*

Dr. Bedros Altouni—*physician to the seven villages.*

Antaram Altouni—*"Mairik Antaram," wife of Dr. Altouni.*

Margoss Arzruni—*silk-weaver, disciple of Oskanian.*

Asayan—*chorister, disciple of Krikor.*

Samuel Avakian—*tutor of Stephan Bagradian, and adjutant of Gabriel.*

Ashod I Bagrathuni—*ancient Armenian king (fl. A.D. 885).*

Avetis Bagradian, the elder—*founder of the family fortune, grandfather of Gabriel.*

Avetis Bagradian, the younger—*elder brother of Gabriel.*

Gabriel Bagradian.

Juliette Bagradian—*Gabriel's French wife.*

Stephan Bagradian—*Gabriel's son.*

Captain Brisson—*French naval commander.*

Nazareth Chaush—*mayor of Zeitun.*

Djelal Bey—*Wali or civil governor of Syria.*

Djevded Pasha—*commander of the Turkish army against Persia.*

Enver Pasha—*Turkey's Minister of War and most popular field marshal.*

Colonel von Frankenstein—*chief of staff, Turkish Fourth Army.*

Hagop—*a cripple among the boys.*

Haik—*a leader of the boys and the scout corps.*

Hoffmann—*German vice-consul in Alexandretta.*

Hovhannes—*Gabriel Bagradian's cook.*

Jackson—*American Chief Consul in Aleppo.*

Jemal Pasha—*general commanding the Army in Syria.*

Thomas Kebussyan—*mayor of Yoghonoluk.*

Kevork—*"the sunflower dancer," half-wit refugee from Zeitun.*

Sarkis Kilikian—*deserter from the Turkish army.*

Krikor—*apothecary of Yoghonoluk.*

Kristaphor—*Bagradian's steward.*

Dr. Johannes Lepsius—*German pastor in charge of Armenian rescue work.*

Manushak—*graveyard dweller, spey-wife.*

Gonzague Maris—*Greek-American visitor to Musa Dagh.*

Vahan Melikentz—*Armenian serving in inshaat taburi.*

Missah—*Gabriel's valet and butler.*

Prof. Nezimi Bey—*member of the Islamic order, "The Thieves of Hearts."*

Harutiun Nokhudian—*Protestant pastor of the village of Bitias.*

Nunik—*graveyard dweller, spey-wife.*

Chaush Nurhan—*retired sergeant of Yoghonoluk.*

Hrand Oskanian—*dwarf, village schoolmaster.*

Osman—*head of Jemal Pasha's bodyguard.*

Agha Rifaat Bereket—*old Turkish friend of Avetis Bagradian and a religious mystic.*

Rössler—*German consul-general in Alexandretta.*

Sato—*refugee orphan from Zeitun.*

Monsignor Saven—*Armenian Patriarch.*

Hapeth Shatakhian—*village schoolmaster.*

Shushik—*a widow, mother of Haik.*

Talaat Bey—*the Minister of the Interior.*

Ter Haigasun—*chief priest of the district.*

Tomasian—*master-carpenter of Yoghonoluk.*

Aram Tomasian—*his son, pastor in Zeitun.*

Hovsannah Tomasian—*wife of Pastor Aram.*

Iskuhi Tomasian—*sister of Pastor Aram.*

Wartuk—*graveyard dweller, spey-wife.*

Rev. E. C. Woodley—*head of the American mission in Marash.*

GLOSSARY OF ARMENIAN
AND TURKISH TERMS

Agha—*a title of great respect.*

Aghil—*Turkish sash.*

Ansariyes—*Armenoid race of Syrian mountaineers whose Mohammedanism is considered suspect.*

Araba—*a covered cart, a cab.*

Baksheesh—*a gratuity, a tip.*

Bashi—*a major.*

Bedel—*tax paid in lieu of army service.*

Bedouin—*nomadic desert Arab.*

Berazik—*a little cake spread with grape syrup.*

Bey—*a governor of a province; also a title of respect for military officers.*

Bimbashi—*a lieutenant-colonel.*

Burnous—*a cloaklike garment and hood woven in one piece, worn by Arabs.*

Caliph—*literally the "successor" of Mohammed, the spiritual and temporal ruler of Islam; the Sultan of Turkey.*

Catholicos—*head of the Armenian Church.*

Charshaffe—*the veiled garment of Moslem women.*

Chetteh—*armed irregulars, hooligans.*

Chibuk—*a long Turkish smoking-pipe.*

Dashnakzagan—*Armenian nationalist party, supporters of the Young Turks prior to the Great War.*

Direm—*measure of weight equal to 3 grammes.*

Effendi—*the courtesy title of a gentleman; Turkish equivalent for Sir or Esquire.*

Endjumen—*meeting of the Turkish cabinet.*

Entari—*long outer smock.*

Ermeni millet—*"the Armenian people."*

Feredjeh—*Moslem woman's veil.*

Ferman—*decree issued by the Sultan.*

Giaour—*infidel, Christian.*

Ginkahair—*godfather (Armenian).*

Hamam—*public steam-bath house.*

Hamidiyehs—*Abdul Hamid's irregular troops of pogrom inciters.*

Hanum—*form of address for women; Madam, Miss.*

Hekim—*doctor.*

Hoja—*religious college.*

Hükümet—*headquarters of an administrative district, of a kaimakam.*

Inshaat taburi—*labour battalions, depôt soldiers.*

Irade—*written decree of Sultan of Turkey.*

Ittihad—*the Young Turks' "Committee for Union and Progress," the official name for the Westernization movement which led the Revolution of 1908.*

Janizary music—*after the music played by the Sultan's janizaries, a special body of Turkish infantry disbanded before the middle of the nineteenth century.*

Kaimakam—*civil governor of a kazah or administrative district; equivalent in military ranking of a lieutenant-colonel.*

Kangni—*ox-cart.*

Karagös—*the Turkish shadow-theatre.*

Kayik—*rowboat for ferrying...*

Kazah—*an administrative district; subdivision of a sanjak or region.*

Kebab—*broiled or roast mutton.*

Kef—*languor, the dreamy state induced by drugs; hence, peace, quiet.*

Khan—*caravanserai, inn.*

Khanzir—*swine.*

Khavass—*armed constable, servant, or courier.*

Kiafir—*infidel.*

Kismet—*fate, destiny.*

Kolagasi—*Turkish staff captain.*

Komitaji—*member of a Balkan guerrilla band.*

Konak—*an official residence or government house.*

Lokum—*Turkish sweetmeats.*

Medjidjeh—*silver coin worth 19 piastres or 84 cents.*

Mevlevi dervishes—*Islamic fanatics.*

Millet—*people, nation.*

Mohajirs—*refugees.*

Muafin—*police chief.*

Müdir—*minor civil official in charge of a nahiyeh or sub-district; equivalent in military ranking of a lieutenant.*

Mukhtar—*mayor.*

Mülasim—*lieutenant.*

Mullah—*a learned teacher, expounder of the law of Islam.*

Münadir—*drummer, herald.*

Mutessarif—*civil administrator of a sanjak or region; equivalent in military ranking of a colonel.*

Nahiyeh—*administrative sub-district; subdivision of a kazah.*

Nargileh—*pipe for smoking through water.*

Oka—*Turkish measure of weight, about 2¾ lbs.*

Onbashi—*sergeant-major.*

Padishah—*one of the Sultan's titles; as an adjective, equivalent to "imperial."*

Para—*coin worth 1/40 of a piastre, or 1/9 of a cent.*

Pasha—*an honorary title placed after the name, given to officers of very high rank both civil and military. The stress falls on the second syllable.*

Piastre—*silver coin worth about 4½ cents.*

Raki—*ardent spirits usually flavoured with anise.*

Redif—*military home guard.*

Sanjak—*large administrative region, coming in order of scope between a kazah (dis-trict) and a vilayet (province).*

Saptieh—*gendarme.*

Selamlik—*the reception-room of the Turkish house.*

Seraglio—*residence of the Sultan, or official palace of the government.*

Seraskeriat—*the War Ministry.*

Shalwar—*baggy Turkish trousers.*

Sublime Porte—*the government of the Turkish empire.*

Sura—*a chapter of the Koran.*

Tar—*Armenian guitar.*

Tarbush—*turban made by wrapping a scarf around a fez or red cap.*

Tekkeh—*Moslem cloister.*

Teskeré—*passport for travel in Turkish interior.*

Tonir—*brick oven dug into the earth.*

Türbedar—*holder of exalted office, "guardian" of the tombs of sultans and holy men.*

Ulema—*a Mohammedan college or body composed of the hierarchy.*

Vartabed—*Armenian ecclesiastic.*

Vilayet—*chief administrative division of the Ottoman Empire; a province.*

Wali—*civil governor or prefect of a vilayet or province; equivalent in military ranking of a general.*

Weli—*Islamic holy man.*

Yailadji—*mountaineer.*

Yayli—*two-horse coach.*

Yüs-Bashi—*major.*

Zikr exercises—*Islamic devotions, practised by dervishes.*

Zilgith—*ancient Turkish battle-cry.*

predictable
biased
boring
badly written
inconsistent (kill)